I0713540

Maeve's Raid

Stephan Grundy

TLS

ISBN13: 978-1-959350-17-0

Set in: Georgia 11pt, Fairy Tails 24pt

©The Three Little Sisters
USA/CANADA

Prologue: Fedelm

This is a tale of two ever at war: woman and man, dark and light, north and south, night and day. This is a tale of a proud queen and a proud hero, of tiny acorns of strife bursting from a contented earth to grow into mighty battle. It is a tale of Ireland, never at one with herself, but torn apart again and again, and of the greatness springing from those gaping wounds between the warp and weft of history. Thus I tell it; I, Fedelm, prophetess and poetess of Connacht. I am Fedelm. I hide nothing. Some say the tale of the cattle raid started with Cú Chulainn's birth, telling marvel stories of him; a swallowed worm getting a woman with child, the god Lugh appearing in a dream, prophecies and portents all around. One hero never made a war.

Cú Chulainn was born to strife, with the hero light burning about him, yet he was a single champion, not a leader of armies; it was not he who first set out to dye the Connacht host crimson red. Others begin the story with the simple things that every wedded couple, the crofter and his wife in their tiny mud daubed hut, the king and queen in their great stone halls, know. Idle pillow talk growing to argument. Argument to rancor. Rancor to challenge, and challenge resounding until nothing else can be heard in their world.

That is nearer the truth. Yet the pillow talk in Cruachan would have subsided, forgotten, were it not for the battle of two others weaving the doom of so many brave men. I shall tell how it truly began. I am Fedelm. I hide nothing. The síde, as every child knows, held Ireland before the human race came to these shores. We fought and made treaty with them, winning rule above this land, while they rule below, dwelling in the mounds that we call síd.

They are shining and wise, with arts and skills beyond our own; their very pig-keepers are magicians. The tale begins with two pig-keepers of the síde. Friuch was swineherd to Bodb, king of the síd on Femen Plain in Munster. Friuch was named after the boar's bristle; he was dark and bristly, quick of words and temper. He was a close friend to Rucht, swineherd to Ochall Ochne, king of the síd at Cruachan in Connacht beneath Cruachan fort. Rucht was named after the boar's grunt; he seldom spoke more than that. He was fair and well kept, but slow of speech and slower to anger, though he never forgot a slight.

When a mast of oak and beech nuts fell thick in Munster, Rucht would grunt to his pigs and lift his crook-stick and drive them southward, rustling through the first autumn leaves to where Friuch sat bristly and dark on a fallen log or tree stump, and their pigs would snuffle and feed together, and when the mast fell in Connacht, it would be Friuch who drove his swine northwards, until the two herds joined like noisy black rivers jostling together, and Rucht lifted his hand and grunted to his friend, bearing a pot of good mead to greet him.

We see the folk of the síd seldom. On some nights; Beltaine and Samhain, most often. They ride pale in the light of moon and stars, and wise folk keep from their paths. They prefer their hills, where the hidden light flickers on craft-wrought gold and silver and gems beyond compare, and they feast and sing as if the clumsy Milesian hordes had never come, forgetting how time passes above. Yet a pig keeper must watch his herds outdoors, and those who watch may be seen. As a little girl in Connacht, I hid in the autumn woods one night when the beechnuts had fallen thickly and moonlight slanted silver through the dry leaves, hoping for a glimpse of Rucht and his swine. First the pigs of the síd gave voice; I knew it was no common swine I heard, for their grunting sounded up through my feet like deep horns shaking the earth, trembling through the old oak where I crouched.

Then I saw moonlight glimmering from dark hides, as though they rose wet from the forest mold; cloven hooves shone sharp and black as bloodied swords in the night, and pale fire sparked in tiny eyes. Each bristle shimmered like moonlit foam, the síd-swine's backs rose and fell like the waves of the sea. I clung to the rough bark of my branch, biting back my breath. My heart hammered in my ears, and my body shook; I feared I would lose my hold, fall and be trampled. Then I saw the brightness behind the swine, and ceased to think or fear. Rucht the swineherd of Cruachan síd. His face was fine, carved ivory with spun gold swirling about it; a snake of pale light twined his crooked staff. He wore a swineherd's dark square bratt, but his tunic and breeches gleamed silver as woven moonlight, and a green stone burned from the pin that held the bratt to his shoulder.

I never knew if he saw me; he passed by, driving his swine. I sat in the tree and wept for longing when they were gone, until cold and damp soaked me to the skin. I could hardly climb down for the shivering, making my way back home bent and bereaved as an old woman. I lay in a fever three days; but when its hot grip broke, my eyes were clearer and brighter than before, so that some called me Fedelm of the Síd; and poetry came to my tongue: it is no chance that this tale comes to me, of all singers and seers. So we knew Rucht in Connacht, as they knew Friuch in Munster. We left food and drink for them, and sometimes they blessed those who had gifted them; and when Connacht folk spoke with Munster at night and told tales over the fire, each boasted of their own síd's swineherd And whenever two are measured in words; Rucht and Friuch, Maeve and Ailill, Cú Chulainn and Ferdiad. Trouble soon comes of it. So a great mast fell in Munster one year, and Rucht came south with his pigs. As always, Friuch made him welcome. No men heard what they spoke, but I, Fedelm; gifted with vision in Connacht, studying it long in Alba, I know what they said. Friuch greeted Rucht with gladsome words, as always, but this year there was a sour tinge to them, like the first taint of mold in bread.

"Ah, is it you?" Friuch said, running a hand through his dark bristly hair. Then he laughed as though to take the sting from his next words. "Men are trying to cause trouble between us: I heard it said that your power is greater than mine." He tilted his head with a wide-mouthed grin.

"It is no less," Rucht grunted.

Friuch laughed again. "That is something we can test. Look, I shall cast a spell over your pigs. They may eat all of this mast they like, but won't grow fat, while mine will."

When Rucht drove his lean flanked pigs back to Cruachan síd, laughter was heard ringing from the mound, sharp laughter, such as wounds somewhat to hear, and more to receive. Ochall's folk said it was a bad day when Rucht set out for Munster, for clearly his friend Friuch had the greatest power. Then anger gave Rucht a tongue.

"That proves nothing," he said. "We shall have mast here in turn; I'll play him the same trick."

If Rucht's power suffered with his pigs, his foresight did not: the next year, the mast fell thick in Connacht, and Friuch and his swine came northwards. Then Rucht did as he had been done by. Friuch's pigs withered, their ribs standing out beneath the bristles while Friuch tore at his dark hair until he looked as mangy as his swine. Then it was said that they were matched in power.

Kings of the síd, like kings of men, do not care to have their servants wasting their goods for private matters. So Bodb dismissed Friuch, and Ochall dismissed Rucht. Bereaved of pigs and place, each because of the other, they met in the woods, and fell to bitter quarreling. They flew up into the air as two eagles, to shriek and bite and tear at each other. The next part of the tale I learned as all folk may: through the stories others tell. We often hold gatherings beside a síd, and Femen is one of Munster's favorite gathering places.

Now a few folk at the Beltaine fair were remarking on the terrible babble of the two birds above them. As they spoke, they saw a man coming up the hill. He was tall, wrapped in a dark cloak, with a dark hood pulled down over his face so that none could look straight at his features. Guests and strangers are holy, so they were swift to make him welcome.

He took the greeting cup, saying, "Hail to you, men of Munster. You do not know me, and see me seldom, but I am Fuidell mac Fiadmire, steward to King Ochall."

Then he looked up and remarked, as any man might, "Those birds are making a great noise over there. One would think they were the same two that kept this up in the north for all of last year." And at his words, the birds took human shape, and everyone knew the two pig-keepers. The Munstermen hastened to hold out mead in beaten silver goblets and scurried to bring food, but Friuch would not drink nor eat. "You can save your welcome," he said. "We bring you but war-wailing, and a fullness of friends' corpses."

"What have you been doing?" Asked Ochall's steward. His blue eyes darkened to grey, and a note of worry might have sounded in his voice, though it is hard to guess with the síd.

"Nothing good," said Friuch. "From the day we left until today we spent two full years in the shape of eagles: a whole year at Cruachan, and a year over Femen Plain, so that all, north and south, have seen our power. Now we shall take the shape of sea creatures and live two years under the water."

Then they turned their backs on each other and strode away, one to the great river Sianann, one to the river Siur; and Fuidell was gone like a shadow when the light shifts, his cup empty on the ground. Soon afterwards, the stories trickled in from the Siur: two great long-necked water-beasts, with horses' manes and pikes' teeth, rising to thrash the river to bloody foam. Then boats pulled into shore and those who dwelt near the river closed their doors and turned their backs, fearing to see such things. A year passed; they were seen in the Siur no more, but boatmen on the Siannan told of lashing black tails and seaweed-maned necks spraying gouts of blood, whipping the great river to red froth.

Next they became two stags, each gathering up the other's herd of young deer and tearing at his dwelling-place with hooves and horns, so that the forest looked as though madmen had hacked it with swords. Then they became two warriors gashing each other; then two phantoms, terrifying each other; then two dragons pouring snow upon each other's lands.

I was fourteen that year, just come to womanhood; I remember huddling close to the fire, and running as swiftly as I could to get back inside when my father sent me to bring in more baskets of turf, and between the cold and the endless peat smoke, we all wheezed like leaky bellows even in the middle of the summer. The year's winter ended; when the Beltaine fires melted the snow around them, the clouds melted as well. Friuch and Rucht dropped from the air, shrinking from great misty dragons to little earthen maggots. Friuch the dark fell into the river Cronn in Cuailnge, where a cow of Dáire mac Fiachna drank him up; Rucht the fair dropped into the well-spring Garad in Connacht, and was drunk by a cow belonging to Queen Maeve.

Their life swelled in the cows' wombs; the cows gave birth to the two great bulls, Finnbennach the White-Horned of Ai Plain, and the Brown Bull of Cuailgne , and the strife of the swine-herde of the síde gave birth on Maeve and Ailill's bed, to the bloodshed and red battle and death of the Cattle-Raid of Cuailgne. I am Fedelm: I hide nothing, and I see much, what is to come as well as what has been. This is how it began. I shall tell how it went on, and how it ended; and of what came after the end. The telling that the world remembers is a man's, and one who felt himself harmed by Queen Maeve. He left the story of her suffering at the Ulster king Conchobar's hands to others, and made a petty shrew of the woman who would defend her queenships holiness.

Ulster's Druid Cathbad, who raised his king to rape and worse in contempt for women – perhaps Cathbad had his desire, in the end.

For the time came when the heroes sung in tales were all men, and the names of Maeve and Boudicca were spoken only as the least afterthoughts. The Cattle-Raid of Cuailgne was told to celebrate the greatness of the Ulster heroes Cú Chulainn and Fergus, with the advice that, "It is no surprise if a herd led by a mare goes astray and is lost". at its heart, this tale was always the story of a woman's loss and a woman's loves and a woman's quest. If the pig-keepers of the síde began the strife, Queen Maeve ended it through her own sorrows, with her own strength, as only the greatest of heroes could. A Druid knows each hour propitious for something: this is the hour to restore the queen to her throne.

Maeve

"The wife of Felim Mac Dall was serving drink to Conchobar and his men when the child in her womb gave a great cry. Cathbad the Druid prophesied that she would be the greatest beauty in Ireland, but that her beauty would bring death and ruin to Ulster. He repeated this at Deirdre's birth. King Conchobar's warriors said she should be killed, but the king had her raised deep in the forest, seeing no man save himself...One day, when Naoise son of Uisnech was hunting, Deirdre saw him and fell in love with him.

She put a geas on him, obliging him to steal her and flee to Alba with his two brothers. Conchobar tracked the sons of Uisnech down and sent Fergus mac Roech, whose honor all trusted, to pledge them a peaceful homecoming. Fergus bore a geas forbidding him to refuse any offer of hospitality; knowing this, Conchobar arranged for him to be delayed on the way. Fergus sent his son Fiacha with Deirdre and the sons of Uisnech as proof of his honor. Conchobar slew Fergus' son and had all three of the sons of Uisnech slain, taking Deirdre to his bed by force. Fergus left Ulster thereafter and came to Queen Maeve of Connacht, Ulster's greatest foe."

Maeve stretched out on the pillows of the great royal bed, welcoming the cool of the early autumn air stroking the fine glaze of sweat on her body. Heavy drops of rain pattered on the thatch, a miserable drenching for those outside, but pleasant to hear indoors in the warm afterglow of their lovemaking. Beside her, Ailill lay with his head propped up on one heavy-muscled arm, grinning foolishly beneath his thick red-gold mustaches. He reached for the gold goblet of mead on the bedside table, swallowing deeply and passing it to his wife. Maeve drank, letting the cool sweetness trickle down her throat to kindle warmth in her belly as the last shivers of pleasure faded between her thighs.

Love-play was pleasant at any time, but always best for her when she and Ailill came back to Cruachan fort; the height of her strength, the heart and seat of her rule. Ailill's gaze swept over Maeve, and she arched her back a little. At forty summers, when many women were bent and wrinkled grandmothers, Maeve knew she was still as fine as any woman in Connacht. She was not one of the bird-boned creatures that grew thin and hard with age, nor had she put on more flesh than the sleekness of her heavy breasts and sturdy hips demanded. She had been raised to command in battle, and could hold her own against almost any champion in her guard.

That training kept her arms and belly and breasts firm where farmers' wives drooped and pouched and sagged. Even the faint eggshell-crackling of white lines bearing her babes had left across her stomach was invisible to all but the keenest searching. Truly, Maeve thought, Ailill had done well to wed her, though a king might have his choice of maids all his life. Eight children between them; and Maeve's courses still came monthly, so that she could yet be fruitful if she desired. The corners of Ailill's lips turned up, the lines about his blue-green eyes crinkling.

"What are you thinking, my darling?" Maeve inquired, comfortably sure of compliments. She handed the goblet back to him; he filled it again, drank, and gave it to her.

"It is true what they say," Ailill mused happily. "Life is good for the wife of a wealthy man."

Maeve considered the whorls of gold filigree-work on the goblet; looked up at the painted planks partitioning off their bedchamber, twining swirls of red and yellow and green spiraling over smooth white oak. The bed was carved of red yew with ornamented bronze facings shining golden in the light of the chamber's torches, piled deep with eiderdown pillows and furs, fox and wolf and even bear. Outside she could hear shouts of laughter and warriors' deep voices.

Her men at their feasting, with gold and bronze glittering from their sword-hilts and heavy rings shining on their arms, sworn to fight and fall for their queen. Inside, three skulls bleached to clean bone and ornamented with polished bronze, Ailill's trophies, the heads of mighty men he had overcome in single challenges gazed dark-socketed down at the rulers, their old boasts silenced now in death-wisdom set to Connacht's service.

"True enough," Maeve said, taking another swallow of mead.

"And likewise for the husband of a wealthy woman." She swept her heavy fall of golden hair from under her shoulder, gathering it up to trail thickly across her breasts and belly. "What put that in your mind?"

"It only struck me how much better off you are today than the day I married you," Ailill said.

Maeve saw the quirk of her husband's mouth, and knew that he was sticking her with a pin to see if she would jump, the worst fault, she thought sometimes, in an otherwise fine man. Instead of drawing herself up in indignation as she would have when she was younger, she casually pushed herself up on the thick soft pillows and said, as if it were nothing, "I was well-off enough without you."

Ailill laughed and beckoned to the serving girl Lochu who stood silently in the corner. She began to plait up his thick red-gold hair into the complicated braids that he favored, and he turned back to his queen.

"Then your wealth was something I didn't know or hear about. Except, of course, for your woman's things, and the loot and plunder your neighbors kept making off with."

Maeve's jaw tightened; she barely kept from gritting her teeth. She was long used to Ailill's teasing, but he was touching too deeply now. Had another man spoken so to the queen of Connacht, blood would soak the straw on the floor.

"Not at all," she replied, trying to keep her voice light. "The high king of Ireland was my father; Eochaid Feidlech the steadfast, the son of Finn, the son of Finnoman, and so on back to Aengus Turbech. He had six daughters, and myself, Maeve, highest and proudest of them. I outdid all in grace and giving, in battle and warlike combat. I had an hundred soldiers in my royal pay, all exiles' sons, and the same of freeborn native men; for every paid soldier I had ten more men. That was our ordinary household." She paused. Ailill was still grinning.

"My father gave me a whole province of Ireland, this province, ruled from Cruachan fort. Which, as you know very well, is why I am called 'Maeve of Cruachan'." Maeve smiled to herself.

Her name meant more than that, not only queen, but land-goddess, the intoxicating mead cup of sovereignty. Ailill was a Leinsterman, and some mysteries were only for the Cruachain to know.

"They came from Finn the king of Leinster, and Coirpre Niafer the king of Temair, from Conchobar king of Ulster, and Eochaid Bec, to woo me, and I wouldn't go. For, as you remember, I asked a harder wedding gift than any woman ever asked before from a man in Ireland: the absence of meanness and jealousy and fear."

"Oh, indeed," Ailill said, his smirk softening. He reached out to stroke Maeve's hair back, but she was not ready to forgive him yet: it would take more than caresses to wipe out his words.

"If I were to marry a mean man, it would be wrong, because I am so full of grace and giving," she pressed on.

"It would be an insult if I were more generous than my husband, but not if we two were matched. It would be just as wrong for me to marry a timid man, because I myself thrive on all kinds of trouble." Ailill laughed out loud, throwing back his head so his plaits swung free of Lochu's hands and the serving girl had to snatch at the gold wires to keep from dropping them.

"It is an insult for a wife to be more spirited than her husband, but not if the two are equally spirited. If I married a jealous man, that would be wrong too, for I never had one man without another waiting in his shadow. So I got the sort of man I wanted: yourself, Ailill of Leinster. You aren't niggardly or jealous or sluggish. When we were promised, I brought you the fairest wedding-present bride could bring: apparel enough for a dozen men, a chariot worth three times seven bondsmaids, the width of your face of red gold and the width of your left arm of yellow gold." "So", Maeve said, driving in her point as if she had just lured her husband's shield aside with a complex feint, "if anyone causes you shame or upset or trouble, the right to compensation is mine, for you're a man in a woman's service."

Ailill's mouth tightened as the hot flush of angry satisfaction warmed Maeve's belly. Now he was paid for the slur on her clan, and, more importantly, reminded that Connacht was hers alone, kept by the law that governed marriage rights by portions brought. She expected Ailill to fall silent, or turn the matter away with a compliment to her. Ailill answered, his voice light as hers had been, though suddenly they were locked in struggle over the rule of Connacht.

"By no means. I have two kings as brothers, Coirpre in Temair and Finn over Leinster. I let them rule only because they were the elder, not because they are any better in grace and giving than I. I never, in all Ireland, heard of a province ruled by a woman save this one; and that was why I came to take the kingship here, in succession for my mother Mata Muiresc, Mágach's daughter. Who better for my queen than you, daughter of the high king of Ireland?"

Ailill reached out to stroke her again, his big callused fingers tracing lightly down her arm to stir the little golden hairs with a familiar tingle. He was truly a fine man, his shoulders and chest heavy from many years of sword play and wrestling and his belly-muscles rippling like a youth's; his cock, softening, still bulked large in its nest of red-gold curls. Now, fair as Ailill was to look on, and though his touch stirred her, Maeve found herself turning away. Her sweat chilled suddenly as she thought:

Is there no end to the pressing of men? She had long delighted in her husband, and in the many other men who had pleasured her since she divorced Conchobar. The short harsh marriage of her fourteenth year and the brutal revenge Ulster's king had taken upon her afterwards still echoed deep in Maeve's mind, calling up the grown woman's anger to wipe out the young girl's fear.

Nor had she forgotten Conchobar's men laughing at her, their jests turning a marriage of honor into shameful captivity. I shall not be helpless again: not before strength, and not before words.

"It still remains," Maeve said, "that my fortune is greater than yours."

Ailill opened his eyes wide as if in amazement and said, "You surprise me, Maeve. No one has more belongings or jewels or treasure than I, and I know it."

"Is that so!" Maeve snapped. The bedclothes spilled onto the floor as she leapt to her feet. "A man's words on the pillows are cheap enough, but when all is laid out and counted, we shall see which of us is the greater. Lochu, attend me; your mistress would dress."

The bondsmaid paused, looking from Ailill to Maeve. With a little gesture of pushing responsibility from herself, she laid Ailill's thick plaits over his shoulders and trotted to find the dress that Maeve had abandoned. One garnet-set bow-pin glinted bright gold where the two rectangles of blue and green-checkered cloth met on the right corner, but the other had fallen off; Lochu had to scuffle in the fresh-laid reeds on the earthen floor, dark hair tumbling about her plump face, before she could dress her queen.

Ailill raked his fingers through his half-braided hair, pulling it out into a great ruddy cloud around his head. All the laughter was gone from his face. He yanked on his breeches and tunic, fastening the royal bratt; the square mantle dyed in stripes of seven rainbow colors such as only a king could wear, sunrise red through brilliant gold through the deepening blues and purples of night with a gold ring-brooch that shone from his right shoulder like the sun. Lastly he bent to the bronze-bound chest where he kept his finest treasures, working the catch between the two hollow gold knobs at the ends of his torc so that he could twist the collar's heavy wrought-gold halves aside and back around his neck.

"Take note of these, Lochu," Ailill said. "Since my queen would prove which of us is the greater, let no finger-length of bronze wire be left out of the reckoning." He lifted his voice, shouting for his own servants, while Lochu tied shoes of bronze-ornamented doeskin onto Maeve's feet.

For a moment Maeve's heart faltered within her. Her pride had run ahead of her thoughts: she was not truly sure how matters would weigh out. She had the advantage in land, but a ruler's wealth was what could be carried in the slow yearly procession from hall to hall and fort to fort; gold rings and bronze goblets, enameled horse-bits and iron cauldrons, cattle and sheep and swine.

Sovereign queen of Connacht, she had taken Ailill as her third husband, but the Leinster prince had come rich to the marriage bed, and his wealth had waxed since. *Yet I will have the victory, however it must come: I will not let any man take from me what I have defended from men all my life.*

"Go out to the servants unpacking our wagons, Lochu," Maeve ordered. "Tell them to set the queen's belongings in one heap and the king's in another. Send to our shepherds, our swine-herds, our cattle herds; let them tally and reckon and match our animals for worth."

"As you wish it, my queen," said Lochu, her face impassive. She had been the daughter of a minor chieftain of Munster, taken in a raid six summers ago; she was a proud girl who kept her own counsel.

Maeve went over to the bronze chamberpot by the wooden partition, lifting her skirts to squat. Her piss frothed out with a mighty hiss, loud against the metal; she could feel Ailill's seed dripping out, washed away by her own strength, and the relief in her belly was not only from the ease of emptying herself.

"You have always been a woman of great potency, Maeve," Ailill said admiringly.

Maeve wondered if he would follow by displaying his own prowess from the advantage of his standing height: Conchobar had never been able to hear her piss without emptying his own bladder to prove his strength the greater. Ailill held back, perhaps unwilling to get into a second contest with her on the same day. Perhaps: the faint knowing smile was back on his broad face as Maeve cleaned herself and shook her skirts back down, and that unnerved her.

Ailill smiled like that when he yielded to her in anything; he also smiled like that when he was so certain of the upper hand he hardly needed to speak. Has he counted our goods before? Maeve wondered. Did he plan to challenge me just before Samhain; does he know what he is doing? Ailill could never have managed the immense task of valuing their belongings without Maeve knowing, so she smiled back at him before picking up her mirror. Maeve's own image gazed back at her from the polished bronze: her face somewhat long, but tender rather than bony, thick golden hair smoothed sleekly back.

The half-moons of dark blue pigment that brightened the blue of her eyes had smeared up into her fair eyebrows; the red tingeing her cheekbones was not paint, but anger. Maeve cleaned her face, then applied fresh pigment to her eyelids with a little brush, and lastly set a torc of her own; a thick twisted ribbon of heavy gold, about her neck. Furious as she was, and shaken, and worried, if she must admit it. Maeve's folk would not see her as less than a queen. Although Maeve and Ailill had just arrived that morning, the servants who traveled before them and the folk of Cruachan itself had been readying Cruachan's great hall for weeks.

Fires had long since banished any mold; the hall smelled of roasting meat and wood smoke and the sharp burning-pine scent of the torches that ringed it, of fresh thatch and damp hounds and damp wool drying slowly in the warm air, all the rich smells of life greeting Maeve at the heart of her realm, this fort where she had been named queen and where she ruled above as surely as Ochall ruled in the síd below her feet. The royal dwelling was more than thirty-five paces wide, a huge round structure of wood with a high-peaked thatched roof held up by a ring of long slanting beams, with a lower ring of heavy posts inside around the tables.

In the middle burned a large fire, two bondsmen turning a spitted pig over it. Plank partitions around the sides made a few rooms. The bed chambers of the rulers and their most honored guests, but for the most part, it was a single hall, where all could hear and see whatever came to pass. Maeve's daughter Finnabair sat at the end of one long table across from her brother Maine Ceat, the two of them playing fidchell with pieces of gold and silver upon a board of reddish-purple yew wood. The other six Mainí were nowhere to be seen out in their chariots, or training at sword-play. Maeve's wolfhound Baiscne ambled up to her, leaning his heavy black head against her waist.

Maeve caressed his rough fur, already thinking, "Baiscne is a hound of worth, but Ailill has Liath, and one could not find a sliver of difference between them. Baiscne was born in the house of Donn; his lick is healing, he stands beside me at Samhain when I make the offering and follow the track below; and when he grows old, he shall vanish and come back young. Liath was sired by a hound of the síd; he has lived twenty years and is still in his prime, and there is never a wolf or deer that can escape his jaws, once Ailill has set him on the track". As Maeve walked towards her seat, Fergus mac Roech came up to her. He was a handsome man, a few finger widths shorter than Ailill, of a height with Maeve, but sturdily-built and powerful.

His red-glinting chestnut hair tumbled in waves down his broad back, held back from his face with a gold headband; he wore a tunic checkered in shades of red and yellow and orange, embroidered with gold thread. Red enamel and yellow gold gleamed from the man-shaped hilt of Fergus' sword, and twisted gold rings adorned the heavy muscles of his forearms. A pale scar scored a streak of white down from one prominent cheekbone through his close-cut brown beard; his nose was arched like an eagle's beak, giving him a look of fierce pride, and his eyes were a keen grey.

Though Fergus was twelve summers older than Maeve, none would guess he bore a grandfather's age. When she had first seen him at Emain Macha, when she was fourteen and he twenty-six, Fergus had seethed with barely-leashed power, like a stallion lunging against his chariot-harness. His strength had not lessened, but deepened, so that even when he stood still and spoke quietly, Maeve could feel its thunder echoing within him.

"What is it you are doing, Maeve?" The Ulster exile asked. "Your servants are in an uproar, running about and heaping goods as if phantoms drove them. Has some treasure of yours been stolen?"

"Ailill and I were speaking of wealth, and we are set upon seeing which of us is the greater," Maeve answered. "He has said words that cannot be answered otherwise."

Fergus shook his head. "I do not think Ailill was the only one that spoke, but my counsel was not asked. As you have shielded me from Conchobar's wrath, I would give you good advice in turn: it is not well when husband and wife strive against each other, or when men and women make war between them.

If it were not for such battles, Deirdre might live yet, and I would yet dwell in Ulster."

"And yet you have not found it so ill with us," Maeve said, smiling at him. "Have I not heaped you with good, with bronze-fitted chariots and torcs of gold, and made you welcome among the nobles of Connacht in every way. You, and your dear friend Dubthach, and my son Cormac whom you brought with you? Have I not given you the best of everything, the finest cuts of meat and the strongest winter mead?"

She rested her hand on Fergus' forearm, feeling the hard swell of his muscles. His nostrils flared slightly, like those of a bull scenting a cow; he met her eyes, then shifted his gaze.

"All of this is true. Thus, I would advise you to give over this strife between yourself and Ailill. Neither of you will win any good of it."

"For shame, Fergus!" Maeve said, staring straight into the Ulsterman's sea-gray eyes. "Would you turn down a challenge from any man at a crossroads, even were it Cú Chulainn himself?"

Fergus' eyes half-closed, his mouth tightening; Maeve thought of a cloud's dark shadow passing across a brooding crag. "I took Cú Chulainn on my knee when he was a child," Fergus said slowly.

"How should I fear him in manhood, for all his mighty feats? Yet if we met with reason for challenge, friendship might find a way to resolve the matter without shame. Do you love Ailill so much less?"

"I am not such a woman as Deirdre, waiting helpless for men to save or torment her." I had more than my fill of that in Conchobar's hall, Maeve thought to herself, feeling her cheeks flush with old shame. Though Fergus might see high temper reddening her face. "I love Ailill, but that does not mean I must suffer all he would say or do. I swear to you by all the gods of the Cruachain, even unto Crom Cruaich and Crom Baiscne, that it was he and not I who started this between us."

"I believe you," Fergus answered. "Though I think you decided to finish it. In any case, I have said my say. I shall speak to Ailill as well, but I doubt that I shall get farther with him.

He is not so rashly proud as some, but there is a core of iron at his heart. If he has not backed down, I do not think he will."

As Fergus strode towards the king, Maeve noticed that fewer folk were in the hall than before, and those were crowding towards the main door to see what was happening. Even were she minded to take Fergus' advice, there were too many witnesses for either queen or king to back down now. 'Put a bold face on what you cannot hide', her father had told her. 'That is the pride of the ruler, never to accept shame. For if you are shamed before your folk, they will no longer follow your rule'. Her tall black wolfhound at her side, Maeve walked out proudly to the measuring.

The storm-squall had already swept east. Looking towards the river, Maeve could see the rain like a grey curtain, but shafts of afternoon sunlight shone golden through the breaking clouds to the west, touching the dark trees and fields below the rise of Cruachan síd with glowing spots of brighter green, glossing the rain-slick posts of the palisades ringing the foot and top of the great fortress-mound inside its ditch and earthworks, and the two wooden watchtowers at either side of the path sloping up to the mound's height.

'My land, and a fair land', Maeve thought, breathing deeply of the clean damp air. Ulster had its wild mountains and gorges; Munster and Meath their low rolling fields, and Meath its fair pastures and high peaks by the sea, but Connacht, from its thick inland forests to its rocky bog lands by the sea where peat-dark lakes mirrored the sky in deep gleaming purple-blue, shining from the brown marshes like gems in tarnished copper under the brief brightness of the sun between storms. Maeve's Connacht, fruitful, yet untamed; wild, yet welcoming to its dwellers was the fairest of Ireland's five lands.

'If Ailill has any rule here, it is only because I allow it to him, as Connacht allows the plough in her fields, yet keeps woods and mountains for herself. I am the land, red-sided Maeve of the Cruachain as well as Queen Maeve: no man can do more than pass over me'. Her feet set firm on her own earth, Maeve lifted her right hand and lowered her left, uttering a chirping call. The Queen's wren fluttered down from the thatched roof of the great hall, but wavered in flight, hesitating before landing upon her hand. Maeve looked into the dark glass-bead eye that regarded her from the smooth grey feathers.

'What do you see? She asked silently. Have matters been weighed out already?' The wren chirped, but Maeve could make nothing of it. Sometimes, with her full power upon her, she could understand the bird's cries and fluttering, but not always: she was queen, not a 'ban-drúi or ban-fili' trained in th. Omens of the air-traders. 'Still, she came to me. My might is not so easily set aside!'

Little clinging paws scrabbled at Maeve's left hand, her pine marten scampering over Baiscne's back to her shoulder like a rivulet of silky brown and cream fur. Its cold nose nuzzled her neck, paws tickling through her hair as though she might have nuts or dried apples hidden there for it.

Her three beasts comforted Maeve, her heart beating more slowly and strongly and her breath flowing easier. The hound of the Underworld; the bird of the air; and the pine marten from Uaigh na gCat, the cave leading from the green earth into Cruachan síde: they had come to her when she first sat on the limestone pillar that was the pole-star of Cruachan's rule.

The first Baiscne had been her father's gift, but when the first wren settled upon her hand and the first marten ran up the stone to sit on her shoulder, then all had seen that Maeve bore the goddess' name rightly, as Cruachan's true queen. The wagons by the eastern side of the hall were mostly unloaded, the servants dividing the heaps for queen and king.

All the things that Maeve and Ailill had brought on their royal procession were being set out on the sheep-cropped grass. Goblets of bronze and gold, drinking-horns with smooth jewels set in bright metal around their rims, buckets and tubs of wood and iron pots, jugs and wash-pails and vessels with handles, everything down to spoons and toiletries, laid out to be judged.

"Who shall decide the measure between us, should it come to a question?" Ailill asked.

Maeve considered it. Had Fergus not seemed set against their challenge, she might have suggested him. "Let Senchán be called to judge." Her voice was as indifferent as she could make it, though she knew the Druid's word would make their contest irrevocable. No less than all my folk, from noble warriors and noble women to the youngest goose-boy, have already done by witnessing.

"Is not a household quarrel a trivial matter for Cruachan's elder Druid?" Ailill said.

"I do not think so," Maeve replied coldly. She raised her voice. "Mac Roth!"

Her messenger was there almost before she could take another breath. "You called me?" He said. Mac Roth was tall and very lean, red-haired and narrow-faced. No runner in Ireland was his match, and Maeve sent him on all her errands of note.

"Aye. Go you to the Druid Senchán, and tell him that we would have his aid."

"So I shall," said Mac Roth, and darted off into the curious throng.

Maeve watched as the heaps turned into neat rows. Their iron cauldrons were laid out by size, from the two great pots that could scald and seethe a whole boar down to the smallest bowls for mixing herbals and fine dainties.

Her gleaming basin of riveted bronze plates figured with the shapes of gods and beasts, made far in the east, was matched by Ailill's, worked only with spirals and twining lines, but adorned with red enamel and stones. Men were wagering now; she heard blunt Dubthach, who had come from Ulster with Fergus, bawling, "My best dagger against a bronze mirror that King Ailill wins!" And the deep voice of her eldest son Maine Orlamh answering,

"My sword against your dagger for Queen Maeve!"

"You are taking a great risk here, Mother," Finnabair said quietly beside Maeve.

Maeve looked down at her one daughter. Finnabair was shorter and slighter than her mother, the slim white length of her gold-ringed arms showing that she had never trained at sword-play. Her hair was fair as Maeve's, hanging to her hips, her eyebrows and lashes pale white around light blue eyes, and her features fine and delicate. Finnabair was not fierce of spirit, but practical; though she was but sixteen, Maeve often found it worthwhile to listen to her.

"Sometimes rulers must do so," Maeve answered. "Your father gave insult and challenged me: was I to yield before him?"

"Of course not...but..." Finnabair bit her full lower lip, looking down at the ground. "It might have been better if what was said between two had stayed between two."

"Such can seldom be the case," Maeve answered regretfully. Lochu and one of the menservants were counting out wooden bowls and trenchers now, large and small, fine-carved and plain, and still she and Ailill seemed matched, chariot-horses striving to outpace each other but yoked neck to neck.

'I am sure I have more horses. The tally of our sheep was to have come in this month; I do not know…'

"It will make little difference, in the end," Finnabair said finally. "We all know that even though this is a question of law. Even though the law says clearly that whichever brings the lesser goods to a wedding is in the other's service, however this turns out, you will still be ruler-queen in fact, and Father king-consort. Your voice will still be loud when his is quiet, and Connacht will still look to you for rule." She gestured at Maeve's animals. "Who could deny the signs of your power?"

"Mayhap," Maeve said reluctantly. 'If they do not desert me…' She thought there was truth in her daughter's words, but did any woman ever truly know a man?

Was there a hidden ember of fierceness in Ailill, long-banked by his place as third son and consort to Connacht's queen, that had only waited this wind to blow it into flame as the cold wind whipped his flame-bright hair about his head? He watched, grinning, while the servants unloaded and counted and matched their household goods, knives and spoons and cups, each for each, and Maeve wondered again if her husband had baited her into a contest in which he knew he could not come off worse than before.

She looked back at the posts ringing the base of the great mound, each topped with a head taken by Cruachan's rulers. The oldest skulls, legacy of Maeve's father's wars, were weathered to grey bone like beech-wood left long to season; the newest were still mottled with blackish-brown tatters of shrunken flesh, the last strands of hair fluttering like dirty cobwebs. Sometimes raids were successful, the Connacht forces returning with cattle and captives and a new bag of heads to mount in triumph; sometimes they failed, and the trophies were taken by men such as that blow hard braggart Conall Cernach, who claimed that he slept every night with the head of a slain Connachtman under his knee; but every man who looked empty-socketed from Cruachan's posts had found that Maeve, and her father before her, were not to be defeated.

Ailill set his trophies where he pleased. Some were mounted along the causeways leading over Cruachan's ditch to watch whoever came in or out, and those he was proudest of adorned the interiors of the royal halls of Connacht, but this ring was only for heads taken by the Cruachain rulers themselves. Silently the heads watched, silently guarded, silently pondered their bone-hole sight of what lay beneath the small round houses of baking and brewing, the larger houses where warriors and servants slept, and the open ring of polished and carven tree-trunks to the west between the Black Boar's Furrows, where the Samhain offerings were made and the gods and dead called every year to feast among the living.

'How long will Senchán take to get here?' Maeve wondered.

The chief Druid of Cruachan was hale and hearty despite his years, but seldom hastened, save when a propitious hour must be heeded at once. He would not leap to her call like a hound, and even Maeve knew better than to gainsay his word. Senchán had taught Maeve since she was a golden-haired child sitting on his sturdy knee and begging for stories, and always been her staunchest supporter, protecting her time and again from the Ulster druid Cathbad's magics and deceits. Surely he would come as a strong ally, true to his office's pride, but more than willing to help?

So: a very little time for swift-running Mac Roth to reach Senchán's oak-grove; then, if the Druid was in his hut or the holt nearby, a fair length of time for him to walk to Cruachan. Senchán would not be seeking herbs or visions in the further mountains on the day of his queen's return, Maeve was sure, unless there were an hour of might that he must heed.

"O queen," Lochu said, breaking Maeve's thoughts like a clay pot beneath a hammer, "the household goods are laid out and reckoned; will you hear the word of your stewards?"

Maeve looked at the two great loads of goods spread out upon the ground as a merchant would spread his wares at a fair, save that no merchant could have hoped to match the wealth of Connacht's rulers. Her stewards Scenb and Rann stood beside them, two large swag-bellied men with graying hair. They, and their brother Fodail, had served her father, and Maeve knew she could trust them.

"O queen, O king," Scenb said. "We have counted and weighed and valued. by the gods of the Cruachain, there is not one pin's difference between the goods of Queen Maeve and King Ailill."

Fodail nodded his heavy greybeard head. "No Druid could tell you truer than we, who have tallied your possessions year after year, and set them in their places in Cruachan after each Lughnasa."

Ailill laughed. "Are you satisfied, my wife? It seems to me that the honors are even between us."

Maeve looked at the gathered throng. The warriors and their wives in their bright cloaks of interwoven colors, the servants in their plain well-dyed tunics, the common folk in their homespun of grey and brown and white, brightened here and there with a strip of colorful embroidery or a tunic of faded yellow or green. "I do not see our treasures of gold, nor our fine cloth of many colors and checks and stripes, nor our clothing of wool and linen and silk. Nor have the weapons we own been counted up, neither javelins nor swords nor bronze-rimmed shields."

Lochu looked up at the sky. The bright shafts of sunlight had faded to a faint golden glow over the near fields; the green of the farther fields, and the low dark mountains beyond, were shadowed and muted by a drift of heavy purple-gray cloud misting the land beneath it with scattered grey veils of rain.

"O queen," the bondsmaid murmured, "perhaps it were best if we laid out the cloth within the hall."

"Go and do that. You yourself will gather my cloth and clothing and treasures. Be certain that not one thread of silk, nor linen, nor even the coarsest hemp escapes your gaze, nor the tiniest bronze pin." Maeve touched the smooth gleaming bronze of the bondsmaids collar; a collar easily mistaken for the torc of a high-born woman; it was no little thing to be in the service of the queen of Connacht. "Understand me, Lochu: I will not lose to any man."

Proud and self-contained as Lochu usually was, now the bondsmaid flinched slightly, a look of fear shimmering across her round face like heat wavering up from a fire.

"As you say, my queen."

"As for this," Maeve said, waving her hand at the piles of drinking vessels and cauldrons and gear. "if it has all been reckoned rightly, then take everything to its place again. Hasten, before the rain drenches it all! And do not neglect to grease the iron against rust afresh; the grass is wet."

Two tables were hastily cleared inside, and the heaping began again. The shining shields, painted red and blue, gold and black, around their plates of figured bronze and bright-scoured iron were taken down from the walls; javelins and thrusting-spears with their elaborately shaped bronze butts were lined up, and swords and daggers laid out, each beside its carven or metal-mounted sheath. Ailill's scabbard was tasseled with speckled gold, his sword-grip wound about with twisted gold wire; but Maeve's was adorned likewise, and though her grip, being smaller, bore less gold, the little curved arms and legs and head-pommel were set with fine red garnets gleaming like great blood-drops.

Both blades were Gaulish-forged, wrought with layer on layer of soft iron and hard-cutting steel; Maeve's was the lighter, but bent the further to spring back undamaged. The huge fair-haired brothers Braen and Láréne stood guard where Fodail weighed out the gold and silver and bronze treasures, looking sternly at any hands stealing too near. Maeve could not help her pride: here was proof of their swiftness in trade, goods from fabled Rome and beyond; but more worthy of pride was the best of the plunder from the other provinces of Ireland.

She and Ailill were open-handed: no man who shed blood for Connacht went home without at least a pair of gold earrings for his wife or gold buckles for his shoes; but the plunder-portion of king and queen befitted their state. The Leinstermen mined their gold, and the men of Munster their silver: through trade and raid, it came to Connacht, and now it was laid out here, glimmering on the table like the sunlight-burning surface of a lake broken into an hundred shining ripples by a leaping silver shoal of fish.

"Good health, Queen Maeve of Cruachan; the blessings of gods and men upon thee," a deep voice rumbled beside her. Maeve concealed her start, turning to look upon Connacht's eldest Druid.

Senchán was broad-built and middling-tall, his shock of curly white hair and beard bushing around bright blue eyes and a lumpy nose, his skin brown and wrinkled as a walnut. He clasped Maeve's wrist in greeting with an oak-hard hand, gnarled and calloused from fifty years of wandering outdoors to gather herbs and speak with the gods and síde and spirits of wood and water. Although the swell of his wide belly pressed against his white linen robe, there was still more than enough strength in the ancient Druid's heavy shoulders to grasp a sacrificial ram by its horns and hold it for the knife, or to knock in a bull's head with a sledgehammer.

Most often Maeve saw him smiling; he was not smiling now.

"I had already turned towards Cruachan fort to greet queen and king when young Mac Roth came like a deer pursued by wolves, saying you had need of me," Senchán went on. "I see he spoke truly."

"Can you tell me what will come of this?" Maeve asked.

She had learned to speak and sing as she had learned to spin and cast spears, to embroider and to lift a shield: it was shame for a child of royal birth to be tongue-tied and scant of words or weak of voice. Yet now it took all her skill to keep from sounding like a silly village girl asking who would be her husband. Senchán breathed deeply, closing his eyes and turning his bearded face upwards, as though to look past the thatch and the smoke darkening the hall's high peak.

"Much," he answered. "A red rain over a host; plunder and triumph, heads hanging on sword-belts and chariots shattered and the wailing of women. I see the eagles that screamed over Cruachan síd ten years ago; two sea-beasts gashing each other in the water, two stags locking horns, two warriors hewing flesh from each other and blood spraying all the land. I see two phantoms, one dark and one pale, gaze and touch alike in terror, and hear them keening in voices no living man ever raised. Two dragons twist in the snowy sky, and fall into snowflakes, each flake the same, broken into two and fighting against itself until one gains victory, over and over, until every province of Ireland is reddened with that blood. There is a doom upon. Síd below and fort above; there is a doom upon the land about, a fate laid upon the hour when love becomes battle. If you triumph, it will not be without great trial and great cost; neither drúi nor fili will find victory easy to weigh in the end. Even the bards will find little lasting treasure in this clash of heroes, though they are usually the surest to win reward when the mighty join battle."

Maeve waited, but Senchán said no more, though he stood staring up beneath his closed lids and breathing with the deep steadiness of a sleeping man. At last she ventured, "That is much to spring from a matter such as this."

"Aye," Senchán murmured. His eyes slowly opened, blue irises rolling back down into the blind whites.

"The greatest often springs from the smallest. If Nes had not, in a girl's sportiveness, asked Cathbad what the passing hour was good for, Conchobar would never have been conceived, and a great deal of trouble saved. Although," the old Druid added, his bright eyes glittering like wind-ruffled water, "I have never been sure that Cathbad would have told that truth if Nes had not been the prettiest girl in Emain Macha, and no other nearby who might begot a king upon her. Had she been hook-nosed and hunchbacked, I think she would have heard that it was a good hour to spin and keep her gaze to the ground. Even when we studied in Alba," Senchán mused on, "Cathbad always was something of a sneak. He never lied about his divinations, but sometimes he was scanty with the truth."

Maeve shuddered in revulsion. She remembered Conchobar's chief Druid all too clearly: tall and gauntly thin, dark-dyed hair sleeked down tight to a snake-narrow head, and harsh bony fingers pinching at her thighs when it first became clear that she was pregnant. Cathbad, Maeve thought, had taught his kingly son much the worst of his ways towards women.

"Do you see Ailill trying to raise a host against me?" She asked, pitching her words beneath the babble of the hall so that no other could hear.

"I do not know," Senchán answered in the same low tone. "I dipped into the lake to catch a frog, and fastened my fingers on the tail of a water-horse. This contest shall be over in the next few days; but what springs from it...that must wait until the Samhain divinations, if more has not made itself clear by then. Now," he said more loudly, "you have asked me to judge. Let some of these strong men move aside to let a feeble old Druid near enough to see what he should be judging.."

Maeve snorted softly at the Druid's words; he belied them himself by vigorously plying the polished golden oak of his thick forked staff to clear his pathway. Maeve and Ailill's foster-son Etarcomol turned with an upraised fist, but dropped it when he saw the Druid, moving hastily away. The men who were quicker of thought or luckier got out of Senchán's way before he could prod or thump them. If a Druid were annoyed, the blows of his staff could deal far worse than bruises: even the excitement of the contest was not enough to drive that simple prudence out of mind.

"There is twice the weight of gold in this torc of the queen's that there is in the one about Ailill's neck, for the king's is hollow beaten metal, and this is solid twisted wire," Scenb was saying.

Fodail shook his head. "Weight alone is not all worth. Look at Ailill's torc, how leaves and vines twine it in cunning raised spirals, every fingernail's-breadth carefully textured by the smith's tiny hammers, while the knobs on the ends are all covered with the finest filigree.

Few fairer pieces have ever been seen in Eriu; the craft and the beauty of it are worth more than weight. Yet it is light, that is true, and the terminals on the queen's torc are also finely wrought with little serpents and coils of wire," he added hastily under Maeve's gaze. "It is a hard thing to judge, indeed."

Etarcomol's raucous laugh rang out over the buzzing babble of talk. "Hard to judge, when you would please both contestants," the young man shouted. Maeve frowned. Neither she nor Ailill had found a way to curb their fosterling tongue, and as he had grown into his height and dark arrogant good looks, he had gotten steadily more insolent. Still, she reminded herself, we taught him the skill with a sword to stand up to the challenges he provokes; and he is loyal beneath his words.

Senchán turned about to stare at him. "The truth," the old Druid said mildly, "is often hard to find, and should be pleasing to all, though it is surprising how often that is not the case. if you are studying to be a second Bricriu, with a tongue sharp enough to split a rock in two, you should not be surprised if someday it is you yourself whom your tongue has split into pieces."

The young man flushed and turned away. If he replied, it was too soft for Maeve to hear and Senchán ignored it, looking at the torc in Scenb's hand and the one about Ailill's neck. He raised a bushy eyebrow to the king, who twisted the terminals apart and handed the hinged gold neck ring to him. "Lighter than I thought," the Druid said, weighing Ailill's collar against Maeve's.

"If a contract were being paid, it would be set by weight alone; but this is a work of great beauty indeed: there are not many who would sell it for thrice its weight in gold. In fairness, I must say they are matched."

A few mutters growled here and there at Senchán's words. Men who had lost their bets, Maeve suspected, but none would question a Druid, although she might curse his fairness. Why had he not kept to the letter of the law? Her wren gave a worried chirp, pecking softly at her right ear. Maeve drew her belt-knife and sliced a piece of wheaten bread from a half-eaten round loaf, breaking it up in her fingers and alternately holding up small pieces for her bird and giving them to her marten to take in its paws and nibble.

Her restlessness had spread to the animals; after a few pecks, the wren rose chirping to circle the rafters, dropping a splotch of lime before it came back to her hand, and she could feel the marten scrabbling a tangle into her hair. Only Baiscne sat still and steady beside Maeve. The black wolfhound's head leaned warm against her hip, and she ruffled his coarse fur with her fingertips. Senchán stood back, leaving most of the judgement to the stewards, but stepping in when they came to points they could not unravel.

Gold and silver, bronze and copper: Maeve and Ailill were matched as they had been in household goods, and the same with the bolts of cloth and fine-stitched clothes. Purple, blue, black, green, and yellow; plain grey and many-colored; yellow-brown, checked, and striped: the dyes and the weaves were measured against each other, silk against silk and wool against wool, the beauty of the embroidery submitted to Senchán's eyes; and all were even. The Druid took longer over the weapons, querying Fergus now and again: the long training that a Druid underwent from boyhood seldom left time to learn war-craft. A few Druids fought, but they were rare; and had Senchán cared for sword and spear and shield, he would have been heir to rule rather than wisdom.

"Once more I must judge you matched," the Druid said at last, thumping his staff on the ground. "Maeve, Ailill, the sun is setting. Will you give over, and shrug out of your knot with the nightfall?"

Maeve looked at her husband's grin. "I have proven that what you said this afternoon was wrong, that you did not and do not bring more wealth to this wedding than I. Is that clear enough?"

Ailill laughed. "We have not yet counted cattle. I brought one-third of the great royal herd of Leinster with me, and they have grown strong and many; my sheep surge into the meadow like a frothing sea of white wool, and my swine have eaten out half your woodlands. I think you are some way from proving my words wrong yet, wife."

"We shall see!" Maeve snapped. "Tell our herders to drive our cattle from the hills, our sheep from the mountains, our swine from the woods. Then we shall know which of us has the greater wealth."

"As you wish," Ailill said, spreading his big hands as their warriors cheered and stomped and laughed, new bets flying afresh. Senchán looked troubled. She wondered if he had tilted his judgement to bring it out evenly, yet she had watched each decision herself: she could not challenge even one of his statements. 'What does he want to avert?'

"Then take your struggle up on the morrow," the old Druid said. "This night you shall feast together and bed together, Queen and King in Cruachan. Let the harp sound for the gladness of heroes, song for the joy of warriors; let any man who strives against another do so without edge or point of sword, for this night is ill-omened for the shedding of blood."

He took Maeve's hand in his own horn-hard paw, placing it in Ailill's and leading the two of them to their low silk-cushioned couch at the southern side of the hall as though he had just made sacrifice and called blessing for their wedding.

"And now," Senchán said softly, "will you give an old Druid some refreshment, or has your quarrel driven all memory of hospitality out of your minds?"

Maeve blushed furiously for shame, that she had been so eager for Senchán's counsel as to forget his proper greeting. Even in the flickering flame-light, she could see Ailill's cheeks flushing beneath their dusting of golden freckles. "Rann!" Ailill roared. "Bring a fair goblet of white bronze bound with gold, and fill it with our finest mead; to welcome this wise Druid on our harvest-time homecoming."

"And bring the fairest-adorned plate of silver, with slices from the boar's loin and the finest wheaten bread; let me thus welcome my old friend Senchán to my harvest-time homecoming," Maeve added.

Ailill had not outdone her in wealth that day; he would not outdo her in generosity that night.

The homecoming feast went on late into the night. The harpers sang, bronze strings ringing sweetly through the hall; Dubthach and Eochan wrestled until Eochan's shoulder popped from its joint and Maeve had to pull it to rights again, but, though the warriors of Cruachan emptied their share of mead, and ale-vats that night, none drank so much as to forget the Druid's warning.

Maeve herself drank deeply, but found no easing. Her head stayed clear with worry and foreboding, and several times when she had meant to empty her gilded horn, she had stopped instead with the vessel halfway to her mouth, trying to remember and reckon the last tallies she had been told of her sheep and cattle. Despite Senchán's advice, Maeve did not offer Ailill the warm friendship of her thighs that night: if he could scorn her straight after lovemaking as he had that afternoon, then let him go with none but bondsmaids and village girls to sate him! As for herself, but as she looked about the raucous horde of their warriors, she did not see a single one who pleased her.

Though the rath's floor was strewn with sweet herbs, heaped with bales of fresh-scented hay for sleeping, the men's sweat reeked stronger than those pleasant smells, whisking her back to her first night in Ulster with the warriors of the Red Band laughing and cheering Conchobar for the blood he had splattered on his young wife's sheets. 'That was long ago, Maeve told herself, and I am no longer that miserable girl: men have given me more than enough pleasure in the years since to make up for that pain'.

Still, the beard-bristling faces about her looked too coarse for her liking; her skin prickled hotly, the silk-softened linen of her under dress chafing her like rough wool. She wanted to lash out, to snap at all of them, and did not know why. They were good men all, and more on her side than Ailill's. She drained the last sweet drops of mead from her horn, banging it down on the table, and rose to go to bed.

Maeve did not notice the soft footsteps keeping pace with her own until she swung open the wooden door to the royal bedchamber, and found that Finnabair was in her way. "What is it you want?"

"I would speak with you, Mother," the girl said firmly.

Maeve was in no temper for her daughter's fancies, but she beckoned her in anyway. Lochu was pattering about, replacing the charred rush lights with fresh; Finnabair waited until the bondsmaid had gone out before she said, "Mother, why are you making so much of this?"

"I told you already. Your father insulted me and mine, and challenged me for the right of true rule here: how else should I answer?"

Finnabair shook her head, white-gold hair rippling down her back like a sheet of pale silk.

"Save such words for the men in the hall, Mother. They may butt heads and bellow like bulls, but you have told me often enough that women should know better. There must be more reason to it than this, or else those who dwell below Cruachan fort have stolen your wits.

Do you really think that, even were Father proved to have brought more to the wedding than you, he could or would usurp your right?"

Maeve sighed deeply, her breath fluttering the little golden flames of the rush-lights on their tables. In the dim light, she might have been looking upon her younger self; her heart weakened, like a wickerwork dam giving way where the sticks had softened through in the water.

"Not usurp, but destroy," Maeve murmured. "I was born to be Connacht's daughter and queen; thus I was named Maeve, the land's goddess in flesh. Yet in Ulster…"

Maeve fell silent. In all her years as queen of Connacht, she had never spoken of how it was to be Conchobar's bride in Emain Macha. That was long behind her: she had hoped those memories buried, but now she could feel them pressing up in her again, harsh and hard as rocks working out of the earth to jut from a newly plowed field. Then, Maeve had longed for a woman's comfort and not been given it; now, her daughter said quietly, "You have never spoken to me of Ulster, Mother, save that I know how you hate its king."

"Conchobar forced me," Maeve said reluctantly. The words came scratchy from her mouth, like old bones dug up with the dirt still on them. "I had meant to give myself to him as a wife; he forced me as a slave so that I bled and wept every night for the first month, wretched as any new-taken bondsmaid. More so than most, for I had hope of love at first."

Conchobar had stood a full head above her own height, and was so fair…hair shining like polished gold in the sunlight, a close-cropped golden beard shimmering bright along his face; eyes like blue crystal and the strength and grace of a leaping stag and a voice as rich and sweet as the deepest string of a harp.

Maeve had drawn in her breath sharply at the first sight of his beauty, her homesick tears forgotten as she praised Lugh that such a man could be wedded to her.

"He was fair to look on, yes, the very dream of a true king. I expected kisses and caresses; I was a little frightened at first, having been untouched before my wedding, but..." Her heart had pounded beneath the layers of silk that draped her. Her breaths coming swift, when the two of them were alone in the flower-garlanded bedchamber at Emain Macha.

She had sipped the sweet mead and giggled nervously, looking up at him

Through her lashes, and he had knocked the cup from her hand, hissing, "No woman laughs at me. Take off your clothes." Startled, she had drawn herself up and said,

"I am your wife, not your bondsmaid. Take off your own, and then perhaps..." Then Conchobar had wrenched her arm, tearing her dress from her.

Trained at sword-fighting, Maeve had known how to slip aside from the power and weight of grown men in shield-presses, but this ferocious grasp was different: she had felt suddenly helpless as a small child against his huge strength, weak with fear and shock. Conchobar had flung her down on the bed hard enough to knock the breath from her body, then, as she lay gasping, shoved her legs apart and himself in, twisting her wrists in a painful grip so she could not wriggle away from the ripping pain of his cock stabbing her dry parts. The blood had made it easier, but he had still cursed her as he thrust. Finished, he had yanked the bed cover from beneath her, stamping into the hall to brandish the sign of his victory without a single word to her.

"He was as brutal as any man still fired from hard battle," Maeve said at last. "And a bondsmaid will get sympathy from her sisters who know her misery, but the women of Ulster hissed from the corners of their mouths in bitter jealousy.

They would not give me salve for the pain between my legs. Instead, as soon as Conchobar went to take the Ulster king's first night with another man's new-wedded bride, I found nettles in my bed. The next day they laughed at me and asked if I burned and itched so grievously for the king that I could not sit still for a moment."

Finnabair stared wide-eyed at her mother. "I never dreamed..." she whispered. "I would never have thought that you could be handled so."

"Nor had I, till it happened. There was nothing I could do, alone in a strange fort with no friend, no ally, not even my own serving maids. Ulster is a men's land: their women fight among themselves the more bitterly for having nothing save their men to take pride in. Yet even then, I was still Maeve of Cruachan. Conchobar would give me no finger's length of rule in Ulster, fearful that if I got a crumb of power or freedom, I might let another man taste that sweet honey that never lessens however often it is shared. He could not break me: I knew my land was my own, as truly as the blood in my veins; that I would come back, and have all that I had been torn from. Even bearing Cormac, and, Danu help me, though Conchobar's seed sired him, I loved him from the moment I felt him squirm beneath my heart, even then, I knew who I was and must be, if not Conchobar's brood-mare.

I mourned my first son as I suckled him, because we would have to part so soon. I could not have left him," Maeve found herself saying, the words trickling out against her will like a few last drops of milk from her breasts,

"Save for what Senchán said on my wedding day: that I should find a love in Ulster and leave him, but that he would come back to soothe my tears, and all be well between us."

"Cormac did come back to us," Finnabair murmured.

"Aye, he did, though none save a Druid could have guessed at it. It is sure that my babe was the only man in Ulster I could have truly loved then..." Maeve swallowed hard.

" What has that to do with this?" Finnabair asked after a little time. "Father is nothing like the king of Ulster. Has he ever sought to force his will upon you? Or do you think he would?"

"Even the best-known man is a mystery. Yet, it is not Ailill's will that matters now. If I had let his words pass unchallenged, if he should prove to have the true right of rule, then it does not matter whether I speak before the folk, or he does, or his fool of a horse-groom. It is a matter of myself: this thing that might seem so little, this quarrel that seems so foolish to others, but if I am not true queen of Connacht, then I am not Maeve of Cruachan. The few light words of a man who meant no harm will have destroyed what Conchobar could not break with his cock nor his fists nor any of the harshness with which he sought to rule me. Do you understand, my daughter?"

"It still seems pointless pride to me," Finnabair said slowly.

Maeve looked down at Finnabair's pale tender-cheeked face, so like her own, yet with her clear blue gaze uncomprehending, as if the síd-folk had made a changeling with eyes of silver-backed glass and skull filled with peat-moss to set in Maeve's place. "You do not understand. Let me tell you, then.

There is something about a woman's power that sets men on, whether they be like Conchobar or like Ailill. Fearful or sure, cruel or kind, a man can accept another man as his better and be proud companion and second. Have you not heard the Ulstermen boast of Cú Chulainn?, What man will speak so of a woman? And after I divorced Conchobar, he went to great trouble to catch me alone."

Finnabair's mouth opened. "Did he...?"

"Oh, yes," Maeve said bitterly. "Such a man, to overpower and rape a fifteen year-old girl. He had to prove that I could not escape him through law, that he could take me at his will."

"Was this known? Did he not have to pay compensation?"

"I told no one. I felt dirtied, ashamed. It seemed to me that if I spoke, that if others knew what he had done to me, I would never be free of him in my life. I have never gone alone without weapons since, even when I only step into the bushes to piss." Maeve paused, breathing deeply until she could feel the ragged edges of her throat knitting to smoothness again.

"Ailill has never taken a woman by force in his life, not even a bondsmaid Yet, here at the heart of my power, he could not keep from boasting his own rule over me, and if I had not challenged his words, it would have made them true. Perhaps if I had come to womanhood more softly, I might have been content to do as other women, guiding the bulls where I will as they bellow themselves masters of the pasture. To let all that I have fought for so long, all that upheld me to fight, be stolen away with a few laughing words. It is the worse that the matter seems so small, that it will mean little to Ailill however it turns out.

Indeed, it is not the great blows that do the worst harm, for they call up strength to withstand them: a foe can be fought. Rather, it is the littlest things, not worth raising a hand against, that gnaw the strength of the heart until nothing is left but a crumbling shell of bark, ready to totter. Do you understand?"

Finnabair said nothing, but the beginnings of tears gleamed in her gilt-lashed eyes. "Think," Maeve said gently, "of how matters went with Deirdre at the last. She endured it when Conchobar slew her beloved Noisu and his brothers; she even endured going back to Conchobar, and far worse suffering with him, I am sure, than I did. Do you remember what happened to her?"

"I have heard that after a time, Conchobar asked her whom, besides him, she hated most, and she said Eogan mac Durthacht, whose spear had drunk Noisu's life. He proposed to give her to that man for a year, and then reclaim her."

"Even that she was steeled to endure," Maeve said.

"She could not fight, she knew only to trust in men, for Conchobar had her raised to know nothing else. Yet many a woman, or man doing great deeds under the Morrígan's bloody eyes on the battlefield might envy her strength, for all she proved able to bear. On the way to Eogan's dun, riding in Conchobar's chariot with her hands and feet bound. Conchobar laughed at her. She had seen her lover slain; been beaten, raped, abused as no one should suffer, and borne it all.

Yet when he said, 'This is good, Deirdre. Between myself and Eogan, you are like a ewe between two rams'

Then, for those few words, she flung herself head first from the chariot and broke her skull on a rock. Men wear their pride outside like crabs, all armor and crash. A woman's may be a single hard core, hidden too deep for any but herself to guess at it; but when that core is gone."

"I wish," Finnabair said, her voice the delicate pipe of the little girl-child she had been before her breasts flowered, "that all of this had never come to pass."

"So do I, my daughter," Maeve answered.

"Does Father know what Conchobar did to you? If you could tell him, if you could make him see what his teasing has brought back to you, I know he would withdraw."

"Out of pity?" Maeve asked sharply. "That would be the worse: it would make the victory Conchobar's at the last. I overcame. How many women, handled as I was, learn pleasure in the bodies of men afterwards? I taught myself that, for I would not let Ulster's king spoil my womanhood, any more than take my pride. Should I now make myself helpless before Ailill by depending on his good heart, though he is truly good-hearted, to restore what he has taken, to let my self be but a gift from his hands? That would be a greater loss than to challenge and fail."

Trembling, Finnabair reached towards her mother; Maeve embraced her daughter gently. 'I have never spoken to her thus. Is it cruel, to lay such a burden on her small shoulders. She is sixteen, well of an age to wed. Better she learn hard wisdom by listening than by feeling it beaten into her stroke by stroke, without reason or explanation until she can winnow them the pain. Or maybe, since she has a quiet spirit, and more sense at sixteen than I had at twenty-six, none of this will touch her more than need be; perhaps she will pass more easily through womanhood's trials than I'.

At last Maeve let her daughter go. "Good night, and sleep well. Do not think too grievously on these matters: things should be set right in the next few days."

"The gods grant that it be so," Finnabair replied gravely, and bade her mother goodnight.

Maeve stood with her hand on the open door, looking around the hall. She did not see Ailill, likely he had gone off with another woman. If he brings fleas back to me, I shall scrub him clean with a horse comb! She thought, trying to rekindle a spark of anger to light the gaping emptiness inside her. Maeve felt hollow, weak, as though her courses had come and passed in a single cramping, painful rush. For years she had not spoken of her time in Ulster, nor thought upon it save fleetingly.

Seeing Fergus' face across the room, as she had seen it then, he had only grown more handsome with age, in his craggy way, sent a curious pang through her, like the twinge of waking from a familiar nightmare. Maeve remembered coming in tears from her first night with Ulster's king: Fergus had spoken kindly and she had looked bleary eyed at him, wondering if he might be the love the Druid had prophesied.

I am Maeve of Cruachan, queen in my own fort, Maeve reminded herself. Fergus is no longer Conchobar's man, and he had best have forgotten my shame'. Defiantly she walked over to him.

"I thought you had gone to bed, my queen," the Ulster exile said, returning her smile. Him, weathered skin shone ruddy in the torchlight. He had drunken well, as a man ought at a great ruler's board, but he was some way from being drunk.

"Not yet." Maeve had only to lift her hand for Lochu to put her gilded drinking horn, brimming with mead, into it. She nodded; the serving maid filled Fergus' cup, and they sat down together.

"The feasting is fine here in Cruachan," Fergus said, his eyes lingering on her.

"I should hope so," she replied. "It is always a joy, coming back to my home after Lughnasa."

Fergus took a swallow of mead, but Maeve could see the dark down turning of his lips in his close-trimmed beard.

"Save for your quarrel with King Ailill."

Maeve made herself smile, hiding the trembling of her lips with a sip from her own vessel, and swallowed hard.

"It is only a matter of pillow-words," she said, as lightly as if she could believe it. "Hardly something for a man such as yourself to take to heart."

Fergus shook his head. "Once I took a matter of words and sovereignty lightly, as a game to slip a Druid's prophecy. We all laughed when I pretended to give the seat and name of Ulster's king over to young Conchobar, I most of all, making jest as if it were Samhain and he the amadan joking upon the throne. When the year was up, the folk of Ulster, yes, even men I had trusted, said 'What Fergus sold, let it stay sold; what Conchobar bought, let it stay bought.' And so he is king of Ulster still, and I, am here, and my son in his cairn, because of it." He stared moodily into his silver cup.

"Why did you stay in Ulster afterwards?" Maeve asked.

She had wondered for years what could have kept Fergus in the kingdom from which he had been tricked. It was no surprise that he was an exile now; what amazed her was how a man like Conchobar could have held his loyalty so long. Before she would not have dared to ask. Now, it seemed to her that she had to know.

'Am I readying for my own defeat?' Maeve wondered, chilled in spite of the thick warmth of fires and bodies. Still, she asked, "How could you, having been treated so shabbily? And when you knew what Conchobar was?" She would have fallen silent then, but her speech with Finnabair had weakened the gates of her mind.

"You were the one man in Emain Macha," Maeve whispered, "who sought to lighten my sorrows, instead of laughing to worsen them. Why did you stay, when you knew?"

"Somewhat from pride: though beaten, I would not slink away like a dog. Maybe I hoped to regain my kingdom someday, though I knew what the Druids had prophesied. Even in his earliest youth, Conchobar was the image of a king, better in fighting than any save myself, or, later, Cú Chulainn; to look upon him was to know.

Well, you saw him yourself. Then, later, I came to see that he was a king worth serving. The folk of Ulster willingly allowed him such powers and freedoms as they had never allowed me, nor any other man. Though I no longer had the pride of rule, there was the pride of the Red Branch. Such a fiann: brothers bound.

The finest fighters in Eriu. Though I had lost my kingship, it was worth remaining to be part of such a thing." Fergus reached out as though to take Maeve's hand, then drew his arm back.

She recognized the gesture: he had done the same in Ulster once, reaching to comfort her, then pulling back before Conchobar could see and take it amiss.

"You could not have understood then, but maybe you have seen since what it means for men to win each other's acclaim, to trust all to each other in fighting and come through together, proven brothers in blood and steel?"

Maeve nodded slowly. She had been a battle-queen for twenty-five years; she knew well how pride and danger knit men together, and the bards had sung more songs of Fergus' prowess in the Red Branch than they ever had while he held the rule of Ulster.

"They are my brothers yet," he went on, staring off into the drifting veils of fire lit smoke as they stirred and curled about the moving bodies of those men who were still awake and walking about. "Though I am exiled, they are still my brothers by blood shed and shared, and Cú Chulainn my son of the heart. I would not have left them by any choice."

Though Maeve tried to hold her face still, Fergus must have seen her thoughts then. He turned back to her, his remote melancholy eagle-gaze softening.

"Maeve," Fergus murmured, so quietly that only they themselves could hear, "I know your memories are far from mine, and how you suffered in Emain Macha. I wish I had been able to ease your sorrows then, and I can not expect you to understand the fellowship and glory that I felt there, or think on what Conchobar made us, when all you saw was a man who, whose hour of conception made him a great king and leader, but a wretched husband."

He paused, draining his silver cup and drinking deeply again when one of the bondsmaids refilled it.

"I have lain in the pangs of Ulster as well." Fergus was staring at the table now, as though the feathering grain of the oaken planks were ogham lines spelling out some deep secret. He could not meet Maeve's gaze as he spoke, and his tone was flat and dead, like the voice of a broken slave who was once a warrior.

"How could Conchobar, young and fierce to prove himself in battle, not wish to prove himself likewise to a girl who might someday see him curled and moaning in the agonies of a birthing woman when he should be leading a host upon the war field? Even as a maid, you were sharp-tongued, and proud of the skills you had learned from your father's war band."

"Conchobar laughed when I offered to face him with a sword," Maeve whispered.

"What might you have said, when you could lift a sword in Ulster's need and the king could not? No fighting man of Ulster has not suffered what no man should know, aching breasts, womb tearing from within, and known that others had seen him shitting and moaning in the straw, unmanned most deeply at the very moment when he most needed to be a man. Blame Macha for the curse she set upon us, for I know, if no other in this fort does, that you understand how it is to overcome shame."

Maeve matched Fergus' draught, setting her hand on his forearm. Now she meant only to comfort, but she could feel the thick muscles swelling with tightness beneath her touch, as though he would flinch, but was unwilling to pull away.

"Maybe I do," she admitted. "Yet you are an Ulsterman, and you have never treated a woman as Conchobar has."

"I was not destined from the hour of conception to be the greatest king in Eriu, the leader of the best war band ever sworn, but, for all that, unable to rise from the pains of child bed to defend my land." Fergus' mouth tightened, and his fingers clenched on the cup, the heavy muscles of his arm writhing beneath Maeve's hand. "I do not excuse Conchobar.

It grieved me to see how he used the women he claimed, and I, in my pride, my joy at the brotherhood of the Red Branch, and my love for my foster son Cú Chulainn when he came, was blind to the knowledge that a man who treats women so could treat men just as ill when they stood in his way.

Until he thrust his sword through my son's body because Deirdre's lover stood behind him, and opened my eyes with that stroke. I; Conchobar betrayed my honor of word and name with the same deceit that brought my son to death at his hand. Yet my battle-brothers still would not see, though their king was proven a betrayer."

Fergus sighed, his hand opening, and for a moment Maeve saw the weight of age sagging his eagle-keen face. "Maeve, I stayed with Conchobar until I could not because I am one who can live well enough, if not wholly content with less than all my will fulfilled.

In my youth, I might have thought that weakness; later, I came to see that it could be strength as well, and if being what I am has not always brought me happiness, at least I have not brought so much sorrow to all those around me as have those who do not know when it may be well to yield to a friend.

If Ulster's king had such wisdom, I would be in Emain Macha yet. I do not know if such counsel can aid you."

He drained his cup and rose. "Good night to you, my queen."

Maeve watched him stride away, broad shoulders swinging. Her warriors gave way before him, though they would jostle each other for place: no man in her troop was unwilling to give Fergus his due as champion, though the Ulster exile took care not to tread on the hem of Ailill's bratt. Her speech with Fergus had made Maeve thoughtful. As Lochu undressed her, Maeve wished that she had asked him to come back with her.

Fergus had the look of a man who needed companionship, and this would have been a good night to have a man in her bed, to take her thoughts from all that the day's doings had churned up in her heart like mud in a roiled pond, and he knows something of how I feel, she thought. He has felt a game turn to destruction around him; he would not take me lightly, nor think that, because I lie beneath him, I have given in to him.

I wish I knew what holds him back. It would be fine to be have a bull that rams through the gate for a change, rather than one that lets his cow lead him about by the long way'.

Until Cormac quickened beneath her heart, Fergus had been Maeve's one brightness in Emain Macha, though then it was a girl's silly hope. As queen, she had flirted with him lazily since he came to Connacht. She could almost smell the desire on him when she came near, a hint of faint dark muskiness that matched the widening depth of his black pupils when she looked him closely in the eyes.

Perhaps it was time to tell him straight out. Maeve shifted gently beneath the covers, breasts nuzzling against the soft linen and thighs stroking silkily together as she slipped gently into sleep, thinking about strong forceful hands on her hips and grey eyes looking into her own and wavy chestnut hair mingling dark-ruddy with her own torrents of gold.

It took several days for the herds to be assembled on the fields below Cruachan síd. The lowing of the cattle and baaing of the sheep sounded endlessly, like wind and sea booming through a cliff cave in the stormy winters of the western shore. Some of the wide green meadows were white and grey with sheep covering them like a low thick jostling fog, and others surged dark and ruddy with the shining backs of well fed cattle.

Half a day's walk from the fort, the swine of the queen and king filled the woodlands so that there was no hunting nor any sound of stags bugling, only the low muttering grunts and rustling of the pigs rooting through fallen leaves for the year's first mast. There were fewer eager watchers for the counting of the herds than there had been for the weighing of the goods, because the village folk were busy at the hard labor of harvest.

Maeve and Ailill's homecoming feast at Cruachan could not give more than a day's reprieve, with the clouds scudding over the sky and the brief gusts of rain always threatening to become storms that would soak and spoil the sheaves.

The Connacht warriors made enough noise for more than their number, shouting back and forth among the sheep and cattle as they drank and made their bets.

They were all skilled raiders, and each man thought himself the best judge of which beasts he would fight for the chance to drive away.

"That great ram of the queen's is worth one of the fairest bondsmaids by himself!" Oll shouted to his brother Oichne.

"Which one?" Oichne shouted back. "Ask anyone: Maeve has her choice of all the best rams!"

Maeve smiled: no lie or insult in that! Looking away from the two brothers; fine men themselves, their well-built bodies clad in close-fitting tunics of blue-green herringbone wool and the silver torcs about their necks setting off their white skin and black hair and deep blue eyes, her gaze lingered on Fergus. Oll and Oichne were sky bright mountain lakes; chestnut-haired Fergus in his gold-embroidered crimson cloak was a sun of darkening fire, and Maeve could not help staring at him a little longer than she had meant to, or perhaps no longer than she had meant to.

Fergus turned his head and saw Maeve watching. The narrow white scar on his cheek sprang out more sharply against his flush, but then his mouth curled into a slow smile. Maeve's own smile widened in answer. She was about to take a step towards the Ulsterman when his eyes flickered sideways towards Ailill, who stood laughing at some jest, and he looked abruptly away from her.

Maeve shook her head angrily. This is not Ulster, Fergus! She thought. You know the tale of what wedding gift I asked from my husband. What is it that puts such a man as you in fear?' For all Oll's praise, Ailill had a ram to match the leader of Maeve's great flock; when their chariot teams and horse-herds were brought in from pasture and paddock, Ailill's equaled Maeve's from that springs last born pony to her finest stallion. The swine were tallied, and Maeve had one great boar, but Ailill had another.

At last it came to the cattle, and there the betting was the fiercest, who would have most and who finest, with other wagers as to whose herds had grown the most by raiding and whose by breeding, and Cormac Mael Foga's son gave Fraech mac Fidag a shallow wound in his left thigh over a bet whose terms they remembered differently after the fact. Maeve and Ailill stood on the man high grassy ring-ridge of the Bull's Fort next to the break in the ring by a shallow pool where the cattle were led in one by one beneath Senchán's gaze.

Now and again the Druid would prod a broad back to see how deep the fat lay, or run his hands over a massive haunch. Senchán had never been on a raid, but it was he who had chosen the offering cattle year upon year, since old Laegaire had died and the Druids of Connacht had named him as the wisest among them. With tempers running so high, Senchán had taken this judgement upon himself, and no one dared to argue.

"That is the last of the cows with calves, and the last of the gelded oxen," the Druid said. "Let us go to the paddocks where the bulls are kept now."

Maeve and Ailill followed him, their two wolfhounds pacing steadily beside them, and the host of their warriors thronged eagerly behind. Each of the bulls had his own enclosure, but Senchán walked in without fear.

"Sa, sa," he crooned to Maeve's black bull, stroking a hand along his horns and looking into his eyes. "You are a fine beast, yes, you need not fear me yet, you have a long life ahead of you, and many calves to sire." Ailill's red bull plunged and snorted until Senchán caught his gaze, then walked over meek as an ox awaiting the harness. So it went again and again; only once did the Druid have even to raise his staff. "Thus far," Senchán said, stepping out of the last paddock, "you are as matched here as elsewhere, with nothing to choose between you. Will you give over now?"

Ailill's grin widened. "I am not done. This is the last of the paddocks, but there is one bull in my herd that we could not drive along, lest good men bleed for forcing him where he did not wish to go.

Come you now, and see if Maeve has anything to equal the White Bull Finnbennach!"

The name went through Maeve like a stroke of lightning, bursting soundlessly in her ears and behind her eyeballs. She drew herself up angrily. "Finnbennach is mine! The calf belongs to the cow, as our laws have always said, and it was to my cow, not yours, that he was born!"

"So he was," Ailill said calmly. "He came over to my herd as soon as he was old enough to know how to mount a heifer, for he would not be ruled by a woman. If you think you can lure him away again, you are welcome to try."

"You would not say that if it were just after Imbolc and the cows coming into season, instead of a moon past Lughnasa," Maeve answered bitterly. Her muscles trembled with the strain of not striking her husband in front of their warriors. Ailill might have meant to cheat her from the beginning, but he would not make her a laughing-stock as well: those mocking words, he would not be ruled by a woman, burned her as if she had squatted to piss in a patch of nettles.

She swallowed hard, as if she were trying to gulp down a rock. "In a matter of law, a Druid may give advice. Senchán, what is the law when a cow bears a calf that goes to another herd?"

The Druid drew a deep breath, looking Maeve in the eye. As soon as he began to speak, the queen knew what he would say. She had heard that regret in his voice only once: when she, suddenly betrothed and about to be wedded at fourteen, had asked him to save her from being sent as peace prize to Ulster.

"The law says that the calf belongs to the cow," Senchán said, but Maeve heard, 'There is nothing I can do to halt this'. "Yet when you drive away the cattle of Ulster, they become your cattle; and if a bull leaves one herd for another and will not go from the second, then he belongs to the owner of the second herd as surely as if he had been taken in a raid. The White Bull Finnbennach belongs to Ailill. Unless you own his match, the king has bested you."

'You must be Conchobar's wife and queen: uphold yourself proudly, for the honor of the Cruachain, Senchán' had said to the young Maeve in that tone of voice; though he had spoken of honor, it had begun her year of shame and misery. Yet even then, the Druid had held out hope: 'If all goes so ill you cannot bear it, and you are willing to set yourself at odds with Ulster, then the law still allows you to divorce your husband, however wrathful he be'. now there was nothing but silence beneath Ailill's genial laughter. The laughter of a man winning a small wager over ale, not of a king winning victory over a land, silence, and the sympathy in Senchán's blue eyes, which was more than Maeve could bear and the White Bull himself, the best of her own herd: how had he so betrayed her?

She thought of her last sight of him: broad back and powerful haunches gleaming like ivory in the summer sun, huge spreading horns dagger sharp, but turned peacefully down as he munched the rich grass.

Maeve had not marked which field he was grazing in, or whose cows he companioned: he had been hers, as Ailill was her consort; all beneath her queenship. She opened her mouth to tell Senchán that Finnbennach was his for the Samhain sacrifices, and shut it again.

'The Bull has stolen even that right from me. Better he had died beneath the Druids' knives last year, better' She might send warriors in secret to shoot the White Bull down, cut him to pieces and cast them in a bog, and let Ailill think that the Bull had deserted the king's herds as he had the queen's. Maeve already knew that would avail her nothing, nor regain her loss. Nor would it even be vengeance, but only spite, and though Maeve knew herself hot-tempered and vengeful, that much was beneath her. She turned her back and walked away even as Ailill called out merrily,

"So Finnbennach is the last piece set on the king's side, and the game is done!"

Maeve strode along furiously to keep from shivering, trying to blow the ember of anger in her cold breast up to a good hot flame. Ailill had played with her, if not from the beginning, then certainly there at the end. His game was not that of king to queen, but of man to woman; the game that Conchobar had played with brute harshness, first with Maeve and then with Deirdre, Ailill played with laughter and good nature. 'If I thought I could pay you back by dragging Fergus behind that hawthorn thicket', Maeve said vengefully to her husband beneath her breath,

'I would have his breeches down and his cock up me faster than a mare's tail can swish away a fly! Before all the gods of the Cruachain, by Brigit and Dagda and Donn of the Underworld, I never thought I would regret wedding a man without jealousy in his heart!'

Head down as if she walked hoodless into the cold teeth of a storm, Maeve did not see Mac Roth until she stamped straight into him. The lean runner staggered from the impact, whirling around ready to fight. Maeve would have welcomed the smack of fist on flesh, the chance to take all her anger out upon a man, any man, but her messenger dropped his hands at once.

"Matters have gone ill," Mac Roth said softly. "May I do aught to aid Maeve of Cruachan?"

"You may..." Maeve was about to snarl that he might spend a week of love-play with a sow. Then she remembered that, of all the men of Connacht, Mac Roth traveled the swiftest and most widely, hearing more news than any traveling bard or satirist.

"Mac Roth. You may indeed aid your queen. I would have you go out, to travel across the land of Eriu, or indeed to Alba if you must, or Gaul or Rome: where-ever you must go, to find me a bull that is the match of Finnbennach."

Mac Roth's little orange mustache twitched, as though he would smile but doubted whether Maeve would bear it yet.

"I know where to find such a bull, and better. In Ulster, in Cuailgne, in the house of Dáire mac Fiachna, dwells the Donn Cuailgne, the Brown Bull of Cuailgne."

Maeve's heart leapt like flames under the bellows. A vast relief washed over her, untangling her limbs like the release of the fiercest love play; she could barely keep her trembling legs upright. "Then go there, Mac Roth!" She cried out gladly.

"Ask Dáire to lend me the Donn Cuailgne for a year. At the end of the year, I'll give him fifty yearling heifers and the Donn Cuailgne back. If the folk of his land think ill of losing their jewel, the Brown Bull, you may offer him this: if he comes with the bull himself, I'll give him a portion of the fine Plain of Ai to match his own lands, and a chariot worth thrice seven bondsmaids, and my own friendly thighs on top of that."

Then Mac Roth did grin at her. "Dáire would be a very great fool to turn down such an offer, and I have never heard that he is a fool. He can be a proud and touchy man, but when bespoken fairly, he is willing to answer fairly. If no phantom whispers evil in his ears, I think that you may count the Donn Cuailgne as good as yours."

"Go to Scenb, and tell him where you are going, and that I say he should provide whatever you need." Maeve drew a silver ring off her left arm and a gold ring off her right. "Take these for yourself, for it is you who shall save the Cruachain from this shame. Hasten now: I would have no moment wasted!" Mac Roth bent the rings tight about his wiry arms and sprang off towards the fort, dashing over the grass with the long legged swiftness of a wolfhound after a hare. Her thighs and belly trembling with relief, Maeve watched him go until she was certain that no tears would flow from her eyes, then turned and walked straight to Ailill, looking proudly up into his face.

"You shall not have long to praise your own wealth above mine," she said. "I have sent for the loan of the Donn Cuailgne, and I have heard it said that he is not only the match of Finnbennach, but his better."

"Ah, well, we shall see," Ailill said. "Meanwhile, it will rain soon. Our herdsmen must take the beasts back from paddock to fields, lest they eat up all the winter's hay before Samhain. I myself would go into a warm and pleasant hall to take my ease. Will you lead me into your hall?"

With the sureness of her victory before her, the whole matter seemed, Maeve did not know how, to shrink and shrink as suddenly as it had grown, like an autumn toadstool sprung suddenly huge, only to wither to dust and slime in the sunlight as soon as it was plucked. Looking back at the last few days, she might have been in the grip of a high fever, or the agony of child bed.

She could remember what was said and done, the ghastly driving fury and misery of her struggle, and yet the pain itself seemed as distant from her as wounds taken by another in a bard's song, her last anger at her husband draining from her like the dregs of beer from a broken vat.

Yet it shook me from my heart outward, Maeve thought. 'How am I so unsure in my strength? Ailill's teasing is the least of fires, quickly kindled and quickly out. This time, it seemed to catch upon a dry peat bog, to smolder and smoke until it burnt the world around me. Still, I have won: the Brown Bull is as good as mine'.

Ailill would never struggle longer than he found diverting, and Maeve could tell he was already bored with the whole affair, and he owed her pleasure now to make up for the annoyance he had given. Once she sat atop him, his thighs clenched tight between hers and his cock hard in her body's grasp, it would drive out the last echoing memory of Conchobar's weight forcing her legs open, her pleasure washing away the faint remembrance of the stabbing pain that had angered her so greatly.

"If you come into my hall, you will not be allowed to take your ease there. It will be hard labor for you, and drops of sweat flowing from your head until you have no more left."

Ailill put his arm about Maeve's waist, caressing the under curve of one breast.

"I've rested soft for too long; such work will do well to harden me." Maeve had spoken soft and teasing, but her husband's voice was loud, and as they began to walk along the muddy road leading into the fort, Maeve saw Fergus looking suddenly away. What is the matter with him? She wondered again. If he would lie with me, why does he not say so instead of blushing like a lad younger than Finnabair?'

For a moment, her desires kindled hot by the days of worry and nights of turning away from Ailill, Maeve imagined calling Fergus to wait his turn outside their chamber and come in to plough her as soon as Ailill had tired. The thought of rising open and aroused from her husband's body to have Fergus tumble her onto her back. In turn was enough to make her thighs loosen warmly as she walked.

If Maeve had never had a man without another waiting in his shadow, it seemed too much. Though she would not forgive Ailill completely until the Donn Cuailgne grazed among her cows, to ask the second man to step into the light before the first one's face. Though Maeve 's body was growing warm and moist already, her nipples tight beneath the sleek crimson silk of her gown, some little seed in her heart was still uneasy. A mushroom might spring up and die in days, but as soon as the autumn rain moistened the mold again, a whole ring of toadstools could stand overnight in its place.

Fedelm

The beds in the school of drúi and fili in Alba are small, narrow, and hard; the students live chiefly on beans and black bread. This, so we are told, teaches us to cast aside the needs of the body for the sake of the soul: we should be nourished by the poetry and tales graven into our heads by day, and think nothing of our rumbling bellies at night. I do not think that any one of us, lying awake in the darkness to the sound of gurgling entrails and loud sleep-farts, did not also learn that spoken truth may not be all of the truth. Beans and black bread are cheap, but the Druids of the school receive a good price for teaching each student. Yet each of us could be advisor to a great king some day: thus we learned more of the ways of men. I think it was done with forethought rather than greed, for our teachers were as thin as we, and farted as often.

You who live in the halls of kings, eating smooth wheaten porridge
with swine or sheep roasted afresh every few days, cannot guess
how such a diet as ours stirs the bowels, and how we looked forward
to those days when we could sleep without the constant rumble and
volley of bean-eaters' innards. There was good cause for the narrow
hard beds, as well.

On comfortable quilts filled with duck down, sleep sucks down the
body before the mind;

We had to learn to still our thoughts and give over the worries of
our days. When waking thoughts are stilled, and the pain of back
and bowels is laid aside, the soul may roam.

Then vision comes, and understanding. I lay in my hard bed,
blotting out the straw sticking into my hip and the noises around
me as surely as I blotted out the gurgle in my own innards, when
I found myself rising above the thatched roof of our sleeping-hall,
naked before the brilliant stars. I felt no fear or cold. The night was
very bright, the stars coming down to touch the North Sea on the
eastern horizon; I knew that there was nothing near that could hurt
me, though my teachers had warned me of phantoms that might
assail the traveling soul.

I had a goal: my heart longed west towards Eriu, and I chanted
Amargain's riding-song. I call the land of Eriu! Eriu, I call thee!
Even as I murmured, I sped west over the waters: I had thought to
go back to Cruachan síd, to see with the eyes of vision what I had
seen once as a child, but fate chose my path. I had just reached
land when I heard the voices within the hall, and must draw near to
listen.

"There's no doubt, the man of the house here is a good man,"
one was saying. I recognized the accents of my homeland at once,
though I was still far to the east in Culaigne. I sank down past straw
and cobwebs, drawn to the burning red eye of the fire in the middle
of the guest-house.

"A good man, in truth," another said. A tall thin redhead, lean and
graceful as a stag in winter: the queen's messenger Mac Roth. The
other, shorter and fairer, I did not know, but Mac Roth would not
be sent out without good cause, and I knew I had not come here by
chance.

"Is there a better man in Ulster?" The first asked.

"There is, certainly," Mac Roth said.

"His leader Conchobar is a better man. It would be no shame for all Ulster to give in to him. It was well done for Dáire to give us the Donn Culaigne. Did you see how he leapt when he heard Queen Maeve's offer, until his cushion burst under him? That is very well, for it would have taken the four strong provinces of Ireland to carry the bull off otherwise."

Then a third man came in, the door banging loudly behind him. He was black haired and stocky, his face flushed; Dáire had not been short with his guests on drink.

"What are you speaking of?" He said.

Mac Roth repeated the conversation. The dark haired man grimaced, then laughed.

"I'd as soon see the mouth that said that spout blood! We would have taken the bull anyway, with or without Dáire's leave!"

As he spoke, three more men came in. Two were servants in plain bratts pinned with iron, one carrying meat and cheese and bread and the other bearing a large pot and cups. The third wore a tunic of red and yellow stripes, with checkered trousers and a bratt of black-heathered blue wool pinned with a large bronze brooch: this would be Dáire's steward. His broad face was anger-red, and foreboding shimmered through me; it seemed that I could feel a huge stone grating from its place on the mountainside.

He spoke no word to the guests; at his gesture, the servants put the food and drink down roughly, ale slopping over the side of the pot, and marched out. A shadow in the night, I followed them to where Dáire sat at his ease, a silver bound drinking horn in his hand. He was a well-fed man, with ginger hair and beard and the ruddy complexion of one with a high temper; the lusty grin fell from his face as the other man began to shout.

"Did you give our treasure, the Brown Bull of Cuailgne, to Maeve's men?" The steward bawled.

"Yes, I did," Dáire said. "I don't care what the Ulstermen think; I was offered a price for his loan that would be enough for any man with seed in his loins."

"That was not a kingly thing to do," the steward reproved him loudly. "It is true, what Maeve's messengers said just now: if you hadn't given him up freely, the hosts of Ailill and Maeve, and the cunning of Fergus mac Roech, would have had him without your leave."

Shouts of fury went up at that from the men all around. One thick voice called, "Give nothing to the Mare of Cruachan!" And another screaming, "Let the Connachtmen try, and see what welcome they get!"

Dáire's own face darkened, and he slammed the tip of his drinking horn down on his table hard enough to scar the wood, a shower of golden mead fountaining out.

"Is that so?" He cried. "Is that so? By our gods, nothing leaves here unless I let it! They are lucky men who spoke so boldly: save that I do not murder messengers or travelers or other wayfarers, not one of them would leave here alive. I won't give up my bull to them, and if they have the brazen daring to come and ask for the Donn Cuailgne after speaking such words, I shall tell them so!"

Now the hall wavered in my sight, the light of fire and torches shimmering to colored sparks and the warriors' cheering fading to a deep buzz as though I stood within a beehive. I had been out longer than I should. Only the turning of a great matter, balanced on that single point, could have kept me so late.

Hastily I turned my face towards Alba, letting light and huts and the faces of the men drinking in Dáire's hall fade into bright fog, and chanted those words which a drúi or fili must know to come safe from soul-wanderings, until at last I felt the relief of my body solid and warm around me, the mattress hard against my hips and shoulders; I took nine deep breaths, settling myself back into myself. Then I rose, wrapping my hooded cloak about myself and buckling on my shoes.

I would be needed at home when Queen Maeve made war on Ulster. I had dreamed some days ago of Maeve and Ailill in their bed, of lovemaking becoming battle: the dream was true, as true as the words of Maeve's messengers. Mac Roth was right, it would take a great host to carry off the Donn Cuailgne; and the other one was right too, that if Maeve were not given the Bull freely, she would take him by force. Our eldest teacher, the high Druid Cernach, had a house of his own a little way from the student quarters. The night was black and rainy, the wet wind tearing at my hood so that I had to clutch it tightly to keep the rain off my hair, but my feet knew every track through the muddy grass.

I dreaded waking Cernach, but I feared he would be more angry if he found I had not come to him at once. However, the light of his fire still burned high, gleaming golden through the cracks of his door: if Cernach had not banked it yet, he was likely to be still awake. I lifted my hand to knock, then let it drop. What if he were out on journeys of his own, or deep in some meditation or working? The students were forbidden to disturb their masters, and yet if I did not tell him now.

"Come in!" The Druid called as I wavered at his threshold. I lifted the latch and stepped inside. Cernach's hut was small, filled with the tools of our calling. Dried herbs brushed against my head; hides and bones were heaped and scattered everywhere. The high Druid himself, gaunt and grizzled, sat crouched by the fire, his tall bony body slumped under his shaggy white cloak, looking keenly up at me.

"You have not come here for any little thing, young Fedelm," Cernach said. His dry clear voice still bore a trace of the music of Eriu; he had dwelt in Alba for near sixty years, but he was a Leinsterman from Clon Meala. "The night is restless, a storm gathering; it wraps about you, and your eyes are dark with it. Now tell me what wind blows you to my door."

My tongue hesitated in my mouth for a second; but I had been training for years as a ban-fili, fit to speak before kings. It did not take long to tell my vision, and the dream that had gone before, which I had mistaken for simple homesickness, and, though I did not say it to Cernach, the sight of Ailill's mighty golden body stretched naked on his pillows, his softening cock still massive between his legs, had led me to think that perhaps my own desires had given birth to some of the images in my mind.

"What do you wish to do?" Cernach inquired, his blue gaze fixed firmly upon me.

"You are far from finished with your training. You have a great gift and you have been diligent, but do you think yourself ready to prophesy for a ruler?"

"This prophecy has come to me, whether I would or not," I answered. "I would gladly give it over or turn it aside, for I think that before it is played out I shall have seen things that I would not wish to see. Yet it is upon me like a cloak: I cannot cast it from my shoulders. I would go home to Connacht, until Maeve has taken the Donn Cuailgne or her host has been beaten back in shame. Then I shall come back to my training, and not depart until I have passed my trials and my time is done."

Cernach brushed the strands of grizzled hair back from his deep-creased forehead and stared at me. The hairs prickled on the back of my neck, but I did not lower my gaze: I could feel the strength within me surging, like the flames of the hero-light leaping up from a warrior in battle.

"So be it," the elderly Druid told me at last. "Go back to your bed and sleep well. Tomorrow we shall outfit you with clothes and chariot and horses, and the tokens of your place that no man may dare to molest or hinder you upon your way, and you shall begin your journey home. May Brigid bring you there soon enough for Queen Maeve to heed your words!"

This was far more than I had hoped. I had expected a grudging permission to leave my studies for a few months, perhaps a bit of passage money to pay my way to Eriu, but Cernach meant to send me off as if I were already a full fili, going to bear the words of the Druids to a great ruler. It was too much, and it made me uneasy; but I could only give him my grateful thanks. I made my way back to bed, as Cernach had ordered, but in this way I could not begin to follow his command: the first glimmer of grey dawn through the smoke hole found me wide awake as if it were high noon.

Maeve

The harvest season was busy around Cruachan, as the land-folk struggled to bring in the shocks of wheat before the warm weather gave way to storm again. Though much of the summer had been damp and grey, Lugh must have joyed in his sacrifices. Day after day dawned bright and clear, and Maeve was often able to cast off her bratt and stand bare-armed in the sunlight, looking towards the east and wondering when Mac Roth would return. The warm confidence she had felt sending him off had not lasted.

Now and again, Cruachan's queen felt as though she were teetering on a plank above deep cold water; once in the night, she woke in a clammy shroud of chill sweat and tangled damp sheets, though the memory that had frightened her slipped from her mind like a dark tail slipping into a river before she could see its shape. Mac Roth had left as the moon began to wane.

The morning after the first new moon, Maeve decided a hunt would ease her mind. For going into the woods, she wore crimson breeches under a long tunic of herringbone woven violet and blue, her masses of golden hair braided back and bound with gold wire so that they would not hinder her running between bushes and trees. She carried three light sharp casting-spears, her sword at her waist; Ailill was armed likewise, but Fergus bore bow and sling.

"The first shot will be yours, with such weapons," Ailill said genially to the Ulster exile. "Is your arm strong enough to bring down a stag with a sling-stone?"

"A blow that will shatter a man's skull will do the same for a deer, if he is hit sound and square," Fergus answered. "Cú Chulainn is able to stun geese with his sling without touching them, just from the wind and thunder of the ball's passing. If I never learned that feat, I can at least kill what I aim at."

Ailill shrugged. "As you will."

Finnabair drove Maeve's chariot: light and lithe, Maeve's daughter was a fine driver, though Maeve had another charioteer to guide her horses in battle. Cuillius drove Ailill's as he had for years. The little man had a greatly skilled hand on the reins, and was as faithful to the king as the big grey hound that ran easily beside his vehicle. Maeve's horses were golden, and Ailill's black; Fergus' steeds gleamed ruddy roan in the sunshine, high necked and high-stepping and swift. Past the fields and low hills ahead, a few early autumn-burning trees laced the woods with red and gold like amber beads sewn onto a green cloak, bright beneath the cool blue sky.

"Shall we race to the woods?" Maeve asked. "The horses will have long enough to rest while we hunt, and it will do the hounds good to stretch their legs before we sight a stag."

Ailill looked over at her chariot, then at Fergus. "I think that you have the advantage, for your horses draw a lighter burden. It is a fair day for riding."

Fergus only smiled slightly, nodding to his own charioteer. The roan horses broke into a run. "Foul!" Maeve cried, laughing as the beat of her own horses' hooves quickened into a full gallop,

Her chariot skimmed swiftly down the road after the Ulsterman, Ailill's team pounding behind. Maeve balanced easily as her chariot's wheels bounced and leapt over the old dry ruts in the road: a lifetime of practice behind her, she could hit any target three times of three with a flung spear from a chariot at full speed. The wind tore the breath from her grinning mouth, stinging pleasant tears into her eyes, as Finnabair urged the horses onward. Down the long track from Cruachan síd they drove, flower starred green meadows and half-harvested fields of golden grain and brown stubble blurring about them; Liath and Baiscne barked joyfully, their long legs outpacing the burdened horses. Maeve and Finnabair were coming up swiftly on Fergus now. His charioteer glanced back for a second, cunningly swerving to block the road, but Finnabair was ready for him.

With a great jolt Maeve's chariot lurched off the track, slowing for a heartbeat before surging on in a single burst that brought her level with Fergus. The Ulsterman, too, was grinning, his long chestnut hair blowing out behind him as he stood easily in his chariot. He shouted to Maeve, but the wind tore his words away. As the golden horses pulled by the roan, Fergus picked up his sling, pointing to a pair of low flying geese ahead. He whirled the leather strap, and the leaden ball sang past Maeve's ear.

One of the geese dropped to earth as the other rose up with a faint mournful honk of surprise and sorrow. Another sling ball hummed past; the second goose fell, but Maeve was well in the lead. Her chariot swung full speed around a curve in the road; she shifted her weight, bracing herself, and laughed like a girl.

At last Finnabair pulled them up where the road wound into the eaves of the wood. The horses were breathing hard, their heads lowered and sweat darkening their glossy golden sides. Heedless of the smearing pigment on her eyelids, Maeve wiped the wind tears from her face and looked back as Cuillius twitched the reins to swerve viciously in front of Fergus' horses. The two roan steeds leapt aside, the chariot bouncing hard enough that Fergus staggered, though he was able to keep his feet, and Ailill raced ahead in the moments it took Fergus' team to recover.

"That was well done!" Said Finnabair, her cheeks foxglove pink and eyes shining brightly. "I am glad Fergus was gentler with us; I might not have kept us from spilling if he had done that so closely."

"You managed to pass him out well enough." Maeve was about to add that it was a pity Finnabair would not drive into battle, but remained silent. The girl had inherited every drop of the Cruachain strong-mindedness, and there was no point in nagging at her for something she did not want or need to do.

"I did, at that," Finnabair agreed happily as her father's team thundered up and the Ulsterman's horses slowed. "Will you get out, Mother, so I can walk the horses before they get stiff and chilled?"

Maeve picked up her casting spears and leapt down.

"That was good driving," she said to Cuillius, who lifted a hand in acknowledgment, the little brown man was not one for much speech. Fergus' chariot turned aside, and the Ulsterman leaned down over the edge once, then twice, picking up the geese he had shot. 'He has a good eye, Maeve said to herself, and I do not know any of our champions who could have hit a bird with a slingshot at that distance'.

"I see you have brought a prize for the winner," Ailill said to Fergus. Not only had Fergus downed the birds, but now that he was closer, Maeve could see that he had neatly broken the head of each. Fergus looked sharply down at the king, then tossed the two geese into Maeve's chariot.

"As you like," he said. "Are you ready to go for bigger game now?"

"Of course," Ailill replied. His red gold hair had come undone from one of its plaits, wind twisted into wild shapes. "I shall not be surprised if we find a good red stag in his bed this day."

Leaving their charioteers to walk the horses, the three of them went on into the woods. The leaves rustling above them were yellowing one by one from the first whisper of the coming winter; blackberries hung heavy and dark from thorny-sprawling bushes beneath the bright red sprays of rowan berries and the deep purple black flatlets of elderberries.

A soft cool breeze murmured through the trees; Maeve heard the gurgling of a spring off to the left, and birds calling overhead. The two great dogs, black and grey, sprang up before them; Liath made a dart at a squirrel, but the little red creature fled up the gnarled trunk of an old oak, stopping on a branch to chatter indignantly at them.

The three hunters went on, their silence broken only by bird calls and dry leaves and sticks crunching beneath their feet. Ailill moved well in the woods, but Fergus glided almost soundlessly, his tread so smooth and natural that he might have been walking the hard-packed earth of a hall's floor rather than stepping over leaf-hidden stones and fallen branches.

The hunters slowed, casting about for spoor, hoof prints, torn earth, or the rough white marks where a stag had torn at the tree-bark with his antlers. The wolfhounds were little help now; they must sight a quarry before they could run it down.

"There!" Said Ailill, pointing to a patch of damp ground. The great stag's hoofmarks stood deep and clear in the rich loam. "If we follow these, we shall find him in his bed."

The three of them cast about silently. They lost the stag's path twice in thick tangles of brambles and downed tree limbs, but found it again each time. Maeve's breath came quicker as they traced the stag's trail between trees and stones, past dull clumps of mushrooms and brighter stands of toadstools. Once she paused to pick a small cluster of flared golden trumpet-mushrooms, though

Fergus frowned at the delay. Maeve put a finger to her lips, no telling how close they were to their quarry!

And pantomimed sleeping. If the stag were deep in his daytime rest, a few moments of standing still would help lull him, so that he did not hear the hunters pacing like a wolf pack on the trail. Overhead, something rustled loudly through the branches; Maeve glanced up to see the dark tail of a pine marten vanishing into the golden leaves of a great beech.

Fergus had a ball in his sling, but Maeve shook her head, and Ailill pointed ahead to where an oak's dark gnarled bark was marred by ragged slashes of raw wood, the stag's marks claiming his land. Gold glinted from the king's thick red braids as he nodded, hefting a throwing-spear in his right hand: 'this way, come on!' Now they walked staggering their paces; no beast would walk in unbroken rhythm, without stopping every few seconds to test the wind.

Long dark scars, pungent with stag's urine, slashed the fallen leaves. More trees were marked by his horns, and his tracks, with the smaller hoof prints of at least two does, criss crossed the trail everywhere.

Ailill's Liath stood with nose in the air, tail quivering with excitement. A lesser wolfhound might have barked; Liath only looked up at his master, begging leave to run. Ailill's eyes met his hound's with the same look of eagerness, intent on the hunt as few men could be. Something was passing between her husband and the síde hound, though that was a chamber into which Maeve could never tread. Baiscne paced soundless beside her. Maeve could feel his trembling readiness, and she opened her mouth to silence the quickening pants of her own breath. Her bladder felt tight, but this was no time to ease herself. She drew a deep, slow breath, and stepped forward to follow the clearest set of tracks.

'Almost upon him!' Maeve thought, her heart pounding. Fergus' mouth was drawn to a tight grin, his heavy shoulders and the cording of his muscular forearm taut beneath his hand's easy grip on the sling. His grey eyes flickered, taking in everything in single glances; waiting for the one glimpse that would unleash his coiled power into the single point of his sling stone. Ailill's hand found the balance point of his spear as he scanned trees and trail. For a second Ailill and Fergus locked eyes; then, without speech or gesture, they stepped forward together, spreading out to cover the area like two bodies guided by a single head. Watching them, a shiver of excitement trembled in Maeve's belly: two magnificent men, bright haired Ailill and dark ruddy Fergus, moving together like wolves long part of the same pack. 'And I the bitch wolf between them', Maeve thought, pacing in softly to cover the ground they had left to her. Someday, I shall.

"My queen!" A man's voice shouted from a little distance. "My queen, do you hear me?"

Off to the left, still behind a thick palisade of trees, but close, so close, they would have had him in another few moments. Branches broke as the stag heaved himself from his bed and lumbered a couple of steps into a run, the sound of his hooves fading into the woodlands. Fergus cursed violently and let his shot fly. It thudded deep into a tree, a few dead leaves fluttering from the trembling branches. Ailill jabbed his spear point into the earth; the wolfhounds barked and leapt.

"What fool shouts at me when I am on the hunt?" Maeve screamed back. "We were nearly upon a great stag when you roused him. By the gods of the Cruachain, you had best have a good answer!"

Maeve heard the sound of light footsteps brushing over damp leaves and snapping twigs; before she could say any more, her messenger Mac Roth stood before her. "My queen," he said, looking her in the eye, "forgive me that I spoiled your hunt, but it was your order that I go as swiftly as I might, and return as swiftly as I might, allowing no man and nothing to hinder or delay me."

"Well, then, what is the news?" Maeve asked, biting her words off sharply to keep from screaming.

"Dáire says that he will not give up the bull, no matter what we offer."

Maeve felt as though a great fist had knocked the wind from her body; she had to fight to keep from folding at the middle.

Mac Roth's face seemed strangely clear to her eyes: the little orange mustache over thin lips and stubble chin; the weathered lines about his eyes and deep creases on his forehead, the hollows beneath his narrow cheekbones. A spare face, hard as a whip, with no softness to slow him on his journeys about Eriu. She could also see the fear in the green-streaked grey of his eyes, the little black holes of his pupils shifting nervously. 'This is a man of worth, who has served me well and long, Maeve reminded herself. Even if his error has lost me the Donn Cuailgne, if I send him to be hung up and have his feet beaten with willows, he will never run as well for me again'.

"Why not?" Maeve asked, proud of the calm in her voice, and on her face, as she listened to the tale of how her men had boasted in Dáire's guest house. 'I should have sent Mac Roth alone, as I first meant to do. Dáire would have taken care of moving the ox for me, with no more of my men needed'.

She had judged as seemed best then, and had not stayed a great queen by moaning over what she might have done. When Mac Roth was done, Maeve let him wait a few moments, his sweaty face glimmering in the sun dappled forest shadows. She could see the nervousness flickering in his eyes, tightening his hands; but the strings of her own guts twisted and drew more tightly within her, and she had to swallow twice before she dared speak.

"We don't need to polish the knobs and knots in this, Mac Roth," she said at last, even and casual as if she were giving him a message for her swineherd to have an additional pig knocked on the head and sent up to the fort for dinner. "It was well known that the Brown Bull of Cuailgne would be taken by strength if he wasn't given freely. Taken he shall be."

Fergus' keen face darkened as he listened to Maeve's words, his grey eyes shadowed by thought. Maeve thought of how he had spoken of his brothers of the Red Branch, of how his face lighted when he spoke of his foster-son Cú Chulainn. 'He has better cause than anyone to wish vengeance on Conchobar. Mayhap this fight will bring Ulster's king into his reach, or mine!' Ailill grinned.

"Well, Mac Roth, if you have spoiled our hunt for one quarry, you have brought us a better one. It will take a goodly host to win our way through to Cuailgne, and it will be a mighty cattle-raid. That carries off the Donn. It has been long enough since the rulers of Connacht claimed their share of kine and heads and treasure, has it not, my queen?"

"Indeed," Maeve answered, smiling. She breathed deeply, stilling the quivering of her belly-muscles. This is not the disaster I feared, she told herself. It is a chance at glory, to wipe out my shame. I shall lead the great raid, riding into danger, sharing out the plunder. I shall prove myself the queen of Connacht to whom my folk look for all things: men are not the only doers of song-worthy deeds.

"Hasten back to Cruachan fort, Mac Roth. Tell my cooks there will be a feast tonight; gather the warriors from their houses, and let the harvesters know that when their day's work, there will be meat and ale in my hall. Then eat well, and rest well, for tomorrow, you shall be traveling the roads of Eriu again."

"Whatever I may do in payment for this failure, I will," Mac Roth answered sincerely, and ran from her. Maeve looked at Ailill and Fergus.

"We shall need a great host, indeed, to take the Donn Cuailgne from Dáire," Fergus said. "It is a long way from Cruachan to the mountains and coast of Cuailgne, and much of that through Ulster: the Ulstermen will not greet a Connacht host as friends."

"The Ulstermen will have little to say about it for a time," Ailill grinned. "Do Macha's pangs not come upon them still with the onset of need, leaving them helpless as a woman in labor? How long is it?"

"Usually nine days and nights," Fergus admitted. His high cheekbones flushed; Maeve thought of how bitterly he had spoken to her, and regretted that Ailill had reminded him of Ulster's shame. "Yet there is geas against slaying them then, unless the slayer would take Macha's birthing pains himself: such a killing would be no better than striking down a woman in her bearing."

"There will be no need to strike the Ulstermen down, when they already lie moaning in the straw," Maeve answered. She had to bite the inside of her cheeks to keep the smile from her face. Her spite might be meant for Conchobar, but he was only a phantom here: it was Fergus, standing behind his former king's shade, who would take the thrust.

"It means only that we can come and go unhindered, and take what we will on our way. Yet, if you cannot stomach war upon the lands of the king who drove a sword through your son, or if you still count Conchobar and the Red Branch such friends that you cannot raid in Ulster, you have my leave to stay behind in Cruachan until we drive the Donn Cuailgne home."

The scar down Fergus' cheek flashed livid white against the blood darkening his keen face; Maeve. Felt the anger beating from his grey eyes like torrential rains driven into her face by the storm wind, sending a thrill of wariness and excitement through her. He lifted his hand as if to grasp her by the neck of the tunic, then clenched his fist and let it drop.

"Is this how you repay me for opening my thoughts to you?" Fergus growled softly. She did not answer, only met his eyes: if there was shame in what she had said, it was none but his own. "No man would say such a thing to me and escape unbattered," he went on, more loudly.

"How should I tolerate it from a woman?"

"Do not tolerate it," Maeve answered, her heart hammering in her breast. She did not look away from Fergus' deep grey eyes nor let herself blink; nor did the trembling of her legs reach her voice.

"I said if, not since. Come to lead our host! You know the lands of Ulster and the warriors of the Red Branch better than any Connachtman; you shall have vengeance for your son Fiacha, and for the dishonor Conchobar set upon you when he trapped you between geas and word. We all have debts to pay here, of many sorts."

Fergus stared into her eyes a moment longer, the flush paling from his stark cheekbones like sunset fading from bare mountain crags.

Maeve knew he was thinking of the girl, weeping and uncomforted, she had been in Emain Macha, or perhaps of Deirdre. Fergus took a step back from Maeve, looking up at Ailill.

"Is this your will as well, King Ailill, that I go with you to guide the hosts of Connacht through Ulster? Is this my payment for the safety you offered me?"

"Not payment, I hope, but friendship," Ailill answered.

"We gave you guest-right and sanctuary because you were in need, and a good man pursued by a king who has been no friend to us and not much better to the best of his own folk. I hope you do not think that the rulers of Connacht weigh up their hospitality in pennies to demand it back again! No, Fergus, you are our friend, beside whom we have set our swords to fight.

I hope you will come on this raid because it is an undertaking of glory, to be remembered in the songs of the bards, and I would have my friend Fergus sung of. Will you not come with us for the joy and the fame of it, Fergus, and the chance to come back with cows and bondsmaids driven before you, a string of battle-won heads hanging from your belt, a sack of fine plunder weighting your chariot, and your name ringing in the mouth of every bard and fili in Eriu?"

Ailill smiled, holding out his hand to Fergus. The Ulsterman looked from the king to Maeve, then back at Ailill. With a sudden fierce gesture, he turned to grasp Ailill's wrist, his fingers clamping tight as the talons of an eagle. Ailill's heavy freckled forearm bulged in turn, returning the grip; then he whirled Fergus into his embrace, holding him tight.

"By Lugh and the Dagda, I'm glad to have you with us!" The king cried. "Come, we've frightened off all the game and the nearest mead is in our chariots: let's have a drink upon it, and go home to Cruachan to set out our pieces for this game!"

Fergus' mouth twitched as though he were trying to hold himself back. Then an unwilling chuckle crept out, and at last he laughed heartily until the corners of his eyes were wet.

"Ailill," he said at last, "there is no king in Eriu like you. I have lost much in coming here, but your friendship, and yours, Maeve, has been no little thing to gain. I shall help to lead your armies upon this raid as best I may."

Finnabair

Nerves tingling, Finnabair watched her mother come from the woods with Fergus and Ailill on either side of her, the two wolfhounds pacing them like a matched pair of black and grey shadows. When Mac Roth had dashed down the path towards Cruachan without even turning his head towards her, Finnabair's heart had stuttered in her chest with fear. Had the stag gored one of the hunters; had they started a wild boar, or a wolf-pack, was her mother, or father, lying with the bright life-blood soaking into the autumn leaves. all three seemed hale, bright-eyed and laughing in spite of their quarry's escape.

"Perhaps Mac Roth was only sent to tell the cooks the hunters failed, so they must slaughter a pig or sheep for tomorrow's meat?' Still the little knot of ice in Finnabair's belly did not loosen. This was not the rueful or chaffing laughter of hunters who had failed their kill, but the loud wild hilarity of warriors about to ride, grievously outnumbered, into battle.

Fergus and Ailill vaulted into their chariots; the charioteers clucked to the horses, and they began to trot towards Cruachan. Maeve waited until their figures were small on the road, then climbed into her own vehicle and said to Finnabair, "Drive slowly, my daughter, and take the long way around. I have things to say to you that are not for the ears of any man, and such are best spoken in the open air."

They set off at a slow walk. The soft breeze brought the rich scent of new-cut grain across the gold and brown of the fields, a fair day for hunting, but, to Finnabair's mind, fairer for simply walking through the meadows, gathering the last summer flowers and eating ripe blackberries. The queen's wren twittered above Maeve's head; and now Finnabair almost thought that the bird called, 'Finnabair, Finnabair, Finnabair'. Had her hands not been busy on the reins, she would have stopped her ears. Cruachan's holy queen sometimes heard counsel in the wren's voice, but Finnabair never wanted to. Maeve lifted her hand; the wren circled down, its little claws gripping her finger, then walked up her bare arm to her shoulder, and twittered again, Finnabair.

"Have you thought, these last months, on what manner of man you would marry?" Maeve asked.

Finnabair looked back, the horses were ambling along slowly, and needed little guidance. She bit her lip. 'I knew this day must come, she said sternly to herself. I never wanted to be a warrior: but sword-wielder or not, one who truly wishes something must be willing to fight for it. If I cannot say what I need to now, when will I be able to? Out with it, Finnabair, or prepare to give up your desire'.

"There is one man whom I would marry if I had my choice," Finnabair said, her own breath and heartbeat so loud in her ears that she could hardly hear her own words. "That is Rochad mac Faithemain, I know he is a man of Ulster, who has fought against us before. When I saw him among Ulster's emissaries at the Samhain fair last year, I felt my heart beating together with his. He spoke kind words to me then, and said that if ever you would give leave for me to marry him, he would gladly take me as his wife. I told you of it then, and you said…"

Maeve sighed. "I said that, though you had reached the age of choice a year ago, you were still too young to be wedded. I said also that you would forget him in time, as many brave and handsome men, the sons of kings, came to display their feats for you and to court you; that one man met at a gathering, high-born but not royal, would hardly keep your heart long. Was I so wrong? And what of Fraech, who has asked for your hand more than once? He is one of Connaught's best-born men, fair to look on: one could easily believe that he was born of the síde, and lover to one of their queens, as the tale has been told of him." Maeve smiled at her daughter. "Indeed, I thought that your heart had turned towards him already."

"That was before I met Rochad." Finnabair bit her lower lip, looking down at the blue-painted boards of the chariot's floor. True, Fraech was golden and síde-fair, and a redoubtable warrior. Two years ago, she had stared cow-like at him whenever he came to feasting in Cruachan, and dreamed endless dreams of him rescuing her from peril; but he had hardly looked at her.

Rochad was tall and gangly and plain, but when he met Finnabair's gaze, his hazel eyes grew liquid and sweet as honey melting beneath the summer sun, and she knew that he saw nothing in all the world but her face. Not her birth, not her wealth or Maeve's expectation that she would be queen of Cruachan in time; not even the rounding curves of her slim body. Alone of all the men who had already tried to win her favor, Rochad only wanted her, to dwell by his side in his little northern fort, happy and far from the trials of great kings and queens.

"Mother, you use men as you will, glad in love-play as in battle. I think I cannot bestow my heart so easily."

Maeve's tender cheeks were still pink as if with excitement, but the wild hilarity that had lighted her face as she came from the woods had faded. Her blue eyes were like the sky's reflection in a black peat-pool, hiding whatever lay beneath. Nor did she speak to contradict Finnabair. Finnabair knew her mother: when Maeve did not show her feelings at once, then something was amiss. The cold tightened its grip on her entrails. Better to find out the worst, than keep trembling in fear of it.

"Yet I also do not think Mac Roth came with good news, for there was fear in his face when he went into the woods, and when he came out, he fled as though all the phantoms of death were tracking him. Tell me what is in your mind, Mother, and I shall tell you what I am able to do to aid."

"This is how matters stand," Maeve began.

Finnabair listened in silence, only occasionally looking forwards to twitch a rein as the golden horses paced quietly along the dirt track way, and the cold crawled like hemlock from her belly to her heart until she shivered within. Her mother's face was pale and intent: what she was saying clearly gave Maeve no joy.

'Is she remembering Conchobar? 'Finnabair had never known Cruachan's queen to shirk her duty because it was hurtful before; Maeve would not now, yet the pain in her mother's face led Finnabair to speak the final words herself.

"You need a great host, you must have something to promise to kings and the sons of kings beyond the plunder of a cattle-raid where the greatest prize is already spoken for."

"That is so, my daughter. Look: I have sworn by Brigid and by the gods of the Cruachain that I shall not do to you as was done to me, I shall not marry you off against your will, and least of all to an old bull whose delight is to make heifers into cows by force. Yet, you cannot help but know this, the offer or hope of a woman as fair as yourself is more than enough to disorder the minds of most men, so that we can ring-lead them as if they were three-month calves. If you would not learn sword-skill from me, I think I have managed to teach you enough of a woman's arts to make up for it."

"Indeed you have, Mother." Finnabair sighed softly. "And I know what I must do. You will offer me to one man, or to several; and I must smile at each of them as though he could be my love, must promise myself with the gaze of my eyes and the touch of my hands and the shifting of my breasts and hips inside my garments, all without speaking any words that would tie me down." Finnabair swallowed hard, the heat of her unshed tears loosening the choking lump of ice in her throat. "Mother, if it comes to it, will you swear again that I will not be given against my will?"

"What is sworn once," Maeve said thickly "need not be sworn again: I keep my word."

"Save when it is truly needful to break it," Finnabair answered, her voice dropping to a whisper. "You trained me to hear the whispers of folk in peacetime, to know the shifting of alliances and the deeds of kings and queens.

I know that you will keep your word where you can, but there have been times..."

"Times when a man's pride or unbreakable oath or iron geas would have been my destruction, and Connacht's," Maeve sighed. "A woman must be practical; a woman who would rule, three times as much."

'Yet you were willing, and are willing, to push my father's challenge to you farther than he ever could dream of taking it!' Anger flashed through Finnabair; she thought she kept it from her face, or at least Maeve did not seem to notice.

The queen's wren chirped sharply from her shoulder, the sound going through Finnabair's eardrum like a needle-stab. If Cruachan's queen were proven second to its king in law, and thus no longer sovereign queen and land-goddess. What, save the king's kindness, kept her from being handled as Maeve had been in Ulster?

Finnabair knew her father would never behave as Conchobar had, but she did not wonder that her mother might fear nonetheless. It was amazing enough that Maeve had ever allowed another man to touch her, after that wedding and rape.

"This I will swear," Maeve went on. "I will do the best I can to keep you unwed until you have spoken again with the man you love. Then, if you truly love him enough to cast aside queenship, well, you have seven brothers, any of whom might rule and sire a daughter. I would choose, if I could, to have a queen here after me, but Rochad mac Faithemain could never be your consort."

"Because he is not of kingly blood like Father, or like Fergus?" Finnabair asked.

Maeve started straight up as though her daughter had jabbed her with the long pin of the silver ring-brooch holding her cloak. "What brings Fergus to your mind?"

"Only that he was king of Ulster before Conchobar tricked him, and could be king again if you would have him so. I had thought that was why, though the bondsmaids giggle about his great manhood and strength between their sheets every night, you had not yet lain with him."

Maeve's mouth dropped open. Finnabair felt a guilty stab of pleasure, suppressed it at once. *What she must ask of me causes her pain enough. Why am I seeking another hole in her hauberk?*

"Fergus is an Ulsterman, and shy with me, for he thinks in his heart that Ailill is such a king as Conchobar, who caused death and destruction among the best of his war band because one woman preferred lying with another to lying with him. While Ailill and I are wedded, my king has nothing to fear from Fergus, however often I might spread my legs to him," Maeve rallied.

"Yet you have not," Finnabair answered. Then she knew what she was trying to say, and why. "Those few little words, while Ailill and I are wedded, are very great ones to Father, I think."

Maeve's pale cheeks flushed foxglove-pink, her blue eyes widening as she drew a quick hushed breath. "I shall think on that," she whispered.

'Had you not thought on it before, Mother? Finnabair wondered. Is your love for my father so great, that you turn from what would hurt him even without knowing it, as a mother turns in her sleep to comfort her babe without ever waking to know it cries?

Rochad's face came back to her, each line unspeakably dear, hazel eyes like sunlit forest pools, his wide mobile mouth, the endearing crookedness of his long nose, his little orange chin-beard incongruously bright next to the dark brown tangle of his long curly hair.

Will we know and love each other so well after twenty-five years of marriage, my love, if we are able to marry? How could I be a worthy bride to you, if I failed my own mother and the queens that came before and will come after her? Even, mayhap, our own daughter.'

Maeve straightened her back, her voice strong again.

"We are speaking of you now. I have offered all I can: will you consent to do what you must, even as I shall, to hold our host together for this raid?"

Finnabair looked directly into her mother's eyes, bracing herself for what she must say.

"I am a daughter of the Cruachain. Whether I go with Rochad, or stay to rule after you, I would see the right of the queen of Cruachan upheld. if my brothers can risk their lives in your raid, can I do less than they?"

No tears fell to Maeve's cheeks, but Finnabair saw the clear bright water pooling in her blue eyes, the quivering of her mother's lips as though they strained between smiling and weeping.

"Not less, but more," Maeve said, her voice half-choking. "They are but seven swords, eight, if we count your half-brother Cormac, whereas you will bring a host far greater than the one Cormac leads to our raiding, and the finest of heroes. O, Finnabair!"

Finnabair dropped her reins to embrace her mother. Her own face was damp against the soft violet-blue wool of Maeve's tunic, and Maeve's own tears fell warm and unashamed on her daughter's hair.

Maeve

"The Tuatha de Danann were a fair people, skilled in every form of magic and craft. After they defeated the monstrous Fomorians in the second battle of Moytura, they ruled Ireland until the human children of Mil sailed from Spain to challenge them. The Tuatha de Danann resisted the human incursion with all their spells, sending a magical wind to halt the invaders' ships beyond the ninth wave; but Amairgin the bard sang a charm that calmed the waters so that the children of Mil could make landfall. Then the two tribes did battle, and the race of humans was victorious; it is said that they won through the use of iron weapons, which did great harm to their foes. It was agreed then that the Tuatha de Danann should go into the Otherworld, ruling Ireland below the earth as the children of Mil ruled above, and they were thereafter known as the síde from the mounds in which they dwelt. Many gateways remained by which each race might pass into the other's world, most notably at Beltaine and Samhain. Some of the Tuatha de Danann, such as Lugh and the Dagda, were hailed as gods and gave help to humankind; others were sometimes friends and sometimes foes, but always powerful in magic, and perilous in their dealings with the children of Mil."

Maeve and Ailill sent out their messengers across Ireland: to all the under-kings and lords and holders in Connacht, and to Ailill's six brothers. They sent to Cormac Connlongas, Maeve's son by Conchobar, and the other Ulster exiles in Connacht; to Leinster and Munster and Meath the messengers went, like a flock of pigeons startled out of a tree and scattered across the skies. They bore promises of plunder to some, of revenge to others, and where Maeve knew it to be the sole lure, the hint that Finnabair would wed only a man she had seen win glory in the Great Raid. The messengers rode or ran as the moon waxed to full; by the time it was waning, the first hosts were pitching their tents on Ai plain around Cruachan síd. Maeve stood with Senchán looking out as another troop came marching across Ai plain from the east.

"That is Cormac's host, I think," Senchán said to her.

Maeve looked at the foremost ranks, an hundred men in speckled cloaks, with cropped hair and knee-length tunics, full-length shields and long grey stabbing spears. The troop of an hundred behind them were better-dressed, in dark grey cloaks and red-embroidered tunics that reached their calves, with hair tied back on their heads, bright metal glinting on their shields, and five-pronged spears in their hands.

Still, her son by Conchobar should be better turned-out: exile as he was from his father's land, Maeve had given him plenty of lands on the fruitful Ai plain, and she had never heard it said that Cormac lacked the pride he should have.

"I do not see my Cormac there," she replied to the old Druid.

Senchán's bright blue eyes twinkled from his windswept white curls.

"Wait a little, and you shall."

As the third troop came over the slight eastern rise, Maeve nodded. There were only fifty, yet every man wore a purple cloak and a red-embroidered hooded tunic reaching to his feet. Their hair hung loose, trimmed to the shoulder, and they carried curved scallop-edged shields. Each had a spear like a palace pillar, adorned with elaborately-shaped butts and mounts of bronze, and a sword hung by every man's side. One stood taller than the rest: thin stripes of red and gold brightened his purple cloak, the bright gold of a torc glinted about his neck, and a silver fillet held back his waist-long brown hair.

"I see him now!" Maeve said happily. It had never ceased to gladden her that the son Conchobar had forced on her, then torn from her, had come back to her in the end.

She raised her voice, "Scenb, Cormac and his troops are here. See that a welcome is made ready, that I may greet my son and his men as is fitting."

Soon enough, Cormac strode into the great hall. He was a tall man in his middle twenties, raw-boned and strong, clean-shaven and long-haired. If Maeve had wished to, she could have seen an echo of Conchobar in the craggy knobs of his face; but his lively blue eyes and long cheeks were all hers, and his expression had none of the closed meanness of a king who had been told, all his life, that he had the first right to every good in his land. Instead he grinned openly, hastening to Maeve's silk-pillowed bench and clasping his mother in an embrace that almost swept her off her feet. She hugged him back tightly. Whenever she looked upon Cormac, she felt the joy of his return.

'My first son, companion beneath my heart, the only good of my time in Ulster, praise Danu that you have come back to me, Senchán's prophecy of my love's return fulfilled!'

"Well-met, Mother!" Said Cormac, looking down into Maeve's face, he was a good half-hand taller than Ailill. "My men are tired of ease; it was a day of fair omens when you gave us something better to do than lie about drinking and looking for bondsmaids to pursue. How soon do you mean to march?"

"The Druids tell me that, whenever it may be that all our allies have arrived, we must wait until after Samhain to set out if we wish to see Ai Plain again."

A look of brief disappointment shadowed Cormac's rough features, but then he grinned again. "There are worse things than two weeks of guesting with you, and it will do my men good to try your guards at swords and spears and other feats. How many more hosts are coming?"

"I am not certain yet," Maeve said. "Come, sit down and let your sister bear the good mead to you; greet your brothers, and we shall tell you all the news as we have it."

Finnabair carried mead to them in a pair of silver goblets adorned with gold bead-wire work and set with purple gems, and Cormac lifted his drink to his mother. "Well-met again, and well-found after so many years," he said softly. Despite the strength of his face, Maeve could see the little boy he must have been, as the round shapeless features of the babe she had wept to leave slowly lengthened and grew closer to a man's, the young boy's face tight with longing for a mother about whom his father would not speak save to curse her, perhaps wondering if he himself had been the cause of her going. 'O my son, I hope someday I can make it up to you for the years we lost!'

"Well-met and well-found, my son," Maeve answered, sipping from her goblet. The mead was strong and dry beneath the rich scent of honey, flavored with a complex blend of herbs that poured smoothly over the tongue. "Do you find life here to your liking?"

"Indeed I do. The fields of Ai Plain are richer than those of Ulster; our cows grow fatter and give more milk here, and the grain ripens more swiftly and sweetly. It is a good land, save that our lives have been too peaceful of late to please a warrior, and you have kindly solved that matter for us," Cormac answered. "You gave me a fair dun, but its walls lack foemen's heads to prove our strength. That, too, we shall remedy now! So tell me: who shall fight beside us on this raid?"

"King Ailill's brothers will send their forces, Coirpre and Finn must hold the Samhain feast for their own folk in Leinster and Tara, but they will join us along the way. The full three hundred of the Galeóin troop from north Leinster are already camped here, and five of the seven kings of Munster have agreed to come as well. Of course, there are yourself and Fergus and your Ulster exiles, so that we may say that the best of all the provinces of Ireland are gathered to take the Donn Cuailgne."

Cormac frowned at that praise, and shifted uneasily. "Fergus and Dubthach and I are all mighty men, who have proven ourselves against the great warriors of Ulster before.

I am not sure that I could have bested Cú Chulainn when I left Ulster, and he has had time to grow since; and there were other warriors of the Red Branch against whom I could find it hard striving, though Fergus might not."

"Are those fit words for my son?" Maeve asked indignantly. "Did Conchobar raise you so?"

Cormac shook his head. "It was Fergus who taught me to speak boldly of what I could do, and not to boast of what I could not. He is a fool who claims he can out swim the fish, or out fly the hawk."

Maeve sighed, and nodded. "There is wisdom there, certainly. I have heard many tales of Cú Chulainn: is he truly so great a hero?"

"I do not know how many of the tales you have heard are wild fools' songs, and how many are true. I was in the boys' troop when he took us on, one against thrice fifty. Not one of us could get a hurley-ball past him to the goal, or block his shots when it was his turn to cast; nor, though the oldest of us were twice his size, could any one of us wrestle him down. The measure between us never seemed to shrink, though I had reached a man's full size while he was still a child of ten."

"Hmm," Maeve said. "Still, he is but one man." And the pangs of Macha will be on Ulster, she thought, though she did not speak it. Her son was, she thought, enough an Ulsterman still that it would be wrong for her to remind him of the land's shame.

"Aye. As for Conchobar's other warriors, some might be hard striving for me, but in the end, I think, it would be their heads hanging from my chariot prow rather than mine cut from my shoulders."

"Well-spoken," Maeve praised him. "Now I would not ask a guest, and less so a kinsman, to begin to think on war right away, but if thoughts of peace have become such a burden to you, perhaps you would rather give me your advice on our march through Ulster?"

Cormac rubbed thoughtfully at the faint shadow of stubble on his shaven jaw. "If Ailill and Fergus were here, where are they?"

"Fergus has gone down to greet his old friend Dubthach, I think. I do not know where Ailill has gone off to, but he should not be long. Well, we shall wait for them." Maeve nodded to Aengus, her favorite among the harpers, and he settled himself on the end of the nearest bench, cradling the ruddy polished curves of his harp in his lap like a lover, and began to pluck at the strings of shining white bronze, their bell-bright music ringing clear through all the sounds of talk and laughter in the hall.

Maeve and Ailill awoke on Samhain to the sound of men and women chanting, "Turn about, and turn about! The year is over today!" Rough hands tumbled the two of them out of their bed; all the folk of their hall stood about, those just outside the wooden partition shouting, "Where is the queen? Where is the king? Bring them out, the dawn awaits!"

Shivering in the damp chill, Maeve quickly put on a dun gown and black bratt, fastening them with a simple copper pin; Ailill wore a knee-length grey tunic and dark bratt to match his wife's.

Then Maeve pointed at her bondsmaid Lochu.

"There is the queen! Let us dress her as befits her state, the queen of Cruachan!"

The women surrounded Lochu, Finnabair undoing the plain pins at her shoulders and Maeve kneeling to pull off her simple hide shoes while the other women rifled the queen's clothes-chest. Lochu flustered and fluttered her hands, but could do nothing against them. They put Maeve's feast-day dress of blue silk embroidered with gold and silver over the bondsmaids head, pinning it with Maeve's elaborate gold brooches. It was only a little too long: Lochu was a tall woman, and a few more pins brought the hem up to keep it out of the mud.

They wrapped her in the queen's many-colored bratt, the long fringed tail going five times about her body; set Maeve's arm-rings on her wrists, put Maeve's thickest gold ribbon-torc about her neck, and crowned her with the queen's embossed gold diadem. Lochu glanced wildly about, but Maeve snatched the pitcher of mead from her bedside table, filling her goblet to the brim.

"Drink this, o queen!" Maeve encouraged her. "It will give you strength for the day."

Lochu nodded silently and drained the cup. A tinge of pink touched her round pale cheeks, and she forced her trembling mouth into a smile. The groom Conla whom Ailill had chosen to take his place was enjoying his part more. Both king and amadán, fool, he shouted at Ailill with great gusto, "D'you think that's straight, you lazy lout? What kind of manservant are you? Fix that pin higher on my shoulder, or I'll have you beaten with willow-withes until you can't stand on your feet for a year!"

Ailill roared with laughter, hastening to follow the amadán-king's commands, while Fergus held Ailill's silver-bound drinking-horn up for Conla to slurp down the contents in a single noisy gulp. They had chosen well this year, Maeve thought as she and Ailill brought the two out of the royal bedchamber. Lochu and Conla might have been blurred castings of the true king and queen: while both were a little shorter than the originals, Lochu's hair more brown than fair and Conla's more bronze than red-gold, from a distance, they might easily have been mistaken for the rulers of Connacht.

"The Queen! The King!" Everyone shouted to greet them.

"Aye, that's it!" Conla roared, drawing Ailill's sword from its scabbard at his waist and waving it about wildly.

"I'm the best king you ever had, I'll lead all the raids, and no Connachtman will ever lose his head to a foe while I rule the army! Yes, and if you have a maiden or a wife who can't bear, bring her to me.

My seed is strong enough to raise a thousand men from an empty field, and I'll still be swinging and shooting when every other man in Eriu has faltered and drooped."

Senchán took the hands of Conla and Lochu, leading them to the silk-cushioned bench where Maeve and Ailill took their ease on every other day, while Finnabair and her brothers,

Ailill and Fergus and Cormac, scurried about to serve them.

"You, girl!" Conla shouted at Maeve. "Your king is hungry, go to the cook house and get me some hot griddle-cakes, and mind they're dripping well with honey."

Maeve took a silver platter from her steward's hands and hastened out, smiling to herself. Samhain was the feast of turnabout, for a time; and if Lochu was silent while Conla ruled, that too was turnabout, and fitting to the season between one year and the next. The wind caught Maeve's hair and the corners of the short servant's brat the moment she stepped outside, whipping them back wildly.

She glanced eastward: the rising sun glowed baleful red behind orange fire-streamers of cloud, and she could just see the darker masses of clouds scudding across the lightening sky.

A brief shower of rain spattered her face; barefoot in the thick-trodden mud of the fort, Maeve found herself shivering like any bondsmaid, eager to hurry to the warmth of the baking-hut. Most of the army was encamped about Cruachan, their tents by those of the merchants and peasants who had come to the great fair.

The shapes of tent and bothy were dark in the growing dawn, but fires burned here and there as the earliest risers cooked their breakfasts, and Maeve saw the occasional human shadow passing over the points of firelight, dark and vague as if the dead had also risen early.

The Druids and their helpers were already bringing the first beasts up the western hill towards the Black Boar's Furrows: two pairs of man-high ridges sloping downward from twinned pools, each wide enough for several folk to walk abreast, far enough apart for a goodly throng to assemble between them. At the base of the hill stood a ring of posts like the hall's own, but open to the gods and the sky. There the offerings would be given; the Druids would make their divinations, and ask the blessings of all the gods from Cromm Cruaich to Brigid, that the cows' udders flow richly with milk and the fields grow thick with grain next year.

Calatín, holding a rope strung through the bronze nose-ring of a great white bull, 'and if I had known how Ailill would use him, I would have made sure that the Druids took Finnbenach last year!' Maeve thought sharply, led the animal into the holy ring, followed by the young men with sharp iron goads who stood ready to guide the bull as needed.

The baking-hut was delightfully warm after the sharp cold wind outside. Graine already had a high stack of cakes baked, and was just about to turn another lot on her big iron griddle. She started to rise to her feet, but Maeve laughed her down, handing her the silver platter to fill. "Remember that tonight is Samhain, I am only a serving maid for this time."

The cook smiled. She was a lean woman, a year or two younger than Maeve, but gray-haired already, her face creased with the lines of good nature. "You have come to fetch breakfast for the king and queen. Who is it this year?"

"Conla the groom, and Lochu."

"Conla will play his part well. He is a born amadán, that boy, what of Lochu?"

"She, is well enough, though perhaps she fears what will befall, with our host about to go to war."

Graine's smile dropped abruptly, and she looked down at her griddle, busying herself with the long turning-fork for a time.

After a while, very quietly, she said, "Is Lochu right to fear?"

"How should I know?" Maeve replied. "I am but a bondsmaid at the moment. Only the Druids can answer that question, and I have never known them to do so before, until the time itself has come."

When Maeve brought the griddle-cakes back to Conla, the fool-king swatted her hard on the rear. "Ha, you're a lively wench!" He called out. "I'll have you in my bed tonight; the king can have any maid he pleases. What of you, my queen? Which of these lusty young rams will you choose?"

Lochu glanced narrow-eyed at Maeve, then looked around. "I will have Fergus!" She said with sudden spirit. "There is a lover fit for a queen!"

Fergus reddened, laughing. "Are you sure you are strong enough to bear my weight in a bed?" He asked her. "Seven women in one day seldom satisfy me; do you think yourself my match?"

"They say thirty men in one day cannot satisfy the queen of Connacht," Lochu replied. Her cheeks were bright red; though she was not slurring her words yet, Maeve guessed that Finnabair and her brothers had gotten a good deal of mead down the fool-queen. "We shall see how well you manage it."

"If you wear me out, there is a better man than I," Fergus answered. He pointed to Ailill. "That big horse-groom there, I hear from every woman in the hall that he is a lover worthy of a queen."

Ailill laughed and grabbed his crotch, shaking it at Lochu. "If you choose me second, be sure you will pay for it. There will not be enough of you left to use as a belt-pouch by the time Fergus and I are both done with you."

The rough mockery went on while the hall filled, Connacht's noblemen and their wives, and the kings and champions who had come to ally with Maeve's host, coming in to pay their jesting respects to Conla and Lochu. Early as it was, the drink flowed freely, Samhain was no time to be sober, and soon Maeve could barely move for the press of merrymakers in the great building. Then the silence spread out from the door like ripples through a pond. The gathered folk surged back to form an aisle down the middle of the hall to where the fool-king and -queen sat in tipsy state. Senchán in his white robe, and Calatín in his black, stood in the doorway.

The older Druid carried only his staff, but the younger one, tall and grizzle-haired, bore a long glittering knife in his hand. Behind the Druids stood nine men bearing the great bronze serpent-curved horns of war and ritual, the embossed disks at their ends glittering brilliantly above their players' heads. At Senchán's gesture, the players drew breath, sounding their trumpets as one. The deep blast rang out, shaking the timbers of the hall; then cut off sharply when the Druid signed to the horn-blowers again.

"Come out, o king; come out, o queen," Senchán called, his old voice sweet and melodious through the sudden silence. "It is time to make the offerings, for the sake of the land."

Conla's voice was thick with mead now, but he stood without aid. Ailill's many-colored brat had slipped sideways on his shoulder, the glittering chains of his sword belt hanging askew. His ruddy-brown hair was rumpled up into short spikes; yet it seemed to Maeve that there was a certain dignity to his drunken voice as he answered.

"King and queen we were named, king and queen we are. We hear you, and we come." He held out a hand to lift Lochu from the bench. She swayed on her feet, leaning against him as the two of them walked unsteadily down between all the staring eyes of their folk, around the fire in the middle of the hall, to join the two Druids.

The procession wound out of the hall, across the field and up the low-sloping hill to the Black Boar's Furrows and the holy ring of pillars where the white bull and black boar and golden stallion waited patiently by their keepers' sides. The three trials stood within the ring: two great wooden tubs of water, their sides higher than a man's arms could reach; two planks on high posts, with nooses fastened above them; and two paths laid out in a circle around the inside of the great ring. Senchán and Calatín led Conla and Lochu to the ladders by the sides of the barrels.

"King and queen pass over water," the Druids chanted, and the rest of the gathered throng, pressing close to the ditch in which the pillars were set, took up the chant, their massed voices deep and inhuman as the sound of waves beating against the shore. "Over water, over water, over water!"

Slowly the fool-king and fool-queen pulled themselves up the ladders. Maeve was close enough to see the sweat springing out on Lochu's brow, the fixed terror on her face as a gust of wind billowed Maeve's cloak out from her body. Two narrow planks lay across the tubs: it was the will of the gods now, whether Conla and Lochu would cross or drown.

Conla swept Ailill's colorful brat up in his arms, almost dancing out as the chant,

"Over water, over water!" Went on.

Lochu froze a moment. Yet if she stayed too long, the young men who had walked beside the bull would turn their ox-goads on her. Drunk as she might be, she knew that: she had seen it in years before. The bondsmaid-queen took a sharp sobbing gulp of breath, then inched out over the tub.

Once a rainy blast of wind sent her staggering, and Maeve thought she would fall, but she managed to catch her balance again, crouching down tearfully to cling to the far edge of the tub. Ailill's amadán had waited for his queen. Together they climbed down, and up the second set of ladders to the platforms where Senchán and Calatín stood with the gallows-nooses in their hands, ready to lay over the torcs of king and queen. With gentle hands, the Druids pulled the knots tight enough to hold, if not to choke, turning the two royal sacrifices to face their second trial. The planks over water had been two hands breadths wide; these planks were less than the width of Maeve's palm.

"King and queen pass through the air," the Druids called, and the folk took it up, their voices shivering through the sounds of wind and spattering rain. "Through the air, through the air!"

Conla had the wit not to look down: he walked the narrow path with the gallows-noose around his neck like a drunk man trying to prove himself sober by walking a straight line; and when one foot tried to slip on the wet wood, he was already swinging it out before the other.

Lochu trembled and swayed like a birch-sapling in the wind, her face shining wet with tears and rain. Maeve could not turn away, for she knew that Lochu walked above death in her place: if the gods demanded a queen's life, Lochu would lose her own for Maeve's sake. 'And yet what good would my death do the Cruachain, save open the door to Ulster's raiders? Maeve asked herself. Whether Lochu lives or dies, I will make my own offering in just a little time, and one that she would not dare in my place if she could.' At last Lochu reached the platform at the other side;

Calatín lifted the noose gently from around her neck, helping her down the ladder to the ground where Conla waited to take her hand.

"King and queen pass under blade," sang the two druids, and once more the throng answered their call, voices harsh and clanging as the shouts of battle. "Under blade, under blade!"

Now Calatín and Senchán each bore a sword, which they lifted above the fool-king and fool-queen. A drummer began a slow, steady beat; Conla and Lochu began to walk the path sun wise around the holy ring, while the two Druids, blades held before them, walked widdershins. Druids and royal couple passed at the eastern point of the ring; the Druids raised their blades over the others' heads, shoulders tense. Maeve's nails bit painfully into her palms; she tasted blood in her mouth from anxious chewing at her cheek.

The gods had spared the sacrifices from the threat of famine, and the threat of plague; but the last trial was the threat of battle, and that, even the children must know it by now!, Was the greatest danger to the folk of Connacht in the coming year. Soon, soon, the paths would cross in the west again; the gods would speak to the two Druids, and they would strike or hold their hands.

"Under blade, under blade!" The crowd roared. Maeve's eyes blurred. It seemed to her that she could see only the gold of her own hair, the red-gold of Ailill's, as Conla and Lochu came round to the west again, standing face to face with the Druids, white and black.

The blades blurred, flashing through the air. Amadán-king, bondsmaid-queen, the two of them dropped still to the earth, and Maeve felt the shock through her own heart.

It was a moment before her sight cleared enough for her to see the two unbloodied locks of hair the Druids were holding up, Senchán's short and red-brown, Calatín's longer, the brown-gold of ripening wheat.

"The king falls, the queen falls, the gods take their share for the coming year. Who will rule in Cruachan now, when the new year begins and the nights grow long?"

Maeve and Ailill came forth, gravely bowing their heads as the Druids' helpers took the royal cloaks and gold torcs from the couple lying on the ground in exhausted relief and robed the rulers again, setting Maeve's glittering gold diadem back on her head. Maeve did not have to call Baiscne; he was already there, his black shoulder nudging against her hip. When she lifted her hand to her folk, her wren fluttered chirping down to her.

Her marten ran out of the multiply-wrapped folds of her long brat to her shoulder, and she heard the cheers acknowledging her, "Oró, Maeve! Oró, Maeve of Cruachan!"

The threefold offering came next: the white bull for the Dagda, the black boar for Cromm Cruaich, and the golden horse for Lugh of the Many Crafts. Her head still ringing with the rushing power of her rebirth as queen, Maeve barely saw the bright blood flowing into the earthen trenches, only felt it as another stream of might among the many streams rising and weaving through the ring of pillars, converging upon her and sinking through her bare feet into the earth again. Though she had drunk little that morning, Maeve was as unsteady on her legs leading the procession back to the hall as Lochu had been stumbling out to the holy ring.

She was deeply grateful when Finnabair thrust a piece of honeyed bread into her hand, murmuring, "Mother, you must eat, or you will faint before the day is out."

After the sacrifices came all the games of feast and fair: the champions of the three allied provinces and the exiled Ulstermen strove at spear-casting and wrestling, at racing on foot and in their chariots, and at showing off their feats of battle, from the salmon-leap to springing across the points of spears. Merchants hawked their wares, their voices raucous as crows in the springtime; the scattered showers of rain were not enough to dampen anyone's spirits.

As the day waned, the sun reddening in the west, the laughter became louder and shriller, the dancers flinging themselves and each other about so vigorously that they often tumbled into the mud. Maeve could feel the night rising like a great wave, the dead pressing hard against the doors of the Otherworld. The sun was no more than a red glow through the darkening grey clouds on the western horizon when the Druids came into the great hall once again.

The fire in the middle of the hall had been left to die to embers; now the servants cast water upon it, letting the last coals hiss themselves to death. Again Maeve and Ailill followed the white-robed men out in silence to the holy ring. All through Cruachan fort, and on the encamped plain about it, the fires were dead, dying with the last of the old year. Wood stood heaped in the middle of the holy ring, but no flame burned there yet; Senchán, wrapped in the white bull's hide, stood facing Calatín, who wore the skin of the black boar. Silently they waited for the sun to set.

The last light died slowly, slipping into night. Calatín spoke, his voice deep and hollow as though it came from the bottom of a black cavern. "Summer ends; the year is dead; the dead come back to their homes. What welcome do their old friends give?"

"Our kin and friends are welcome, however they visit and where-ever they now dwell. Let the need-fire kindle light through the worlds, guiding clan to clan and kin to home," Senchán replied.

The old Druid crouched down, his hands moving swiftly and surely in the gloom; Maeve heard the hissing of wood turning fast against wood. It was too dark to see the first wisp of smoke, but she smelled the faint scent of burning even before she saw the ember, glowing as if the cloud-dulled sun had kindled a single spark in Senchán's care.

The Druid wrapped the little coal swiftly in a nest of dried grass, lifting it to his lips and blowing steadily until the flames suddenly sprang up. He dropped the burning ball of grass at the edge of the heaped wood, feeding it with dry twigs, then little sticks, then larger ones, until the fire leapt before him, its shadows patterning his white robe beneath the white bull's hairy hide.

"The fire dies and is reborn; the doors of Donn's house stand open; the dead come back to life. Take flame, and open doors, and welcome the wandering ghosts with meat and drink!"

Maeve and Ailill stepped forward, each lifting a burning brand from the fire. They bore their torches back to the great hall together. The central hearth had already been cleaned and new wood laid, from kindling at the bottom to the solid logs that would burn warmly all night.

Pine-needles and dried leaves crackled up at once as queen and king thrust their torches in, followed by the slower sizzling of the fire taking hold along the larger sticks, whipped up by the wind gusting straight from western door through eastern door. This night, however cold it got, those doors would not be closed: the ghosts must be free to pass, and the path of the síd-folk must not be blocked. Baiscne lifted his head, looking at the darkness outside, and gave a bark of welcome.

Maeve shivered: her hound could see what she could not, and the dead were quick to rise this night. The servants moved to set the tables, inside and out. They bore great platters with mounds of steaming roast pork and cheeses the size of chariot-wheels, creamy yellow and white with veins of blue; they heaped up loaves of white wheaten bread, and bronze bowls filled with sweet apples and little hard pears, with the last picking of blackberries, for after this night the Hag would sour them on their branches, and dark sloes mixed into honey.

Hazelnuts for wealth and fruitfulness, and sweet breads made with apples and nuts; all were set out for the living and the dead. No one sat at the white-draped table by the far wall: the food there was for the ghosts, and their wrath would fall on any living who touched it. A second plate of food and a full goblet of mead lay beside Fergus' own, and three more by Cormac, for Fergus' dead son, and for Noisu and his brothers Ardán and Anle. It seemed to Maeve that the spaces on the benches before those platters were not wholly empty, though she could not tell if the returning spirits filled them, or only the grief of the men who had failed to protect the slain.

Finnabair danced in the ring of folk about the fire, her golden braids swinging as she whirled in the embrace of a horse-masked man; Maine Feidhlim danced with a woman whose face was covered with blacking, but whose left breast hung out of her green gown. Maeve ate and drank sparingly, her belly tight within her. She passed bits of meat to Baiscne and her marten, bread to her wren, letting the soft sounds of the beasts' nibbling fill her ears like the humming of mead-drunkenness, and waited. Dark as the night was, even indoors where she could not see the least glimmer of stars through the flowing clouds. She could feel the moon rolling on through the sky. She did not need her black hound's bark to tell her the time had come.

Carefully Maeve rose from her seat, making her way through the travelers. No one would ask where she went. Ailill had drunken himself merry, and one woman would do him as well as another now; Fergus had drunken himself sad, sitting and staring at the empty place beside him. Her sons were all dancing about the fires, or else doing another sort of dance between the blankets. As for Finnabair, no telling what fancy might take a young woman on Samhain, but that was her own affair.

Maeve skirted the shadows of the bonfires, taking the western path down the hill. She had brought no torch: her feet knew the way, and her marten scampered before her, its pale fur a faint shimmer in the dark as it led her to the cave from which it had risen. Lest she fear misstep, she had Baiscne to guide her. Her hound from the house of Donn, protector against all that lay beneath the earth. Uaigh na gCat lay a fair walk from Cruachan síd, beneath a blackthorn tree at the foot of a small embankment.

Even in daylight, it was easy to miss; but the gleam of the marten's fur suddenly disappeared. Into the earth. Maeve crouched on all fours, feeling for the opening. The broken stones were wet and slimy beneath her hands as she crawled into the low, narrow space.

She knew this part of the cave as well as she knew the road that led to it: a few paces on, she could rise to a crouch, and a little further in, she was able to stand, carefully reaching above her head to be sure she had made the higher part of the rocky passage. Slowly she felt along the slippery rocks with her feet, crouching and bracing with her hands to ease herself down the two low drops in the narrow cave's floor. Neither was more than a step's depth, but in the dark, with the slime-covered irregular stones flooring the passageway, she could easily fall and crack her skull. Further along, the cave's floor rose sharply again. Maeve crept up it on hands and knees until it began to level, then rose to her feet once more.

She was not sure, she never was, just when she had passed from the outer reach of the Cave of the Martens to the way beyond it, the way that led into the depths of Cruachan síd, but now that she was upright again, she held herself proudly. If those who dwelt here saw her fear, it would go badly for her indeed. On Maeve walked, straight as if it were she who trod the narrow planks above water and through air now. She kept one hand on Baiscne's head, that he might guide her through the turnings beneath the earth. The thick silence faded to a humming about her head; she seemed to hear unearthly laughter behind her, a cruel cold laugh shivering up her back. In the utter blackness, her eyes began to cast ghostly glimmers against the dark.

Once, out of the corner of her gaze, she saw a goat's golden eyes and heard a sound like a horse nickering through the throat of a man; once something icy touched her back, and she had to choke her gasp of horror. She was Maeve of Cruachan, Connacht's queen, her strength won through pain and fear and struggle: she walked steadily on. Slowly, Maeve could not tell when, or how, the strange sounds in the blackness faded to faint music, swelling sweetly to lure her on. The wet stink of moldy stone gave way to a fragrance of apples, fresh and ripe; at the end of the dark hallway, golden light glimmered. Yet, though she wanted to run towards the lure, she trod as evenly as before, matching pace with the black dog behind her, till at last she stepped into the brightness of a green summer's day, and saw the one she had come to see waiting for her.

"Welcome to thee, Maeve," said King Ochall.

The king of Cruachan síd was taller than Maeve. His hair hung to his knees, waving in a play of golden light as though it were wrought from a thousand strands of gold spun finer and softer than spider-silk. His skin shone bright as moonlight; his eyes, pale blue as the sky at dawn, drew her as if he had flung an hundred tiny iron hooks into her heart and was pulling it from her body. Yet there was no pain or sorrow in looking upon him, save that of longing for his beauty.

Maeve clutched her fingers tightly in Baiscne's coarse wavy fur, staring back at King Ochall. It was said that no living man or woman could withstand the síde-beauty in their full glamour, but Maeve on Samhain, in Cruachan, was more than a woman.

She was Maeve of the Cruachain, bearing the right and the strength of the land within her, and that even the síde-king could not fully enchant or master.

"I am glad to visit thee, King Ochall, for so long as Samhain night lasts in the world above Cruachan síd and no longer. I am come to make our alliance as my father did, that Cruachan síd and Cruachan fort dwell in peace and gladness together, the heart of the rule of this land."

Ochall looked down at Maeve and smiled. Maeve felt her nipples tightening with desire, hard points tugging at the melting softness of her breasts with an almost painful pleasure. Her inner thighs throbbed for Ochall's touch, her belly aching for him to fill her.

"You are fair as ever, Maeve; I will lie with you. Yet, and you know it, you cannot bring to me what you did. You are not your land's sovereign as you were, nor the woman that you were: your husband rules your wedding. If you become my client, ruling Connacht under me, I shall give you all in my power of what you desire, and we shall seal that bargain instead.

"You need fear no shame in this: was not your own mother Croderg once handmaiden to Queen Etain, serving under King Midir?"

Ochall moved his pale hand gracefully, and his glimmering green raiment was gone, leaving only the white beauty of his body to blind Maeve's eyes. She felt the hot tears of unfulfilled longing spilling over her cheeks, the hot dampness between her legs, and she wanted, grievously, to say yes to the síde-king's offer. She held firm to the last shreds of her pride, though they sliced her heart like shards of broken iron, and said,

"I shall be client to no other ruler. As for my own rule: I have gathered a great host, and if we do not come home with the Donn Cuailgne, to reclaim my right and strength, I shall not come home living. if you will not recognize that, then this I vow: never again in my life shall I lie with a man who thinks me less than his match, be he of the sons of Mil or of the Tuatha de Dánann. If that ends our alliance, then remember, King Ochall: it was you who first gave scorn to me."

Ochall frowned. Suddenly he seemed stern and terrible to Maeve, and he no longer stood there naked, but clad all in shining silver mail, with a white-flaming sword in his hand.

"If you will not take what I offer now, then do not come beneath this hill again. Those above will regret your rashness, but keep the lands above while you can hold them. Though that may not be so long as you think!"

The flash of his sword through the air was a stroke of lightning; the thunder that followed after hammered Maeve into darkness, blind and deaf. For a moment she felt nothing: then there was cold mud soaking through her dress at the knees, cold wet stones slipping under her rock-torn hands, and Baiscne's cold nose prodding anxiously into her neck. Bruised and breathless, Maeve clung to the great hound, pushing herself up to her feet.

"I am Maeve of Cruachan, and Connacht's queen," Maeve whispered to her hound through gritted teeth, even as she had murmured through tears to Cormac in her womb. "And now I know what I had guessed at before: if ill comes of this raid, or this war, it is still better than if I had meekly accepted Ailill, or any man, as my ruler. At least now I have a chance to win back what his ill-thought words stole from me; whereas, had I given in, I should be not only Ailill's mere consort, but bondsmaid without hope to King Ochall. Let us go home now, my hound, and sleep as we may. There is much to do if I am to regain what I have lost!"

Fedelm

To look at, the land of Eriu is not so different from Alba. Only the weather is a little softer: it might have been a moon's turning before Samhain instead of near a fortnight afterwards when my chariot's wheels rattled on the causeway that led towards Cruachan in the dawning brightness. I rode through thick woodlands, the ruddy leaves of oak and the gold of beech brightening the brown ash-trees beneath blowing grey curtains of rain; between low hills and green fields splotched here and here with red and dun and white cattle, heads and horns lowered as they steadily sought out the last of the good summer grass.

I had not been accustomed to riding in a chariot when Cernach sent me on my way from the Druids' school, but in the long journey across Alba and Eriu I had learned to balance while standing, bending my knees with the shocks and only grasping the edge with one hand when the iron rims of the chariot's wheels clattered and bounced over the great logs that formed the track ways through bog and fen.

Nor did I still fear that a jolt would throw me into one of the peat-dark pools that glimmered back the sky's pale grey light to either side of the track way: Eochaid was a skilled driver, as skilled as any of the school's servants. I had been away for ten and a half years. Little had changed to the eye since my childhood, but as I watched the fine rain sifting over the familiar roadway and hills, I seemed to see a pattern of uneasy light swirling and weaving everywhere, as though the land were lit faintly within by a wind-whipped fire.

I thought of my bold words to Cernach, and my heart trembled a moment. In my childhood, the sight of a swine-herd of the side had whelmed me near death, and into the gifts of vision and filidecht. As a woman, I better knew the might of what stirred beneath Cruachan, and though a Druid's heart must be stauncher than any warrior's, her flesh more enduring and her will firmer. I had to clutch the chariot's edge and breathe a few deep slow droughts of air to strengthen the roots of my body and stop their quivering.

Then it seemed that all the faint unseen lines of light whirling beneath peat and pool, field and forest and the rough wet wood of the track way, swept into a single rippling current that flowed, not towards Cruachan and Maeve's host, but sharply to the right where the log road gave way to solid ground again.

That way, I knew, lay the house of Calatín, the younger of Cruachan's Druids.

"It must be, I thought, that I should speak with him before I set eyes on Maeve and Ailill in the flesh once more. He may have learned something of this that I do not know".

"To the right, Eochaid," I said.

My driver glanced back and nodded, his narrow black-mustached face pale under the folds of the dark bratt he had drawn around his head against the rain. He did not speak: Eochaid the Cat could not speak, save for a wordless yowl. Some students said he had truly been turned into a spotted cat, struck with a wand of shape shifting for some offense; and that, when he came to the school to beg his human form again and make amends, it was found that the spell had been laid either wrongly, or too well. Others said he was still enchanted, that only his voice had ever been stricken, and might yet return when he had served whatever time was set for him. Yet others claimed that he had been a fighting man struck in the throat with spear-butt or haft, so that no scar showed, but his voice was ruined; and thus had come where he might receive care, and where no man could reproach him for surrendering war for service.

Be that as it might, his hands were light on the reins of the fine matched grays that pulled my chariot; and were any brigand so foolish as to lift hand against a ban-drúi, Eochaid's sword was more than a match for one, or several. 'You will be riding through battle, Cernach had said. None would harm you willingly; but who can say where a sling-ball or spear may choose to strike once it has gained the freedom of the air?' In any case, after ten years in the close confines of the school, I had been not ready to ask for guesting at a farm, or find an ale-house for a night's bed.

Though Eochaid had no human voice, his gestures spoke clearly: between that, and the awe of crofters and ale-hosts when they saw a ban-drúi with a guard in a fine glittering shirt of Gaulish link-mail such as a king's son might wear, our travel had been pleasant and easy. Too pleasant in one way: my first feast of pork and the last fresh summer cheese after years of beans and black husk-bread had delayed us for two days. Neither the seeds of fennel, dill, and caraway I had Eochaid crush and steep in hot water, nor all my skills of body-mastery, could do much until the rich food had all made its unhappy passage out. The broad-faced farmer and his sweet plump wife had hovered in undeserved terror, lest I think that they had poisoned me and take some dreadful vengeance.

They did not, I suspect, breathe easily again until I left them with my blessing upon their home and flocks, going on my way with the rueful knowledge that satisfaction may sometimes be harder to bear than denial. Calatín's house lay a good walk northward from Cruachan fort, the track passing through the beech woods where I had seen Rucht and his swine before it swung around a tall hill and into the grove of hazels where the Druid dwelt. Not all Druids are alike in skills, though all know some of every wisdom-art. Some are gifted at word-craft or vision; others at harp and song and the tales of those who went before us.

Some are skilled at law and judgement, and some, though those are rare, know best the arts of magic. Most Druids in full training can call or turn weather, storm and wind and fog; that I could do, though my control was still imperfect. Some can make their visions so real that they appear to the waking eye in the full light of day. The greatest, I had heard, though never seen, could wreak such transformations as that rumored of Eochaid, to strike themselves or another with an enchanted wand and change the one struck into a beast: thus Math ap Mathonwy, once king in Alba, had done with Gwydion and Gilfaethwy, a transformation so complete that one bore in turn to the other a wolf-cub, a piglet, and a fawn.

As a child, I had believed Calatín's skill so great, and kept well out of his way when he passed my family's steading in his white robes.

At fourteen I knew no greater terror than when I stood trembling under his keen dark gaze, waiting for him to judge whether I was worthy to send to Alba. There, I had heard that, if he were not quite so mighty as I had feared, he nevertheless had a high repute in the magical arts.'I must calm myself; I must not meet him trembling like a new student before one of the high Druids'.

I knew that I likely looked well, even after riding in the early winter damp. Students were allowed no mirrors, nor might we darken our brows and lashes, redden our cheeks with berry juice, shadow our eyes with blue woad, or any of the other things folk do to make themselves look well. I smiled to myself.

Before I went to Alba, I would have thought such things beneath the notice of a Druid, whether woman or man. as I prepared to leave, Eithne, the eldest of the ban-drúi, took me aside and explained the importance of looks.

"The wise would pay as much attention to the ugly and ill-kept as to those of fine appearance. Yet if all folk, or most, were wise, what need would there be for Druids?" She had said to me. "And you are young and fair, hence must take pains to make men look on you with awe rather than desire, and keep women from striving against you. Use no colors on your face! Thus you may seem above trying to draw men's eyes, but you are gifted with fair hair and dark brows and lashes; you have by birth the hues others strive for. If you are well-dressed and carry yourself as I teach you. You will seem like a veritable woman of the síde-folk. I have never let a half-trained student pay such attention to appearance before. it seems that, ready or not, your task is on you. You may be half-trained; you shall not go half-armed."

Eithne had not boasted unfairly. The first time I saw myself in a mirror, the first time in ten years, I hardly knew myself. The woman looking from the polished silver was beautiful: fine-carved features, broad forehead and high cheekbones tapering to a pointed chin, with brilliant blue-grey eyes edged by soft black lashes under sharp-arched dark brows, white skin framed by a wealth of golden hair. When the burdensome rope of braid that had hung down my back for years was brushed out at last, it fell about me like a softly waving cape.

Then Eithne thumped me hard on the back of the head, for I had lost control of my face, lips parting in surprise and eyes widening. "A fine garment, but you will change it soon enough!" She scolded. "Do not let yourself be taken by the sights that dazzle the unwise; you know the body's beauty is a snow that melts to nothing when the sun strikes it."

Chastised, I had composed my face. Still, in the depths of heart and womb, I kept remembering my vision of King Ailill lying golden and magnificent beside his queen, and wondering if – though the body be but a garment that is changed again and again – such a maid as the mirror had shown might draw his eye. That thought had not wholly left me as I neared Ai Cruachan, but I carefully pushed it down beneath Eithne's teachings. I had braided my long fair hair into three plaits instead of the simple braid that kept it in order while I traveled, winding two tresses about my head and letting the last fall to brush the backs of my knees.

From the school's bounty, I wore a mantle of green heathered with colors, pinned over my bosom by a gold brooch, and a hooded tunic embroidered all over with red interweaving; my sandal-buckles were gold. I used no berries to redden my cheeks or lips, but the cold ride would have brought the color out in my face, bright as foxglove blossoms against my pale skin.

Still, I could not keep my fingers from twitching. Lest they betray me, I drew my lace-weaving from the bag at my feet. Cernach's personal leaving-gift to me had been a bordering rod of silvered bronze with seven strips of red gold at the sides. As I touched it, I could feel the power thrumming hard within the metal. I could not help looking at the bunching of Eochaid's shoulders beneath his dark bratt and wondering, 'If I touched him with this rod, would it transform him again into a cat? That would be a wonder, here in Eriu. We call martens tree-cats, perhaps because they are the closest likeness that the sons of Mil found here; but I never saw a true cat before I went to Alba'. The urge was almost overwhelming: I have found few things harder than reining in power when it springs easily to the hand.

Like water, power carried casually often spills on the user's own feet. It would have been an ill deed to treat a good man in my service so, and foolish in any case. If it failed, I would be an idiot for having tried, and if it succeeded, twice so, since neither a cat nor I could drive the chariot. As we drew nearer to Calatín's house, my nervousness faded into a shimmering tingle throughout my body; it almost seemed to me that I was floating as in vision.

I did not know whether the Druid's power was so great as to bear me up even before I saw his hazel-grove, or whether it was I myself coming closer to some turning of power. Eochaid swung us expertly around a sharp bend in the path, and the world blurred to a rainbow of pale light in my eyes, save for the woman staring at me from the warrior-seat of her own chariot, woad-ringed blue eyes wide and lips slightly parted. I knew Queen Maeve at once from childhood glimpses; and had I not seen her naked in my vision?

She wore a long red tunic and bratt embroidered with glimmering threads of gold and silver and silk; an embossed band of ruddy pure gold held her yellow hair back from her face. She gazed at me, her pupils swelling black as if from fear or desire; the blue paint about her eyes was stark against her pale skin. Her broad shoulders strained as if she were forcing her hand not to drop to the gold-adorned hilt of her sword. I had words made ready for this meeting, but Maeve spoke first.

"What are you doing here, maiden?" She asked.

My speech shifted in my mouth, smooth as a salmon in the water.

"I bring advantage and good luck in your gathering of the four strong provinces of Eriu against the land of Ulster on the Raid for the Bull of Cuilagne," I said, and knew that I spoke the truth.

Maeve looked at me carefully, for quite a long time.

When she spoke her words were very measured, as if she spoke indeed to one of the síd-folk, and a single word amiss might lead to disaster and worse. "Why should you do this for me?"

"I have much cause, for I am of your folk, though lowly born."

Once more Maeve considered deeply. I could see the faint furrow between her darkened brows, and it seemed to me that I knew the thoughts roiling like springtime salmon flashing through the deep waters of her mind. She had asked me two questions already. The third, she was thinking, would tell her the truth of what I was and what I wished of her.

"Who of my people are you, and what is your name?" The queen asked me at last.

"That is not hard to answer with truth. I am the seeress Fedelm, called by some Fedelm from the síd of Cruachan, and I am a ban-fili of Connacht."

The tightness in Queen Maeve's shoulders eased. She would have known when I went to Alba, and perhaps remembered some word of me in my childhood: even a great queen's stronghold is not so large that the least of its folk are wholly unknown to her.

"Whence have you come here from?" She asked.

"From Alba, after learning the skill of prophesy."

Maeve blew out a quiet breath. Though the shadow about her eyes seemed to darken, her gaze lit the more fiercely, like a hunter who, thinking his antlered quarry lost, rounds a copse of brambles in the woods to find his stag standing poised before him again. "Do you have the form of divination?" Her voice was low and rich, so that I wished I might hear her sing, and she controlled it almost as well as a trained bard. Still, I had learned to listen.

Beneath the queen's commanding voice ran a tiny harmonic shiver: the very faintest hint of a young maid's hope and fear in inquiring about a might-be husband, or a young mother's, asking the fate of the babe in her womb.

Now I understood. Maeve had been to Calatín, and he had not told her what she needed, or wished, to know. I had been sent for this. Senchán was famed for wisdom, the younger Druid for magic.

Though, as full Druids, both must be competent diviners, neither was unusual in prophetic skills.

"I have," I answered.

"Look then for me, and tell me the outcome of this deed I have undertaken."

Now Maeve's voice was fully under control, holding only rulership and strength. Nevertheless the echo of her last words haunted me. Though a Druid's first allegiance is to her school and fellowship, few of us do not have a second faith to our land and ruler. Since none would dare raise hand to a single drúi, let alone all the druid together, that second faith usually plays the greater part in our deeds when we are gone into the world. I had in my bag of herbs a precious tiny phial of glass traded from the South, full of a draught I had compounded myself.

Valerian to still the body, hemp flower and fey-caps to open the sight to the Otherworld, and vervain to cleanse and make holy ward: when one looks into the realms beyond the hills we see, the folk there may look back, and many are no friends to humankind. As I stooped to find the phial, even before my hand closed on its smooth surface, the blood rushed to my head in a dizzying gush. Weaving with Cernach's rod had brought me half into trance: now unseen wings beat about my ears, and my sight shimmered into swirling brightness as the wheeling sun glinted a myriad of sparks from the corselets and spear-tips, steel sword-blades and bright bronze shield-studs, of the host of the warriors of Ireland. All shone brilliant red, lit as by a shaft of sunlight through a river of water-clear blood.

I felt like a drinking-skin, overfilled with mead to spurting or bursting. Maeve's question tightened my throat so that only a thin stream of words could flow, answering what was asked.

"Tell me, Fedelm, ban-fili: how do you see our host?"

"I see them crimson with blood; I see them bathed in red."

"That cannot be true augury, for I have heard from my messengers that Conchobar already lies in his bed in Emain, struck down by the pangs of Ulster: we have nothing to dread from Ulster's men speak truth, Fedelm, ban-fili: how do you see our host?"

I might be angry with the queen later for her doubt. Now the vision swelled within me as though I were a harp's sounding-board thrumming with the resonance of its deepest string; naught else touched my mind.

"I see them crimson with blood; I see them bathed in red."

"That cannot be true augury. My messengers say Cuscraid Mend of Macha, Conchobar's son, lies in his bed in Inis Cuscraid, writhing in the pangs of Ulster: we have nothing to fear from Ulster's men."

Despite Queen Maeve's words, I saw the fear-shadow sweeping across her eyes like the veil of rain under a swift-blowing storm cloud. Mirrored deep within her gaze were eight strong young warriors and a maiden, then nine babes, Maeve's heart twinging with the sweet pangs of suckling at her breast; then children with wooden weapons, each clash of training-blade on shield ringing through her in a bolt of pride and terror, bolts striking keener than the swords' fine edges as the boys grew to wield the steel of men and she saw their faces grinning beneath spatters of blood.

It seemed that I could feel each pang as my own. Echoing and trembling in my maiden womb, and I could not tell whether I shook from longing or from fear. Only Maeve's words, strict as ritual must call for, and that is why! Drew me back to the greater vision.

"Speak truth, O Fedelm: how do you see our host?"

"I see them crimson with blood; I see them bathed in red."

"Surely that is not true augury! Eoghan, Durthach's son, lies in the pangs of Ulster in Rath Airthir, and Celtchar, Uthechar's son, at his fort in Lethglas, and a third of the Ulstermen with him. My messengers bear word: we have nothing to fear from Ulster's host. Fergus son of Roech son of Eochaid stands with us, and thirty hundred warriors with him. Speak truth, O Fedelm: how do you see our host?"

Maeve's voice shook with fear and anger, her right hand shadowing her glinting sword-hilt. I might have feared her, had the vision not tightened its grip on my throat so that only the truth could force its way from me.

"I see them crimson with blood; I see them bathed in red."

"Surely," Maeve said, lifting her hand again and forcing herself to stillness, "this is not as it seems to you. For when Erin's men shall gather in one place, there shall always be quarrels and broils over how they shall be ordered, in the vanguard or the rear, at the ford or the river, over who shall be first to kill boar or stag. Look now again for us and speak the truth, Fedelm; tell me, Fedelm, how do you see our host?"

"I see them crimson with blood; I see them bathed in red."

Then the poet-words came upon me, but I barely heard them spurt from my mouth: the swirling vision filled all my world and thought. A man moved whirling through the host, sparks flying from his chariot's wheels. The hero-light shone about his head, radiance hiding his face as truly as a cloak of deep shadow, save for the needle-keen stare of his dark eyes through the brightness, seven points of power burning many-colored from each pupil. His mantle flowed red; he held two bloody spears in one hand.

Many wounds gashed he pale muscle-etched skin of his half-naked body, some straining the stitching that closed them until they leaked thin droplets of blood where each thread drove into flesh, and some gaping fresh. It seemed to me that he turned and writhed, coiling and striking like an immense serpent, a monstrous shape of flickering shade and white flame against the slow-moving crimson host around him. The great snake's black tail lifted as a huge cruel-barbed spear, the red streamers of blood spattering from its head interwoven with sharp dark trails like harsh sorrow scoring a king's face. Light swirled about the short-bladed sword he wielded, so swift that he might have held four swords in each hand.

He rose and rose again, swelling and warping into a shapeless shadow of terror, setting his foot on every hill; it seemed an hundred heads dangled like a truss of berries in his grip. His brightness-hooded head reared back and he howled. Hill and earth answered him in turn, and then I knew him: Setanta called Cú Chulainn, the Hound of Ulster.

Though he was but one, and sorely hurt, he scythed through the host of Ireland to the sound of women's keening, their cries rising high and eerie to drown out the deep war-calls of the men. Warning or unshakable foresight, I did not know. Even the wisest cannot always know such things. Yet I spoke as I saw. I knew that the words came from me in the well-trained forms of poetry, as molten gold must pour into the shape of the mold or be wasted; but only Maeve knows what they were.

Maeve

The weaving-rod fell from the young prophetess' hand, rattling against the wooden floor of her chariot. The maiden's body sagged abruptly, but before the queen could cry out, Fedelm's charioteer had whirled to catch his charge about the waist and lift her in his arms. He dropped the reins; the well-trained horses stood firm as rocks while the charioteer jumped lightly down and carried the seeress over to Maeve, her long golden braid looped over his arm to keep it out of the mud. He looked pleadingly into Maeve's face, but spoke no word. *Is he an idiot?* Maeve wondered. No: lines of intelligence marked his clean-shaven face; his carefully-shaped black mustaches showed careful tending, and his green-gray eyes were bright and sharp.

She looked for scarring on his throat, saw none. *Under a geas he wants me to help her.* Maeve pointed back towards the Druid's house, tightening the sinews of her wrist to keep her own hand from shaking.

"Calatín's house lies that way. Put her in the chariot, and follow me."

Finnabair's face shone pearl-white against the bright red and blue checks of her hood for a moment before she turned to the reins of Maeve's horses again. She drove without speaking, and Maeve was glad for that. The queen felt trapped between two bronze shields ringing with the clangorous beat of swords, her own questions and the prophecies poured out upon her echoing ceaselessly inside her head.

'Many part with their kin and friends here today, and from their homes and lands, fathers and mothers. Unless every one return unscathed, it is upon me that they will cast their sighs and their ban, for it is I that have assembled this levy. I see them crimson with blood, I see them bathed in red. Yet there goes not forth nor stays at home any dearer to me than we are to ourselves. On to battle now he comes; if ye watch not, ye are doomed: this is he who seeks you in fight, brave Cú Chulainn. Speak truth, Fedelm, ban-fili: how do you see our host? Gore shall flow from warriors' wounds, long shall it live in memory; bodies hacked and wives in tears." How do you see our host?" The man in his red cloak sets his foot on every hill...I know full well this host shall be smitten red by him', and Calatín's words warred against and interwove with those Fedelm and Maeve had spoken, a glittering golden thread through crimson and shadow: 'Whoever comes not back, you yourself shall come'.

The grove of hazels was leafless already, a thicket of slender living wands thrusting up like a host of spears trembling in the rain-spattered wind. Maeve had risen well before dawn and reached the Druid's door as the first light began to glimmer in the east. Though a heavy sweep of clouds dimmed the morning brightness to pale grey, Maeve could see the Ogham lines carved on the door posts of the round hut beneath the dripping edge of its peaked thatch roof, and the dark stain on the threshold-stone where the piece of sacrificial swine's flesh that Calatín had gnawed to gain his prophecy had rested. 'How long was I listening? I must hasten: it will not be much longer before the host is ready to march'.

Maeve tapped the doorpost as Fedelm's charioteer came up with his mistress cradled in his arms. The girl breathed deep and even, her delicate triangular face serene. Maeve had seen men sleep thus after the shock of a deep wound, and awaken in good heart afterwards. She hoped it was the same with Druidcraft. Calatín opened the door. The Druid was no longer wearing his white robes, only a striped bratt wrapped around his lean body. His young wife Nuagal nestled lazily among the blankets and sheepskins of their bed, pale blue eyes heavy-lidded over a faint sated smile, and the rich smell of their lovemaking hung heavily on the air. 'How long was I listening? Maeve wondered again. Or perhaps a Druid has other skills than poetry and magic and law, to satisfy a woman so well and quickly when time presses.'

"Bring her in," the Druid ordered. "Nuagal, leave her have the bed: she has greater need than yours."

Nuagal rolled out of the bed, hastily wrapping her mantle about herself, and Fedelm's charioteer laid the girl down. Calatín bent over the young prophetess, peeling each eyelid back in turn as if she had received a head-wound, then setting his long hand lightly upon her pale throat to feel for the pulse's beat.

"Fedelm prophesied. Did she take any draught beforehand, or rub an ointment between her eyes?"

"She did not. It seemed to me that she was reaching for something in the bag at her feet. Then she stood again, and a strange light shone from her eyes, it was as if each had three pupils glimmering with power. I asked her my question, and she answered, and then she began to speak at length of the vision she saw." And if you don't know that I doubted or disliked her augury, then perhaps I do not need to tell you, Maeve thought: Calatín was touchier than Senchán when it came to the rights and privileges of a Druid.

"Indeed. Well, I remember when we sent Fedelm of Cruachan síd away to Alba ten years ago. I had not seen a more promising young foreseer, and betimes word of her progress has come back to me. She should not be here, for she has ten years and a season yet before she becomes a full Druid. Yet I see that she is no runaway, but has been sent out with the school's bounty and its blessing, and I felt Cernach's token in her hand even as she rode here. There are great matters stirring, and she stands near to the heart of them."

As he spoke, the Druid began to dress himself. He did not put the robes of his ritual office back on. Those he would only wear for sacrifice or judgement or other ceremonies, but instead took blue-dyed trousers and a yellow linen tunic from the large chest beside the bed.

"How soon will she recover?" Maeve asked.

"In a very little time. She is only stunned, with no harm done. Nuagal, be ready to feed the girl when she wakes. When she has eaten, send her back to Ai Cruachan in her chariot as fast as she may come. If her head aches, give her a draught of the herbs I use for such occasions, and send her when she is recovered."

Calatín pulled a corselet of jingling iron links out of the chest, working it onto his arms and then flinging them over his head so that the mail-shirt slithered into place on his wiry shoulders.

Then he took a sword in a scabbard mounted with dark garnets in bronze work, girding it about his waist with a gold-worked leather belt, and shook the chain mail again so that the belt would take up some of the weight, as if he were a warrior used to bearing such gear every day. He wrapped the heavy woolen brat around his shoulders over the armor. The heavy silver brooch that pinned it shone fair in the grey light from the open doorway, but the dark gleam of the mail-shirt underneath seemed a truer promise of what lay ahead. Maeve could not quite bring herself to ask what more Calatín might have seen, to make him give up his Druidic inviolability for the armor that both warded and marked a warrior.

She knew that he was a surprisingly fine fighter for a man of his calling, and more than surprising for his age, more than twenty years older than herself. More than once she had come to his hut to see the Druid stripped to the waist with lean muscles moving tight under his sallow skin, leaping and joining among the rustling hazel-branches as lithely, powerfully, and precisely as any young hero who had trained with Aoife or Scathach. It was rare that a Druid should be a man of weapons, but not unknown, and it was also said that Calatín would have been a champion as great as any in Connacht or Ulster if he had not been called to magic and learning.

"I have summoned my sons to this raid as well," the Druid said, bending to shrug the straps of his large wicker pack onto his shoulders. "The time may come when you are glad of our aid."

Maeve was about to frame some remark that she was always glad of Calatín's aid, but the way his black brows knit over his raven-keen eyes forbade her to speak.

'How many sons will lie in their blood because of me? She wondered. His...or mine? Someone's, without doubt, and each as dear to their mother as my own are to me. They pass bright to the Otherworld, and will come back to the earth we see again. That little lessens the sorrow of their going, when we see the beloved body hacked and gashed about with wounds, and the dear eyes that gazed into our own gleaming blind and still as fracture-clouded glass. Still, no one in my host has come bound or dragged in chains. Heroes will fight for glory and treasure and pride, whether they gather in a great army beneath a leader, or quarrel over the hero's portion in the hall until only bloodshed will serve to settle it. I sent out call and cause, but every sword-bearer camped by Ai Cruachan is there for reasons seeming good to them, for me, there is reason enough.'

Maeve

When Maeve arrived back at Ai Cruachan, the sea of warriors' tents around the great fortress-mound's lower palisade was gone. Chariot-horses stamped and arched their necks, neighing eagerly. The hard cold wind shattered the clouds, their swift-moving heavy shadows mottling the low green fields and dimming the brown-forested mountains with ragged scatterings of sun-silvered rain; fresh-washed winter sunlight glittered from helms and armor.

Here and there a standard-pole rose above the host, the polished bronze of the standard-figures, boar and bull, horned serpent and Fergus' mighty horse, the marten of Cruachan, shining like gold over the warriors' heads. The gilded bronze of the leaders' helm-crests glowed like molten fire, 'Just such a glow as Fedelm saw, when she spoke of the hero-light around the head of our foe!' By the standards stood trumpeters, their long curved horns like a row of glittering bronze eels arching out of the water.

Most fighters wore helms and armor, but there were many whose lime-washed hair stood up in fearsome crowns of pale spikes, and a few standing bare-chested and laughing at the winter cold, their white skins ornamented with blue whorls and lacing of blood-stanching woad.

Two chariots broke off from the main body as Finnabair drove her mother up the road. Ailill's helm was gold-washed above his long ruddy-gold hair, and the mantle about his armored shoulders was bright crimson. Standing in his chariot, he looked a magnificent figure. Fergus was a little shorter than the king, but the bronze horse cresting his helmet raised his height above Ailill's, and his mail over padded leather exaggerated the bulk of his shoulders and chest to awesome proportions.

"What word of foretelling do you bring back for us, Queen Maeve?" Her husband asked formally. For once, Ailill was not smiling, his handsome features grim beneath the gilded rim of his helmet.

"It is a raid of blood and heroism we go on," Maeve answered. "The hosts will be reddened; we will face a strong foe. Yet what warrior ever won glory in cutting down swineherds?"

Ailill and Fergus both nodded.

"True, that Ulster's men lie in their pangs, and cannot stand against us on the way in," Fergus said. "An army of this size, at this time of year when the light lessens swiftly and the roads are thick with mud, cannot cross to Cuailgne in nine days, let alone back. Nor do you, or you would not have summoned to yourself the men of the four provinces of Ireland."

"And women," Maeve murmured, looking over the heads of the host to the gleaming bronze deer-standard of Flidais Foltchain, who had come with a troop of her men, though she had left her husband Adammair behind to tend her lands and beasts, and wagons piled high with butter and grain, hard-pressed cheese and smoked meats to feed the host on the way. "As you should know yourself, Fergus."

Fergus' grey gaze followed Maeve's. A rare grin lit his face; he ducked his head, as if pretending to be an abashed youth.

"It is true that Flidais and I have gotten along well enough before," he murmured.

Ailill leaned over from his chariot to thump the Ulsterman hard on the back, his fist thudding against Fergus' mail hard enough that a lesser man might have called it more a blow than a friendly buffet.

"And may you do so again, my friend! When battle is close to hand, there are few reproaches regarding who enters which tent in the night, is it not so?"

"Enough of this," Maeve said crisply. "The days grow short, and the march is long. The chariot-steeds are yoked, the wagon-horses harnessed: time we were on our way! You go back to your men, Fergus, and I shall take my place at the head of Connacht's warriors. Ailill, are your troops drawn up beside mine?"

"As always." Ailill's mouth curled into its usual lazy grin under his bright mustaches.

"Then let us go."

Maeve's war-gear lay carefully wrapped in layers of wool at the bottom of the chariot. She unwrapped it now, shrugging on her mail corselet and belting her sword to her side. She set the helm on her head, the helm of Connacht's ruler, its two short straight horns and nibbed cap of ancient bronze remounted on good Gaulish iron and bound with gold about the brow in her grandfather's time. Finnabair urged her mother's horses on. The two golden steeds trotted through the host, tossing their heads with excitement, though they were too well-trained to shy or pull sideways against their bronze-mounted yoke.

Maeve lifted a short casting-spear from the bottom of the chariot, holding it above her head so that all might see Connacht's queen was ready for war. Men shouted greetings as she rode through the host, voices keen with excitement. The provinces of Ireland had not mustered together thus in their lifetimes, and few here did not have a score to settle with Conchobar and Ulster. Maeve's own troops stood between Ailill's Leinstermen and her son Cormac's threefold host. The former were all large men, with a few female champions who over topped Maeve herself.

They seemed a troop of giants; Maeve almost expected the earth to shake as they moved. Singly, Cormac's men were not so awe-inspiring; but together, with matching hair and cloaks and armament, they seemed mightier than their numbers. The more so when they began to march, for the fifty men of her son's elite guard lifted their feet and put them down all together, like one man multiplied to many by a Druid's incantations. Though their eyes slid sideways as Maeve rode past, they kept their close discipline; when Cormac, in his chariot at their head, lifted his spear in a salute to his mother, they raised their spears as one.

"Oró!" Cormac shouted, and his men echoed him. "Oró, Queen Maeve!"

Excitement flushed Maeve's body as the deep voices hailed her. Her fingers tingled, gripping the spear; her morning's misgivings melted away, and the world took on the sharp-edged clarity of battle soon to be joined. The rising of the hosts of Ireland from Cruachan would not last long, but this first glow was something to cherish: its memory would warm the army well on the wintry march.

"Oró, Cormac Connlongas, my eldest son!" Maeve called back. "Sharp are your spears and keen your arms, and that is well, for there are great deeds to be done!"

The eight best chariots in Connacht, with the finest steeds and best charioteers, bearing Cruachan's mightiest champions, ringed Maeve's own chariot. That was her habit in battle: it kept a space clear about her, that she not be blinded by dust, but could see, as well as possible, how the battle moved and where she should command her troops to press or withdraw. When a sudden shock was needed, she and her guard could thunder down like a flight of eagles stooping from the mountain's peak. Many a man had striven to break through their cordon, to win the head of Queen Maeve of Cruachan.

She and her guard were bait for the best warriors, but none had ever snapped at that bait without scathe, and the heads of several men who had tried now stared hollow-socketed from the trophy-posts that ringed Cruachan's fortress. Now all were in place. Maeve signaled to the two trumpeters who stood to either side of Cruachan's gilded marten-standard. Their long curved instruments rose in unison like the bronze-adorned horns of a noble bull, the thin embossed disks on the end catching the sunlight and flinging it about in brilliant sparks. Three deep blasts rang out, and the hosts of Ireland began to march towards Ulster.

Though Maeve began the march in the lead, when she had held her position long enough for all to see and know her, she began to circle around and through the host. She marked whose weapons had been polished that morning, whose already showed the first dull bloom of rust; she saw who marched and rode in good order, who scrabbled along in a mob; and where men quarreled among themselves or between clan or sept or province.

It was no easy thing to keep such an army in close form, and she knew it would grow harder as the exaltation of marching out wore off. Some walked barefoot or in ragged shoes: she marked them as well. Even hardy folk could lose toes to the frost, and the queen's bounty could easily stretch to the care of common soldiers. Baiscne paced beside her when Finnabair drove fast, leaping up to curl in the bottom of her chariot when she slowed. He might be from the house of Donn, but he was still a wolfhound, and would sleep more than half the day if he could.

Maeve's wren fluttered about her: she hoped its flight would hint some sign of what was to come, but no understanding was given her. When the western sky began to redden, Maeve signaled her trumpeters to call a halt. The host did not stop easily, nor all at once, but ground to rest piece by piece. Maeve's own servants began to put up her tent, but she would not allow her chariot to be let down nor her horses unyoked until she had rounded the whole camp, although she oversaw the last of it only by the light of torches and camp fires.

Ailill's tent was beside Maeve's, Fergus' next to Ailill's, with Cormac and his seven half-brothers camped by Fergus. On Maeve's other side were the tents of Finnabair and Flidais, and a fourth had been raised behind her. She was about to ask who had come uninvited to the royal camp when she saw the firelight glinting oddly from the green-gray eyes of Fedelm's mute charioteer, who stood armed and threatening outside the tent: the ban-fili must have caught up with the host along the way.

Maeve's sons were nowhere to be seen, either reviewing their own troops or washing off the mud and sweat of the day's ride before they ate; but Ailill, Fergus, and Finnabair were all seated on stools about the fire between Ailill's tent and Maeve's, where Lochu was turning skewers of thick-cut lamb on a spit. Maeve's belly cramped with hunger at the scent of the roasting meat. She had gone fasting to Calatín, and had only managed to cram down a few hard oatcakes in between her surveillance of the gathered host. Baiscne, too, lifted his great head to sniff the air and nuzzle hopefully at Maeve's breast.

Finnabair handed her mother a silver goblet. Maeve sipped the sweet mead, careful not to drink too quickly. There was a silver platter with a half-destroyed loaf of bread and part of a round of cheese on the ground between the two men: Maeve sliced off a good helping of both, while another servant brought a stool for her and a large platter of bones and offal for Baiscne. The cheese was excellent, not hard and dry as winter cheese often was, but white and creamy with a hint of fennel; the bannock was toasted brown without the usual camp fire charring. Her marten scampered up, raising itself on its hind legs and bracing its forepaws on Maeve's shins to beg for tidbits.

"Flidais was here not long ago," Maeve said indistinctly, clearing her mouth with a sip of mead.

Ailill laughed. "You are wise as a Druid," he said, the good humor in his voice taking the sting from his sarcasm. "Yes, she left this food, and said she would be back after tending to her own men." He paused. Maeve waited for the question she knew must come, marshaling her thoughts to the answer.

Fedelm

I had woken a little past noonday, to find myself in Calatín's hut, and the Druid almost ready to be gone. I had quailed under his gaze at first, but his kind-voiced young wife Nuagal had quickly put me at my ease. it is harder to fear a man, even a Druid of high magical skill, when you have seen him kicking through the rushes and peering under the bed for a lost shoe. Calatín was a tall man, but wiry and thin: his weight hardly slowed our chariot as we rushed to catch the host. He was a good companion on the ride, asking after the health of the old teachers and a few of the younger ones with whom he had studied.

He inquired about my studies, but gave none of the harsh criticisms of my half-trained state I had feared, only said, "Well, if Cernach thought you fit for this, he is likely right. Still, I should like to know what caused that choice, and what you remember of the vision you spoke for Maeve."

When I had told him, he nodded, and did not speak for a time. During the day's march, I caught glimpses of Maeve circling around and through the army. She stopped occasionally to speak to her warriors; once I saw her break up a fight between two nobles, pounding her bronze spear-butt sharply on their helms and backs and shouting until they gave over. She never came close enough to speak with Calatín and myself, and I was not sure she saw us.

When the army halted at Cul Silinne, I asked Eochaid to put my tent behind Maeve's. The child I had been, peering awed from behind a door when the queen rode by, cringed at my presumption. As ban-fili, I had the right and duty to be there; for the honor of all Druids, I should ask no leave. Still, I could not bring myself to sit between King Ailill and Fergus where they lounged beside the fire. I watched from my tent as Maeve passed the guard and the withy-wall about the royal camp at last, settling by her husband.

A fair couple they looked: Ailill had washed and dressed his long hair already, so that it shone like new copper, the leaping shadows of the flames softening the interwoven colors of his mantle. Maeve was still armored beneath her red cloak; her fair hair was braided about her head, and if a day under her helm had matted or disordered the thick tress, the glitter of her ruler's diadem hid it. I had to still myself as for trance to pay attention to what they were saying, numbers and gear, who could not march beside whom for the sake of old blood-feuds that might leap from ember to flame in an instant. Druids know something of war: none would dare assail us or our holy places, but those who would counsel kings must know a king's business.

Druids have turned the tide of battle more than once. Sometimes in full fight: calling down terror and the aid of those who delight in blood and fear against the foe, or summoning such storms or fog that no man could see who stood within weapon-reach. More often, by cunning means: the storm turning the foe's road into a quagmire, the river swelling to become unfordable, the mice or mold devouring the enemy's food. Though all arts are learned a little with the others as one might nibble on bread and cheese with ale before a feast, the main banquet of magic is for the third seven-years of learning. I was not here to cast battle-spells or advise war-leaders on tactics and supply, but to offer visions of those things that sense and experience and wit could not foresee.

Now, I listened to learn. Ailill drew Maeve skilfully, like a spinner teasing soft strands of wool into a smooth thread; but when Fergus broke in, I heard the clash of flint on iron and saw the sparks leaping up. The tiny wrinkle between Ailill's bright brows eased then; he would stretch his long legs and drink like a farmer who hears hard-battering rain ease into the good soft mist that nourishes the young seedlings. Finnabair watched and listened, now and again asking a thoughtful question. She was unarmed and without armor; and her slim white arms showed no warrior's muscles or scars; but I guessed she was thinking towards a day when she might advise husband or consort, and I paid close attention to the answers she received.

"I trust you are learning from this," Calatín murmured in my ear.

I started sharply. "I...believe so."

"That is well. Maeve is a wise war leader, who can keep such a host as this pointed towards one purpose. Her heart is a rock-strewn river in flood. She cannot see all its depths or hazards, and a river in such turmoil may spill over its banks to its loss. Watch and listen well! This night is well-omened for those who would strike against their foes. On such a night, one should aim one's anger with care."

Then he was gone. I told myself that I should not be vexed that one so skilled in magic could hide himself from my senses, even when I had been looking up into the shadow of his face half an heartbeat ago. it was hard not to feel galled that I could be deceived like any once-born herder of sheep. However, though I was not full-trained and had only a little magical lore, that did not mean I had to be a fool.

Calatín had no clear reason to sneak here. If he had walked to Maeve's camp and fire, he would have been welcomed with food and drink, his counsel heard with great attention. Hence, he did not wish that. Whatever he meant to come of his visit to the royal enclosure must come from me. He had left me a riddle to unravel for my training? Did he mean to teach me along the way. He would hardly hazard a great matter on such a purpose, unless, for my gifts or some other reason, he knew that I would be able to see something that he could not. The first step was to guess what.

'How am I different from Calatín? I doubt this is a matter of training, except as we are gifted in different ways. Very well: I am the more gifted in vision, and perhaps more skilled in poetry. I am young and virgin; he is old, at least in his fifties, twice-wedded with grown children. I am late-come from Alba, where he has not been for more than twenty years. Some news or new thought in the schools. Word travels swiftly between Druids, and while we may keep wisdom from the hands of those who cannot be trained and trusted, we seldom keep it from one another. I am a woman, and he a man: and is that not near the root of this matter?'

The advice he had given me was to watch and listen. Every Druid knows that, as the young salmon must grow in the deeps of the sea before it can flash silver in the flood. Wisdom is often nurtured in hiding before it springs up to the knowing mind. I watched, and listened, and waited by the riverbank to see what might glimmer forth.

Maeve

"Cruinniuc boasted that his wife Macha could run faster than any horse of the king of Ulster. The king heard, and demanded that she fulfill Cruinniuc's boast, or else he would slay her husband. She was heavily pregnant, and begged to be allowed to give birth first; the king refused. Macha turned to the warriors of Ulster, pleading, "Did each of you not have a mother? None would aid her. So she raced the horses and beat them, giving birth to twins at the finish. As she lay there dying, she set this curse on the king and men of Ulster: that however great need was upon them, they should suffer the same pains that she herself had suffered in her labor. It is thought by many that Cruinniuc's wife was the same as she who raised the royal fortress of Emain Macha, the horse-goddess and land-goddess of Ulster."

While Maeve, Ailill, and Fergus had done a great deal towards arranging how their troops should be arrayed on the march, according to tribe and sept and province, so that the cantreds should work together, but each man stay with his comrades, friends, and kin. There was little point in bringing up the matter of supplies until she heard Flidais' laughing voice at the entrance to the withy-fence around the royal camp.

"Let me in now, Ferdiad, and mayhap I shall let you in unchallenged another time to a softer enclosure!"

"You are encamped within by Maeve's friendship and honor," the Connacht champion replied somberly. "How then should I challenge or keep you out?"

"A good boy, that Ferdiad, but far too serious," Ailill remarked as Flidais walked towards them.

She had clearly paused to wash after seeing to her men. Her wondrous wealth of long hair tumbled free over her broad shoulders and down her back, carefully brushed but still dark with water, so that its spectacular sunset flame was dimmed to a rich copper glow in the firelight. Although her sword was still belted at her waist, she had laid aside her jerkin of hardened leather and iron plates, and was dressed as befitted a queen, in a long dress checkered in blue and green, woven with gold threads and embroidered with red and yellow silk. Flidais was shorter than Maeve and ten years younger, trim-waisted but buxom and strong. More than one bard had admired the fitness of it, that the under-queen who bore Ireland's finest breasts be known for the wealth of milk and butter and cheese flowing from her land.

Her face was broad and slightly freckled, but pretty, especially when she smiled; and she smiled often. Nor was she shy with the friendship of her thighs, though no man held power over her. She had once laughed to Maeve, "Whatever men may think of their cocks, and a fine one is good to find, no doubt, they remember too seldom that it is a tool needing a skilled user, not a Druid wand to enchant all it touches."

Maeve was surprised at how relieved she felt to see Flidais, as though Ailill and Fergus had been pressing her in an unfair combat of two to one.

"Still, he is the best single fighter in Connacht, with the strength of the Fir Bolg from whom his forebears came," Maeve answered. "I have seen him do many feats that no other could match."

"And have you found his feats matchless elsewhere?" Ailill chuckled. "He is such a fine lad, surely you have not let him go untried?"

"I think Finnabair is more to his taste, if he does not prefer the pleasures of his schooling-days," Maeve replied. 'If only Ferdiad would court her, and she would forget this Ulsterman who has stolen her heart like a prize cow! If she will not wed Fraech, Connacht's champion would be a fit consort for her, who should be queen in Cruachan after myself.

Ferdiad keeps his own thoughts, and shows his passion only in battle-skill. This is no time to further the matter, when we must hold Finnabair's troth as a glittering lure for those who need playing, while Ferdiad is already bound as our champion.'

"Wouldn't that be a pity, now?" Flidais said, seating herself on the empty stool next to Fergus and setting her hand lightly on his thigh. " I think you are right about Finnabair, for did I not see his glance stealing towards her through the fence once or twice already this night?

"You might find him a fine playfellow indeed, my darling," she added to Finnabair, "if he could get over his shyness. I'm doing my best for you there, but he is a hard stone to crack."

Finnabair blushed deep crimson, but Fergus smiled. "It is hardly kind of you to tease Ferdiad," he chided her affectionately. "How do you think that young pup could handle a woman like you?"

"Sure, the young pups are the best for teaching new tricks. a man who is quick to learn feats with sword and spear is likely to be quick to learn elsewhere." Flidais' full breasts heaved as she sighed, tossing her head so her hair rippled down her back like a great cloak of burnished copper.

"Well, my own warriors are bedded down like babes, if babes keep a guard rota, I always suspected mine did; I hope these lads won't wake me thrice a night. You want to know how we are supplied. I cannot see how we can get in and out before the Ulstermen recover from their pangs. My best guess is that we are provisioned for two months, or four if, as I am sure we will, we plunder Ulster as we go."

"Four months!" Maeve said. "This raid should be a matter of weeks at most. We should be in and out long before a month has passed. Before two months, even if we had to crawl on our knees! Whether Conchobar lies in his bed or stands in his chariot, surely we cannot be delayed so long."

"Likely so," Flidais agreed. "I hope and expect so. I have never seen raid or war spoiled for lack of provisions, and there is no telling what may await us across the border. In any case, if we eat Ulster bare, it will be to our good and their harm. if this raid goes as speedily as we hope it may, we shall still have the food and can feast well from now until the new milk comes in."

"Shall each leader feed their troops from their own first?" Maeve asked, "Afterwards it would seem that they were our clients, and that will sting their pride. Rather, we shall host the cantreds in turn, two or three at a time.

Thus they will stay in good heart and friendship, and there is nothing like companionship and fine food to strengthen warriors on a cold winter march."

"There speaks Brigit's daughter!" Ailill said. "May she bless you as you pour out her blessings!"

"How could it be otherwise?" Flidais answered. "A cow that is well-milked will give more milk for it, and food and drink are better for being shared with good company. In any case, we are not likely to run short of supplies on the way. It is true that the wagons will slow us, but less than if we had to stop more often to forage for so many. it would be well to think now on who shall guide us, and find the swiftest paths between here and Cuailgne, and seek tidings in advance of our host."

Maeve looked at Fergus, Ailill's head turning with hers as if they were a well-matched chariot team. The low firelight threw Fergus' hawk like nose into sharp relief, deepening the shadows about the bones of his strong face, and the scar that cut through his beard gleamed red as a fresh-cut wound.

"I held the kingship of Ulster for seven years: no man here knows its land and folk better than I," he said slowly.

"And I owe a great vengeance to Conchobar. Indeed, I have been long from Ulster in exile and enmity; and did I not agree to fare on this raid with a whole heart, or as well as I might manage?"

Flidais' hand stroked his leg, her round face soft with comfort. She would offer him a mother's breast, Maeve thought, and if he knows his heart's needs, he will have the sense to pillow his weary head there. Fergus did not look at the milk-queen, only put his own hand over hers to hold it still.

"Then you will guide our host?" Maeve said, careful to let no harshness or challenge into her words.

"Go before us to find tidings of the land and folk, of who is ready to meet us and who is not ready and who will give way to us?" Added Ailill.

Fergus sighed. "I will do that," he said. "For our friendship, and my vengeance."

It seemed to Maeve that, for the first time, she could hear Fergus' age weighting his voice. That made her both uneasy and frustrated. She wanted to take his head to her breast and caress him; and to shake his shoulders until his teeth rattled.

She knew Fergus' word was strong, but how would it be when he came to the land where he had first ruled, then found the fellowship of the Red Branch compensation for his loss? Friends he had fought and swayed and drunk beside, who had saved his life, and whose lives he had saved: how deep did those currents run? Deep, from the way he had spoken of it. How would it be for him, to raid and slay in the land to which he had once sworn his life, though that land had cast him off?

'I would be easier in my heart, if I thought Flidais had twined him in her wonderful hair. If I could capture him between my thighs, I would feel the more sure of him. A shiver of warmth ran between Maeve's legs, like a ripple over a stream. Or perhaps it is I who needs a good bedding; Ailill knows how to please me as a harper of many years' training knows his instrument, but Fergus, how deeply do I desire him? If only I had taken him to me earlier! Much would have been simpler then'.

"If I am to choose the ways and guide our host, then I should go and think," Fergus said abruptly. "And perhaps consult with the other exiles. Several may remember what one has forgotten, and it has been some time since I set foot in Ulster."

He carefully lifted Flidais' hand from his leg. Maeve could not tell whether he gave it a little promising squeeze or not, and walked off to his tent.

"It is a hard thing for a man to fight against those who were his friends, whatever ill may have befallen him," Ailill murmured. Her husband's eyes narrowed as he watched the tent-flap close behind Fergus' broad back. The exile had not taken a lantern; no light showed through the thick wool of the shelter. Whatever Fergus was thinking on, he was doing it in the dark. "If he betrays us, there is little hope.

Fergus is not one to betray those who have treated him well, but I fear he is of two hearts here. I do not say we should mistrust him; but I do not think we should put all our trust in him either."

It was rare indeed for Ailill to speak so directly and seriously, and that made Maeve the more uneasy. She thought of what Finnabair had said, of the thing that seemed to lie between herself and Fergus as surely as a drawn sword. 'Ailill has no jealousy over that which can be shared a thousand times and always made sweeter; but kingship is another matter. Is it that which wakes his mistrust, or is it only good sense, when I could hear the sorrow in Fergus' voice myself?'

"It may be so," she answered.

Ailill turned to Flidais again.

"If Fergus is or is not of two hearts, it is certain that the heart in him is downcast this night. Perhaps you should remind him where cheer and friendship may be found."

Maeve expected her friend to answer with a bawdy jest and rise to follow Ailill's suggestion, but Flidais shook her head.

"He has no mind for me tonight, and I am not such a fool as to offer my fields to a man who will not plough. I wish that Adammair were with us, but someone had to stay behind to see to the beasts and land. Perhaps you should take your own advice, and rejoice in what you have."

Ailill stood, holding out his arm to Maeve.

"Shall we, my dear? It is a long way we have to go, and we shall rest the better for a bit of joy now."

Maeve shifted uneasily on her stool. Though the moon was near full, she felt as though her courses might come upon her at any moment. Her skin prickled uneasily, as though the little itchy halms of reaping-time had worked their way under it; her breasts and the soft folds between her legs felt heavy, as if with desire, but there was no pleasure to it. She longed for Ailill's mouth warm on her body, for his big powerful hands stroking her and the hot satisfaction of his man's spear filling her until she cried out with delight.

Yet, at the same time, the thought of his touch rasped her like a blacksmith's file scraping against her nipples, and Baiscne growled so softly that Maeve felt the sound rather than heard it.

'Is it Fergus I want? Yes, I want him; but I could not go to him now. My legs are sore from standing in my chariot while I raced about the army, and I have had no time to think about the prophecies I heard this morning, nor am I sure I want to.

I do not think I could bear the touch of any man this night.'

"It has been a long and weary day," Maeve answered her husband. "I am like to feel more myself when I have slept. Perhaps we shall rouse the host in the morning!"

"My own champion is ready to be roused for battle at any hour," Ailill replied lightly. "As you will. if you will not, then I am for sleep now. So should you be, if you are too tired to use your blankets for anything better!"

"In a little time," Maeve said.

Flidais was quiet until Ailill, too, had disappeared into his tent. Then she murmured, "Is there more than meets the eye, that neither you nor Fergus, of all folk in Eriu! Will have company this night?"

Maeve drew in a sharp breath.

"It has been a long and weary day," she repeated. "Has there never been a time on you when you wanted none but yourself in your bed?"

"Usually once a month, when the pains of my courses are on me." Flidais' blue-green eyes glanced up to the clipped silver coin of the Moon, then back to meet Maeve's gaze. "Have yours come late, or early? I have a mix of herbs that will soothe the cramping and give you a good night's sleep."

My courses could be coming early, Maeve thought. It was a comforting suggestion, that no more than that might be amiss with her. 'My last were a little late, and it is often enough that the spring will stutter and spurt before it fails altogether. If I am no less in strength or wit or beauty for age, still my elder sons have sons of their own, and my youngest child is well of an age to wed.'

"That would be kind of you," Maeve said.

"Well, and I hope it helps." Flidais sighed. "I fear Fergus' troubles are not so easily overcome. I would never have thought he could be so downcast as to want to bed alone."

She blinked, a smile of pleasant memory coming to her round face.

"Indeed, before this I should have wondered if he could. I tell you, a single ride with Fergus is worth seven lesser men in a day, and if his father was as well-armed as the son, there was no boasting to it when he called himself Roech, the Great Horse!"

Maeve could not help laughing a little at that. Between gossip and the closeness of folk, there were few secrets in a royal entourage, and she knew her friend was reporting only the strictest truth.

"No bigger in Eriu, I have heard," she agreed, and Flidais grinned.

"Mother," Finnabair muttered between her teeth. Maeve could almost feel the heat from her cheeks, like a boiling-stone pulled fresh from the fire.

Flidais patted the young woman on the arm.

"No need to be embarrassed, darling. You'll find a man who suits you soon enough. Then you'll find yourself that what is pleasant and good to do is also pleasant and good to speak of. Since everyone else is sleeping alone, and, it has been a wearying day! I suppose I shall go to bed, and hope for better on the morrow. Shall I send Lochu to make that tea for you?"

"That would be well."

Maeve and Finnabair sat in silence until the serving maid came back with a dark-glazed mug of steaming brew. The herbal mixture tasted slightly bitter, but clean and refreshing, scouring the thickness from Maeve's mouth. Still, it brought her no ease.

"You are deeply troubled, Mother," Finnabair murmured.

"I am," Maeve confessed. "This is no little thing we are doing, and the omens are uncertain." She told Finnabair what had befallen that morning. The girl listened, her delicate face grave.

"Still," Finnabair said when her mother stopped speaking, "it is worth the doing, for your own sake, and your vengeance on Conchobar." Finnabair's jaw tightened; she looked as fierce and resolute as any warrior going out to do single battle. "For what he did to you, is it not worth it, that his lands be laid waste while he lies in Macha's pangs? Let him feel the fair repayment for rape!"

Maeve felt a hot spurt of surprised pride. She had never doubted her daughter's love; but to see Finnabair so angry over a harm to her mother was like a warming-stone laid against rain-chilled feet, and, though the girl had not said it aloud, it was Maeve's shame that Conchobar's crimes against her had gone unavenged so long, 'and who has avenged Deirdre, bereft, ravaged, mocked, and driven to her death? I never met her; but suffered Conchobar's brutality even as she. Had I not been Cruachan's heir, with many swords to support my divorce, I, too, might have forced some young warrior to flee with me: Deirdre's sorrows could have been mine. How could I not feel her in my blood, and seek to avenge her?'

"This night," a soft woman's voice said, "is well-omened for those who would strike their enemies."

Maeve whirled on her stool. Fedelm stood behind her, white robe and pale hair gleaming in the firelight, and her gold-inlaid weaving rod in her hand. The prickling under Maeve's skin shivered into a tingle of anticipation: This was a ban-drúi dressed for a ritual.

"My enemies are still out of sword-reach," she said slowly.

"Are you certain?" Flickers of red firelight gleamed from the unsheathed steel of the young woman's blue-grey eyes, her gaze stabbing deep into Maeve's.

'Now I must tell the truth to myself. I am still angry with Ailill: why else would I not have gone to him tonight? I am angry with Fergus for his endless holding-back. He wants me, and I him, but he will not lie with me; he is our friend, one of my oldest, in truth, for did he not do his best to ease my travails in Conchobar's hall? Agreed to share in this raid. Ailill has the right of it: half of Fergus' heart still belongs to the land and folk of Ulster. Yet I would bring no harm to either of them.'

Ailill had struck her deeper with a jest than with any spear, wounding the root of her soul. Because of that wound, Maeve would sleep alone in her war-tent tonight instead of curled warm in his strong arms. Though she had seen and dealt many deaths, she could not imagine his great golden body hacked and drenched in blood. Not even in the depths of night, when the worst fears crawled like slugs tracing their cold slimy trails over her bedding. For all that lies between us, I love him. Something had twinged in Maeve's heart at Fergus' pain that night, as a harp string would shiver untouched when its mate on another instrument was plucked.

'I am not sure that we can trust him; yet I love him. Perhaps I would love him the less if he could cast Ulster from his heart so easily.

It is not that he lacks faith, but that he is too faithful, even to those who turned from him.'

"I am quite certain," Maeve answered at last.

"That is well. For a curse spoken with a divided soul may strike where you did not wish, as an ax's blade may turn if the haft is grasped with slippery hands. If you are whole of heart and will, it has come to me how I may aid you. Follow me."

"I would go too," Finnabair said as the ban-drúi turned.

Fedelm looked back over her shoulder, eyes wide in her triangular face. "Truly? Do you understand what it is we would do?"

"Well enough. I am maiden, and royal. Once I thought no man could dare lay hand on me against my will. Nor has that happened, but now I know what might befall. I have a debt for my mother's sake." Finnabair's voice was grim and stern as Maeve had never heard it. A sudden sense of loss, and fear, caught painfully at Maeve's pride and love like a tangle of brambles. 'My last child is grown. My daughter, whom I thought would be safe all her life. I was disappointed when she refused the sword, but relieved as well. She may be safe from sword and spear, but I cannot keep her safe from her own womanhood, and all that must go with it. Indeed, asked her to play a grown woman's part on this raid; how can I do other than accept her right to do so?'

"Then come."

Perhaps Fedelm had cast a Druid's spell of passing unseen upon them. It seemed to Maeve, her eyes light-blinded from the camp fire, that she could not tell whether they walked through the enclosure's guarded opening, or passed through the woven withies as though they were a low bank of twining fog. Ferdiad stood with his spear in his hand, gazing around with the alert look of a champion who would treat the simplest guard duty as a purpose worthy of his skill, but his blue eyes darted past like a dragonfly over a stream: he did not even nod in acknowledgment to his queen.

Baiscne paced shadow-dark and silent beside Maeve; she rested her hand on his warm shaggy shoulder so that he might steady and guide her, as if she were tracing the Samhain track from the Cave of the Martens down into Cruachan síd once more. Her wren did not fly by night, but her pine marten stayed curled around her throat like a warm torc of fur, and Maeve felt the power thrumming through its soft length.

The three women glided silent through the camp like eels in the depths of a peat-black stream. Away from the tents and fires, withy fences and blanket-covered bothies of woven poles, the night seemed wholly dark: only the Moon gave a shifting, cloud-tattered light. Dead grass, wet from the day's rain, soaked Maeve's shoes and the hems of her long tunic and trousers, tangling sharp-edged along her chilled ankles. She felt a faint cramping in her womb, as if her courses were, indeed, starting early. Slowly Maeve's eyesight resolved, until trees and bushes showed black against the darkness. A few faint stars glittered between fast-moving ragged clouds; the cold night wind bit into the iron links of her corselet, and she shivered her thick bratt close about her.

The itchy unease she had felt earlier strengthened into a prickling over her skin, a wild tingle like sleeping with a new man for the first time, as if Fergus were to touch my hand, and gesture towards the bed, or the fierce tingling down her arm when her sword-blade clashed in blood-hungry earnest with another warrior's steel. Before Maeve, Fedelm moved like a swan on a still pond; beside her, Finnabair stumbled, but kept the pace with fierce determination.

Maeve heard the rushing of the little river before she saw it, a soft purling that was almost lost in the whispering of the leafless thicket-branches along its edge. Shadowed by its banks, it seemed a cleft of bottomless darkness, save where the Moon's wavering light caught a gleam of silver here and there along the stream. Fedelm led them along the river, then turned towards it again, down a little slope that ran between the sharper drop of the banks. Maeve and Finnabair followed until the ground softened between their feet and the cold mud sucked at their sandals and soaked icy into their numb toes.

Fedelm held out her hands to them. At first Maeve thought the seeress' palms were painted black. Then she saw the two little heaps of blackberries, and the darkness around the ban-filid's mouth. It was after Samhain; the touch of the Hag was upon the fruit. Maeve took the berries from her right hand, and Finnabair from the left, and they ate. The taste was very sweet, but edged with sourness, tingling upon Maeve's tongue as if the blackberries had begun to ferment where they grew.

"Conchobar and his men lie in their pangs," Fedelm said. "Yet Macha's curse will not hold them forever: they will rise ready for war before our host has set eyes on the Donn Cuailgne."

"If they are ready for war, we shall give it to them!" Maeve said. "Our host lacks nothing against theirs, not strength nor skill nor numbers. She remembered what Fedelm had said that morning, and the chill within her did not come from cold wind or cold water.

"There is much you do not know yet, and much that has not been shown to me," the ban-drúi answered calmly. "This has been: would you speak before the gods and those who dwell in water and wood and hill, to set your curse on Conchobar?"

"I would," Maeve answered. With those words, though the strange shivering excitement in her did not dim, she felt herself suddenly eased, as though she had vomited up something that had festered in her belly for far too long. "I would have him feel the pain he has given; I would have him know the fear and shame that he has set upon others, and know what it is to be held helpless in suffering with no surety of relief. Yes, him, and all those men of Ulster who laughed at me in my travails, and still snigger behind their hands at the words that drove Deirdre to her death!"

"And you, Finnabair. Are you set on this?"

"I am!" Maeve's daughter declared bravely. Fedelm did not say anything, only stared at her until Finnabair dropped her eyes. "I… after my mother told me what had befallen her, for the first time, I knew what it was to fear the strength of men. It seems to me that there is no answer for that fear, save to match, in some way, that strength with some power of my own, or else to accept that I am ever at the mercy of whoever is mightier of body than I." She held out one arm, white and slim as a birch-bough.

Weaving and playing fidchell built little muscle; but in the moonlight, she might have been holding out a sword-blade. The steel stronger, despite its slenderness, than any bulk of bone and flesh.

"Then speak, and may Macha and Brigit and the Morrígan all hear you."

Maeve drew in a deep breath of icy night air, sweet and strong as winter mead. It thrummed through her like the sound of a thousand voices raised in song; the words flowed from her mouth like ale bursting from a keg kept too long stoppered, above the deep drone of Baiscne's low growl.

"Conchobar mac Nes, I curse you! You who bear your mother's name, yet bring ill to all women who stand before you, I curse you! I curse you in Macha's name, I curse you in Brigit's name, I curse you in the name of the Morrígan! Harmer of women, may you know our pangs. May the Hag who touches the berries set her hand upon you; may you have no ease from suffering while she stalks the winter land. My maiden's blood unkindly shed rises to curse you; the blood of my womb from your rape rises to curse you; Deirdre's blood and brains upon the stone rise to curse you."

Maeve stopped, panting hard, her mouth dry and her eyes streaming furious tears. Finnabair spoke, "Conchobar mac Nes, I curse you in my mother's name and in my own. For the shadow you have lain across our lives, for the shadow fallen on my heart, I curse you: lie in your pain, and know that what you suffer past the doom Macha laid, you have brought on your own self."

Fedelm raised her wand, and it seemed to Maeve that its gold inlay glowed as though it had just been drawn from the fire, burning of itself against the Moon-tinged darkness. She began to chant: the words were simple, but each line rode hard upon the next, pounding into Maeve's head like hoof beats hammering down upon hard earth, beating against her ears like clubs pounding on a great skin drum.

"Morrígan and Macha,
Macha of the battles,
Battle now is dawning.
Dawning, pangs of Ulster,
Ulster's men shall suffer,
Suffer, what they dealt out,
Dealt out women's weeping,
Weeping, may they lie there,
Lie there without rising.
Rising, hosts of Eriu,
Eriu come for vengeance,
Vengeance fierce to Conchobar
Conchobar in the birth-bed!
Birth-bed without ceasing,
Ceasing not in frost-hold,
Frost-hold keep you fettered.
Fettered, hosts of Ulster,
Ulster, trod by Morrígan,
Morrígan and Macha!"

The ban-fili was breathing as hard as Maeve and Finnabair by the time she finished, moonlit sweat sheened over her bone-white face and running about her staring dark eyes. Pointing her glittering wand north-east, towards Emain Macha, she slashed it violently through the air, its brightness trailing a lightning-streak to flash behind Maeve's eyelids when the queen blinked. Maeve was still trembling, but now it was the fine tremors of exhaustion quivering through her.

Her head and all her muscles were aching, and her sinews felt unstrung, as though she had fought to collapse, or given birth. Without a word, Fedelm turned to walk back towards the camp. The ghostly smoothness of her gait was gone; she stumbled awkwardly over the heaps and tussocks of dead grass.

Maeve leaned on Baiscne's shoulder to keep herself upright, her other hand clutching Finnabair's, mother and daughter staggering like a pair of drunks in the dark. The men guarding the perimeter of the camp peered suspiciously at them, but Fedelm's white robe and Maeve's gold diadem silenced their mouths.

Thankfully, Ferdiad had been relieved and gone to his own rest, and the man who replaced him had the sense to turn his face away when he saw the ban-drúi with the other women trailing after her. Back in her tent, it took Maeve two tries to shove a torch's end into the bronze holder nailed to the central pole, and Lochu had to come and unfasten all her pins and buckles for her.

When Maeve stripped off her under-breeches, she saw a few spots of blood; but when Lochu brought her a cloth steeped in warm water, the cloth came away clean. Maeve felt oddly certain that the breech clout her servant fetched her would not be needed either. Still, a woman's courses are often irregular at this age; I should wear it just in case.

The thought soothed her a little. Whatever might have passed at the riverbank, or might come to pass in this great raid, simple matters must still be dealt with whatever magic or mysteries lay in the inner folds of her womb, Maeve knew very well that coming into her courses with no preparation would make a mess.

She crept into bed, curling up beneath the thick wool blankets with Baiscne stretched out warm beside her and her marten nestled at her shoulder. As she was falling asleep, she heard a soft sleepy chirping from the roof-pole. 'The creatures of my sovereignty are still with me; I am still queen, Maeve thought, and slept well and deeply then.'

Fedelm

Once the exaltation of our working faded, I found myself shivering beneath my thick wool blankets, as if my body no longer gave out any heat to warm them. I was too tired to rise. I drowsed shivering all night, and awoke fog-eyed and sleepy to a hard glitter of frost-crystals everywhere, save where feet had trodden the white gleam into dead brown grass and cold-hardened earth, and a ring around the fire where the frost had melted from the ground. Miserable as I felt, it was a wonder to see the woven withy-fence transformed into a shining hedge of ice, thorned brambles, and the coverings of tents and bothies shining like beaten silver in the pale winter sunlight.

'We called the frost, and the frost came; we ate the blackberries claimed by the Hag of Winter, and she rides with us. Surely the Morrígan rides on this raid. Did we do well to call her? Or only as we must, as fate and the hour set? It is sure that, friend or foe, she will be no easy travel-companion.'

Calatín said no word to me of what we had done. I was certain he knew, it must have reverberated through the Otherworld as though we had beaten a drum mighty enough to shake the very leaves from the trees.

He spoke of other things, tales of elder days or herb-lore, telling me the secrets of each plant. Sometimes one of his sons would circle our chariot. Then I saw a love in the old Druid's bony face that I would never have believed before; his pride in the rangy young men with their war-harness and spears, very like their father, though softer of face; and beneath that pride, a tender fear and hope that reminded me of what I had seen in Maeve's eyes as I prophesied.

'Is it worth it, to be a mother or father? I wondered. To send a child out to war, wishing their glory and fearing their pain or death?' I began to understand why many Druids never married, saving their love for their lore. Yet, now and again, I would think of a babe in my arms, a child with red-gold hair suckling at my breast, and a little pang ran through my womb. To my surprise, the host of Eriu moved more slowly than Eochaid and I had in our chariot. In song, armies swept like eagles. Ours was more like a great hedgehog: thick with gleaming steel spikes, but ambling here and there, pulling itself clumsily over rocks and hillocks, turning constantly from its path. Certainly we followed no straight track to Ulster.

Though I had never traveled more than two or three days' journey in my childhood, I had studied the main pathways from Maeve's fort to Cuailgne before I came back. Fergus, in the army's van, seemed to be turning where I thought we should go straight, and going straight where I thought we should turn. I thought of the conversation I had overheard. Again I wondered, as Maeve and Ailill must too, where the heart of Ulster's exiled king lay. Was he delaying us, or were there dangers afoot of which I knew nothing, and he the only safe guide through? I wanted to ask Calatín. He had begun to speak of weather magic, staring gravely into my eyes as he warned of its dangers.

"Rain now means drought elsewhere; a storm steered wrong may bring a great flood. First you must learn the patterns of the land and the air and clouds, and how to feel the forces behind them, not all can be urned, even by the wisest of folk." I nodded, drawn in by his dark gaze. "See that wispy breath of mist above us?"

I looked up. I could just barely see the faint stream of white haze against the cold clear blue of the sky, thinner than any tatter of fine silk.

"In as little as a day or as much as three, mares' tails will stream over the sky. Then any farmer could tell you that they are the outriders of a great host of clouds. By then it would be too late to turn that host, though now it might be done, if this were an ordinary storm. Listen to the wind that blows about us! Soft here, it keens fiercely in the upper air: more than rain rides the sky-steeds from the northeast."

I drew in a deep breath, listening. What might have been easy to hear alone on a hilltop with only breathing and heartbeat in my ears, was something else in the middle of an army. Chariot wheels creaking and harness jingling; many footfalls, some few marching in unison, but most following their own rhythm; men's voices, and some women's, jesting or complaining or just talking.

I felt like an ant trying to stand still amid the bustling streams of ants pouring around and through the nest.

Slowly the discipline of my training prevailed, until the noises faded to a faint watery rushing. Then I heard the breeze rustling through dry grass and leaves; and above it, like the high note of a bone flute, the keening of the icy upper airs.

Stretching my senses further, I almost heard the thin wild voices in the distance, and then a great flock of crows flew up from the rimmed brown stubble of the field to our left, their black wings a sudden rushing that overwhelmed my sight and their gabbling cries sending a sharp stab of ice down my back. I swayed, nearly losing my grip on the chariot's rim as it bounced over a frozen rut in the road. Calatín's strong lean hand caught me, holding me effortlessly upright, his thin mouth twisted in a rueful half-smile.

"You learn swiftly," he said. "And no doubt will learn even faster on this raid. I hope, for I am uncertain of my legacy."

I only nodded; I had no idea what I could say. Was the hour of his death spoken, or had he seen some sign of it? Or was it only his knowledge that Druids, like all that lives, must someday put off their garments of flesh to be reborn and relearn their lore over and over, greater each time, yes, but never with less struggle in the doing? And even a Druid who had fared often in the Otherworld might feel the fears of the flesh at the prospect of death for himself, or his sons.

"And we shall see what we may do to turn the storm, while one may stand against it. If not turn, then delay, until we are come to some better place to shelter.

You will watch, and listen, and learn."

So I did, that night: Calatín and I walked out in the icy moonlight, wool-wrapped shoes crunching sharp on the frosted grass. Though his voice was too rough for a true bard's, it was powerful and well-trained, singing the winds and calling them to lay easy, singing the storm clouds and calling them to let down the weight of their burden over the sea. I graved every word he sang in my mind, focusing all my training to be sure that those incantations could never leave me. What one writes, one may lose; what one learns, one has forever: so the Druids have known since our folk first rode out of the world-distant eastern mountains.

"The weather will be colder, while it stays clear." Calatín said when we were back in his tent. "This will be such a winter as we have not seen in my lifetime." Exhausted, he stretched on his pallet and let me cover him with all his blankets.

Eochaid had brought hot water, and I ground the herbs for a simple restorative tea: mint and honey for strength, meadowsweet and willow bark for the headache he was surely suffering. When it had finished steeping, the bronze goblet was still too hot to hold in my hands. I wrapped a length of wool about it; he let the wool fall, holding the burning cup between his palms.

"We will travel all the faster for it: frozen earth will slow us less than snow or mud. We shall need to do so. I feel power rising against us, a single will in the way of our host; and a half-cloven stick is easy to split."Do you mean Fergus? I wanted to ask. Calatín downed his near-boiling tea as if it had been a draught of cool water, then lay back and closed his eyes. I tiptoed out, leaving the old Druid to his rest. As Calatín had promised, the skies stayed clear for the next days, though the cold bit to the bone. After the trials of my training, I had thought myself hardy. At the end of my first seven years, I had spent my night in the stone box of chill water with a rock upon my chest, chanting every song or lay asked of me: few in Maeve's army could have done the same.

Riding in the jolting chariot day after day, until my bones rattled like sticks under an old woman's dry skin and my kidneys began to ache with every lurch, eating no set foods at no set times, the weight of battle ahead pressing my mind – that was something else. Nor could I use the herbs that quieted pain and strengthened the blood's flow through sore muscles, for not only would that be yielding to my body without good reason, but I would need all my supplies once the fighting began.

I slept like the dead every night, so that Eochaid must shake me to rouse me in the morning, and only my pride kept me from showing Calatín how fragile my control was becoming, and yet, if slowly, my mind learned to put these new sufferings aside, and my body hardened to the rigors of the march. By the time we had passed into the drumlin-lands, where the tiny hillocks rose so close together that the land looked like a heap of brown eggs in a basket, I had gained the strength to bear the chariot's endless lurching, though each time we drove down the little slope of one drumlin and up the next, I had to hold tight against the fear that this time the chariot-poles would crack and the horses bolt.

When we entered Ulster at last, I felt the first wave of power beating against us. It seemed everywhere, like a long wave crashing against the shore. Yet it seemed to me that I could sense a single will, keen and bright as a hard-forged spear-tip, pressing piercingly against me. It was then, as we neared Iraid Cullein, that the army slowly ground to a halt, piece by piece and troop by troop. Calatín let out a slow breath, then said to Eochaid, "Take us to the fore."

On the journey, I had seen a good deal of shouting and occasional blows exchanged when one chariot would try to force its way ahead of the others. Even armed and armored as he was, only a blind man could have mistaken Calatín for anything but a Druid. Foot soldiers and high-born in their chariots alike moved out of our way when they saw his uplifted wand of polished wood. In front of the host, I saw Fergus and Ailill ahead of the rest, dismounted with their guards near them.

The fields on the left had given way to a great oak wood, the dark gnarled trunks mottled with patches of frost. To the right lay a wide marsh, impassable at this time of year. Thin cataracts of ice blinded the dark pools scattered through it, and the mossy tussocks of peat were crusted hard, but the weight of men and chariots would break through at once into the sucking mud. The broad way between was clear, save for a single standing stone, gnarled and grey, like the great finger of some monstrous being thrusting from the torn and bitten earth.

Crookedly atop it, a strange crone's winter-bitten garland, lay a thick peeled sapling of pale oak bent into a hoop and fastened with a peg. Thus my earthly eyes saw. Then Calatín touched me lightly on the forehead with his wand. The stone shone deep red, its root glowing darkly up from the depths of the frozen earth; the tip of a dragon's great tail, and the hoop that crowned it coruscated a brilliance I had seen before: the hero-light that had burned around the head of the man in my vision, so bright that I could not see his face. This was his track and his sign; this was the first warning of our foe come upon us. A chariot-bridle rang behind us, and Maeve's high clear voice called out, "Why have we stopped? Why are you waiting here?"

She and Finnabair drove out to join the others, the queen's nine guards behind her, but she did not dismount, only looked down at the two men.

"We are waiting because of this spancel-hoop," Fergus answered heavily. "The peg is graven with ogham. It says, 'Come no further, unless you have a man who can make a hoop like this with one hand from one piece, excepting only my foster-father Fergus.' I know Cú Chulainn did this. See, how the grass is torn up, the clay cut by hooves to the bedrock? His matchless chariot-horses grazed here."

Maeve shrugged.

"By what right may one man stop a host? Anyone can cut and carve a sapling, and write it with a challenge that can hardly be met. Who can say it is more than a fool's boast?"

Fergus reached up and lifted the spancel-hoop from the stone.

"You Druids, tell us. What does this hoop mean to us? How many set it, and what shall befall if we pass it without meeting the challenge?"

Calatín's mouth twisted in an odd half-smile. He took the hoop with his fingertips, as though the brilliance I saw burned with heat in truth.

"Read the ogham, Fedelm, and hide nothing."

At first I saw only brightness. Then the shape of the peg that fastened the oaken hoop began to darken, though the ogham writing still glowed like a row of white finger-marks of power, the tree-lore distilled down to an array of simple straight and slanted lines. Fergus had read what any high-born man's learning might show him, the simple sounds and words. I read beyond and beneath them.

"A hero made this, a champion cast it," I said, my eyes mazed with the glowing might of the hoop. "He left it as a trap for warriors, a way block to kings wrought and cast with a single hand. One hand and one eye, standing upon one foot: thus he made it, that none might gainsay him. It is wrought true, and no fool's boast. Unless there be a man other than Fergus who can match this champion's feat, we can go no further on this road. If we ignore it and pass by, the fury of the maker would reach us, were we locked in Cruachan with all its strength. If we pass without matching this feat, we will see deaths by morning." I stopped, panting heavily. Sweat prickled my brow, chilling as it ran down my face.

Maeve's fair brows drew together, her blue eyes sweeping over her guard.

"Ferdiad," she said. "You studied with Cú Chulainn under Scathach and Aoife. I have heard that he was your shield-mate, but you were the elder, and it was he who served you by day and night. I think most tales of this youth have grown as tales do. I have heard one thing said that may easily be believed: that if any man in Eriu is his equal or greater, it is either Fergus or yourself. Can you match this feat of Cú Chulainn's?"

Ferdiad shook his head, his wavy golden hair whipping beneath his helmet's rim. In full daylight, I had to own he was as handsome a man as I had seen. He was taller than Ailill, heavier of chest and shoulders but narrower of waist; supple, but awesomely powerful. A close-cropped golden beard set off his clean sharp features; his eyes were such a deep blue that they almost looked black until the sunlight glanced to show their depths. His armor bulked his form even mightier, wax-boiled leather, hard as horn, strengthened with iron plates and set with glossy grey flakes of flint interspersed with the purple gleams of amethyst and the sunlit brown of cairngorms. I could not help wondering how old it was: had it belonged to one of his ancestors in the ancient days, before the Tuatha de Danann came to Eriu?

"I often overcame him when we were learning the skills of war, though then he was the younger and I more schooled. In this matter, it is like the Fir Bolg and the Tuatha de Danann again. I have the greater strength, he the greater craft and agility. I could pluck and bend such a sapling with one hand, more easily than he. I could not shape and peg it while standing upon one foot with one eye shut."

Maeve clicked her tongue thoughtfully.

"It would not be well for our blood to be spilled so soon in this province, now that we have crossed into Ulster. Indeed, it would be far more pleasing to spill another's blood and besmirch him red."

Ferdiad looked Maeve straight in the face, the little muscles of his jaw clenching under the short-cropped golden bristles.

"Cú Chulainn is my foster-brother, beloved friend, and sworn shield-companion. Whoever fights him, it shall not be I, though I would hew down the rest of Ulster's host without a thought. Nothing in Eriu could force us to lift swords against one another."

Maeve glanced sharply at him; then her eyes slipped sideways to Finnabair for a moment. Her daughter stood with her white-blond hair veiling her face, staring at the great wood to the left of the standing stone as if she expected a host of men to run from it to her rescue at any moment.

The queen looked back at Ferdiad. Her black wolfhound sat up suddenly in her chariot as though the shadows had gathered and come to life beside her, and she rested her hand on his great shaggy head.

"Nothing?" She said softly. "When Maeve of Cruachan holds what is fairest in all these lands?"

I saw the flush that pinked Ferdiad's cheeks, but that might have been the cold. In any case, he did not flinch or look aside from her gaze, but answered through clenched teeth, "Nothing."

Ailill coughed, then spoke as Maeve turned to him, his voice even and firm as he looked up at her.

"We shall not ignore this challenge, nor shall we spend our warriors early. I believe that great wood is Fid Duin, and we are near the narrowest part. If we turn a little south and go through there, it may delay us slightly. it will save having to pass here, and with no lost lives where there need not be."

'There is a king indeed', I thought, looking from the searing brightness of the spancel-hoop to the gentler gleam of Ailill's long red-gold hair. Even now, there was a faint smile on his lips beneath his sweeping mustaches. Still, I had no doubt that Maeve would bend to him in this. It would have lowered me, and hence all Druids, in the eyes of the serving women if I were to stoop to asking the questions another woman might. I could not help thinking, 'A king who is so careful of the hearts and lives of his men, would he not be as tender in bed with a maiden?'

Maeve

"At last we are on clear ground again," Maeve said to Finnabair as the last of her host emerged from beneath the empty branches of the winter trees. It had been two days of hard travel, as much time spent hacking through thick tangles of woody brown bramble-vines and heavy thickets as moving forward. She had wanted to shout at Ailill for suggesting it, but she knew that it was the ruler, not the counselor, who bore the responsibility.

Finnabair shuddered.

"I thought I would be glad to be away from those trees, but now that I look at the sky, I wonder if we would not have done better to stay in shelter another day or two."

Maeve glanced up. The sky had been winter-clear for days, with only the finest strands of thin white mist scattered through its cold height. Now it looked like a pale sea, streaks of white clouds streaming and roiling everywhere like storm-tossed foam.

"I will speak to Calatín," she said comfortingly. "Be of better cheer, my daughter. We have beaten Cú Chulainn's challenge, and there is a good road ahead."

Finnabair might have been about to speak, but then the shouting reached them, like a wave of sound rolling back from the vanguard of the army.

"Attack! Ulster's men are attacking!"

Finnabair's lips parted, the wind-brightened color draining suddenly from her face. "..."

"Ask later!" Maeve snapped. "Down – Munremur, drive me to the front, as fast as you may."

Her daughter leapt out of the chariot, and her battle-driver vaulted lithely in, snapping the reins. The horses surged forward as Maeve slipped on her shield and drew her sword; Baiscne ran baying by her side, and her guards struggled to keep the pace and hold her formation around her. Maeve's vanguard was drawn up in defensive lines. Slingers stood to left and right. Weapons dangling heavy-weighted from their hands; warriors held light spears ready to cast, heavy spears stabbed into the earth where they could be snatched up in a heartbeat as the enemy closed to hand-range.

"Out in front!" Maeve ordered. Munremur obeyed, wheeling to slant before the first line. Then the queen saw what had stopped her host. There were two chariots there without drivers or riders. The horses stood still, heads down and snorting foam, reins loose about their ears.

As Maeve's own vehicle rumbled closer, she saw the four headless corpses slung and tied like deer, gaping red neck-stumps still spattering bright trickles down the chariots' ribs on either side. She turned to the front line.

"Who are these?" She asked.

"Mother, they are Eirr and Indell, the sons of Nera, and their drivers Foich and Fochlam," Cairbre answered, still holding his place. "They had gone before us to see what might lie in our way, and they found out.

The sons of Nera were fierce fighters, and should have been able to outpace most pursuit. We think the men of Ulster have risen, and there must be a great multitude of them waiting ahead."

Maeve looked at the men before her. Three of her sons by Ailill were in the front line, the other four in her guard. Cormac was at the fore, his purple-cloaked elite troop to either side of him, and Fergus with his exiled Ulstermen; Ailill, she knew, was in the middle of the army, holding it with the strength of his voice and arm lest any panic or try to break into frenzied attack.

'Has it all gone wrong? Wondered. Our curse astray, and Ulster ready for us. Did Fergus betray us after all, and this raid to end in failure and shame?'

She bit back tears of fury, made her face stone. She was Maeve of Cruachan: she would not give in to fear of what might be, even with the brutal mockery of those four corpses in front of her. She had the Ulster foe to deal with, and this was a matter for which a Northerner was most needed.

"Fergus…"

Fergus' grey eyes found hers, his rugged face lighting with sudden fierce excitement. Maeve's heart leapt to that brightness like a salmon to a flashing lure, a fine trembling rippling through her body.

'No. To Ulster, Fergus is exile and foe. I must send, Brigit help me, but I can see no other way, nor would any other have as much chance of living through this if all has gone awry. If it has, then he, at least, will survive. They will not kill their own king's son, estranged though he be'. "Cormac."

Cormac met her gaze, his blue eyes steady beneath his helm's gold edge. He grinned.

"Mother, my men and I will go forward to see what awaits. We will not be taken so easily as these, I assure you!"

Maeve wanted to draw him to her bosom and hold him as if he were still the babe who had been her only comfort so long ago. Instead she stood straight and said,

"My son, I trust in your bravery and skill, and wisdom. Go forth, and we will follow. Not so close that we can be seen at once, but close enough that, should battle await, you will not have long to hold."

Cormac and his men marched forward. Cormac's gilded helmet flashed and darkened as the racing streamers of clouds tumbled past the sun. Maeve waited until she could not make him out any longer before she signaled her army to move forward. Although Maeve strained her ears, her nerves jangling like harp-wires seeking their tuning-notes, no sounds of battle came to her as the host of Eriu pressed on to the banks of Turloch Caille More where the river flowed deep and fast.

There, the tracks o. Cormac's troop turned towards the right, up towards the ford. The nails of Maeve's right hand clawed at the gold on her sword's hilt as though she would strip it bare, but she kept her mind on what she knew of the land and how Ulster might defend the ford. Now she could see the speckled cloaks of Cormac's rearmost troops. There were no woods nor hills that might hide an army of Ulstermen near the ford, only a dry brown meadow strewn sparsely with trees.

She turned to Cairbre and said, "Ride swiftly back, and tell your father and the Druids to come forward."

"At once, Mother!" Her son's driver wheeled his chariot, swerving through the throng behind.

Cormac's men parted to let Maeve and her guard through. A four-pronged fork of wood stood in the shallow water, the trunk as thick as a man's thigh and the branches so broad that a chariot could not pass through the narrow ford on either side. Each jutting limb bore a man's head, the branch-tips protruding from their mouths like swollen and bloodied black tongues. Thin rivulets of blood dribbled from their severed necks, eddying pink into the clear ripples below. Four pairs of wide dead eyes stared at Maeve in blind astonishment. At first glance she could not tell the blood-caked hair of the two warriors' beards from the darkening scab-beards of the young drivers, but all dripped slow red drops into the river.

"One man did this," Cormac said grimly. "We sought his tracks. There was but one chariot, with a single warrior and a single driver, and their trail turns eastward. There are ogham letters graven upon the wood. They say, 'A single man cast this fork with one hand. Go not forth from here unless one man of you throw it with one hand, with Fergus excepted.'"

Maeve looked at the bloody trophy-pole and smiled grimly. "This, at least, we may pass. Fergus, I see nothing here that keeps you from pulling it out, to begin with."

Fergus was staring at the head-mounted fork as well. Maeve could not read his face, nor guess at his thoughts, but he made no move towards it.

"Fergus, tell me what is in your mind," Maeve commanded.

Fergus had not remounted his chariot since he got out to hold the center of the foot force. Now he looked up at her. A momentary blink of anger scarred across his face; then his grey eyes shuttered like a hawk's at twilight.

"Let us wait for the Druids," he answered. "I am not minded to gainsay a geas laid by a man who can do what this one has done."

Maeve wanted to lash him with her tongue, to shame him for his slowness, or for aiding the foe's means of delay. 'How can I trust him? She asked herself again, as she had asked so many times. The answer was always the same. He is Fergus mac Roech, and loyal beyond reason, and brought up the same gnawing question in turn, to whom?'

Yet she could not say Fergus was wrong. Severed heads were as much a prize of war as gold or cattle or bonds folk: Maeve had often come back to Cruachan with several hanging from her chariot-pole.

She had never seen slain men's heads set contemptuously thus. 'They might have been deer-heads, or sheaves of corn: not the seats of four human souls. Two of them only drivers, beardless youths! What manner of man has no care for his victory save that it cause fear?'

It was not long before Ailill arrived, Fedelm and Calatín's chariot beside the king's. Ailill gestured his chariot-driver to ride a little way into the ford, so that he could look more closely at the great fork, murmuring quietly. Maeve could not make out the words, but she heard the sorrow weighting his voice like soft snow. Still, his face was calm as he turned back.

"What have you men of Ulster called this ford before now?" Ailill asked Fergus.

"It was called Ath Grenca."

"Now it shall be called Ath Gabla, the Ford of the Fork. Eirr and Indell, Foic and Foclann, shall not be forgotten, though their slayer seems to have held their deaths worth little."

While he spoke, Ailill was staring hard at Fergus. The exiled Ulsterman looked aside, blood staining the prominent bones of his cheeks, he had grown gaunter, Maeve marked, on this journeying. Instead of challenging the king's gaze as he had hers, Fergus turned to the two Druids.

"Tell us of this," he said.

Calatín considered the head-fork coolly. Fedelm stood trembling, face greenish-white and hand stopped halfway to her mouth. Maeve opened her mouth to order the girl away; Calatín shook his head. It was not Maeve's habit to take orders even from a Druid, but this was a Druid's own matter.

"One man cut this fork with one perfect stroke," Calatín said. "And one-handed he flung it into this ford. Like the spancel-hoop that turned us aside, it was a deed of a champion's power; and like the spancel-hoop, we may not pass until we have matched the challenge."

Ailill looked at the grisly trophy-pole.

"I am amazed by the man who could have so swiftly slain these four and set this post. See, they still bleed, and the blood has barely jellied where it lies thickest."

"Be more amazed," Fergus said grimly, "at him who could have cut and sharpened this tree, root and trunk and branches, with a single stroke, and flung it one-handed from his chariot to sink so deeply. The bottom of this ford is flagged with grey stone: no sword dug that hole, but the force of the cast drove it in. Someone must draw it forth before we prove if that throw can be matched."

'Now we shall see', Maeve thought. "As you are a man of our host, Fergus, I charge you to do so. The ogham said nothing of who should pull it out, only who should equal the cast."

Fergus sighed. Maeve saw his great shoulder-muscles bunching beneath the dull iron of his hauberk, as though he were even now fulfilling the arduous task.

"Give me a chariot, and I shall."

"Let these heads be taken from it first," Ailill broke in. "Let them be washed, and wrapped in good linen, and kept after the arts of the Druids. Nera will wish to see his sons tended in death; Foic's wife and Foclann's mother will keen over them, but at least they shall be honored."

Calatín nodded to his mute driver, who wheeled him to the middle of the ford. The horses stamped a little at the smell of blood, churning the water, but they were battle-trained and did not shy as the Druid set to his task.

The heads came off the branches with a nasty slurping crunch, and Maeve noticed that Fedelm had vanished. Just as well, she thought. The young woman would see many slain before the raid was over, but this cruel taunt had been an unpleasant initiation into the trials of war. By the time the Druid's chariot had returned to shore, Fergus had mounted his borrowed one and was already splashing through the water. Reaching the fork, he grasped the thick trunk with one arm and crouched down, driving upward with legs and back. Maeve heard the little links of his hauberk grating against each other, then the creaking of wood, and a sharp shattering sound: the force of his lunge against the post had driven his feet through the chariot's bottom.

"It could have been better made," Maeve said. "Bring a sturdier."

The next chariot shattered, and the third as well. Fergus' lips were drawn back in a snarl of effort, or a smile? It was hard to tell, but Maeve could feel herself growing angrier and angrier as she watched. At Fergus, or at the man who had set the post: she did not know, but Fergus was here.

"Enough of breaking our chariots, Fergus. Do you mean only to delay our host until the Ulstermen rise from their pangs to offer battle?"

Fergus glared at her, grey eyes blazing. The thin scar running through his beard shone purple with effort, as though the blood were about to burst afresh from it. He was soaked from the neck down, standing waist-deep in the icy water amid the rubble of the broken vehicles, and sweat ran freely from beneath his helmet-rim.

"Bring me my own chariot, and I shall show you!" He snarled.

One of the Ulster exiles drove Fergus' chariot forward – its poles were sheathed in bronze, and bronze horse-heads glittered like gold at each corner. Fergus leapt in with a single water-spraying bound, grasping the post one-armed like a lover again, and surged heavily upward. This time, there was no sound of splintering or even creaking, only a series of tiny sharp cracks as several of the fine iron links gave way across his straining back. The post rose up slowly and steadily, its branches lifting above Fergus' head as if the tree's growth of twenty years were pressed into a few moments.

Then the Ulsterman had it free, cradling it in his arm and bearing it back to Ailill and Maeve.

"One stroke, indeed," Ailill said. " Cú Chulainn."

"Aye," Fergus answered.

Her fury baulked in one direction, Maeve turned towards Calatín.

"Why is Ulster's champion not laid out by the pangs of Ulster?" She asked. "Or have they failed already?"

Calatín shook his head.

"The pangs of Ulster endure, longer than ever before. Cú Chulainn is free of them, for three reasons. He is no Ulsterman born, no heir to Macha's curse. He is but a beardless boy of seventeen: even were he born to Ulster, he would not suffer the pangs until full manhood. He has never harmed a woman in the way of a man. Indeed, in the fullest height of his battle-frenzy, he must turn aside from the sight of a woman's naked breast, and his fury be cooled. Thus there is nothing in him on which the wrath of the goddess may grip."

Soaked to the skin, Fergus was shivering hard, but his voice was steady.

"Cú Chulainn defeated the war-teacher Aoife, and took the pleasure of her thighs as ransom for her life. Is that not harm?"

"Not as it happened," Ferdiad broke in.

The champion of Connaught had stood silent in his chariot at the head of Maeve's guards while Fergus struggled to lift the post. It was not like him to speak uninvited, but he went on passionately.

"It was a fair fight, and anyone defeated in challenge may offer ransom or accept a condition.

Aoife chose to lie with Cú Chulainn, and she did not hold it against him, nor seem displeased after: I think that was not the only time for them."

Calatín sighed.

"You have some things to learn about the hearts of women. As you say, Aoife accepted the challenge freely, and chose freely. If she bore resentment or regret, or sorrow is to come of it. It is human resentment and human sorrow: the gods have no hand in it. Cú Chulainn is free of all that is laid on Conchobar and his Ulstermen, and thus stands to oppose us, a hero, if a youth, alone."

"A youth alone, if a hero," said Maeve firmly.

"However strong and agile his body may be, he has but one. He has dodged around our host rather than bring us to open battle, and at seventeen he is hardly a man. How, then, may he hold out against many warriors long-tried in battle?"

"The deeds that he has done from childhood…" Fergus began.

Maeve cut him off with a gesture.

"Enough. We may hear of them later; we shall not delay here any longer. Ferdiad, you boasted of your strength earlier. Can you match this feat of Cú Chulainn's?"

Ferdiad smiled.

"Give me the fork."

Standing in his chariot, Connaught's champion gripped the bloody trunk with one hand, heaving it up above his head. The thick forked pole began to spin with ponderous grace, gaining speed swiftly as Ferdiad whirled beneath it, his powerful body uncoiling like a whip cracking out. It arched into the air as swiftly as a light javelin, sailing more than halfway across the ford.

A fine spray of water misted it as the point drove downward, and Maeve felt the deep shuddering crack of shattered stone echoing up through her chariot's iron-bound wheels into the soles of her feet. Fortunately, Ferdiad had aimed his cast to the very side of the ford, so that the host could pass easily through. The golden-haired Connaught man grinned at his queen, all his solemnity gone for once.

"You will find that my boasts are never ill-founded," he said. "And if they were, you should not have made me your champion. As I said before, I will not fight Cú Chulainn. if he chooses to set trials of strength, he will find, as he always did, that I am his better there."

"So may it always be!" Maeve agreed, smiling back at him and thinking, *I wish Finnabair could have seen this. He is a far better match for her than that Ulsterman with whom she is infatuated!*

The wind had been strengthening; now it eddied back into her face, a fine gust of snow stinging her eyes.

"Forward, the host! Fergus, take my cloak, you, and you, give him yours as well."

The ice bit brutally through Maeve's hauberk the moment she stripped her cloak off. Fergus, hero though he was, shivering so hard he could barely take it, his blue lips too frozen to utter more than a vague whisper of thanks. He made no protest as Maeve's guardsmen helped him strip down, their backs shielding him from the snow-laden wind. Fergus' muscles stood out stark against his white skin, bunched and trembling against the cold as the men hastily rubbed his limbs dry.

Even thus chilled, with his manhood doused in freezing water, he was magnificent: Maeve could not help staring until the guards had bundled Ulster's exiled king in several cloaks and huddled close to share their bodies' heat with him. Maeve turned to Calatín as the first chariots splashed over the ford.

"Where is Fedelm?"

The Druid pointed to a little copse of trees.

"There, I suspect. You should not disturb her."

He spoke pretentiously, but Maeve had seen plenty of young warriors puke after their first battles. If there was any great Druidic secret to Fedelm's disappearance, it was only the knowledge that Druids, too, could lose their breakfasts. She snorted, getting out of her chariot to walk to the copse.

Fedelm was on her knees in a pile of dead leaves, retching dryly. Her eyes were red-rimmed as she looked up, her hair hanging about her greenish-pale face in wild fair tangles. With all her trained composure lost, the ban-fili might have been no older than Finnabair. A sudden rush of pity and tenderness swept through Maeve, and she knelt beside the girl. Fedelm did not resist the older woman's embrace, resting her head on Maeve's breast; Maeve could feel the shudders racking her body.

"I'm sorry," Fedelm gulped. "I should have been able to control myself, I should have…"

"Hush, hush," Maeve murmured, stroking the girl's disheveled blond hair. "There is no shame in being sick at your first sight of a man's death." Fedelm's kin were peasants, who would bear arms only if Cruachan were grievously pressed in battle: the ban-fili would never have seen anything like Cú Chulainn's grisly message-fork.

"I have seen young men twice your size and fully war-trained in no better state. Now you are past the worst: you shall not have to turn away another time."

"Calatín, he froze me with his wand to keep me from throwing up before the host, then sent me off beneath the cloak of his power, that none might guess what I had to do. He will be so angry, that I could not master myself, that I was about to shame our school and order before the warriors, he will. "

"He will not," Maeve said firmly. "He is war-trained himself, and has seven sons, all fighters. He knows as well as any, that it is hardly more common to pass your first war-deaths with your breakfast in your belly than to make it through a day's battle-training with no bruises. Come, are you able to stand?"

With Maeve's help, Fedelm got shakily to her feet, pulling her colour-flecked green mantle tightly about her against the cold. "Thank you," she murmured.

"Do not worry," Maeve told her. "We should hasten now, for the weather is worsening and I wish to press on as far as we can this day."

Fedelm's swollen eyes opened wider.

"We cannot! The storm is full-come upon us. Calatín and I have been struggling to hold it off. Now it is breaking, and this the least part of what is to come. We must make camp on the other side, as quickly as possible, or we shall lose half our army to the cold."

For a moment Maeve wavered, impatience pricking her like a charioteer's goad. Yet the weather was worsening, and what good was a foreseer if one did not listen to her?

A deep, mournful howl echoed through the woods, shaking a heavy scatter of thick snow from the bare trees. Looking through the gathering whiteness, Maeve saw Baiscne sitting upright in her chariot, sniffing the harsh northeast wind.

"So be it: I will give the orders. Come on." Maeve took the girl's hand. Something rattled in the icy branches. Maeve looked, and saw her marten running down a tree towards her, a streak of pale brown and cream against the grey bark. She held out her free hand, and the marten leapt to it, its tiny claws snagging in her hauberk as it scampered up her arm to nestle its welcome warmth against the chilled skin of her neck.

Both she and Fedelm were shivering in earnest now, and they ran for the chariot together, shielding their eyes against the stinging lash of snow and wind.

Maeve

Ailill had halted the host; servants and warriors scrambled to
throw up tents and hastily lash bothies together, cursing the snow
that piled up faster than they could scrape the ground clear. Instead
of the usual royal enclosures, several of the larger tents were pitched
closely in the middle of the camp. Maeve's hauberk felt as though
unkindly síde-folk had transformed it to ice on her body. Though
Fedelm bore no metal armor to suck the heat from her, she was
a hand span shorter than Maeve and much lighter. Spasms of
shivering passed over the girl, her teeth chattering.

Maeve had to lift the ban-fili from the chariot; then the foreseer's
knees gave way, and Maeve scooped her up in her arms and ran for
the nearest tent. It seemed blessedly warm inside, though the puffs
of Maeve's breath showed reddish in the firelight. Two of Flidais'
servants were tending a large cauldron.

Next to it was a mound of blankets streaming copper-glittering
red hair mingled with dark. Flidais and Fergus looked up at Maeve.
Flidais grinned, but Fergus' grey eyes were still unfocused, and he
barely had the strength to move his head.

"I've ordered as much hot stew and ale to be given out as we can
manage," Flidais said, her voice surprisingly even for a woman
who was lying naked against Fergus' bare body. "Fergus is out of
danger, I think. He can feel all his fingers and toes again, and he is
beginning to warm up."

Maeve looked down at the two on the floor, feeling a flash of, not
jealousy; even Flidais could not drain Fergus to exhaustion for long.
Envy, rather, that the other queen lay there so casually and would
undoubtedly raise Fergus' spirits to more soon, while Maeve was
hedged from the friendly pleasures of his body by this tangled maze
of feelings and rights.

Still, this would be Flidais' time for him in any case, Maeve
consoled herself. The milk-queen could depend on her followers
to feed the host, while Maeve could not personally turn aside from
them any longer than she absolutely must, in such a crisis. She set
Fedelm in front of the fire. One of Flidais' guards, a wiry woman still
in full war-gear, was there with blankets and a steaming mug, taking
the ban-fili's shoes off to rub life into her stone-white feet.

A little of the hot drink spilled over the cup's rim as Fedelm's shaking hands closed on it, then the girl's chin lifted and her fingers clamped down hard and steady. She will be well, Maeve thought.

"Your cloak, Queen Maeve," a servant said. Maeve stood by the fire till her hauberk heated before donning it. Under the heavy wool, the metal would be like a warming stone in a cold bed, for a while. The color was coming back to Fedelm's face already. As Maeve rose to her feet, the young foreseer looked up at her.

"My queen, guard yourself well, and have a good care to your warriors. We called to the Morrígan and Macha, but Nemhain and Badb ride in this storm."

As if in agreement, Baiscne licked Maeve's hand, then howled again, his deep call drowning the blizzard's rising noise for a moment. The sound cleared Maeve's head, driving back the trembling fear in her limbs that she had not acknowledged until it was gone. Her marten curled about her neck; on the other side, she felt soft feathers, hard little feet scrabbling at her skin, and a quick light heartbeat as her wren emerged from the cloak's folds to nestle in the crook of her shoulder.

'They are here because I need all the strength of Maeve of Cruachan', Maeve realized. 'What Fedelm said just now, it is no bard's fancy.'

"I will be wary," Maeve answered. "You, have you learned the arts of healing?"

"The arts of the body, in any case, though I have only a little of the deeper lore."

"Then, when you are recovered, prepare yourself to do what you may. There will be many who need restoring from the cold, and likely no few cases of frostbite." For I have never seen or heard of such a storm, save from a few old men telling tales. The wind flung snow brutally into Maeve's face as she stepped out. She blinked desperately to clear her eyes, wiping tears away before they could freeze and drawing her mantle about her head. Her guards stared shivering and wild-eyed into the moaning whiteness.

"Get inside and get some hot food," Maeve ordered.

"You will be no help if your hands are too frozen to grasp a sword. if we cannot fight in this, then no foe can attack us." She touched each man on the shoulder as he passed. Strength flowed out of her into each, like hot mead streaming from Brigit's cauldron. "When you are able, go spread these orders. Let no man go away from his fellows until the storm has stilled: it would be easy to become lost in this." And friendship always lessens fear.

"Let all gather about the chief tents, and let each leader of a troop see that there is food and one fire for his own. Do not let each kindle a fire in his own shelter, or we will soon run out of wood to little gain."

"It shall be done, my queen," Ferdiad answered.

Maeve walked onward, squaring her shoulders tightly and squinting her eyes against the bitter buffeting of the storm. Although she knew it was but a little past noontide, the light had faded to the deep grey of twilight, with nothing to be seen past a couple of paces but shadows in the snow. Someone jostled her, recoiling with a man's terrified shriek. Maeve saw the dark wideness of his eyes against his drained skin, like the pits in a dead man's face when the crows had been at him, and grabbed his arm before he could flee in panic.

"Have no fear!" She shouted over the keening wind. "I am your queen: no harm shall come to you."

The young man . his dark beard barely a scurf upon his throat and chin – stared wordlessly at her, but Maeve felt his straining muscles easing in her grasp.

"Come with me, what is your name?"

"F-Fiacha mac Finnchad, my queen," he stammered.

"Come, Fiacha. There is much to be done tonight, if we are to weather this storm safely, and every stout heart and strong hand will be needed. My guard are busy: you will take their place for now."

The youth straightened, his voice growing firmer. "I am at your command, my queen."

With the snow already halfway to Maeve's knees, there was no way to drive a chariot around the camp. Nor would Maeve have tried: as the storm's howling rose and fell capriciously, she could hear the terrified whinnies of the army's horses. 'There first. If our steeds panic beneath the Nemhain's breath and break free, we are likely to lose them all, and good men and women with them". As she and Fiacha lowered their heads to force their way to the nearest pen, the snow beat against Maeve like a multitude of white crows battering her with fierce wings, the wind ripping at every bit of exposed skin like cruel beaks. She could feel the terror riding the gale, its keening raising the specters of battle-panic.

Even with her hand on Baiscne's shoulder, her marten and wren against her neck, feeding their strength endlessly to the core of warmth within her, she almost quailed when she stared into the snow too long and thought she saw a cruel skull-gaunt face glimmering in the whiteness. Further away, someone screamed, or was it the wailing of the wind?

'I am Maeve of Cruachan, and I will not give way to fear. For if I do, the whole host is lost'.

Each cantred was supposed to see to its own horses, penning or tethering them to graze as the night's camp allowed. In the haste of making camp this day, Maeve guessed that several divisions had worked together to throw up a wicker fence around the whole herd. The horses were a plunging, squealing mass within. As she watched, one big grey reared to batter down the flimsy withies.

"Down!" Maeve cried, stretching out her arm towards the stallion. Once more she felt that flow of warm strength from herself: the animal came down on all fours, tossing its snow-crusted mane.

"Macha, lady of horses," Maeve murmured. "We called you in fury; you came as our ally. Be our ally now!" Taking a deep breath to steady herself, she gathered her strength. The wicker fence was as high as her shoulder.

Though she had never learned all the great feats, she could salmon-leap as well as any warrior of Eriu. She did not try a running start: the deep snow would hinder more than help. Instead she bent her knees, driving all her strength down into her legs to fling her body over, twisting in the air to come down in a deep crouch.

A fleeing horse's shoulder bumped Maeve, knocking her down in the snow; she rolled frantically to get out from under the flying hooves and came to her feet.

"Stop!" Maeve shouted at the frantic horses. Her voice cut through the wailing wind as she lifted both hands in a gesture of soothing. "Stop, be calm. I am here, and nothing shall harm you!"

The horses eddied around her like a torrent of huge tumbling boulders. Any stray hoof could have crushed her bones, or knocked her down to be trampled, but none touched her. Instead, some distant part of her mind watched in silent amazement as she reached out to stroke the ice-spiked hides, drawing up the warmth beneath them, and the horses calmed beneath her touch as Fiacha had. Maeve followed the wicker fence around until she came to the gate. The leather straps that held it had frozen solid already, crackling ominously as she opened it. Several grooms stood outside in a tight cluster, clutching bags of grain to themselves as if to build a bulwark against the terror of the storm.

"Feed the horses now, and then get to the main tents for something hot," Maeve told them. They stared at her, awe driving fear from their faces as they realized that the herd no longer plunged in wild panic, but milled quietly, beginning to scrape at the deep snow to get at the dead grass beneath.

"Oró, Queen Maeve!" One of the grooms breathed, his words almost lost beneath the keening wind. "It shall be as you say, our queen."

Maeve turned back towards the larger tents herself, meaning to see what Ailill was doing and be sure that all was going as she had ordered before she made her full round of the camp. Then she heard the screaming, though it was a few moments before she could make out the word, "Fire! Fire!"

Maeve ran towards the sound, Baiscne pacing her and Fiacha floundering in her wake. The flames rising from the small tent lit the snow with an eerie shifting red brightness, as though the swirling flakes burned from within with a fire that gave no light. A man stumbled howling out, cloaked in fire and his head wreathed in flames, falling and rolling in the snow even as he screamed. Maeve reached him in moments. One of Ailill's Leinstermen, she thought, though it was hard to tell under the black charring and raw blisters where his hair and beard had burned. His brown eyes wandered, sliding vaguely over her face.

"I heard orders," he moaned. "The voices, in the dark needed fire, more fire and more. "

"Hush," Maeve said. He whimpered in pain, but did not try to speak. The burns would be agonizing, Maeve knew, and he would be scarred forever.

He had gotten out in time, and the snow had been a mercy. If the Druids could keep the deep scorches from festering, he would live, and fight again. It was long past dark when the wind eased at last, the howling that had struck fear into her host fading away to distant moans. Her guard had rejoined her, Ferdiad and Maine Cairbre breaking a trail for her through the snow. So much snow, knee-deep on Maeve in the thinnest places, with some drifts rising over her head; and the tents and bothies were no more than a thick cluster of white hillocks by now. As the terror of the storm faded, the strength that had carried Maeve through it sank back. She shook with exhaustion, hunger, and cold, but did not let it show as she made her way among the warriors and servants who huddled over their bowls of hot stew and mugs of hot ale around the great tents.

The tents with the fires were crammed full of people, but Maeve saw torchlight glowing faint through the walls of Ailill's own shelter. She wanted food, and the comfort of her husband's warm arms and warm bed, and there was no more that she could do or needed to among the host this night. Ailill was not alone. Flidais and Fergus were with him, and Finnabair and Cormac, and Connla mac Laegaire, the leader of Munster's under-kings.

"It is Maeve who will choose whether we attack this fort, or not," Ailill said as she walked in. "And you may present your case to her now."

Ailill sounded and looked as weary as Maeve felt. He, too, had gone among the host to reassure them, with only his own courage and such strength as he gained from her touch to sustain him. She had seen him struggling in waist-deep snow to raise tents that had collapsed from the weight on their roofs, once digging bare-handed in a deep drift to pull men from a fallen bothy before they smothered. Connla looked up fiercely at Maeve.

"There is hardly a case to present. The matter seems quite clear to me, and to the other kings and leaders who have come on this raid as well."

Munster's chief under-king was a wiry-built man, brown-haired and brown-eyed, with a short reddish-brown beard. He was dressed in a clean bright-striped tunic, his hair plaited and beard and mustaches groomed to neat points, with a heavy gold torc about his throat and gold rings on all his fingers. Maeve liked him little: he was argumentative and vain, touchy about his rank and privileges, and she had often thought that if she were Munster's ruler, she would sleep less well with him at her back. Still, he led a strong cantred, and if she offended him, she risked losing many of the Munstermen.

' I look forward to the day you learn you will never have Finnabair, no matter what hopes we hinted at when we talked you into joining this raid!' Maeve thought.

"What matter is this?" She asked, her voice as mild as she could make it.

Connla leaned forward, jutting his sharp beard at her like a spear-point.

"You promised us plunder, and glory, and vengeance on Ulster. Yet we have been marching for weeks, and not taken a calf or copper bracelet; and for glory and vengeance, we have seen only a boy's tracks and that...thing he left us." The under-king's dark eyes slipped aside, as if looking away from the memory of the sight.

'So I was not the only seasoned warrior disturbed by the Hound's head-post', thought Maeve. That matter was best left to lie.

"Although the way has been longer than we hoped, we are into Ulster now, and it is not a province lacking in riches or the chance for battle. Why bring this up now?"

"Cormac tells me there is a strong and wealthy fort, Rath Echach, less than half a day's march from here, if we turn a little aside. Now, we of Munster have had enough mysterious messages and foes lurking about the edge of the host. Nor did we come to huddle like sheep in the snow while our foes gather to slaughter us. We shall take Rath Echach tomorrow, and you can come with us or not!"

Maeve's ice-numb fingers closed loosely about the hilt of her sword. Only the realization that she could not tighten her hand enough to get a proper grip kept her from drawing to meet his challenge. She did not know what she would have said next, but Fergus broke in. He was still pale, heavily wrapped in blankets, but his hands no longer shivered and his voice was steady.

"I came to win the Donn Cuailgne, and to strike a blow against Conchobar. I have heard that the men of Ulster still lie in their pangs, far longer than ever before.

What glory is there in taking a stead defended only by boys and such women as have chosen to learn war-skill? I see no need to turn aside from our road."

"Our road!" Connla scoffed.

"You have led us around in circles; you led us through the drumlin-land instead of around it, which broke so many chariot-poles that we have hardly any spare shafts left. How did Cú Chulainn, your foster son, find us so swiftly?

It was Cormac, not you, who told us that there was a prize ready to our hand here; and Cormac will tell us that, if we had taken the straight road in, we would already be leading the Brown Bull home. Is that not so, Cormac Connlongas?"

Maeve's eldest son bit his lip, staring at the fire and winding his long knobby fingers together. At last he said,

"I would have chosen a straighter track, but Fergus knows Ulster better than I. Yet it is true that we have had little reward for much effort. My men, too, are eager for battle and plunder. There are few warriors of this host who are not ready to strike back after the insult and deaths of this morning. If this night is not to steal their strength altogether, we must rouse their hearts again."

Flidais nodded. "That is so. Moreover, our supplies are lower than I had thought they would be by now. Not one person in this host, from the highest nobles to the lowest slaves, went unfed or lacking in hot ale or mead this night. That was needful, but not without cost to us, if there is much chance of further delays. Rath Echach could replenish our wagons well enough."

Her anger cooling already, Maeve thought on what the others had said. Already sure he had the upper hand, Connla was not even watching her. Instead he gazed at Finnabair with the faint smile of a man about to close his bargain and lead a prize heifer away. Maeve itched to strike him, but forced her hand from her sword-hilt. Cormac's blue eyes were bright with eagerness; Ailill only looked tired and Fergus.

Some trick of the firelight, under-shadowing the bones of his face and veiling the marks of battle and age, showed him for a moment as a young man in pain. Maeve knew how little he wanted the folk of Ulster to suffer for his vengeance, how this new suggestion must tear him. Yet he would not beg, nor plead his cause with any weapon but plain words and good reasons, such as they were.

As for Maeve herself, the thought of slowing now was almost unbearable. She had felt the storm's fear, and seen the shame gathering in its wake. She, better than any save her Druids, knew just how close they had come to breaking that night: battle would in truth hearten her army. She also knew that the aftermath would be uglier than usual, as the fighters strove to drive the memory of terror and ice from their hearts with blood and fire, and, inevitably, rape: no ruler's command could prevent it.

'Maybe the fear and fury must be loosed before this host turns to devour itself, as will happen when warriors need a foe to battle and there is none to hand. Maeve disliked where her thoughts led her, but could find no better turning from that trail. Then a shaft of sunlight fell across it. She smiled.'

"That is all true," she said. "And moreover, this boy-champion, this Hound of Ulster, if he has not fled, is it not likely enough that he is guesting there? What youth would pass a night such as this outdoors if there were a steady-going of his friends nearby?"

"Cú Chulainn would and could," Fergus answered. "The fire in him. Such cold is nothing to his heat." Melancholy and pride tinged Fergus' voice like wormwood and honey mixed together in ale, but a smile tugged at his lips, as though he could not help his joy in his foster-son. Then his mouth straightened into a hard line. "But," Fergus added, his words dropping like stones, "Cú Chulainn might have stopped to guest at Rath Echach. For it is a geas upon him that he never refuse an offer of meat or drink. If he passed there, he will have halted there."

'We are tearing you apart between us, like two hounds with a single piece of meat, Maeve thought. I wish it were otherwise. I cannot send you back to Cruachan without shaming you, nor do I dare risk your parting from us, when such love still ties you to Ulster and the Red Branch.'

"We may hope for the best," Maeve said briskly. "My Cormac, I will send you and your men to spy out the ground tomorrow. Now, I think we are all weary: if there is to be battle, we should get to bed."

"True enough," Cormac agreed, unfolding his rangy length and pulling his tunic's hood over his golden-brown hair. "You shall not be disappointed in my troop, Mother."

"I know that," Maeve answered, smiling and embracing her son.

Fergus rose without a word. Flidais took him by the hand. "A wise choice, Queen Maeve," she said softly. Fergus' mouth tightened, but he left with her all the same.

"You should be going to bed as well, Finnabair," Ailill said. "If you are to keep enchanting half the leaders of this raid with your beauty, you must have your rest."

Finnabair's mouth twisted. She spat into the fire.

"I would gouge out my own eyes if it would keep me from having to wed Connla!" She hissed softly, glancing towards the tent door as if she feared to be overheard. Nor, indeed, would Maeve have put it past Connla to stay and listen a moment.

Maeve laid her hand on her daughter's shoulder, as she had comforted her warriors in the storm's terror.

"Whatever passes, that shall not happen," she murmured. "So long as he believes it, we have him and his men; and we may need them all. You have done very well. With any luck, this will be over by Imbolc, and you can wed as you choose.."

"May it be so!" Finnabair answered fervently, and left Maeve and Ailill alone.

Maeve went to her husband, leaning into his warmth. Ailill put his arm about her shoulders, lifting a gilded goblet to her mouth. The hot mead seemed to melt Maeve from within, easing the shaking tightness of her limbs and unknotted her stomach. Ailill helped her take her hauberk off; he held her while she ate and drank, and when his big hand moved gently under her tunic to support the weight of her heavy breast, Maeve arched her back and smiled at him.

Fedelm

After Maeve had left Flidais' tent, I sat gathering my strength as the warmth flowed to my limbs. Even by the fire, I could feel the cold fury of the storm leaching the heat through the thick hides and wool. Snowy wings battered the tent walls, the clawed wind struggling to rip the tent-pegs free like a fox digging out a nest of baby rabbits to devour, leaving us naked to cold and fear. Yet, half-trained though I might be, I was still a student of the druid.

I could no more leave Connacht's host without protection than Maeve, unwounded, could abandon them on the field to be crushed by a host against whom they had no defense. I breathed from the core of my body, and murmured the ancient words that were both meditation and blessing, reaching out with my deepest senses to those mighty things that lived and did not change, from which all grew and was wrought.

"Brightness of sun, whiteness of snow. Fire's strength and lightning's swiftness; depth of sea and steepness of rock and steadfastness of earth."

Power came to me with each phrase, the bright and the dark and the strong. My roots ran deep, my mind reached to the Sun shining fair above the storm; and from the corner of my eye I saw the steady golden glow about myself as my warding-strength rose from within. Flidais was kissing Fergus now, moving gently under the heap of blankets. They, too, were beginning to glow like coals blown to brightness beneath the ashes, their heat giving the tent a better warmth than the fire.

The lovemaking of kings and queens has power: I did not need to touch the servants tending the great cauldron, for as Flidais warmed Fergus to strength and health, a touch of that fire spread out to all her folk, and gave virtue to the food and drink she poured out so freely. It was well that I had warded myself before stepping outside. To walk into that storm with the sight of the druid was to step into the Otherworld raging like a winter sea, waves of furious terror battering the steep stone walls of my mind. The Nemhain and the Badb, those wild battle-crows who are one and three and many. Their might seethed through the furious eddies and gusts of snow-heavy wind, uncaring of who had called them, only seeking to terrify and devour.

A black-clawed hand clutched at me; bone-stark death-faces with black pits for eyes and long-gaping mouths took shape from the snow and dissolved again. Things misshapen and cruel shadowed the edge of my sight. A huge monster with one eye, one foot, and one hand; a beak-faced hag with streaming hair and frost-blue talons; a gaunt black goat-headed man with huge blind moonlit eyes; the twisted shapes capered and gibbered, keening their madness and seeking to maze me from my path as the blizzard buffeted me. I did not know if the cries I heard came from the crazed host, or the army of Eriu, but one voice rose above the rest.

"Hear ye, listen to what shall come of this war. A dark march to the Brown Bull, one man to do the deeds of a host. Once two pig herds were friends; now crows shall drink a cruel milk. The rivers shall rise; the hard raiders shall herd men, and man's meat lie wherever the Warped One may reach!"

I set the words in my mind, but closed them away. Only time would show whether I had heard a true foretelling, or deception shaped to engender fear: the wights of the Otherworld do not lie, but entangle and deceive with clever words beyond earthly measure. I heard the wails of living folk as well, but did my best to shut them from me, seeking the light of Calatín's tent. Yet always, pacing me, a single great black shadow followed me, its shape veiled by the raging snow.

Like any cottager fearing the wrath or humor of the síd-folk, I drew my little belt-knife an inch from the scabbard, gasping at the burning cold of the frozen iron blade on my fingertips. The black thing did not turn away, so I turned to look straight at it, my heart hammering in my chest. To face the creatures of the Otherworld gives them strength, but only thus can they be truly defeated. If one's own power is great enough. I sucked in a throat-freezing gasp of snowy air. The thing that followed me was longer than three horses, slimmer than one. At first I thought it was a great worm, slick and black in the snow.

Then I saw the chewing mandibles, the chitinous tail raising dark and threatening above its head. The derg-daol, the black-blood beetle: called Nemhain's Horse by those who dared to speak her name, the black narrow-bodied stag-beetle bears the spirit of terror to battle, and burrows into the corpses to feed afterwards. On its back I could not see the rider clearly: only long grey hair streaming, and a ragged garment of snow twining and whirling around a hunched woman's form. If I quailed or fled, the Hag of Terror would have me; and whether she ate my mind, or the derg-daol chewed into my body, it would be the same in the end. I stood my ground with the snow and wind tearing at me, and faced Nemhain and her dreadful steed, calling up every spell of fortress and will that I knew.

At last, because I had mastered my fear, or perhaps only because it was the hearts of warriors that were her proper prey. Nemhain's gaze left me; her black mount slither-scuttled away, leaving me to the other phantoms swirling at the edge of my sight. It seemed that I wandered for a very long time, until my feet were numb and I could no longer feel my fingers clutching my mantle about me. At last I saw the shimmering brightness spreading in rings through the snow, like ripples over a pond, and the warped dark storm-figures faded to shifting shadows where that brightness passed. Calatín sat cross-legged and naked to the waist in his tent, a flickering torch casting a muffled light over his gaunt face and the sharp ridges of his ribs.

Patterns of deep blue coiled over his shoulders, turning the angular bones and wire-strands of muscle into a haunted landscape of crags and gorges wound with dark serpents. I did not dare to speak, for I could tell that he was deep in trance. I paused, uncertain whether it would be better to try to lend him my strength, or whether even that would disturb his mind: should I go elsewhere, and strive with such lore and might as I had to do what I could without his counsel?

If I could even ease the ferocity of the weather a little, it would steal some of the power from the Badb howling with the storm, and give a little relief to the terrified host caught in it.

The old drúi did not look up at me, slowly, every muscle of his body under control more perfect than any warrior's or dancer's, he uncoiled his legs, stretching out his feet. Without hesitation, I went to him and took them into my lap. I had never performed this rite, nor trained for it, but I knew that I could do what was needed. For I was a maiden untouched in body by any man, and thus he could join my power to his own and, reflecting it back and forth between us, make it greater than either of us could manage alone. I did not need to know what he did or how he shaped it: I had only to be unbroached, and willing, and strong enough myself that his working could not drain me to my death.

Like a greater river drinking a smaller, Calatín swept my thoughts into his own. I looked down upon the camp, and nothing was hidden from me. Maeve shone like a white pillar-stone in moonlight. Through her wren, the strength of the heavens gleamed down into her. The hound Baiscne drew up the great dark roots of the Underworld; and her marten scampered to link the two in an arching shimmer of power. The stone was half-undermined, teetering on a rim of earth where little creatures dug and scrabbled: the might that made her Maeve of Cruachan.

Queen and goddess, balanced precariously on that gnawed foundation. Still, she stood now, a beacon of courage in the seething sea of wind and snow and terror. Near the center of the camp, Ailill was a great golden oak: not so mighty as his wife, but strong enough to shelter those around him under his branches. The cries of Flidais' and Fergus' joy drowned the storm's keening, Flidais' cauldron poured out a flood of bright honey-milk, strengthening all who drank there. The lesser kings and leaders, they too were fires against the dark, shining staves upholding their folk against the cruel storm.

We, even a ban-fili cannot truly show such things in words: I can say only that the mighty river that the two of us were poured into the host; the stone ring-fort that we were sheltered them; the bonfire that we were gave them warmth and strength and comfort, and slowly, the host of the Nemhain, the assembly of the Badb, the specters clawing chilled flesh and keening with fanged mouths next to cringing ears. They began to fade. The storm wind still wailed, the snow fell no less thickly, but the terror over the camp rolled slowly back, like a great ninth wave breaking on a staunch cliff to sigh exhausted and harmless down the beach again.

Calatín withdrew his cold bony feet from my lap and coiled them under himself again, passing a hand first over my eyes, then over his own. He arose, settling the white robe of ceremony over his bony bare shoulders.

"Well-done," he said. "Take that smaller chest there, and I will take the larger. We have done what we may for the spirits of the host, but their bodies will need tending."

I followed the drúi, squinting and bending nearly double as the wind-hurled weight of snow smacked into me.

The cold was gone from my limbs: I tingled with warmth and life down to the tips of my fingers and toes, though I had lost the wool wrapping my shoes and my legs sank into the snow past the knees at every step. As we waded through the thick drifts, I concentrated on storing that feeling: the strong beat of my heart, the thrumming exaltation like a wind that blew the fire of my spirit to burn the fuel of my body; I knew now why so many of the druid were so lean. There was, indeed, a great deal of healing to be done.

Most of the damage was frostbite: Maeve's servant Lochu melted cauldrons of snow for us to steep herbs in, soaking and rubbing feet and hands and ears with the concoction. For worse cases, Calatín showed me the incantations, the movements and pressures of the hands, to coax stubborn blood back into deep-chilled flesh. When those failed, we took sharp knives to cut away the black patches of frozen meat, and towards the end of the night, sometimes bone-saws to take off dead toes and fingers before they could spread rotting death through the body.

There were a few burned men, who had not heeded the queen's order not to light fires in the smaller shelters. One was only lightly scorched, face and hands blistered as if he had fallen asleep in the summer sun: we sent him off with a handful of snow and a scolding. Two were more badly burned: those we treated with ointment of comfrey and marigold spread carefully under soft bandages. One was charred like a roast that had fallen into the fire, hairless and oozing and horrible, moaning through bare teeth cooked half to chalk and trying to writhe. Calatín lifted his wand, touching the burned man between the eyes, and he slumped silent. Mercifully dead, I thought: but Calatín turned to me.

"You know how to make a clean sacrifice. It is the same with a man. His garment cannot be mended: free him of it, that he may find peace for now, and a better one after."

I swallowed hard. I had always known that the time might come when my hand must shed a human life, as offering or message or blessing to the gods. What one prepares for in holiness, and knows one can do in the exaltation of ritual, is not the same as what one can set oneself to in cold blood.

"Would you leave him to suffer? Even my spells cannot hold him in sleep for long."

I wanted to ask, Could you not do it? I knew better. I had shamed us once already that day. I would not do it again; for my own pride, and because I had not, after all, wholly lost my fear of the old drúi.

Then I recalled how Maeve had spoken to me, when she found me vomiting in the dead leaves like a silly child. The comfort of her embrace, and her voice, so calm and sure, "Now you are past the worst: you shall not have to turn away another time."

Eochaid was just coming into the tent with another load of wood, shaking snow from his wet dark hair at the door. I gestured to him. A warrior who had seen mortal wounds before, he knew what I needed at once. He lifted the burned man's body and carried him outside, that the blood not foul tent or bedding; I passed a whetstone over the edge of my knife to be sure of it, and followed him. It was still dark when Eochaid forced a path through the thigh-deep snow to the Druid's tent.

Though thick cloud still hid Moon and stars, the storm had passed, only a few big flakes drifting gently down. Midnight was long gone: the first servants were already striking tents and readying breakfast around Cormac's encampment. Heavy cloaks hid the warriors' armor, but they sat by their little camp fires sharpening weapons and checking their gear, moving with steady purpose.

"There will be little sleep for us tonight," Calatín told me.

"There are herbs to grind and ointments to make for tending the wounded, and I must also teach you spells of blood-stopping and healing for cut flesh and broken bones before morning: there shall be battle tomorrow."

I ached to the bones, but looking at Cormac's troops, I could not doubt my teacher's word.

"I shall be ready for it," I said.

The flickering light of Eochaid's torch showed Calatín's mouth harsh as a sword-cut, his eyes gleaming black stones against the pale blur of his face. "See that you are."

I feared that he would speak of my morning's disgrace, but he kept walking. After a little time, I realized that he had: by the most subtle of means, leaving my own mind to shape the words. I was learning from him, I thought, more swiftly than I ever could have in Alba. Though the lessons had proved harsh, with likely more sorrow to come of them, I could not wish them unlearned, but some small part of me hoped that I would not see more of the battlefield than the wounded we strove to heal.

Maeve

Maeve spat out a mouthful of blood and gummy saliva, leaning on her shield and breathing hard. *I knew this would be ugly fighting,* she told herself. Wordlessly Maine Feidhlim handed her a water skin. She rinsed her mouth, spat again, and drank deeply. Rath Echach had been a fair hill-fort, a ditch and a palisade of sturdy oaken timbers ringing the chieftain's hall and the huts around it.

Now black smoke curled up from the half-charred palisade into the dull grey sky. The trampled snowdrifts were dark with mud and blood; Maeve could hardly tell the corpses from the heaps of stained snow. A few fallen still lay shivering and moaning, but not for long. The battle-frenzy was still on some of Maeve's warriors, who stabbed down at the wounded like children gigging frogs. Behind some of the huts, women were screaming and crying, or keening in pain.

"Boys, farmers, slaves, and battle-captives," Feidhlim said. "And a few female warriors. If only they had given up, or at least not tried to frighten us away!"

Maeve nodded. The women of Rath Echach had armed their youths and slaves. They had bound their hair beneath their chins like beards, shaking spears beside the men who shouted threats. Their deception had worked, the fighters of Eriu had believed the settlement's full force arisen, but that had only whipped the attack to greater frenzy.

Maeve's army had charged, firing the palisade and burning the gate while rocks and sling-balls whistled around them. Had every warrior inside been hale, they would have had no chance against the host gathered to meet Ulster's full might, or any fraction of those numbers, if that fraction's hearts roared as mightily for blood as the hearts of those who had seen the Hound's mocking head-post and passed the night in the open under Nemhain's frenzy. It had been a slaughter more brutal than any Maeve had seen, with nothing of glory to be gained.

"The Hound was not here. Let us see if there is anything worth taking in the hall," Maeve said.

The great hall of Rath Echach was like one of Maeve's own, but smaller and poorer. Some of Cormac's men were pulling the hangings from the walls and stripping the armor and jewelery from the corpses of the women who had made their last stand in the doorway.

Several Munstermen stood around a broken cask, streams of mead funneling golden down their beards to mix with the blood splashed over their faces and clothes. Most of the rooms around the edge were open; a few had been cleared by the simple means of smashing the plank partitions with axes. Suddenly a scream rang out from one, the ragged scream of a woman in child bed, but harsh with the depth of a man's throat. The sound scraped down Maeve's spine, but she ran towards the room. Cumail, one of the Munster under-kings, stood with his sword raised over the bed. Maeve hit him low with her shield-shoulder, driving him into the wall hard enough to splinter the thin planking as her sword-pommel smacked his right wrist. His blade spun away as he struggled. Cumail was heavier and stronger than Maeve, but she had him pinned off-balance.

"You fool!" Maeve screamed at him. "You dung-brained, beetle-souled, goat-licking idiot! Would you bring the curse of Macha on yourself, and mayhap on all our host? Would you dare the wrath of the Blood-Hags again, so soon after." Maeve could not speak of the night before; she knew that none of them would be able to, perhaps not ever. She let her anger carry her past the shuddering memory to snarl, "Were you not a king yourself, I should have killed you on the spot."

Cumail licked his lips nervously, the blood-frenzy fading from his pale blue eyes; Maeve was close enough to smell mead on his breath. One way or another, she thought, the Battle-Crows will have their due: terror, madness, and blood. When that must befall, better to be slayer than slain.

"I...The fury had me," the Munster under-king stammered, looking aside.

"Get out," Maeve said. Cumail staggered under his own weight as she stepped back, then the big man made for the door without another word.

The man on the bed was unwounded, though he writhed and groaned. Maeve was not sure he even saw her. Her birthings had all been easy enough, or so the midwives said. She remembered the pain still, and wondered how the Ulstermen could have survived so long; she could not help her pity for them.

'Because Macha's curse will not let them die, nor allow them ease, these are the folk who chose Conchobar as their king, when they could have had Fergus: do they not pay the price for their choice?'

Maeve stood a moment. There was a bronze cup of water on the table by the bed. She took it up and drank. Then, moved by she knew not what, held it to the lips of the man who lay there.

He raised his head to gulp gratefully, droplets running into his unkempt red beard, whispered something in a voice broken by much screaming, and let his head fall back as if that much effort had exhausted him.

"Well, it is done," Ailill said from the doorway. He was splashed with blood, a fine spattering of it standing out like a spray of dark freckles across his long straight nose and broad cheeks. His mustaches hung bedraggled with blood and sweat, but Maeve could see no sign of a wound on him. The king opened his mouth to speak again, then looked downward.

"Oh." Ailill fell silent. In the sudden quiet, Maeve heard a soft suckling noise from the floor, and followed her husband's gaze.

A woman's body lay there. She wore a helm, but no armor; a sword lay by her hand, but her dress was pulled aside from one breast as if she had been giving suck. She had carried no shield. Even in death, her left arm was crooked around her baby. The child still nuzzled at her nipple, one side of its face damp with its mother's milk, the other side shining red with the blood that had spurted from the great gash between her sword-side shoulder and neck. The wife of the chieftain in the bed, Maeve guessed, fallen defending her husband.

The strong muscles of her bare arm and shoulder marked the dead woman as a trained warrior, but who could fight half-naked with an infant at the breast? The baby was only a few days old: its mother would barely have recovered from the birthing, no doubt why she was in here instead of holding the hall-door with the other female warriors. Ailill closed his eyes tight, as if to shut out what he saw, or force back tears.

"You know," he said softly, "I have female champions in my own troop; I have never complained when you beat me three rounds of five in sparring. Yet, when I see such a sight, I must wonder…"

"If women should fight?" Maeve said harshly. Her tongue went to the gap between two of her back teeth. Conchobar had knocked the missing one out when he caught her training with his guards. She had never known if he had clouted the side of her face to keep from spoiling her looks, or whether it had only been chance that he had not smashed in her front teeth instead.

"This one chose to die defending her husband and child: Cumail, the gods-cursed fool, was about to murder her man in his bed. If she had not, what good to her?

She would most likely have been slaughtered after being raped. At best, carried off as a captive. What chances would you give that the man who took her would not bash the babe's head against the wall, rather than be encumbered with it on the march?"

Ailill did not answer. Instead he carefully moved the dead woman's arm and disengaged her child from her breast. The babe began to wail; Ailill jogged it soothingly in his heavy mailed arms.

"There is surely a woman with milk somewhere in our host," he said. "I will see to it."

Maeve nodded. Her throat was suddenly too thick to speak, but she put a hand on Ailill's forearm, squeezing gratefully. He leaned forward to kiss her, careful not to crush the baby between their armored bodies, a familiar position, between man and wife with eight children of their own. When Ailill was gone, Maeve stood there a moment. Shortly she would repeat the orders that must be hammered into some heads again.

Enough able-bodied women and slaves left to care for those warriors lying in their pangs, enough food left to get them all through until summer: it was no wiser to dare Macha's wrath by letting her victims die of neglect than by slaying them outright. For now, Maeve looked at the dead woman in the bloodied straw, at the man who lay doubled up, moaning and clutching himself, his blunt features twisted with pain and his red hair rucked into dark sweaty spikes. She did not know if he would remember her words, nine times she had given birth, and never been able to recall more than a few fragments of what the midwives had said but she spoke anyway.

"Your wife died bravely, protecting you," Maeve murmured, "and your child will be cared for." There was more she wanted to say, or so she thought, but the words would not come to her.

A heavy footstep startled Maeve. She whirled, grip tightening on her sword. Had Cumail gathered his courage to meet her with weapons? She wanted to fight; and she hoped with all her heart for Ailill to return, that his embrace might loose the storm within her which the brutal slaughter had not released. Fergus stood in the doorway. He, too, was bloody from the wounds of others.

She could see no hurt on his body, but tears had carved clear streaks through the soot and grime of battle on his face.

"Maeve Leathderg," he said: Maeve Red-Side. Not the title of the human queen of Cruachan, but the goddess: sometimes kind mother, sometimes red battle-hag. Maeve waited for Fergus to curse her, or fear pangs through her. *Did one of my children die in this fight? Has he come to tell me of it?*

Ulster's exiled king only stood there, gazing at Maeve through smoke-reddened eyes as though he had never seen her before. The muscles of his jaw jumped under his soot-darkened beard, and he squared his broad shoulders as though he were steeling himself to some fearful task. With a movement so startling that Maeve almost jerked her sword forward to spit him in reflex, Fergus lunged to throw his arms about her.

Her own arms went around his broad back to crush him against her armored breasts. Fergus' lips found hers, hot and urgent, breath mingling in harsh pants as they devoured each other's mouths. Maeve's heart hammered against Fergus' chest, sharp stabs of pleasure radiating from her tight-pressed nipples to waken an answering pang in the depths of her womb. As suddenly as Fergus had clasped Maeve, he let her go; but his fingers trailed a moment over the bloodstained hand still clutching her sword-hilt.

His grey eyes were alight with wild longing, with desire and burning sorrow, or was that what Maeve felt herself, and thus saw mirrored in him?

She was unsure, and the more so when he turned without a word, back stiff and steps stumbling.

'Why now?' Maeve wondered. 'What could be in his mind? Why, of all times, now? When he might indeed feel cause to hate me? She had no answer to that.

Maeve cleaned her sword with a handful of straw, then searched her mantle for an unbloodied corner and dampened it in the cup of water to finish the job. Whatever Fergus was thinking, she could not neglect her duties as queen and war leader any further. She had lingered here too long as it was

Fedelm

To my sneaking relief, Calatín and I were not ordered to take part in the attack on Rath Echach. Instead we waited in our chariot with our chests of herbs and bandages, a good half-mile away.

"A skilled slinger with a strong arm can hurl a ball with killing force up to almost a quarter-mile," Maeve had said to us. "No one would choose to aim at a Druid, but I will not risk losing either of you to a stray ball. , Calatín, I have not asked why you came armed on my raid, nor why you are armed today. Nevertheless, if you have no strong reason to fight in this battle, I would have you wear your robe of office so that what you are may be known from a distance, should Rath Echach send scouts or warriors to harry our flanks. I do not think they have enough fighters to do so, but..." The Druid had bowed his dark head and agreed.

We watched from the top of a low hill near the fort. The snow-laden branches of a thick beech grove hid most of what happened from us. Still, we saw the smoke rising black against the pale winter sky. Thin dark threads at first, rapidly thickening into a heavy storm cloud-pall. Gouts of white steam leapt between the trails of smoke as last night's snow hissed away beneath the flames. Above, ravens wheeled and croaked their delight at the slaughter within the burning ring of timbers, circling lower and lower.

In their cries, I heard the echoes of the Nemhain's storm; I shuddered, knowing that the battle-frenzy would be upon those within.

I had sung of it a thousand times, but now I had seen the bloodied corpses and severed heads, and felt the terror that could turn to slaughter-madness as easily as a salmon flopping from side to side in a creel. The wind was blowing in our faces. I could smell the heavy smoke; the burning was tainted with scorched blood, and I thought I could hear the faint cries of battle. Calatín stared keenly as the flames crawled higher on the timbers, high enough that we could see them over the whitened treetops. I wondered what more he saw, and if he regretted that he were not wielding his sword today.

None of the teachers in Alba were so warlike; had they been, they would have been out in the world of kings and battles. I had expected that Maeve's army would take half a day or more to break into Rath Echach. In fact, though the Sun rose late at this time of year and the assault had not begun until after dawn, it was still well before noon when Maeve's long-legged messenger Mac Roth came loping back. His lean face was smeared with soot and blood, dark streaks of filth matting his red hair. He was not breathing hard from his run, but when he halted, he stood with the sloping hunch of a deeply exhausted man.

"It is time to come up and tend the wounded," he said.

"Though we took little enough harm." He looked as if he might say something more, but pressed his lips tightly together and glanced away.

'Did he see me about to cast my stomach before Cú Chulainn's head-fork? I wondered, shamed and angry. Does he think I am too weak to bear the sight of the wounded?' If so, the tall runner kept his thoughts to himself, pacing beside our chariot as Eochaid urged our horses forward.

An awful stink attacked my nostrils as we rode between the half-charred timbers, past the shards of the broken gate. My eyes, bleary from lack of sleep, began to water. I had expected the heavy stenches of burning oil and wood, the coppery odor of blood and the unnerving savour of cooking flesh: one smells as much at the Samhain rites, although the meat there is usually what is fit for humans to eat. The Druids who perform sacrifice are far too skilled to open an offerings bowels, nor do we do so when searching the organs for omens, a careless stroke of the knife could destroy the knowledge we seek, and usually sweet herbs are burned to cover the slaughter-stinks. I had learned many songs of red blood flowing until victors and slain alike were drenched.

None ever mentioned what I, who had learned divination by the innards of beasts and helped my father butcher and clean pigs, should have known: the battlefield stinks of shit. I breathed in very slowly, reminding myself that foul as the air was, I would take no harm from breathing it, and I must not disgrace myself again.

I forced myself to look at the corpses strewn through the foul slush of mud and blood, the crows hopping black from body to body.

'Entrails are entrails, I told myself, and when the greatest matters are afoot, only the entrails of men can answer what must be asked. It was not only shame for our order that made Calatín angry at my weakness yesterday.'

Already my nostrils were dulling to the smell, the blood flowing back to my head as my breathing steadied. When Eochaid stopped the chariot, I climbed out without hesitation. I had to wonder why the head-fork that had sickened me so profoundly, when today I could look upon bodies far more badly hacked about and mangled. Perhaps, as Maeve had said, it had only been the shock of the first time, so that now I was ready to face such deaths.

Or perhaps it was not the slaughter, but the wrongness of the heads being left thus: as if the slain were worthless, their skulls not holy trophies, but only a message of mockery.

'I know the fear and shame that led to this slaughter, I thought, stepping over a severed arm half-buried in the red snow, its fingers curled up as though it would still cling to a weapon's hilt. I felt the Nemhain's touch last night. What could have moved the one who left those heads mounted on the ogham fork? Did he think that, if he frightened us enough, a whole army would flee from a single man?'

Then I heard what I could no longer put aside: the women's screams and weeping coming from behind the nearest hut; a man's voice, thick as a drunk's, calling,

"My turn next!"

"Can we not help them?" I asked Calatín.

The Druid looked down at me, his black eyes like water-polished stones.

"No. Do you think the men who did this slaughter are able to listen even to a Druid's word yet?" He waved a long arm; several crows squawked and flapped into the air, then settled again.

"The Morrígan has no pity, and she has not yet released her grip here. A great curse may lie on any man who slays a Druid; the bards may satirize him until the flesh peels from his bones with shame, but that will not do you, or me, any good if one in the raven's talons strikes us down. Come along: it will settle you to do what you can."

As Mac Roth had said, Maeve's army had taken little harm. Less than a score had been slain or wounded too badly to live. Of the latter, their friends had mostly delivered the stroke that freed them of their damaged bodies already, for which I was quietly grateful. Most of the defenders of the fort had been brutally slaughtered.

I could not look on them without sorrow. They must have battled bravely, with no chance of winning. At least my breakfast did not threaten to rise, and I was able to set steady-handed to sprinkling powdered woad and yarrow on bleeding wounds, stitching and binding and giving careful tiny spoonfuls of hen bane-seed concoction to those in the most pain.

It was not long until our first wagons rolled through the broken gate, and Calatín and I helped the wounded into the wains prepared for them. I had just turned from supporting the last warrior's splinted leg as two of his friends lifted him for me when I saw Ailill coming towards me. I almost did not recognize him. His fiery mustaches drooped bedraggled and tattered; his elaborate braid had come undone and his hair hung in tarnished copper straggles about his face, matted with sweat where his helm had rested, smeared with blood beneath it. In his arms, held carefully against his broad armored chest. I blinked twice before I was certain of what I saw. He was carrying a baby. A very small baby, newborn or close to it.

"Fedelm," Ailill said. Dull and tired as his voice was, the sound of him speaking my name sent a thrill cutting through my own exhaustion. I looked up, meeting his gaze. It seemed as if a shaft of sunlight shone through the grey clouds, brightening his blue eyes to a water-dazzle of brightness.

"King Ailill. What may I do?" I had to fight to keep my voice steady, reminding myself that I was a ban-fili and a Druidic student, not some farm maiden to quiver and giggle under a noble warrior's gaze.

"This is the child of the chieftain here. His mother is dead: he will need a nurse. By choice, not one of the women who survived to be captured. I would have him raised as a fosterling, not a foe."

"I will see to it," I promised, reaching out to take the baby from his arms.

For all the grime on our hands, mine stained with faded splotches of blue and yellow and green from a night of grinding herbs, Ailill's blotched dark with soot and dirt, and both smeared with blood. When his fingers touched mine on the baby's wrappings, I could not help a tiny shiver of excitement at the closeness. Ailill looked down into my eyes for a moment, and a slight smile touched his lips, a ghost of his usual good cheer.

His big hand gave my small one a little squeeze, then he relinquished the child to me.

"Thank you," he said, and turned away, leaving my heart pounding faster than it ought to have.

I looked down at the baby. It nuzzled close, seeking my breast. Its face looked as though it had been very hastily washed, smears of blood still faintly visible. I cuddled it close to me, its small solid weight comforting against my body, such a little thing, so warm and harmless, like a pup or newborn piglet! 'I had best find a woman with milk to care for this child soon, I thought, or else I will never be able to let it go. There are others of the ban-drúi who bear children in their training years. How not, when we would be well past the age of safe birthing by the time our schooling is finished?'

"Have no fear, little one," I whispered to it. "King Ailill has taken you under his protection."

Flidais was overseeing the men carrying kegs of drink, wheels of cheese, and joints of smoked meat out of the storehouses. She looked up as I approached. Although she had washed face and hands, and her wonderful hair hung in clean wet ringlets down her back, her armor, like that of the rest of the warriors, was still dribbled in drying blood. A darkening bruise shadowed her left cheekbone.

"What have you there, Fedelm? Ah, the poor little mite. Mother killed, was she? Well, give the babe to me, and I'll see it gets looked after."

I shook my head, holding the child close. "King Ailill told me to see to it."

Flidais gazed at me searchingly, then grinned. "Oh, it's like that, is it? Ailill wouldn't be my first choice of the men around here, but be like Fergus is too much for a young maid like you."

'If Fergus ever looked at me as a man to a woman, I think I should run away and hide in a deep cave, I thought. I wanted no part of his grim sorrows or the consuming fire of his passion; I wanted, I do want King Ailill! What other man would come out of smoke and blood with a babe held gently in his arms?'

Flidais patted me on the shoulder.

"I expect you'll have your chance somewhere along the way. So long as you have the courage to let him know that you are a woman, and not an untouchable ban-drúi, who might turn him into a stag or boar for his impertinence!"

I felt the tightness in my shoulders ease, and smiled back at her.

"I have not such skills yet, even were I minded to do such a thing. Can you tell me if there are any nursing women with the host who might be willing to look after this child? Ailill said he would have him raised as a fosterling."

"Ailill is almost too sweet-natured to be king. As well for him that Maeve does not flinch from doing what is harder. Suithchern the wife of Lóch Mór mac Mo Febis is still nursing her daughter. She is very fond of children. I don't doubt that she will be happy to take this one in, especially knowing that King Ailill's favor comes with it. You'll find her in the Leinstermen's camp, ask anyone there.

I had no trouble finding Suithchern, whose husband was well-known in the Leinster host. Lóch's wife was a pretty young woman, rather plump, with a thick coil of honey-brown hair wound about her head.

She was sitting outside her tent with her little daughter at her breast, both swathed in a heavy blue, and yellow-checkered blanket. When she saw me, her round face turned pale and she rose at once.

"May I be of aid, fili?" She inquired breathlessly. "Is something wrong, is my husband hurt?"

"Not to my knowledge, and I have just come from tending our wounded. No: King Ailill gave me charge of this motherless babe, and I am told that you might be willing to care for him."

Suithchern looked at the child in my arms, her face softening. "Of course I will! Has he a name?"

"None that I know."

"Then I shall call him Conall, and raise him with my own daughter."

I gave little Conall into Suithchern's free arm. She pulled the blanket aside: beneath it she was naked to the waist, her own child suckling happily at one full breast. She put Conall to the other, and he immediately snuffled about until he got the nipple in his mouth and began to drink.

"Such a handsome babe, no doubt that he is well-born! Thank you for bringing him to me."

"It is kind of you to take him," I said stiffly.

I felt an odd empty ache in my own heart, my arms strangely light without their small live burden. At least I have fulfilled Ailill's trust in me, I thought, and that was a little consolation. Maeve's host feasted that night, but in our own camp rather than in the hall where we had raided.

Some of the warriors still seemed wild from the day's fighting, so wild that I had to hide my fear and return their gazes with all the cold force I could muster when they looked at me.

Others were subdued, or grim; I heard a number of mutterings along the lines of, "Women and boys, is this the best Ulster can give us for glory?" Only a few heads had been taken, all beardless and long-haired. I did not like to look at the raw eye sockets and the marks of the crows on them; but they, at least, were mounted properly in a place of honor, as warriors who had given a good fight deserved to be. Ailill seemed to have regained some of his usual cheerfulness, but his laughter still sounded rather strained. 'He is trying to put a good face on it for the rest, I thought. Does Maeve know what it is costing him?'

I glanced at him as seldom as I could, but my gaze kept coming back to the clean sweep of his profile in the torchlight, his straight nose and strong chin and the bright flashes of blue from his eyes; and I could not help wondering what it would be like to undo his elaborate braids and run my fingers through the thick waves of his red-gold hair. I thought of Flidais' advice, but had no idea of how follow it. 'If I were Maeve or Flidais, I could simply walk up to him and offer him the friendship of my thighs.

I believe I would curl up with embarrassment and turn myself into a hedgehog before the second word was out of my mouth.' I breathed deeply, gathering all my courage, and made myself stand and walk towards Connaught's king. When he looked up and smiled at me, my throat dried like a strap of raw leather left in the sun. Had I not learned the arts of song and speech, I should not have been able to get any sound out at all.

"King Ailill," I said with all the formality of my training, "I have given the babe to Suithchern, the wife of Lóch Mór mac Mo Febis. She has named him Conall, and is caring for him as her own."

Ailill's smile widened.

"Well done, Fedelm. Thank you! I shall see that they are well-rewarded."

For all my skill in word-craft, I could think of nothing to say that would not sound like an idiot's babbling, so I nodded and walked towards my tent. Tomorrow we would march again, and there was no telling what waited upon the journey. For all that had passed in the two days before, I slept well and deeply, and rose refreshed. The clouds had passed, the Sun glittering bright and cold off the snow.

The land sloped gently downward until we came to a broad plain, a field so fair and white that I had to slit my eyes against its dazzle, as if we had slipped into the Otherworld somewhere along the way. Only a few small groves of gnarled oaks and grey smooth-trunked beeches broke the brightness, scattered here and there like snarls of dark wool from a careless weaver's basket. At the edge of the plain glittered a small river, silent beneath its clear coat of black ice. Beyond, the land rose into low hills and ridges, like a great white blanket rucked up into wrinkles.

Two tall weathered stakes marked the ford-point: between them lay a mighty oak, the gashed wood of its trunk startlingly pale against its damp black bark and its branches clawing at snow and air as though, dying, it still struggled to stand. I could see the light flickering around it, and knew that we had found Cú Chulainn's next trap. As we got closer, I saw the long white stripe where the bark had been peeled away and the gleaming ogham letters. Yet it seemed to me that there was not so much strength here as in the two previous charms. I let my eyes unfocus, and the dark lines took shape against the glow of the dying wood.

"Let none pass this oak until one man has leapt it in his chariot at the first attempt."

Calatín's thin lips curled into a smile.

"He could not except Fergus this time. It is as I hoped. The Hound is but a boy, and no Druid: he has power, but Cathbad has only given him a little training in its use.

He drained himself mightily for the spancel-hoop, a good deal for the fork of heads, and there was little left in him for this effort. Hereafter he will have only the strength of his body, at least for a time."

The leaders of the host had come up while we were speaking. Calatín repeated what he had told me.

"That is good news!" Maeve said, her tender cheeks flushing pink. "Shall we call Ferdiad again?"

Fergus looked at her, his grey eyes sparking like steel on flint.

"Ferdiad is a mighty fighter, but not a great charioteer. I myself shall do this." He spoke as if to challenge Maeve, his voice hard as ringing iron. Her flush deepened, but she was still staring at him as he gestured his driver out of his chariot.

"Clear me a path," Fergus ordered. "I must have enough length for the horses to reach full speed."

As the warriors and servants set to trampling and shoveling, Calatín bent down to murmur in my ear.

"Courting a queen such as Maeve is not like courting an ordinary woman, or even a ban-fili."

I felt the heat in my cheeks. How much did my teacher know of the paths my thoughts were wandering? Yet maybe Maeve was better suited to Fergus than to Ailill. Proud, turbulent, fierce. I admired, perhaps even loved her, for those qualities that frightened me in Ulster's exiled king; I had to admit, the two of them seemed well-matched. 'Would she forsake Ailill to take Fergus for her own king? Does Fergus think she might? Would he, as rigid in his loyalty as he is proud, accept if she did? Ailill is a Leinster king in his own right, if a lesser ruler than Maeve; could he not find a woman better-suited to him?'

I silenced my roaming thoughts. None of those matters were properly my business; not yet, and maybe not ever. Fergus had driven to the end of the cleared track; now he was urging his horses on. At first they moved slowly, hooves sliding a little on the hard snow, and my hand tightened on my weaving-rod. There had been two broken chariots already, and one horse that had snapped its leg and had to be given mercy. I could not deny Fergus' magnificence in that moment. As his horses gained speed, his chariot lurched and bumped precariously over the trampled snow; but he stood with reins in one hand and the other uplifted, his heavy-muscled body swaying as lithely as a willow-wand with the chariot's movements.

His chestnut hair flowed back over his broad shoulders; his eyes shone brilliant as sunlight on steel, and he grinned like a boy as his steeds pounded into a full gallop on the slippery track. My breath caught in my chest as he thundered up to the oak, torn between terror of horses screaming as they fell, bone and wood shattering together, fresh blood spurting onto the snow, and the sheer beauty and power of horses and man and chariot daring a feat that I had never seen nor heard of any man achieving before.

The reins cracked; the horses' haunches surged into a mighty leap. Behind them, the chariot wheels left the ground, Fergus swaying forward as if to add his own great strength to the jump. Up and over!

I heard a great shattering noise: the oak's trunk, as thick as a tall man's height, hid what had just passed on the other side, and I thought for a moment that my fears had come true. Then I saw Fergus was driving on through the ford, a glass-bright shower of water and clear ice spraying up around the horses' hooves and chariot wheels as he gradually slowed, wheeling through the snow on the other side of the river to face Maeve and wave to her in triumph.

"It is done, and the Hound can no longer block us!" Maeve cried. "Get this obstacle out of the way: on to Cuailgne now!"

Maeve

The sunlight on the snow dazzled Maeve's eyes, leaving only the sight of Fergus swaying forward in his chariot as it took flight, leaping over the huge oak's trunk like something from a tale of the eldest days. She could feel Cú Chulainn's spell snap, her foe's will giving way like an overstressed chariot-pole cracking suddenly in two. She felt as though she had quaffed a pitcher of strong winter mead on an empty stomach: the blood rushed to her spinning head, her heart leaping like a salmon in spring. She raised her hand in answer to Fergus' gesture of victory, not sure whether she meant to hail his deed or beckon him to her. The way was clear now. The worst is over.

"It is done, and the Hound can no longer block us!" She shouted in triumph. "Get this obstacle out of the way: on to Cuailgne now!"

Fifty strong warriors trotted forward, grasping the great oak's branches and heaving. Flidais rounded the hacked base of the trunk, then said something to her charioteer.

As she crossed the ford, Maeve felt another pang of envy: was it the other woman who would enjoy Fergus in his moment of victory. Surely Flidais would not lure him off when the army should be marching, with a foe so close? Even a swineherd could kill a hero, if the hero were naked with his face to a woman and his bare back to the world. For all Maeve had come to hate Cú Chulainn, the boy was no swineherd. The milk-queen got out of her chariot, walking in a slow half-circle around the edge of the ford, casting further and further around with her head down, like a hunting-dog on a trail.

Flidais and her husband Adammair, Maeve remembered, might be the two greatest hunters in Eriu: even Senchán and Calatín admitted that they knew no Druids so wise in the ways of beasts in the woods. Flidais shook her hair back, a waterfall of shining copper flames in the pale sunlight, and crouched down carefully. Then she rose to her feet, twisting her upper body to look back across the little river.

"Maeve!" She shouted. "Over here!"

Finnabair shook the reins, and their horses rounded the base of the oak. Baiscne gambolled beside them, barking like a puppy as they forded where Fergus' chariot had shattered the thin clear ice, his lashing tail splashing water everywhere. A few icy drops splattered Maeve in the face.

She could feel them warming to the heat of her skin as they struck; she would not have been surprised had they hissed away like raindrops in a bonfire. Finnabair drove skilfully to Flidais, careful not to disturb what the other queen had found.

"What is it?" Maeve asked.

"Look at these tracks here."

Maeve looked, but all she saw was chariot-tracks through the deep snow: the marks of two large horses' hooves, and the ruts left by iron-bound wheel-rims.

"The Hound was here in his chariot; but surely we knew that already," Maeve said, trying to keep the nettle-prickle of irritation out of her voice.

"These tracks are fresh. Very fresh, and Cú Chulainn is not traveling in any great hurry. Hero or not, no earthly horses could make good haste in this snow, nor is he pushing them. These are not the tracks of animals laboring for speed in bad footing, and he seems to be going straight upriver, along the bank. A few men in swift chariots could catch up with him, even now."

"And clear this nuisance away," Maeve agreed thoughtfully, glancing back as the men at the oak bent their backs together and the huge tree slowly began to slide over the snow.

"Whom might we send? Ferdiad will not fight his foster brother, nor Fergus his foster son."

Flidais grinned.

"Ask Fraech mac Fidaig to go. He is swift in his chariot, a skilled tracker, and a champion of duel and battlefield as well. Has he not been trying to court Finnabair for some time? He will be glad to show his strength for her, in hopes that she will look on him with favor."

"If I thought he were the man for me, I would not need such proof," Finnabair muttered, her eyes downcast. "Two years ago, I might have wished to marry him, but not now."

"Well, you hardly need say so to Fraech. Mayhap when he has brought back Cú Chulainn's head, we can play fidchell to see who shall reward him first! Fraech claims that he shall never fear death in battle, for he has lain with Queen Úna of Cnuic Síde Úna, who shares my rule beneath my own lands.

And by Brigit, I well believe it, for his beauty, Fraech!" Flidais shouted across the river. "Fraech, are you ready to win a name for this raid! Over here, and bring a few swift riders with you!"

A single chariot wheeled out from the mass of soldiers, nine others following it. They plunged straight across the ford. Maeve noted the speed and ease of their movements, but the foremost was the best, and Maeve looked approvingly at the agile balance of the warrior standing behind the driver.

"What would you have of me, my queens?" Fraech asked as his chariot came to a sudden halt, snow puffing up from the red horses' hooves and the bright-scratched iron rims of the wheels.

Maeve had seen the young Connacht chieftain enough times before, and knew that he was fair to look on; but now his beauty struck her like a hammer-blow. Fraech was tall and lithe as a willow-whip, with the broad shoulders and sinewy wrists of a lifetime swordsman. The hair flowing beneath his helmet was golden as a field of yellow flag-blossoms in the summer sun; his high-boned cheeks were bright pink in the icy air, his eyes the deep greenish-gold of a woodland in the warm light of summer dawn. Warmth rushed between Maeve's thighs; her nipples, already tight with cold, brushed tingling against the smooth linen of her leine. Yet her shiver held fear, as well as desire.

This was not the surging heat of passion she had felt at watching Fergus leap the oak, but a faint echo of the keen irresistible pleasure that had ravaged her body and soul beneath King Ochall's gaze, far below the mound of Cruachan. Ochall had sought to seduce her to his service, to finish what Ailill had begun with his pillow-challenge. Baiscne's tongue licked Maeve's hand, warm and wet; his rough shaggy head butted against her arm.

The great black hound was standing on his hind legs with his huge forepaws braced on her chariot's edge, and he nuzzled her insistently until she put her hand on his head. As when Maeve walked the ring to go beneath Cruachan, Baiscne's touch steadied her. She drew a deep breath: the dizziness passed, and Fraech was no more than an unusually fair young warrior.

"These are the tracks of the Hound of Ulster," Maeve said. "Go before the host, you and your friends. Find him, and kill him. He had little care for the heads of our men, but we shall tend his with all honor to him, and to the warrior who slew him!"

"I shall do that," Fraech answered. He tapped the shoulder of the slim ruddy-haired boy who drove his chariot. The horses surged forward in a tight circle through the deep snow, a shower of white spraying from beneath the chariot's wheels, and he drove forward. His nine companions, who had waited at a slight distance, fell in behind him in a perfect formation.

"If Fraech slays Cú Chulainn, there shall be nothing barring our way between here and the Brown Bull," Maeve said with considerable satisfaction.

Even without the oak tree blocking the way, the ford was narrow. No more than three chariots could pass at a time, or nine men on foot or one wain. It took Maeve's host a long time to cross. She waited with Fergus, Ailill, and Flidais at the base of one of the little hills, watching the endless march of men and horses and wagons like a draught squeezed through the narrow neck of a water skin to splash in a bright spreading pool over the snow-whitened land on the other side of the river.

"How long do you think it will take Fraech to find the Hound?" She asked Flidais.

The other queen shrugged her sturdy shoulders, her large breasts shifting beneath her rippling hauberk. "How long is a rope? All we can do is find out."

Fergus said nothing, but stared upriver. Fraech and his men had long since passed out of sight behind a tree-covered ridge: there was nothing to see but low snowy hills and the fine white-and-gray tracery of snow-layered branches. All the exhilaration of Fergus' leap had drained from his craggy face. Now the harsh winter light carved deep furrows across his forehead and about his eyes, and he rubbed absently at the thin scar cutting down his cheek. His foster-son, Maeve thought. She thought of her own fosterling, Etarcomol.

His sharp tongue and arrogant ways made him hard to like, but if foe-men were hunting him down, and she must stand as friend and ally to those who had sent them, that would be no easy thing to bear And she knew that Fergus loved Cú Chulainn dearly. I wish there were some way to spare Fergus this, she thought again. There was none. She had been over that ground again and again, as if she were searching the floor of a hall for a lost bracelet; if no glint of gold had rewarded her before, she was unlikely to find it now.

"I shall not wager on it," Ailill said, smiling at her. "There would be too much sorrow in the loss to pile another loss atop it, and joy enough in winning that a ring or cup of mead would hardly be worth adding. I have heard of Fraech myself, and he is both a skilled and a cunning fighter – and has the luck of a síde-queen's lover. Surely a boy of seventeen will hardly be a match for him."

The last of the wagons and servants were crossing the river when Maeve saw the small line of chariots crawling black over the ridge. Ten chariots, but one had only a single man in it. 'Perhaps he continued the chase alone. If Cú Chulainn saw them coming, and fled on foot among trees and broken ground where a chariot could not easily follow, or if Fraech were wounded in the fight, a leg wound that keeps him from standing, perhaps.'

Maeve's heart already lay heavy as an ill-baked loaf of bread in her breast as the chariots of Flidais' warriors came closer, the icy breeze bearing the whisper of their soft keening across the snow to her. Finnabair swallowed hard, looking back at her mother with tears pooling in her blue eyes.

"Though I did not truly wish to wed Fraech, he was so fair, and brave," she murmured. "If it were Rochad that had been slain thus, I do not know how I could bear it."

"As a woman must," Maeve answered her softly. "Or anyone who loves another. Had Fraech not been brave, he would not have met his death this day, but nor would he have been so fair."

Flidais nodded, wiping the tears from her own face.

"Give me a little time here. I will call my men to gather stones for a cairn, to honor Fraech and lay him to rest by this ford for now. When we can, we shall bear him back to his own clan's lands in Connaught."

Fraech's charioteer halted before Flidais. The champion's corpse had been laid in the bottom of the chariot. Fraech's helm, armor, and weapons were piled beside him, his green cloak swathed about him. No blood stained the garment, nor had any weapon rent it.

Only a little pink-tinged froth bubbled from his mouth; that, and the water-logged hair slowly freezing to the chariot's wood around his head, showed how he had died. Flidais leaned over the chariot's edge, wiping Fraech's lips clean with the corner of her own bright-striped mantle and gently kissing him.

"How did it happen?" She asked.

"We came upon Cú Chulainn washing by the river's edge," the youth answered, his voice choked with tears.

"Fraech told us to wait behind, and he would fight Cú Chulainn in the water. It seemed a sensible plan. The Hound is a small man: it should have been easy for Fraech to take him off his feet in deep cold water. We laid a fire so that we could dry him as soon as he came out, and Maeslir and Maeslach took their armor off beneath their cloaks, standing ready to warm him between them. Then Fraech took off his own armor and went up to Cú Chulainn. Cú Chulainn said, 'If you come any closer, I shall have to kill you.' And Fraech said, 'All the same, I shall come to you in the water and you shall have to fight.' Cú Chulainn shrugged, looking right up into Fraech's face. There was a hand span and a half of height between them, and said, 'Choose your style of combat, then.'"

Fraech answered him, 'Each to keep one arm around the other.' We said nothing. We were certain Fraech would have the victory, for his arms were so much longer, and however agile or good a swimmer Cú Chulainn might be, the advantage in grappling should have been to Fraech.

"They fought in the water, each with one arm around the other; Fraech could not throw the Hound, however they strained and swayed. At last Cú Chulainn crouched and got Fraech by the knees and bore him down. They both disappeared, but Cú Chulainn came up on top, and pulled Fraech's head up. Cú Chulainn said, 'Will you let me spare you?'

Fraech answered, 'I wouldn't have that said', and heaved upward, trying to get his feet under him. Then Cú Chulainn pushed him down, and held him down; and when the Hound carried Fraech to shore, he was dead. I heard him say, 'You have died a champion's death: let your companions bear you home.'"

"Not one man thought to kill him then, when he had just slain your friend?" Maeve asked. "There were nine warriors there, and ten charioteers: did you just let him go?"

One of Fraech's companions spoke up then.

"Queen Maeve, Fraech would not have thanked us for falling unfairly on Cú Chulainn after that fight. The Hound took the challenge bravely, granting terms that gave Fraech the advantage, and they both strove with great honour. Nor did Cú Chulainn treat Fraech's body with anything but respect."

Maeve wanted to scream and rail at him, but she knew she could not gainsay his words. Who would follow her, if she were not seen to care for the honor of her warriors as well as their victories?

"You acted rightly," Maeve forced herself to say, though the words scratched and stung her tongue like a mouthful of fresh nettles and grit. "Gather those who loved Fraech to keen over his body, and lay him out as he ought to be: others are already preparing his cairn."

The eerie wails of mourning women rose over the snowy hills as Fraech's fellow warriors piled rock on rock, the cairn-ring rising like the wall of a miniature fort. His friends who had gone with him dried and combed his wet streaming hair until it shone bright gold again, pulling his armor back over the cold limp corpse and adorning his neck and arms with twisted silver rings. Others brought up a keg of mead, a joint of smoked ham, and a wheel of cheese; Flidais set a silver goblet inlaid with gold in his hand, and others brought gifts to lay about him as well.

When Fraech had been thus dressed and provisioned, Calatín stepped forward. The Druid had put on his white robe again, and held his wand in his hand, ready to speak the words that would guide Fraech to the western sea and the House of Donn, and perhaps back to this earth in time. Baiscne leaned heavily against Maeve's leg. She felt, more than heard, the low sound rumbling through the black wolfhound's deep chest. He was staring towards the southwest, every muscle in his body taut, as though he had spied a wolf or deer and were about to leap, or as though he recognized a threat to his mistress.

Maeve looked about, trying to guess what her hound was staring at. The nearest hill in that direction was well within sling-range: was Cú Chulainn even now aiming a ball at her head, perhaps one of the fatal missiles the Druids compounded from brains mixed with lime. The snowy hill was bare, and the Hound of Ulster no Druid to stand unseen in plain sight. Maeve heard a soft gasp beside her. Fedelm was staring in the same direction as Baiscne, her lips slightly parted and blue-grey eyes open wide. Maeve still could see nothing but the dazzle of sunlight on snow, but a chill marched up her back.

Whatever the wolfhound and the ban-fili saw, it was moving, coming closer. Maeve rested her right hand on her sword-hilt, her left on Baiscne's shoulder. Whatever it was, she would not flee. She did not see or feel whatever passed, but she saw Fedelm and Baiscne turn their heads to watch, their eyes following the unseen to where Fraech lay within the rising ring of stones. Flidais, sitting by his body with her hair veiling her face in shadowed fire, raised her head for a moment, then bowed it again. Foreseer and hound stared as, whatever they saw, moved away, while Calatín stepped back and men lifted more stones to raise the ring higher. When Baiscne's tight muscles eased under her left hand, Maeve swallowed and spoke quietly to Fedelm.

"What did you see?"

"I saw a troop of women, all clad in long green tunics. They were tall and very fair; their faces shone so that I could hardly look straight at them. The woman who led them wore a diadem of gold. Her hair was like bright-burnished copper and streamed to her ankles, and it seemed to me that her face was much like that of Flidais to look upon, if Flidais were so beautiful that it might break your heart to see her. They gathered about Fraech's body, and the leader said to Flidais, "He was yours for a time; but now he is mine again." She lifted him up in her arms, and they bore him into that hill there."

Maeve could not speak, nor did she want anyone to see her. She got out of her chariot and walked towards the nearest grove of trees, as if she merely meant to relieve herself. Behind a tangled thicket of holly, its glossy dark leaves hiding her from any eyes that might be watching, she crouched down to hold Baiscne with all her strength, trembling as if she had just come off the field from her first battle. The great hound licked her face, his tongue startlingly warm against her cold skin. 'Whoever comes not back, you yourself shall come'.

Now Calatín's promise rang with terror: now Maeve knew what, more than rule or life, she could lose on this raid. For if Queen Úna of Cnuic Síde Úna, who ruled the lands below Flidais' green fields, could claim her fallen lover, might King Ochall not do the same? The Druids taught that the flesh was a garment, put on and cast aside, but the soul went on endlessly. If Ochall took Maeve now, she would be his bondsmaid forever, beneath the hill that had been the seat of her own sovereignty.

"Protect me, Baiscne," Maeve whispered into the wolfhound's soft black ear. "Guide me safe to the House of Donn when my time comes, and back to rebirth as may be." Baiscne leaned comfortingly against Maeve and licked her some more. She clung to him until she stopped shivering, then rose to return to her army.

Finnabair

"When Cú Chulainn, then known as Setanta, was almost seven, Culann of Muirtheimne gave a feast. Culann's hound was better than any in Ulster, so fierce three chains were needed to hold it, and when it was loosed, no man nor wolf dared assail Culann's herds. Setanta was to come to that feast, but he forgot the time while playing, and came late. Conchobar was asked if there were any other guests following him, but forgot that Setanta was coming. So Culann loosed his hound. When Setanta came along, the hound sprang at him. Setanta attacked it with his bare hands, clutching the beast by the throat-apple, dragging it down and choking it to death. Culann was greatly grieved, for he had held that hound dearer than anything in his land, the guardian of his life and honor, the shield and shelter of his goods and herds. When he said so. Setanta replied, 'I will rear you a pup from that same pack. Until that hound grows up to do his work, I will be your hound, and guard all Muirtheimne Plain. No herd and flock will leave my care without my knowing it.' Thus Setanta gained the name Cú Chulainn, the Hound of Culann."

Although the sky had cleared and the sun shone so white upon the snow that the Druids were kept busy making washes of eye bright for the reddened and swollen eyes of those who had stared at its brilliance too long, the cold held its tight grip on the land.

The heaviest of the snow had fallen around Cúl Sibrille and Rath Echach: as Maeve's host slogged eastward, the thick blanket over the earth thinned from knee-deep to ankle-deep, and the army moved more swiftly for a time.

Finnabair drove as carefully as she could, hands clenched on the reins and fear-sweat soaking slowly through the linen and wool of her clothes: chariots were built for speed in raid and war, or for carrying nobles over good roads in summer, not for pushing through snow where the innocent layers of white hid rocks and fallen branches in the path, and only the slightest dips in the surface might betray a deep wheel-breaking rut below.

She knew that the army as a whole was pressing on faster, but, more and more often, someone's chariot-pole would snap or wheels crack or twist their iron-shod rims; and each time Finnabair heard the sound of wood breaking, she had to force herself to rein in carefully rather than jerking the horses to a halt in fear that her own chariot was about to pitch over and be dragged.

The store of replacement shafts, already badly depleted by the rough passage through the drumlin-land before Cul Sibrille, was near-gone; every evening now, the sound of metal hammering on metal rang out through the harpers' songs as the smiths beat wheel-rims and chariot fittings back into shape.

'If I asked my mother, she would let me ride in a wagon, Finnabair thought more than once. Though I am no warrior, I am no coward either. If I do not dare to face edged weapons, I shall not quail from what I can do!'

Ath Froich was several days behind them, and Maeve had just directed her daughter to skirt the Munstermen's cantreds when Finnabair felt the front left wheel strike something under the snow. The horrible snapping lurch flung Finnabair sideways, so that she had to clutch the chariot's edge to keep from being thrown free. Baiscne leapt out, barking wildly and dashing about in a shower of snow.

The startled horses tugged mightily at the reins, so that Finnabair had to haul with an effort that felt as though it were cracking her arms from her shoulders to keep them from bolting and dragging the chariot behind them. One shaft had cracked right through, its decorative bronze mounting shattered.

The right-hand horse swerved violently sideways, and Finnabair gasped at the pain. "Out, Mother!" She panted.

She was losing control, she could feel it. The horse on the left pulled hard away, wrenching against the surviving shaft and spinning the broken chariot into a tight skidding half-circle. Its strength did what Finnabair's own could not, hauling its mate back into line. She tugged sharply, several times, and the horses slowly halted to stand in place, their breath coming in harsh puffs of white steam. Maeve dismounted, her strong hands taking Finnabair around the waist and lifting her down carefully. Maeve's guards had all halted, getting out of their own chariots and hurrying towards the women.

"I'm sorry, Mother!" Finnabair said, tears choking her voice. "I didn't see anything under the snow, the horses went right over without stumbling…"

Maeve embraced her daughter. Finnabair could feel her slight body trembling in her mother's grasp, but she was not ashamed. There were several men in the wounded-wagons with broken bones from similar accidents, and a Munster warrior and his charioteer had been killed two days ago when their chariot's wheel hit a large hidden rock and horses, vehicle, and men went over together in one smashing fall. Baiscne came up and leaned against them both, his big head resting warm above Finnabair's hip.

"Hush, it's all right," Maeve murmured. "None could have done better. You did well to keep the horses from bolting." Her mother's grip tightened. Finnabair winced and hissed through her teeth. "Are you hurt?"

"My shoulder hurts." Finnabair worked her left arm, frowning. A sharp pain shot up through it, but she could move it easily enough, though she could feel the swelling of her shoulder tightening it already.

"It isn't broken, not even out of joint, and the pain is already fading a bit."

"Well, we shall get you to the Druids while our chariot is being repaired," Maeve said comfortingly.

"Is all well?. Maine Orlamh asked anxiously, coming up to them with his brothers Feidhlim and Cairbre close behind him. Ferdiad held his position, but his eyes kept darting towards Finnabair.

"My chariot will need a new shaft, and your sister's shoulder is wrenched, but there is no great harm done," Maeve assured him. "If you can take her up in your own chariot and find the Druids."

A sharper voice broke in. "Of course you will let me through! Finnabair may have been hurt."

Finnabair closed her eyes, just for a second. She should have known Connla would not be far away.

"Remember we need him, Finnabair," her mother whispered under her breath. Finnabair gave her a slight nod.

My brothers can not reproach me for not sharing their danger. At least they do not have to play up to a weasel who speaks like a man!

Ferdiad stood in front of Connla like a man of stone, glaring down at the Munster under-king with his jaw set.

"The queen said she has taken no great harm," Connacht's champion said through his teeth. "Her brothers are with her: she hardly needs anyone else crowding around."

Finnabair hoped that her mother would send Connla away, but Maeve sighed, "Let him through".

The Munster under-king hurried towards them. "Finnabair, my darling," he exclaimed. "Are you injured? Do you need help?"

When Connla made as if to put his arm about her, Finnabair turned her shudder into a wince of pain, only slightly feigned; her shoulder was throbbing nastily now. "Careful," she murmured, dropping her eyes. "The horses pulled so hard, I have hurt my shoulder."

"Then you must see the Druids at once!" Said Connla. "Come, give me your other arm, and I will help you to my own chariot."

"Surely one of my brothers..." Finnabair started. Leave me alone, the gods curse you! I could have died there, I hurt, I want to be home and safe and away from you!

"The queen's guards should stay with her," Connla insisted. "You are so light, you will hardly slow my driver. What were you thinking, Queen Maeve, to risk Connacht's greatest treasure thus in your chariot?"

Finnabair kept her gaze down, lest the Munster under-king see any trace of her anger in her eyes. Maine Cairbre was opening his mouth, and Finnabair found herself hoping that he would put a stop to Connla's clear intentions, but Maeve spoke first.

"Save for battle, Finnabair is as good a charioteer as any in this host," Maeve answered evenly. "And she is lighter than Munremur, hence less strain to the horses when the road is bad."

Maeve's mouth was still open, as though she would say more but a sudden shattering crack struck through her words. Another chariot broken? Finnabair thought, glancing about quickly and crouching to spring out of the way of bolting horses. It had been too close. "Oh," she said softly, her hand to her mouth and the tears starting to her eyes as she looked down towards their feet. Baiscne lay there his long black limbs sprawled in the utter relaxation of a sleeping wolfhound. One brown eye gazed unmoving up at her; steam rose around the shaggy black head, from the pool of hot red blood in the snow, and something thicker and grayish-pale leaking with it.

"Baiscne," Maeve whispered. The queen dropped to her knees, carefully lifting her dog's broken head as though her hands' warmth could bring him back to life. Something dropped from the shattered skull: a rough grayish sling-ball, dark with blood and brains. Finnabair had seen brain-balls before, held up by warriors swearing extravagant oaths against their foes. Baiscne is no mortal hound, or was he? Can such a missile have slain even the hound from the House of Donn? Who could have thrown it and why?

"Where..?" Maeve began.

"No one is in sight, and the closest woods are near a third of a mile away," said Orlamh. Finnabair's eldest brother was standing almost on top of them, his body tense as though he expected another shot at any moment. "No slinger I know..."

"The Hound of Ulster," Maeve said. Her voice cracked into tears; she bowed forward, but Finnabair saw the clear drops falling into Baiscne's fur.

The dog's pink tongue lolled lifelessly, his brown eyes open and glazed as those of any deer or boar ready to be gutted and packed back to the hall. 'This is not Baiscne's first death', Finnabair reminded herself.

She had been a child of ten when the weary, gray-muzzled old dog had limped from Cruachan hall into the night; she had risen from her bed at dawn to be knocked over by the greeting of a young black wolfhound, who answered to Baiscne's name and, save for his age, could not be told from the one who had disappeared.

"When he grows old, he returns to the House of Donn, and comes back renewed; this is the second time since I took my queenship. He will return for you as well, when you are queen in Cruachan," Maeve had told her daughter. Finnabair had never had reason to doubt the truth of it, though even then, it seemed to her as though she felt the queenship, not as a thing to strive for, but as a burden like the weight of distant storm clouds pressing on the air about her.

Baiscne had never been slain before, nor, from what her mother said, had he ever left a body behind. 'Can he come back again?' Then, worse: 'Will he?'

Finnabair was not queen of Connacht, nor did she want to be. She was Maeve's daughter, with the right if she would take it. Looking down at the great black hound's body in the snow, she felt a strange icy emptiness within her, an odd sagging unbalance, like the roof of a hall from which one of the pillars had suddenly collapsed. 'And if I feel this, what does my mother feel?'

There was little need to ask. Maeve's shoulders shook with a deep sob, and she held Baiscne's cooling corpse as if he were a fallen man.

"How like a woman, to take on so," Connla muttered to one of his guards. "It was only a dog."

Connla's words struck Finnabair like a drop of soured cider falling into a pail of milk, protesting her sorrow and the trembling aftermath of her terror and pain to anger in an instant. Maeve's hand moved towards her sword-hilt, and Finnabair wished for just a heartbeat that she, too, were skilled with weapons, to pay Connla back for what he had said. 'Even if I could fight him, we would have war with the Munstermen in our midst, and that we cannot afford. Mother, hold your temper: I have not suffered this man's attentions so long to have you kill him now, and risk all we came for.'

"Listen, you..." Orlamh said angrily, turning his head to glare at the Munster under-king, though he kept his stance braced in front of his mother. The biggest and strongest of Finnabair's brothers, Orlamh was generally also the quietest. Ailill's red-gold hair had become fierce fox-red in him, and though his temper was even slower than their father's to rouse, it was awesomely ferocious when it did.

'Now I must be peacemaker, though I would love to see my brother or mother cut Connla down here and now.'

"Baiscne was no mere hound, but dearly beloved to us," Finnabair said, keeping her voice soft. The words poured slippery as oil from her throat; she half-despised herself for it, but someone must show good sense now. However shameful it might be, she had the power to make Connla do what was needed.

"If you were to seek my favor, you would send your men out to beat the woods for this dog-murderer who calls himself Cú Chulainn, and bring his head back in answer for this insult." She drew a deep breath, aware of Connla's gaze on the heaving of her breasts.

"It may be that I would seek to wed the king whose champions could do such a deed." Mother, I trust you will get me out of this if he succeeds! "And I am hurt. Will you take me to the Druids, or must I ask one of my brothers to leave his post?"

"I will, of course." Connla raised his voice. "Noisu, Fachtna, Aengus! Gather our swiftest warriors, and go bring me the head of this insolent whelp who has slain the queen's hound! Now come, my dear," he added coaxingly. "My chariot is coming; I shall lift you up into it, lest you hurt yourself further, and I will see to it that all is made well for you."

"Thank you," Finnabair murmured demurely.

"Mother, you should move back from here," Maine Orlamh said urgently to Maeve. "Cú Chulainn is probably long-gone, having missed his shot, and what wonder, from such a distance? He must know that we will be hunting him. Nevertheless, he is but a boy and might linger in hopes of one more chance."

Maeve's gaze went to Baiscne's body once more, and Finnabair's followed. If she half-closed her eyes, he could be sleeping, sprawled in the white snow as if it were the warm sheepskins that covered a hall's cold earthen floor. 'I am sorry, Baiscne, she thought. I did not want you for myself, I am sorry, but I would never have seen you slain, only passed to one more suited for rule than I.'

"There is nothing you can do for him now, Mother," Cairbre added. "Let Orlamh take you into the midst of the host. Feidhlim and I will see your chariot repaired, and lay your dear hound to rest as if he were a fallen hero. Hereafter this ridge shall be called Drum Baiscne."

Maeve bent her head once more to kiss Baiscne's muzzle like a little girl, as Finnabair had often seen her mother do before when she thought no one was looking.

"Farewell, and come back to me, my faithful one," Maeve whispered in the wolfhound's black ear. Finnabair's lips moved silently in her own prayer: 'Come back to my mother, for she loves you.'

Connla's driver steered up to the ring of guards, who parted for the two of them. Finnabair let the under-king take her about the hips to lift her into his vehicle. She hoped that he would take her shudder for pain, though she knew herself that it was fear. He was strong enough to do as he would with her, if he were not afraid of offending her kin, and she could not fight him. Even her mother, trained at weapons and wrestling, had not been able to fight off Conchobar's rape.

The horror of that revelation haunted Finnabair whenever a warrior looked on her with desire; and feeling Connla's powerful hands lifting her body lightly into the air brought it home so that she trembled with terror and anger. It seemed to her, as well, that his grasp lingered a little longer than it should have. It was not so long that she could take offense at it, but she flinched away as the wiry man vaulted into the chariot behind her.

"Is aught wrong?" Connla asked.

Finnabair composed her face, smiling wanly at him. "Only a little pain; the horses really wrenched my shoulder quite badly. Come, take my hand to steady me."

If she gritted her teeth as the chariot lurched into motion, Connla did not see it. Instead, he spoke all the way to the Druids' wagons, how this loss would be avenged by Cú Chulainn's death, a hound for a hound; how it would be safer for Finnabair to travel with him than to round the edges of the host in her mother's chariot.

Finnabair smiled and nodded and murmured meaningless words. Rochad, she thought, 'I will have earned our bridal as surely as any hero who brought an hundred heads to the wedding. Brigid grant you understand what I have had to do, that you do not hear tales of this and think me faithless!'

Finnabair did not know which of the Druids she would rather have had tend to her. She had always been afraid of Calatín, but she was also loath to face Fedelm. How could the ban-drúi feel anything but contempt in seeing Finnabair play up to Connla?

Whether Fedelm knew the truth of the matter, or thought Finnabair so shallow of heart as to be drawn by any man with a kingly title who would fight as she lured him, either must seem pathetic, if not downright shameful, to a woman who had found her own place in the realms of wisdom, without need to fear or charm or deceive any man. In any event, Calatín was alone in the wagon with the wounded, salving and wrapping a Munsterman's deeply-slashed leg, his breath murmuring over the injured limb.

Finnabair could not make out what he was saying, and even Connla did not dare to interrupt the Druid, but eventually he looked up. Calatín's dark piercing eyes seemed to take in everything at a glance, as though he read the depths of Finnabair's heart. The intent look on his face did not change, but Finnabair felt strangely comforted, as though he knew all that she was doing and did not think the less of her.

"Finnabair is..." Connla began aggressively, but the Druid cut him off with a sharp gesture.

"Come here, Finnabair, and let me look," he said calmly. His long fingers probed at her shoulder, and Finnabair bit back a hiss of pain. "It is only wrenched, but you should not drive for a few days yet, and should move it as little as possible. Here, I have a salve to speed the healing and a draught for the pain, and then I will wrap it for you. Connla, step back, I cannot work with you crowding so close."

The Munster under-king waited while Calatín tended to her, tapping his fingers on the edge of the wagon in an irregular rhythm that made Finnabair want to slap his hand. *He would let me, but what if this raid goes truly ill? If my parents and brothers are killed and he lives, I would be at his mercy. I cannot risk anything that might anger him.* The thought was more bitter than the concoction Calatín gave her to swallow.

She did not know if the faint glow in her belly was from the Druid's herbs, or her anger. When Calatín was done, Connla smiled at Finnabair, carefully taking her right hand to steady her again against the wagon's movement.

"Will you ride in my chariot now?" He asked. "I promise we shall go as slowly and carefully as you might wish."

Finnabair shook her head.

"I am far too sore, and Calatín's draught is making me a little sleepy," she demurred. "I would rather ride in one of the wagons, though perhaps not here with the wounded."

"Then I shall find you one more to your liking," Connla said. "In the meantime, here is something to cheer you. I plundered it from Rath Echach; I had meant to keep it for later. Let it bring you joy now, and I shall dream of the day when you serve me our wedding-mead from it."

He drew a small silver goblet out of the pouch at his waist. It was a precious piece, clearly traded from the craftsmen of the far South. Embossed upon it was the figure of a half-naked woman reclining on a couch with a bunch of large berries in her hand: a fair treasure, and suitable for a king's gift, or wedding-cup. Finnabair hoped that he took the hot flush on her cheeks for a blush, and the trembling of her hand as she accepted the goblet for maidenly modesty.

Connla ordered the wagon-driver to halt, lifting her down as he had lifted her up. This time, Finnabair was sure that his wiry hands lingered a little longer on her hips than they needed to, but she still could not object.

'And if it were Rochad handling me so, I would not wish to complain. I think to Connla I am like this goblet: a thing to be shown off, perhaps treasured for its value, but at the end, handled or disposed of as he will. Perhaps I am treating him no better than he treats me, but I have seen my mother and father together all my life, and I know there is more to hope for between men and women.'

"Ah, here are my mother and brothers," Finnabair said in some relief as Maeve and her guards came up. "I thank you for your tender care, but you must leave me to them now. I shall rest in a wagon for the remainder of the day's journey, and though we may not wed until this raid is done, perhaps if you come to our encampment tonight, I shall serve you mead. Go now, see to your men, and if you can bear me word that the Hound of Ulster is slain or taken, you shall have as great a joy of me in turn."

Connla looked disappointed, but mustered a smile all the same. "So may it be, my dear."

"Is all well?" Maeve asked her daughter when the Munster under-king was out of earshot.

Finnabair grimaced. "Well enough. Calatín says I am not to drive for a few days. Connla gave me this." She lifted the goblet, holding the stem between the tips of her thumb and forefinger; she would sooner have carried a chunk of dried cow-dung.

Maeve sighed. "Well, you must keep it for the time being. You did very well, my daughter."

"Thank you. I wish, poor Baiscne! It is a shameful man, who makes war on animals."

"I think that shot was more likely aimed at my own head," her mother said grimly. "It is good fortune, that we were far enough away for even Cú Chulainn to miss his mark."

Finnabair felt herself paling. She had not let herself think of it, but it could have been her mother lying in the snow with her skull broken open, or herself, if the Hound of Ulster had aimed a little more awry. 'I want to go home, she thought again. I believed that if I never took up a sword, I would be safe from violence. I was wrong: no one is safe, not an unarmed maiden nor a hound. Yet I will have Rochad, whatever I must do to win him. I will see Cruachan's queenship restored: our daughter may yet desire what I would lay aside'. As she had several times before, Finnabair repeated her resolution to herself. She did not know if she believed it, but she would hold to it.

Maeve

When Maeve was seated by her fire in the camp's royal enclosure that night, and remarked on her narrow escape, Fergus shook his head.

"I do not think he missed. I have seen Cú Chulainn hit smaller targets from further away. I believe that he meant it as a warning, and perhaps a boast."

"What manner of boast is it, to kill a dog with a brain-ball?" Maeve snapped. Her deeper fear; that Cú Chulainn had struck knowingly at the remaining roots of her rule. That must remain unspoken, lest by planting the thought in others' minds she lose all she was struggling to keep. Fergus himself could testify that there was more to sovereignty than blood or right.

"You know why Ulster's champion is called Cú Chulainn, though his name is Setanta?" Fergus asked.

"I have heard the tale," Maeve replied grimly. "Though I hardly believe that a seven year-old could truly have warded Culann's flocks and lands as well as a mighty wolfhound."

"I saw him slay the great dog myself. I thought I would die of sorrow when it sprang at him, for there was no way that Culann could have opened the gate in time for me to save my foster-son. He did not need my aid. Even then," Fergus added softly, "he was very good with a sling. I think he slew Baiscne to tell you that the Hound of Culann would guard Ulster as steadfastly in his seventeenth year as he guarded Muirtheimne Plain in his seventh. For Cú Chulainn would not shoot to kill a woman, even an enemy queen and war leader, save in the greatest need."

Maeve took a last bite of meat from the pork rib in her hand, then reached down with the bone, and stopped halfway. There would be no great jaws to take it daintily from her fingers, nor warm tongue to lick the grease from them afterwards. She swallowed hard, rubbing the back of her hand across her eyes. Connla's men had come into camp late, cold, wet, and swearing.

"We thought we had found his tracks in the wood at one point," one of them had said, "but he was long gone, and there were no more tracks to be seen. We might as well have been hunting a ghost." To Maeve's relief, the under-king of Munster had retired in high dudgeon: his presence at their fire tonight would have been more than she could bear.

Ailill put his arm around Maeve to comfort her, and she leaned against him for a little while, but she could not turn her heart away from the thought of Baiscne's body stiffening and growing cold on the ridge where her sons had raised his cairn. The memory of her hound's limp corpse was still with her as she went to sleep alone, sorrowful in the silence where his quiet breaths had always been. Her bed felt strange without Baiscne's weight, and her feet were icy without his furry warmth.

At last Maeve slipped from her dark wakefulness into a deeper darkness. Then it seemed to her that she was wandering lost and naked in the black maze that led beneath Cruachan síd, the dark passage that turned and turned and yet led nowhere. Things whispered wordlessly just beyond her hearing; something silky and cold as an ice-frosted cobweb slid across her bare shoulder, and she bit back a scream.

It seemed as though she had been wandering for ages, searching for some glimmer of light in the darkness, some hint that she might reach Uaigh na gCat's opening to the green earth again. At first the gleam before Maeve was no more than a phantom flickering against the backs of her eyelids as she blinked against the dark. Slowly it brightened: she hastened towards it, hoping with all her heart that it was the light of dawn she saw.

Brighter and brighter the light grew, Maeve's hopes waxing with it. Then she saw what stood at its heart, and stopped dead.

"Maeve," King Ochall's musical voice sang. "You have come to me at last." He was naked, his pale body shining as if it had been wrought from fine silver.

His manhood stood erect, a perfect white column swelling smoothly at the pink-flushed tip, inviting her hands to caress its silken hardness, to guide it into herself. Her tight nipples ached with desire, twinging down through her body; a cool breeze brushed against the moisture dewing her upper thighs as her legs moved involuntarily apart. Ochall's dawn-bright eyes met Maeve's; the keen bolt of pleasure that went through her felt as though he had pierced her with a thrust that ran through her entire body, leaving her breathless and gasping.

"My bondsmaid," he crooned, "my servant." He reached out to her.

With all the strength that was left in her, Maeve wrenched herself away, turning and stumbling back into the dark on unstrung legs, her whole body shaking so that she could barely stand. Out, she must get out, where was Baiscne? Her hound would lead her free, would guard her from the beings that watched in the blackness beneath Cruachan síd.

Maeve awoke, gasping and drenched in sweat, her body still trembling with dreadful reluctant excitement. She was alone in the dark, and Baiscne was dead. It took a long time for Maeve to steady herself enough to grasp the bed frame and lever herself to her feet. She could go to Ailill's tent, or Fergus.

"No," Maeve said aloud to herself. She spoke very softly, so as not to waken Lochu, but the sound of her own voice made her feel better. Instead, she slipped out the door. The camp fire had burned down, the coals' glow hidden under the ash, and the only torches to be seen were those of the guards outside the wicker enclosure. The Moon was nearly full again.' A month since we set out, Maeve thought, trying to turn the heat raging within her to anger, and still we have not even reached Cuailgne!'

Maeve walked back between the tents, where no one was likely to see her. Pulling up the hem of her leine, she squatted in a snow-drift. The sudden jolt of ice on the heat of her tender parts shocked through her like a blow. She bit her lip to keep from crying out, but sat there until she began to shiver. Then she raised up a little and let her bladder go.

The powerful hot stream warmed away the bitter bite of ice between her legs, hissing fiercely out to melt the snow beneath it: Maeve imagined she could see the steam rising, and felt comforted in her own strength. Rising again, Maeve looked at the low-sailing Moon. Nearly full' My courses did not come upon me with the dark', she thought. After those first few drops of untimely blood, there had been no more.

The cold was gnawing deeply at her now, and her knees hurt from squatting. For a moment, Maeve felt altogether wretched, as though her fears and her sorrows had gathered into a great army to overwhelm her. Aching with age, her spring dried and body soon to wither, her right to rule wounded if not destroyed, 'and shall I be remembered as the woman who led the hosts of Eriu to destruction for her own pride? If we can be hindered by one man, what will become of us when the hosts of Ulster arise from their pangs?'

Maeve straightened her back.

"Whatever betide," she whispered, "I am still myself. That cannot be taken from me, unless I myself should surrender it; as I will not."

She was still shivering hard, but from cold, not from the power of her dream. 'Dream? Maybe; or maybe Ochall still sought to seduce her to himself, even now and from so far away. With Baiscne gone, I refused him, and with none other than myself to strengthen me. I would sooner wander lost in the dark places forever than be bondsmaid to another!' In any case, she had been sitting in the snow on a bitter-cold night with only a thin linen tunic over her. Her dream-sweat was beginning to freeze in the garment, and her feet and fingers had gone numb.

Maeve hurried back into her tent, bundling all her covers around her. It was a measure of her terror, she thought, that she could actually welcome the needling pains as the blood came back to her feet and hands, savor the trembling of cold and its slow, easing as the thick blankets of wool and sheepskin warmed around her. Still, she had won the victory, and that was enough for this night. When she awoke with the first light of dawn creeping about the edges of her tent, Maeve lay still for a little while.

Something rustled in the corner, and her heart leapt with joy: Baiscne had returned, after all. It was only Lochu, sitting up and rubbing the sleep from her eyes. Cruelly disappointed, Maeve wanted to shout at her, but nothing that had happened was the serving woman's fault. She started up again at the next noise, but she already knew that sound: her marten running down the central tent-post. Maeve held out her arm, letting the little beast scamper up to curl in its usual place by her neck.

It was warm, and comforting in its way, though she could not help thinking, 'If Cú Chulainn had to slay one of my beasts, could it not have been you, or the wren, rather than Baiscne?' She drove the thought from her, stroking the marten and murmuring affectionate words to it.

Baiscne's death was no more its fault than Lochu's, and only a fool would let what she had lost spoil what she had left. Suddenly Maeve felt a sharp pain in her shoulder, and choked back a cry. As if it had heard her unkindly thought, the marten had nipped her hard, sinking its teeth through linen and skin and flesh. A small dark blot of blood was already spreading on the light fabric of her tunic. She grasped the marten firmly, lifting its long body off her. The beast's wild dark eyes looked into her own; its brown muzzle was stained with Maeve's blood. Maeve realized that she was trembling, that she was suddenly afraid of the little animal from Cruachan síd.

'It is Ochall's beast as well as my own, and now he is close to being my foe', she thought. Angry, frightened, shamed at her own fear, her shoulder aching sharply from the animal's bite, Maeve tightened her hands to twist the marten's neck.

'No. I have lost one of my animals to our foe; will I slay another myself? If I give in to my fear, if I cast away the living emblem of my rule because I have not the courage to bear it, I might as well be Ochall's bondsmaid already.'

Carefully Maeve set the marten on her shoulder. She could not help thinking of how close its sharp teeth were to the great blood-vessels in her neck, nor still the following thought: If Ochall wants me badly enough, would this creature from Uaigh na gCat slay me, that he might carry me back to his síd.

Maeve had already made her choice: the queen's marten would ride on her shoulder until it decided to slither down and be off on concerns of its own, as always. At her guards' urging, Maeve kept well within her host that day, rather than riding around the edges as was her usual habit. Now and then, a dog would bark and Maeve would look around sharply, but it was never Baiscne.

'He did not come with the dawn, as he always did before. I must accept that he is gone from me', Maeve told herself, and forced herself to turn her mind to other things. The days were growing very short now: it would not be long until Midwinter.

'When we shall lose another three days, for what the daylight is worth at this time of year!' Maeve thought bitterly. Yet that made it all the more important to feast her host well when the time came. Winter was no time for raiding, and even if Rath Echach had been a better victory, the cold and strain of travel in this harsh winter would be wearing the triumph thin already.

Maeve's smiths and woodworkers had repaired her chariot so cunningly that only the missing piece of bronze mounting showed it had been broken, and replaced the other shaft as well. Everyone had been warned once more to look closely at their chariot-poles before setting out in the morning, but the army was nearly out of shafts, so there was no replacing wood that might have weakened unless a crack was clear.

The host was traveling through a thick forest, perhaps two miles from the place where Fergus thought they would be best to camp for the night, when one of Maine Orlamh's shafts snapped through. At least, surrounded by foot-soldiers and wagons as they were, he had not been going fast enough to be in any danger. He climbed out of the chariot and stood considering it.

"Well," Maeve's son said, "there are plenty of shafts around us. Come, Fertedil, we shall go cut some. Mother, let my brother Dáire take my place, and we can catch up after you have made camp."

"I would rather you took more men than a young charioteer with you," Maeve told him.

Orlamh laughed.

"The Hound of Ulster may be able to throw a sling-ball half a mile, or ten miles, but even he must see in order to shoot. In these woods, any man who wants to challenge me will have to come within reach of my spear. I shall be glad enough of that, if Cú Chulainn is willing to meet my challenge! Indeed, if I knew he were there, I should hunt him down myself."

Fraech was as certain, Maeve thought. Her son was more imposing than Flidais' champion, a great oak of a man, she thought affectionately.

Cú Chulainn was a little fellow, by all reports. She leaned over her chariot's edge to kiss her son.

"Be careful, and be sure that Fertedil watches your back: remember that the strongest can be slain by surprise."

"Can be, but shan't," Orlamh said, grinning. "I'll be back with you by nightfall."

The host stopped to make camp a little before sunset. They were well away from the woods, though the rise and fall of the land made it impossible to find a place where a skilled slinger could not fire a ball at them and disappear behind a ridge or hill.

Maeve was towards the rear of the army, with Ailill and his Leinstermen, when Mac Roth came dashing up to them, his freckled face taut with fear and sorrow.

"Orlamh," Maeve said, her heart fluttering in her breast like a wing-shot bird.

Her messenger nodded. "Fertedil is coming back alone."

Ailill tapped his charioteer on the shoulder. "Move, now! Out of our way!" He shouted. His chariot creaked alarmingly as the youth wheeled it in a tight circle. Munremur looked uncertainly at Maeve.

"My queen, you ordered me to stay in the midst..."

"Go!" Maeve screamed at him.

Though their wheels skidded on the trampled snow and muck, Munremur kept the chariot under tight control, their horses leaping forward to catch up with Ailill. Her guards and her husband's struggled to follow, but Maeve and Ailill were both past caring. They reached Fertedil just as the charioteer was coming up to camp. The youth's blotchy freckles stood out like a thick spattering of mud on his pale face; his brown hair hung tattered and disheveled, and he was laboring along in the army's slushy track as if he had been running for miles.

His hands were raised oddly behind his head, holding. Maeve closed her eyes, but could not shut the sight from her mind. Orlamh's head was set upright as if it were sprouting from the charioteer's shoulders behind his neck, her son's mouth fixed in a snarling grin beneath his thick red mustaches. His bright hair was all straggled and dark with blood, and a long trail of blood had flowed down Fertedil's back.

Ailill threw back his head and keened, a sound all the more mournful and horrible from the depths of a man's chest. Maeve joined him, the cry bursting high from her throat, and for a moment there was no sound in the world but the dreadful harmony of their wailing for their slain son. Ailill stopped to draw breath first.

"What happened?" He said, his voice as raw as if he had been weeping for days.

Fertedil lifted Orlamh's head with shaking hands, giving it over for Ailill to cradle in his arms as he had once cradled the red-haired infant. His voice breaking and cracking like that of a boy five years younger, the charioteer told his story. Maeve wanted to put her hands over her ears and close her eyes, but she could not.

Her son was dead, and she would know how it had come to pass, whatever it cost her. Instead, she put all the strength of her mind into seeing, to understanding, what had happened. Orlamh and Fertedil had gone a little way into the wood, far enough to find a good thicket of straight trunked holly trees. Someone else's charioteer was already cutting and stripping shafts there.

"Oró, and what are you doing out here, with the army over there?" The youth had inquired.

"Cutting shafts for a broken chariot, like yourself," Fertedil had answered. "I'll help you with yours, if you'll help me with mine, and my master will keep watch to be sure no one attacks us by surprise. Would you rather cut, or trim?"

"I'll do the trimming," the other boy had said. So, while Orlamh had paced around them to guard, Fertedil had made to cut down two good straight trees. While he was chopping the second, the other charioteer drew his sword and whisked off the bark and branches of the first in less time than it took Fertedil to sever the slender trunk.

"This isn't your usual work," Fertedil had said, frightened.

"Who are you, then?" The youth had asked, peering closely at Fertedil.

"I am charioteer for Orlamh, the son of King Ailill and Queen Maeve. You?"

"I am Cú Chulainn. Don't be afraid; I have no quarrel with unarmed charioteers, unless they make one with me. I will see about your master, if he dares."

And Cú Chulainn had fought Orlamh, and killed him. Fertedil could tell Ailill and Maeve little of the fight:

Maeve suspected that he had hidden with his eyes closed. Afterwards, Cú Chulainn had beheaded her son and shaken the head towards her host, then set the head on the charioteer's back and said,

"Take this with you and keep it like that all the way into the camp. If you do anything other than carry it on your back into the camp, I'll break your head with a stone from my sling."

Although the tears were streaming down the faces of Orlamh's three brothers as they heard this, and the mouths of the other guards were twisted with grief, they all still stood with their shields up around Maeve, as Ailill's guards did around him. Maeve opened her mouth to order the guards in closer around Fertedil, but she was too late. She heard the whistle of the stone tearing through the air, ending in a flat horrible crack, and the young man dropped bonelessly to the ground.

"After him!" Maeve shouted, pointing in the direction from which the shot had come. "After him, every man who dares, and Crom Cruaich take champion's challenges and fair fight!"

Ailill's bull roar echoed her high shriek.

"After the Hound of Ulster. Now, while there is still light to kill him by! Dáire, Ferdiad, you stay to shield the queen; the rest of you, go!"

The guards leapt into their chariots, thundering off. Behind the shields of Ferdiad and Maine Dáire, Ailill moved close to Maeve, staring down at his grievous burden, then at Fertedil lying dead on the ground with his skull shattered.

"He didn't need to kill the charioteer," Ailill rasped, as though his last cry had broken his throat.

"No. Since he cannot face our host in battle by himself, he means to break our wills instead."

Ailill's face spasmed, tears running down his cheeks to drip into Orlamh's blood-matted hair.

"He will learn how wrong he is," Maeve's husband said roughly.

"My son, my son. I swear by the god of my clan, Cú Chulainn will pay, in death or an equal measure of sorrow, before this raid is done."

They walked back to the camp in silence. Maeve wanted to speak, or weep, but her eyes burned hot and dry, as though she had been staring at the treacherous brilliance of sunlight on snow all day.

"I will see to what must be done," Ailill croaked when they came to Calatín's tent.

"Our son will come home with us. Go. Rest, and mourn, and I will come to you when I am able."

Her throat too choked to speak, Maeve nodded her thanks. Ailill knew her as well as a man could know a woman: knew that she would want to be alone with her grief for a time, away from the eyes that were always on a queen, able to be only herself.

Lochu was waiting in Maeve's tent with a platter of bread and cheese, a golden goblet, and a bronze pitcher of mead. The sadness on the bondsmaid's face told Maeve she had already heard the tidings.

"My queen, I grieve, as well," Lochu murmured.

"Orlamh was always kind to me. Eat, and drink, and weep as you can."

Maeve lifted the goblet. The cold metal was already furred with frost; the sweet mead slid down her swollen throat, icy and strong.

"It is better to weep," Lochu added. "Believe me, I know."

Maeve looked at her servant as if seeing the young woman for the first time. She had been a chieftain's daughter, Maeve remembered, had seen her father and brothers slain.

Yet she had been brave, if silent, when she was brought to Cruachan as plunder, and Maeve had never heard her speak ill of her captors.

"Have I ever treated you badly?" Maeve asked.

Lochu shook her head, her golden-brown hair tumbling about her face. "Never, my queen. You chose to take me in when I might have been forced to far worse. In your service, I have never been forced to lie with a man I did not want, nor kept from a man I did. You have not beaten me; you have clad and fed me as well as ever my own clan did, or better.

Save for bearing the name of a battle-captive, I could hardly have done better than being your attendant: enough high-born girls have been glad to serve beside me in your company, though they gained more honor by it.

"And yet, I know what it is to lose those one loves. I tried not to weep when I was taken, but the longer I held it back, the worse it was in the end."

Spontaneously Maeve reached out, clasping Lochu by the hand. The other woman's fingers closed tightly on her own, and at last the tears came to Maeve's eyes.

Fedelm

Cú Chulainn continued to harry our host as we crossed Breg Plain, casting balls from his sling and ambushing those men who came out to hunt him. if he had thought that he could frighten or warn Maeve away, it was not so. Though he had murdered her beloved hound and slain her son, and once managed to creep close enough to shoot her pine marten where it curled about her neck, it seemed to me that she did not fear death; though she did, at least, keep wisely to the middle of the host thereafter.

As for Ailill, the loss of Orlamh struck him more visibly. I could see him struggling to show his former cheerfulness and keep heart in the host. When he was by himself, or with only the other leaders, he would fall silent, clasping his hands on his knees and staring grim-faced and resolute into the fire. I thought back to what Flidais had said, "Ailill is almost too sweet-natured to be king. As well for him that Maeve does not flinch from doing what is harder." She might have mistaken Ailill's easy manner and warm heart for weakness; whether Maeve did as well, I did not know, but I knew better.

'Cú Chulainn does not know either, I thought at times, but he has as much to fear from Ailill as from Maeve now, or more. She is the storm wind, but he is the rock: beware, when the rock moves in anger!' Calatín spent most of his time teaching me all he could, as if he would pack ten years' lore into a month of long nights. I learned much, most I did not fully understand, but when I said so, he would nod and say,

"Keep it safe in your mind: there will come a time when you do understand."

Nevertheless, I had some moments of freedom. I spent most of them with Suithchern. Though she was not a woman of great learning or wit, it was a pleasure to sit with her and tend Conall and Clothra.

Often she would nurse one child while I cuddled the other, talking of simple things: the best herbs to soothe a colic or calm a fretful baby, when they should crawl and when they should walk, how her husband had chosen her from the women of their chieftain's household and how he had courted her, all those things that I had chosen, without thinking, to give up when I went to Alba.

The ban-druid may bear children during our studies, but there is little place in a student's life for courtship; Suithchern was two years younger than I, but wise in a life where I was but the newest child.

"How do you draw a man's eyes to you?" I asked her one evening. "Do you speak boldly, or look away if his gaze falls on you? If you know a woman who has won him before, is it best to follow her example?" Though I could not imagine any way in which I could possibly resemble Maeve.

Suithchern shifted on her stool, wrapping a corner of her blue bratt over Conall's head lest he catch a chill while he nursed.

"A man who likes apples and has had none for some time will generally snatch at cider," she remarked. " a man who has had a great deal of apples lately will often be better pleased by a dish of blackberries on occasion. Is there such a man in your heart?"

I blushed and looked away, and she chuckled kindly.

"As fair as you are, I think you have little to worry about. Many things move a woman to first love, but the first path to a man's heart, and other parts! Is usually through his eyes. I think Conall is full. Will you burp him while I feed Clothra?"

I passed her daughter to her and took Conall, wrapping my own mantle about him before I bent him gently over one arm to pat his back. He was already heavier than he had been when Ailill brought him out of the slaughterhouse that had been Rath Echach, strong and healthy. He gurgled a little as I patted him, then rewarded me with a healthy belch.

I wiped a dribble of milk and froth from the corner of his tiny mouth with one of the soft linen cloths which, Suithchern assured me, a wise mother always had to hand. He gurgled again, then bubbled softly further down, the inevitable smell arising. Fortunately, his breech clout had caught all the mess this time, and I had grown deft enough to change it and wipe him with another damp cloth while he squalled before the stain soaked through to my white robe.

"It's hard learning the ways of a body again, after the Otherworld, isn't it, little one?" I murmured to Conall, rocking him to quiet him. "Harder still being a babe in arms who cannot walk or even crawl, if you remember anything from before."

Conall's cries gradually trailed into little whimpers, as though he had it in his mind that he should be crying, but had already forgotten why. I jogged him gently on my knee. "Who were you before this, I wonder? Did I know you before I left and came back myself?"

He looked up at me. Like all infants, his eyes were blue as though they still reflected the skies of the Land of Summer; but it seemed to me that he saw me clearly. His little lips opened for a moment in what might have been a toothless smile, and my heart turned over.

I wished that I could take him back to Alba with me; but I had no milk to give him, and even if I could find a nanny-goat in milk at this time of year, it would be cruel to take him from Suithchern now. Suithchern's eyes were half-closed with pleasure as she nursed her daughter.

"It is more trouble following Lóch to war with babes at the breast, but I cannot say I am not glad of it," she mused. "They are such a delight, well, when they are not cackling or puking or screaming to awake one from a deep sleep after a day's march! And," she said, glancing aside nervously, "whatever this Cú Chulainn is capable of, I hear that he is at least unlikely to assail a nursing mother with her babes."

"Fergus says that he does not strike down unarmed women or servants," I reassured her. In truth, though the white robe was usually only worn for rituals, I had begun to put mine on more and more often.

Judging from what the Hound of Ulster had done, it was hard to guess what more he might dare, but I thought that even he would shrink from striking down a ban-drúi. Calatín never chided me for it, though he himself, as if in defiance, continued to wear his warrior's gear.

"Aye, so the Ulstermen all say. The Munstermen have already ordered that their unarmed followers march at the edges of their cantred, as if they were a palisade around the warriors."

I had heard that; and noticed, too, that while Maeve had not given such an order, there had been a slow inward movement of the fighters while the army was on the march.

Suithchern shuddered.

"I wonder if he is a living man at all? It seems at times that we are haunted by a neim-mairb, coming unseen to steal the life and vanishing again before any can strike him down. Have you noticed that the guards and patrolers no longer dare to go by one and two, but by twelve and twenty? The nights are so long and cold now; but sometimes I am afraid even to sit by the fire, because the warriors say that doing so makes one an easy target for a shot from the darkness."

"Cú Chulainn is certainly a living man," I assured her.

A little of the fear lifted from her face. She trusted my word, because she thought of me as a ban-drúi: to a woman like her, it meant little that I was ten years from finishing my training. Fortunately, she did not ask me what manner of man he could be. I did not know myself: I remembered the hero-light that had hidden his face in my vision, and the curling tail of the dragon.

"I am sure that you, or any who are not fighters, have little to fear from him. He seeks to defend Ulster and to win glory, and there is none of that in killing unarmed women."

"Still, he killed the queen's hound, and her pine marten. What threat could they have been? What glory did that win?

Orlamh's poor charioteer, to make him carry the head like that, with the gore running down his back! He could choose any of us for something horrible next: I almost think I would rather die."

As though she could taste her mother's fear, Clothra let go of the nipple and began to wail. Suithchern paused to soothe her. Wiser in the ways of infants than I, Suithchern managed to get her daughter's head out of her bratt before Clothra spewed out a fountain of sour milk. Suithchern patted her on the back to keep her from choking, then wiped the babe's face and returned her to the breast. The familiar task had brought some color back to her own cheeks, and I thought I might be able to ease her a little further, for I had learned in my studies that reason could be a great antidote to many troubles of the soul.

"Surely your husband has brought back heads of his own as trophies?" I said. "And have you not helped him to clean them? What Cú Chulainn did to Orlamh's charioteer; it was cruel, to make him bear the head of the man he loved and served, and worse still to shoot him down for what seems little cause to me. Being made to carry a friend's head is not truly more gruesome than carrying a foe's, is it?"

Suithchern shook her head. "It is not even so much what he did that time, as what he might do," she said stubbornly. "He is a derg-daol, which creeps about and spits, until it burrows into the flesh to suck the blood, bringing the worst of ill-luck to the living and fattening on the dead." I shuddered myself at the memory of the lean black corpse-beetle I had seen in the great storm, Nemhain's Horse.

I could neither reason with Suithchern's argument nor deny it, and so I changed the subject, saying, "Clothra seems a bit gassy tonight. Would you like me to make up some dill-water for her again?"

"That would be very kind of you," Suithchern answered. I could hear the relief in her voice: I only hoped that I had not worsened her fear by encouraging her to tell it. Sorrow shared is often lessened; but now I was seeing, by day and even more by night, that fear shared is more likely to be magnified.

Perhaps my own fear was magnified as well, for, when Calatín finally finished with me that night, I found myself lying awake late. The disciplines I had learned could loosen and ease my body, but had less effect on my mind. While I recited lays and lists to myself, my thoughts ran in the deep groove of memory; but when I finished each one, my mind went back to the shining warped shape of my vision, and I wondered again what he was doing that night.

Creeping about the hills looking for a good chance with his sling, or lying in wait for the unwary, perhaps: he had not yet started picking off the camp's guards, but, as Suithchern had showed me, there was more fear in thinking on what he might do than what he had done.

At last I decided that there was no point in lying and wondering. If Cú Chulainn could have done me harm in vision before, he could not now:

I believed Calatín's judgement, that he had crippled himself at least for a time in his efforts to block us by enchantment and challenge. My breaths deepened and slowed; my body faded from my awareness.

The lodestone will move to the strongest metal: for those who are gifted with foresight, however well-trained, a great power or happening will often draw us away from the lesser, unless the strictest rites be followed, and sometimes even then.

I had meant to search the hills and woods for the Hound of Ulster; instead, I found myself drawn away beneath the swift-waning Moon, over the faint gleam of frosted fields and trees black and slick with ice, to the mountains of Cuailgne rising round-headed above the lashing winter ocean.

Though the mountains dropped sharply to the water on their northern and eastern sides, they sloped gently towards the landward side of the peninsula; and on one of their fields, the shapes of many cattle bulked dark and thick against trampled mud and scattered snow. There I saw a standing stone, the frost on it like pale lichen in the moonlight, and by it dozed the greatest of the cattle.

This, I knew, was the Donn Cuailgne, in the field where he had been brought to winter. His ridged black horns spread so wide that a tall man might have lain between their tips; lying on the ground, his shoulder was hardly lower than my own, and were he to stand, his back would rise above my head.

Each breath that snorted from his huge nostrils struck against me like a storm wind blast, so that I could hardly steady myself. I moved carefully behind him, lest he open his eyes and gaze on me, for there was more power in him than I wished to dare. A darkness passed over the face of the Moon, blackening all for a moment, and swept past again.

Though I had no breath to hold, I waited silent as a vole when the owl glides overhead. Only the barest fringe of a black feather brushed me. I had felt that touch before: the wild rage, the thirst for blood. The great raven circled; the fifty heifers in the field huddled close, too frightened to run from the shadow winging over them.

The Donn Cuailgne raised his huge head, his horns like two immense oak-branches against the moon, and looked up as the raven swooped down to roost upon the standing stone. Her voice shuddered harshly through me: a raven's rough call, but full of unearthly music and wild sharp-edged power.

"Dark one, are you restless? Do you guess they gather to slaughter? The raven cries aloud: foes stream through the fair fields to ravage. Now learn, I discern: men's remains on green plains, hosts ground to dust; the raven raging among corpses of men. Affliction and outcry, war over Cuailgne: death of sons, death of kinsmen, death!"

The Morrígan rose, her wings beating an icy downward gale. The Brown Bull lumbered to his feet, his heavy head swinging as though he sought a foe to gore. It seemed to me that the plain trembled beneath his feet as he trampled a slow circle about his heifers. Resolute and sure, he began to walk away, with the herd following him. He was leaving the field of Temair Chuailgne, of that I was certain, and it was in my mind to shadow him until I knew where Maeve might find him.

Then he raised his horns high and bellowed, an awesome deep sound that shivered through earth and air like a mountain-high wave, sweeping me up and casting me away as though I were no more than a twig upon the stormy ocean. For a moment I flailed in blackness and terror, sure that the strength of that bellow had driven me so far into the night that I should never find my way back to my body, but must wander lost between the worlds until

I might chance upon another path. Yet I gathered myself, and found the glimmering silver trail at last. Although my limbs felt chilled and sore when I tried to move them, I was so grateful to be safe in my body again that I nearly wept. If I had learned less than I had meant to or hoped, at least I knew that the Brown Bull could not be easily found, but we would have to search for him. While that was not the knowledge I had wanted, it was knowledge we needed; and that would have to do.

Maeve

Midwinter's Day dawned clear, cold, and bright, the sky arching unclouded above the army's camp like a steel shield polished to a pale blue gleam. While Midwinter was not one of the great holy days, it was a time for celebration. Maeve had feared it would be hard to keep her warriors alert and on watch, but her concerns proved groundless. For all folk reassured each other that the Hound of Ulster would surely have left to guest and feast the longest night away, few in her army let down their guards too far.

Full-armed fighters with glittering spear points patrolled each cantred's encampment; though cauldrons of hot mead and cider hung over camp fires here and there, much of her host was sober. The exceptions were those young men making up the procession winding through the camp, the Hunters of the Wren, the boys of the White Mare. The youths had arisen at dawn to kill a little wren, hanging it from a cross-ended pole decorated with bright ribbons; they bore the slain bird before them, the promise that winter's rule must wane.

Many of the wren-hunters were masked with the basketwork or wooden heads of stag and boar and bull. The man in the middle bore a great bronze trumpa, playing as he walked with the horn's curving stem and glittering disk rearing high over his head. Though this was not the music of war, the resounding high blasts that could be heard clearly two miles away, the singers had to call out with full voices to match the strength of the horn-player's lively tune.

At the rear of the procession, the White Mare, a wickerwork horse's body large enough for two men to fit inside, covered in white cloth, with a horse's skull mounted as her head, pranced and capered to the singing and the rumbling thump of the bodhrans the paraders carried.

Maeve's own bird had stayed perched on her shoulder since dawn: it knew she was its safety on this day. Now it twittered softly in her ear, its song a delicate fluttering above the men's deep voices and the boys' high ones. The White Mare circled up to Maeve; Ferdiad and Maine Cairbre moved aside to let it bear its luck close to Connacht's queen. The Mare's foremost bearer moved the sticks that made the skull's jaws snap, lunging playfully at Maeve. Even that did not startle the wren from her shoulder; nor did it take wing when Maeve snapped her own jaws back at the White Mare.

Around her. The guards all laughed, and Maine Ceat shouted, "White girl, Connacht's red-sided mare is a match for you!"

The Mare's tail, a long stiff broom of plaited rye straw, flicked from side to side. The white-covered figure leapt and whirled away, as the Mare sought out another to greet. A little way from Maeve, Fergus also stood watching as the rear of the procession passed by him, staring intently at the antics of the White Mare. Maeve expected that the wicker-beast would charge at him next, or perhaps turn about and lift her tail, pretending to beseech him to mount her: surely the horse-players could not resist jesting with the son of the Great Stallion. The White Mare passed Fergus by without so much as turning her bony head towards him. The Ulster exile stared after her with a hard-set look of sorrow on his face, grey eyes befogged with longing? Thoughtfulness? Maeve could not tell.

'The land-goddess of Ulster shows herself as a white mare, too', Maeve thought. More than ever, she felt the emptiness at her side where Baiscne should have been; the winter air was cold on her left shoulder where her marten should have coiled. Only her wren was left. She stroked the little bird's head with one finger.

'If I had never come on this raid, if I had made peace with Ailill before the matter went too far, no, I should have lost everything in that moment, though only drúi or síd-folk might have seen it at first. This raid is not my destruction yet, for all the sorrow it has brought: it is still my hope'.

Fergus still watched the White Mare. The sharp winter sunlight threw the lines of his craggy face into deep relief, and the little glimmers it sparked out from deep in his thick chestnut hair might have been the gold of youth or the silver of age. 'He is not the only one aging. My courses have not come upon me again . I wish I could go to him now'. Maeve did not know whether she wanted to comfort Fergus, or be comforted. He had already lost all that she was losing, though he had learned it in a moment's cruel stroke instead of this slow black beetle-nibbling.

He, too, would know what it was to reach for the outward signs of his power and find nothing, to reach into his soul for ruler-might such as had flowed from Maeve in the storm at Cul Silibrinne and find it empty. Though Maeve had refused all her life to give way to fear, she did not dare cast deep into her own soul now.

It was not needed, this was the day of the wren-boys, not one of the great feasts where the queen must link folk and land and gods, and she could not yet bear what she might find.

'You alone, Fergus, of all our host, know what it is that I feel and fear'. The procession wound between tents and hide-covered wicker bothies, more youths joining it as it went and raising their voices in the wren-songs. Other folk thrust cups of drink to the dancers, mead and ale and cider: it was good luck for a wren-boy to accept a draught from one's hand. Maeve forced herself to smile. There had been little enough luck for her thus far, but the Sun would turn in the darkness this night to start her summer ward course again: matters could turn for Connacht's queen as well. 'Why not?' Maeve thought.

She went to a steaming cauldron, taking a cup from the nearest servant to dip in the large pot. Breathing the rich honey-scent that rose from the hot mead was almost enough to make her head swim by itself. 'I am still Maeve; I am still the cup-bearing queen.' As she made her way back towards the long winding line of dancers, something seared across the line of Maeve's jaw, and she heard a small dull thump next to her ear. She touched her face, feeling the sharp burn of a narrow graze running straight along the line of her jaw. Bright blood smeared her fingers when she brought her hand down, too much blood.Maeve already knew what she would see, but she had to look.

Her wren's little body lay on the frozen ground. Its head was gone, torn off or destroyed utterly by the shot, she could not tell. 'How could he have seen me clearly enough to shoot?

I am in the middle of our host; if he arched a shot over our heads, even Cú Chulainn could not have aimed so precisely.' Maeve touched the graze on her jaw again. It was straight as a knife-slash: that shot had come from close by. Her guards had their shields up around her now. Before any of them could draw breath to speak, Maeve shouted with all her strength, her high voice cutting through the wren-songs. "Cú Chulainn is in the camp!" She drew her sword, but she was surrounded by a wall of strong backs on every side now, and three of them were her sons: she could not bring herself to beat her way through.

"Let me through!" Maeve raged as someone else called, "Cú Chulainn is among us!" Others took up the cry. Swords flashed from their scabbards, and suddenly warriors were running everywhere and shouting wildly. A large dark-haired man tore the mask from one of the wren-boys; the others were hastily pulling off their own wicker-heads to show their faces.

"Let me through!" Maeve shouted again, grabbing Ferdiad's massive shoulder.

Connacht's champion did not look at his queen, only kept scanning the swirling chaos of armed men about them as he answered,

"We shall not. It is you whom the Hound seeks. He has already struck at you thrice: by the gods of my clan and the ancient ones of the Fir Bolg, he shall not do so again!"

Maeve's fury was a strong draught of winter mead, filling her trembling limbs and sick heart with a welcome flush of heat.

"How could this happen? You, of all men, should know the Hound on sight. Were you not watching, or did you hold your tongue to keep from giving him over to me?"

"I did not and would not do that!" The golden-haired champion replied. For all the anger in his voice, Ferdiad still did not turn to face Maeve, but held his guarding-position with his shield up before her. " Many of the wren-boys were masked, and who would have thought there was cause to fear them?"

"Who, indeed?" Maeve retorted sharply. "How could Cú Chulainn have gotten into our camp in the first place? A man of his fame."

"A small, dark-haired youth?" Ferdiad answered. "How many such are there in our host, as charioteers and servants? No man knows every other in this army; and who would question, say, a youth coming out of the woods with a couple of new-cut chariot-poles?"

'Even Orlamh mistook the Hound for a charioteer.' Maeve's heart twisted with fresh grief. She looked at the limp tiny bundle of feathers, blood pooling where its head had been, and swiped at her tears with the back of her bloodied hand. She had gutted men in battle, taken their heads; there was no reason for sickness to twist her belly as she gazed on the beheaded bird. Nor could she fall to her knees and weep. Connla's words at Baiscne's death had been harsh, but reminded her of the truth. A ruler could not show weakness, thrice as true for a queen, and thrice more when the weakness was real.

"Every guard, henceforth," Maeve told him, her voice harsh and grim. "He could have killed me more easily than my wren. That sling-ball came in low and straight: he was not fifty paces away."

The sound of Ferdiad's sigh was lost in the shouting around them, but Maeve saw his huge shoulders heave and fall.

"My queen I failed in my duty to you. Send me away, if you will."

"No." Maeve's fury was already fading, leaving only dull sick sorrow behind. "I need Connacht's champion on this raid. I had no thought that the wren-boys might hide a foe in their midst, nor did anyone else." She bent down to pick up the little feathered corpse, what a tiny thing the wren had been!

She missed Baiscne most grievously. When Cú Chulainn had shot the pine marten from her shoulder, she had been ashamed of the thin thread of relief woven with her mourning. For the power beneath Cruachan síd was also one of the great roots of her own rule, and even though the síde-king might know her weakened and seek to take advantage, the risk that came with clinging to her strength had seemed better to her than the certainty of abandoning all.

'He has raped away the beasts of my power, Maeve thought. Is it contempt that has kept him from shooting me myself, or is there something he fears will come to pass if he slays me? Or could he not strike me directly while hound and marten and wren were there to take the blows?'

Furious, heartbroken, and impatient, Maeve waited in the ring-fort of her guards while her army hunted Cú Chulainn.

"Get him, get him," she murmured, not knowing if it was an order or a prayer.

The queen winced slightly as tents toppled beneath the onslaught and she heard the cracking of a wicker bothy-frame. Occasional yelps of pain broke the baying cries of her warriors. 'No surprise, Maeve thought unhappily. With so many men running with their weapons out, there must be accidents'. it would be worth the losses if Cú Chulainn could be slain. 'His head, next to Conchobar's, on the pillars of Cruachan! She thought. Then my losses would be avenged. Orlamh...' At last the clamor began to fade. Fergus came up to her, a broken wicker stag-mask and a sling dangling in his hands. The ring of Maeve's guards parted to let him in, then closed behind him again.

"He was disguised as one of the wren-boys," Fergus said.

Maeve nodded. "Ferdiad thought that was likeliest. He slipped behind a tent or bothy to shoot at me, then dropped his mask and sling...even joined the hunt for himself, until he could get away?"

"It seems likely. Is that your own blood?"

"A little," Maeve answered, touching the graze on her face again. "Most of it was my wren's."

Fergus looked at the little corpse, shaking his head. "You should come and wash yourself, lest it be thought that Cú Chulainn harmed you. I will watch the queen for now," Fergus told her guards. "Even were Cú Chulainn to still be hiding among us, he will not assail her, while she is with me."

Maine Cairbre and Maine Feidhlim glared suspiciously at the Ulsterman, but Ferdiad said, "That is true. Cú Chulainn is Fergus' foster son, and he would rather be beaten on his soles with willow-whips from Beltaine to Samhain than dishonor Fergus' protection. Our queen will be safe with him; safer, perhaps, than with us," he added, his voice strained and unhappy.

Fergus clapped the younger man lightly on the shoulder.

"You could not have foreseen this, nor did I. Henceforth, unless Queen Maeve is with me, keep your shields up around her."

Maeve let Fergus hand over the mask and sling to Ferdiad and take her by the arm. He held her gently, but she could feel the huge strength lurking behind his light grip as he steered her alone. Maeve kept her head up, careful that her feet did not falter.

No one would have cause to think that Cú Chulainn's sling-ball had done her any great hurt; only she, and perhaps her Druids, would know the deeper harm of that stroke. As shaken as she was, Maeve did not notice at first that Fergus was leading her on a long route around the camp. 'So that I can be seen, she thought. I should have washed my face first.' At the edge of the camp, Fergus spoke quietly to two of the guards. His grasp on Maeve's arm tightened a little, firm and comforting; but instead of turning back among the host, he started out across the thin strip of frost-paled dead grass that separated the army's camp from the nearby woods.

They had nearly reached the first low-growing tangles of dark holly when Maeve's head seemed to clear. She halted in her tracks, staring at Fergus.

"What are you trying to do?" She demanded. "Are you taking me to…" To give me over to Cú Chulainn? She wondered. She could not say that to Fergus' face, nor even believe it. "Is Cú Chulainn out here?"

"Not to my knowledge. He has struck his blow; we will not find him so easily, nor will it be in his mind to seek us here, and if he did, he will not strike while you are with me." Fergus' voice was quiet and certain, his hawk-proud face set in a mask of calm, but a little vein throbbed in his forehead.

"Yet no one can break wind in an army camp without everyone hearing, and I would be with you alone."

His grey eyes met hers, dark and hot as iron warming in the forge. A shiver ran through Maeve's body. She had wanted Fergus, and he her; Brigid and the Dagda might witness that it was still so. They walked between the frost-whitened trunks of tall ash-trees and glossy holly-thickets. A single bird twittered somewhere above; the only other sound was their shoes crunching on the fallen leaves. They climbed up a little rise, skirting a hollow and half-rotten log, its crumbling blackness locked beneath a thin scum of ice. When Maeve looked back, her army was altogether lost to view.

"Fergus," Maeve whispered, and reached out to caress his face, feeling the thin slick line of the scar on his cheek cutting through the short-cropped hair of his beard like a river running between thick trees. Her fingers tingled at the touch of his skin, chill, but with a deep heat banked beneath.

"Maeve." Then Fergus grasped her in his powerful embrace, fastening his mouth hungrily on her own. Though his lips were cold, his tongue seemed almost burning-hot as it caressed her, and Maeve tightened her own grasp on him, her breaths coming hard and fast. Sweet fire flared from her womb, her nipples and the soft flesh between her legs swollen and tight with sudden urgency.

Sword-calloused hands sure even in his haste, Fergus stripped off his mantle and her own, laying them down on the hoar frosted leaves. The icy air brushed pleasantly over Maeve's heated flesh as she pulled off her long scarlet tunic and trousers, standing bare before him.

A sharp pang of doubt pierced her: 'am I too old? Am I no longer fair enough?' Fergus's fingers tore at his sword-belt and ripped his breech-strings in trembling urgency.

His spear jutted thick and awesome from his loins, a single crystal drop glittering at its end. Maeve reached for him. She could not wrap one hand all the way around his manhood; its hot silky hardness seemed to burn like a bar of iron drawn from the fire.

"Now, Fergus!" Maeve panted. The thoughts whirling in her head 'Be with me; drive out my fear and sorrow and loss; pour your own into me, and transform it into delight, if only for a moment', could find no better voice than that. "Now!"

Fergus pulled Maeve down on top of their cloaks as he thrust deep into her. Her flesh tightened on him in one exquisite spasm, powerful as the pangs of childbirth. Fergus' mouth opened, gasping, dizzied for air. His face contorted in what might have been ecstasy or deathly pain as he pushed himself in again and again and she arched to meet him.

Each time he beat against the roots of Maeve's body and his heavy stone-sack slapped against her raised buttocks, her body resounded to his thumping blows like a great drum, rising louder and louder as she thrust up to meet him. His hands closed on her breasts, stroking and squeezing; the waves of pleasure battered back and forth through her body until she felt him swell and pulse and spill a hot wave, and screamed in absolute release.

Fergus did not withdraw straight away, but moved carefully to lie beside Maeve, still deeply nested between her thighs. His grey eyes were soft now as he looked at her; the harshness of his face eased, and it seemed to Maeve that she gazed at the young man who had been king of Ulster.

"Maeve," he whispered, his voice drunken-thick. "Will you take me for your own?"

Maeve's body was still trembling with small internal quivers, her limbs flopping warm and relaxed. She barely heard Fergus' words through the slowing beat of her own heart, and they made little sense to her. "For your own?" She repeated drowsily.

"If Ailill were no longer your husband, then what would the White Bull or the Brown mean to you? This raid has been costly enough; we could end it, and I..."

Fergus was not drunk on mead, but on her flesh, Maeve knew. His tongue, and heart, were loosened all the same, and his wit cast aside like a burden.

"No," she murmured. "Our host will not go home without plunder or utter defeat. I could command it, but our allies would pay no heed now. Nor would it change matters for me if I cast Ailill aside, "and," Maeve added with sudden understanding, feeling again all that had passed between them, "it is not I you truly love, but the White Mare of Ulster."

Fergus grunted, a deep soft noise as if a sword-point had just punched into his guts and he were only waiting for the pain to start. Maeve knew she had touched the truth, and closed her eyes. Tears slid hot down her cheeks, stinging fiercely on the sling-ball graze along her jaw. How long has he been thinking this? She wondered. 'Since the raid on Rath Echach, when he called me by the land-goddess' title? And if his hope was so great that a man of his age and wisdom in leading warriors could blind himself to our position. How cruel to dash it?'

Fergus lay silent. Maeve could not speak either, but she bent to kiss him, the salt of her own tears mingling with the sweetness of his mouth. She still held him inside her; carefully, so as not to lose him, she shifted her position until she straddled Fergus' powerful thighs and slowly began to move around him again, her golden hair falling over her shoulders to brush the broad taut curves of his chest.

"If we cannot be king and queen," she said, "at least we may comfort each other."

Fergus shook his head, his eyes grey pools of rain. Maeve could feel him swelling huge within her again, his hips starting to answer to her rhythm. She gasped and cried out, pushing herself down on him harder and faster. His arms locked tight about her once more, and he drew her head down to kiss her deeply, murmuring something into her mouth that she could not make out.

Fedelm

Calatín had given me leave to spend Midwinter's day at my own pleasure. It was a strange feeling, to stand with a goblet of hot cider in my hand watching the wren-boys and their White Mare capering and singing, and knowing that, if only for the space of this day, I was free to do as I would. Free from study and healing, free from the burdensome mission my visions had laid on me. It had been ten years since I had been able thus to turn a moment from the long track of Druidic training.

Now I found myself unsure of what to do, but enjoying it greatly. I hummed along with the wren-boys' lively song, admiring how they leapt and kicked and sang to the tune of trumpa and drum, like young goats prancing from sheer delight. Then, somewhere behind the wren's procession, I heard Maeve screaming,

"Cú Chulainn is in the camp. Cú Chulainn is among us!" In a heartbeat, all the laughter and song dissolved into shrieks and cries of rage. A big warrior banged against me as he barreled past almost without noticing me, dashing the cider from my goblet. I stumbled, trying to regain my footing, and someone else shouldered me aside, the hardened leather and iron plate of his armor bruising-rough against my back.

"Out of my way, bitch!" He shouted.

I backed as close to one of the tents as I could, trying to draw myself up into a semblance of Druidic dignity. Bitch! I would speak a satire that would raise blisters on every inch of his flesh,

That would. I did not know the man's name, had not even seen his face, only a brown shock of hair and beard. It might have been Cúr mac Da Lóth, that ill-tempered fellow whose pinching fingers I had learned to fear at thirteen. I thought that was even likely, but I could no more lay a curse without clear knowledge than I could speak a legal judgement against a man on the basis of a fleeting glimpse and a ten-year old grudge.

Nor had he given me bad advice. I seemed in the middle of some mad battle with no clear friends or foes, as the warriors of Maeve's host turned inward. Everywhere I looked, men were running about with drawn weapons, swords slashing through the frosty air and spear-shafts swinging about as their wielders whirled, as often or not clouting the men behind them. Two men and one woman, all big and armed. Ailill's Leinster warriors, I thought, charged up to the tent where I stood.

The broader of the two men, a giant with thick black hair curling out from under his helmet, roared, "Get out of the way!" He reached for my arm, but this time I was ready, stepping aside and fixing him with a stern glare. His broad-mustached face cleared, his jaw dropping. "You! I'm sorry, but please move, ban-drúi! The Hound may be hiding inside a tent or bothy; he shot at the queen."

I could not help flinching. If Cú Chulainn was able to get into the camp unrecognized and shoot at Maeve, then every one of us must live at his mercy, and we had seen the worth of that already. I moved aside, and the three Leinster fighters barged into the tent. Within, a woman shrieked in fright, or perhaps indignation; on the way out, one of the warriors must have knocked against the center pole, for the fragile structure slumped at a precarious angle behind them.

All I could do was try my best to dodge the large bodies hurtling about me and make my way towards the royal enclosure and Calatín's tent. Someone's spear-shaft caught me on the back of the head, dazing me and bringing the tears to my eyes. I heard a youth squealing in pain, and the sound of blows thumping hard into flesh before a man shouted,

"That's not him, you fool, I know that boy. Keep looking!"

'I should have worn my white robe', I thought, stumbling towards my teacher, and safety. At least the men guarding the leaders' tents had not given in to panic. Maeve's son Maine Feidhlim was in charge of the guard here. He took me gently by the elbow, steadying me and guiding me in past the wicker fence.

"Is my mother all right?" He asked anxiously. For all his size, I realized, Feidhlim was younger than I, his reddish-gold mustache a thin sketch of his father's and his blue eyes wide in a softly freckled face.

"She was able to raise the cry after the Hound of Ulster," I said. "I did not see her, but her voice was strong and I heard no pain in it: I doubt she is hurt."

"How could he have gotten in among us?" Maine Feidhlim asked. "Our camp is well-guarded…"

I thought of a beetle burrowing, small, black, and baneful, into flesh, and shuddered, for I already knew the answer to the young prince's question.

"Would you recognize Cú Chulainn if he stood before you?" I asked. "Has anyone here, save those who have dwelt in Ulster before, seen his face?" I shivered again, for it came to me that I myself did not know what Cú Chulainn looked like in the flesh.

Only that he was short and slight, dark-haired, and beardless, as the boy I had heard screaming no doubt was. If he stayed out of the Ulstermen's cantred, the Hound could have been traveling with us for days, waiting his chance to strike. I shivered. Derg-daol, Suithchern had called him, the black-blood beetle of ill-luck and terror and death: the likeness could not be denied.

"Fraech's companions saw him," Feidhlim said, "and…" He shut his mouth, his jaw tightening beneath its scattering of fine bronze hairs, recalling his brother's death, I guessed.

Save those who had watched the fight between Fraech and the Hound, no one who had encountered Cú Chulainn on this raid would be able to tell of it, unless their heads were made to speak.

"Every youth who looks something like him must be vouched for and watched," Maine Feidhlim said, the thoughts struggling slowly from his mouth. "Charioteers and servants must stay with their own cantreds, where they are known. Else…" He did not finish, but I followed his trail well enough. If one young man could be beaten in mistake for Cú Chulainn, how many others had been?

Or killed, when the shock of realizing that our foe had slipped among us was so great that our warriors could batter a ban-drúi in their rough haste?

"Else he turns us against ourselves, and makes enemies of our own," I murmured.

My head was aching quite nastily where the spear-shaft had banged against it, and I could feel several other bruises beginning to stiffen my shoulders and arms. Feidhlim looked unhappily out at the camp, where the clamorous hunt continued. A number of tents had been toppled and bothies smashed already; I could see one man lying limp on the ground, and a couple of others nursing wounds and trying to keep clear of the running and shouting.

"Are you harmed?" Calatin's dry voice asked behind me. I started sharply, my hand going to my mouth to stifle a little cry.

"Ah…no," I stammered, turning to face my teacher. "Only a little bruised."

Calatín had put on his white robe, and held a pale wand of polished wood in his hand, the very image of a Druid serene in his power.

"Cú Chulainn is gone. Now I must go out to bring what calm I can and see to the wounded. Go to my tent, tend to your bruises, and drink some of my wife's good mead if it please you. I shall not ask more of you this day."

Nuagal's mead was very fine, rich and sweet-scented, but dry on the tongue, pleasantly flavored with meadowsweet and a dusting of powdered hemp flowers. By the time I had downed my second goblet, the ointment I had put on my bruises, comfrey root and marigold and yarrow, simmered with beeswax and flax-seed oil into a smooth green paste, already seemed to be easing the stiffness, and the pain at the back of my skull was a distant memory. The shouting and bashing outside the royal enclosure had largely died down when I had finished my third cup, and I was feeling warm and easy in all my limbs.

Even discovering that the sleeve of my fine purple dress had been torn in the scuffling and there were mud-stains upon it was no more than a prickle of irritation now. 'I can wash and mend it easily enough. In such a camp as this, there is no doubt that one of the kings' or chieftains' servants will have purple thread to lend me'. Still, I knew I ought to change clothes, wash my face, and comb my hair before I went where others might see me. I was just stepping out of Calatín's tent when I saw Ailill's charioteer Cuillius coming towards the king's tent, a naked sword in his hand. I froze, the tent-flap in my hand, murmuring the words Calatín had taught me to turn the eyes of others aside.

'What madness is this? I thought. Is Ailill in danger within – or does his charioteer seek to kill the king?' I looked back into the tent, eyes searching for something like a weapon.

Calatín had either borne his sword hidden beneath his robe, or hidden it well, but I knew where he kept the sacrificial knives. Glancing back out for a second, to make sure I was not too late, a spark of light from the gleaming hilt of the charioteer's sword caught fire in my eyes. I blinked, and stared.

The Gauls made the best blades, but only one man in the host bore a Gaulish sword with such a hilt, a man of gilded bronze, his head forming the pommel, ball-ended arms curling out for the upper guard and legs curved as quillions. It was Fergus' sword; and the charioteer was not striding like a man in the grip of fury or madness or enchantment with the weapon's hilt gripped to attack, but holding the blade uncertainly away from himself, his eyes lowered and darting like one who brings bad news to a powerful man.

'Is Fergus dead? Did he trust Cú Chulainn to return his love, and find himself wrong?'

Silent and unseen, I followed Cuillus to the door of Ailill's tent, standing just outside so that I could listen, and act, if my first thought had been right. If nothing else, I could stand before Ailill to protect him as a Druid.

That inviolability might go unnoticed in a maddened horde of warriors, but no single man could mistake my status, if he were in his right mind, I thought. Still, I would do what I could.

"Well," Ailill said calmly as his charioteer stepped inside.

"Well, indeed," Cuillius answered, voice trembling a little. "Here is your sign. I found them lying together in the woods, as you thought."

Ailill laughed softly, a familiar sound, but edged with a new keenness. "Fair enough. She does it to keep his help on this raid, no doubt. Now, keep this sword well. Put it under your chariot seat with a piece of linen around it."

I did not pause to hear what more was said. Instead I slipped back to Calatín's tent. It hardly seemed to matter anymore that my sleeve was torn and my hair disheveled. There had been no need for me to fight or speak for Ailill's life. Light as his voice had been, I knew he was wounded, and that I might give aid. I filled my goblet, carrying it carefully before me in both hands. At the door of Ailill's tent, I set aside the charm of passing unseen, and stepped in before my trembling legs could betray me. Cuillius had gone, and there was no sign of Fergus' sword anywhere. Ailill sat alone on the edge of his bed, his bright-braided head in his hands.

He glanced up as I came in, blue-green eyes dazed and dark pupils wide, as though he had just taken a wound to the head.

"What is it you wish, Fedelm?" He said courteously. "Have you come with a prophecy for me?"

I held out the goblet to him. "The woman who bears you this goblet wishes to offer her friendship, and bring you joy, my king."

Ailill reached out. His fingers covered mine on the white bronze stem in a firm, gentle caress, but he did not take it from me yet. "Are you sure, Fedelm?" He murmured. "You are half my age, and I believe you are maiden still. Would you give me that gift?"

"I would," I answered.

Despite the mead I had drunk, my mouth was dry, my heart hammering a wild river of blood through my veins. Ailill was so fine to look on! No stripling, but a man in his full strength. Though the late sorrow of his son's loss had grooved new furrows about his mouth, his face was still carved by years of laughter and a warm heart. He took the goblet from me and drained it, then drew me in to sit in his lap. I felt small in his powerful embrace, but at the same time very safe, and I could also feel his rising manhood pressing against the backs of my thighs.

As I had dreamed for weeks, my arms went about Ailill's neck, my hands feeling for the silver wires that bound up his intricately-twined braids. One by one I loosened them, combing my fingers through his wealth of thick red-gold hair. Even in the tent's dimness, it gleamed like a fall of precious metal, but so soft, far softer than I had ever dreamed, like a thick bundle of fine silken threads. Ailill's lips touched my mouth, warm and gentle, the wings of his mustaches stroking across my face. I felt as though I were melting within, and yet at the same time I could feel my limbs trembling with a strange urgency, and pressed in closer to the muscular hardness of his body.

Ailill's large hand stroked down across my breasts, caressing and teasing my left nipple. A keen pang of pleasure fluttered through me from his touch; I found myself arching my back to press harder against him, and throwing back my head. He kissed me, soft and tender, all down the line of my throat, the warmth of his lips shivering through my whole body, the sweet moist throbbing between my legs resonating like a harp's sounding-board to a bard's caress on the strings. Slowly he drew my dress up over my head as I moved to help him, leaving me naked upon his lap.

"So young, and so fair," he whispered. "Fedelm, are you truly sure...?"

"Yes, yes!"

I reached between his legs for the hard staff of his manhood, grasping it with sudden urgency.

"Careful," Ailill gasped softly. "That is not a tool for rough handling, yes, there!"

My hands were uncertain, fumbling on his breech-ties, but at last he stood free and proud. I had seen men upright before, hard to avoid, in the closeness of our narrow bunks at the school, and more so in an army camp, but I paused for a moment, awed at the broad ivory column rising from its red-gilded nest, the shape and flare more perfectly turned than any craftsman could manage. 'Can I truly take all that inside me?'

I wondered; but it was no real fear I felt, only a playful likeness that goaded my excitement higher. I stroked him with the tips of my fingers, the skin stretched over his hardness was so silken and fine that I could hardly believe it, the heavier fold about the swollen tip as soft as a newborn lamb's ear. I reached down further, caressing the soft skin and light covering of hair that hid Ailill's heavy stones from view, and he moaned, gently pulling me back upon the bed.

His head bowed, suckling softly at one nipple; one hand played at my other breast, his other hand moved between my legs, touching the little kernel at the threshold of my gateway. A thrill of pleasure that drowned out all the rest shot through me, and I cried out, moving my hips to the gentle rhythm of his hand as he stroked me and slowly pressed a single finger inward.

"Oh, yes!" I whispered. "Yes, Ailill!" Simple words for a ban-fili; but maybe we are all alike, when overcome with such pleasure that nothing save our lover exists in all the worlds. Ailill seemed to know everything that could no longer find words to shape it in my mind, for he guided my delight with such a tender and cunning strength that I felt only a single sharp bite of pain as he eased into me, and that was gone in a moment, lost in the deeper convulsions of pleasure that shook through me again and again, until he thrust with a greater urgency that drove me to fling my head back and cry out with no words at all. Then he stiffened above me, and I felt a greater wash of heat and wetness through the sweet moist place where we joined.

Shivering with the echoes of delight, the sweat slowly cooling on my skin, I thought: Now I am no longer a maid; now I have Ailill's seed within me. Brigid grant that it kindle!

Ailill kissed me again. "You have given me a wondrous gift, Fedelm. Is all well with you?"

"It is very well," I answered. I did not think I could stand; the muscles of my thighs were still quivering, and my limbs felt all unstrung. Ailill pulled the coverlet over us. I had not noticed how chill the air was until the warmth of the blanket covered us both, but I cuddled closer to him.

Eventually, though, it had to end. Deftly and gently, Ailill helped me to clean myself. There was less blood than I had expected, only a little lost among the black-and-brown heathering of the blanket, and a few smears on the whiteness of his belly and my thighs; there was more of a mess where his seed drained out as I sat up. When we were both fully dressed, Ailill embraced and kissed me once more.

"It will be well between you and Maeve again," I said, leaning my head back to look up into his brilliant blue eyes. I did not know whether I spoke from true foresight, or from hope for his sake, but his gaze softened a moment, the softness of the faint mist that cloaks the first sight of land between even the brightest sea and sky.

"Thank you," Ailill whispered. There seemed little more either of us could say, but I leaned my head on the powerful muscles of his chest, listening to the soft rhythms of his heart for a moment.

Maeve

Flidais had spoken true, Maeve thought, when she had said that lying once with Fergus was worth any seven times with ordinary men. She ached a little within as they walked back from the woods, but it was a warm and pleasurable ache; her body felt heavy and relaxed, and she wished for nothing more than to lie down and sleep while the pleasant thoughtlessness of their lovemaking was still on her. Striding beside her, Fergus was silent.

His face had hardened again, and Maeve could not tell his thoughts, though he had muttered something about having done wrong to Ailill. 'He knows now that I will not forsake Ailill for him. No harm was done; and perhaps this was needful. Still, I wish that I could have eased his heart longer, and not had to deal him more pain.' Maeve's guards met them as they came into camp, taking their places around her with their shields up, and she forced her thoughts to the matters at hand. The hunt for Cú Chulainn had wrought more devastation than she had seen at first. A number of tents had been destroyed, and at least one was burning.

The White Mare's wicker framework lay woven in on its side, its white covering torn and muddied and the horse-skull's lower jaw missing. Calatín, clad in the white robe of his office, crouched over a body on the ground, rising as the queen neared him.

"Two dead, and several badly injured," the Druid said. "And the Hound escaped cleanly, though I had to call Ferdiad to make sure that this was not the one we sought."

Maeve glanced at the body. She wondered how Ferdiad could have been sure: the face beneath the cropped black hair had been battered into an oozing mess.

"This cannot go on! What manner of creature is he, to kill and turn us on each other thus?"

"A wise one, for all his youth," Calatín answered dryly. "For only thus can one man, even though a hero, fight an army. We are barely two day's march from Cuailgne, and it is time for you to bend your thoughts to how you may find the Donn Cuailgne, since Fedelm says he has left his pasture."

"I shall call a full council on the morrow," Maeve said.

There was no more celebration that day: the host of Eriu was busy repairing the damage it had wrought upon itself, and no one was minded to see maskers.

Inside the shield-ring of her guards, Maeve was already frustrated: tall as she was, her sons and most of her champions were even taller, and it was hard for her to see much between their broad backs and long oval shields. Nevertheless, she went about the camp, doing her best to ease the minds of her warriors and turn their thoughts towards the plunder that would be had in Cuailgne and the glory of winning the Brown Bull for Connacht. Evening came early, on the year's longest night, and Maeve returned to the royal enclosure as the sunset began to flush the evening sky like a blush on a maiden's white cheek.

Fergus was just going into Ailill's tent ahead of her. Maeve paused, wondering if she should be worried. She knew that she had done Ailill no wrong, but Fergus might think differently, and he had sought and even hoped, though he only spoke of it for a moment, to take her husband's place. Eavesdropping was an unworthy skill for a queen; but she had learned the way of it in Ulster, to survive, and she had not completely forgotten how to listen while pretending to do something else altogether. She settled down before the fire, calling Lochu to bring her spears for sharpening, and listened while she began to hone her sword.

"Missing something, Fergus?" Ailill said, his voice light with jest.

Maeve's whetstone stopped in mid-stroke. She held her breath. What has Ailill done? The first thought that went through her head was a gruesome image of Fergus deprived of the mighty stallion's emblems from which his power still rose.' No, Fergus would not have let that happen without a fight. There would have been war between his Ulster exiles and Ailill's Leinster folk, before...'

"It seems that I am," Fergus said heavily. "You called me here to play fidchell with you; I hardly need a sword for that."

"Nor for your feats in the wood, it seems. Seldom does a hero lay his sword aside for combat as you did this day." Ailill laughed heartily. As well as Maeve knew her husband, she could still hear no trace of anger in his voice. 'Either he is truly without jealousy, even for Fergus, or he feels that he has the upper hand now: he will tease Fergus until he is tired, and then let the matter go, as he always does unless he is pressed. I have not learned all his depths, not after more than twenty years of rule and raising eight children together'.

"Now sit down and we shall play fidchell, if you are recovered from your woodland drunkenness. Don't be surprised: I know, better than you, what Maeve's cup does to men. There is no need for us to quarrel, there are mares aplenty in the camp."

Maeve bit her lip, hardly noticing Lochu with her spears. The bondswoman laid the weapons on the ground by her and crept away. 'Now Ailill is going too far, to twit Fergus with his loss of Ulster. She rose to her feet. It may be that I can stop this before Ailill's humor forces Fergus to fight him. I do not know which would beat the other, but I know that I would not see either wounded or slain.' Yet when she stepped into Ailill's tent, Fergus was sitting down on the stool, while Ailill lounged on the bed.

Her king's fidchell-board was on the little table between them, the bronze board with its graven squares gleaming dull in the torchlight, the gold and silver pieces pegged into it sparking with flashes of bright red fire as Ailill took up the gold king piece, turning it in his hand and setting it down again in the king's home-square at the center. Fergus' face was flushed with anger, his thin scar shining dark crimson and the heavy muscles of his shoulders bunching, but his hands lay empty on the table. Then Maeve saw what Ailill had been referring to.

Instead of the gold man-hilt of his Gaulish sword, a rough-carved piece of wood jutted from the scabbard at Fergus' side. 'He cast his sword-belt away in his eagerness for me, Maeve recalled vaguely. While I lay sated, he walked into the wood, saying he had done Ailill a wrong, and when we came back, he stayed on my left, so that I would not see his sword was missing.' Maeve opened her mouth to shout at Ailill.

How dared he spy on them, and shame Fergus so. She knew her husband's ease was deceptive. He could draw and strike from where he was in a single murderous motion, and if Fergus was unarmed, he was still a mighty man to contend with. Fergus moved one of the silver attackers a square along the edge of the board without looking up at Maeve, but Ailill raised a hand to greet her. "Have you come to play fidchell with us, Maeve?" He asked casually, shifting one of the four inner defenders a square along on the other side.

"As may be, but my mind is more upon the Brown Bull."

"Perhaps it ought to be, since we are but a day and a half from Cuailgne now, if Cú Chulainn does not find another trick to deceive us with," Ailill added, his voice hardening.

Fergus looked vaguely at the silver peg-man in his hand, setting it down on the board next to one of the outer four defenders. A skilled fidchell-player herself, Maeve could see no sense to his second move. Perhaps Ailill did not either; he moved swiftly to set another of his defenders on the silver warrior's other side, trapping it between two gold pieces and plucking it from the board. The two men played for a little while. The advantage was often to the attackers, with their greater numbers, but Ailill was unusually skilled on the king's side. H

e played fidchell very like he fought. Secure in his skill, he took few risks, carefully marshaling his defenses to block his opponent's threats rather than trying to take every piece he could, but striking with lightning-deadliness when he saw a devastating move clear. That was often the best way for the fidchell-king to reach the board's edge in safety, or for Ailill to kill his foes. The two men were usually a good match, Fergus pressing as fiercely as Ailill defended, but Fergus was hardly paying attention to the game.

"It isn't right," Ailill said in a satisfied manner, moving his king piece down the clear path to the edge of the board, and victory, "that death should take this sweet little king on his coppery board tonight. Indeed, it seems to me that without your sword, it is hard for you to strike a good blow, though you have struck your only blows on this raid without it, thus far."

Fergus glanced up from beneath lowering dark brows. "Aye, I lay with Maeve. I have heard it said that she chose you for your lack of jealousy, as well as your open hands and noble blood and prowess in fighting. Mayhap you should prove that now."

Maeve spoke up before Fergus could go further.

"We are one troop, with one enemy. Truly, Ailill, there is no need for you to worry whom I share the friendship of my thighs with. Has that ever come between us before, any more than I have chided you for sharing the king's blessing with my women?"

"Not ever," Ailill answered. "Still, it seems to me that Fergus has no need of his sword here. He does not wish to raise it against the folk of Ulster, nor his old friends of the Red Branch; and it is not he whom Cú Chulainn threatens. What does a scout or guide need with a sword?"

The muscles along Fergus' jaw tightened, but his grey eyes, black in the dimness, slid to the side. 'He feels truly shamed, or his pride would have brought them to blows before now', Maeve thought.

"I am little willing to slaughter old friends, or raise my sword against those for whom I was once the shield," Fergus answered. " I came, not only to aid you, but to win my vengeance against Conchobar. I did not battle him for the kingship; I was loyal to him, as I have been to you. Fiacha's blood, and that of Uisnech's sons shall cry out until I redden my blade in Conchobar's own, and for that, I must have my own sword!"

Ailill grinned. "Well, when Conchobar rises to do battle with us, I shall give it back. Until then, I think you have shown that you are as well-armed as you need to be, isn't he, Maeve?"

To any other man, Maeve would have answered that Fergus bore a mightier weapon than he. If Ailill were indulging his taste for sharp jesting, he would deserve it. if he felt hurt by what she and Fergus had done well, he had borne enough sorrow on this raid. She would not add to it, not in this tent where Orlamh's head lay, preserved with herbs and salt and oil and waiting to be brought home.

Fergus, whatever moved him, his shame, the remains of his friendship with Ailill, or perhaps a whisper of relief at his enforced freedom from fighting in Ulster, nodded his head curtly.

"Perhaps that is fair," he said. "In any case, I suppose I can do nothing about it."

Ailill raised a bright eyebrow.

"Maybe you could. If our oaths still hold…"

"As they do," Fergus answered, and though his voice was still rough-edged as a sword after a hard battle, Maeve was certain she heard a tinge of relief in it.

Ailill stood as Fergus left the tent, and Maeve tensed. He had never laid an angry hand on her, never struck her at all, save with wooden weapons when they sparred, and she usually gave a little better than she got. His shape and stance, a looming male figure, with the torch behind him so that the shadows hid his face, awakened fears she had thought long slain. Conchobar, striding into their bedroom; his fist crashing into the pit of her belly, driving her air out in a gasping wave of pain; his rough grasp half-jerking her arm from the socket as he flung her face-down onto the bed.

"Maeve, what is wrong?" Ailill asked, stopping.

Maeve realized that she was breathing fast, her hand tight on her sword-hilt, too tight, her fingers almost numb and her arm aching with tension; she could not have struck a good blow thus had she needed to. Maeve forced her hand loose, pressing her palm flat against her thigh. Instead of striking or fleeing, she stepped into Ailill's gentle embrace, his familiar touch, his scent, so different from Conchobar's.

'He needs this, as do I, Maeve thought. Fergus sated me well; but Ailill knows how to arouse me again. Perhaps, if there is truly aught amiss between us because of this day's doings, lying with Ailill now will help to heal it'. Maeve wanted to tell Ailill that she had refused Fergus' offer, that it had been doomed before the Ulster exile ever voiced it, but that would mean letting him know what Fergus had hoped, and then there would never be peace between the two of them.

"You are my husband and my king. Drink from my cup," Maeve said.

Ailill lowered his mouth to hers, kissing her passionately, but carefully, as though he must drain a goblet in one draught without spilling a single drop of the precious mead. Maeve could not truly guess what would come after; but for tonight, at least, it would be well between them.

Perhaps Cú Chulainn felt he had done enough harm for now; or perhaps the wall of Maeve's guardsmen, with their shields raised to protect her from arching shots and their broad bodies between her and closer attacks, was enough to dissuade him. In any case, he made no assaults the next day. Maeve called a full council for that evening. Flidais set out a great feast in the royal enclosure, and Finnabair circled between kings and chieftains, filling their cups and speaking with each of them, though never too long with any one.

Flidais had wanted to kill one of the swine from Rath Echach, but Maeve forbade her. Men had come to death-blows over a champion's portion before, and while it was well for the leaders of the cantreds to vie for success and glory, she wanted them to compete in gaining victory on her raid, not in striking each other before they had even crossed into Cuailgne.

"Now it seems to me," Maeve said when everyone had eaten well and sat with cups or goblets of mead in their hands, "that we would do well to divide our host. Fedelm tells me that the Brown Bull has left his pasture, and it will not be easy seeking him through the mountains of Cuailgne, nor easy driving him back.

Dáire mac Fiachna put insult on all the folk of Connacht when he refused us the Bull and swore that we could not take it from him by force of arms; and to answer that, I mean to see every holding in his land stripped of cattle and wealth and every captive we can take. One part of the army must turn to that task, while I go myself to capture the Brown Bull."

"The men of Munster will raid!" Connla said fiercely. He raised a ringed fist in the air, gold bracelets jangling down his scarlet sleeve. "Let Connacht herd the Bull, while we do the fighting."

"Such as it is, with Ulster's men still in their pangs," Ailill remarked. "Though it is true that there is no knowing when they will rise again, for their torment has gone on longer than was ever known before: they could leap from their beds tomorrow."

Fergus shook his head, his chestnut hair rippling over his wide shoulders.

"Not so. They will lie in a deathlike sleep for a little time, when the pangs end. We shall know before they rise. Now I shall charge you again, before any forget: do not harm any man who groans under Macha's curse, lest you bring it down upon yourself and your folk! Take what you can, but do not leave the men of Ulster to starve or lie untended in their pains. For that, too, will draw the goddess' wrath."

Cumail shifted on his stool, thick sandy brows beetling over his pale eyes. Connla laid a hand on his arm.

"It is good advice, whoever gives it," the Munsterman said to his fellow under-king. "Cuailgne is a rich land: there will be more than enough for all of us." The other chiefs of Munster were stirring as well, but Connla's dark look quieted them.

"Remember, as well, that we have come on this raid as one army," Maeve told the Munster kings sternly. "You will share in the renown of the Brown Bull's capture; we will share in the spoils of Cuailgne, as is the custom. Ailill and Flidais shall lead the harriers around the mountains, while I take my part of the host after the Bull. The Ulstermen under Cormac and Fergus shall come with me, for some of them know the land here and can more easily guess where the Donn Cuailgne is wandering." And Fergus, and the rest, will be spared the sight of their country folk harried and led off in bonds.

Ailill looked sharply at Maeve, then Fergus, his mouth tightening. he would not argue, not with Connla ready to leap on any weakness like a weasel pouncing on a wounded bird.

"Aye, that is how we must go about it," he said. "And that is easily done, for our host is already divided into cantreds, each marching and camping with its own, under its own leader. So be it: Connacht to the Bull, Leinster, Munster, and Meath to the harrying."

Connla leaned forward, hunter's eyes gleaming in his narrow face.

"What of Finnabair? Surely she should go with the harriers and see our deeds of arms; bull-herding is no task for a noble maiden."

Before Maeve could take offense, Finnabair stepped forward, tossing her long golden hair back and setting a delicate hand on Connla's shoulder.

"It is kind of you to think of me," her soft voice said. " I am my mother's charioteer in all save battle. I will not leave that duty unless I must, and driving through the mountains of Cuailgne, it is best that the queen's chariot bear as little weight as possible. Be sure, I will hear of your deeds, and those who do best shall have the highest place in my thoughts."

Connla grunted, but subsided. Then there was only the talk of the roads and paths to be followed. Cormac, who might have been Ulster's king after Conchobar, knew every fortress in Cuailgne, and had at least a rough guess at its strength.

"I wish that we could slay Dáire mac Fiachna, for his insults to my mother," the young man added. " Macha's doom protects even as it harms: I think the land-goddess of Connacht is a better one." Cormac's grin lightened the craggy knobs of his face to beauty, and Maeve wanted to embrace her son, even as she winced inwardly at his words.

When the other leaders had gone, Ailill sat staring into the fire, tugging at the end of one of his looping red-gold braids and wrapping it around and around his forefinger.

"This arrangement does not please you," Maeve said tentatively.

Ailill dropped his braid, meeting her eyes.

"I would sooner take my Leinstermen with Connacht's warriors. What if Ulster's men recover while our army is split? If Connacht alone could surely defeat the northern host, we should not have had to ask our daughter to charm Connla and his ilk."

"They are the very problem. I do not trust them without one of us there. Flidais is a good leader, but not, I think, the one to keep the Munstermen under control." Maeve rested her hand on her husband's thick forearm, feeling the play of his hard muscles beneath the skin. "There is no one in all this host whom I trust as I trust you."

Ailill gave her a long, considering look. "No one?"

"No one," Maeve replied firmly.

He sighed, smiling.

"If I am doomed to lose to you, I should like to see the Brown Bull's capture. From the tales of his size and fierceness, he will not prove easy to take, and more tales will come of that. Maybe I would like to know if he is Finnbennach's better, before we must set them to battle! It would be well for our herds, if we had both the Brown Bull and the White to service our cows."

"Maybe so. All the same, I cannot see any choice if our host must split, except that you must take the leadership of one part and I the other. I would have our sons go with you."

Ailill looked into the fire again, wrapping his bright-striped bratt more closely about himself as if the night's bitter cold had suddenly bitten him deep. The folds of the heavy mantle over his shoulders gave him an odd hunched look.

"You think that Cú Chulainn will follow you into the mountains."

"Yes."

"It will be easier for him to shoot unseen there."

"I am well guarded, so well guarded," Maeve added bitterly, "that I can barely see what is happening in my own army. In any case, it is I who has the leadership of this raid: should it not be I who takes the greater part of risk, if there is risk to take."

"He has shot close to you thrice, but not struck you, although he could have. Even though..." Ailill fell silent again. Maeve had never been certain whether Ailill knew exactly what her three beasts were to her. He was king and consort; but it was a different thing, to have felt the current of might that made her, at times, both queen and goddess: she would never know if he could truly understand.

"It is my risk." And more so than you can know, if Ochall's claim on me still holds now that the marten of Cruachan-below is dead.

Ailill shrugged. "Well, if it must be so, it must. I know better than to hold you back when your mind is set. As you love me, Maeve, I would suffer a great deal, rather than lose you."

"I shall take every care," Maeve promised. An unworthy suspicion was still niggling at her, like a rat gnawing into a grain-sack. "And if your part of the host finds the Donn Cuailgne..."

"I swear by the god of my clan that we will bring him to you alive and well," Ailill said. The fine lines at the corners of his bright blue-green eyes crinkled as he smiled at her.

"We would look like Eriu's greatest fools, would we not, if we came all this way on this raid, then slew the mighty bull we meant to take before he had a chance to come home and service all our heifers?"

"Aye, we would," Maeve agreed, grateful, for once, for Ailill's way of making light of the most serious things. Another man, Fergus, say, might have roared in anger and hurt at the hint of her suspicions, and driven them in the deeper thereby; Ailill's laughter eased her heart.

Maeve awoke to Lochu's sniffling as she came in with the pot of warm water for her mistress to wash in. "Whatever is the matter?" Maeve asked her bondsmaid.

Lochu tossed back her head, scrubbing the back of her hand across her eyes. "It is the maids of the kings of Munster," she said. "When I went to draw water for you, they pushed me aside. They said that the ones they served would be going into danger and battle, whereas the ruler I served was content to drive away cattle and never blood a blade; so they should go before me to draw unmuddied water."

"Did they, now! Did their masters tell them to speak thus?"

Lochu lowered her pale gaze.

"I do not know," she mumbled. "My queen, you may not know this; but a bondsmaid must take pride from the one she serves. You have always treated me well, and your service is not without honor. Servants jostle for place as warriors do. I think they may have overheard somewhat, taking it for a weapon in their own hands. Yet, if I have served you well, I would ask your help. I have accepted being a captive, and striven to do my best with what my fate decreed, but I will not accept scorn of those who were lower-born than I, the more when it insults you as well."

Maeve considered the girl for a long moment. Lochu's eyes were puffy and swollen, but the muscles of her jaw clenched in anger beneath her soft flesh. Her bronze-gold braid was half undone, the hair unraveling down her back like a careless spinner's thread fraying into loose wool again, and her plain brown bratt and dress were wet in spots. Still, for the first time, Maeve could see that Lochu had been born a chieftain's daughter: she stood prouder than she had in the queen's place at the Samhain ritual.

"Nor shall I accept it," Maeve assured her. "When you go to draw water this evening, you shall bear my own diadem again, as a sign to all of the rights that my rule gives you, and a sign that any who scorns you, captive or free, shall answer directly to me! The kings of Munster shall know that naught that is mine may be handled lightly, not in words or in deeds."

Lochu took Maeve's hands, her tear-stained face lighting. "Thank you, my queen!" She said. "If I had to be taken, I could have asked for no better service than yours."

Fedelm

"When Cú Chulainn took up arms for the first time, his battle-fury came on him for the first time as well. He wished to fight every man in Emain Macha to the death, but Conchobar sent the women of the fortress, even his own wife, out naked to show him their breasts. Cú Chulainn hid his face from them, and the warriors of Ulster were able to grasp him and plunge him into cold water. The first vat burst asunder; the second boiled with bubbles the size of fists; and he warmed the third until his heat and its cold were equal: thus was his fury quenched."

I spent Midwinter's evening and much of the longest night helping Calatín with the aftermath of Cú Chulainn's assault on our host. I had been lucky, I realized, to come off with no worse than a few bruises. Broken bones, cracked skulls, a few burns, and the boys who had been beaten before someone who knew them spoke up to save their lives. Now I understood why Calatín had restrained me at Rath Echach: some forms of madness are impervious to even a Druid's authority, or fear of a future curse. Others can be healed with herbs, or spells and songs, or even strengthening words at the right time.

Nemhain had wounded our warriors' souls: now Cú Chulainn had spread his infection deep through them, the terror that turned our hands against each other and woke men screaming and reaching for their weapons at any noise in the night, that we could help, if not wholly quell. The cure could not be accomplished until the Hound was dead, but at least we could ease the symptoms. The trumpa players, who should have been readying to greet the dawn with songs of joy and celebration, were gathered instead at the wounded-wagons through the night, blowing the slow deep harmonies that vibrated through wood and flesh, aiding the healing of mind and body.

I had brought my harp, its cherry wood sounding-board thrumming to the low power of the trumpas as I plucked and strummed the six strings of silver wire stretched down its narrow length, my voice, trained and strong as it was, like a thin flute tracing the melodies of healing above the deep horn-song.

Calatín salved injuries and doled out droughts of Valerian and primrose and cowslip, with a pinch of mistletoe for those who seemed worst stricken, only the lesser mistletoe of the apple; but a powerful herb nonetheless, for those not trained in its use. With each dose, he traced a sign above the drink. I saw its faint fox fir glimmering streaming beneath his fingers to light the cup with power, and realized, through the concentration of playing and singing, that I would not have been able to see so clearly, nor recognized the sign, before coming on this raid.

All is not ill, I thought. In truth, for all the pain and fear in the wagons that night, I could not be sorrowful. For even now I felt the deep pleasure in the secret places of my body, aching softly like a fledgling bird's wings after its first flight, and there was still a trace of Ailill's seed sticky on my thighs.

I smiled to myself as I took a deep singer's breath and began to weave the next phrase, pouring the warm glow of joy I felt out into the words and music to soothe the troubled minds around me.

Calatín, between patients for a moment, looked up at me. The old Druid's harsh, careworn visage softened, breaking into a grin. The expression was there and gone so swiftly I almost thought I had imagined it, but I knew that my teacher knew what had passed that afternoon, and that he approved. Tired as I was from the long night's healing, my joy lasted through the next day. We had come to the edge of the ocean, marching west into Cuailgne. The wind from the sea was raw and cold, blowing down the bay on the south side of the wide jutting spur of land to spit tiny needles of salty sleet into our faces.

Far ahead, I could see the dark rise of Cuailgne's mountains, almost hidden by the low-hanging clouds. Calatín, as ever, showed no sign of exhaustion from the night's work, nor did he shiver from the cold or curse the dashing sleet as he wiped his eyes clear. I, the hearth-fire glowing within me was enough warmth to make the icy sea-wind no more than a light chill against my skin. We stopped for the evening by a broad stream running between the gray-brown skeletons of cat tails, where the land sloped gently down to the dun sand of the beach and the low white-capped waves lacing the iron-gray sea. Usually Eochaid went to draw our water alone, but, when I could, I would help Suithchern with the children as she filled buckets for herself and her family.

I took Conall, wrapping him well in my purple mantle and nestling him on my hip as I walked, and she carried Clothra under her own bratt of checkered green and yellow, the yoke of buckets resting easily over her sturdy shoulders. Eochaid the Cat walked beside us, silent and watchful as always. Though we paid him little attention, I felt safer with him beside me: he would have saved me a few bruises, had I not told him to stay with Calatín the day before. In truth, I was uneasy at being so exposed. We were safer here than in the middle of the army, with only women and charioteers and unarmed servants, none of whom were likely to draw the Hound's wrath. Suithchern darted a sideways glance at me from under her long dark lashes, then smiled slyly.

"Have you found the pleasure of the man who likes apples?" She asked.

My hot blush drove out the wind's chill from my cheeks, and I found myself glancing down at a clump of matted dark sea-kale that lay in an icy crumple on the sand.

"Oho, I see you have. Did you find pleasure of it?"

I could not help my foolish grin.

"That is very well," Suithchern said with the contentment of a married woman and mother. Then her plump face grew serious again.

"Do you know if you do not want a child of him, do you know what herbs? I have a supply of my own, that I hardly need since I am still nursing, I could lend..."

I raised an eyebrow at her. "Oh! I'm sorry, you're a Druid, of course, you know far more about such things than I ever will. It's just easy to forget sometimes, with, you understand, women's things, you seem so like any girl..."

"Be easy, Suithchern," I said. "True, I am new to much of being a woman...but less so than I was!" We grinned at each other.

"That is very well," she said again. "Do you think...are you bearing? Do you want to?"

"Oh, yes," I sighed.

"Will he marry you?"

I laughed and shook my head. "I should not think so. Nor, in truth, do I wish to marry him. I have my studies; I could not give them up, even – especially! To be a king's wife."

Suithchern sucked in a breath, her brown eyes shining. Her round cheeks were already pink with the cold; now they grew pinker with excitement. "Is he a king? Which? One of the Munster rulers?"

I laughed again.

"Hardly! I would not touch a single one of them. Connla is a weasel, Cumail a brute, and none of the others are any better. In any case," I added dryly, "they are so busy panting over Finnabair, I could strip naked and lie in their beds as a foot-warmer and they would never notice."

"That is certainly not true," Suithchern chided me merrily. "Finnabair is fair, yes, as fair a maiden as one could ask for a queen's daughter to be, but have you never seen your own face?"

"Ah, but Finnabair may come with the queenship of Cruachan," I answered. "I could be as fair as Etain, and she as ugly as any Fomorian hag, and I think Connla would still turn away from me to wed her. Nor have I any mind to be leman to a man I do not love."

"So, if not one of the Munster kings, then who? Fergus? I have heard that there is no man in Eriu to match him between the sheets."

"Oh, no! I have heard all I need to of Fergus' mighty manhood. He may be very well for a woman like Flidais, but I fear he would tear me apart like a bull trying to service a squirrel. He is old enough to be my grandfather, and I cannot say that I even like him, let alone want him."

"Oh. One of the Maini, then? They are certainly handsome lads, good-tempered and well-mannered. Looking at them, one can see how Ailill won Maeve in his youth. Especially..." She fell silent, but I knew what she would have said: it was Orlamh who had truly looked like his father come again.

"Ailill is not old," I rebuked her. I meant to keep my voice light, but some of the passion I felt must have seeped in unknown to me.

The yoked buckets over Suithchern's shoulders, still empty, luckily, tilted alarmingly as she put a mantle-shrouded hand to her lips.

"Ailill? You slept with our king?"

I nodded, smiling helplessly with pride and delight. I knew such a thing was better kept to myself, but...' Any road, I have never heard it said that Ailill was slow to love a woman who wanted him, nor that Maeve ever took umbrage of it, as she hardly could!'

"You slept with King Ailill," Suithchern repeated, as though she could hardly believe it. "Wasn't, weren't you frightened? Or was it he who asked you?"

"I asked him. I went into his tent. I was a little drunk," I confessed. Suithchern giggled.

"It is often best so, when one is set on losing one's maidenhead. you liked it? He was good?"

"Oh, yes. Yes, he was, I knew he would be." Embarrassed as I was, I could not help enjoying such talk, for the pleasure it recalled to my mind, and my pride in the courage the deed had taken.

"Do you think you might be bearing?" She pressed. "Ailill will provide well for you and the child, if so. Look at the care he has taken for Conall, after all!" She shook her arm so that her bratt slipped down a few inches and I could see the gleam of twisted gold at her wrist.

"I hope I am," I answered.

"With all my heart I hope, May Brigid make it so!" I had missed my courses at the dark of the moon, while I was still a maiden, but that was nothing unusual for me, or for most women under the rigors of an Alban student's diet. "It may be that I will know in a week or so. I will ask nothing of Ailill save the pleasure of his company again, if we can. I am well able to stand on my own, and I will not be the first ban-drúi to bear a child during her training years."

A sharp gust of wind from the sea caught Suithchern's buckets, and she had to wrestle one-handed to keep them balanced on her shoulders without dropping Clothra.

She blinked icy spray from her eyes. "Strange," she mused.

"Calatín has his wife and many sons, yet one never thinks of a ban-drúi bearing children. I am so happy for you! Brigid bless you; and if you haven't caught this time, may you have many more chances. If you have, well, may you have many more chances yet, before you grow too ripe to risk it!"

We were almost at the stream now, giggling like a pair of little girls. Warm beneath her mother's mantle, Clothra gave a little burbling giggle of her own, and Conall gurgled happily, as though the babies felt our delight. Eochaid ignored us as though he were deaf as well as mute, too busy scanning the low land about us for any possible threat, or, perhaps, too embarrassed by our talk to look at us. Near the ocean, the stream side was thick with charioteers watering their horses, and herdsmen with their cattle and swine. We turned our backs to the cold sea-wind, walking past the animals to where the women and servants jostled for position: the further upstream, the less roiled and muddy the water would be. They parted to let us through.

"Isn't that Maeve's servant Lochu up there?" Suithchern said, pointing with her chin. "Look, she's wearing the queen's diadem, and has two guards with her. Do you think Maeve has freed her, or...?"

I blinked. The queen's bondswoman was indeed wearing the ancient ribbon of embossed gold that marked the power of Cruachan's queen. Even in the swift-fading evening light, it was bright against the tarnished bronze of her hair, and she walked with the pride of one nobly-born. Of course Maeve would hardly be attended by a servant of common blood; but Lochu was usually so quiet and self-effacing that, like Eochaid, it was often easy to forget she was there at all. I had never realized that she was almost as tall as the queen; but now she stood with her back straight between the two guards, no more than a hand's-width shorter than either of the big men.

"I would know more of this," I said quietly. "Let us draw water beside her. I am a ban-fili, and Maeve's foreseer!" I added, when Suithchern would have hung back from the place of honor.

The Munster kings' women, a bright gaggle in their mantles of green and yellow and blue with bracelets flashing silver from their wrists, glared as we walked through them, but did not dare to argue with me. We were almost to Lochu when I heard the whirring in the air, like a wood-pigeon flying low and fast. At first I thought it was a bird startled from its nest; but the sound ended in a low dull smack, like the sound of an axe meeting hard wood.

One of Lochu's guards had already leapt the stream with his sword drawn, pelting as hard as he could towards where a tiny dark figure was just vanishing into the twilight. The other was down on his knees, and Lochu, who had stood so proudly with the queen's diadem on her head, was on the ground. I tore off my mantle, wrapping Conall and thrusting him into Eochaid's arms. A few paces from Lochu, I slowed. I would have been too late had I been standing by her side. In the center of her forehead, the grainy grey curve of a brain-ball bulged out like an eye in warp-spasm, rimmed by a slowly-welling line of blood. Maeve's gold diadem lay on the ground, shattered by the blow.

"Cú Chulainn slew Orlamh in fair fight," I said, though I did not know to whom I was speaking. "Orlamh's charioteer disobeyed him, and striking at Maeve was a deed of war's demand. This death is nothing but shame to him; and by the Dagda and Ogma Sun-Poet and Lugh of all the arts, I shall see that shame fall on his head."

I picked up the three pieces of Maeve's broken diadem, the warmth of Lochu's flesh already fading fast from the thin gold in the chilly wind, and walked back to Eochaid and Suithchern.

"Eochaid, help Suithchern to draw her water, Calatín and I can wait our turn. I charge you most strictly to keep her as safe as you would me, and her babes as if they were my own. There is something that I must do, and I must do it now."

I turned on my heel, pacing into the camp, so full of rage and sorrow that I could hardly think. Yet I was a ban-fili: the roaring river of feeling was already flowing into the well-wrought channels that I had built for it, the shapes of words and the power they raised and crafted and aimed to strike more surely, and over a longer distance, than Cú Chulainn's sling.

I let that tide bear me where I knew I needed to go. Many things I had seen and heard were gathering into shape, random notes suddenly coalescing into a single chord. I found Fergus, not in the royal enclosure, where he might have been expected at this time of evening, but almost to the edge of camp.

Maeve's broken diadem, I kept hidden beneath my mantle.

"Come with me," I said to him.

Fergus looked down at me, his dark brows lowering. He was twice my size, and one of the most skilled warriors in Eriu, but he watched me warily, like a man in the woods who rounds a tree and finds himself staring into the eyes of a wolf.

"What do you wish, ban-fili?" He asked.

"Come with me," I repeated.

I walked towards the edge of the camp where the guards went about twelve by twelve, and Fergus followed me, his feet rustling slowly through the thin dead grass. One group of guards came up, hands hovering near their sword-hilts as if they meant to challenge me. As soon as they were close enough to see my face, they halted and edged away.

I kept walking until we were well out of hearing distance, and the camp was a mass of grey and black shadows in the darkening twilight. There was just enough light left for what I needed to do. A poet's tongue is as simple folk suppose a tree-cat's tail to be: soft and silken-furred, yet with a claw hidden at the end to rip and tear when needful. Now it was time for the claw.

I turned to face Fergus, drawing the shattered diadem from beneath my bratt.

"Do you know this circlet?" I asked him.

Even in the thickening gloom, I saw the blood drain from Fergus' weathered face, leaving him grey as a corpse.

"Maeve," he breathed. "Ah, Maeve, if only…"

Another time I might have felt pity: now my rage was all I knew.

"Not Maeve." Before Fergus' heart could beat relief, I pressed on. "The queen lent her diadem and guards to Lochu, why, I do not know, but she wore it when she went to the stream for water. The ball that shattered it broke her skull: she lies dead here at the edge of the sea, a bondswoman who did no harm and never offered another threat or defiance. Let alone the champion of Ulster! Yet he slew her from afar, without giving her so much as the warning he gave Orlamh's charioteer, nor any chance to defend herself, or live."

Fergus flinched back from me, his face twisting in pain and his thick-muscled shoulders hunching.

"My heart's son," he whispered. "To do such a thing. He could not have known! You say Lochu was wearing the queen's diadem, and attended by her guards?"

"Yes."

"In this light, at a distance. He must have seen the circlet, and thought that he was shooting at Maeve," Fergus said dully. "He would never have killed a bondswoman by choice, that is not in him."

"Tell that to Lochu," I bit out. I wish you could go after her on her way to the Summer lands and tell her now.

"As for Cú Chulainn, I know you have been leaving the camp to speak with him."

I had not known before I said those words: but they came from the same place as my visions, and I was sure of their truth. I saw the tiny flinch of Fergus' mouth, and knew I had struck home. He was, after all, a warrior and once king: he straightened his back, grey eyes glaring down into mine.

"I have told him nothing that would do us harm!" He snapped. "Cú Chulainn is my foster son: it gladdens my heart to speak with him, and I will never do him ill, but I have not betrayed Maeve."

'Even leading us on the roads that led round about instead of straight, and through the drumlin-lands?' I thought. Knowingly or not, Fergus had betrayed us, but that was not my matter to deal with.

"When you tell the tale of this raid, you may say whatever of that you please," I snapped. "For now, since you are the one person who speaks to Cú Chulainn without harm from him, and knows where he is, you shall bear him this message. Tell him what he has done; tell him of the blameless woman he slew because he could not bother making sure of his target. Then tell him this." I drew myself up to my full height, breathing from the roots of my body.

If I could not bind the Hound from harming us forever, I knew, as surely as I knew what had passed between the síde-swine herds of Cruachan and Femen, that I could hold him now. The poet's vein at the back of my head, that secret river of blood running through the darkness, pulsed with power, swelling and roughening my tongue with venom. I could feel the curse pressing within me like a skein of raven-dark wool winding thicker and thicker, words ready to spin and weave into a garment of grievous harm, should Cú Chulainn dare to work that one more deed which would give me spindle and distaff and rod on which to shape my wreaking.

"Tell him," I said, my voice ringing deep from within my chest, as though my whole slim body had become a great bronze horn, "that if he lifts hand or weapon or word of enchantment against us while we seek the Brown Bull in Cuailgne, that I shall cast this shame back on his head threefold. He shall no longer bear the name Hound, but derg-daol shall he be called, and friend and foe alike hold him in loathing.

My satire shall raise the blisters on his face, dark as the black-blood beetle, red as fresh-spilled gore, and white as a dead man's cheek; it shall slough the skin from his flesh, and the flesh from his bones. Nor can he withstand it, not though he were the greatest hero that ever trod the green lands of Eriu, nor though the mightiest Archdruid stood to protect him. For now Cú Chulainn has slain a woman unarmed without cause; and though that be no geas upon him, yet as it was once said that his refusal to do such deeds was his honor, now that he has done it. It is his shame!"

Fergus was too proud to cringe from me, but I saw, as no warrior ever would, the terror and pain in his eyes, as though I had flayed his face with burning whips. For himself, or for his foster son? That I would never know; but he drew himself up again.

"I will tell him," Fergus said, his words falling heavy and dull as the tolling of a leaden bell. "And I do not believe that he will strike against this army again while we are in Cuailgne. As for you. You are a ban-fili, and even the strongest arm cannot contend for long against such words."

Fergus turned his broad back on me, walking, not back to the camp, but off into the darkness. The Sun's light had failed almost wholly now; the Moon, near-dark, was only the faintest silver glimmer through the low shifting clouds, but he moved surely, as though he knew where he was going. I let him go: I had one more task to do, though my heart shrank from it. I did not see Maeve in the royal enclosure, although Ailill, Flidais, Finnabair, and three of the Maini, Feidhlim, Ceat, and Dáire, were sitting about the fire, their bright heads like a ring of gold catching the red fire-glow here and there.

Ailill smiled up at me as Ferdiad passed me through the gate. My warm rush of delight fed my anger: should Lochu not have had her own part in such joy?

"Come and be welcome, Fedelm," Ailill said to me. I smiled back at him, but shook my head, a bitter pang passing through me. Had matters gone otherwise this evening, I might have been able to sit down beside him, even, for Maeve was not jealous, shared the warmth of his arms.

"I must speak to the queen," I replied regretfully. "Where is she?"

Sadness passed across Ailill's strong features like the shadow of a dark cloud sailing over a sunlit meadow.

"Maeve is in her tent. If you can ease her heart, or make her see that Lochu's death was no fault of her own…"

Flidais nodded silently; Ailill's children only looked aside. Even then, I could not help glancing at them and wondering. Would his seed grow so strongly inside me, breeding a tall son or daughter with fire-tinged golden hair, with his firm chin and high cheekbones and bright blue-green eyes? Or would we blend like gold and silver melted together, one lending ruddy yellow richness, the other its pale bright hardness, to create something new, yet fair as both. I had my duty, and more: I could not help Lochu, but at least I could do my best for Maeve.

I paused at the queen's tent-flap. Ailill had given me leave: I squared my shoulders, walking in. A single leaning torch burned inside, its end thrust carelessly between the sheepskins that covered the ground into the earth. Maeve sat on the bed, her head in her hands and her two thick golden braids hanging down to hide her face. I did not hear her weeping, but her shoulders trembled slightly.

It took her a few heartbeats to realize that she was not alone. Her head snapped up, and she glared at me like an angry badger disturbed in its den. Her face was reddened, but whether that was from crying, or only the ruddy glow of the torchlight, I could not tell.

"What are you doing here, Fedelm?" She snapped. "What do you want?"

Even a good dog will bite its master, if its pain is great enough; I could guess at Maeve's, and took no offense at her words, or her tone. I straightened the torch, pushing it down to secure it as well as I could, though I lacked the strength to shove it more than an inch or so into the hard earth.

"I came to bear this back to you, and to speak to you," I said softly, bringing out the three shards of her diadem again.

The fine raised design, a pair of gently-curving lines swelling in waves to enclose a wide-spaced row of sun-circles, caught the firelight, the gold's bright glitter stinging water into my own eyes.

"I saw Lochu fall; I would have saved her if I could. I have sent my word – the word of a ban-fili, to the Hound of Ulster. Even he will not dare to gainsay it, for the shame that is on him, whether or not, as Fergus thinks, he did this harm unknowing, thinking that he shot at you."

"I set my diadem on her head at Samhain," Maeve whispered, staring beyond me. "If the gods had called for the queen's death, she would have fallen as royal sacrifice. Why now, and not then?"

I closed my eyes, reaching within for that knowledge that had filled me earlier, for the bright gate that let in the flood from poet's vein to tongue. I heard only emptiness resounding, as though I stood alone within a high-arching cave, neither the whisper of wind nor the beating of waves nor the twittering of birds to guide me, not so much as the dripping of water on stone.

"I do not know," I answered. " I do know this: it was not you who killed her. Unless..." One need not always be a foreseer or a Druid to know that danger, or death, lie in one's way.

The simplest of folk, though they be otherwise blind to the unseen world, may feel it when they stand at that crossroads where the straight path leads on to the House of Donn and the Summer lands beyond. Though Maeve's beasts of sovereignty were all slain, she was, or had been, Maeve of Cruachan: it was no wonder if she understood more than common folk. I said no word of those thoughts, but Maeve seemed to know what was in my mind. She looked up at me, her long face haggard with sorrow and worry.

"No. I did not feel I did not send her to die for me. Lochu said the women of the Munster kings scorned her at the waterside; I gave her my diadem and guards, for the sake of what pride she had, and for my own pride, for it was I whom they insulted through her. I swear to you by Crom Cruaich, I did not know nor guess what might befall."

I laid my hand on her shoulder, feeling the tension thrumming through her solid muscles.

"Then you bear no guilt. Believe me, my queen. There is only one to whom blame may fall in this; and I have seen to it that he knows it, and shall pay the price."

"What price is that?" Maeve asked. The slack muscles of her face were already tightening again, her mouth firming in anger, but that was better than the awful aged sadness I had seen there for a moment.

"Have you called the Hound's death upon him?"

"That I could not do," I said regretfully. "What I could do, I have. He will not, I think, strike again at us while we are in Cuailgne."

"If you have achieved that, then you have done well." Maeve told me. She sighed deeply.

"And yet Lochu is dead. She had served me for seven years, and I never knew more of her than those few glimpses she showed me upon this raid. Nor did she, alone of those who have died thus far, or are like to die after this, choose to come, but came by my command. Yes, I have sent men and women to their deaths before, even by misjudgment: everyone who leads in battle must sometimes bear that knowledge. Yet they were warriors, who followed of their own will and knew the risk any who obeys another's orders in war must take. Lochu was a servant, and I meant only to do her a good turn."

"If she had the choice?" I asked. "Would she have followed to serve you here? Even taken the risk of death in your place, if she had known?"

"She did it once before, when the risk seemed greater. No, I do not think she would have stayed behind to be simply another bondsmaid in Cruachan, if the choice had been hers. She was a chieftain's daughter, not born to service, and proud.

More so than I would ever have guessed; and part of that was in the silence she kept in the place where her fate set her. A little like Fergus, in that way..." Maeve fell silent again, her face grave and thoughtful.

"Fergus! My queen, do you know, he has been going out to speak with Cú Chulainn in the evenings?" I clenched my hands at my sides. I had not meant to bring her that word, not on this night, but, hearing her speak so of the Ulster exile, I could not have kept his shameful secret any longer.

I expected Maeve to leap up, reaching for her sword-hilt. Swearing vengeance and death on Fergus, perhaps; at the very least, naming him traitor and outcast. She only sat there, and after a little time, she lowered her fair head again.

"Yes," she said, staring at the white heap of sheepskins under her bare feet. "I know."

"You know? You still trust him? Let him come and go as he will. Let him guide your host?"

"Yes."

"Why?"

"He is Fergus. He will not turn against those he loves, to whom he is sworn, Cú Chulainn is, after all, his foster son, dear to him as his own blood. Nor will he turn against us, for we are likewise bound. I think," she added sadly, "that of all of us who are engaged in this matter, on either side, it is he who suffers worst, for there is no death, of Eriu or Ulster, that he does not feel, nor will there be any victory in which he can take joy."

"Have you been lying with Fergus?" The question slipped out before I could stop it. Horrified at myself, I bit my tongue, but it was too late.

Instead of shouting at me for my presumption, Maeve looked up again, smiling like a young girl for a moment. "Indeed, I have. Oh, do not look so shocked, Fedelm! When you have known the pleasure of a man's love..." She stopped, her smile widening. I knew that my face was controlled, and cursed my fair skin, that seemed to show my every feeling in a flush of warm blood. "Ah, you have, and just lately, I would guess. Who?"

Twice, our hot-tempered queen had surprised me; I did not think she would again. Ten years of schooling did not wipe out fourteen years of childhood awe: I dropped my gaze, and mumbled, "Ailill."

Maeve laughed, a warm heartfelt laughter.

"My dear Fedelm! Did you think I would be angry with you, or Ailill, over such a thing? No wonder, well, never mind that. Be sure, I shall never bear you ill-will for this. Rather, I would tell you that you could not have chosen a better man to relieve you of your maidenhead. I can swear that there is no kinder nor more patient lover in all the five provinces, nor one better able to teach a young girl pleasure."

Her eyes closed, her breath hissing softly through her lips as if an old memory were coming back to her, but I could not tell whether it was one of joy or pain.

"Indeed, I should not object were you to wish a place as Ailill's adaltrach, for a young woman of your wisdom and skills would be a help and an ornament to Connacht."

I blinked. I felt as though I had stepped off a sheer cliff, expecting to plummet and smash into the rocks below, and instead found my feet firmly set on soft grass.

"I...you..." I stammered.

"Could I have sought a man free of jealousy to wed, if I myself were tainted by it? What Ailill is to me, and I to him..." Maeve paused, her blue eyes pale and distant in the torchlight. "Though he may indeed be angry with me at the moment: I do not know."

"He sent me in here, hoping that I could give you some comfort," I said. "I do not think he is truly angry with you, for whatever reason."

"And yet he has cause to be. If I had not led our army here, Orlamh would still be alive. Our son, what guilt do I bear there?"

Maeve's voice was raw as a raven's croak, asking me that question. It seemed to me that I could hear it echoing back to her earlier words, and further to that morning outside Calatín's house; I heard my queen's voice in my mind, though my ears had never heard her speak the words: 'There are many who part with their kin and friends here today, and from their homes and lands, fathers and mothers. Unless every one return unscathed, it is upon me that they will cast their sighs and their ban, for it is I that have assembled this levy...'

"What guilt does any ruler bear, who leads the folk out to war?" I asked quietly.

"Some might say, the guilt for every warrior dead and every man or woman or child led into captivity, foe or friend. Others might say that each makes their own choices and takes their own risks. Though you are a mighty queen, you are but one. Could you have taken Ferdiad by the scruff of the neck and dragged him all this way by force? Each of the men and women who has come to war upon Ulster: could you have compelled them all by your own strength, if they were unwilling? Your own troops may fight to your will, and even force others to obey you; but who makes those warriors multiply your strength so many fold, save they themselves? And I have seen how this army moves. Seventeen cantreds, with the cantred of the Galeoin the eighteenth spread among them, and each with its own leader: it is all you and Ailill, Fergus and Flidais and Cormac, can do to keep them in some order. If they all rose against you, they could destroy you as easily as a river in full flood destroys a weir of willow-branches. It is also true that they would not be here if not for you. You have been a ruler for many years: how many men have followed you to their deaths before? Is it so different, that one is your son rather than another's? It feels different, surely, when it is you and not another woman bereaved."

A sudden rush of fear and grief twinged in my womb, as though I echoed Maeve's own feelings in the child of whose very being I was still uncertain.

"Can you say that it is so, before the gods?"

"Yes," Maeve whispered, "...and no. Do not think I have not thought all these thoughts before, or asked myself these questions, even as we set out, when you saw our host dyed crimson-red. My coracle is on the crest of the rising river now, and I must go on, or be overwhelmed."

"That, too, is true. Here are my last questions. Would Orlamh have stayed home, if he knew that he would be slain on this raid? And if, knowing it, he had chosen to come. Then would you have denied him a man's portion – or a hero's?.

Maeve reached out and took my hand, wrapping her long fingers about my smaller ones. Her grip was icy; the bitter sea-wind crept in through the tiniest cracks, even in a queen's tent, and she had not bothered to have her servants, of course not! Bring in warming-stones. She held me for a long time, her grasp slowly warming and easing.

"Thank you, Fedelm," Maeve murmured. "I do not know how many of our questions are answered. I am ready to go on, at least. That is no small service you have done me."

"Shall I ask Ailill to come in to you? I think he wishes to, and I think it would do you good."

Maeve gave a small half-laugh of surprise.

"I...yes, I think so. Thank you."

Maeve

"When the Tuatha de Danann came to Ireland, they found it inhabited by the Fir Bolg. The Tuatha de Danann were fair and swift; the Fir Bolg were a folk of great size and strength. The two fought at the First Battle of Moytura, and were evenly matched, doing such harm to one another that both agreed on a truce: the Fir Bolg to go into Connacht's rocky western lands, the Tuatha de Danann to hold the rest of Ireland.

Thereafter the Fomorians, a monstrous race from the sea, assailed the Tuatha de Danann, and were defeated at the Second Battle of Moytura; while the Tuatha de Danann were beaten in their turn by the sons of Mil, and made their royal halls in the Otherworld beneath the síd-mounds.

The lesser kin of all three races lingered in those wild places that no other claimed..."

Before the armies parted the next morning, Maeve went to seek out Flidais. The milk-queen was busy at the wagons, making sure that a fair share of the provender she had brought would be going with the Connacht cantreds, perhaps more: the other parts of the host could replenish their supplies by raiding. Flidais' wonderful hair was bound up into several braids, plaited into an elaborate interweave that flashed brilliant copper whenever a stray shaft of sunlight struck through the low-hanging clouds. She was fully armed, but the bratt wrapped around her shoulders was striped with crimson and violet, blue and green and yellow, and pinned with the great gold disk-brooch that was one of her clan's oldest treasures.

"Flidais, I would speak with you before we leave," Maeve said.

"Of course," her friend answered. "Is all well with Ailill?"

"As well as it may be, I think."

Flidais coughed into her fist.

"I was sorry to hear of the death of your bondsmaid. It was an ill thing Cú Chulainn did, to strike her down! Now there is not a servant or woman-follower in camp who does not tremble when they go to the water, nor are the servants willing any longer to arrange themselves by the edges of our host, for they no longer feel themselves safe from the Hound."

"Fedelm tells me that he should not strike while we are in Cuailgne," Maeve said grimly. "I ought to have told you earlier, but I feared to spread word too widely, lest he prove me wrong. What if he is so bound to protect Ulster, that he has no care for his good name nor the curse of a ban-fili?"

"Ah, no." Flidais shook her head. "The Hound is very young, and it is in my mind, from the tales Fergus has told, that his name as a hero is worth even more to him than the fate of his king. Did he not take up weapons at seven, because he heard Cathbad say that the youth who took his weapons on that day would be famed in Eriu forever, though his life would be short? Even then, Cú Chulainn said it was a fair bargain; that if he achieved fame, he was content, though he lived but a day on the green earth. A young man who speaks thus at seven will not cast his good fame away at seventeen."

"I hope it is so. That was not why I sought you. Rather, Fedelm tells me that the Brown Bull has left his home pasture in Temair Chulaigne, that the Morrígan warned him of our coming, and he would not be driven off like common cattle in a raid. Now you, milk-queen, huntress, know more of the ways of kine and deer than any other in Eriu. Where is he likely to have gone to hide from us?"

Flidais tugged at one of her glistening red braids, her eyes glinting like pure blue glass beneath half-closed lids.

"If a stranger challenge an ordinary bull in his field, he will defend himself: however great the might arrayed against him, he will not imagine himself the loser. Yet I have heard the Donn Culaigne has the pride of a king and the wit of a man. I think he will go into the mountains, to his summertime búailed, and hold the best of those places as a fort. Beware: what you see as a trap for him, he may see as a chance to slay your folk. Do not let him trap you! Let your herdsmen be careful when they approach him. An ordinary bull may flinch if a man charges him shouting in turn, but the Brown Bull will not be fooled by our height on two legs: he knows full well the measure of his strength, and that of a human. You had better have some strong ropes plaited as well, if you are to bring him along. Most of all, beware of harming his heifers. Rather lure them, and if he does not follow peacefully, at least he should not flee you too swiftly, but turn his mind towards freeing them."

"That is well to know." Flidais smiled. "And I shall look forward to our next meeting. For I have never seen a bull as fine as the white Finnbennach, but if the tales of the Donn Cuailgne are true, there has never been a bull such as he in Eriu, nor Alba, nor Gaul, nor the lands from which the sons of Mil sailed! Indeed, it may be that when all this is over, I shall ask you for his services for my fairest cattle as well."

Maeve gave Flidais a quick hug.

"If a flock of wild birds were grazing on Ai Plain, I'd give you one and share another; if the salmon were swimming in the weirs or river-mouths right now, I'd give you one and share another, with the three proper herbs: cress of the stream, marshwort, and sea-herb. I would stand for you in the ford of battle, as we have stood beside each other before; and if we reach home safe with the Brown Bull, you may bring as many of your cows and heifers as you please for his service. Like Fergus..." Maeve smiled with the faint echo of pleasure that still twinged in her womb at the memory of his lovemaking,

"I think the Donn Cuailgne has more than enough seed to go around."

"Ah, indeed," Flidais replied with an answering grin, "and it is no hardship to share bull or man with you. Mayhap Fergus will have learned a few new feats by the time I next lie with him!"

Maeve's portion of the army turned inland, towards the edge of the mountains, while Ailill's followed the sea-road westward. Maeve turned in her chariot to watch them go, until the last of the crimson cloaks and glittering spearheads was lost in the thin mist seeping up from the ocean.

"Do not worry, Mother," Finnabair said, expertly guiding the chariot-horses around a curve in the path. "Father and my brothers are well-able to guard themselves in battle, and I have heard it said that, with the men of Ulster still in their pangs, this will be as easy a raid as ever a warrior followed."

"That is true. I think it is we who have the more dangerous part, though there be no swords drawn."

Maeve fell silent, looking towards the low fog-shrouded mountains. For all both Fedelm and Flidais had said, and much as she had hated being walled about by the ring of her guards' bodies and shields, she felt uncomfortably naked now.'And if everyone is wrong about Cú Chulainn? ' She thought.

'If he has chosen to cast away his honour for Ulster's sake. Fergus did as much, when he refused to fight for the throne that Conchobar stole from him; and men may think ill of us in later days, that we used Finnabair to lure men onto this raid with no intention of ever giving them the prize for which they think they fight. Is it in Cú Chulainn to think as a king, or only as a champion? And if he will sacrifice his name for his land. If he knew that it was not I, but Lochu, at whom he fired, and sought by that to break my will, as he sought by killing my hound and marten and wren, would Finnabair not be his next target?'

Maeve sighed. "I almost wish that you had not chosen to come with me."

"Why set the lure in a salmon's mouth, if he will leap into the net all the same?" Finnabair said. "I think that the Munster kings will not give up their lust for me because I am out of their sight, and I am weary to death of pretending for them."

"That is not it. It is the danger."

"Mother, all this raid are in danger! If not from sword or sling-ball, from cold or breaking chariots or simply from being in the midst of an army. You told me before we started that I would have my part to play, and that you were proud of me for it. Do you now wish me cowering at home?"

Maeve bit her lip. Finnabair's words were too much like Fedelm's had been, speaking of Orlamh's death the night before. As then, she could not deny it. If her heart cried out to say, "Yes, take a company of guards and go home; we can lie about you to the Munster kings, or whoever we need to, just as well if you are not here", she could no more do that than, if Finnabair had wished it, she could have forbidden her daughter to take up sword and spear.

"I may not say that. Come, let us see if we can find Cormac: he may know where the likeliest of the Brown Bull's summer búailed is."

Cuailgne's mountains sloped up gently from the southeast. At first the rise in the land was so gentle that only the white puffs of the horses' breath panting a little harder from their nostrils showed it. Soon the ground became more uneven, small plateaus of dull brown grass ringed by sharper slopes, with the track ways winding here and there up their sides. Cormac had often guested with Dáire mac Fiachna in his younger days, and gone with the other lads to admire the Donn Cuailgne.

"With us he was gentle, and even allowed the boy-troop to play upon his back. He was young then, and tamer: few bulls grow sweet-tempered in their full age," her son had warned.

"Any road, his favorite summer pasture in the mountains was Dubchoire, for he loved the sweet waters of the tarn called the Black Cauldron. I think it likely that he may have gone there first."

As their path climbed, Maeve began to feel a prickling at the back of her neck. She found herself glancing about, waiting with every nerve on edge for the sound of a sling-ball whirring through the air. Once or twice, she thought she saw a small dark shape darting behind a rock or ridge in the distance, but nothing happened: if Cú Chulainn was following them, he was biding his time.

The day waned slowly, tendrils of mist winding down from the clouds overlaying the tops of the mountains. Once their track plunged into a low lake of white fog caught in the bowl of a plateau, so thick that Maeve could barely see the necks of her chariot horses. At least the Hound cannot see to shoot at us, she thought. That was little comfort: he, or anything, could come out of the mist at any moment.

Then Maeve heard the creaking of chariot-wheels coming up beside her, and set her hand to her sword-hilt, watching the shadow near her. She could just make out the shapes of the horses, and the three figures in the vehicle.

"You are well-clad in iron," Fedelm's voice said softly.

"You need not be afraid."

The Druids' chariot came closer, until their horses were side by side with Maeve's own. Maeve could just see the purple of Fedelm's mantle, the gold of Calatín's, and the deep green of their silent servant's, all muted by the greyish-white cloud through which they drove.

"What do you mean?" Maeve demanded. She suspected she knew. There were many wild places in Connacht, and each held its own watchers and guarders, who were seldom friends to human folk.

"These mountains are as thick with the geniti-glinni, the glen-spirits, as any in the world. I have already caught glimpses of bocánach and bánánaich and wild siabra watching us from the higher places. It seems to me that you will do more harm to Dáire mac Fiachna by taking the Brown Bull than you may have purposed. For the Bull's bellow drives away all those who creep among the rocks and lurk in the high glens. None of them can stand against his cry, the strength of it nearly cast me myself into the dark places! Thus he holds these mountains safe for the children of Mil to pass."

"Should I care if the mountains of Cuailgne are safe for human folk when we have left them?" Maeve asked, angry with herself for the chill that traced down her spine like the caress of a cold damp hand, trailing a runnel of goose flesh behind it.

"Not in the least," Calatín said calmly. "Rather, the sooner we have gained the Donn Cuailgne, the better.

For whether he bellows in anger or greeting, he will drive those who watch us away, and we shall be the more sure of our safety in these high winter places until we have left them."

Maeve shrugged, hearing the comforting jingle of her Gaulish hauberk's iron links. "Well, you are the Druids," she said, doing her best to sound unworried. "It is for you to deal with such matters."

"So we are doing," replied Calatín. "Halt your horses for a moment."

The horses shied and pulled at the reins a little, stamping uneasily on the hard ground, but Finnabair managed to stop them. The old Druid leapt lightly from the chariot, whispering softly as he came up to them. To each harness, he tied a small bundle of herbs and twigs with a piece of red thread, then reached up to tie a like bundle around Finnabair's wrist, and after hers, Maeve's.

"What is it?" Maeve asked curiously. She lifted her wrist up to sniff at the dried plants. They smelled odd and musty, though not unpleasant.

"The seven herbs of ward: vervain, eye bright, speedwell, new blossom, mallow, yarrow, and self-heal, all noon-plucked on a day of the full moon," the Druid answered.

"While you wear it, you are safe from any harm at the hands or weapons of the folk of hill and wild. I have not so much that I can deal it out to all, but I have done what I can. Cormac is already full-warded, as you are. Fergus does not need my aid, for some trace of that kingship that was his clings to him yet, and even the wild ones of Ulster honor it. You," Calatín added quickly, "they recognize as a foe, and moreover a great one. They do not much love the children of Mil who dwell here, and they fear the Brown Bull; yet they hate us more than either."

'Is he salving my pride, or telling the truth, or both?' Maeve wondered. it seemed to her, indeed, that she could feel how unwelcome she was in these high lands.

"Then we shall depend on the two of you to ward us while we are here."

"One thing more," Calatín said, vaulting lithely back into his chariot. "Do not, as you value your life, let your horses tread where you cannot see the ground, or break into a run. Where the wild folk cannot touch directly, they will deceive and terrify. Against that, there is no protection but good sense and strength of will, and being forewarned.

Follow no lights in mist and dark; once we have made camp, do not go out of easy sight of your tent; and go nowhere alone, not even to make water."

The Druid tapped his driver on the shoulder, and their horses veered away. Others were coming up on either side of Maeve now, and she was glad that the fog veiled her relief when she saw Cormac's unmistakable tall, rangy silhouette to her left, and Fergus' broad-shouldered shape to her right.

"A pity we didn't come here in summer, Mother!" Cormac called. "The mountains are still foggy then, but fair and green, without this endless deep chill. Have the Druids seen to you?" He lifted his sword-arm, which bore a bundle of red-tied twigs similar to the ones Maeve and Finnabair wore.

Maeve raised her arm in return, saying,

"You never told me of this danger, neither of you," she added, slanting a sharp glance across at Fergus.

"I did not know," Cormac replied. "We only came up here to see the Brown Bull and his heifers, and slept peacefully in bothies under the sound of his lowing. That is why we have been searching for you all this time.

Your chief herdsman Lothar has found the tracks of many cattle leading upward from here; it looks as though I guessed rightly when I thought the Donn was going to Dubchoire."

"Well-done, Cormac!" Maeve cried. She had not known how constricted her chest had become until now, when it loosed with the blessed ease of tight iron bands releasing and she heaved in a deep sweet breath.

"Will we reach him before evening?"

"At this rate, it will be late tomorrow," Fergus answered. "We shall have to make camp soon, for the mountain mists bring darkness early up here. I am not minded to risk pushing horses or men, considering the advice your Druids have given."

"No. A little further on, perhaps."

Slowly they climbed out of the lake of mist, up a low slope and into another dry mountain meadow. The clouds were rolling down from the tops of the mountains, trailing through the tops of the few bare scrubby trees that raised their gnarled branches as if to dare the harsh sea-winds to uproot them. All the while, Maeve's sense of being watched grew.

She had been a warrior twenty-five years, and had never felt that odd prickling at the back of her head when there was not a foe watching her with destruction in his mind. She tried to drive it from her, but the memory of Lochu's dead face with the sling-ball bulging grey as brains from her broken forehead kept coming back, the bondservant's bronze hair paling to gold and her rounded features fining to Finnabair's delicate face. Finally Maeve could bear her fears no more, and asked Finnabair to drive alongside Fergus for a time. When they were close enough that only their charioteers could hear them, she said,

"Fergus. What did Cú Chulainn say, when you told him it was Lochu he had slain?"

Fergus' grey eyes widened slightly, but he showed no other sign of surprise. Nor did he try to justify himself; perhaps he did not feel he needed to. He said only,

"He was shamed, and grieved. He is no willing slayer of unarmed women. Fedelm's word will hold, while we seek the Bull in Cuailgne."

Maeve only nodded. At another time, she might have shouted at him, or cursed him as at least half a traitor, but here in these unfriendly highlands, she had no heart to quarrel with him. Instead she said, "Perhaps this would be a good place to halt for the night."

"I think so. We will hardly be able to go further today."

Maeve stood and watched while her cantreds made camp. Ferdiad came to take up his watchful position beside her; she felt as though both of them were standing guard together. Once, on a higher slope, she thought she saw something move, a grey rustle, the brief shape of a goat-horned head among the rocks, but when she looked straight at it. It was gone. Calatín and Fedelm walked about as the servants took the lengths of woven willow from one of the wagons that had come with them, lashing them together into fences and the frames of bothies.

Now and again, one of the Druids would tie something to the wickerwork, or sprinkle a pinch of a dried herb with a few whispered words.

"I thought this would be the easier part," Ferdiad murmured to Maeve. "I wondered that you should come to herd the Brown Bull rather than leading the war-party. I think it is well that you are here."

The big warrior's winter-pale skin seemed tightly stretched over his cheekbones, his blue eyes shadowed as if he had outlined them with berry-juice, then smeared his hand across his face before the color had dried. For all Ferdiad's awesome strength, there was something boyish about his wide eyes and tip-tilted nose; the slight fuzziness of his short golden beard betrayed that he had not borne it for long. *He is barely twenty: he has fought in battles, but he is still hardly more than a youth.* Now he looked at Maeve anxiously, and she thought that he might be remembering the night of the storm at Cuil Sibrille, and how she had quieted both horses and men beneath the terror of the Nemhain.

"Others came for the plunder of Ulster, but this is my raid," Maeve answered. She rested a hand on Ferdiad's arm, feeling the tightness of the powerful muscles beneath her light grasp. "Do not fear."

For all Maeve willed it now, she could feel no strength flowing from herself into Ferdiad; her words were only words. Nevertheless, her champion managed a smile.

"I do not. Men before me have met many creatures with swords and strength; did not my own ancestors of the Fir Bolg strive undaunted against the very Tuatha de Danann? The watchers of Ulster's lands shall not dismay the champions of Connacht."

"That is well-said," Maeve approved. She stood watching beside him as her cantreds kindled their fires. Fires barely large enough to take a trace of the evening chill from them. There was little wood here, and though plenty of old cow-dung lay scattered about the mountain meadow among the fresh, the wet air here kept it from drying. At least Flidais had sent most of a wagon load of good turf with them, but they could not use it too freely: there was no guessing how long it would take to find the Brown Bull.

The mist hung fuzzily about the small fires; from twenty paces away, it blurred them into the faint fairy-light of a will-o'-the-wisp. Now Maeve understood Calatín's warning about staying close to her tent a little better. If anyone wandered off, it would be all too easy for the watchers to lure them to their deaths with the slightest deceptions. Maeve, Finnabair, Cormac, Fergus, and the Druids all had their tents and camp fire within a smaller enclosure.

Although night and cloud shrouded the mountains, Maeve could still feel them rising above her, and was grateful for even the little fire's fuzzy glow. No one felt much like talking, but Finnabair brought out her harp, slim fingers coaxing pleasant strains of music from the six strings of glittering silver, and it seemed to Maeve that the sound eased her as much as the firelight. Still, the darkness beyond their ring pressed close and unfriendly, and she found herself longing for human warmth.

'It is strange, she thought: I had no doubts about lying with Fergus when Ailill was in the same camp. Now he is away, and hardly likely to be sleeping alone, and yet, does he lie wondering if I hold Fergus in my embrace, or find more pleasure in his friend's bed than in his? If Ailill is indeed still Fergus' friend: his laughter hides his thoughts better than another man's face of stone. It is cold here, and Fergus glows warmer than that drizzle-damped fire.

Maybe it is as Calatín said, that a trace of his kingship hangs about him yet, that he is still holy enough to turn aside the hate of goat-horned bocánach and pale bánánaich.'

Maeve rose and went to Fergus. At least she had done well in bringing him. The harshness of his hawk-like face had eased, as though softened by mist and firelight; and when his grey gaze turned on her, she felt heated rather than scorched.

"Will you share my tent?" Maeve murmured in his ear.

Fergus' hand came up, trapping her own in his strong warm grasp. A smile curled his lips. "I will."

Yet as Maeve gripped Fergus' strong body with all the power of her thighs to pull him hard into her, although he filled her almost more thoroughly than she could bear, she still felt curiously empty. Each thrust he made struck a shower of pleasure-sparks through her like an iron hammer beating hard against a flint boulder, but she held no kindling for those sparks to light in, no wood or earth to feed the fire. Even as her body tightened about him over and over again, as her breath came hot and rough with pleasure and she almost saw a faint glow about Fergus' body in the chill darkness, she thought: 'Something is missing, however I may want it. Is this what Fergus felt, lying with me at Midwinter?'

When they had done, and were lying beneath the thick woolen coverlets in each others' warmth, such a sudden and bitter sorrow came over Maeve that, had she not trusted wholly in her Druids' power to ward and the iron knife stabbed into the earth beneath the tent's entrance, she would have been sure that a bánánaich had somehow crept in to lay her white-ice hand on Maeve's heart and whisper her curse of cold and weeping madness into the ear of Connacht's queen.

If I am still Connacht's queen, with the signs of my rule all broken before me. No smith in the army would even try to mend Maeve's diadem with the rough tools of wood, and iron-work they had brought, nor been certain that they could even with the finest tools in their homes. The ancient gold circlet was still shattered in three, and might never be whole again. Lochu, who was both a trophy of battle-victory and, though I hardly knew it until too late, the very embodiment of loyalty, lies dead. The diadem might be mended someday, but however she return to this world, she shall not come back as we were. Was my queenship not in her, as well?

Maeve

The dawn came in thick fog, an icy mist that stole deep into Maeve's bones and left them aching as if with age. Still, the Brown Bull was ahead, and that was enough to drive away her melancholy. Clad only in a short tunic and breeches, long golden braids pinned tight about her head, she stepped outside the tent and began the round of those warrior-feats she knew. At first her muscles and sinews were tight with chill and she moved slowly.

She had neglected her daily training on the march, though the effort of keeping balanced and loose-bodied in a swaying and jolting chariot, a skill nearly as deep as instinct, had compensated to some degree and kept her from stiffening too badly. Soon the blood began to pump through her limbs, warming her.

Then her fingers grew nimble on sword-hilt and spear-shaft, her body stretching and twisting easily, until she finished by leaping nearly head-height from the ground into a full somersault, striking out four times with her sword before her feet touched down lightly on the earth again. At some point, Fergus had come out to watch her.

He raised an eyebrow.

"You have not failed in training with the years," he remarked.

"I have heard that it is easier for a woman to keep her litheness into age than a man, if she be not too worn with childbearing."

Maeve started to flare, then thought again of the courses that had not come to her at the last dark moon. Nor had she felt the slight tenderness of her breasts and heaviness of belly that usually presaged her bleeding yet, and the next dark moon was almost upon them.

"I did not mean to say you are aged!" Fergus added quickly. "Perhaps it is for myself I speak. I have lost none of my strength, but on such mornings as this, I hear the voice of every bone that has ever cracked in my body, crying out that I have treated them ill; and only true need could drive me to close these hands on my weapons before the Druids' salve has finished soaking into them."

Maeve looked at her lover's powerful hands. Last night, Fergus had caressed her body with a young man's strength and ease, but in the veiled grey light of the foggy morning, she could see the crookedness of often-broken finger-bones and the swelling of his knuckles, like gnarled boles on sturdy branches.

'For all his vigor, he is past fifty: a grandfather's age, Maeve thought. Is it any wonder that he cannot sunder his heart from young Cú Chulainn, the nearest he has left to a son?'

"Even youths move stiffly after a night sleeping in this cold mountain mist," Maeve said. "I notice it was no boy whom the Hound excepted from matching his feats. Come, get some hot porridge and honey into you, and you will surely feel ready to face the Brown Bull."

Fergus smiled at her, one of his rare sweet smiles with hardly a tinge of sorrow about the edges. Maeve wiped the cooling sweat from her brow with the corner of her heaviest bratt and pinned the purple-edged square of checkered crimson and blue about her shoulders before the morning chill could steal her loose-muscled warmth from her again.

Soon Maeve's troops were on the march again, following the deep-stamped tracks of the Donn Cuailgne and his herd of heifers further up into the mountains. The fog thinned as they climbed, shifting veils passing over the high meadows and slow-rising ridges of earth and stone. Maeve was careful to keep her gaze ahead, and to pay no attention to the tricks of mist and rock wavering in the corners of her eye, nor the occasional wave of creeping prickles around her back.

Far away, a sound like a great horn's deepest note belled through the fog. Faint as it was, Maeve felt it vibrating up through her chariot's wheels. As if it had been a signal to whatever watched from the cloud-shrouded ridges, the unnerving sensation that something was staring angrily at her eased, a darkness she had hardly noticed the tattering and vanishing like clouds beneath a strong wind from the sea.

"Ulster is waiting for us!" Ferdiad said, motioning his charioteer to swerve closer to Maeve and Finnabair. "That was a war-horn blowing."

"No," Cormac called from Maeve's other side. "That was the voice of the Brown Bull."

The sound came again, the deep bellow gaining power and resonance. The hairs on the back of Maeve's neck stood up again as it thrilled through her, the blood beating more keenly in her veins. If I had known the Donn Cuailgne was such a treasure, I should have sought for him long ago!

Lothar came trotting back to his queen. Maeve's chief herdsman was just past middle age, his thick curly brown hair strewn richly with silver and his face deep-creased and brown as well-worn leather, but his bare feet were hard as horn and he moved easily over the rough ground.

"We are close enough now. The Brown Bull left his scat by the side of the track, such a mound could only be his! It is still warm. My queen, I would advise that we leave the chariots here and come up on foot. He is more like to see horses than men as challengers. If we are lucky."

"Let it be so," Maeve said. "Finnabair, you shall be in charge of the charioteers and servants, save for my herdsmen. Keep Calatín close beside you; but Fedelm shall go with me, in case her sight should be needed. Should aught go amiss, your duty is to see that all those who are left behind make it safe out of these mountains and back to our main force. Follow Calatín's advice if you can, but remember that you are a queen's daughter, and that the rule is yours here until I return."

"I shall do that, Mother," Finnabair said. Her face was very pale, but set in resolution. Maeve nodded, her heart swelling with pride. 'And she thinks to waste herself on a minor chieftain of Ulster? Though she is no fighter, she has the soul and mind of a queen'.

Maeve went at the fore of those she had chosen, with Fergus, Cormac, and Ferdiad beside her.

Thrice fifty fighters, the best of her own guard, Cormac's purple-cloaked elite, and those Ulstermen who had come with Fergus into exile, and twenty skilled herdsmen, all bearing looped ropes of triple-plaited osiers, walked four abreast up the path. Lothar walked a little ahead to follow the tracks, though it was hardly needed. The thin winter grass had been bitten nearly down to the earth, then trampled down by the heifers; but for all the lesser cattle that had walked behind the Brown Bull, his hoof prints were still stamped so deep that the dew pooled grey in the bottoms of the tracks.

Maeve and her men came up a slope and around a ridge of stone to the edge of another plateau. This time, the bellow from the mist seemed to vibrate through the very mountains around them, deafening as if they were standing in the middle of an hundred trumpas blasting a single war-note. Maeve's whole body trembled with the resonance, her hauberk jingling a faint belled counterpoint.

She drew a deep breath, and stepped forward onto the Brown Bull's meadow. At first she only saw the milling heifers, the nearer ones an array of hues, red and grey, white and brown and black and spotted, the further ones misted to colorless boulders. The sea of cows parted, lumbering away to either side.

The Brown Bull heaved himself out of the mist like a whale rising from the ocean, his hide dark and slick with fog. At first his huge head seemed misshapen, a third horn sprouting black and thick from his forehead between the two sweeping in mighty curves to either side. Then the raven perched on his head took wing with a croak of mocking laughter, rising into the foggy air and circling out of sight. Maeve stepped carefully forward, hands at her sides with the palms turned forward in a gesture of harmlessness.

"Brown Bull, come with us, for we mean you no ill," she crooned. "We shall bring your heifers with you, and give you three hundred more, each fairer than the fairest cow-maid here.

"We shall lead you to the finest pastures of thick green clover, and in the winter you shall have your fill of hay that is sweeter than honey-mead. Come, leave these harsh lands, and come with us."

As she spoke, her herdsmen spread out, ten to each side, their ropes of plaited osier wound about their arms with the ends dangling. The heifers lowed, shifting uncertainly. These were not their herders, but men brought them food and led them to good fields: why should they not trust? Then the Brown Bull bellowed in rage, his deep voice shattering the air.

He lowered his great head, heavy fore hooves tearing great divots of icy mud and dead grass from the earth, and began to lumber towards Maeve, picking up speed with each step. Maeve drew in a deep breath. She had not wanted to test herself thus, but she had calmed the horses in the very teeth of the Nemhain's storm. Surely the power of Maeve of Cruachan was a match even for the Brown Bull of Cuailgne?

She forced her shaking legs to take a single step toward the charging Bull, stretching her hand out towards him and reaching within for the streams of power that had flowed through her before, From the roots of the earth, from the depths of the sea, from the bright heights of the heavens. Even with the Brown Bull thundering down upon her like a mountain descending in rage, Maeve closed her eyes for a heartbeat, clawing desperately inside herself for the queen's strength as she shouted, "Halt!"

There was nothing, but the earth trembling beneath the hammering hooves of the Brown Bull as he charged upon her, the wickedly sharp tips of his great horns poised to gore and toss, platter-sized hooves pounding mud and grass as they would pound her body into red ruin.

Now he was almost on Maeve: flight would enrage him further and she could never outrun him, but she knew he could not be bluffed into sheering off. Instead, she lunged into his charge as he dipped his head to begin his murderous hooking toss, grasping one horn with both hands.

The rough surface tore at her palms as she leapt and twisted in mid-air, flinging herself up over the Brown Bull's head, but she kept a death-hold on the horn as she scissored her thighs around the dew-slick hide of the Bull's neck, clutching him more tightly with her legs than she had ever clutched a lover in the heights of passion. Maeve pulled at the horn she held with all the strength in her back and shoulders as the Brown Bull slowed in bewilderment.

"Get him!" She shouted breathlessly. "Catch him, now!"

The men with the ropes ran forward together, but the Bull was already wheeling, heading straight for Lothar. Maeve's herdsman did not run: he feinted forward, shouting, as 'if this were any vicious bull; but Flidais said that would not work!'

With a supreme, sinew-cracking effort, Maeve wrenched sideways at the horn she held, trying to pull the great beast's head away as he hooked at the man before him. Lothar leapt back, but stumbled as he came down; and all Maeve's strength was not quite enough to keep the Bull's horn-tip from tearing across the herdsman's belly.

Lothar's entrails tumbled out in a wave of gleaming pink before the bright blood sheeted down to veil them, and he crumpled. Maeve's effort had swung her sideways, the trampled ground whirring sickeningly before her eyes as she felt herself sliding off the Brown Bull's thick neck. In another moment she would dangle helpless from his horn, for him to toss and trample as he would.

She drew her legs up under her, pushing off into a desperate leap and curling in the air. The point of her right shoulder slammed into the earth; she rolled to her feet, ready to leap again or die. The Bull was charging the line of men.

Red misted Maeve's eyes, and every joint and sinew in her body screamed with pain as she saw the bodies flying, the blood and flesh scattering across the field, and then the Brown Bull was past, charging off along the winding path that led higher into the mountains until the fog closed to hide him from view.

Maeve dropped to her knees, shaking dreadfully, her jaw clamped tight to lock in the sobbing scream that beat against her throat. Strong arms went around her shoulders, lifting her to her feet. She bit back a cry of pain. She tried to blink the blood from her sight, saw her son's face swimming in a pale wash of red.

"Mother?" Cormac Connlongas said anxiously. "Mother, are you all right?"

"All right?" Maeve's voice caught in her throat, coming out in a halting half-sob. "No. No."

"Fedelm!" Cormac shouted. "Over here!"

"No," Maeve said again. This time her words came out clear and strong. "Let her tend those who have taken grievous hurts. I am only..."

'Only bereaved, of my rule and my hope of winning it back'. Maeve knew for certain, now, that the power that had come to her with Cruachan's queenship was gone; and the knowledge was far worse than the fear of it had been.

"Only bruised," she said firmly. "This time the Brown Bull has escaped us. We have his heifers, and I do not think he will abandon them altogether. He may resist for a time, but sooner or later, he will come to us, and we will catch him."

Cormac blinked at her in wonder. "Surely Eriu has never had a queen so brave as you, Mother! I thought for a moment I must watch you die, and then, when you leapt between the Donn's horns. The bards will sing of this for generations!"

Maeve's mouth twisted. "The bards sing of deeds that win victory, or death. I managed neither here. Come, let us see what we can do for our wounded."

In his brief passage through Maeve's men, the Donn Cuailgne had left twelve dead on the meadow, four so badly wounded that there was no hope of saving them, and two with several broken bones. The heifers lowed and shied at the smell of blood, struggling towards the road where their bull had gone, but Maeve's surviving herdsmen were already driving them back and roping them. Maeve herself could barely walk, waves of pain shooting out from her right shoulder at every step: her left hip felt as though the marrow had been rasped out and molten bronze ladled into it. Fergus took her left arm, and together he and Cormac helped her to sit on a low boulder at the side of the field.

"Cormac, would you tell Finnabair to bring up the chariots and wagons?" Maeve said. "I think we can go no further today."

"Of course, Mother," Cormac said. He trotted off, and Fergus sat on the boulder next to Maeve.

"There is nothing worse," the Ulster exile murmured, "than watching one who holds a piece of your heart face death, and being unable to aid. you are well set among the heroes of Eriu."

He passed her a water skin, and she sipped at it. It was full of apple wine; the drink might have been good, but the blood and the sharp copper after taste of fear in her mouth seemed to sour it. Maeve rinsed her mouth, spat, and drank again.

"He did not heed me," she said quietly.

"He is a creature of Ulster."

"Do not try to comfort me. I know..."

Fergus said nothing more, but he took Maeve's hand in his and held it until Fedelm and Calatín came to bind her injured shoulder and smear her cruelly aching flesh with salves. Under the surprisingly gentle strength of Calatín's long thin fingers and Fedelm's delicate touch, the pain eased back to a dull throbbing ache, but the heartsickness it left in its wake, like a seaweed-tangled corpse abandoned black on an empty beach by the ebbing tide, almost made Maeve long for her bodily agony again.

Fedelm

My queen had taken no lasting harm of body from the Donn Cuailgne. A badly wrenched shoulder and strained hip were the worst of it, as well as a few lesser sinews pulled and a great many bruises. The herdsman the Brown Bull had gutted had not looked at me with such pain when, too hurt to do more than open and close his bloody mouth wordlessly, he had signed for me to free him from his mauled flesh and show him the path to Donn's house and rebirth. I would have given Maeve a sleeping draught, and woven spells of easing over her, but when I reached for the package of henbane seeds, Calatín shook his head. I said nothing then; but later, when we had done all we could for the injured and sat in our tent, I asked,

"Why would you not let me give the queen a sleeping draught?"

Calatín sat cross-legged, pressing the point of his chin between finger and thumb. He had not shaved that morning, and the silver that speckled the prickling of black on his narrow jaw and lean cheeks gleamed in the torchlight like a scattering of salt over his face.

"Because," he said at last, "if her strength is seen to fail, then there will be little hope. Maeve must stand or fall on her own now. There is nothing we can do for her, save to keep from harming her, even through good will."

"What do you mean?" I asked.

He only said, "Recite for me the shapes of Amairgin."

Bewildered, I spoke from habit, the words rolling smooth and practiced from my tongue. "A wind on the wave; a wave of the deep; the ocean's roar. Stag of seven battles, hawk on cliff, ray of sunlight, greenest of plants. The wild boar; the salmon in river, the lake on the plain. The word of knowledge, the point of the spear; the lure beyond earth's end."

The next morning, I went to Maeve's tent at dawn. The two maidservants who had taken Lochu's place were already mixing meal and milk for porridge and heating water over one of the wretched little fires that were all we were allowed to make while we must depend on the fuel we had carried with us.

"How is it with the queen?" I asked softly.

The older one pressed her thin lips together, shaking her head; the younger merely looked aside.

"I have brought more balm for her hurts," I told them.

"She hardly seems to need it," the older woman replied.

"Is Fergus with her?" I asked. Perhaps the Ulster exile's melancholy was not what Maeve needed, it would be far better for her to have Ailill with her now, if she could bear to face him after losing the Brown Bull. Perhaps Fergus' body could offer her the easing that I did not think his spirit could, although the thought of trying to make love with hips as wrenched as Maeve's had been yesterday made me wince with sympathy. Ailill, I thought, might be able to manage such a thing, but not Fergus.

"No," the older woman said, glaring at me through narrowed eyes. "And I am sure the queen would thank you for keeping such thoughts to yourself."

Even a ban-drúi knows some battles are best not fought. I turned my back and walked to the tent. Inside, barely lit by the faint glow from the smoke hole, Maeve stood naked, slowly twisting through a variety of stretches. I drew in my breath sharply. Even in the low light, I could see the huge bruises flowering dark all over her. Her body was more black than white. I did not know how she could move, let alone balance on one leg with the other raised straight above her head, her swollen cheek pressed against her bruised thigh. The breath hissed between her teeth in pain, between mine in worry.

"My queen," I said, as respectfully as I could. "You strained your hip yesterday. If you keep on with that, you will tear it, and not be healed until weeks after your army has gone home again."

Maeve whirled on the ball of her foot to face me, lowering her leg slowly. Even her left breast was swollen and dark with bruising; I recalled that was the side she had pressed to the Brown Bull's neck.

"Who are you, to say that to me?" She demanded. "What do you know of a warrior's training?"

"Very little," I admitted. " I know a fair deal of healing, and I know that if you do not rest now, you will do more harm to yourself than the Bull did to you."

Then a thought came to me: when I had salved Maeve's hips and thighs yesterday, I had seen a few spots of blood and thought her courses were beginning. She was wearing no breech clout, and even in the faint light, I could hardly have failed to notice blood between her legs when she turned to face me.

"My queen," I said. "I should look at you more closely, for I fear you may be injured within."

Maeve's long face drew into a tight mask. "And is there any help you can give for it?"

"A poultice without, and I have some herbs that may help within. Has there been blood in your piss, or only from your womb?"

The queen blinked, as though I had suddenly changed the subject. "Neither. My courses did not come last month, nor do I feel them coming on me now, though the Moon is almost dark."

"Ah." My shoulders eased, as though I were setting down a heavy weight. Maeve's skin was still smooth, save a few creases about the eyes, her breasts and belly firm, but she was a grandmother of a good age. It was little to be wondered, that her courses should have slowed or stopped: those few drops of blood could be wholly natural. "Any road, will you give over straining your body and let it heal?"

"If I had been stronger yesterday, better able..."

"You were strong and able enough to deal with the Brown Bull when he would slay you, and I think no other in Eriu could say that," I told her. "We should rest here for two or three days, for you should not be either riding in a chariot or walking."

"I shall not rest!" Maeve hissed. "I have been told, often enough, that the Donn Cuailgne has the wit of a man. If we were hunting a man through his own mountains, found and lost him, would we give him two or three days free to escape? Fedelm, you may be a ban-fili, and Calatín a full drúi of many years' skill, but this is not Emain Macha, where even Conchobar may not speak until the Druids have had their say. Unless you be set to oppose and ban me with all your powers, we shall go on."

Maeve glared at me, one blue eye gleaming half-shut out of the bruising on the left side of her face, the other still reddened from the little blood-vessels that had burst in her struggle with the Bull. Mayhap, for her own good, I should have threatened satire, enchantment, or Druid's ban; and I was greatly tempted to do so, but I thought of what Calatín had said about harming her through good will.

"You must do as you think best," I said. "At least do not deliberately tear those muscles that are weakened! Or you will be crawling after the Brown Bull on your hands with your crippled legs trailing behind, or carried helpless in a wagon like a bundle of turf. Let me rub you with this salve, and bind your shoulder again, and then, if you must, you can lead your cantreds onward again."

Reluctantly, Maeve lay down on the bed and let me salve her bruises and sprains once more. The ointment of comfrey, mallow, and end-bit scabrous would help her heal quickly, though it would do little to dull her pain. I had brought powdered meadowsweet and willow bark for a tea to ease the queen's hurts, but as determined as she seemed to be to drive her body beyond the capabilities of human flesh, I was not inclined to make it easier for her to harm herself. Despite her bruises and injuries, Maeve rode in her chariot at the head of the host that day, following the Brown Bull's deep tracks.

Although I winced in sympathy at every jolt, she showed no sign of pain: the rigid clench of her jaw might as easily have been iron-hard determination as an effort to keep from groaning each time her light vehicle lurched on the uneven mountain paths. Whether for the fodder we offered or because we were going in the same direction that their bull had gone, the herd of heifers trotted along obediently with us, and I overheard several of the herdsmen saying nervously that the Donn Cuailgne would surely be back for them. Maeve had sent out a number of scouts to sweep the many little meadow-plateaus that lay hidden between the mountains' sloping rises, and I was not surprised when she said to me,

"Fedelm, can you divine where the Brown Bull is hiding now?"

"I can try," I answered. "I cannot approach him in dream, for no spirit can stand against his bellowing; but it may be that I can reveal him."

So, when we had stopped for the evening, I sat upon the bull's hide that Calatín had brought with us; I chewed a piece of flesh from one of the Brown Bull's heifers. My right hand held my gold-inlaid weaving rod; my left, a dried scarlet pimpernel, root, leaves, and flower. Before me, in an elegant-waisted stone brazier whose upper cup was no bigger than my two cupped hands, glowed a piece of turf upon which smoldered a handful of yarrow and mugwort leaves, sending up curls of pleasant-scented smoke into the air, smoke that would ward me, body and spirit, and aid me in my vision.

The smoke thickened, its soft grey mist blotting out the sullen red glow of the turf. The taste of bloody meat in my mouth grew sharper, a ringing copper pang through my head; it seemed to me that my whole body was beginning to vibrate like the bell-disk of a bronze trumpa.

"I call thee, Brown Bull," I murmured thickly. "Donn Cuailgne, I call thee! Broad your horns, strong your back; heifers made fruitful, hooves earth-scarring, bellow of might! Brown Bull, I call thee! Mountain-warder, warrior's pride, wit of man, raven's friend; Donn Cuailgne, I call thee!"

The grey mist before my eyes parted as though the wind from the sea had caught it. For just a moment, I saw the Brown Bull as from a great distance, standing on the rounded crown of a low mountain, his head and horns silhouetted immense against the starlight. He swung his head, sniffing the wind, then turned northwards, lumbering slowly down the gentle slope, and it seemed to me that he was heading along the mountain range towards the deep bay to Cuailgne's north.

Then the thread of vision snapped, like a strand of wool spun out too fine to hold the spindle's weight. The smoke clawed at my throat, driving me into a harsh wheezing spasm of coughs; my eyes burned and stung, and my head was beginning to ache as though a spiked iron band were tightening about my skull. I wanted nothing more than to take a painkilling draught, perhaps even a henbane seed, and tell Maeve what I had seen in the morning when I was recovered. I thought of how fiercely she had borne her own pain that day, and I could hardly do less for her.

Staggering to my feet and spitting the stale taste of blood from my mouth, I made my way to the queen's tent. Maeve lay with Finnabair rubbing the salve I had given her into her body. Bleary-eyed as I was, I noticed that her bruising had already gone down somewhat, although her breath hissed through her teeth every time her daughter touched her.

Maeve sat up abruptly when she heard me enter, though I could see the pangs it cost her. "Have you seen the Brown Bull?" She asked.

"He is going northward through the mountains," I told her. "If we follow him, he must turn or be driven down to the shore. He may mean to go there in any case," I added, thinking of my childhood among the herds. "There is little good grass this time of year, especially so high. Whatever his powers be, a bull of that size needs a great deal of feeding: he will find more to eat where the winter storms have tossed the sea-kale on shore than he will in the mountains."

"Well enough. We shall follow the track you have given; and you shall seek him every night, how far ahead of us is he?"

"My queen, I could not tell."

"If we do not come on him tomorrow, you shall seek to discover that as well."

The pain in my skull had grown so great that I could hardly see or speak: tomorrow I would be limp and near-useless as a piece of raw hide soaked in lime water for a week. I nodded slightly, and caught my head in my hands as it exploded with pain; for a moment, I feared that something had burst within, as can happen when one goes too far beyond one's strength.

I whispered, "I shall do my best." I walked from the tent as carefully as I could; I felt as though my brains had been smashed into thin liquid, sloshing agonizingly within my skull at each step.

By the time I reached our own tent, tears filled my smoke-stung eyes so that I could hardly see. Calatín took my hands, guiding me in, and lifted a cup to my lips. I drank the cool bitter draught, and let him lead me to the bed and ease me down. Calatín allowed me to perform the same divination for two nights following.

Twice I saw the same thing: the Brown Bull was still heading north, though his path wound about from meadow to meadow, mountain to mountain, so that our road was slow and difficult. His tracks were easy to follow: thrice we found the shards of a wicker bothy-frame that he had stamped to bits, and one evening we actually heard the faint echo of his lowing in the distance, but he was long-gone by morning. On the fourth night, when I went to get the sacrifice-knife, Calatín was already standing with his hand on the chest where we kept such tools.

"No," he said. "I have told Maeve you have gone beyond your strength, and shall go no further."

"Is it not my choice?" I demanded. "I know that I can bear more, and I will not have it said that a ban-fili in Druidic training failed in her duty through weakness or cowardice."

Calatín's thin lips pressed together, though I thought the corners turned up slightly. "First, I doubt you can tell us more than we know already.

Maeve may wish to ask the same question again, hoping for an answer she likes, but she will not get one for some time. Your skills are hardly needed to track the Brown Bull, whose tread marks his passing on stones, and leaves his prints stamped a hand span-deep in the high pastures. Secondly, your hands shake too badly to wield the knife tonight, nor would I trust you not to overturn the brazier and set our tent on fire. You have lost flesh; the shadows beneath your eyes are so dark it looks as though I have been beating you. Thirdly..." The Druid's smile broadened. "Thirdly, it may be your choice to risk your own life. Is it just your own life that you are risking?"

I drew in a shaking breath, pressing a hand to my belly. "Am I...?"

"I do not know," Calatín said. "The Moon is beginning to wax now, and I have not smelt your woman-blood, and it is possible, is it not?"

"Yes," I whispered.

"Well, then. Eat properly this night, and rest, and do nothing until I say you are ready again. If you feel like casting up your food, tell me. I have a remedy that Nuagal finds infallible when she is bearing."

"My child," I whispered, touching my belly. Something seemed to flutter at my touch, as though a lark beat its wings within me in great excitement, or fear. If I were bearing, I thought of the long journey back to Alba with a babe in my arms, of the maddening effort of studying with a child at my breast, crying to be fed or cleaned or petted, and my heart faltered.

'Do I really want this? If I am, and I may not be, it is new in the womb; I must choose now, to drink the tea of tansy and mugwort and small-flax and cast it out to seek a new house, or not. Dear Brigid, I have been breathing the smoke of mugwort these past nights! Please, please, let that not have harmed my baby!'

"Eat, and lie down," Calatín said. "There is no more for you to do this night."

I obeyed the Druid's orders, but I could not sleep. Warm beneath my blankets, breathing the damp chill mountain air, I lay on my back with my hands on my belly. I did not dare seek for deeper sight, lest I harm what might be there in looking for it. I envisioned it in my mind nonetheless. If a child were growing within me. Every Druid knows how a babe is shaped. At first the new-returned soul is formless, a wave of salt water and blood.

From that hidden sea comes a worm; the worm becomes a fish; the fish a beast with four legs and a tail, horse or swine, kine or deer, wolf or hound; there is little telling, but the soul knows its own shapes. At last the beast becomes a human being, a perfectly formed child, unless something should go amiss in the womb. Terror and guilt rose about me like a river, swirling and sucking at me like a black whirlpool: what if it were already too late, if I had done my babe some irreparable harm by straining to divine after the Brown Bull?

I prayed that night to Brigid with all my heart, now in a fili's perfect troigithe, the words of poetry fermenting up from the cauldron of my mind like half-brewed mead fizzing up in a great wave when one casts an apple into it; now in the simple, heartfelt prayer of any farmer's daughter: 'Dear Brigid, let my babe be all right!' I felt better the next day, my over-strain passing swiftly from me. With my health my awareness rose again. Maeve was growing gaunt, her tender cheeks long and haggard and the furrows about her mouth sinking deep and harsh. She had not spoken more than a few words to me since Calatín had refused to let me prophesy any further; she spoke chiefly to her scouts, the refrain,

"Have you seen the Brown Bull?" Echoing in my head as though she cried from mountaintop to mountaintop.

All the while we sought the Bull, the watchful hate of the glen-folk beat on our host like a constant icy wind from the heights above us. When the gales blew in from the sea, moaning through the mountains, I heard their voices crying and mocking, endlessly prophesying death and despair.

Calatín and I did our best to ward Maeve's warriors, to keep the creatures of the glens and heights outside our camp, but the longer we stayed, the harder they pressed us; our supplies of the herbs that kept them at bay were dwindling swiftly, and there would be no getting more at this time of year. We had been nearly ten days on the Brown Bull's trail when the night of dreams came. It seemed to me that I had left the camp, picking my way along the rise of a stony ridge to stand alone in a high frost-coated pasture, white mist swirling about me.

First I heard rustling and whispering to either side, then shapes began to form. The bocánach, lean dark manlike figures with starved ribs showing through thin black hair, crept from the fog first; goat-headed and goat-hoofed, they stared at me through the rectangular pupils of yellow wind-seeing eyes.

Behind them glided the pale bánánaich, thin white fingers trailing like birch-twigs and black hair twining in tangles like nests of starving adders.

Among them stood the small lithe figures of the siabra, those willful and wild lesser kin of the síde-folk, with mist turning the fair-haired dead skin-pale, and frosting the darker heads like white lichen spreading on black bark. The bánánaich murmured; the siabra sang a high eerie harmony: I did not know if it was unearthly beauty or unearthly terror that raised the prickles on the back of my neck.

"Why are you here, Fedelm, ban-fili of Connacht?" bocánach and bánánaich whispered beneath the singing, a unnerving chorus that crept dry and sickening along my skin.

"Go away, go home, leave these mountains to their dwellers, or you will surely die here."

I drew myself up, my weaving-rod gleaming bright in my hand as though it reflected the Moon's light even through the mountain mists.

"Show me where the Brown Bull is going, for you have as much desire to see him gone as we do to take him from you."

Rusty laughter crackled around me.

"We do not help intruders; thrice over do we not help foes."

A bocánach capered close to me, tossing black gnarled horns and reaching crooked fingers towards me. His cock extruded from the sheath between his scrawny dark legs, thin and barbed as a tiny black casting-spear.

"Do you think the babe in your womb still lives? Come, I shall give you better."

"You are too old already for a first bearing," a bánánaich rustled, her stick-thin fingers sweeping bony to stir the mist around her white face. "Your womb has grown misshapen; your babe is dead within you. Cast out the corpse tonight, or you will surely die with it."

I put my left hand protectively over my belly. I felt cold within, as though my body were an empty water skin filling slowly from an icy stream. I held my weaving-rod like a whip, and called,

"Get hence, go from me! I shall not listen to you nor hear you; your words of ill-omen are but moaning of the wind." As they laughed, I brought the rod down, and it seemed to me that bright lightnings flashed from it; thunder crashed, and the rain poured sudden down, scouring the meadow bare and empty.

I woke in darkness with a fist stuffed into my mouth as though I had been stifling screams. Shifting beneath my blankets, I felt the wetness slippery on my thighs, and my heart stopped with a vicious jolt that shocked through my body. My courses, or? Terrified of what I might find, I reached down carefully.

The blankets were slightly damp under me; there had been no great gushing from my womb, but so early, there might well not be. If there were ever a child there at all, I reminded myself sternly.

I ran a finger across the inside of one thigh, brought it to my face and sniffed. No blood; only sweat, musty with the stink of fear.

The geniti-glinni had haunted and frightened me, and the fact that they had been able to push through the protections Calatín and I had set up and the trained walls of my mind was near as frightening as what they had said, but if I were bearing and not merely a little more irregular in my courses than usual, my child was still safe in my womb.

"I shall keep you so, little one," I whispered.

Carefully I began to weave my wards around myself again, the complex word-rhythms and the rhymes and half-rhymes of amas and uaithne and uaim rising from the poet's vein pulsing at the back of my head to blend with the passes of my hands over my body. At last I felt myself as secure as if I lay within a palisaded hill-fort ringed by warriors, but it was still a long time before I could bring myself to sleep again. When I rose in the morning, I soon saw that no one, save perhaps Calatín and Fergus, had slept more easily than I.

A brisk icy wind from the sea had blown the crawling mountain clouds away in the night. In the bright winter sunlight, Maeve's warriors all looked pale-faced, stiff-moving, and silent as corpses set into Bran's Cauldron to rise armed and walk again. I thought I heard some muttering behind my back, and in truth, looking on their white faces, I felt my failure keenly. They had trusted Calatín and I to ward them: did they now fear that our strength was giving out. A worrying thought, would that fear turn to anger or madness, as it had in the raid on Rath Echach? It was Maeve who spoke to me first, her voice harsh and rasping.

"Have you seen the Brown Bull?" She asked. "Others dreamed last night: did you?"

"I did not see him," I answered. "His track is still easy to follow."

The bruises on Maeve's face had faded to yellowish-green, like a smear of kale against her white skin. The circles beneath her eyes were pouched out, dark and cracked as old leather. Her ill-tended golden braids looked harsh and dry as winter straw: she might almost have been a mountain hag herself. 'There is no solace I can offer her, I thought. Either we must find the Bull, and find some way to catch him, or not'.

"Go, and do what you can," Maeve said roughly. "Come back to me when you have more knowledge."

Her dismissal stung more than it ought, but I went to help Eochaid finish packing our things in the wagon that carried the tents and chests and such things for the royal enclosure. I had nearly reached the wagon when Ferdiad loomed suddenly out from behind it, blocking my way. I stared up at him.

"Forgive me, ban-fili," the young warrior said, stepping aside. " I... These mountains are wearing on me. I grew up in the rocky coast lands of the west, and am used to the unseen regard of those who dwelt here before the children of Mil. At home, those who watch are my own elder kin. Here, I feel only hatred from the crags, and I dreamed ill last night. I would have you read the dream for me."

"Tell me," I said, feeling more confident. If I could do nothing for Maeve, at least I could aid Ferdiad.

"I dreamed that I stood at the edge of our camp. Finnabair came walking out of the mists to me, all gowned in white, her golden hair blowing about her head in the wind and a cup of gold in her hand, as though she were calling me to a wedding. As I reached for the cup, a scarlet stain spread over her gown like blood; her hair darkened to the blue-sheen black of a raven's wing, and it seemed that blood dripped from the cup onto her hand...And then I cried out, and awoke."

For all Ferdiad's height and massive muscular breadth of shoulder, I saw his mouth trembling slightly beneath his short golden beard as he spoke, and he shivered inside his silver-embroidered blue bratt.

"I have heard that the siabra can take many shapes, some fair and some hideous," I said slowly. "It is in their minds to frighten us away, since they cannot harm us directly while we stay within the wards that Calatín and I set each night. Or perhaps the maid you saw sought to lure you outside, and grew angered when you did not rise from your bed to follow her, as our charms should have prevented and did prevent."

"So what I dreamed had nothing to do with Finnabair?"

"Nothing, save, perhaps, the hopes and fears of your heart, on which siabra and bánánaich play as a harper upon the strings."

Ferdiad relaxed, the great muscles of his shoulders lowering and his strong features easing.

"That is well to know. If, this night, you could give me some herb or spell to keep it from happening again..."

"I will do my best," I reassured him. He left me comforted, but my thoughts were not easy. It is said that the síde-folk never lie outright, though they may deceive and mislead until one thinks that sky is earth and white is black.

Such a thing has never been said of the lesser dwellers in the wild places, who often seek to lead travelers to their deaths by any means they may. Yet that does not mean that they cannot tell the truth, or show it. I could not help wondering if Ferdiad's dream betokened ill to come for him over Finnabair: it takes no Druid's wisdom to know that when many men set their hearts on a woman, life may not be without danger for the one who gains her. Nor, though I should have known better than to brood on it, could I help but wondering if the little worm or salmon-fingerling in my womb were already lying still with the blood festering about it, ready to claim my life as well.

There knowledge was my friend. If the bánánaich had spoken truth, Brigid forbid, it was early enough that all would pass from me of its own accord. if she had lied...no words or powers of a foe would delude me to cast my child from my womb, or from its growing house of flesh. Calatín and I worked late that night, weaving the strongest spells we could against those who assailed us from the high rocks and meadows. Perhaps, thus banished, they whispered at the edges of my dreams that night; but I slept soundly nevertheless. It was only when morning came that we discovered two men missing, a guard who had wandered away from his comrades in the night and a scout who had only come back after dark the evening before.

"They were called," Calatín said grimly. "For all we can do, there are too many minds here, and the bocánach and bánánaich have touched some more deeply through their fear than others.

All we can do is set our spells as we may, and warn each man and woman to look to their comrades and keep them from wandering in the night, even if they must knock them down and bind them."

We found the guard's body at the base of a long steep slope, caught in a dry tangle of bare thorn bushes. His blood streaked face looked as though it had been clawed by cats, his body broken from dashing against the rocks. He might have been running, and tumbled long and hard in the dark – or seized and battered by something stronger than a man. We never found the scout, and I knew that was the worse for our host. It was that evening that Fergus came to me as soon as we made camp.

"Fedelm," he said, "I know that you have little love for me, and cause to hate my foster-son. You are true to Maeve, and I have thought that the two of you are friends."

"That might have been said," I replied cautiously. "What is it you want?"

"I want you to help her. I fear for her as I never have before, I fear that she is driving herself to death, or madness. She eats little, and speaks little, save to ask after the Brown Bull, and though she tries to hide it, I can see that she is still in much pain."

"If I could help her, I would. I think. I think she is not mad, at least not yet. Nor do I think that you are telling me all you know."

"I have told you all I can," Fergus said. His mouth twisted, as though an old wound had stabbed a shaft of pain through him again. "Think on it, if you will. For myself. I would see her find peace of mind and heart, not face the Bull once more."

Fergus spread his arms as if he were standing before Maeve to protect her, his red and gold bratt blowing in the wind. 'To protect her from the Brown Bull, or from herself? I wondered. He has not done greatly well at either. Perhaps that is because she needs no man's protection'.

"I shall help my queen do what she must," I answered softly. "As to what is best for her, I think she may know that better than any other."

The next night we lost three men, and found two bodies in the morning. One, like the first, seemed to have fallen a long way. Roen the singer, who had come to tell the tale of the hunt for the Brown Bull, as his brother had gone with Ailill's army to sing of the raiding, was naked, stiff, and cold, as though he had wandered out unclad and frozen to death. The bunch of dried herbs that I had tied to his wrist with red thread myself was gone. "He must have cast it away," I whispered. I remembered the eerie music of the siabra: had its beauty lured the singer where fear could not drive him?

Five were gone the night after that, but they had all been on guard duty together. I could not help wondering if they had truly been lured by the watchers, or if they had decided to desert. Though the Brown Bull was still wandering here and there, he had kept to his northward track. As we followed his path around the last rises in the land, we could already see the low dark mountains rising on the far side of the northern bay.

It would not have been a long walk to the shore, if the guards had left of their own accord. Nor would it have surprised me. The mutterings behind my back had grown darker; the least noise always seemed to startle two or three men into spinning about with their swords drawn.

I did not doubt that there would be fighting and deaths among us, if we did not find the Brown Bull or he did not choose to leave the heights soon. With only the single stony mountain-head to shelter us from the ocean, the winds blew harsher and colder. When Calatín and I had finished our nightly working and gone to our tent, the torch Eochaid carried showed frost-crystals sparkling on the inside of the hides that covered its frame. I was about to speak when Calatín held up a long hand to silence me, cocking his head with a small smile.

"Do you hear it?" He asked.

I held my breath, listening. At first I heard only the low keening of the wind and the faint rumbling of the sea. Then I heard what he had: deep and far, the lowing of the Brown Bull.

"We shall sleep in peace tonight," the Druid said. "...That is, if it is not already too late."

"What do you mean by that?"

Calatín only shook his head, and would say no more. As for myself, it seemed that I could already feel the cold that had tightened nightly around me loosening. I knew that bocánach and bánánaich were fleeing the sound of the Donn Cuailgne's voice.

'As close as we are, mayhap this dreadful quest will be over tomorrow, if we can catch him, and live.'

Maeve

Maeve lay sore and uneasy in her bed, as she had every night of the hunt for the Donn Cuailgne. Her bruises had faded to a pale yellowish staining on her skin, and the little broken blood-vessels of her eye had healed, but her shoulder still shot a pang of agony through her whenever she lifted her arm, and she had to force herself not to limp on her strained hip. Perhaps Fedelm had been right to advise her to rest.' She was quick enough to take that advice from Calatín herself, Maeve thought angrily.

With the aid of her foresight, we might have been able to trap the Brown Bull long before this, and even he, great Druid that he is and with seven sons of his own as well, could not be certain that she is with child'. The wind keened over the mountaintop, a lonely, empty wail. Alone in the queen's great tent, hidden by the darkness, Maeve let a few hot bitter tears seep down her cheeks at last.

'This has all been a waste and a loss: we shall wander after the Bull until every one of us is dead. I shall not give up until then! What more have I to lose?'

There was another sound on the wind now, so deep and far away that Maeve was not certain whether she truly heard it, or only hoped. A great horn's call, or the lowing of the Brown Bull. She held her breath, waiting. Yes: there it sounded again, as though the Bull were bellowing to a heifer across the bay.

'It may be too late to bring me hope', she said silently. 'I will have you nonetheless: I have not come so far to turn back now.'

She strained her ears, trying to hear whether the Brown Bull were moving closer, or further away. She could not tell, but, lying in absolute silence and listening through the wind, she heard the murmuring of men's low voices at the back of her tent.

"Surely she sleeps now; she looked more than half dead today."

"If she had died when…" Maeve could not make out the rest, but her instincts flared awake like a banked turf fire bursting into sudden flame under a powerful gust of wind.

She rolled quietly out of bed, snarling in furious silent pain as her injured hip took her weight for a second. Drawing her sword sent another shock of pain through her shoulder, but the arm would hold. She lifted her shield with her left hand, moving soundlessly on bare feet to the side of the tent where she had heard the voices. For a moment there was nothing: then the unmistakable whispering sound of a knife cutting a long slit downwards through wool and leather. Maeve judged height by the noise; just as the blade reached the level of her knees, she stabbed through and down with the spear, putting all her weight behind it.

She felt the blade punching through flesh and ribs as the man below her screamed in agony. Maeve let go of the spear-shaft; pain flared in her hip, but she was almost too angry to feel it. She burst through the slit, striking to right and left in a single fluid motion. Her blade caught in something soft on the right side, ripping out and through. To the left, it rang against metal, and she saw a sword glittering in the moonlight and heard a man's harsh panting above the others' moans.

"Raiders!" Maeve shouted as she fought. "Guards, to me!" The man still standing was good, his short sword flashing in quick arcs and sharp straight hacks.

His shield-rim smashed a glancing explosion of brilliance across her right eye; as her shield came up, a line of cold fire licked up her left thigh, warm blood trailing after it. Half-blinded, Maeve chopped down brutally, and his sword went flying from a half-severed hand. Her left arm punched out hard, slamming the edge of her own shield into his face. Her enemy staggered, his shield-guard wavering open, and she struck reflexively with a rising stab, her point slicing into his belly and tearing upward. Panting, Maeve dropped her shield and pressed her left hand to her bleeding leg as her guards ran up with torches... only six men, where she had set nine that night. Ferdiad was in the lead, his sword naked in his hand and his blue eyes staring about wildly.

"Where...?"

Maeve pointed at the ground. The first man still rattled like a gigged frog; he gave one last twitch and fell limp. Her blade had opened the second man's throat. He lay face-down in a wide pool of dark blood that drowned his features.

The one she had gutted was still moving. His dark eyes blinked; his mouth worked as he tried to speak, a thin line of froth dribbling into his ruddy beard.

"Madwoman," he grunted. "No, true queen." He struggled to rise, pressing his good hand against the ground.

Then a fresh rush of blood spurted out of the wound, bright even in the torchlight, she must have nicked one of the great arteries inside him, and he slumped back, dead.Maeve bent to look more closely at the faces.

"These were my own guardsmen," she said grimly. "Ferdiad, how did this come to pass?"

"My queen, I swear I do not know! I trusted these men, I would never have let them take this post if I did not." The big young man paused, and Maeve saw water pooling in his eyes. "Now I have failed you twice. Send me to herd your swine, if you will. I am not worthy to be your champion."

"No. It was the duty of the Druids to protect us from the madness-whispers of the glen-folk. If they could not tell that something was amiss with these guardsmen, how could you? Have this carrion hauled away and call Calatín to see to my wound, it is not much, but I think it will need sewing. Then go back to your post, Ferdiad. I still trust you." As much as I can trust anyone here.

"Thank you, my queen," Ferdiad whispered, the sheen of a tear on his fair cheek.

Holding her wound shut with her left hand, Maeve limped around her tent and back in. Despite her words to Ferdiad, she kept her sword out in her right, though now that the bout of battle-fury was over, she was unsure that she could even lift it to shoulder-level. For a brief moment, the bright red madness had freed her from herself; but it had already drained away, leaving the copper-sweet smell of blood clogging her nose and throat like a nauseating medicine, her hip and shoulder throbbing with agony, and her heart beating with slow sickening thuds.

'No queen, he said. I have tried my best to hide it; but what one man sees, another will see soon'. Maeve did not let herself grimace at the pricking of the needle and the pulling sensation of the fine sinew drawing her skin together over the cut, though the sharp stinging on top of all the other pains reverberating through her body was almost unbearable.

"Was it the madness of the watchers that took them?" She asked Calatín as he tied off the last stitch.

The Druid looked up from where he knelt, his dark gaze curiously intimate and unfathomable. "If I do not summon their ghosts before they have fled too far, we shall never know. Is that your wish?"

"I...no. No."

Whether bocánach and bánánaich and the wicked little siabra had whispered treason in her guards' minds, or whether the men had thought it on their own, Maeve knew enough of the truth, as she had learned when she sought to summon the power of Maeve of Cruachan against the Donn Cuailgne. 'Tomorrow I shall face the Brown Bull again. Even if we capture him with rope and spear, and bring him home to be judged against Finnbennach; and even if he should prove the greater, can that restore what I have lost? Will my folk follow me long enough to get him home?' Maeve refused to ride in the wagon with the other wounded as her host followed the curving track down the mountain to the bay.

Instead, she sat in the back of her own chariot, clenching her teeth at each bump in the road as they passed between patches of white mist and grey light. The icy wind blew salt and seaweed into her face, stinging her swollen eye and split brow.

They were nearing the Brown Bull now, his lowing ringing out through the thin sea-fog like a deep horn calling ships to shore. 'I do not have to face him myself. I cannot run, nor leap: none will call me coward if I let my warriors and herdsmen take him. Surely I have done enough!' For Maeve was afraid: the last time she had come closer to death than ever in her life.

Then she had been hale; while this morning, she had needed to use a spear as a crutch to hobble to the chariot, and let Ferdiad lift her in. They reached the foot of the mountain, rounding it as the Brown Bull bellowed once more. He was very close, his voice drowning out the sound of the wind-whipped waves beating on the shore.

"Stop, Finnabair," Maeve said. "We shall walk from here, and you shall stay behind in charge of the charioteers and servants once more."

Finnabair nodded, pressing her mother's hand tightly between her own.

"May the gods of Cruachan watch over you, Mother," the young woman murmured.

"May it be so," Maeve replied, though she knew it would not. The gods of Cruachan had abandoned her with the loss of her rule. She had only herself, and whatever loyalty lingered among her warriors.

Then Maeve had to wait for Ferdiad to leap from his own chariot and take her by the waist.

Her champion lifted her as if she had been a harvest straw-doll, easily raising her over the chariot's edge and settling her carefully on the ground, supporting herself until she could balance on her good leg and get her spear braced to hold herself up.

"Get the men into order, Ferdiad," Maeve said. "You and Cormac and Fergus know the array we have planned: see to it."

"At once, my queen," Ferdiad said.

Maeve's army moved slowly along the seaweed-strewn beach. Each man held a spear and a rope; the swiftest runners were nearest the waves eating their way up the sand, ready to block the Brown Bull's path if he should try to swim across the bay. From down here, the mountain they had just crossed rose steep and sharp, its rocky sides strewn with clumps of white cloud clinging here and there like a stone on which sheep had been scratching themselves. A rainstorm was moving swiftly from the north, grey already drowning the tops of the dark mountains on the other side.

The tide was coming in, rising around the low patches of rock that scaled the bay: soon they would be no more than little slicks of darkness against the white-foaming grey water. The sea-mist was thicker as they rounded the base of the mountain and followed the beach southward. The Donn Cuailgne's lowing seemed to come from all around them, echoing back and forth off cliff and water as if two great bulls were challenging each other from either side of the host.

When the Brown Bull lunged from the fog, he came with breathtaking swiftness, a huge horned shadow scattering men about like sticks in a child's game.

Cormac, Fergus, and Ferdiad had all avoided the first charge: they shouted to their troops, ordering them into a five man-deep ring about the Bull with spears grounded and sloping inward like the sucking-toothed mouth of a giant lamprey, as if to stop a chariot charge. Maeve would not have the Donn Cuailgne slain, after seeking him so long. He would have the wit not to ram himself into a spear-point; even horses usually had more sense.

"We have you now," Maeve panted, limping painfully along beside Fedelm. The ban-drúi frowned up at her, an oddly stern expression on her delicate face, but Maeve had no time for that. "You stay back!" Maeve said to her. "There is no need for you to risk yourself." Fedelm halted, but Maeve went on ahead, grimacing at every halting step until she stood about fifty paces behind the ranks of fighters, far enough away that their backs could not block her view of what was happening within the circle.

The Brown Bull stood in the middle of the ring of spears, swinging his heavy-horned head back and forth in search of an escape.

"Step in!" Fergus shouted. "Step!" The warriors with their spears and ropes strode another pace inwards, then another, bracing their spears after each advance, slowly tightening the ring around the Bull.

The great beast shifted from foot to foot, stamping a great fore hoof deep into the sand as he readied himself to charge again.

"Hold fast!" Called Fergus, and the armed men crouched to brace their spears more tightly.

It seemed to Maeve that she could see the gleam of angry intelligence in the Bull's black eyes as he sought his way out, looking over the heads of her men from water to mountains. Then his raging gaze fixed upon her and the strength went from her legs, so that she had to clutch tight to her spear to keep from dropping to her knees on the coarse sand.

"I will not turn from you in fear!" Maeve whispered fiercely. "Conchobar beat and raped me for a year, and I still had the courage to defy him and leave. Though I could not withstand him then, I did not flee when he assaulted me again. Nor, hard as it was, did I let his memory drive me to the fear of men afterwards. Brown Bull of Cuailgne, I shall not flee you either." She pushed the spear hard into the sand, forcing herself upright to stare into the Bull's eyes.

Swifter than any beast so great should have been able to move, the Brown Bull lowered his head and charged forward. For a moment Maeve thought he would run straight onto the spears, but he swung his head in a hooking motion, casting the points aside in a single powerful sweep. A couple of spear men managed to drop their weapons and leap away; the others, unbalanced, fell, screaming as the Bull trampled them, bursting from the circle. Maeve straightened to meet him.

He was not charging her. His gaze was fixed straight on Fedelm, her small white-robed figure almost lost in the thickening grey mist. The blood burst hot down Maeve's leg again as she ran to place herself between the Brown Bull and Fedelm. The Bull skidded to a halt ten paces from Maeve, his tail switching back and forth and puffs of white snorting from his huge dark nostrils, head down and horns moving in swift threatening hooks.

Her swollen right eye burned as a trickle of fresh blood ran down into it from her split eyebrow, clogging and darkening her sight.

"You and I," Maeve panted. "This is between us; Fedelm followed you at my will: you may not have her, save you go through me." Her heart was suddenly, strangely light. She knew she would die now, and she no longer cared; she still felt empty, but it was the emptiness of a vessel scoured clean.

Whatever waited beyond, whether the death of Maeve's pine marten had broken Ochall's tie to her so that she might fare unmolested to the House of Donn, or whether there was another battle past this for her, she was ready for it. Others had paid the price for her queenship long enough: that, too, was the cost of leading; but now it was her turn. Maeve would die, and Cruachan be freed of her empty rule. With her death, the power could pass living to Finnabair, and the land have a true queen again.

"Come on, then. Kill me if you can, for I shall pursue you while I live, until one of us falls to the other."

The Bull lifted his head, black eyes staring deep into Maeve's. She stared back, all fear and anger gone. There was only the moment between them, and her will, purer than the gleam of a single fine-honed spear-tip: to die, rather than give ground. She waited, squinting against the pain in her right eye with all her weight poised on her good leg, to see what the Brown Bull would do. The great head lowered, horns nearly sweeping the sand.

In the next heartbeat, he would be on her, goring and trampling and crushing. Maeve drew her last breath, tasting the unutterable sweetness of the damp salt air.

Her blood muttered and rushed against her eardrums: she could hear nothing else. He did not charge. Then Maeve realized what she was hearing. The Brown Bull had begun to munch a clump of black sea-wrack that lay on the strand before him, its tiny bladders popping and crunching as he drew its long flat fingers into his mouth. Unable to believe it, Maeve still stood staring as Ferdiad walked up beside the Bull and tied his rope of thick-plaited osiers around the man-thick dark neck.

Watching in amazement, she saw the Donn Cuailgne lift his head slowly, walking behind her champion. Ferdiad led the Bull to Maeve, pressing the end of the rope into her hand. She closed her fingers over its rough scratchiness, still unbelieving. The Brown Bull stood there, docile as any suckling calf; and when she took a halting step, he moved with her.

"Oró, Maeve!" Someone shouted. The rest of the host took up the cry, "Oró, Queen Maeve! Maeve of Cruachan!" Until mountains and sea resounded with it, and the Brown Bull lifted his head once more to bellow acknowledgment. Maeve barely felt Fergus and Cormac coming up on either side to support her. A spattering of rain struck her face, cold and pure, washing the burning blood from her swollen eye. Each breath she took was rich with salt and seaweed and the warm earthy scent of the Brown Bull; even the pain shooting through her from hip and shoulder and the torn stitches on her bleeding thigh seemed keen and sweet.

'I am alive, Maeve thought in wonder. Still queen of Cruachan; or at least I may be again.'

Fedelm

I waited only long enough to see Fergus and Ferdiad lift Maeve into a wagon, settling her to sit as a queen in her high seat on the waxed hides that covered cheeses and ale-barrels as Calatín began restitching her thigh. This time Maeve did not protest the wagon: her open eye had the dazed, water-clear look of one whose soul has begun the journey to the Otherworlds and been called back suddenly. I had seen it on candidates emerging from the last bardic trial, body numb from icy water and the weight of stone, eyes blinded by a night of darkness, stumbling and blinking in disbelief at the sunrise brightness.

I remembered coming forth thus myself: each long yellow leaf clinging to the branches of the ash-trees sharp-edged as a sword, each blade of brown grass keen-tipped as a spear, the pale blue light of winter's first morning stinging my eyes full of brightness, so that it seemed I looked at everything through a piece of clear rippling glass, all unreal, yet, like a vision, brighter and truer than anything in waking life. I had felt every blade of frosty dry grass scratching the soles of my feet, the smooth coolness of my fine white linen robe slipping over my skin with each movement; the thrilling caress of winter wind on my damp face.

Hence, I knew what Maeve felt now: come back from the death she had chosen and met, with the cheers of her warriors still ringing between mountain and sea, it would be a little time before she was truly herself again. I would need to see that she ate before too long, to seal her soul back into her flesh, but for now the best thing was to let it settle. I...When the Brown Bull's gaze had met mine, I, too, had known myself dead. I had seen the flare of recognition and fury in his huge dark eyes, as though he were at last certain of the one who had been spying upon him. His anger had struck me a blow as heavy as his bellow had when first I sighted him in my visions, stunning me as if his great head had already crashed into my chest.

Even for the sake of the child that might be in my belly, I could not move, only stare helplessly as he thundered towards me. I will never know if I might have recovered quickly enough to spring and clamber up the rocks piled at the edge of the strand before the Bull reached me, or not, because Maeve put herself between him and me, with only a spear she was too injured to use. Perhaps she moved in despair, at seeing the Brown Bull about to escape her warriors for the second time; perhaps. Even Maeve herself might not know; how could I.

Had she stopped for a heartbeat's thought, the Bull would have been past her to attack me: she would have been safe. 'And that, I thought in a rush of awe and love, is a true queen'. Maeve's wagon began to move, the Brown Bull walking behind as if he were guarding his own herd of heifers. The warriors were all staring at their battered queen in her triumph, so I slipped quietly aside behind a row of armored backs, down to a piling of rocks with the waves foaming white about its base, and climbed carefully down to wash.

The warm wetness on my thighs might have frightened me at another time; but I knew what it was; I was only glad that at least my bowels had held against the Bull's glare. Nor did I reproach my flesh for its weakness. If my soul had not been able to stand against the Brown Bull's might, how should my body not have been shaken to the roots?

We followed the strand back around the edge of the northern bay, skirting the feet of the mountains. The road back through the mountains was straight if one traced the paths in the sand, but with wagons and chariots, it would be easier and swifter to go around. After I judged that enough time had passed, I told Eochaid to stop our chariot so that I could get out.

"You are going to see that the queen eats?" Said Calatín.

"I am...unless you think I should wait a little longer?"

Calatín's narrow mouth curved into a small smile.

"Your sense for the hour grows stronger. Had you not known to go now, I would have sent you. Take this." He reached into his belt-pouch and drew out a small phial of deep purple glass, filled with some dark liquid.

The tiny bottle itself would have been worth a gold arm ring or two; I was sure that its contents were the more valuable.

"This is an extract of white-flowered poppy, sent to me by our kin in Gaul who trade with the southern folk. It is far stronger than our own red poppies. Give Maeve three drops of it, for when her spirit is altogether reseated in her body, her injuries will begin to cause her needless pain."

I thought once more of my bardic ordeal, how even the stabbing agony as the blood warmed my feet and hands again had seemed only another of the keen sensations that swept through me; and how, when the exaltation of being recalled to life had passed, I had fought not to whimper as every shudder jarred my bruised chest and cold-knotted muscles almost past bearing.

"Ah, you understand," Calatín said softly, his dark eyes gazing down into my own. "I, too, have felt what it is, to pass from my body to the Otherworld, and to be flung back again when I had set one foot on the ferry to the House of Donn and one eye on the brightness beyond world's end. Go to our queen, now, and do not fear that you will harm her. For sometimes the flesh must feel pain to strengthen and free the spirit; but when the spirit has won its battle, then the flesh may be soothed."

I went to fetch some food for the queen, and made my way to Maeve's wagon on foot. The Donn Cuailgne turned his head, one huge dark eye glaring sideways at me. "I am here to aid my queen," I said softly to him. "Let me pass, Brown Bull, and do me no harm, as I mean none to you and yours."

He made a low grumbling noise in the depths of his massive chest, but looked away. As slowly as the oxen pulling the wain walked, it would have been easy for me to haul myself over the edge empty-handed. With a bag of food and a tall clay jar of cider, it was more of an effort, but I managed. Maeve sat with her back propped against a stack of round cheeses under a thick hide.

More cheeses, sewn tightly into their waxed linen shrouds, supported her injured leg; her sword-arm was bound up against her chest. The right side of her face was brutally battered, her eye the thinnest glint of blue in the swollen purple-black mass and her eyebrow standing out incongruously golden against the bruising.

Calatín had washed the blood from her face and restitched the gash through her split eyebrow; the discolored swelling glistened with ointment. She would heal, and be as fair as before. For now, between that and the faint yellow-green stain of the old bruises on the other side, Maeve looked as if she had fought a dozen over matched combats without respite.

At least the bruising stopped above her jaw: I would not have to offer her the humiliation of having another cut and pound and soak her food into paste. Maeve's right arm twitched against the bandages as she tried to reach for me without thought, and a spasm of pain passed over the untouched parts of her face.

I carefully measured out the three drops Calatín had prescribed into a little silver spoon and held it to her mouth. She grimaced and shuddered as she swallowed, then winced again with pain at the movement.

"Have you something else to drink?" She asked. "I have never tasted so bitter a draught!"

I passed Maeve the jar of cider, steadying it as she lifted it left-handed, letting the golden stream flow as if she had gone thirsty for days. Mayhap she had; I knew she had hardly been eating.

"You must eat as well, my queen," I said firmly. I drew out the food I had brought for her.

White cheese with caraway seeds sprinkled through it; reddish-black strips of smoked venison glistening with salt, and twice-baked journey bread, still crisp and free of mold in spite of the fog and rain. Maeve began to worry at a bite of jerky, wincing as the movement pulled against her swollen cheek. She was lucky that neither her cheekbone nor the ridge of her eye had broken.

The blow must have been a glancing one, for a strong warrior could smash facial bones with a shield-rim as easily as with a more heavy weapon.

Maeve did not speak, but ate steadily: I guessed that, renewed from death to life, she was also recognizing her body's hunger for the first time in days. I sliced the cheese and broke the journey-bread into pieces for her, and after a time, as Calatín's potion began to work on her, she relaxed a little.

"My queen," I said when she had finished eating, "you saved my life."

Maeve took another long swallow of cider, then passed the jug left-handed to me. "I suppose I did," she said, her voice soft and a little bewildered. "I saw that the Brown Bull was going for you, and, well, I could not let him have you. You have come so far for me, and struggled to the limits of your strength. I had not been kind to you these last days, though Calatín was right when he told me that you should not keep on searching for the Bull by magic."

"You drove yourself harder," I answered.

"Still…I hope that I did no harm to you, nor the child in your womb."

"Calatín told you that?" Is he more certain of my pregnancy than he professed to be?

"Aye, he did. Do not be angry with him: I would not have listened otherwise. You carry Ailill's child, or may.

I…have come to think of you as something of a daughter, or a younger sister." Maeve's voice was thick, the black apple of her good eye widening in spite of the sunlight slanting down between the heavy drifts of cloud to gleam from her crown of golden braids. The tightness of her face had eased, the deep furrows carved by the strained days and haunted nights smoothing as I watched, as though Maeve grew younger before my eyes.

If Calatín had not told me what was in his phial, I would have suspected henbane seeds and nightshade. I resolved to pay close attention, lest I should need to use the Southern poppy-draught on a patient sometime myself.

"Is the pain gone?" I asked.

"Yes, it is gone. For the first time in so long, Fedelm, why did the Bull halt then? I could not fight him or run, and I was ready to die."

"You no longer had any fear," I answered, and knew it true, as surely as the hidden river of blood pulsed in the poet's vein at the back of my skull.

"Because he had never seen anyone, living or a creature of the Otherworld, who could face his wrath without a trembling heart; but you feared neither him nor death, so he knew he could not defeat you. You were willing to die to protect one of your own folk, without a second thought. Would Conchobar have done as much? Or any ruler in Eriu?"

"Fergus would," Maeve murmured, "and Ailill, perhaps."

"I think Ailill would, but it is not he in whom the might of the land lives."

"And so," Maeve mused, "I live because I was willing to die, and the Brown Bull has acknowledged me." I heard the drowsy satisfaction in her voice, but a faint chill prickled over my skin, as if in answer to the distant blast of a war-horn.

"You will not have the victory until you have brought him to Cruachan, and he has proven himself against Finnbennach," I warned her. "It is a long way back; I could not bind Cú Chulainn outside the borders of Cuailgne. There is no surety that you, or the Bull, or any of us will return to Cruachan."

"I know..." Maeve whispered. The slit of her right eye had closed altogether; her left lid drooped. "Calatín said I would come back, but not how or when.

Perhaps such fore telling are a marsh-wisp flickering its light across a misty bog at night, a guide that may lead on a safe way or into the sucking mud's embrace, with no telling which..." Her eye closed, her head sagging. I thought she was falling asleep, but she jerked upright and looked at me again. "Fedelm, are you truly carrying Ailill's child?"

"I hope so."

"That is well. Do you wish me to tell him of it?"

"No...At least not until I am certain. Then, yes, I would have him know. Only if he will be glad of it! If not, then I will rejoice enough in what I have, without giving him trouble of mind in return for the gifts he has given me."

Maeve smiled sleepily. "If you bear Ailill's child, he shall be glad of it. As I said before, if you wish to be his second wife, I will welcome you joyfully. If you go back to Alba first, you will go laden with wealth, to raise your child as befits a king's son or daughter; and you shall always have any place with us you wish. Ailill loves his bairns; he has never let one go uncared for, however light-hearted its besetting might have been, and I will bear no more. Two dark moons have passed on this raid, and my courses have not come down. Only a few little spots of blood, the night we cursed Conchobar."

Maeve spoke drowsily, as if deep in trance, but I was wide awake, the blood thrumming in my veins. We had called on the Hag, and I had missed my courses as well.

"What of Finnabair? Do you know if she...?"

"I think they did not come on her last month, I think I should have known, for she often has painful cramps. Not as bad as some women, who must take to their beds for a day or two, but enough that I would have noticed when she drove me. This month..." Even through the soft blurring of the poppy juice clear on Maeve's face, I could see the muted echo of guilt, and hear it rustling behind her soft words like a tree's dry leaves in the autumn wind. "I do not think I would have noticed."

"Hard though the way has been, this part of the raid is over, and you victorious," I soothed. Maeve had earned her rest, and needed it. "Sleep now, and heal."

Maeve sighed gratefully as I came behind her, moving the cheeses and helping her to lie back with her head in my lap, as if she were my own child. I gently stroked a few wisps of golden hair that had come out of her braids back from her forehead, careful not to touch the dark stains of bruising on her face. She stirred a little, as if in protest.

"You need not fear that I will think you weak for taking comfort," I whispered to her. "I have never seen anyone bear up as bravely under sorrow and hurt as you, my queen."

Maeve sighed again, a faint hiss of air. As strong as Calatín's southern potion was, I wondered if she would remember anything that we had said between us when she awoke.

The muscles of Maeve's neck eased, resting the full weight of her head upon my thigh, limp and trusting as Conall when he had gone to sleep after a feed. I looked tenderly down at her. Someday, Brigid willing, before next Samhain! I would hold a babe of my own so; and watch him or her grow from babe to child, youth or maiden, and thence to woman or man. I hoped with all my heart that my child would not suffer as Maeve had. Yet, I thought of the pains I had endured in my own training; a warrior took bruises and slashes and broken bones as a matter of course.

If my child were to achieve aught, it would have to learn pain in plenty. Girl or boy, I did not want it to be a coward or weakling; but I did not know how I could watch my little one pay the suffering of bravery and strength – battered as Maeve now was; immured in the stone coffin of icy water and struggling to sing with a great stone on his or her chest as I had been; hacked about on the battlefield, screaming in childbirth.

I was not even certain of my pregnancy, let alone my maybe-babe's sex; and yet the thought of the pains that might come to it years from now tightened my belly with fear and brought tears to my eyes. Now I understood how torn Maeve was between her pride in her warrior sons and her fear for them; why, though Orlamh's last fight had given him a brave death by his own choice, his loss still racked her with guilt. She was still his mother: she could not and should not have kept him from the risks of the battlefield, but her heart still cried out that she should have protected her son. We were three days rounding the foot of the mountains.

With the Brown Bull's lowing lulling us to sleep at night, we had no fear of the hate of bocánach and bánánaich, nor the spite of the little siabra. Now that Maeve was resting and eating properly, she healed quickly; by the time we reached the plain, though her bruises still stained her face with a sickly rainbow of blue and yellow and green, the swelling was almost wholly gone, the gash through her eyebrow healed so clean that one would have to look very close to see the faint line of pink scarring.

She still limped slightly, but was able to ride in her chariot again, though, Calatín insisted that her sword-arm stay bound up for a little longer. It was not until the third day that I got a chance to speak with Finnabair alone.

She took great pride in doing a charioteer's duties, even those that one so well-born might easily have left to the servants without criticism; she was rubbing down and grooming her mother's golden horses when I came up to her and said, "Finnabair, I have a question I must ask you."

Finnabair glanced sideways at me, pushing a coil of fair hair from her forehead. "Ask away."

"Have your courses come upon you since we began this raid?"

She looked harder at me. Since that flare of hard fury when we cursed Conchobar, she had kept her strength well-hidden. We had spoken in passing, but perhaps I was too aware that she was Maeve's daughter, or she, that I was a ban-fili and Druidic student. Or maybe it was only that Finnabair was as quiet as Maeve was outspoken and Suithchern eager to giggle and share her thoughts with a friend, though when Maeve's daughter carried cups to the war leaders with her fair eyelashes fluttering, or played up to Connla and his ilk, it was easy to think of her as less than her mother.

Now her blue gaze was cold and bright as the sunlit winter sky. "I am not with child. I have not lain with any man."

"I know that," I said, speaking as carefully as I would to a strange large hound standing in my road with its hackles raising.

"I do not mean to pry, nor am I suggesting aught. It is as ban-drúi, or at least ban-drúi in training, that I ask: have your courses come upon you?"

Finnabair drew herself straight up, the silver currycomb held lightly in her right hand like a dagger. "Why do you ask?"

"It may be of some importance. So, I ask thrice: have your courses come upon you?"

Finnabair regarded me a little longer, but finally turned back to working her comb carefully through the flaxen tail of one of the horses. "Yes," she said without looking at me, her voice slightly muffled. "I missed the first dark moon, and the second, but they began yesterday. I did not ask Calatín for aid, for Flidais knows that my blood often brings pain on the first day, and she gave me herbs for it when we set out."

"I see, thank you," I said, and turned, thinking that Finnabair would not wish to speak further.

"Wait!" Maeve's daughter said, lowering her currycomb again and looking straight at me. "Why is such a thing of any importance? Is it to do with the men of Ulster, and how long they have lain in their pangs, so much longer than any have heard of before?"

"It may be," I said regretfully. Frost on the land; frost in our wombs; the Hag's cold touch. If that grip were easing. "We can only wait and find out."

Maeve was of an age for her womb to dry; my courses had always been irregular, and Finnabair was not accustomed to the hardships of such journeying. What nature shapes always has meaning, but sometimes the message is not directly for us.

Still, if the force of our curse were beginning to fail, the men of Ulster would begin to arise, with Conchobar's own men at the end and the king himself last of all. I would have to warn Maeve: now that we had the Brown Bull and a good share of plunder, for the forts and villages we had passed along the coast and the mountains feet all bore signs that they had been well and truly looted, we would do best to travel home as quickly as we might, without any of the detours and delays that Fergus had tricked us into following on the way to Cuailgne.

Maeve

By the time Maeve's part of the army reached the plain at the foot of Cuailgne's mountains, the greater portion of her host was drawn up there. She could see the glitter of standard-poles and chariot-mountings, spear points and helms, from a great distance, a shifting sparkle under the clear winter sky like a thick dust of gold and steel over the plain. As she came closer, the glints of metal separated, shining above the bright colors of warriors' mantles.

Even so far away, it seemed to her that her host, freed for a time from Cú Chulainn's assaults and turning homewards with their plunder, had found new heart. She could not see faces yet, could barely make out the shapes of bodies and limbs, bu. something in the way her folk stood and moved told her the creeping blackness of fear had left their blood. Maeve was riding in her own chariot again, with the Brown Bull following behind her and his heifers, every one in calf! Trailing after.

Her sword-arm was still bandaged, but the Druids had sworn the binding would come off in a few days, and her bruised face, bad as it was, would hardly be a shocking sight to those who were used to war and training for war. The standard-pole that upheld the gilded bronze pine-marten of Cruachan was fastened firmly to its socket in her chariot. If she still felt a pang every time she looked at the sleek glittering form, her shoulder chilling where the live marten had once curled silky and warm, at least the sight of Cruachan's emblem no longer gnawed her with hopeless loss as it had since Cú Chulainn's sling-ball had smashed the little animal from her shoulder.

In the middle of the great host, nine bronze serpents reared suddenly up, their flared disks catching the sun in a shattered ring of brilliance. The great trumpas sang, deep and powerful, some holding the lowest notes and others' voices rising above. Behind Maeve's chariot, the Brown Bull lifted his head and bellowed greeting, the earth-trembling bass of his lowing weaving seamlessly into the tune, catching it and magnifying it as the horns' disks caught the higher notes and cast them out to be heard over miles. Despite Fedelm's half-remembered warning, Maeve's heart swelled with delighted triumph. A small of chariots detached itself from the army ahead, charging towards Maeve's cantreds.

She saw the glitter of Ailill's gilded helm-crest, the bright golden and ruddy-gold heads of their sons in the chariots around him. All six of the boys, alive and well, she smiled in pride and relief, but not without a twinge of pain: with Orlamh dead, she would never count them again with quite the same delight.

"Oró, Maeve!" Ailill called as the seven chariots pounded up to her. "Is that the Donn Cuailgne I see behind you?"

"It is, indeed," Maeve answered.

Ailill's driver cracked the reins, racing ahead of the king's sons and wheeling dangerously close to Maeve's own horses.

As he slowed, Ailill leapt from the chariot, tumbling exuberantly in the air and somersaulting up to his feet with agility surprising in such a large man.

"You are well-returned, by the gods of my clan, Maeve, what happened to you?" Ailill's laughter had dropped from his bright-mustached face like an unpinned mantle slithering away, leaving only shock and concern.

Maeve drew in a deep breath, looking for words to tell him how it had been, on the winding haunted ways through the Cuailgne mountains. that unbearable nadir of despair, as though she had finally sunk to the bottom of a deep icy well...when she had realized that the trust of her folk, the last thing that had made her a queen, had broken.

She could not deny it to herself, but she would not speak it aloud, even to the man who had been as much a part of her as her right arm for over twenty years. She said only, "Three of my guardsmen were driven mad by the mountains' watchers, and attacked me. I defeated them all, but one managed to strike me with his shield before he died."

"And your arm, how badly injured is it?"

"Hard-strained, and perhaps slightly torn. That hurt I took when we first met with the Brown Bull, and is a little thing against what might have befallen me under his horns and hooves. Let Fedelm tell you the tale, if she will."

"Fedelm? What of Roen, who went with you that he might compose your part of the tale?"

Maeve sighed.

"He is lost too. The bánánaich, or perhaps the siabra, called him in the night. We found him naked and cold, and he had cast away the charm that would have warded him from them."

Ailill grimaced, his blue-green eyes crinkling wryly.

"His brother Roi, who came with us, is dead as well. We were caught in a flood crossing a river; many chariots were swept away and men drowned, our poet among them. Well, perhaps Fedelm will sing our tale, or another: there are harpists aplenty among our host. You, daughter?" He said to Finnabair. "Have you survived unscathed?"

Finnabair also paused before answering, her eyes distant and clear as the winter sky. Maeve wondered if she were weighing the terrors of their search against mere hurts of the body; but when Finnabair spoke, her voice was lively.

"I have, Father. I was hardly in danger, for Mother left me to tend the chariots and servants. I did not see her leap onto the Brown Bull's neck at the first, nor overcome him at the last. Perhaps that is as well, for my heart would surely have failed in my breast."

It saddened Maeve a little, to hear Finnabair speaking to her father in the same soft and guileful tones that she would have used to the kings of Munster. Ailill only boomed out a great laugh, reaching up to tousle his daughter's hair.

"Save your nose-ring for the poor fools who court you; I know better than to be led by it. I am glad that your mother took good care of you, for you are the dearest treasure of all that is fair in Cruachan."

His strong face sobered again, though his accustomed grin still flickered about the corners of his mouth.

"And you are well-come now, for Flidais and I have been wrangling with the kings of Munster about the sharing of our plunder for a day and a half. Since you are here, we can sort matters out quickly enough, and be on the home-road before evening."

Maeve nodded, turning to wave her troops on again as her sons came up to greet her. Feidhlim, Cairbre, Dáire, Ceat, Sin, and Eochaid: the six surviving Mainí swarmed about their mother as if they were small boys again, asking questions one on top of the other, until Maeve had to laugh and wave them off as if she were beating at midges.

"Enough, enough! Tonight there will be time to tell you everything!" Or everything that can be told.

The plunder of Cuailgne had already been sorted by the time Maeve arrived. Fine cloth in many colors, ornaments and cups of gold and silver and bronze, and bright-shining weapons lay in heaps on the plain, reminding Maeve uncomfortably of the reckoning between herself and Ailill.

Herds of cattle and horses milled in wicker enclosures, and in another stood a large group of women and boys, some weeping or glaring in sullen defiance, the captives of noble blood, and others, most likely those who had been bonds folk before, simply waiting with the patience of those who knew that their future was unlikely to be much different from their past. Maeve's herd of heifers looked a small thing, next to what the rest of the army had won on their sweep around the peninsula, but the Brown Bull towered above all, the gloss of his dark hide in the sunlight making the piles of plunder tawdry by comparison.

Flidais was waiting with the seven under-kings of Munster. She hurried forward to embrace Maeve as soon as Maeve's feet were on the ground, her long cape of shining red curls falling about them both; but she could not turn her gaze from the Donn Cuailgne.

"You have not had an easy way, it seems, but what a bull!" She exclaimed. "I have never seen his like. Even the aurochs of Gaul is not such a magnificent beast, nor has it such sweeping horns. Truly he is worth the trouble of this raid!"

'In more ways than I can tell you, even you, my sister-queen', Maeve thought.

"It is a pity that he cannot be divided with the rest of our plunder," Connla broke in. "For now that I see the Brown Bull, I think that you have won more than your share, even though we did battle about the whole of Cuailgne for ours while you were traipsing unhindered through the mountains."

"Unhindered?" Cormac said dangerously, leaping from his own chariot to glare at the Munster underling. "We faced things that I hope you will someday know, while you fought farmers and boys and those few arms-bearing women of Cuailgne, to win as much glory as you did at Rath Echach."

Undaunted by Cormac's wrath, Connla merely looked up at the younger man.

"We took the part of battle, and you did not, though I see by Queen Maeve's face that you did not all escape unscathed. Let us not quarrel over such things! I only seek to see that all is distributed fairly, and that those who were parted hear properly of each other's deeds," he added, looking at Finnabair.

Finnabair lowered her golden lashes, looking modestly away from the Munsterman. Maeve guessed that it was as well for Connla that her daughter had never sought to learn weapons-skill.

'And she has him well and truly by the nose-ring now, as Ailill said. What will befall when she must turn loose of it at last? We will do well, to make sure the man she marries is strong enough to defeat Connla and his allies outright if need be.'

"Well, all that we have won is sorted and counted," said Flidais. "And I..." She gave the Munster underlings a hard look... "have divided it evenly to be shared between all our cantreds, as we agreed at the beginning that all plunder, save only the Brown Bull himself, should be, in fairness, while the Brown Bull is yours without question, it may be that his,heifers, which I mark are all with calf – ought to be divided out among the host as well. Though we should not separate them until the Brown Bull is back in Cruachan, for I doubt he would take well to being deprived of his brides so soon."

"We have captured plenty of other heifers to put to him," Cumail said eagerly.

Flidais shook her head. "That is a matter for she who holds the Bull to decide. It is not a part of the army's plunder: we knew that from the outset."

Connla and his fellow under-kings complained a little longer, but it was clear to Maeve that they were only posturing. As the wagons of the various cantreds rolled in, Maeve walked a little aside with Flidais.

"That was easier than I expected, from what Ailill said," she murmured.

Flidais sighed, running her fingers through her thick red hair.

"You see the tuft of the cow's tail, and mistake it for a mouse. I thought several times that it would come to fighting here on this plain. If we were not so far from home, or if Connla did not hold such hope of Finnabair and yet know that you could still pull her away at the last moment. You are lying to him, aren't you?"

Maeve snorted softly. "Do you truly think I would marry my daughter to that man? If she loved him, I would still be against the match; but she despises him. I would cut him down myself first."

"Aye, and I would help you. Be careful. He means to come out as the chief hero of this raid." Flidais lowered her voice still further. "Your poet Roi died when the river-flood caught us, true, but I am not altogether certain whether his skull was truly crushed by wreckage in the water, or whether one of the Munstermen saw an opportunity then."

Maeve raised her brows, although the right one pulled painfully against the bruising and the little cut through it.

"Surely not! Roi was a skilled poet, if not a Druid-trained fili. Even Connla would hardly dare to have him assailed so."

"The vengeance of poets is only a threat when one knows a name to be satirized," Flidais said darkly. "And I, well, I recalled what you told me of Cumail at Rath Echach, so I kept a close watch on him. Twice he had to be restrained from harming Ulstermen in their beds, not, thank Brigid, with the sword this time, but he could hardly be held back from using fists and feet. I think he has little fear of curses, and a great love for killing and hurting; and such men are more dangerous than any others."

Even Cú Chulainn feared Fedelm's word, Maeve thought. She nodded slowly.

"Well, the Munstermen are a large enough part of our host. I would rather have them with us, and thrice rather not be weakened by fighting them while we are still on the road home, with it unknown when Ulster's men may arise. Still, if it comes to it, we can deal with them by force of arms."

"Indeed."

As the army swung into movement again, Maeve's sons surrounded her once more. When they heard the tale of her guards' treachery, they all insisted that none but themselves should guard their mother in future. Maeve laughed with pride and embraced them, but added,

"Ferdiad shall be with you. Though he failed to keep me as safe as he wished, that was through no fault of his own, and I would not have him feel that I was setting him aside. Remember, my sons, that a ruler must care for the pride of her, or his, followers as well as their bodies; and I think that Ferdiad's pride was more greatly harmed than my face. Now, if you would guard me, come with me, for I must speak with my Druids."

When Maeve had found Fedelm and Calatín, she climbed down from her chariot, and motioned the Druids down as well.

"Let us walk together a little way, for I would speak with you quietly, our charioteers to either side of us, and my sons surrounding us without."

Calatín nodded, handing Fedelm down carefully. Maeve noted with approval how easily he lifted her; Fedelm was no more than middle height, and slim-built, but she might have been a small child in the Druid's wiry grasp. Calatín leapt down lithely and paced beside her, waiting for her to speak.

"It has come to me," Maeve said, the words tumbling eagerly from her mouth, "that Fedelm by herself, skilled ban-fili, but not yet a full-trained Druid, was able to ban Cú Chulainn from assailing us within the bounds of Cuailgne, just as he was able to force our host to another road with a single spancel-hoop. That being so, is it possible that you two, perhaps together with the other Druids who have come with the kings and queens of our army, might be able to hold him altogether from harming or delaying us further?" 'Why did you Druids not think of this already, while Orlamh still lived?' Was Maeve's next thought, though she managed to keep her tongue behind the bit of her teeth. Calatín sighed and shook his head, his narrow face mournful.

"The powers of a Druid may seem boundless to one who has not known what it is to wield them, but stricter rules that bind us than any that guide the doings of other folk. Fedelm was able to bind Cú Chulainn because he slew, though unknowing, an unarmed maidservant. It is not magic that has held him back, or not much, save for that which springs from a fili's words, but his own shame. Even if it were wholly magic, such things cannot work without justice to shape them, any more than words are poetry without the structure of foot and rhythm and rhyme. Cú Chulainn could work against us as he did because he was able to set a challenge that few others could match, and it cost him grievously in soul-strength to exclude Fergus. Had he not been able to equal his own challenge, he could not have made it to us. Nor, since Lochu was slain by accident, could Fedelm bind Cú Chulainn longer than it has taken to find the Bull, nor can your curse upon Conchobar last longer than the grip of the Winter Hag. All power is shaped and defined by its limits; but without those limits, there is no power. If Cú Chulainn performs no more infamous deeds, and I think he will be careful where his sling-balls strike in future, there is nothing we can do." The Druid paused, fingers rasping over the grizzled stubble on his lean jaw. "If he were tricked into eating the flesh of the hound that is his name-beast and sigil. Then he would lose strength and luck altogether; then he would have to fall. I do not think he would come to such a banquet here, nor trust unknown meat from our hands."

"So there is nothing you can do?" Maeve asked sharply.

"For now, this raid has become a matter of swords and spears again. If I think that I can strike a good blow, I assure you that I shall; if there is aught that I can do by my arts, I shall do that too. This is my counsel for now. Leave thoughts of magic aside, and prepare to defend your army from the Hound by the strength that you have in this world, for it is in this world that the others are anchored."

"I thank you for your counsel," Maeve said politely. She would sooner have grabbed the tall Druid by his wiry shoulders and shaken him until she got a better answer, but the greatest rage of her life had never risen high enough to drive her to such foolishness.

Maeve

Unhappy as Maeve was with Calatín's advice, she knew better than to disregard it. Her army passed the standing stones that marked the borders of Cuailgne well before sunset. The moment they crossed that border, her sons and Ferdiad closed and lifted their shields around her, so that even if the Hound could creep into the middle of Maeve's host, he would have no clear shot.

Maeve hated feeling so trampled and blinded again, a captive in the middle of her own army, all the worse after the exaltation of riding through Cuailgne with the Brown Bull behind her, but her victory would do her no good if Cú Chulainn broke her head, and her return to Cruachan were only as a corpse or a babe reborn in later days, even now, she still did not know if Ochall could come for her after death.

Although Maeve had half expected Cú Chulainn's next attack the moment she passed the mark-stones, the army marched on and made camp in peace. Her sons and Ferdiad guarded the royal enclosure, coming to eat one at a time. They had wanted to stand guard all night, but Ailill had pointed out that if they took it in shifts, there would never be enough of them watching to do any good, and if they did not, they would be useless the next day.

Maeve and Ailill's foster-son Etarcomol took his turn, on the understanding that if he started any quarreling among the guardsmen he would not be allowed to stand with them again; and so did several of Ailill's nephews and younger cousins from Leinster. Maeve herself had little fear of another betrayal. Her boys and Ailill's kin took such pride in their duty that she could not gainsay them; and Ferdiad stood the straighter for being the only man in that company not tied to the royal house by blood or fosterer.

'Though perhaps he hopes the day will come, if only Finnabair would turn her gaze towards him, and forget that accursed Ulsterman...' Maeve was lying in Ailill's arms, drifting off into a comfortable sleep, when the commotion began outside.

Distant shouting, growing louder and nearer as more took up the cry; the Brown Bull's shattering bellow, the sound of running feet. She cursed and rolled slowly out of bed. Gentle and skilled as Ailill was, and she could not have endured more vigorous handling yet, her hip still throbbed, and her shoulder was beginning to ache sharply again.

"Where do you think you are going?" Ailill asked. She heard the wood and rope of the bed's frame creak as his weight left it, followed by the rustling as he pulled on his clothes in the dark.

"Our camp is being attacked! What else should I do, but go to deal with it?"

"Our foe's chief target, and your sword-arm still bound to keep you from injuring it further? There is bravery and duty, and then there is stupidity. I know if I ordered you not to go, you would have to. I am not such a fool, and so I ask you to stay.

I'll beg, if I must!" Although Maeve could barely see her husband's silhouette hulking black against the darkness, the pleading in his voice was unmistakable, and she thought he was pulling hard at his mustaches as if to rein in his own rashness. "Please, Maeve. I could not bear to lose you; and none could name you fearful, after all you have done."

"Connla could, and no doubt will," Maeve said grimly. " I have no wish to risk my head for the sake of impressing him; and while he thinks Finnabair is nearly in his grasp, he will at least keep his whispering quiet. Yes, Ailill, I will stay this time."

"Thank you." Ailill bent to kiss her, his warm mouth and soft mustaches sweeping gently over her face. Maeve heard the sound of him buckling on his sword belt. The tent-flap opened; for a moment he was silhouetted against the low-burning camp fire outside.

"You are ringed all around her tent? Good, stay there!" Ailill said to her guards, and then he was gone into the muffled sounds of shouting and running, leaving Maeve to pull on tunic and trousers and try to fasten her mantle-brooch one-handed, then to sit in the dark and worry with runnels of sweat chilling on her brow in the icy winter air.

She thought about calling for a torch, then thought better of it. There was no sense in risking a light that might make her tent a clearer target. *My sons are outside, and Ailill.* Maeve's fists tightened hard enough to cramp, her jaw clenched and aching. Her guards would not come into the tent with her: it would be too easy for someone outside to fling a firebrand at it.

To leave her kin and loved ones outside, while she sat in the nearest thing to safety her camp could afford, that was far harder to bear than battle. It seemed an endless time before Ailill at last came back, stamping his feet and swearing.

"May Crom Cruaich eat that wretched little siabra's soul, if he has one!" He shouted. As long as they had been married, Maeve had almost never seen her husband so angry – or at least not showing it so clearly.

"What is it? What did he do?"

"He has been running about outside our camp with his sling, now shooting from here, now from there. None of our warriors would go after him with less than twenty companions, and thrice seven men to catch one in the dark…" Ailill sighed and sat down heavily, as if all the strength of his anger had flowed out in that single breath. "I would sooner that all the hosts of Ulster had come against us in open battle, where we could see to fight. We cannot pull all our fighters into the tents and bothies, then he might do as he pleased in our camp; and yet whoever walks outside armed is a target."

"Where is Fergus?" Said Maeve coldly.

"He is with his Ulster exiles. Before you ask: no, the Hound is not shooting at them. He can tell them from the rest: I put some of my own Leinstermen among them, and he picked them out like red currants in a bowl of blackberries."

Ailill's frustration and grief seemed to drip from his voice like drops of water falling from a soaked sheepskin.

"What, then, can we do? He can kill an hundred of us a night, if he chooses, and there is no way for us to chase him down."

"Send one of the servants to fetch Fergus. If anyone who knows how to deal with this, it is he."

Fergus came swiftly. He bore a torch with him, of course, he is safer if Cú Chulainn can see his face, Maeve thought, her heart bursting with anger. Like Maeve and Ailill, he seemed to have leapt abruptly from his bed; his chestnut hair hung in a long ruck down his back, and his checkered mantle of scarlet and gold was on wrong-side out.

"He is your foster-son," Maeve said before Fergus could open his mouth. "And you have been speaking with him. Now you will speak with us. Tell us how to deal with this scourge on our host."

Fergus' mouth tightened. He touched the hilt of the wooden sword that had filled his scabbard since Midwinter, not a warrior's gesture, but as a man might touch a charm against ill luck, or a token to remind him of a vow.

"Cú Chulainn does what he can for Ulster's sake, since no other is able. Should he come alone against an army with sword and spear in the daylight, and be slaughtered to no avail?"

"We could hardly object to that," Ailill said dryly. "Surely there must be some middle ground by which he can save his pride, and we our warriors? After all, we are not marching on to raid Emain Macha, but have begun our journey homewards."

"With the Brown Bull, and the plunder of Cuailgne," Fergus remarked. "Is he to let you go, with that shame upon the face of Ulster? Would you leave the matter, were Finnbennach in the foe's camp?"

Maeve and Ailill looked at each other. Ailill's mouth was tight with anger, but it seemed to Maeve that she could see her husband's defeat in the creases of his brow and the tired droop of his eyelids. For that, she would gladly have killed Cú Chulainn an hundred times over.

"You have been speaking to the Hound. Very well: speak to him again, and find out what he will have. I shall not give over the Brown Bull, but beyond that, perhaps we can come to terms. He is not an Ulsterman born: if he came over to us, I should set him beside Ferdiad as Connacht's champion; whatever Conchobar's gifts, I should give them twice over. Fedelm, whose word abashed him – instead of satire, she should make praise-poems, that his name should ring out an hundred generations from now. Indeed, we should give him Finnabair, whom all men desire, as his wife. Though he slew her brother, it may be that his skill and bravery have earned him that greatest sign of peace."

Ailill's ruddy eyebrow twitched, a sign Maeve knew well: Are you lying? Her left shoulder moved slightly in return: Maybe: we shall see what comes of it. Fergus looked keenly from one to the other, as though he knew that some hidden speech was passing between them, though he could not guess its meaning.

"I will speak to him," the Ulsterman said carefully, "if you will tell me more clearly what you wish me to offer."

"Very well. He shall be compensated for the damage done to Ulstermen, as the men of Eriu best adjudge. He shall have entertainment at all times in Crúachan, and wine and mead shall be served to him, and he shall come into my service and into the service of Ailill, for that is more advantageous for him than to be in the service of the petty lord with whom he now is." Fergus sighed.

"I shall take him those words, though I think no more scornful and insulting speech has been spoken on this raid than to call Conchobar a petty lord. If he does not accept?"

"Then let him be offered those of the cattle that have milk and those of the captives who are base-born, and let him cease to ply his sling on the men of Eriu and let him allow the hosts at least to sleep. If he will not have that, then offer all the dry kine of the herds and all the noble among the captives, so that he ceases his slinging against the men of Eriu. If he will come over to us, then the champion's portion shall be his, and Finnabair his bride."

Fergus' brows furrowed. "It seems to me that there are many men whom you have given reason to hope for that latter."

"If any disappointed suitors wish to fight over the matter, I am sure Cú Chulainn can deal with them himself, if he is worthy to be our daughter's husband?"

Fergus gave a short harsh bark of laughter.

"You can wonder that? I shall take the terms as you have given them, though I advise you not to expect too much in return."

Had Maeve's sword-arm not been still in its bindings, she would have struck Fergus. 'You comforted me in the depths of my sorrow, and I you, Maeve thought. You sought the Brown Bull with me; you said I held a piece of your heart. This youth Cú Chulainn is not even of your blood, and yet you show me scorn for his sake, despite all I thought we shared: why?'

And despite her anger, she could not look at Fergus' powerful shoulders without remembering his strength and vigor driving her pleasure, nor gaze at his stern face without remembering it lighting in youthful joy as he leapt his chariot over the oak, and softening with care and hope when they had lain together.

Even now, she quivered within at the thought of caressing his strong-muscled body, running her hands through his thick chestnut hair and drawing him into her; and that made her angrier than before.

"Go, and take our terms to Cú Chulainn before he disturbs our sleep further," Maeve said, coldly as if she were speaking to a sullen and slothful bondsman.

"I am sure you can find him swiftly enough: you always seem to have done before."

Fergus' grey eyes glinted red in the torchlight, and he opened his mouth. A shattering bellow burst through the tent, so loud that it seemed to drown Maeve's sight in blackness for a moment. The tent-poles shook; the bed-frame rattled silently beneath the stunning sound. For a strange heartbeat, Maeve thought it was Fergus who had shouted; then she realized what it must be.

"The Bull!" She cried, her voice thin and distant in the ringing echo of the Donn Cuailgne's bellow. "Cú Chulainn is attacking the Brown Bull!"

Now Maeve would not be stayed; she grasped her sword left-handed and ran out of the tent. Cursing, Ailill and Fergus grabbed their shields and followed her. Her guards leapt to take their places around the three of them, their shields raised high and Ailill and Fergus' straight overhead to form a tortoise's shell over Maeve, while their own flesh protected her from any lower shots. The smoke of the torch in Fergus' right hand curled dark beneath the shields, stinging Maeve's eyes and scratching her throat. Maeve heard a loud crackling sound, followed by a long snapping and smashing.

"Let me see, gods curse you!" She shouted. Ferdiad and Etarcomol shifted just far enough apart for her to get a glimpse through the crack between them, seeing the massive dark shape smashing through the withy-weave about the royal enclosure. The whole fence had buckled, twisting and falling beneath the powerful hooves, and a swift twinge of fear bit into Maeve: had the Brown Bull decided to turn back to Ulster. The Bull halted before her guards, lowering his head to Maeve as he had before, and stood quiet there in front of the ruin he had made. His breath snorted from his huge nostrils in white puffs, and the firelight reddened the thin steam rising from his shining dark coat in the icy winter air, so that he looked like a very monster from the depths of the underworlds.

"So, so," Maeve said softly, her knees weak with relief. "You are safe with me, and I with you."

"I shall go to see what has happened," Fergus said.

"I think we shall all go. It may be needful for you to enclose me in a walking fort, but I shall not be a prisoner in the middle of my own army when such things are happening! Buide mac Ban Thai was guarding the Bull with his troop of twenty-four picked warriors: we shall see what he has to say."

Beneath the unwieldy shield-fort of her guards and husband, Maeve moved to the enclosure where the Brown Bull and his heifers had been kept. That fence, too, had been smashed beneath the Bull's hooves; some of his heifers were still milling uncertainly, but the hoof-furrowed icy ground showed that most of them had made a panicked flight together into the camp.

"Over here," Ferdiad said, and the guardsmen walked Maeve along to the right. Buide was on the ground: her guardsmen passed around him and closed again to bring the fallen man safely inside their ring. Buide grunted as he turned his head to look up at Maeve, his homely face twisted with pain and smeared with blood. He lay on his side, the shaft of a short spear jutting from his chest and its darkened blade sticking out of his back.

"My queen," he gasped, coughing out another gout of blood. "He... didn't get the Bull. Was walking with, Murchadh mac Eoghan , thought he was his charioteer, until he asked my name, with an Ulster voice. Then I knew and we traded spears. I kept his gift, and he cast mine away."

"You have done well, Buide. You met Cú Chulainn without fear, and gave the Brown Bull time to escape, and that shall never be forgotten. Would you have me pull the spear out now?"

"Yes, my queen," Buide moaned. He closed his eyes. Maeve bent to brush a kiss across his lips, then grasped the shaft of the spear firmly with her left hand, bracing her feet hard, and drew it out of his body with one swift yank. Blood spurted, staining Buide's blue mantle dark; he gave a sharp cry and thrashed, then suddenly fell limp. Maeve laid the spear over him, gently folding his hands.

"Now," she said, "for Murchadh mac Eoghan."

"We shall not have long to wait," Ailill answered grimly. "Buide's men are bringing him now, though he may be little able to answer questions."

Maeve's guards parted again, and two blue-cloaked warriors dragged a third man inside. The beating Murchadh had taken made all Maeve's battering look like a child's scrape.

His face was a mass of purple and red, his nose flattened to one side and almost lost in the swelling. Maeve could see the white glint of broken teeth beneath his ruined lips; his mantle was covered with blood and vomit, and his arms and legs hung at strange angles. His breath whistled out pitifully through mouth and nose; one eye was closed altogether, the other no more than a shrinking slit of darkness.

"Why did you do it?" Maeve asked. "Did I not give you gold and land and praise for your faithfulness and your sword? How did you come to betray me thus?"

For a moment she thought that Murchadh was beyond answering. Then the words hissed out, thin and slurred and painful through the battered remains of his mouth. "Troops, hunting him. Lost sight of charioteer, went back, he caught me. Said he'd, chop off my stones and spear, thrust his barbed gae bolga into my entrails from beneath, leave me, bleed and die in shame." The mauled traitor's head drooped; he did not have the strength to scream as he sagged broken-boned against his captors' grip, but his soft gasp said all that needed saying of his agony.

Still Maeve felt no pity.

"And now you are the worse off. For you have shamed yourself, worse than the Hound of Ulster could have done in his worst wrath, and you shall die in dishonor and pain."

"Give him to Calatín, my queen!" One of Buide's men said. "Imbolc is coming; let him burn in the wicker, or be slaughtered for Crom Cruaich, that our fields be fruitful and some good come of him."

Maeve glanced at Ailill. He shrugged, his mouth set grimly.

"Do as you will with him. I have little love for seeing such, but less for a traitor's deeds done to his queen's harm and comrades' deaths."

Maeve did not want to ask Fergus' counsel, but she could not help the sideways flicker of her eyes. Fergus' lips were pressed as though he would spit in contempt, with no sign of mercy or sympathy on his fierce hawkish features. Torn between Maeve and Cú Chulainn he might be; but there would be no help for cowards and traitors from him, whomever they aided. 'And if I do not deal harshly enough with this man now, there may be others who think that it is better to risk my wrath than Cú Chulainn's'. The love and loyalty of her folk was a sweet draught for Maeve; to set them in such fear was bitter. She knew, all too well, that a ruler must mingle both cups or swiftly fall, and she had her chance to lay down the burdens of sovereignty with its joys.

"Strip his clothes, and his manhood, from him," Maeve ordered. "Walk him about the camp as he is, that all may see him and know his crime; give his broken legs no more support than you must. When that is done. He chose to be Cú Chulainn's man instead of mine.

Take him outside the camp, and leave him there for his master to tend, if he will. If any other in this army finds Cú Chulainn's service more to their taste, let them go now, and fight against us as honest folk."

Buide's two companions nodded grimly.

"That is well-chosen, my queen," one stated.

The blue-cloaked men dragged Maeve's ruined warrior away, and her guards turned back with her, the Brown Bull still following protectively behind. The remains of the royal enclosure's flattened wicker fence cracked and snapped under their feet as they walked over. Maeve looked down at the wreckage, and suddenly began to laugh, the smoke of Fergus' torch bringing water to her eyes.

"Can you share your jest with us?" Ailill asked.

"I thought, the Donn Cuailgne is a king too. We should have made a place for him here to begin with: no wonder he felt that he needed to burst in!"

It was the weakest jest Maeve had made in her life, and yet it was the funniest thing in the world. Maeve's shoulders shook with her great heaving gasps and her belly was beginning to ache with her laughter, the smoke-stung tears streaming down her face in painful rivulets. Ailill looked at her, taken aback, then suddenly threw back his head and guffawed uncontrollably.

The two of them leaned on each other to hold each other up, like a pair of drunks laughing at something in which only drunks could possibly find any hope of laughter.

Maeve

Maeve awoke to the sound of men's voices, Fergus' deep and rich, Etarcomol's sharp and high.

"Where do you think you are going?" Fergus was asking.

"I am going with you," Etarcomol replied. "Cú Chulainn has crept unknown into our camp twice. Now I will behold his form and appearance, so that we shall not be tricked again."

Maeve sighed, crawling out of her blankets. The cold air shivered a trailing of goosebumps over her skin as the two women who had taken Lochu's place hastily dressed and armed her.

"If you will listen to me," Fergus was saying to Maeve's foster-son, "you will certainly not go to speak with Cú Chulainn."

"And why not?" Etarcomol asked. "What would you say to him, that you would not have me hear?"

"I will say nothing to Cú Chulainn that I would not say even if Maeve and Ailill stood beside me. I know you, Etarcomol. You are light-hearted, sharp-tongued, and arrogant; Cú Chulainn is fierce, valorous, and hostile. If the two of you come together, you will surely fight. Maeve and Ailill have lost one son already; would you have them lose a fosterling as well?"

"And can you not protect me?" Etarcomol asked mockingly.

"Is your arm so weak, or Cú Chulainn so heedless of your honor, that your oath of safe conduct means nothing to him?"

Maeve heard the stifled grumbling noise deep in Fergus' throat. "I can protect you, so long as you yourself do not seek the combat. If you challenge Cú Chulainn, then Lugh and the Dagda witness, what happens to you shall be on your own head and no shame on mine!"

"I shall not seek it," Etarcomol replied.

Maeve stepped out of the tent. "You had best not," she cautioned her foster-son.

"Fergus goes to bring our terms to the Hound of Ulster, and by all honor, there should be no fighting nor challenges on either side until that is done with. True, it would be well for Cú Chulainn's face to be known to more than a few here, but if you provoke him to kill you, that will hardly happen."

"And if I should kill him?" Etarcomol smiled triumphantly at Maeve. "However good he be with a slingshot or from ambush in the woods, I have heard that he is only a little siabra of a man."

Maeve stared harshly up at her foster-son. Etarcomol was very tall and rangy, dark hair curling around an elegantly-planed face. His chin was deeply cleft, and his bright blue eyes glittered from beneath arched black brows, a face to make young women's knees weaken, and young men's fists itch, and Etarcomol knew it. He was a skilled fighter, as he needed to be; but Orlamh had been better.

"He is a fool, who thinks that victory with sword and spear can be foretold by measuring an opponent's height. I will not have you challenging, or provoking, the Hound of Ulster this day." Maeve looked at Etarcomol's charioteer, a handsome sturdy youth with red curly hair by the name of Comgan. "Comgan, I hope that you will aid Etarcomol in keeping a bridle upon his tongue."

The gilla ducked his head, abashed under Maeve's gaze. "As best I can, my queen," he mumbled.

"I do not like this, and would rather you were not going," Maeve stated plainly to her foster-son. "Yet it would be well for one of us to look on Cú Chulainn, and for two to hear how he answers our terms; for neither of you is trained in memory as a Druid or fili, and one may remember what another forgets. So, if I have your word of good conduct, you may accompany Fergus." 'I know you, Etarcomol; and I know that if I do not give you permission, you will go anyway, and then your tongue will get the better of you and you will certainly shame Cú Chulainn into killing you'.

"You have my word," Etarcomol said lightly. "I will come back safe to you."

Maeve gave him a long look. She remembered the small dark-haired boy placed in her keeping, whose tongue often got the better of the other youths until their fists got the better of him. She and Ailill had salved his black eyes and bloodied nose more than once; they had shown him how to fight and wrestle bigger lads, then, when his growth suddenly came in his fourteenth and fifteenth year, how to use his height and reach against smaller fighters. Troublesome as he is, I would grieve to see him dead.

"See that you do," she said at last.

Taking Etarcomol's head between her hands, she pulled it down and laid a kiss on his forehead, as she had bent to do when he stood no higher than her waist. A heavy snow had fallen in the night, but the clouds had passed already, leaving only a few faint white feathers behind. The plain was a wide glittering field beneath the pale pink and gold of the sunrise, the army's tents and bothies like so many drumlins humped up beneath their white covering. The servants muttered and grumbled as they began to shovel the thick wet layer away so they could strike the tents, but Maeve stood looking at it in delight until her guards surrounded her again.

"Fergus has gone to make parley," she argued. "Surely I am safe until his return?"

"No, Mother," Feidhlim said. "There is no telling what the Hound may do. We shall guard you until the matter is certain."

"I shall stay with you, at least," Ailill said from outside the shield-ring. "Move aside, boys, and let me in."

Maeve's sons kept their post while their parents ate. "I wish that Etarcomol had not gone with Fergus," Ailill said, spooning up another bite of the smooth honeyed wheat porridge and chewing thoughtfully on a currant. Maeve had to admit that the older maidservant, Fearbh, was a better cook than Lochu had been.

"So do I," Maeve admitted. "He promised me that he would keep his tongue in order, but…"

"We have heard that song since he was a small lad. I am not too afraid for Etarcomol's life, since Fergus is with him, but if he says the wrong thing at the wrong moment, I fear there will be no coming to terms with Cú Chulainn.

Unless we can do so, either to buy peace or bring him to real combat, I fear there will be nothing we can do except endure his thunder-feats of the sling every night, and lose. He slew thirty-five men last night, shooting and running and shooting from the dark . not including Buide." 'Or Murchadh', Maeve thought. That man's name would not be spoken again, nor long remembered.

"Well, we shall see what word Fergus brings back. I could not hold Etarcomol, for had he not gone beside Fergus, he would have followed behind him, with neither protection nor promise."

"True enough. I am not blaming you."

The pale winter sun had nearly reached her noonday height when Ferdiad said,

"I see two chariots returning." Maeve was about to blow out a breath of relief, but her champion added, "I fear that the news will be ill: Fergus is in one with his gilla, but Etarcomol's charioteer is alone."

Maeve looked at her husband. Ailill's eyes closed briefly, his heavy shoulders sagging. Neither of them needed to speak: Maeve knew her husband's grief, and was sure that he knew her anger. The chariots rumbled up, and beyond the shield-wall around her, Maeve heard Fergus say,

"You may stand aside: the queen is safe for now."

Maeve's sons lowered their shields and stepped aside. Grim-faced, Fergus pulled the cloak off the body in the bottom of his chariot. Etarcomol lay naked and sundered in three pieces, split from crown to middle, with the lower half of his body sliced cleanly from the upper.

A swath of hair was missing from the crown of his head, as though a razor had passed slickly over it.

"Here is your young warrior for you," Fergus said angrily.

"'Every restoration together with its restitution', as the law says."

'Now I know whose side you are on: you let Cú Chulainn kill him!' Maeve thought. Aloud, she said,

"I thought that the honor under which Etarcomol went forth was not the honor of a coward, was even the honor of Fergus!" Her voice was sharp and loud enough that Ailill and her sons winced back from the sound, but Fergus stood fast, the thin scar down his cheek purpling.

"What makes you so angry, wench?" The Ulsterman snarled back at Maeve.

She raised her hand: the only thing that held her back from striking Fergus was the certain knowledge that having him half-hearted in her own camp was better than having him turn altogether to Cú Chulainn.

"Was it fit for the whelp to seek the Hound of battle, whom the warriors and champions of four of Eriu's five provinces cannot withstand him, and I myself should not be sure of coming whole from single combat with him? Aye, I gave him my protection, but he left it of his own accord. After we had spoken with Cú Chulainn and turned back towards the army, Etarcomol lagged behind, pretending his chariot-shaft needed mending and he would catch up with me.

I halted a little further up the road to wait, and then Comgan came and told me Cú Chulainn had slain his master. I came back to the ford where we had met, and found Etarcomol lying thus." Fergus worked his mouth, spitting into the snow as though to clear a foul taste from his mouth.

"And I cursed Cú Chulainn then, for he had set my words of protection aside so lightly. The Hound told me to ask Etarcomol's own gilla what had befallen. I did; and it was clear to me that Etarcomol had earned all he received."

Maeve looked up at Comgan. Etarcomol's charioteer's eyes were swollen and red, though his tears had dried. Now the flush spread over his face to drown the spattering of freckles over his cheeks.

"He would fight, whatever I said to him. Cú Chulainn was little willing to do battle with him, but Etarcomol provoked him until there was no other choice. They began to fight: Cú Chulainn cut away the sod beneath his feet so he fell helpless on his back, and told him to give over for Fergus' sake. Etarcomol said he would fight on. Then Cú Chulainn leapt and passed his sword over Etarcomol's head, shearing away his hair as neatly as any man could do with a razor, and told him to give over and go home. Yet I think the Hound could have done no worse, for now Etarcomol was humiliated, and that he could never bear.

He vowed that the combat should not end until one had spilled the life of the other. Only then did Cú Chulainn strike him as you see, from crown to navel, side to side, so he fell in three pieces and his blood and bowels and lights went into the snow. There was nothing I could do. He had thought to be the first man to meet Cú Chulainn at the ford tomorrow, but he would not wait..."

The young man's voice had grown thicker as he spoke, as though his tongue were swelling in his mouth from grief. With his last words, Comgan turned his head aside and hid his face in his hands. While the gilla spoke, Fergus had covered Etarcomol's body again. Maeve looked at the mounded scarlet bratt with its blue and silver tracery of embroidery, now stained a deeper red here and there.

Though the other women of her court had done most of the work, she and Finnabair had both had a hand in decorating the mantle. Her anger had drained from her as Comgan spoke, leaving only a sick sadness behind. It was not truly aimed at Fergus, as Maeve had thought at first, but at Etarcomol himself, and he would not hear it on his way to the house of Donn. She remembered how she had bidden him farewell, thinking of the child whom Fid and Leithrinn had given trustingly into her care. 'I knew already then, she thought. I could not stop him: he chose his own end.'

"I will bear the news to Finnabair," Ailill said, as if he knew the thought in Maeve's mind. He did not turn to go, only stood there staring at the heap beneath the bright cloth. "The brave fool," he murmured sadly.

"At least none could say that he was a coward, or that he had the least trace of willingness to retreat in him, whatever he faced. Yet I could wish, for the sake of his father and mother, that he had been just a little wiser, and perhaps a hairsbreadth less brave."

Maeve coughed, clearing the thickness from her throat. When they were back in Cruachan, there would be time to grieve, but she still had many other mothers' sons and daughters to care for.

"What did Cú Chulainn say to our terms?" She asked coldly.

Fergus looked down at her. The flush of anger had drained from his face as well, leaving his harsh-carved features pale and sad, but his voice was firm and steady, as though he welcomed the chance to speak of something other than Etarcomol's death.

"He said that he would not accept your first offer. If the Ulstermen had no dry cows, they would kill the milch cows for companies and satirists and guests, for the sake of their honor; lacking noble women, they would take their low-born women to bed and begot children of base blood. As for the second, the Ulstermen would kill all their dry kine for the sake of their honor, for Ulstermen are generous, and Ulster would then be left with neither dry cattle nor milch cattle. Without bondswomen, they would set their free-born women to work at querns and kneading troughs and bring them into slavery and servile work; and Cú Chulainn does not wish his legacy in Ulster to be the reproach of having made slaves and bondwomen of the daughters of the kings and royal leaders of Ulster. Nor will he abandon that king to whom he has sworn his faithfulness, for whatever reward; and there is a woman whom he holds far dearer in his eye than Finnabair, however fair she be. This offer he makes. That one man from the men of Ireland should fight him every day. While that man is being killed, the army may march. Then when he has killed that man, another warrior shall be sent to him at the ford, or else the men of Ireland shall remain in camp where they are until the bright hour of sunrise on the morrow. Cú Chulainn shall be fed and clothed by you while this truce lasts."

'From the sound of it, Etarcomol would hardly have won us an hundred paces, Maeve thought bitterly. If he was not the best fighter in our host, he was still skilled.

"Fergus, Ailill and I must speak together on this. Will you wait here a while, and have your midday meal if you have not yet eaten? By the time you are done, we should have an answer for the Hound."

Fergus nodded curtly. His grey eyes were hard and opaque as flint, but he replied as courteously as she had spoken, as if they were met for the first time at this parley.

"That is well offered. I shall wait until you are ready to speak."

Maeve turned to her sons. Dáire hastily dashed the back of his hand across his eyes, saying in a choked voice, "We shall see to our foster-brother's body, Mother."

Inside Maeve's tent, Fearbh poured goblets of mead for the king and queen, then left silently. Maeve sipped at the cold sweet liquid, wishing that she could gulp it down and follow it with another.

"We are not likely to get fairer terms from the Hound," Ailill said at last. "And better for those who will to meet him one at a time, than for those who will not to be struck down like barley under hail."

Maeve nodded, sipping again. "No one, however skilled, can win every fight, nor come untouched from every one. Yes, we will lose some, and some of our best. We will be slowed, as is his intention. We will not lose many men every night; we will not go night after night without sleep, watching the hope and courage and faith of our folk gush like blood from a severed limb, and sooner or later, Cú Chulainn will grow tired, and suffer wounds. Then he will fall."

"Another brave fool," Ailill murmured thoughtfully, "trading his folk's sure advantage for a hero's fame. You are right: however bravely he defend the ford, he must in time fall."

Fedelm

Calatín and I were in our tent when Cú Chulainn's first sling-balls struck our camp. The old Druid had been teaching me charms by which illusions might be raised in battle to dismay and delude a hostile army, his dark eyes glazed in half-trance as he drew them from the well of his memory to pour them into my own. When the shouting began, his head came up and his gaze cleared.

"Stay here until I come back," Calatín said sharply. He opened his clothes-chest, tossing tunics and trousers carelessly onto the ground to dig out his white robe, throwing it about his wiry shoulders.

"What is happening?" I asked. "Should I not be with you?"

'And would I not be safer with you?' I thought, remembering the tents knocked over and set on fire when the host had given way to fear and anger before. We were in the royal enclosure.

"No. Maeve's guards are around the fence, and Eochaid will make sure that no harm comes to you. You will stay!" Calatín pointed a long bony finger at me. I felt only a gentle touch upon my forehead, nothing like the joint-locking compulsion he could exert if he chose.

I would no more disobey him than I would have shouted in Cernach's face: I sat on my bed, and he took the torch and went out.

I heard shouting and running for a long time. Then the Brown Bull's shattering bellow struck me, knocking me backwards flat on the bed: I lay there panting and staring at the bright lightless patterns of colored fire against the blackness, I did not know for how long, until the tent flap opened again and the torch's fire scorched new light into my eyes.

Whatever had passed outside, it had not disturbed Calatín. Not a hair had escaped the grizzled braid pulled tight at the nape of his neck, and there was a faint smile on the Druid's thin lips.

"Cú Chulainn has failed to take back the Brown Bull," he said. "And that is the greatest reproach and grief and madness inflicted on the Hound in this hosting, for not all his skills or courage or wiles could suffice to overcome our queen in this. By the loyalty of her man Buide, who gave his life to delay Cú Chulainn a moment; and by the honor of the Bull himself, for, as we found, he is no mere kine to be herded by whomever shall lead him, now the Hound has found himself over-matched. Now he will struggle to wipe out his shame in Ulster's eyes; and if he does so with the bravery and arrogance of the youth and hero he is, now we may defeat him."

"May it be so!" I said fervently.

Still, though I had perforce learned something of war, and of warriors, on this raid, I could not imagine what precisely Calatín meant. I had, perhaps, some vague notion that the Hound might stand at some ford or crossroads to place his body against the whole might of our host at once. A few shards of vision from my prophecy to Maeve came back to me, the great serpent flickering against the crimson-dyed army, and the huge warped shadow with an hundred heads dangling by the hair from each hand: I wondered if that was what I had foreseen. In a strange way, it was a relief when I heard the terms that Cú Chulainn had offered, for they were the terms of a man, if a hero, and not a monster or god.

From the first duel at the ford, where Cú Chulainn killed Nath Crantail, our army moved southeast in fits and starts, like a chariot with a warped wheel-rim catching on every rock and crack in the ground. The singers Roi and Roen were dead; so it fell to me to keep the count of the slain. Fer Taidle and the sons of Búachaill; Lúasce and Bó Bulge and Muirthemne and Fir Crandce; The two Artines and the two sons of Lecc and the two sons of Durcride, and the two sons of Gabal, and Drúcht and Delt and Dathen, Te and Tualang and Turscur, Tore Glaisse and Glas and Glaisne.

Cúr mac Da Lóth, that unpleasant fellow, was summoned to Maeve's tent and offered many rewards if he took up the challenge, for everyone felt that if it were he who fell at the ford, it would be a lightening of oppression for the hosts, and that if it were Cú Chulainn, it would be still better. The Hound killed him as well, and no one, to my knowledge, grieved. I could not help thinking, good riddance; I still suspected it had been he who had shoved and cursed at me at Midwinter.

Then Lóth and Lath mac Dabro, Srub Daire mac Fedaig, and Mac Teora n-Aignech fell by Cú Chulainn in single combat. Many in the host had hopes of Ferbáeth mac Firbend, who had fostered in Ulster himself and sparred often with the Hound as a boy; but he, too, died.

The only man who lived of all those who fought Cú Chulainn then was Láiríne mac Nóis, because he was the brother of the Hound's friend Lugaid mac Nóis. Him, Cú Chulainn crushed in his grip and shook and cast away in pain, covered with the stains of his bowels. Calatín and I worked for most of that day to set his bones, poulticing his body and giving him such herbs to swallow as might help to heal all the damage done within.

Yet he would never be able to rise without complaint or eat without pain; the muscles of his abdomen were torn so that his bowels protruded under the skin, and there was lasting harm to the bowels as well: we knew that he would die of it in time. Although we were both exhausted from our struggle to preserve Láiríne as well as we might, when we had washed the ointments from our hands and cleaned the last of the blood and matter from beneath our nails, Calatín said to me, "Now we shall go to the grove of rowans that I saw a little distance back, and cut wattles for your bed this night."

"Is there something you wish me to seek in my dreams?" I asked.

"I do not have your gift of foresight, but I have long studied the lore of finding the hour and day that are well-omened. I know that this night shall be good for visions. A lesser seer must seek them by rite and sacrifice, but I think what is needed will come to you."

The rowan trees stood where Calatín had said, slender and gray-barked with a delicate tracery of snow lying upon their bare branches. The small gold sickle that the druid use for cutting mistletoe and other holy herbs would not suffice for what we wanted.

Instead, Calatín had brought a little bronze-bladed axe, its metal green with age. The Druids at the school had such an axe, which had been used by their forebears for a great many generations: not so old as the great rings of stone that mark the turning of the seasons, yet far more ancient than the ages of the sons of Mil in Eriu, made before men learned the skill of working iron.

The edge was still keen, kept carefully honed over the countless years, and there was no weapon better for cutting wood that must not be touched with an iron edge. Though I had done such work before, and knew how to slice the slender branches cleanly with each stroke, I was sweating in the icy air and panting great white gusts by the time I was finished, my arms aching with the effort. Once a work of power is undertaken, one cannot pause to rest until it is done; nor could Calatín or Eochaid aid me.

I wondered what Calatín expected me to find that night. Yet I knew better than to ask: a little knowledge is often the bane of foresight.

"You need not fear," Calatín said softly, once I had finished weaving the wattles to lie under my pallet. "I would not ask you to do anything that might harm the child in your womb."

"Am I truly bearing, then? Do you know?" I asked eagerly.

The Druid gave me one of his small smiles. "It is early yet. There is no harm in being careful."

It was true, the thought had crossed my mind more than once while I was sweating and heaving the little axe into another sharp stroke. Still, Calatín was not only a skilled drúi, but a father of seven sons. I had no doubt that he knew well what a pregnant woman ought and ought not undertake.

I expected that it would take all my skill at meditating and stilling my mind to get to sleep that night, if I could do it at all. Calatín was wise in more matters than lore. Exhausted as I was, the thoughts racing in my head blurred swiftly, echoing into gibberish as I sank downward, my lumpy pallet growing softer than wool and closing about me like fog. it seemed to me that I wandered in that warm fog until it cooled to evening snow-mist, tingling pleasantly on my face and hands.

A light gleamed through that misty darkness: torch or camp fire or a delusion of the siabra, I could not tell, but I followed it nonetheless until I saw it mingling with the ruddier light of flames.

There, before a fine tent with embroidered hangings, sat Cú Chulainn: it was the brightness burning about his head, hiding his face from me as before, that I had been following. He sat on a stool, honing the head of a spear with quick sure strokes and gazing into the flames.

Although the hero-light about him flared too brightly for me to see his features, or even be sure of the shape of his body, there was something in the way he sat that made me think he had taken more than one wound over the days of fighting.

His shoulders slumped with weariness, and he leaned slightly to one side. 'Is it this that I was to see? I wondered. No one stroke will fell an oak-tree; but if enough men chop for long enough, then one stroke must down it at the last. Has that time come?'

Then my whole skin prickled with wariness; I felt as though a rusty file were stroking over my bones. Cú Chulainn raised his head, looking out into the dark, and I followed his gaze. A woman stepped from the night into the ring of his fire's brightness.

She was tall, very slim and lithely muscled, wearing only a kilt of red and black, a black bratt hanging open about her white shoulders, and a raven-crested helm upon her long black hair; the nipples of her firm little breasts shone red as if her milk were blood. Her face was as fair to look upon as one of the síde-folk: her high-boned features were both keen and delicate, sharp-angled raven-wing brows slanting above blue-steel eyes, sharp straight nose and red lips more perfectly chiseled than those of any human woman.

"Cú Chulainn, do you know me?" She asked.

"I do not know you, though it would be rude to turn a wanderer from my fire on such a night," he answered.

"I am a king's daughter, who am come to bring you my treasures. I love you because of the great tales I have heard of your bravery and your deeds."

I held my breath, the chill of the night air seeping cold through my lungs. Though she had not deigned to notice me yet, I knew that I did not have the strength to meet her gaze. How, then, would any of our warriors withstand the Hound of Ulster if she were beside him? If Cú Chulainn did not know her name, I did, though I would not even think it to myself while she stood there and offered my foe her aid.

"You come at a bad time," he said wearily, like a much older man. "I cannot attend a woman during a struggle like this..

I bit my lip, though I felt no pain, and my teeth seemed to meet no resistance of flesh. Did he not know; could he not see who had come to him?

" I might be a help to you," she said.

"It wasn't for a woman's backside that I took on this ordeal," Cú Chulainn replied, biting off his words with a curt snap of his teeth.

Arrogant amadán! I thought, shocked. Then: 'Fool, yes: but the foolishness of a boy alone against an army, trying to be a hero, and speak like a grown man of war'. Cú Chulainn was foe, and murderer, and a figure of terror in the night...and yet a terrible wave of pity for the boy swept over me, seeing how his warrior's self-sureness flared and flickered desperately now like a guttering torch in a high wind. 'He speaks thus to give himself courage, and casts away the Raven-Queen's favor thereby'.

The steel of her eyes flashed like sword clashing on sword; the black mantle about her shoulders stirred, and I saw the serried rows of sharp-edged feathers. The black iron beak of her helm-crest opened with a croak like rusty metal grinding hard on itself, but so deep that I seemed to feel it running along my spine rather than hear it.

"You shall regret that, when you go to battle at the ford tomorrow!" She cawed. Then she was gone, and I saw only the sweep of a raven's wing fading into the darkness. I woke on my bed of lumpy-bound rowan wattles, gasping in deep breaths of clean cold air and pulling my blankets tighter about my shivering body.

The name I had not dared to think or speak rang in my head: 'Morrígan'. Slowly, as the shaking of my limbs eased, I smiled. Cú Chulainn had scorned the Raven-Queen tonight. Tomorrow, the Hag of Battles would come against him.

Fedelm

The warm sweet scent of honeyed porridge awoke me in the morning. I blinked the sleep from my eyes and uncurled like a hedgehog, rolling onto my back and stretching. I did not hear the sound of sleet or heavy snow on the hides of our tent, but the weather must have turned foul, or Eochaid would not have brought our breakfasts in. I looked up, and saw Suithchern's face above mine, round and tear streaked, her honey-brown hair straggling loose around her shoulders in tangles as if she had been tossing and turning all night. She held a wooden bowl of porridge in her hand.

"I'm sorry your servant let me in. Oh, Fedelm!" She dissolved in tears again.

I took the bowl from her hands before she could drop it, sitting up with the blankets around my shoulders.

"What is wrong?" I asked anxiously, suddenly wide awake with terror. If Conall, or Clothra, were grievously ill, or dead in their sleep, so many things could go wrong with babes at the best of times, let alone when they were dragged about with an army in the depths of a ferocious winter!

"My husband, Lóch has gone to fight at the ford. I thought, if you could do magic to aid him..."

The breath hissed from my body in a soft moan. I set the porridge down carefully on the ground, taking Suithchern's small rough hands in mine.

"Ah, Suithchern," I murmured. "If there were anything I could do, I would do it. If I could ward Lóch against sword-edge or spear-tip, I would do it now and not count the cost. If the druid could do such, we should have done it before, for Nath Crantail or Ferbáeth or the others, well, except perhaps Cúr mac Da Lóth, who pinched my arse hard enough to bruise when I was but thirteen, and would have done it again, I'm sure, were I not a ban-fili."

Suithchern giggled unwillingly through her tears.

"No one misses him. My husband. He is a brave man, a good fighter, but hardly a match for the champions the Hound has already slain. All night, I begged him to stay, until he told me I would only ensure his defeat by keeping him awake with my wailing."

I did not know what to say. I only knew Lóch slightly: a quiet man, lithe and well-knit, with a mass of sandy curls and long reddish mustaches. As to how good a fighter he might be, I did not know; such things were hardly my business. I had heard the names of most of those reckoned great champions in our army, and he was not among them.

Yet I knew Cú Chulainn was growing weary, his wounds, for even if they were all slight, he must have collected a number of them, beginning to wear upon him. Lóch would not truly be fighting alone at the ford: the Morrígan would be with him. Would the goddess' disfavor be enough to bring such a hero down? I did not know.

I was reluctant to raise Suithchern's hopes, lest they dash on the wreckage of her husband's corpse. Still, it tore me to watch her grief, as though Lóch were already dead.

"Let me get dressed, and I can at least come to sit with you and help watch the children while we wait," I said soothingly.

"Even a half-trained ban-drúi knows that many things may happen in a fight. Calatín has told me more than once that the greatest warrior may be undone by a lucky stroke from the weakest. If Lóch is not one of the far-famed champions, neither is he unskilled."

We retrieved the two babes from the woman who had been watching them, and settled down to wait while the servants loaded the wagons for the morning march, the march that Lóch was, most likely, buying with his life. It would have been warmer by the fire, but folk were cooking their breakfast, and I could tell Suithchern could not bear any other company. Someone at the fire had sausages: the rich scents of pork and fat and herbs crept into the tent. My stomach rumbled quietly; I wished that I had thought to bring the porridge with me, but now was no time to leave Suithchern, or complain of something so trivial.

"Come, we shall ride on one of the wagons today," I said to her. "No one will complain if I claim the right."

Nor will they object to you, with your husband fighting at the ford, I thought, though I could not say that to her either. We settled ourselves on top of a wagon piled with tents.

The weather was fair, and Eochaid quickly propped up one of the small tents as a shelter against the wind for us and the children, its owner would not begrudge it to us, or would have more sense than to say so. It was hard to think what to talk about, but at least I had my weaving-rod and my lace making to occupy my hands and occasionally Conall's, the gold inlay on the bronze rod glimmering in the tent's dimness as I looped and knotted the stream of scarlet wool into the growing piece that would, someday, be a shawl.

"When Lóch courted me..." Suithchern said. "He is no poet himself, but he asked a poet to make a song of love for me. He said my hair was like sunlight through a golden stream where trout swim, that my eyes were bright as summer's first bluebells; he spoke of my breasts as two white hills of the Summer lands, that would lure him beyond world's end. After we were wedded, he brought me bluebells every day of spring, to twine into my hair or scatter over our bed. Why is it that men cannot be content with what joys they have, with wife and home and children, but must go seeking after fame as well?"

"I do not know," I answered her sadly.

"My father seemed content with his wife and seven children, his two milch cows and his good fertile sow. He was a farmer born, who never lifted a sword, nor hoped to use his spear for more than propping up the washing, and he did not understand that I was born to poetry and prophecy; I think he was more glad than sorry to see me go." I thought a moment. "Ailill, I think, is another who would be content to live in peace if he could. Though he is renowned as a warrior, I do not think he seeks more than his joys and loves. It is Queen Maeve who would reach beyond that which is already in her grasp, who bears that pride and yearning. Mayhap it is not a matter of men and women at all, but only that we see such desire more easily in those whose striving is on the battlefield."

"Maybe you are right," Suithchern said, lifting her yellow-and-green checkered bratt aside and unpinning her dress to let Clothra suckle, wincing as the little girl's first milk-tooth bit into her nipple. I had given her an ointment to rub on Clothra's aching gums, but the purple shadows of sleeplessness beneath Suithchern's blue eyes were deeper than a single night, however anxious and sorrowful, could tint them.

Conall squirmed in my lap and I cuddled him closer, thinking, with a mixture of excitement and apprehension, 'By this time next year, it could be my nipples chewed by a babe; it could be my own child crying to keep me awake at night'. though I had seen enough women frazzled to the edge of distraction from waking to tend their babes in the night, and had to wash enough of Conall and Clothra's puke and shit from my own clothes, to know better, something within me almost longed for that as well: the mess and lost sleep, too, were part of having a child. If only, but I did not even know if I had missed my courses from bearing, or from the working Maeve and Finnabair and I had wrought; it would be another month before I could begin to guess, and longer until I first felt the certain movement beneath my heart.

Clothra spat the nipple out and wailed, as though Suithchern's fear had soured the milk in her breast. Suithchern tried to bring her to suck again, but the babe cried harder, her face turning red and then an alarming shade of purple. I thought Conall would wake and join her, as he usually did, their high ear-piercing shrieks like an ill-tuned pair of miniature war-trumpas in chorus. Mercifully, he only grunted like a little boar and turned about to settle more comfortably in my lap.

"I think, perhaps I shall walk her, if you stay here with Conall," Suithchern said hastily. She did not have to tell me that she wanted to be alone for a little, or at least away from anyone who would make her feel as though she had to speak to them. I nodded, and said, "I shall watch him."

I whistled to the wagon-driver to stop and let Suithchern off, handing her squalling child down to her. Then I settled down to looping and coiling and knotting, my eyes following the scarlet thread through all its braided twists and turns about the flashing glitter of my weaving-rod. Scarlet and bright, a host in crimson and red, the makeshift shelter's shadow faded sparkling about me, my eyes dazed by the glitter of swords in the sharp winter sunlight, twining patterns of bronze flashing from a shield's mountings; the hero-light burning fierce and brilliant around one warrior's head as he leapt and whirled and struck, the other striving frantically to defend himself, and the icy river water foaming about their feet. Then, as though the snow had risen in a whelming wave, a herd of white heifers stampeded into the ford.

Their leader was huge, near as large as the Brown Bull; her ears were red as the blood-spatters on the snow at the ford's edge, her eyes glinted like keen-honed steel knives. They churned the water into a great froth so that I could not tell ford from flood, buffeting Cú Chulainn ferociously.

He went down; Lóch struck, and a thin thread of crimson swirled through the foam. My heart leapt like a salmon in spring, but the brilliant crown of hero-light rose from the chaos of water and beasts again.

The Hound's shield was gone; he held a smooth holed river-stone, casting it at the great lead heifer's eye. Red blood and clear water spurted; she turned, charging up the bank with her herd behind her. The blood was flowing from Cú Chulainn's shoulder, drowning the gold bracelets on his arm. Lóch struck more often now, slowly forcing the Hound back into the deeper water beside the ford, Cú Chulainn seemed to be standing in a thigh-deep pool with his foe raining blows upon his head, and yet, even without a shield, his sword moved so quickly to block every stroke Lóch made and return his own, that he might have had four hands and a weapon in each.

Then I saw the long black shape writhing downstream, an eel as thick as a man's leg and twice the length of a man's height. Swift in the water as any serpent, the black eel poured herself into the pool where Cú Chulainn stood, twining three coils about his legs to bind him and pull him down. The Hound of Ulster twisted and stamped to free himself, stabbing down into the water. As his sword sank and black blood spurted up to muddy the frothing pool, Lóch stabbed downward as well, a crosswise stroke aimed at Cú Chulainn's chest.

Cú Chulainn writhed desperately aside, but the blade bit in among his ribs, shearing his scarlet tunic open so that the gash gaped white and red into the naked air for a heartbeat before blood poured from it in a flood that darkened the crimson linen. Finish it, finish him! I urged silently. The eel was gone, and though Lóch had cut deeply, I could see that he had not pierced the Hound's lung or heart. Cú Chulainn drove a mighty stroke at Lóch's legs, shearing off a hand span's width of the lower point of his long oval shield as Suithchern's husband leaped backwards. More blood spattered bright red into the water where the tip of his sword ripped along Lóch's left calf, his lower trouser-leg hanging in soaked tatters.

That was not a crippling wound either, but it bought Cú Chulainn a moment to leap flashing from the pool onto high ground, the water frothing about his ankles again. Now Cú Chulainn had regained the advantage. Lóch stumbled back, and I saw the death-stroke flashing in. Before the sword bit, a huge russet shape crashed into Cú Chulainn, knocking him to the side; his blade hissed through empty air. I heard a ferocious snarling and growling as the ruddy she-wolf bared long white fangs to tear at the Hound.

Her one steel-bright eye was narrow and glaring; the other was a broken socket leaking clear fluid into her red fur, and more blood flowed from a long gash across her shoulder, but she snapped at her foe like a crazed thing. Cú Chulainn leapt and whirled and twisted, trying to keep her jaws from closing on him.

Though he dodged her teeth's grasp, her fangs raked bloody furrows across his legs and arms, and Lóch drove in, cutting hard to his side. Then Cú Chulainn gasped in pain. He sprang a body-length away, and the she-wolf bounded after him. Before her paws landed in the water again, the flat of his blade smashed into her foreleg with a sharp cracking sound. She howled and fled three-legged, passing for a moment between the two warriors.

In that heartbeat, Cú Chulainn leaned over to the bank, plucking up the weapon that lay there in his left hand. I could not see it clearly: but it was black and gleaming and barbed, and seemed to curl like a serpent's tail in his hand as he thrust it over the rim of Lóch's shield and deep into his breast. Lóch staggered, dropping sword and shield and grasping at the weapon that pierced him.

Though I could hardly believe it, he was still on his feet, standing in the bloody foam of the ford with more bloody foam pouring from his mouth. He spoke: his voice was no more than a bubbling gasp, but I heard his words clearly.

"Grant me one favor now, Cú Chulainn. Retreat a step from me, let me fall eastwards, not towards the men of Eriu, so, no one says I fled before you, nor shamed Suithchern and my babe, fallen by the gae bulga." More blood bubbled from his mouth and drowned his voice. Still he stood, though I did not know how.

"That is a warrior's request you make," said Cú Chulainn, and took one step back from him. Only then, still clutching the barbed black thing buried in his chest, did Lóch let himself fall forward into the swirling froth of water and blood and mud.

I thought at first that the wail that split my ears was Lóch's charioteer keening his lord; but then I felt the warm wetness seeping into my lap, and dizzily realized again where I was and that Conall had just pissed copiously enough to overflow his breech clout.

"Wusha, wusha, little one," I crooned, lifting him up and looking for Suithchern's basket, with its skin of warm water and the cloths and spare clouts Suithchern kept for such moments. The water had already cooled, and Conall yowled more loudly when the cold damp cloth touched his bare rump. I cleaned and changed him, then rinsed my dress as best as I could, welcoming the brief distraction. At least it was only piss, washing out easily with a good soaking.

The wet front of my dress was chilling fast even beneath my thick mantle, but my training had fitted me to deal easily enough with cold. 'Should I tell Suithchern when she comes back?

I wondered. It will be a while before Lóch's charioteer brings his body to halt our march again; is it kind to let her have a little time of hope, or cruel, to leave her in fear?' A Druid must see and know more of the truth than any other, but also see and know what should be spoken aloud, and what kept in the inner well of silence.'What would I wish for myself, if it were the man I loved who had gone to the ford?'

I thought on that little time. If it were Ailill, I cared for and desired him, yes, but did I love him? Not as Suithchern loved Lóch. Ailill was as dear and good a man as I could imagine, and my heart was set on going back to Alba with his child in my womb. He had not courted me with songs nor brought me flowers; I had not followed him to war with a new babe at the breast because I could not bear to be parted from him for two or three months' time. Yet Ailill was as close to a love as I had known. If I were sitting here even now, wondering if the Hound's sword were stabbing into the sweet body I had caressed, hacking at the powerful arms that had embraced me so warmly, dyeing his wealth of red-gold hair a darker red with blood. I did not know how Suithchern bore it so well.

'Because she must, I thought: because there is no way out save to go on. For myself, I think it must be better to know, though it only be confirmation of grief: a wound cannot be healed until the blade is drawn from it.' The army was still shuffling on, like an adder writhing after its head has been chopped off. It would be a while yet before Lóch's gilla returned with his body and we had to halt. My wagon stopped again: Suithchern was back.

I came out of the little shelter to take Clothra as she hauled herself up. The words I was readying for her died on my tongue like bees in winter: she saw all she needed to know on my face.

"Ah, Fedelm..." she breathed. "You know, already..."

I nodded silently. Suithchern's face crumpled inward, and she sagged to her knees. With Conall in one arm and Clothra in the other, I could not help her up; instead I knelt down beside her.

"He wounded Cú Chulainn thrice, and at least one blow struck deep. He thought of you and Clothra at the end. He asked the Hound to retreat a step, so that he might fall facing east towards the foe, lest it be thought he had tried to flee and shame be brought on you."

"As if I cared!" Suithchern shouted. "As if I gave the smallest mouse-turd! All that matters..."

The loud fury drained from her voice and face like water dropping in a sudden rush from a cauldron whose bottom suddenly gives way.

"All that matters," she whispered, "is that he is not coming back to me."

This was no time to speak of the hopes of rebirth. It was no time to speak at all. I shuffled closer, letting Suithchern throw her arms about myself and the children and sob hopelessly into my shoulder. I set Eochaid to watching the babes while Suithchern and I laid Lóch's body out. The army had halted for the day: no warrior stood ready to follow Lóch to the ford. I wondered if I should go to the queen, to tell her the Hound was wounded and see if the knowledge of that advantage would draw any more would-be champions out.

Suithchern needed and deserved the halt, so that she might care for her husband's body on solid ground and not the jolting back of a wagon. Let Cú Chulainn's wounds stiffen overnight. Lóch's charioteer could tell the tale to the queen, but my care now was for my friend. Together in one of the larger tents, Suithchern and I soaked away the frozen blood that crusted Lóch's tunic and trousers to his body, cutting away the ruined garments. Coming out, the gae bulga had torn a gaping hole all the way through his body.

With Suithchern beside me, I was more concerned to hide the damage than to examine it; but the barbs of the weapon in my vision had been real, shredding Lóch's heart and lungs on withdrawal. Thankfully, his gilla must have cleaned the worst of the mess away at the ford, but the damage that remained was bad enough.

"Ah, my beloved," Suithchern crooned, looking down into Lóch's pale face. Dead, he looked very young in spite of the long unkempt mustaches hanging down over either cheek, his blunt honest features slack as if with a boy's deep sleep. His charioteer must have closed his eyes on the way back, for the lids had stiffened shut.

"Why did you have to go? Why could you not have listened to me, and stayed with those who love you? I never left you, nor would I have you leave me behind, even in war. Could you not have waited, that we might go even to the house of Donn together? How shall I bear this night alone in my bed, while you lie beneath your cairn?" Suithchern looked at me as though I could give her some answer, or help.

"I felt so safe in his embrace at night, so warm and loved," she pleaded. "To sleep in a cold bed without him, to know that he is truly gone from me..."

Clothra began to wail, and this time Conall joined her. Eochaid, sitting on the ground with the two children on his lap, widened his green eyes and gave me a helpless look. They were both lately fed, burped, and changed; I shrugged and murmured,

"Jiggle them a bit, see if that helps."

"Have they not good cause to keen?" Suithchern asked sadly. That question needed no answering.

I had barely known Lóch himself, but the tears were beginning to sting my own eyelids again: I had seen his impression stamped on Suithchern's heart like a bronze brooch pressed into clay, and that shape showed me enough that I must mourn him with her. I stood beside Suithchern that afternoon as Lóch's cairn was raised. Together, we had washed him and plaited his hair and mustaches; we had tugged his finest clothes over his stiff limbs, set shoes with gilded buckles on his feet, and belted his sword at his side. Eochaid had found a joint of meat and a large pot of cider, that he not go hungry on his journey, and we had woven him a bed of yew-branches and covered him with a warm blanket.

If carrying out her last duties towards her husband had not eased Suithchern's grief, at least it seemed to comfort her in some small measure that she had been here to tend him, not stayed behind at home while his body was left to the care of others. I had combed and plaited her thick honey-brown hair, washed her face and helped her dress in her best finery.

Though her eyes were swollen and red, her throat too sore with crying to do more than moan beneath the keening of the other women, she stood straight as the rocks were set about his body. Before they rose too high, we carried Clothra and Conall to the side of Lóch's last bed, and held one to either side, that they might touch their lips to his cheeks and grasp his mustaches one last time.

"Remember your father, my darling," Suithchern said to Clothra, and to Conall, "remember your foster-father. He loved you both, and would have loved you the more, had he lived longer."

Then Lóch's charioteer told the assembled folk of the fight at the ford. He spoke well of Lóch's valor and skill, and recounted his brave last words...but he had not seen the white heifer with her herd, nor the black eel, nor the red she-wolf. I held my tongue as well.

Brave as it had been for him to take the challenge when he was so over matched, it was no doing of Lóch's that the Morrígan had fought beside him. Nor did her aid make his courage any less worthy of acknowledgment, and if his skill was remembered as a little greater than it had been in life, there was no ill done by that.

Suithchern and I might have waited there until the cairn was finished; but it was Clothra's turn to soil her clout, and Conall's to cry himself red-faced until he threw up. One never knows how much souls fresh-returned to this world understand of what happens around them, but it was certain that they could feel their mother's grief, and mine. We went back to Suithchern's tent to clean and settle the children, but they kept up their dual howling keen until our ears were ringing. At last I sent Eochaid to fetch my harp, letting Suithchern take both squalling babes.

I began by playing the strains of sorrow, very slowly and softly, the notes falling like rain, drop by drop, from the silver strings beneath my fingers. Gradually the children's screaming quieted to soft whimpers; quiet tears trailed from Suithchern's eyes as well, as if to soothe the reddened heat of her swollen cheeks. From the strains of sorrow, I played into the strains of sleep. Conall's eyelids drooped, his head rolling back against Suithchern's arm.

Clothra whined a little longer, but then she, too slept, and Suithchern's eyelids were beginning to droop. I set the harp aside a moment, gently easing Suithchern into her bed. Exhausted and heart-shattered as she was, the enchantment of my music had overcome her as easily as a wave pouring over the sand. Carefully I tucked her in, nestling the two children close against her, then settled to my harping again.

I played the strains of sleep again thrice, then, ever so slowly, careful not to break the music's fine thread, plucked the melody of the strain of joy, weaving it faintly through the slow thrumming of the sleep-song. Let Suithchern sleep deeply, and find ease and a little taste of sweetness in her dreams. Though she must wake to pain, at least her healing would have begun.

Calatín was waiting in our tent when I returned, sitting cross-legged on the ground. His tunic was off, his lean chest bare and his eyes closed: he was clearly in deep meditation, and I moved as quietly as I could so as not to disturb him. At last he shuddered, wiry muscles standing out in sharp relief beneath the deep blue whorls etched into the skin of his shoulders. His dark eyes focused on me.

"You have seen much that is worth telling," he said. "Tell me, and hide nothing."

I told Calatín of my dream, and what I had seen of the fight. He listened intently, thin lips pressed tightly together and long bony hands grasping his thighs. His grizzled brows drew close as I spoke of the wounds Lóch had dealt to Cú Chulainn. Though his eyes were still fixed on me, his gaze turned inward. I could see the little muscles working at the edges of the Druid's stern jaw.

"Did I do wrong, not to tell you of my dream and my vision straight away?" I asked anxiously.

I felt suddenly ashamed, that I had let a single woman's concerns, grievous as Suithchern's sorrows were, keep me from the duty that my teacher had set to me. I could have told her that I had work to do for Calatín and left her for a few minutes, at least, while I recounted what I had seen. Surely such a short absence would hardly have mattered to her?

"What is. Is," Calatín replied. "Had you told me in the moment, it would have altered nothing. This was not a day for men to shift the thoughts of gods, nor enchantment to change the fate of heroes. Will you stay the night here, or are you going back to your friend's side?"

I had not thought about it. As soon as Calatín spoke, I realized that I should not let Suithchern sleep alone that night.

If I could not give her the warm embrace she mourned for, at least I could be there if she awoke to her sorrows in the darkness.

"I will go back to her, if you do not need me here," I said. It might be late for me to remember my duties and obedience; but I would try not to forget them again. Calatín shook his head.

"They do not teach this in the schools. You will be a better Druid for what you are learning now from Suithchern. Or, perhaps, with Suithchern." He paused, gazing into the shadows of the torchlight.

"Sometimes I wonder," he mused, "if we do well to start our students so early. Some, like yourself, yes. Your gifts came so strong and early that there was no choice but to take you young, lest you become a danger to others or spin into the madness of uncontrolled vision.

For the most part. You know I was a man grown, wedded to my first wife, before Manannán woke his gifts in me? I had already learned the joy of being woken thrice a night by a screaming child, and the wondrous magic by which a baby can magnify a single mouthful of milk to two bucketfuls of mess, one at each end."

"I had not known." All my life, Calatín had simply been there: Cruachan's younger Druid, but the one all feared, dark magician and maker of bloody sacrifices; whereas most folk loved good-humored old Senchán, who always had time to settle a wrangle over a strayed sheep or mix a draught for a baby's colic.

"Aye. I had gone to the western shore, the leader of a guard-troop on a wagon load of goods to trade for salt. I awoke in the night, it was autumn, close to Samhain. The sky was clear and moonless; the wind howled beneath the white river of stars, and the waves battered the rocky strand, plumes of spray rising up like storm-torn birches from each crashing comber. I did not know why I went down to the sea, nor what might await me. I stood on the rocks with the thin frothy edges of water running higher around my feet with each surge, until the ninth wave, so much greater than the others, rolled in to break over my head. Salt water filled my mouth and blinded me until I could not tell up from down, nor feel my limbs for the cold of the sea, and I thought then that I would die. The water's great arms lifted me upwards, and the breath was sweet in my mouth and the blood warm in my body again. Then Manannán spoke to me as he held me there. All that night, he chanted lore to me, and filled me with the skills of magic, though I was not yet fit to understand nor wield them, that did not fully come until my years of training were done. His waves left me gently upon the shore at dawn. I went home with my troop, and spoke to Senchán, who had come back from Alba a few years before, and to Eoghan, who was then the elder Druid of Cruachan. They sent me to be schooled, and I gave over the blade for the wand, though never wholly: my hands have not forgotten their skill on sword-grip and spear-shaft, nor my limbs the many feats that I learned in my youth."

Calatín rubbed absently at his right shoulder. Always before, when I had seen him unclothed, I had only noticed the dark whorls of the woad-pricking on his skin. Now I looked more closely. There was a knot near the edge of his collarbone where it had once been broken. Though the deep blue spirals nearly hid it, I could see the pale line of an old scar running across his shoulder: he must have been lucky, not to lose the strength of his arm. Another thin silver scar was nearly hidden in the shadows between the deep ridges of Calatín's lower ribs on the left side, and a third, that I had several times seen, but never considered, thinking vaguely that it might have come from some rite of blood-letting, traced down the Druid's left arm from the elbow almost to the wrist.

"There was much that Manannán taught me which I have not passed on to any save you; and much of what you have learned from me, you do not yet comprehend. Once I hoped that my sons might be called when they were of an age, yet there was never any sign of it. Now and then I have thought that I should go to one of the great schools as a teacher for a time, yet it has never seemed right to me, that I should leave Cruachan." Calatín sighed.

Although his lean-muscled body seemed taut and lithe as a young man's, and his face, heavy-furrowed about the mouth and etched with deep thought-lines about forehead and eyes as it was, might have belonged to a stern man of forty years, a moment's pause to reckon from his words told me that the Druid must be past sixty. Indeed, Calatín's eldest grandson was on this raid, not as a gilla to an older fighter, but a full-grown warrior in his own right.

"It may be, that if I come home safe from this raid, that I will do as I have longed to for some while. I would found our own school of Druidry there at Cruachan, and build Manannán a rath in the grove above the Black Boar's Furrows..." Calatín's voice trailed off, but his dark eyes were still watching me as an eagle watches a salmon's silver back rising in the clear water.

"If you do so, and if you find me worthy when my training is done, I would be glad to come and teach those skills of filidecht and prophecy in which my strengths lie," I said.

Calatín smiled.

"I have no doubt that you will be found worthy. Though simple men say that a daughter born with the fili-gift will end it in that line for seven generations, the wise know better. If you are indeed bearing, I should be surprised if your child does not inherit all that you have yourself. Though I have not your strength of foresight, the god did lay his hand on me; and I think that what he has taught to one, he may build on in another in time. Now, go to your friend and comfort her in her grief as best you can. I shall send for you when I need you."

Fedelm

I lay on a hard bed, the bedclothes disarranged about me, my knees spread and raised. A woman's voice at the foot of the bed "But," Suithchern's Said.

"Here it comes!" I felt a strange squirming in my belly, then something slipping between my legs, soft and slick as an eel, and I shuddered at the wet stroking. My sight cleared as the midwife laid her wriggling bundle on my breast. Without thought, I reached to cradle it, and the next, and the next, until my arms were full of four wriggling infants, with two more at my sides.

"Grab them, they will fall off the bed!" I said in frantic terror, trying to reach for those two without dropping any of the others.

Then I saw what I held. A single huge baleful eye stared at me from each infant forehead. I looked on the twisted little forms with horror: each had only a single arm and a single leg, the limbs ending in hands like crooked black claws. The two at my sides were hauling themselves towards the edges of the bed; I struggled desperately to grab them as the others tried to squirm out of my arms.

I threw my head back and forth to scream, but my throat was locked. This was a dream, it must be! If I could cry out, I would awaken; yet though I drew in all the breath I could, calling on my singer's training to open my throat and force the sound up from my belly, nothing came out.

Then a strong hand gripped my shoulder, and I opened my eyes to torchlight and shadows flickering about Suithchern's tent. I lay on my pallet panting and shaking, barely able to focus my eyes on my deliverer as he straightened up.

He was a tall man in a leather corselet with iron rings sewn to it. I could not place the young face beneath the helm, though he seemed very familiar. The lean line of the jaw, the long narrow nose and straight black eyebrows drawn low over dark eyes, young as he was, I realized, he looked like Calatín. This, then, must be the Druid's eldest grandson, Glas mac Delga.

"Grandfather needs you," he murmured to me. I glanced over
at Suithchern's bed. She was still sleeping, curled around the two
babes. She must have risen in the night to feed and change them,
but I had slept too deeply to be awakened even by their crying. I lay
torn for a moment. I did not want her to wake alone, but if Calatín
needed me, I must go.

"I shall wait outside while you dress," Glas whispered. "Be swift."
He had my white robe draped over one long arm; he carefully
unfolded it and laid it over the foot of my pallet.

As I was hastily pulling my clothes on in the dark, I heard
Suithchern stir.

"Lóch?" She mumbled, her voice thick with sleep.

I made my way carefully to her bed, resting a hand on her
shoulder.

"It's Fedelm," I said quietly to her. "Suithchern, Calatín has called
me, and I must leave you for a little time."

"Be careful," she mumbled, pulling the children a little closer to
herself. My heart turned over in my breast, tears stinging my eyes. I
gave her shoulder a gentle squeeze, then stroked her hair a moment,
as if she were my own daughter.

It was a little time until dawn. The sky was clear, the high river of
stars above blurring into an arch of faint blue-white light against
the black sky, with more pin-pricks of brilliance scattered here
and there like seed cast about at ploughing time. The icy wind bit
ferociously at my face and hands; in moments, my nose was growing
numb and my ears ached sharply. Though I had wrapped my feet
and lower legs in thick swathes of bound wool before putting my
shoes on, the cold was already creeping in, the ankle-deep snow
wetting the leather and seeping in icy rivulets through the slits in
my shoe-tops. Calatín and his seven sons were waiting at the edge of
the camp with torches.

Eochaid stood behind them, carrying a large leather bag, a small
cauldron and tripod, and a bundle of sticks; several water skins
bulged from his belt. To my surprise, Calatín was not wearing his
own white robe. Instead, he was fully armed and armored, with a
sword belted about his waist and a silver-inlaid helm shadowing
his face, his eyes gleaming like polished jet from the darkness. Glas
and I joined them, and Calatín led us away from the camp. No one
spoke: I heard only feet crunching through snow, armor jingling and
torches occasionally hissing and sputtering. I breathed deep and
slow, each frosty draught strengthening my inner fires.

Before, I had kindled my body's heat against the winter's onslaught without thinking or knowing: now I called it deliberately, sending the hot blood from my core out to warm numb fingers and toes, soothing my ice-aching ears and thrilling through me so that I hardly needed the heavy purple mantle draped over my white Druid's robe. We walked until we came to a grove of oaks, their huge gnarled trunks looming black in the flickering torchlight and the stars glittering like tiny burning-white gems amid their wide-reaching branches. Without speaking, Calatín took the bag from Eochaid and stood waiting. Eochaid crouched down on the ground in the middle of the grove, laying down his sticks and setting up the tripod with the cauldron hanging from it above them.

He untied the water skins one by one, filling the cauldron, then stepped back. Calatín gestured for his sons and grandson to drive the pointed end of their torches into the ground. Last of all, he lit the fire with his own. The smaller sticks flared so brightly that I was sure he had soaked them in tallow, the larger ones caught more slowly, but burned surely. When the Druid was certain of his fire, he drove his torch's butt down through snow and earth, so that the nine men were surrounded by a ring of nine flames.

Eochaid and I stood outside, silently watching. Whatever the Druid meant for me to do, I would have no direct part in this. Calatín reached into the bag Eochaid had brought, pulling out parcels of herbs. As he crumbled each into the cauldron, I scented them with unnatural clarity, sharp and sweet, clean and musty. Foxglove and donnlus, the king and queen of herbs; the acrid smell of madness-bringing buttercup flowers; meadowsweet, oak-leaves, and broom flowers…and ragwort and ferns. His knife flashed silver in the starlight; a dark gleam of blood dripped onto the three small dried mushrooms in his hand before he cast them into the cauldron, and it came to me what he was about.

The Hound of Ulster was wounded: now, Calatín would create a champion from his blood and from the herbs in the cauldron, as Gwydion had made Bloddeuedd from meadowsweet, oak, and broom; as enchanted swine and the horses of the síde could be made from ferns and ragwort. My heart fluttering as if I had drunk foxglove myself, I forced myself to control my breathing, and my own power, lest I distract Calatín. I had never seen a working of such might nor dreamed of doing one. Calatín had not brought me to aid, but to watch and learn. The knife in the old Druid's hand had been replaced by a wand, the peeled hazel shining white as the new moon against the darkness. One of his sons handed him a round frame-drum.

Calatín beat on it with wand and fisted hand, its deep booming echoing through the grove and shivering through my body. The Druid began to sing, the eerie edge of harshness in his deep voice sending a tingle from my spine through every nerve in my body. I listened carefully, carving each word into my mind as they wove in coils and counter-coils; I could feel the power circling up from beneath the earth like a great dark wyrm, old as the most ancient barrows where it had left its spiraling tracks graven upon the threshold stones.

I lost all sense of time in Calatín's song and the dizzying might that spun up and into the ring of flames and men; but the steam was rising white from the cauldron and the blackness of the eastern horizon fading to deep grey when he gave three sharp blows on the drum with his wand and fell silent. He strode forward, dipping the end of the wand into the cauldron and touching each of the younger men, then himself, on the forehead with the steaming draught.

"Three stems from one seed, arise! Three leaves from one stem, arise! From one springs many: arise, arise, arise!" Calatín cried.

A mass of bubbles rose in the cauldron, streaming down along its sides and into the fire in a great gush. The steam hissed like a huge wyrm in fury, rising up in a great cloud to fill the circle; I could see nothing but flickering pale light and dark shadows through the hot white mist. Then, slowly, it cleared. I stared open-mouthed, slow to believe what was before me. Where nine had stood, now there were twenty-seven, each man become three, I remembered the three mushrooms. There was no time to think too closely on what Calatín had done, nor turn the precise words he had sung over in my mind, but I knew that I would understand his rite when I did. Nine, the original nine?

Pulled the low-burning torches from the ground, turning them over and stabbing them down to hiss into cold blackness in the snow outside the ring, that within was all melted, the ground dry and brown and sere where it had been. The true Calatín was still holding wand and drum: only thus could I tell him from the two who stood beside him. He handed the drum to one of them, the wand to the other, and took a stoppered clay jug from the bag of herbs. I did not need to smell the draught within: that jar was oddly shaped, with four small handles and a broad-flaring base. Even in full darkness and great haste, it could never be mistaken for another.

With great care, Calatín uncorked the brew of hemlock, dipping a rag into it. Each of the men unsheathed their weapons in turn so that he might touch the edges with the poisoned draught, the same that the siabra use on their hidden shot to bring pain and paralysis and sorrow. As we had come silently, we walked back silently.

I was so filled with awe that I could not have spoken. Such a work of magic was given to few to witness: it seemed to me that I carried it within my head like a new-planted child, a fruitful acorn that would sprout and grow into a great spreading oak. The camp had come to life while we were gone, breakfast-fires burning between the tents like an hundred crackling sparks cast by the red flame of the rising sun.

Servants moved about, bearing buckets of water; I could hear the faint crying of infants, the deep voices of men twining with the higher murmurs of women. We still moved without sound, parting the wave of camp-noises. Where we trod, everyone we passed fell silent and stared. Within the royal enclosure, Maeve, Ailill, Fergus, and Flidais were sitting by their own fire, eating and deep in conversation.

Ferdiad was already standing guard by the gate. His blue eyes widened and his jaw dropped as he caught sight of us. Without speaking, he stood aside and let us through. Maeve gasped; Ailill took one look and burst out laughing. Flidais only smiled, almost as though she had been expecting it. Fergus, great warrior, hero, and once king, sat gaping foolishly like a boy at his first fair, all the harshness stunned from his craggy face, and I could not help relishing the sight. 'So you thought your foster-son was a match for all of us, did you?' I thought vindictively.

"I shall go to meet Cú Chulainn at the ford this day, I, and all that is me," Calatín announced.

Slowly Maeve, too, began to smile. Fergus' mouth snapped closed in a hard line, his flint-grey eyes sparking with anger.

"The agreement was for single combat! I shall not permit this... you will have to fight me, and all my men of Ulster, before I let you fall on Cú Chulainn so unfairly, with all your kin and, and..."

"All whom you see with me are stems of my seed, leaves of my stem," Calatín stated. "Blood of my blood, bone of my bone, flesh of my flesh. Who shall say that a father does not live in his sons, that they are not one and the same? As the calf belongs to the cow, the son belongs to the father."

Fergus opened his mouth, then closed it again. He knew, as well as I or any, that there was no argument that would stand against what Calatín had said: no law nor custom would deny its truth.

"Go, then, and may Cú Chulainn repay you as you deserve for this!" Fergus spat. He stood up and stalked off. Flidais half-rose, as if to follow him, but Maeve set a hand on her fellow-queen's arm.

"Let him go," Maeve murmured. "He has cause to be angry, and little joy can come to him from this, however the day end."

Flidais sat back down, and Maeve stared at Calatín's troop. "I never thought to see such a thing in the light of day," she said, wondering.

"How, no, you will not tell me, nor would I understand, I think, if you did. However you did it, this is a wonder and an amazement. I thought those who tell tales of your skill as an enchanter sometimes embroidered their thoughts, but I see now that they all fall woefully short of the mark.

Go, and my blessings on you! Take whatever chariots and drivers you wish, saving only Finnabair, and whatever else you may need, and bring back Cú Chulainn's head."

"I cannot say for certain how this day will end," Calatín said. Though he stood straight and strong in his link-mail shirt, I could hear the exhaustion of his great working soaking heavy and cold through his voice. "This I do know: my seed will be Cú Chulainn's doom. If it is thus fated, it may be today."

"May it be!" Maeve said, and Ailill echoed her.

Calatín turned his head, looking down at me.

"Fedelm, you will stay with the host this day. Do not seek a vision of the battle! There will be great strife in it, of more than our bodies, and I do not wish you to risk yourself. Nor would you be able to aid me in any manner."

"I understand," I said, bowing my head. Suithchern had borne her husband going to the ford, with far less hope than mine. I could surely bear that uncertainty as well as she, and Calatín was not my husband, nor my love.

Though we had slept in the same tent, dressing and undressing before each other's eyes, for almost the whole of the raid, the thought of lying with him had never so much as crossed my mind. It came to me, looking up at the Druid's lean stern face, he had shaved last night, washed his grizzled hair and woven it into a badger-brindled braid at the back of his neck; and I suddenly regretted that I had helped him ready himself, that if he was not husband or love, he had become more a father to me than that simple man who had sired me and tried to raise me as a farmer's daughter.

Calatín had cared for me and guided me. It was not to those strong sons who stood armored about me that he had given his great heritage of lore, but to me: no kin by blood, but closer kin by lore and soul. I stood on tiptoes, taking Calatín's helmed head between my hands. The frost on the helmet scorched my palms with cold, but I did not flinch. Gently, I pulled his face down and kissed his mouth. Calatín blinked, his lips curving up slightly as though the touch of my own had thawed them.

"Fedelm, daughter of my heart," he whispered. "Tend yourself well, and the babe you carry: the blessings of all the gods upon you."

Then he turned, and his enchanted troop of sons and grandsons with him. I watched them go until they were lost among the tents, and Ailill and Maeve and Flidais rose to shout the army into movement, to make as much ground as we could this day, before Calatín's fight was done.

'If he kills Cú Chulainn, who is wounded and bears the Morrígan's wrath, then we shall no longer have to hasten in whatever space of time a man's death can buy us!' Suithchern and I took the wagon again that day. I did not have to say a word: when the driver saw me, he leapt down and immediately began to help Eochaid set up our makeshift shelter, face pale and hands trembling.

My hands went protectively to my belly. For a moment of stark
fear, I remembered the horrors I had birthed in my dream, and
wondered if something within me could already be perceived even
by an ordinary wagon-driver. Then I saw the sleeve of my white
robe falling over my arm: I was still dressed as a Druid prepared to
perform a rite or enchantment. Word of Calatín's great feat of magic
must have spread over the camp. I remembered his quiet anger
when I had almost cast up my stomach from revulsion before the
leaders of the host, and understood better.

What one Druid did cast its light or shadow on all of us in men's
hearts, so deeply that perhaps they themselves did not understand
why they thought and reacted to us as they did. I will be strong
for you,Calatín, I thought. The wagon lurched slowly forward, and
Suithchern unwrapped her bratt, tucking Conall under it so that he
could nurse in the warmth of the thick woolen folds.

She was still pale, her face swollen from long crying, and her
movements were slow. If I had not known her, and her sorrow,
I might have thought from looking at her that she had dived too
deeply into a keg of mead the night before, at least until I came
close enough to realize that no smell hung about her except the faint
aroma of milk and babies, or saw how clear her blue eyes gleamed
inside their reddened rims. Bright as summer's first bluebells, I
thought, and knew that the sadness I felt at that was only a faint
echo of Suithchern's own. .

"Have you eaten today?" Suithchern said timidly. "Or, are you
allowed to?"

As she spoke, I realized that my belly was tight and roiling, on the
verge of nausea. I thought again of the dignity of the druid: I should
tell her I was fasting. I remembered Calatín's clothes scattered on
the floor of our tent, careless of what Eochaid or I should think; and
how I had seen him as a man for the first time as we prepared to
leave Cruachan, kicking through the rushes and looking under the
bed for his lost shoe with Nuagal hiding her quiet smile. Even he
needs someone to be human with: why not I?

"I couldn't eat now," I said. "Perhaps later."

"You really ought," Suithchern persisted. "However you fear for
Calatín, you cannot help him now by going hungry, unless there
is some Druidic reason for it. Eat, and settle yourself. Or, is it
something else?" A faint smile struggled against her tear-swollen
cheeks.

I drew in my breath in surprise. I would have spoken, but the words gagged in my throat, and I found myself stumbling to the edge of the wagon, retching over the side until sparks burst in my skull. Nothing came out but a few strings of frothy spittle; but when I had finished and wiped my mouth, I found that I was feeling better, the racking shudders transforming into a sudden thin shiver of excitement and a smile pulling at my own mouth.

"I think. I think it is," I said. I laid my hand on my belly again as though I could feel the wonder of the new life within, my night's terrors driven back into their underground cave. .

"Ah, Fedelm," Suithchern said. "That is splendid! Will you stay in Cruachan? At least until the babe is born?"

"I must go back to Alba. Likely, I will not even be showing until after this raid is over; there is plenty of time for me to travel safely."

The brief gleam of joy on Suithchern's round face faded back into her sagging grief. "I shall miss you. I would have liked to be at your birthing."

"I wish you could be," I said.

Clothra, who had been sleeping quietly in her blankets, was awake and squirming now. A fold of green wool fell aside, and she began to wail as the cold air bit into her tender skin. I hastened to wrap her up again, picking her up and rocking her.

After a few more squeals, she fell asleep again, the little soft petals of her mouth half-open and a few drops of drool trailing silver from the corner.

Careful not to wake her, I blotted them away. 'I will be doing the same for my own, in less than a year,' I thought, gazing at the babe's face. Her features were so tiny, and so perfect: the miniature nose and ears, the wide bright blue eyes, now closed beneath a spiderweb delicate fringe of golden lashes.' If I birthed the monsters of my dream? If it were a true dream'. I had been sleeping on a pallet of blankets in Suithchern's tent, not on the woven rowan-branches in Calatín's.

One of the first things I had learned as a student of prophecy was how to tell a true dream from the strange weaving of fear and hope and nonsense that the mind, unguided, casts up. Yet now I could not apply what I had learned. As a boy in his first real fight, however long he has trained, may sometimes forget all the skills of hand and foot and eye, flailing at his foes in wild panic; so I could not disentangle the threads of my own feelings well enough to tell if there were a skein of truth among them. I glanced out of our shelter at the Sun, her glow pale yellowish-white as a disk of polished electrum against the sky.

It seemed as though it had been forever since Calatín marched his troop of sons and enchantment off to meet the Hound at the ford, but the Sun still hung low in the south eastern horizon, barely a quarter of the way through her low winter arc. 'Fight well, Calatín, and may the Morrígan strengthen your hand, I thought, hoping that he could feel my blessing. Win this fight, and live!

You cared for my child before I knew I was bearing her; though I will be far away when she is born, I know you will rejoice with me. Live, and found your school, and teach my daughter when I have come back and she is old enough, if the power come to her'.

I did not feel like speech, nor did Suithchern, my heart whirling between joy and fear, hers sunken in sorrow. Yet I was comforted by her quiet presence, like the warmth of a faithful hound curled on my bed, and I thought, I hoped, that mine was some comfort to her. We rode in silence, save for a few murmurs to the children. I had brought my harp, and if none of my skill could aid Calatín now, at least the enchantment of its silver strings could bring easing to the two of us.

Carefully I wrapped Clothra to settle her back into her nest. She did not even open her eyes, utterly limp and trusting in my arms as I tucked the blankets up around her. I took up my harp and began to play, the notes ringing clear and soft through the frosty air. Between the concentration I needed to keep my fingers sweeping over the singing silver wires, and the sound of the music ringing through the air and thrumming through the sounding-board into my body, there was little thought left in my mind to worry about Calatín, or to let myself be entangled in the strings of fear and hope for what I bore within me.

I played, and played. Clothra slept; Conall smiled and gurgled, reaching one tiny hand outside Suithchern's green-and-yellow checkered bratt and waving it in the air, as though he would catch the ringing notes in his little fist. The tightness of Suithchern's face eased as she listened, as though I had won a little slackening in the harsh rope of grief that bound her. I let the music take me, as though I were a swan whose own wing-beats made the wind to bear me aloft.

The harping of the síde-folk, it is said, can enchant a man or woman to dance for an hundred years, until the last mortal bone has fallen to dust. If mine were not so mighty, at least it could hold me enthralled within in its silvery fortress of sound, nearly safe from the whirling storm of my thoughts and the tight quivering of my body. When the first shadow rose sparkling across my sight, I tried to fight it, concentrating harder on the movements of my fingers and the delicate tugging of the silver wires at my nails.

Calatín had told me not to seek him, for my own sake, and my child's, and I would obey. Yet my own music swirled around me like a strong sea-wind rising from a deep cleft in the shore-cliffs. My eyes darkened; I stopped playing and breathed deeply until the day came back. I bent down to lay my harp carefully on a heap of folded tents, and as I straightened, the dizziness overwhelmed me in a maelstrom of darkness and lights flashing scarlet and blue and white.

I could not clear my sight, only watch as the lights brightened to the glitter of shattered ice and rushing water at the ford, the shadows resolving into the shapes of tall lean men surrounding a single small brightness-crowned figure who whirled and parried and struck in a mad blur. I could not tell Calatín from his sons and enchantments, nor did I dare look more closely to see who lay staring open-eyed through the water that rushed over his dead face, or who crawled bleeding towards the bank, his hands feeling at the rocks like a blind man's.

The hero-light around Cú Chulainn's head flared to blinding brilliance, his spinning body a shadow beneath it. As I watched, that shadow bulged and warped. He shook like a tree caught in a river's flood, or a reed in a stream; his body twisted inside his skin, feet and knees turning backwards, and the hard fists of his calf-muscles standing out like great knots on his shins.

Now I could see his head inside the halo of light, but it was already deforming, the sinews of his temples bloating out like great bladders and his face sinking into an horrendous red bowl, one eye sucked in, leaving only a narrow dark tunnel as though a crane's beak had stabbed deep into his face, the other swelling to hang huge from the socket. His cheeks peeled so far back from his jaws I could see the red cave of his gullet, flakes of fire flying from his gnashing teeth; his heartbeat boomed from his gaping mouth like the base pounding of a big goatskin drum.

Clouds of dark steam, flickering red with faint lightnings, rose from his body; his hair twisted and tangled like the branches of a thorn bush. From the top of his head spurted a great fountain of smoking black blood, a boiling and seething liquid pillar. He roared, and it seemed to me that I heard a hundred warriors' voices echoing; that the cry rang through the plain and hills about, and was taken up another hundredfold by all those beings who dwelt unseen there, their high eerie screeches like a thousand bone flutes shrieking above the war-blast of a trumpa-band.

Then the darkness rose around me. When it cleared, I gazed over a misty plain. A small dark-haired man clothed in red stood before a pillar-stone, a sword in his hand and his stance oddly erect. The hero-light still flickered before his face, but when I looked closer, he was drenched in crimson blood, and stood so straight because his body was bound to the standing stone with a rope. Before him capered the monsters from my dream, sallow-skinned, one-handed and one-footed, single black eyes bulging from their sallow brows. Now they were grown to full size, and I could see that three were male, three female.

The hags crouched before a fire where a dog's butchered body turned on a spit; each of the distorted men lifted a spear in his single hand. As I stared in revulsion, their shapes merged, each three into one, and for a moment, I saw through the nightmare figures. A tall, slim maiden with seal-brown hair, long-jawed and long-nosed, black eyebrows straight over her dark eyes; a tall, lean young man whose face, like his sister's, I almost knew. I had seen it that morning. Calatín's face in his youth: this man's hair was brown instead of black, and his features a little softened, but still he could nearly have been brother to Glas mac Delga. Calatín's children by Nuagal. Great in power!

"My seed will be Cú Chulainn's doom." With a single panicked, convulsive effort, I wrenched myself away: for my child's sake, I must not look any longer. The dizziness and darkness threatened to whelm me again, but I strove to breathe deeply, that my lungs might draw my soul more firmly into my body with the cold bite of the winter air. As my head began to clear, I tasted oats and honey in my mouth, chewing and swallowing without thought. I had slipped halfway off the pile of coarse wool I was sitting on; Suithchern had one arm around me, and her free hand held a honey-smeared oatcake to my mouth.

"Fedelm? Fedelm, are you all right?" She was asking anxiously.

I reached for the nearby water skin, washing the crumbling stickiness out of my throat.

"I think so," I said hoarsely. Then, "How did you know what to do?" For she had done exactly the right thing to succor a seer overwhelmed by vision, or a drúi by magic, just as Eochaid would have if he had not been pacing about the wagon to guard me from any outer threat.

"I thought, I didn't know. I knew that if someone rests on a patch of hungry-grass, they grow suddenly pale and weak-looking as you did, and the only cure for that is to give an oatcake or a handful of oat meal. I thought what works against one such thing might work for another."

"Well, whatever you thought, you were right. ," I admitted ruefully, "you were right earlier when you said I should eat." For I should have eaten something as soon as Calatín's ritual was done, to bind my soul tightly back to my flesh: had I done so, I could not have been overwhelmed as I was.

A faint smile glimmered on Suithchern's face.

"Another time I shall be firmer with you," she said, and I smiled back at her.

Then there was nothing to do but wait. I knew I had escaped the vision in time, and taken no harm, to myself or the child within me. I did not dare to play the harp again, nor take up my weaving-rod, lest the twining weave of strings or strands draw me once more into unwilling sight. Instead, I babbled to the two babes, wiggling my fingers for them to grasp in tiny soft fists and letting them pull at the long golden rope of my braid; I told Suithchern of the workings of life at the school in Alba, and of how it would be for me to raise a child while I finished my studies.

"It is not easy for a mother alone," she said sadly. "I wish you could stay at Cruachan, that we might aid one another. There is our house..." Her face crumpled again.

"I do not know how I can bear to live there alone, with Lóch dead. Could you not stay and study..." She bit off her last words, but I heard them as clearly as if she had spoken them aloud: study with Calatín?

I blinked, thinking about it. Calatín was planning to found a school there: what if I were to remain with him from its beginnings? If he lives. It would be easier for me to dwell at home where I did not have to wrap my tongue around the odd consonants of the Cruithne speech; to live in Suithchern's house and have her help caring for my child.

If I went back to Alba, Conall and Clothra would be ten by the time I returned, and I would have lost the chance to see their childhood. Nor would I see Ailill for ten years...and though he was a strong man, who knew what might befall a warrior-king in ten years? If I finished my training at Calatín's school, if he lives, I would bring nothing more than we had already. To be worthy of the place he had offered, the teaching he had given, I must go back to Alba.

"I can't. I'm sorry."

Suithchern nodded sadly. "I didn't really think so. I only hoped..."

Looking at her downcast face, I felt wretchedly guilty. Suithchern was young, and fruitful, and fair; and Ailill would see that she and her babes wanted for nothing. I could not say it now, with her husband less than a day dead. Still, I was certain that there would be another man for her, one who spoke of eyes like bluebells and hair like dark honey and breasts like hillocks of soft churned cream; one who was glad to foster the babe of a warrior who died fighting the Hound of Ulster at the ford and the child that King Ailill himself had brought out of the slaughterhouse that had been Rath Echach.

'If Calatín falls today, who could stand in his stead? I wondered. Who else has been gifted with the lore of enchantment by Manannán mac Lir, and worked for forty years to understand and refine it? So much of what he had taught me, I did not truly understand yet. What if he died this day, if he is already dead, if he was one of the fallen men at the ford?', And all his knowledge was lost with him?

We fell silent again for a while. The Sun crawled up the sky, excruciatingly slow; Conall soiled his breech clout again, and had to be changed. I was leaning over the side of the wagon, sluicing the last of the mess from my hands, when Eochaid tapped me on the shoulder. I looked up into his green eyes. Eochaid met my gaze, his sharp-featured face weighted with the sorrow he could not speak.

Only a harsh meowing noise came out when he opened his mouth, but he put his arm about my shoulders as if to hold me up. Moving slow as in a nightmare, I turned to look behind me. Our wagon was at the rear of the host, the road to the ford clear behind. I saw the chariots in the distance, the horses plodding steadily towards us. Not one held a living warrior standing behind the young gillas who drove. Suithchern was at my other side. I turned to her, burying my face in her warm shoulder for a few heartbeats.

The hot swelling in my throat felt like an abscess, ready to burst in a flood of tears at any moment. I could not weep where so many could see me. Calatín had taught me the duties of a drúi: now that he was fallen, I must be worthy of him.

"Help me down, Eochaid," I said. "I would speak with the charioteers."

Suithchern whistled for the driver to stop, and Eochaid lifted me from the wagon, setting my feet gently on the ground. I stood where I was, lifting my hand and gesturing the gillas to step up their pace. Even at this distance, they could see my white robe, and they urged their horses to hasten. I waited until the young men were gathered around me, pale, hands trembling on their reins. Cold as it was, the fresh slaughterhouse-stink from the burdens their chariots bore was almost unbearable, blood and raw meat and the stench of opened entrails. A small part of my mind wondered faintly that the horses were not shying and bolting at the smell, though of course they were trained to battle.

"Tell me of the fight," I said.

The gillas glanced at each other. Finally a plump freckled youth shook his curly brown hair back and said,

"We did not see it. Calatín ordered us to wait behind a hill near the ford, until he should triumph or all his sons were dead. So we waited, and knew nothing more, until Glas struggled dying around the hill. His bowels were out. He only said one word before he died: fiacha."

"Blame," I echoed.

'Who did he blame? Calatín, because even this dawn's rite was not strong enough to overcome the Hound? Maeve, who began this raid, and accepted Cú Chulainn's offer to save as many of our lives as she could? Or, could he have blamed me? Was there something I might have done, and did not?'

"Then we went down to the ford. Eight bodies were there; the rest had vanished." Vanished back to sprinklings of ragwort and fern, I thought; of meadowsweet and broom and oak, vanished like mushrooms melting into the mold from which they sprang.

Calatín lay in the bottom of our chariot, his long body curled in death. I remembered the knot of the broken bone and the scar I had seen on his sword-shoulder beneath the whorls of woad-pricking. Cú Chulainn had struck in the same place, his sword shearing through the iron links of the old drúi's hauberk, through bone and ribcage and lung.

Though the blood had darkened as it dried, I could still see how it had frothed and spattered out as Calatín had struggled for his last breath, trying to curse his foe as he died?

Calling to Nuagal, across half Eriu's breadth? Or, as so many do, crying for his mother with his last breaths as with his first?

I would never know, and the thought wrung my body with a convulsion of sorrow. I clenched my fists by my side, forcing myself to remain upright until the spasm had passed.

"Take Calatín's sons and grandson on, that their wives or friends may ready them for the cairn," I said. " Calatín himself, you shall leave here with me. Eochaid, raise our tent, and fetch our chests and bags, that I may do what I must for my teacher. Suithchern…" I looked up at her, standing in the wagon with one child in each arm. "I am sorry, but this I must do alone. Thank you for…" For feeding me to bring me safe from my vision, for talking to me so that I was not left wholly to my thoughts, for being beside me, so that I was not alone.

"I understand," Suithchern murmured. "If you need me, you have only to let me know."

I stood by Calatín's chariot while Eochaid and a few of the gillas raised the tent. That done, Eochaid leapt into the chariot, crouching to take Calatín upon his shoulders.

Lean as the old Druid had been, his length made him a burden for the smaller man: Eochaid lurched under the weight and almost fell as he climbed out, but caught himself hard on the chariot, and when one of the gillas reached to aid, he turned with a hissing snarl that might have been swearing from another man's throat. The pale sunlight glanced silver from the wet trails on the Cat's cheeks as he stumbled in to lay Calatín upon his bed: he, too, had come to love my teacher in his way.

I wondered anew who and what Eochaid had been before he took service at the Druidic school. A champion, who would not stay among his brethren to suffer their pity? A king's son who, maimed of throat, could never take the rule? Now I found it easier to believe, had the students' tales of the Cat's transformation been the truth after all?

I could not ask Eochaid, even had his speech been clearer: it would, I was sure, only be more pain to him. Eochaid straightened, looking down at Calatín's body. He reached down to lift the iron links at the hem of the Druid's shattered hauberk, raising a dark eyebrow at me: Do you need my aid? I shook my head. It would be hard work, getting the ring-mail off Calatín's stiffening body, the Hound's blow had driven some of the broken links very deep into his flesh, as well, but it was my task to do, as was that which must follow.

Eochaid nodded, and left me alone to work. I had to remind myself that Calatín would not feel it as I cut the embedded bits of mail from him, nor did I need to fear causing him pain as I soaked and pulled the blood-crusted tunic away from his chest and shoulder. Now I could weep freely, and I did, dashing the tears from my blurring eyes with the back of a bloodstained hand.

At least Cú Chulainn had not taken Calatín's head: that would have been the final loss, and perhaps the worst. Even as I gathered the tools that I would need, my heart shrank from the task before me. Calatín's eyes gazed at me, dark and dull as those of any slaughtered animal. His grizzled hair had come loose from its braid at the back of his neck.

There was no blood in it, but it had dried in snarled tangles, as though he had fallen into the water to die. I combed it carefully and braided it, looking into his eyes as though I might yet see the gleam of life in them. The garment of flesh could not be mended. Yet it did not seem to me that he was altogether gone. I touched my lips to Calatín's cold mouth, as I had done at our last parting.

"I hope I understand," I said to him. "I hope this is what you wanted. I will do my best to see that Manannán's rath, your school of Druidry is raised at Cruachan."

As I had stood beside Suithchern while her husband's cairn was raised the day before, so she stood by me while the rocks were heaped about the bodies of Calatín, his sons, and his grandson. I was not ashamed to take her hand in mine: her own grief was so fresh, and mine so sharp, that we could do no more than comfort each other. When the stones had risen high enough that we could no longer see the bodies within, we turned away. Ailill was standing there; he must have been waiting for some time. He looked down at me, his strong face soft with compassion and grief.

"Fedelm," he said. "I am sorry. If I could have held him back, I hoped that he would have victory."

"He would not have heeded you had you tried," I answered dully. "A Druid who had made up his mind, and done such a work to carry it out, would not have listened, not to the greatest of kings."

"No. Still, is there aught I can do for you? You know you have only to name it."

I looked up at Ailill's dear face, at the sunlight catching a shimmer of light across his elaborate mass of red-gold braids and the softness of his finely-shaped lips beneath the bright wings of his mustaches. I laid my hand on his arm, guiding him without speaking back to his tent in the royal enclosure.

Maeve was already sitting by the fire there, talking in low tones with Fergus. The Ulster exile set his jaw firmly and looked away from me. Maeve nodded, a sad smile on her lips, and lifted her hand as if in blessing as Ailill and I walked into the king's tent.

"Fedelm..." Ailill said.

I could not bear to speak. I laid one finger on the tender warmth of his mouth, then pulled his head down to kiss me. His arms went around me, strong and gentle.

He held me to his broad chest, undoing my braid and stroking my hair while I wept, and kissing my face clean of tears when I was done.

Carefully as if he were trying to lift a spider's web whole without disturbing the fine silky strands, he helped me undress; and for a time, I was able to give myself wholly over to the comfort he offered.

"Would you sleep here this night?" Ailill asked when we lay quietly again in each other's warmth.

"I must go back to my own tent," I told him. "I must go. Suithchern will stay the night with me."

"She is a good woman. If only Lóch, I will see that she and her babes are well cared-for."

"I know you will," I assured Ailill. I wondered briefly if I should tell him yet. This was not the hour; I would know it when it came.

Suithchern came to spend the night with me. If she feared what I kept in our tent now, she did not speak or show it; and Clothra and Conall were still too young to get into the bags and chests of herbs and other things that we kept there. She brought me food: I might as well have been chewing on fallen leaves and toadstools for all I tasted it, but Suithchern made sure I ate all she put before me. When I would have sat in darkness, she brought a torch in; and when I would have stayed awake in grief, she insisted on settling me in bed before she curled up with the two babes.

I still thought I would not sleep, staring into the darkness with the lumpy rowan-twigs creaking beneath me at every movement. The body has its own demands, and I was grievously weary: soon I drifted towards soft darkness.

'I should have taken out the rowan-branches before I lay down, I thought vaguely'.

I was too sleepy and comfortable to move, the thought floating away even as my mind voiced it. I dreamed, and knew that I dreamed. As before, when I had seen the Morrígan come to Cú Chulainn, I saw the fine tent with its elaborate hangings, the fire before it and the young man sitting by it, his face still hidden by the light that glimmered faintly over his features.

This time, he was not honing his weapons, but sat huddled into himself and wincing at every shiver that ran through his body, as if in great pain. The heavy mantles layered over him hid his wounds and bandages, but I could see the end of a wooden splint bound to his wrist. Across from him sat a larger youth, fair-haired and hale, the Hound's charioteer, I guessed, who had brought him away and tended to him.

"Is there any more I can do?" The blond youth said anxiously to Cú Chulainn.

Cú Chulainn raised his head wearily. For a moment I almost caught a glimpse of his face beneath the dimming light, but its flickering cast more shadows than it showed flesh beneath them.

"Go forth, Láeg, and rouse the hosts. Tell them for me in Emain that I am weary from each day's battles, wounded and bloody. It was no physician's hand that smote my right side and my left. Tell noble Conchobar that I am weary, wounded sore in my side; that Dechtire's dear son no longer looks as he did." He coughed, spat something dark to sizzle into the fire.

"I am here guarding Ulster's flocks alone: I will not let them go, but neither can I hold them, standing alone at many fords. Today Fiacha, Fergus' man, came to help me against unfair fighting; but no other comes to aid me. A single log does not burn, nor a single horn rejoice; but two or three together burn brightly, and several make fair music."

He thinks he is dying, I thought. Maybe he is!

"The she-wolf bit me, the eel entangled me, the heifer trampled me. Lóch wounded my liver; the cold creeps through me from the wounds Calatín and his sons dealt me. Why do the men of Ulster not come to give battle, while I am here in sorrow, wounded and bloody? I pledged my pledge; it holds and has been fulfilled, by the honor of the Hound, but the ravens rejoice. Conchobar does not come: it is hard to reckon his wrath. Láeg, there is little more you can do for me here. Go now, go at once, and tell them for me in Emain that they must come while they still can."

He slew Calatín, I thought. My teacher, the father of my mind; how can I pity him? I should be filled with hatred; I should rejoice at the pain of his wounds and the cold of the poison in his veins, and ready myself to tell Maeve that he did not fight Calatín and his sons by himself, but that Fergus and his man Fiacha betrayed us.

Looking at Cú Chulainn's small huddled figure, all I could see was the lonely boy who had, for so long, fought a terribly over matched battle by himself. He was dying now, in any case. At least he was so wounded that he would not fight again for a very long time, if ever. Telling what I had learned would do us no good, nor restore Calatín's sundered body. Now Cú Chulainn was alone by the fire. A great shudder racked his little body; he clasped his hands tightly to his chest, rocking and moaning slightly until it had passed.

I saw a man moving in the fire's shadows, the flames' ruddy brightness gleaming from fair hair, and thought that Láeg must have gone in search of something to ease the warrior's pain. This man was taller than Cú Chulainn's charioteer, and the light on his golden hair was more than the reflection of the firelight. I had seen a swineherd of the síde in my childhood, and been stunned to fever and poetry. Even wrapped safely in the distance of dream-vision, I could barely look on the face of the lord who had come to Cú Chulainn now.

He wore a green mantle, pinned by a bright silver brooch; his tunic beneath was crimson silk embroidered all over with spirals of gleaming red gold. His skin was white as moonlight on the snow, and his eyes glowed as hot a blue as the sky at summer's height.

"This is a manly stand you are making, Cú Chulainn," he said softly, his voice thrumming through me so that it took all my strength to keep from being shaken to blinders.

Cú Chulainn did not look up. "It isn't doing very much," he said, his words weighted with despair.

"I am going to help you now."

Cú Chulainn slowly lifted his head, clenching his teeth in pain. "Who are you?" He breathed.

"I am Lugh mac Ethnenn of the Tuatha de Danann, your father from the síd."

Siabra, I had heard folk call Cú Chulainn when they were angry or would mock him. I had not thought about it, but assumed it was meant to cast a harsh light on his slightness, or else to liken his deeds to the night-shrouded malice of the síde-folk's lesser kin. Maybe no more was meant by those who spoke; but words, and even insults, often bear a truth beyond what the speaker knows.

The Hound of Ulster sighed, letting his head droop painfully onto his breast again. His hands fell to his lap, as though he could hold them up no more. He knows that Lugh has come to take him.

"My wounds are heavy. It is time they were healed," Cú Chulainn murmured.

Lugh laid a moon-burning hand on his half-son's light-shrouded head. "Sleep a while then, Cú Chulainn," he said.

"A heavy sleep of three days and three nights; and while Láeg bears your message to Ulster's armies, I shall guard and tend you."

Cú Chulainn breathed out, a long slow exhalation like a dying man's last breath sighing from his lungs. He slumped and would have toppled, but Lugh caught him, lifting him up and bearing him into the tent. Within, the summer sun's brightness shone from Lugh's face so that I could not look straight upon him. He drew aside the mantles enfolding Cú Chulainn's body, unwrapping the bandages that hid the fearful gashes of his wounds. The pink sheen of his bowels bulged from a long slice across his abdomen, the dark ruddy-brown of his liver gleamed from a deeper cut in his side, and I saw the truth of Lugh's words.

No ordinary man could have lived so long, much less fought, with such injuries. I watched Lugh tend to his son, the brightness of his hands flowing into the wounds as if to clean them. The herbs that the god laid into Cú Chulainn's injuries glowed bright as drops of sunlight; he sang in a deep murmur, and I could not make out the words, but I knew that it was a song of healing. I must tell Maeve, I thought.

We have three days before she must find more men who will undertake to meet Cú Chulainn at the next ford, or go back to each side doing whatever they can to the other. It seemed to me that the thought dimmed Lugh's brightness before my eyes, a dark fog rising between myself and what was passing in Cú Chulainn's shelter, until I knew that I was lying on my uncomfortable frame of rowan branches and staring at the darkness within my own tent.

Maeve

Fedelm came to Maeve as she sat waiting for her breakfast. Fearbh was crouched by the fire baking flat cakes on a griddle, the delicious scents of honey and toasting wheat and berries rising temptingly from it. There was no need to hurry. After Calatín and his sons and grandson had been brought back, no other man had come forward to say that he would fight the Hound. What manner of man is he? Maeve thought despairingly.

How could any warrior stand against twenty-seven skilled fighters, or the might of such a Druid's enchantments, and live?

"My queen," Fedelm said. Maeve wanted to tell the girl not to speak so to her, was Fedelm not the next thing to Ailill's adaltrach, or her own little sister? Remembering what she had seen yesterday, and that Fedelm was Calatín's pupil, she held her tongue.

The seeress stood very straight, like a young guard reporting to his commander. Though Maeve had not seen her weeping, her bright blue-grey eyes were rimmed with red, wide and stark against her pale face, and the shadows beneath them were very dark, as though she had smeared blue woad-pigment about her lids with the unskilled hand of a little girl trying paint for the first time. If Fedelm had slept at all last night, Maeve thought, it had done her no good. She ought to have stayed the night in Ailill's tent so that he might have continued to comfort her grief.

"Is all well with you, Fedelm?" Maeve asked gently.

"I have seen the Hound," Fedelm replied. "He was wounded near death; I thought him dying as I watched. Lugh came to him, and hailed him as son, and gave him healing. Yet he will sleep three days and nights; and while he does, he does not guard the ford, and we may move onward."

Maeve drew in a deep breath, letting it out slowly. Before she had set out on this raid, she would scarcely have believed such a thing. Now, in the light of day, she had seen enchantment multiply nine men by three, illusion or truth, it was still a wonder almost beyond accepting. 'And Calatín almost succeeded. If Cú Chulainn was dying, and Lugh himself came to him, it is hardly fair!' Then Maeve had to laugh at herself. Fairness was for champions' duels, the duels of ordinary champions, not multiplied by magic, nor aided or hindered by gods. From the day Eriu's host had set out for the north and she, Fedelm, and Finnabair had cursed Conchobar, there had been precious little of fairness on this raid, for either side.

"Maeve?" Fedelm said tentatively, her worn delicate features creasing with worry.

"No, there is nothing amiss with me," Maeve assured her. "The news you brought might have been better, but if we have three days in which to press on unhindered, we should take advantage of them."

"Yes. Macha's pangs will not bind the men of Ulster too much longer," Fedelm warned. "While the frost holds, Conchobar will lie in his bed. Imbolc is coming,and the curse will wear off his lesser men first. The Moon is near full: Ulster's men will begin to rise before the white gelding is dark again."

"Then we must make what haste we can."

Fedelm nodded, looking down at the ground and shifting uncomfortably from foot to foot, as though there were something more she would say.

Eager as she was to spring to her feet and shout her army into motion, Maeve waited.

"Fedelm," Maeve said finally, "are you hiding something?"

"I... Cú Chulainn said something to his charioteer. He was in pain, and thought they were alone..."

"Go on," Maeve encouraged.

Fedelm looked at her feet again, but the words finally came out in a rush, like blood bursting from a vein. "Glas mac Delga,he made it back to the charioteers, and said one word before he died. Fiacha: when they told me, I thought he was blaming someone, his grandfather's magic, or..."

" Fiacha is a name as well," Maeve said slowly. The gillas' story had been nagging deep at the back of her mind like a mouse gnawing quietly inside a chest of meal, a disturbance almost too faint for her to notice.

"The name of Fergus' dead son, and also of one of his Ulstermen."

"Yes." Cú Chulainn said.

Maeve closed her eyes. Fergus must have sent his man to his foster-son's aid after he stamped off the previous morning. Breaching the terms of single combat, yes, but though Calatín had upheld his case by the strict word of the law, it would be hard to aim an accusation at Fiacha. 'And Fergus? What aid has he been to us, truly? Would we not have been better off, had we left him at Cruachan.

Now Maeve was back at the same dilemma that had haunted her throughout the raid, circling painfully again and again like a bird with a wounded wing. He could not stay, for his honor; he should not have come, for his loyalties'. Nor could she forget how she had clung to Fergus in the depths of her winter's darkness, or how he had striven to give her what love he could. Cú Chulainn would have died at the ford, and we been free of him, if Fergus had not interfered! If I sent him away now.

What reason could I give? Maeve thought of how her men had handled Murchadh, how the one warrior had told her to give him to Calatín to burn in the wicker. She thought, as well, of those youths beaten to death at Midwinter because they were small and dark-haired and no one had spoken for them in time.

'If anyone else knew that Cú Chulainn survived yesterday because of Fergus, they would beat him to death as well: however great a hero he may be, he could not stand against an angry army. We would have war in our camp: the Ulster exiles would be slaughtered for what Fiacha did, and our whole host weakened. Cormac, my son, would even he escape?'

Maeve felt sick with rage and disappointment, as though she had swallowed something curdled and yet did not dare to cast it up.

Fedelm did not flinch back from her face, but the girl's eyes widened, the tiny muscles at the edges of her pointed jaw clenching tight.

"I am not angry with you," Maeve said. "Say nothing of this, to anyone. It is grievous to hear, but would be more grievous still if it were widely known, you understand?"

"I understand," Fedelm whispered.

"You have done well, Fedelm. Calatín would be proud of you."

Maeve saw at once that she had misspoken, as Fedelm swallowed painfully: Maeve had been a mother long enough to know when a girl was fighting back tears.

"You have done well," she said again, as soothingly as she could.

"Now I shall have a comfortable shelter and bed made up in one of the wagons for you, and you shall rest as we travel. Do you need one of my maidservants?"

"No," Fedelm said. "Suithchern... Lóch's wife...she has been taking care of me."

"You of her," Maeve murmured, remembering how Fedelm had stood by the bereaved woman as Lóch was laid in his cairn. "That is well. Perhaps this is not the time to speak of it, but when her grief has eased, tell her that there is a place of honor for her in my retinue, should she choose to take it. If she marries again, I will see to it myself that she brings a noble portion to the wedding."

"Thank you. That is kind, I will tell her. I think she will be grateful for it: she has little wish to dwell alone where once she lived with her husband."

Maeve nodded. Even when she was angriest with Ailill, she could not begin to imagine how empty Cruachan, or any of her royal dwellings, would seem without his cheerful voice and booming laughter.

"You know what I would offer you, if you choose it. Is there any other thing you desire?"

Fedelm blinked.

"Not for me, but for Calatín. He dreamed of founding a school for Druidry at Cruachan. I was to help him when I had finished my studies. I would do that still. He spoke of building a rath for his god-teacher, Manannán mac Lir, in the grove above the Black Boar's furrows."

"Will you stay to found his school?" Maeve asked hopefully.

The ban-fili shook her head. "Calatín wanted me to complete my training in Alba. Now I must, for though Senchán is hale, he is very old..."

"Well past eighty winters, I believe," Maeve agreed. "Druids are often long-lived; but you are wise not to expect him to last forever. I shall have the wrath built, just as you tell me, and it will be ready for you when you return. With Ailill's child beside you?"

Fedelm smiled brilliantly for a moment. Even through the girl's exhaustion and grief, Maeve thought she could already see a bearing woman's first rich glow tinged Fedelm's pale skin: there must be little doubt now. "If all goes well, I hope so."

Maeve's host marched all through that day. For the first time, Maeve marked what she had been missing without knowing it: men's deep voices and women's higher ones raised in song as they strode along, the lively booming of frame-drums and the occasional bone flute whistling above the beat, and the sounds of laughter rising here and there. She had kept Fedelm's vision of Lugh to herself, for it would do no good to let her warriors know that their foe had been tended by a god. It was enough that they knew Cú Chulainn was too badly wounded to hold the ford, at least for a time.

'When he rises, and comes to the next ford ahead of us, perhaps there will be more who are willing to face him, now that we have shown that he can be harmed'. It was halfway through the next day when Mac Roth came loping up to Maeve's chariot, the breath puffing from his mouth in small frosty clouds. Maeve frowned: she had sent her runner out as a scout, because he could cover ground more swiftly and with better endurance than even the best chariot-team. He would not have come back himself if the matter were not important.

"My queen," he said, "the boy-troop of Emain Macha is coming towards our host. There are only thrice fifty of them, and none older than fourteen, but they are well-armed and grim. I hailed them and asked who they were and where they were going.

They said they were coming to aid Cú Chulainn, so that he would no longer have to fight alone. I laughed and told them to go home and lay their swords aside for their hurleys again. They cast sling-balls at me before I had finished speaking: I was lucky to escape alive."

Maeve looked down at her red-haired messenger. "How far are they?"

"Perhaps an eighth-day's ride in a chariot."

"Go find Fergus and tell him to come to me. Only that!"

"As you will, my queen," Mac Roth said, and dashed off.

It was not long before Fergus' chariot drove up beside Maeve. Fergus stood easily in the middle, his strong legs braced as sturdily as oak-trunks, but swaying instinctively with the lurching of the vehicle, not so much as resting his hand on the edge. Maeve knew that she would never see him in his chariot without remembering his great leap over the tree, and her heart clenched within her. She had meant to speak angrily to Fergus, to shame him to aiding. From the jut of his bearded jaw and the fierce gleam of his grey eyes, he expected the same, but now that he stood before her, Maeve found the harshness evaporating from her tongue like spilled water fading from a warm hearthstone.

"Fergus," she said, "I know this raid has been much sorrow to you, but now there is a chance for you to lessen its harm. The boy-troop of Emain Macha has come, as they think, to aid Cú Chulainn, armed and ready to do battle. Go to them and turn them home again, before they raise weapons to the grown warriors of this army. I would not have the slaughter of children, however fierce, on my hands."

Fergus stared at her for a few heartbeats, then laughed bitterly.

"Ah, Maeve," he said. "I wish I could do as you say. If they are come from Emain Macha, no words of mine will quiet them. To them, I am a traitor, and their king's foe, as I am their king's foe, indeed, and marching with Connacht's army. No, I would only inflame their rashness further." He turned his face from Maeve, but she saw the spasm pass through the heavy muscles of his shoulders, and felt the worse for it. She had meant to offer him balm. Instead, she had ground her foot into his open wound.

"If there is one man in this host that they might listen to," Fergus said, turning back to her, his face calm again, "and I am not sure there is, it would be Cormac Connlongas. For though he is your son and loyal to you, he is also Conchobar's son. For the great awe in which the men of Ulster hold Conchobar..."

His mouth twisted as though he would spit, but he only glanced at the trampled snow beneath his chariot's wheels for a moment.

"They might heed Conchobar's son. Or they might not, and red slaughter take place anyway, but it is certain that no other would have any chance of avoiding it."

"Then I shall send Cormac," Maeve said. "I thank you for your advice, and..." I did not mean to hurt you, she wanted to say; but admitting that she had seen Fergus' pain would make it worse still.

"It is well-done for you to try to head the boy-troop off without slaughter," Fergus said painfully, as if he were drawing his own entrails out through his mouth. "May you be able to!"

Maeve thought Fergus would ride away from her then, but he was still beside her when Cormac's chariot dashed up.

"What is this about Emain Macha's boy-troop, Mother?" Her eldest son asked. Cormac's knobbly cheeks were flushed red from the cold, his blue eyes bright; it lightened Maeve's heart to see him. Quickly she told him what Mac Roth had told her.

"Can you make them go home?"

Cormac frowned.

"Conchobar has his youths trained to be brave, fierce, and harsh of heart. I know many of them. I may have trained some of them, for the elder ones would have joined the boy-troop before I left Ulster.

Yes, I think they will listen to me. I will certainly do my best."

"I know you will," Maeve said warmly. "Take your men, and hasten, before anything can happen that might bring us all more sorrow."

Fergus watched Cormac's chariot turn, and watched still as Cormac's gilla drove him back to gather his troop. His lips were pressed tightly together, but Maeve saw the longing shining through his face, like a flame glowing through the scraped hide of a lantern. Fergus' own son had been a toddler when Cormac was born, Maeve remembered. The two of them would have grown up, played, and fought together; Fergus had likely trained them together as well, as he had raised and trained Cú Chulainn eight years later.

'And he has lost his son, and is parted from his fosterling. What wonder that Cormac should hold some portion of their places in Fergus' heart? Even though he is the son of the man who took Fergus' place' An eighth-day's ride in a chariot, Mac Roth had said.

Cormac's personal troops were foot soldiers: his fifty elite warriors rode to battle in chariots, but dismounted to fight, and the rest would be marching. Maeve did not begin to worry until the Sun was a low red coal glowing against the dimming blue south western horizon and she had to call the army's halt for the night.

'He may still be talking with the boy-troop, for all I know. He knows them, and they respect him: he may even stay the night with them. I wish he had sent a messenger back to let me know!' Ailill had come with Maeve on her nightly round of the army. When she glanced at him, she saw that he, too, was looking uneasily towards the lowering sun. He coughed in an embarrassed manner, stroking the bright flare of his mustaches and turning towards Maeve.

"No matter how fierce the boys of Emain Macha are, I do not think that they could be much of a threat to Cormac's men," Ailill said. "And with Cú Chulainn down, at least for a time, there is hardly any other ill that could befall his troop."

"Still, I wish he were back. So much has gone awry, that it is hard not to fear the worst."

"True enough," Ailill sighed. Then he grinned. " Conchobar has his folk half-convinced that he is one of the gods. How could they assail his son?"

"My son," Maeve said firmly.

"With all his mother's courage and strength," Ailill agreed. "Surely you need not fear. No, you certainly need not fear." He pointed northeast. "See, here they come, after all. Surely that is Cormac's chariot in the fore, with him standing all hale behind his gilla."

The troop was just coming over a low rise in the land as Maeve looked. Although the sky was dark behind them, the snow was still catching a little of the evening light. A wave of relief washed over her as she saw Cormac's rangy silhouette black against the deep blue sky, unmistakable even at a distance.

"Surely you did not think Cormac was in any danger from a pack of boys?" Ailill teased. "Perhaps you were afraid that he might have his nose broken and his teeth loosened by a hurley or a flying ball? I myself was near-crippled at the age of ten when another boy's hurley caught me between the legs."

Maeve laughed. "You seem to have recovered well enough by now. Seven children by me, and how many by other women?"

"Stars in the sky, grains of sand on the beach," Ailill smirked.

Maeve leaned over the edge of her chariot to punch him lightly on the shoulder.

"That is boasting even beyond your measure. I think Fedelm has found your measure quite worthy of her, and I guess you enjoyed showing it to her."

Ailill's grin widened.

"The secrets of the Druids are many, and it is said that the tongue of a fili has many skills that are lacking to ordinary ones."

Maeve only laughed again. Somehow she doubted that an unbroached maiden, even a ban-drúi, was likely to have shown Ailill any feats of the blanket that her husband had not seen before. Ailill drew himself up with mock dignity.

"If you are quite through laughing at me, perhaps we should go and see how Cormac got on with the ferocious warriors of the boy-troop."

Finnabair glanced back over her shoulder at her father, rolling her eyes and sighing, but she snapped the reins to drive Maeve's golden horses on, and Cuillius did the same with Ailill's blacks. Even in the swift-darkening winter evening, Maeve could tell that something was amiss long before they closed with Cormac and his men. Some of the warriors on foot were limping, or leaning against their comrades.

Many of the chariots bore more than one passenger, with both sitting rather than standing; a few others were driven by warriors, their gillas nowhere to be seen.

Now that Maeve was closer, she could see the exhausted slump of Cormac's shoulders, and a sudden ball of cold dread thumped into her stomach like a sling's shot so that the breath hissed out of her lungs.

"Faster, Finnabair!" Maeve said. Her daughter was already urging the horses to greater speed, coming up on Cormac's troop as swiftly as possible: Finnabair, as well, must have noticed the signs that matters had gone very ill.

"Was it an ambush?" Maeve asked as Cormac lifted his head wearily. She caught her breath: his jaw and neck were black with blood, a cruel dark stain on his pale skin, and there was a bruise swelling dark above his right eye. "You're wounded! How badly? Have the men of Ulster arisen?"

"Not too badly, compared to some," Cormac said. "I ducked my head in time. No, the men of Ulster have not arisen." He squeezed his eyes tight shut, pressing his palm lightly over the darkening bruise on his forehead. "Only Emain Macha's boy-troop. They're all dead. May the gods help us!"

Maeve sucked in a sharp breath. She wanted to take Cormac in her arms, to rock him and croon to him and kiss his hurts away, as she had never gotten a chance to do when he was a little boy. He was a warrior and a leader, who could not lay his head on his mother's breast with his men watching.

"How did it happen?" She asked gently. "Would they not heed you?"

Cormac shook his head, wincing as the movement pulled against the long slash across his jaw and neck. The cut was too close to the great vessels for Maeve's comfort, and she wished greatly that Fedelm, or one of the army's other healers, were there to stitch it on the spot.

"They drew up in good order when they saw us. A troop of soldiers in miniature. Follamain spoke for them; he was their leader. I was hardly surprised. At seven, he was one of the most promising children I had seen. I myself put his first wooden sword in his hand, and showed him the first simple cuts..." Cormac's head drooped, then lifted again. "He knew me at once.

Before I could speak, he called, '

There is the traitor who marches against his own father! I have sworn to bring back Ailill's head, with his gold circlet atop it; but I will be glad to start with you. Come, my men, up and at them!' And then they attacked us. We tried to handle them as gently as we could. We struck with the flats of our blades instead of the edges, with the shafts and butts of our spears instead of the tips, trying to knock them down and show them how over matched they were without doing them any great harm.

"They would not stop. They cried 'Cú Chulainn!' And 'Ulster!' And 'Conchobar!' Over and over again; when we knocked them down, they stabbed at our legs and feet. They were only boys, they did not believe they could die, though their friends were bleeding on the ground about them. They attacked our gillas, for all those young men were without armor and not ready to fight.

Some of my men could not strike at children, even armed children striving with all their might to kill them, and so died, or took grievous wounds. Others, seemed to go wild from horror, and then the slaughter began. The boys of Ulster..." Cormac swallowed hard, rubbing the back of his hand over his eyes.

It was too dark for Maeve to see his tears, but she could hear his voice choking as he struggled not to sob.

"Even the worst-wounded fought on. Máel mac Laoghire, he was barely twelve. He was dying, his sword-hand half-severed at the wrist and his blood flowing into the snow. I recognized him and reached down to stop the blood. When I bent close, he drew his dagger with his left hand and tried to open my throat. If I had not ducked my head, so that the blade skidded from my jaw, I would have died with him."

"Ah, Cormac," Maeve murmured. "I am sorry. I would never have sent you, if I could have guessed..." She thought of how Ailill and she had laughed about the boy-troop, such a short time ago, and her belly roiled and clenched, a thin burning strand of bile tracing up her throat. Maeve swallowed hard. Cormac and his men had lived the nightmare; she would not show herself so much the weaker, that she could lose her stomach only by hearing about it.

"It would not have mattered," Cormac said dully. "They were set on battle; they would have fought whoever you sent, and died all the same. All those children, thrice fifty. The youngest were only seven, fighting with long knives and hurleys and toy shields.

It was a hurley that struck me here." He touched the bruise above his eye.

"Carrying hurleys to battle, as if it were a game. I do not know how Conchobar is training his boys now, what he is telling or doing to them, that they should have been so willing to kill and die when they should have been playing ball-games and stealing honey-cakes. The training in Emain Macha was always hard, meant to shape Eriu's finest warriors, but..."

Cormac slumped down once more. Maeve leaned far over to grasp his shoulder, terrified that he had taken a worse wound than the two she saw. "Cormac, have you any other hurts?"

"No. They did not have the strength, most of them, to cut through even boiled leather, let alone Gaulish iron. I am only tired from battle. I knew most of those children."

'Tired, and heartsick', Maeve thought. "Tell your wounded to halt, and come ahead with me. We will send wagons and chariots for those who need them. I would have Fedelm see to you straight away, before your wound opens any further." She could almost see the gash along Cormac's face and neck pulling wider, wide enough to sunder the large vessels that lay so close, the hot blood gushing out in a great flood, his body folding at the waist and collapsing as his life emptied from him. 'Not now, not Cormac, not while I am here to prevent it!'

Against all reason, Emain Macha's boy-troop had managed to kill nearly their own number of Cormac's trained warriors, and twelve gillas as well. Maeve gave Cormac over to Fedelm, who stitched his wound and pronounced him in no danger before tending the other wounded. Most of the injuries, as Cormac had said, were to legs and feet: Maeve cringed away from her mind's sight of how that had come to pass.

Fergus stood quietly while Cormac retold his tale to the army's other leaders: even Connla sat quiet and pale, daunted by Cormac's account. When Maeve's son was finished, Fergus came and put his arm around the younger man's shoulders.

"Come," the Ulster exile said, his voice rough as the nicked and chipped edge of a sword after a long battle. "There is no cure and no help for this. Enough mead will still it, at least for the night. I can think of nothing that will better aid you."

Maeve met Fergus' grey eyes for a moment as he led her son away, and nodded her thanks. She suspected that Fergus was offering the medicine he himself needed. When Ailill's lips twisted and he said,

"Wise counsel, indeed, and perhaps not only for Ulster," Maeve gratefully answered, "I think it would be as well for Connacht, too."

The torch in Ailill's tent had almost burned down, fitfully sputtering gouts of black smoke into the air. Ailill lay on the bed in all his clothes like a great felled autumn oak, his red-gold braids trailing fuzzily over the edge and his mouth hanging open. He seldom snored, but he was snoring loudly and vigorously now, a deep bellowing rasp like the springtime calling of a bull from a distant field. Maeve was little more sober, but sleep was not coming to her. Blearily she lurched to the bed and started undressing Ailill. The knots on his shoe-thongs gave her trouble, but she managed to get his shoes and trousers off. She had to roll him over on one side, then the other, to tug the blankets out from underneath him so she could wrap him against the winter chill.

Moving a man Ailill's size in the depths of drunken slumber would not have been easy were Maeve been clear-headed herself instead of so drunk she had to keep steadying herself on the bed frame; but she would not leave him to sleep on top of the coverlets in the cold, nor trust that the servants would be in so late to look after him. Tugging the torch free, Maeve stumbled towards her own tent. The fires had been banked for the night, leaving only the sputtering torch-flame and faintly misted glow of the stars to keep her from tripping over every little thing in the way.

She stumbled over one of the stools by the remains of the camp fire, and only a quick twist of her hips kept her from going straight into the banked coals. Instead, she landed flat on her buttocks, the torch flying from her hand to hiss out in the mud. As drunk as Maeve was, her fall suddenly seemed absurdly funny to her: she sat laughing like a fool for a little time before she managed to get her hands and feet under her and shove herself up again.

Fearbh and Liadhain had left a torch burning inside Maeve's own tent. Moving with exaggerated care to keep from staggering into the wooden supports to either side of the flap, she ducked in, turning the motion into a headlong tumble to her bed. Her bed was not where she had left it: instead, she went sprawling onto a pile of sheepskins, and her out flung hand came down on a hard-muscled thigh.

"Why, Maeve," Fergus slurred. "What are you doing here?"

Maeve pushed herself unsteadily up, blinking at him. She realized that she must be even drunker than she had thought. She had managed to get turned around after her fall outside, and wandered into Fergus' tent instead of her own.

Cormac was laid out in Fergus' bed much as Maeve had laid Ailill out, though Fergus had either not bothered or not been able to undress him. The exile had piled every spare mantle and a couple of sheepskins over Cormac's gently snoring body: Maeve's son would take no chill in his wound.

"That…" Maeve waved a hand at Cormac, "was a good thing you did. Shit-souled son of a worm Conchobar, sending children to fight us…"

"Don't think Conchobar did that," Fergus said mildly. "Not if he's still in Macha's pangs…but they loved Cú Chulainn, y'know.

The Red Branch's always been close like brothers, so they wanted'a be part of it. Poor little fools."

"Poor fools," Maeve agreed, her head spinning. "It still grips, even here. Even you. Shouldna taken you on this raid, it's done no one any good. Maybe Cú Chulainn."

"Don't know if I've done him any good either," Fergus mumbled. "Tried to do best for everyone, be like a king, even if I'm not anymore..."

'Brigid and the Dagda, he's drunker than I am!' Maeve thought. The mead stirred in the cauldron of her brain, fermenting up an idea.

"Cú Chulainn'sh going to be at the next ford in a couple days, isn't he?" She asked cunningly.

"Probably."

"How many more men you think are going to die killing him?"

Fergus waved a hand, the gesture toppling him over to slump on the sheepskins beside Maeve. "Lots. It'll happen, though. They'll wear him down again, or you'll give up and ambush him, or something. One log can't kindle a fire, one man can't hold an army forever." He lay on his back like a dying man, staring at the smoke-stains at the top of the tent.

"Y'want him to live, maybe you should be the next man to go. You won't kill him and he won't kill you, but if y'sparred with blunt weapons and you got the better of him..."

"Don't think I could," Fergus answered glumly. "I'm too old, just a broken-down old chariot horse. Don't think I was even that good when I was young. Ferdiad might do it, maybe."

"Cú Chulainn's a puppy, only seventeen. You been fighting more than twice as long as he's been alive." Maeve pointed a wobbly finger at Fergus. "Y'just feeling sorry for yourself now."

"Maybe so. All right. Don't think it'll work, but I'll try it."

"Your oath on it?"

"Sure, my oath on it."

Maeve thought Fergus would say more, but after a few moments, he began to snore as well. She sighed, rolling off the pile of sheepskins and dragging as many out to cover Fergus as she could.

'They're all just little boys who need a mother, Maeve thought. that seemed like the height of a Druid's wisdom. Got to remember it. Now, see if I can find my own tent this time...'

Fearbh and Liadain were waiting outside Fergus' tent when Maeve crawled out. Fearbh took the dangerously wavering torch from her hand as if she were a child, the older maidservant's mouth pressed into a thin-lipped frown of disapproval. The two of them helped her to her feet, guiding her carefully past the camp fires coals.

"How'd you know I was there?" Maeve demanded.

"It wasn't hard, considering you were crashing around like a bull in rut out here," Fearbh said acidly. "Queen or not, if your fellow leaders weren't all as drunk as you, there would have been shoes thrown at your head. Come along to bed now, before you get into any more trouble."

"I...am trouble," Maeve slurred. She wobbled badly to one side; Liadain braced herself and heaved her queen back upright.

"You certainly are. Come along, now."

Maeve was barely aware of collapsing on her own bed. She was asleep before Fearbh and Liadan had her first shoe off.

Maeve

As Maeve had expected, her army had only gotten a little distance on the fourth day before her scouts came back to tell her that Cú Chulainn was waiting at the ford ahead.

"Then I suppose we must stop again. How is he? Is he still weary, or showing signs of wounds?"

Brión shook his head, his long brown braid lashing behind him.

"He seemed very lively and hale, and said that he was eager to fight, if there were still any man in your host who dared to meet him."

"Well. We shall see about that. Call Fergus to me."

Fergus did not hasten to Maeve's side, but he was there by the time the army had ground to a halt.

"Fergus," Maeve said without preamble, "do you remember the matter we spoke of in your tent?"

Fergus winced slightly. "Aye. You must have been very drunk to think of it, and I to agree to it."

Maeve nodded ruefully. The army's leaders had all been as green and sick as it was possible to be without dying the morning after; she was only now beginning to feel like herself again.

"Indeed, we were. I did, and you did, and I had your oath on it. Now it is time for you to fulfill that oath."

"We shall see what comes of this, but do not expect too much," Fergus said.

Maeve thought for a moment of asking Ailill to give back Fergus' sword, but she knew the effort would be futile. Moving Ailill once his mind was made up was only a little easier than shifting an earth-fast boulder, and it was not as though Fergus would draw a killing weapon on Cú Chulainn. The Sun was more than halfway towards noon when Maeve saw Fergus' chariot coming back. At Maeve's first glance, her heart nearly stopped in her chest, for she thought his charioteer was alone. Not him, too!

She cried silently. She could almost see the wave of black grief cresting above her head, about to hammer shatteringly down on her. Then the chariot's path curved slightly with the road. There was Fergus, standing in his place behind his gilla. It had only been the angle from which Maeve was looking, and perhaps the fear in her heart, that had hidden him from her gaze. She watched him carefully as he rode towards her.

He stood easily, lightly balanced in the middle of the chariot and swaying with unconscious ease as it jolted along. No broken bones, nor had he taken any hard blows to the head, Maeve thought. 'Did the old stallion out spar the young Hound, after all?' Maeve wondered. Or had Cú Chulainn over matched Fergus so easily that he had not even needed to give him deep bruises? 'Would Fergus have been fool enough, or unwilling enough to do this task, that he would have yielded at a showing of feats?'

It seemed unlikely. While the feats of a warrior were good to practice, training the suppleness and speed and accuracy of stroke that brought victory, there were few occasions in a real fight to leap and somersault and toss a blade from one hand to the other in a whirling circle.

Every so often, a youth new to the royal retinue would try such a thing on Ailill, and he would knock the over-enthusiastic lad out of the air with a wooden training-sword like a hurling-ball. 'If Fergus wanted to lose'

As Fergus neared, Maeve looked more closely at him. For once, his hawk like features were calm, almost peaceful. Whatever had passed between the exiled king and his foster-son, it had clearly been at least somewhat to Fergus' liking. Is that the calm of victory, or of accepting defeat? Maeve wondered. Had she lost such a contest, she would have been furious.

Fergus had managed to live for many years in Conchobar's court after the other man usurped his place. He had somehow learned, as Maeve could not, how to bear the pain of being overcome and go on. 'And it is a different thing to be beaten by a child one has raised and trained than by a foe'. Maeve knew that well: did it not swell her heart with pleasure and pride beneath the prickle of annoyance when one of her sons scored a blow on her in sparring?

Maeve waited until Fergus was close enough to speak quietly before hailing him. If he had lost, even to Cú Chulainn, there was no point in shouting it to the whole host.

"Shall we move on?" Maeve asked.

A small smile played about Fergus' lips. "You shall."

Maeve felt the smile spreading over her own face. "You defeated him, then. Tell me of it!"

"There is little to tell. He yielded to me, this time. You have three more days to march your host. Cú Chulainn will be waiting at the next ford after this, and he will not give way before me again."

"Still, you have bought us more time than any save Calatín and his sons. Well-done!"

Fergus looked at her with an ironic twist of his lips.

"It may be so. You will still have to pass Cú Chulainn in his full strength before leaving Ulster. As you say, I have bought us time."

Maeve spent much of that day, and the next, thinking on what she could do to move Cú Chulainn from their path.

They had worn and wounded him nearly to death before, at the cost of fewer lives than his sling could take in a single night, but also at the cost of much time. That she knew she could no longer afford. She had no doubt that Fedelm had spoken true when the ban-drúi warned her queen that the men of Ulster would soon be rising from their pangs, and though her host was still strong enough to meet Conchobar's in pitched battle, she meant to avoid it if she could. 'For I am growing weary of death.

Orlamh and Etarcomol, Lochu, and Calatín; and all the champions and simple warriors who have fallen. The duels at the ford took only a few each day, but they were the best and bravest, who were willing to face Cú Chulainn. My womb will bear no more children: now I would hold what I have, and must hold it all the dearer. Yet I cannot see any way to get past the Hound, for the one man in all this host who might be able to slay him will not raise sword against him. He must, or else we shall have to fight a full battle. We are still deep in Ulster.'

'Even if we win the first fight, it will be a long and hard way home with the northern warriors all raised against us.'

Maeve thought a while longer, and then went to Flidais' tent. Her fellow queen was sitting at her ease with a silver goblet of mead in her hand, nibbling from a platter of creamy golden cheese and fresh-baked bread of fine white wheaten-meal. The two young noblewomen who had come to serve Flidais on the raid were both with her, plump fair Gráinne combing carefully through the queen's mass of shining copper hair and slim dark Mughain sewing a rent in her purple, and blue-checkered mantle with careful tiny stitches. All three women were laughing, a cheerful sound that lightened Maeve's heart.

"Oró, Maeve," Flidais said. "Sit down, have some food and something nice to drink.

We are running low on the best mead, but we may as well enjoy it while we have a little peace."

The woman who was sewing got up to fill a cup and a platter for Maeve. Maeve sipped at the mead. It was Flidais' best, made from heather honey and aged for years so that the strong taste of the heather had mellowed to a deep rich summery flavor: the scent alone was almost enough to make Maeve's head spin.

"Is there something on your mind, or are you just here for a little rest?" Flidais asked, smiling at her friend. "Gráinne here is a fine harper, and I am sure she would be pleased to play for us."

"Indeed, it would be an honor," said the young woman. "

And a welcome rest from the tangled brambles of this great copper forest through which I am struggling!"

Flidais laughed merrily, shaking out her hair so that it fell about her shoulders and back like a thick mantle of gleaming auburn.

"It is troublesome, is it not? Well, leave it for a time, and take up your harp."

Gráinne laid down her comb and picked up her instrument, settling herself cross-legged on the floor with the pale wood of the sounding board braced between her knee and shoulder. The bronze strings glittered beneath her fingers, her light hair falling over her face as she began to pluck a bright tune. Maeve sat and listened for a while, speaking of small things with Flidais and Mughain.

She could feel the tightness fading from her shoulders and neck beneath the mead's warmth, the soothing harp song, and the voices and laughter of the other women. Even as all she had drunk the night after the slaughter of the boy-troop had not been able to quiet her mind altogether, so her urgency now nagged at her like the aching of a full bladder pressing through an early morning's drowsiness, and she realized that she would not be able to enjoy this little space of peace until she had dealt with it.

"Flidais," Maeve said, "can you keep Fergus distracted tomorrow night?"

Flidais' white teeth flashed. "I am always happy to keep Fergus distracted, and I think I am well up to the task. Why?"

"Can your women keep this to themselves?"

Flidais glanced at Gráinne and Mughain. "Can you, girls?"

"If you wish it, of course," Mughain said. Grainne glanced up from her harp and nodded.

"Well, then…" Maeve told Flidais of her plan. The other queen listened thoughtfully, her head cocked to one side.

"I certainly cannot better that," Flidais said when Maeve had finished. "It will be a difficult thing, but. You might ask Fedelm to join you as well. If a bull will not be lured through a gate, a sharp poke in the rump with a stick can often jolt him forward. A champion who will not be moved by the caresses of the soft side of a fili's tongue can often be moved by the threat of a few strokes from the rough side."

Finnabair

Long before the evening meal at the royal encampment was finished, Flidais led Fergus into her tent. Soon the muffled sounds of their vigorous coupling began to leak from inside the heavy covering of hides and greased wool. Finnabair was no stranger to the noises of lovemaking, no one who had grown up in the royal halls, with their rooms separated by thin wooden partitions, could be; but she found herself blushing all the same. Her mother gestured to the rest of them, herself, Ailill, Fedelm, and Cormac.

"Let us go into my tent, for I would speak without being overheard," Maeve said. When they were all settled inside, Maeve said, "We have no hope of overcoming Cú Chulainn at the ford unless Ferdiad agrees to fight him. Arranging that will be no easy matter, for the love that is between them. I think Ferdiad has another love as well. Though he has said that even Finnabair will not move him to lift his sword against his foster-brother, it is one thing to turn down something one desires greatly when it has not been offered, and another to reject it when it is within one's grasp."

Finnabair sucked in her breath, her face tightening.

"I shall not!" She said.

"I have played up to that weasel Connla for the whole course of this raid, and him all the while thinking that we would be wedded at its end." She felt as though she were spewing up bad food that had lain too long in her belly: once the first spasm took her, she knew that she would not stop until she was empty.

"I have shaken out my hair and borne cups of mead to those many champions whom we would lure to fight Cú Chulainn, and each lay dead in his own blood before another sunset had passed. I am tired of being the marsh light that lures men onto the path to the house of Donn! After the first two or three duels at the ford were done, I knew what would happen to each of the rest, one by one: it sickened me, to promise what I knew I would not fulfill in order to bring men to their deaths. If Ferdiad falls to Cú Chulainn, that will be one too many for me to bear. If he does not, then there will be no way out of it than for me to wed him, for we could not break our pledge to the man who slew the Hound and freed our host. I do not want to marry Ferdiad!"

Finnabair felt her cheeks burning with anger; her golden hair had come loose from its pins on one side, falling half-over her face. She shoved it back angrily.

"I want to marry Rochad, and go home with him to his little peaceful fortress. Where I never have to charm anyone but the man I love, and where people aren't dying around me all the time!"

"Far more will die if you do not do this," Ailill told Finnabair quietly. "If you wed Ferdiad now, you can always divorce him afterwards, and then marry the man you truly want."

Her father's mouth curled ruefully beneath the red-gold sweep of his mustaches, and he ran his fingers over the deep grooves of the twisted gold bracelet weighting his thick shield-wrist, as though tracing the path of his thoughts for a moment, before he spoke again.

"Women seldom see all that is in men's minds, but I can tell you that there is little that whets a man's heart so keenly as seeing the woman he loves gaze at another, and little that shows him the depths of his love so sharply as having her turn again to him thereafter. If Rochad loves you, he will be all the gladder to get you back when he had thought you lost to him."

Finnabair's bowels clenched, her face screwing up painfully.

"How can I break his heart so? We promised we would wait for each other: I know he has waited for me."

Maeve shook her head sadly.

"Your father is right. Rochad will prize you all the more if you have turned from the man who slew Cú Chulainn in single combat for his sake. I swear this to you: if you charm Ferdiad this night, and wed him for a little time when he has won his victory, then Ailill and I will do all that we can to aid you in gaining Rochad afterwards."

Finnabair turned away. 'Do they mean it, this time? She wondered. Or are they only luring me on, as I lured our champions to die at the fords? If so, perhaps it is just. Warriors are often wounded, as they wound, by the sword. I have used love, or at least desire, as my only weapon. Is it not fair, for all those deaths, that I should suffer the same hope, and risk of betrayal?'

"Very well," Finnabair said at last, her voice muffled and choked. "I will do it. Never again, if Ferdiad falls, do you understand me? Never again!"

"You shall not have to," Maeve assured her. "If Ferdiad falls, there will be little we can do except prepare to meet Ulster on the field of battle."

"I will do it," Finnabair said again. "May Brigid forgive me!"

Cormac cleared his throat.

"My little sister is stronger than I," he said unhappily. He clasped his hands, his long fingers working against each other, and drew his lanky legs tight under his stool.

"Mother, I would ask your leave to go. I know this must be done. I am Ferdiad's friend, and I have seen for years how deep the love between him and Cú Chulainn runs. It was not seven days ago that..." His face twisted, his shoulders hunching tightly.

"It may be that I will never be the great ruler that you are, nor the king that my father is. I do not have the strength of heart to watch this, and if I stay, I will only hinder your plan."

Maeve went to Cormac, embracing him. He stiffened, then laid his head against her side as his arms came up to hold her in turn. Even now, Finnabair found it hard to think of Cormac as her brother. He had been a grown man when she first met him; he had not carried her on his shoulders when she was a child, as Orlamh had, nor pulled her braid like Cairbre, nor. It seemed odd, to see her mother holding him so. There was no doubt that he was Maeve's son, and something wrenched at Finnabair's heart as she watched them. 'She hated Conchobar, and yet. If I must marry Ferdiad, if I bear a child by him, will I love it so?'

"My son," Maeve said, "if I thought you might grow to be such a king as Conchobar, I would run a sword through my own heart before I could live to see it.

Go, and find a woman to lie with or friends to drink with; listen to the harp's sweet music, and let your heart be quieted as best it may. It might be that you could aid here, but Finnabair is already paying price enough: I cannot ask more pain from you."

"Thank you," Cormac said, his voice muffled. He held his mother a little longer, then rose and left.

Maeve looked at Fedelm.

"Is there anything you can do for him? The boy-troop, kind Brigid, how I wish I had sent anyone but him!"

"You could not have known, and you did what would have seemed best to anyone at the time," Ailill rumbled. Finnabair closed her eyes. The look on Cormac's face, when he had come back from the slaughter of the boy-troop.' And Mother wonders why I do not want to be a queen?'

Fedelm sighed. "The síde can make the passage of an hundred years seem a moment. Neither they, nor the greatest of Druids, can hasten the passing of time through a man's heart. I know nothing save that to blunt the barbs of Cormac's grief and sorrow and shame. You can only do as you have done, and not ask too much of him if it should come to battle against those who were his dear friends."

Maeve nodded, turning towards Finnabair again.

"Dry your eyes and wash your face, Finnabair; sip some mead to sweeten your voice," she said gently. "Then you must go to fetch Ferdiad back to us."

Ferdiad stood in his usual place, by the opening in the withy-fence around the royal encampment. Although Finnabair knew her footfalls were nearly soundless,

Connacht's champion glanced back at her when she was still ten paces away, the wariness on his face easing a little as he saw her. She forced herself to walk closer...'I should not be afraid of him. He has never spoken unkindly to me, he has hardly spoken to me at all. If he wins this fight, and weds me. He is so big and powerful; could he embrace me without breaking my bones?' Connacht's champion was so well-proportioned that it was only standing near that one realized how large he was, over topping Ailill by four finger-widths and considerably broader of shoulder than the king.

The horn-hard boiled leather and jewel-adorned iron plates of his ancient armour bulked him out even further, though Ferdiad moved as easily in his heavy gear as most warriors could in the lighter and more flexible ring-mail.

"Ferdiad," Finnabair said nervously, "let my brothers take your place here. My parents would speak with you."

Ferdiad's blue eyes widened as he looked down at her. "Can you tell me why?"

Finnabair shook her head staring at the trampled slush of snow and mud.

"Please come."

Even sitting uncomfortably on the stool Cormac had left, the young champion seemed to loom large enough to fill the queen's tent by himself. Ferdiad's blue eyes flicked mistrustfully between Maeve and Ailill as he waited for one of them to speak. 'He knows why he is here, Finnabair thought. Mother, Father, speak well to him: do not leave this burden wholly on me!'

"Finnabair, bring Ferdiad some mead," Maeve said. "He has stood guard in the cold too long while we sat inside at our ease; it is time we honored him as he deserves."

Finnabair quietly fetched Maeve's best goblet, a beautiful cup of gold ornamented with whorls of filigree and small garnets winking glints of dark red in the torchlight.

Fedelm had brought a little keg of the mead brewed by Calatín's wife, a delicious brew flavored with meadowsweet and hemp flower that was even better than the droughts Flidais saved for herself and her friends. Finnabair filled the gold goblet from that keg, bearing it to Ferdiad in her two cupped hands as if to seal a betrothal. Ferdiad's fair cheeks pinked as his fingers touched Finnabair's on the goblet. He glanced aside with a boy's embarrassment, and Finnabair felt herself blushing with shame. In a way, Ferdiad's modesty disturbed her more than Connla's constant importuning, or Cumail's gaze fixed on her breasts.

It was easy to deceive a man she loathed and despised, she could keep telling herself that Connla deserved the day when his hopes of her would be dashed. Finnabair thought, or at least tried to think, that the champions whom she had lured to the ford had not truly been drawn by her, but by the promise of wedding Cruachan's queenship.

Ferdiad. 'Does he truly love me? If I had not met Rochad, could I love him? And if we should wed, Brigid, I do not want to, but I do not want Ferdiad to die either!' To put Ferdiad at his ease, Maeve and Ailill began by speaking about fighting, as any warriors might do about the camp fire, while Fedelm picked up her harp and began to play softly.

It was not long before Ferdiad warmed to the subject, the stool creaking between his weight as he leaned forward to make this point or that. Finnabair listened with half an ear, understanding little. She had learned how to be sure that a fort or war band would not go short of food so long as there was food to be had, by careful planning and storage in times of plenty and rationing in years when the harvest was scant. The details of weapons-play were of less interest to her than the many illnesses of sheep.

'What would I talk about with him in the evenings, if we married?' Finnabair wondered. 'He would be happier married to a woman like Scáthach or Aoife, or a warrior-queen like my mother. Could I teach him that there is more to life than weapons and their use?' Still, she refilled Ferdiad's goblet as often as he emptied it, and after a time, she brought out the last winter apples that Flidais had carefully packed in straw for the journey, holding one between her cupped palms just above her breasts.

"I would share these apples with you, Ferdiad," Finnabair murmured. She could not bring herself to meet Ferdiad's eyes; she knew from the heat of her skin that her pale cheeks had gone from the pink of foxglove to the bright red of hawthorn berries. Ferdiad caught his breath, slowly reaching out to take the apple from her hand. His fingers brushed hers, the lightest touch, and Finnabair shivered.

'If I would be more than a blanket on the bed, I should speak to him, she thought. If I have to wed him, we must speak sometime. It was so easy with Rochad, as though I had known him forever' She could think of nothing sensible.

At last she said, "Ferdiad, you are from the far west, are you not? Tell me of it, for I have never been there."

"It is hardly worth speaking of," Ferdiad mumbled. "There are a great many rocks, and sometimes black peaty pools and bits of bog."

"The Tuatha de Danann did not deal well with the Fir Bolg when they gave them the west," Maeve remarked. "There is no good earth to plant a seed in, nor clean fresh water to sprinkle on it, nor a single tree to give shelter from the endless rain. It is hard to see how anyone lives there."

"By fish and seaweed and salt," Ferdiad said. "I have no wish to go back there."

Maeve smiled quietly. 'She is about to spring the trap', Finnabair thought.

"You would do better to stay in Cruachan, and rule lands upon the fruitful Ai plain, as befits a champion such as yourself. I would give you land and wealth suited to a princely station, free from tribute so long as your descendants dwell there."

Ferdiad's boyish face was already flushed from the mead that Finnabair had poured into him, but now his rounded cheeks grew redder still.

"My queen, my king, I know what you mean by this. I shall not fight Cú Chulainn, not for any land or wealth."

Fedelm dashed her hand angrily across the strings of her harp, the instrument's stinging resonance humming beneath her voice as she said,

"What manner of champion for Connacht are you, if you will not stand against Ulster's best?"

The ban-drúi's blue-grey eyes blazed, two spots of color standing out bright on her pale cheeks. Her long golden hair flew about her face like flames as she tossed her head.

"Calatín went forth when our need called him, and he was a Druid past his sixtieth year, who had not fought for longer than our queen's lifetime. If you had dared to face Cú Chulainn, he would yet live; the lore that he had directly from Mannanán mac Lir would not now be lost to us."

Fedelm drew in a very deep breath, her bosom swelling so that the purple wool of her mantle strained against the arched gold fibula that pinned it.

"And for Calatín's sake, I shall speak a satire against you if you do not go. I shall raise three blisters of shame upon your face, so that you do not dare to let anyone look upon you; I shall sting you with all the poison in the black bag beneath the fili's tongue. For there are many great warriors in Eriu, and more in Alba; but never a Druid the like of my teacher Calatín."

The ban-fili was breathing hard; her eyes had darkened to the bluish-purple of storm clouds, glittering with bright tears. 'By the gods of the Cruachain, she is terrifying!' Finnabair thought. She found herself edging away from the ban-drúi's anger. While Finnabair's parents had to some degree feigned comradeship, and Finnabair knew she herself was feigning modesty and love, she was certain that every grain of Fedelm's furious grief was real.

'And yet I envy her. My only power is to look fair and speak sweet words with no substance; she is as beautiful as I, and yet she need never lie, and even brave folk tremble at the power of her speech. I am no more fit to spend thrice seven years at hard study than I am to wield a sword'. Fedelm struck her harp again, the silver wires singing sharply through the tent, and the hairs prickled up on the back of Finnabair's neck, all her nerves thrumming as if she stood naked before a drawn sword.

'Ferdiad is near thrice her weight and the best fighter in our host. He would be wise to yield to her now, for he has no more chance against her than a mouse against a wolf'.

Ferdiad met Fedelm's eyes without flinching, showing no sign that she had moved him.

"The greatest fili in the world cannot raise blisters on a cheek that feels no shame," he said stolidly. "And there is no shame in it for me, that I should refuse to slay my dearest friend."

'How can I bear to go through with this? Finnabair thought. Have I not done harm enough. The Hound of Ulster killed my brother, and Ferdiad is the one man who can slay him. If I cannot wield the weapons of warrior or drúi, at least I can do this. I must'.

Finnabair closed her eyes. She breathed deeply and raised her arms to push back her white-blond hair, knowing that her breasts would swell out with the movement.

"Ferdiad," she said, "would you not fight for me? For I would wed the man who is the greatest warrior in Eriu. Yet I would not have my brother's slayer to husband, nor do I wish to see Conchobar's champion sit as king in Cruachan when the land-queenship passes from my mother to me." She put a slender hand on Ferdiad's heavy-muscled shoulder.

Ferdiad looked at her, and Finnabair saw the longing flare in his face like a glowing log whipped into sudden flame by a strong cold wind.

His sudden intense regard frightened her, and yet she felt a strange sense of satisfaction: 'powerful as he is, I can still move him'. Slowly as a man moving in a dream, Ferdiad set his own hand on top of Finnabair's, tightening his fingers on hers as carefully as if he were trying to enclose a butterfly in his fist without bruising its delicate wings. 'For all his strength, he is gentle, like my father', Finnabair told herself. 'He would never force himself on me, nor harm me, nor let another hurt me. I would be safe with him, and he would be a good husband to me'.

Ferdiad held her like that for a few heartbeats, then reluctantly lowered his hand again.

"I cannot," he muttered. "I would have you, if you want me. Not at the price of my beloved friend's life. Not even for you, Finnabair."

Finnabair turned away, hiding her face in her hands. Ferdiad might think she wept because he had turned her down; he would never know that the tears in her eyes were from joy. She felt like a sapling that had been weighted down almost to breaking, then suddenly freed from its burden to snap straight again, trembling violently with the shock of release.

"Your loyalty to your friend does you credit, Ferdiad," Ailill rumbled. "It is a sad thing, that Cú Chulainn is not such a friend to you as you are to him."

Ferdiad's head came up. Glancing sideways at him, Finnabair saw the sparks of anger kindling deep in his wide blue eyes. She bit her lip. Careful, careful, Father! She thought. 'I have pushed him hard already; do not arouse him to turn on you!'

"Who says that?" Ferdiad snapped. "I will prove it is not so, in as much blood as is needed to silence such a lie."

Ailill sighed, looking down for a moment.

"I had hoped not to have to tell you this, for the love you bore to Ulster's Hound. You know we have many exiles from Ulster, men who would still have Fergus as king, or could not stomach Conchobar's overweening rule; and some are later-come than others. When I asked among them about Cú Chulainn, and who might have the best chance at the ford, they all said the same. These last two years, it has been his boast that, although you were the stronger and more skilled when the two of you were younger, he has long since passed you in all skills and feats and whatever may have to do with fighting; that he would count it no triumph if his greatest feat of arms were your downfall. Perhaps that was only a boy's rash boasting, for it is easy to measure oneself against another who is far away, but, hearing those tales, I could not help but notice that it was Fergus, not you, whom Cú Chulainn excepted from meeting his challenges. If he had thought you his match, I do not believe that he would not have bothered to mention you then."

Ferdiad rocked back on his stool as though Ailill had struck him with a heavy stone. The flush drained from his cheeks, leaving his face dead-white; his mouth opened, then closed again. His fists clenched, the huge muscles of his shoulders and chest swelling so that the iron plates of his corselet grated harshly. While Ferdiad was still stunned, Maeve stepped in for the killing stroke.

"Twice you failed as my guard," she said softly. "Will you have Cú Chulainn able to say that not only is he the better fighter, but the truer champion of his land?"

Ferdiad cried out, a wordless bellow of pain and anger. He hammered his fists down on his armored thighs with a loud crack. One of the ancient flints shattered in a spray of sparks, and bright red blood welled up from his hand, dripping a scarlet trail onto the iron and leather sheathing his legs. Grateful to have something useful to do, Finnabair was there with a cloth at once. Ferdiad stilled his wounded hand, letting her bind it, but his other fist clenched and unclenched.

"Cú Chulainn should not have spoken thus, nor shall he be able to speak thus," Ferdiad growled through his teeth. "He never knew me slow or sluggish to fight, night or day. Now I swear it by Aengus son of Umhor, who brought the Fir Bolg to Connacht, and all the gods of my clan: tomorrow morning, I shall be first at the ford to fight him!"

Finnabair closed her eyes, her shoulders sagging. If the bargain had not been made for her sake, still it had been made. 'I wish I had not seemed reprieved for a moment. I would never have known how hard I had tried to convince myself I could be content with him.'

Maeve

Ailill lingered in Maeve's tent a little after the others had left.

"Is there any of that mead left?"

Maeve poured a goblet for each of them, taking a deep gulp of her own. "It was a wretched thing we did this night," she said heavily.

Ailill sat down on the bed beside her, wrapping his arm about her shoulders and drawing her close.

"Yes. If I could have thought of any other way, I would have said so, you?"

"Likewise. Well, perhaps Ferdiad will win. I believe he does truly love Finnabair; and she does not dislike him. I would find no fault in it if they were to be queen and king of Connacht after us."

Ailill pulled Maeve's head over to kiss her. "Finnabair has no wish to be queen. Let's oblige her, and live forever."

Maeve could not help smiling at him. "That seems a good plan."

Early the next morning, Maeve and Finnabair came to Ferdiad's tent to arm him and comb his hair, plaiting it into a tracery of elaborate braids that hung like heavy golden lace work. Maeve's champion was even quieter than usual, pale as though he had not slept well; but Maeve marked the stone-hard gleam of his blue eyes from their shadowed hollows, and smiled in grim satisfaction.

Unless Cú Chulainn were willing to name himself the lesser and yield to Ferdiad, the Connachtman would be fighting with a whole heart. Maeve pinned Ferdiad's scarlet mantle over his armor with her own heavy ring-brooch of gold.

"Go with all our blessings, and come back with Cú Chulainn's head!" Maeve told Ferdiad.

As Ferdiad rose, Finnabair stood on tiptoes, reaching up to cup his face between her palms and brush her lips lightly over his own.

"Avenge my brother, and come back safe," she whispered to him.

Ferdiad's mouth curved into a trembling smile. He touched his fingers wonderingly to his lips, looking down at Finnabair. The icy hardness melted from his blue eyes, leaving them clear and warm as a summer sky. 'What a fair golden couple they are! Maeve thought. Win this fight, Ferdiad!' For Maeve wanted Finnabair to be happy, but also to be queen after her, wedded to a man worthy of Connacht's land-goddess.

Ferdiad was no Conchobar: he would love Finnabair, and treat her as the precious jewel she was, never letting any raise an angry hand to her. Nor would Connla, nor Cumail, nor any of the others who had hoped to gain Finnabair for their own, have the courage to stand against Connacht's mighty champion, especially when the Hound's head dangled from his belt. He could bring joy from all the sorrow Maeve's daughter had suffered for her mother's sake, and fulfil all Maeve's hopes for Finnabair, if he won.

"I shall do my best," Ferdiad murmured.

To Maeve's surprise and annoyance, Fergus was waiting in his own chariot beside Ferdiad's, just outside the royal enclosure. He, too, looked as though he had gotten little sleep, his cheeks hollow beneath their hard bones and the morning sunlight casting the furrows on his forehead and about his eyes into sharp relief.

"What is it you mean to do?" Maeve asked him.

"I shall go to watch this duel, to see for myself that all is done as it should be."

Maeve thought of objecting, then shrugged. She had no plans beyond trusting in Ferdiad's strength and skill, and she did not think that Fergus would interfere in a fair fight.

"Then I am going as well," said Fedelm, coming up from behind Maeve. "I think no one will doubt my word and judgement."

Fergus glared down at the seeress from his chariot.

"No one doubts mine, unless they are ready to meet me sword to sword!" He said.

"There is no need for you to go. Ban-drúi you may be, but this is a matter for warriors. You were the pupil of a man who used enchantment and a fine point of law to make a mockery of the single combat of heroes. I have no wish to see such things employed again."

Fedelm's lips tightened. She drew herself up, her slim white-robed figure shining like a plume of sea-spray in the sunlight.

"And should we trust in your honor alone? It has been betrayed before. Once without blame, and once with Fiacha!"

Maeve sucked in her breath. The fili's poisoned tongue had struck Fergus deeper than any man would have dared: his face reddened alarmingly, the thin scar down his cheek flushing a deep purple, so that Maeve almost expected to see the dark blisters blossoming on his skin straight away.

His hand clasped the hilt of his sword, though he held enough self-control to keep from drawing it. Before either of them could say anything more, Fedelm's servant stepped between his mistress and Fergus. Although the man had always been dressed and armed as a noble warrior, Maeve had never taken any notice of him before, since he never spoke and was often doing a servant's tasks.

Now he stood grasping his own sword-hilt, staring fearlessly into Fergus' eyes as though he were royal-born in his own right. For a heartbeat, Maeve had to wonder just who or what he really was; but the urgency of the moment drove the question from her mind. Fergus shifted his balance as though he were about to leap from his chariot to attack the other man.

Fedelm's servant tilted his head back and opened his mouth. The noise that came out was like no human sound, like nothing Maeve had ever heard before: a low, drawn-out, screeching yowl. Even Fergus blinked at the strange cry, and Maeve seized the moment.

"Stop, all of you!" She shouted. "For the gods' sakes, can you not remember that this is a single host, fighting towards the same ends. I know that neither of you will interfere with this duel in any way, or lead any other to do so. The one who does will answer to me!"

Fergus slowly dropped his hand. Glaring, Fedelm's manservant did likewise, but held his ground.

"You shall both witness," Maeve said. "Fergus, you shall see that the duel is carried out with all honor. Fedelm, ban-fili, you shall find the makings of a mighty poem in the river this day.

Mayhap you will recite it at the wedding feast when Finnabair and Ferdiad are married. You shall both go, though it would be well for you to keep a little distance from each other. I do not know how this hate between you has sprung up, but I would rather not see it grow any worse." In truth, Maeve thought she had quite a good understanding of the troubles between Fedelm and Fergus, but this was no time to speak on the matters.

"I will go as well," another woman's timid voice said. Fedelm's friend Suithchern stood there, an infant on either hip and a worried look on her tired face.

"By your leave, my queen," Suithchern added hastily. "Fedelm needs someone to cook for her and such; I think Druids are not taught those arts."

Fergus' brows beetled and he drew a deep breath. Maeve cut him off before he could begin to bellow.

"It is not your affair who Fedelm has in her retinue. You have your charioteer; Fedelm has her guard, or whatever he is, and her attendant. If you wish to bring another, you may. I hardly think you need fear that Suithchern and her babes will weight the scales too heavily against Cú Chulainn in this duel."

The air leaked from Fergus' lungs in a slow exasperated hiss.

"Why not bring the whole host to witness, with the women and servants as well?"

"I suppose they may come, but I will take no responsibility for them. Nor should they expect me to aid them if they cannot deal with whatever they meet by themselves."

"I think Fedelm and Suithchern are fairly well-guarded already," Maeve said dryly. "The Sun moves no more slowly while we stand here quarreling. Have I your oath to keep the peace?"

"I will not swear such an oath," Fergus grumbled. " I will say that I shall seek no more trouble between us, if Fedelm and her guard will say the same."

Fedelm's man shrugged, spreading his hands. His gesture was complex, taking in Fergus, himself, Fedelm, and his sword, but Maeve guessed that he meant something like what Fergus had said.

"I shall not seek trouble either," Fedelm agreed. "I will defend myself if I must."

"Well enough," Maeve told them. "Gather what you need and go. Our host is nearly ready to march."

Fedelm and Suithchern turned back towards their tent in the royal enclosure; Fedelm's servant began to walk towards the area where the royal chariots and their horses, and those of the Druids, were kept. Maeve hastened a few steps after him.

"Try to keep them away from each other," she muttered to him. "I know you are loyal to Fedelm; but we need Fergus as well."

The Druid's guard raised a narrow black eyebrow, snorting softly through his nose.

"We do," Maeve insisted, feeling a bit of a fool for speaking to a mute as if she could understand him.

Fedelm

While three lean people can ride in a chariot in reasonable comfort, as Calatín, Eochaid, and I had proven to our own satisfaction, three grown riders, two babies, and a fair-sized chest of medicines and bandages were almost too much to fit in at all. At least the chariot's jolting proved soothing to Conall and Clothra. Clothra had been crying from gas, but let out a little burp with every lurch until she settled into a satisfied sleep nestled against Suithchern's hip, and Conall, in my arms, looked bright-eyed about himself and seemed to smile as we rode.

"You have ridden in chariots before, haven't you, my little warrior?" I murmured to him.

"There will come a day when you stand on your own feet bearing weapons in one, with your name going before you." I pushed away the thought that, if Conall were riding in his own chariot, other warriors in theirs would be eager to spill his blood: that fear was still years from ripening.

'A daughter, I thought, putting my hand on my belly. A little daughter with red-gold hair, who will inherit my skills of poetry and foresight and the lore Calatín taught me, and grow to be a Druid in Cruachan after me'.

We rode on Ferdiad's left side, and Fergus on his right. Connacht's champion was speaking with his gilla; his voice was low, but anger roiled like heavy storm clouds on his boyish face.

Maeve's great gold brooch burned on his shoulder, and the amethysts and cairngorms set into his armor flashed whenever he moved, glints of purple and golden-brown flaring as the light caught them like the eyes of tiny otherworldly creatures glowing out of the black iron. His helmet was off, the sunlight gleaming from his fair hair as though he shone with his own halo of hero-light.

Looking at his massive figure, crowned with brightness above his dark armor, I saw the strength of the Fir Bolg, they who had contended as equals with the Tuatha de Danann when the gods first came to the land of Eriu, and I wondered how even the Hound of Ulster could stand against him.

And yet it seemed the brilliant red of his scarlet mantle was clouded, as if by a faint haze of twilight mist seething about him. I knew he was angry with us, who had twisted and maneuvered him into this duel; with Cú Chulainn as well, for what the Hound had said, or what Ailill claimed he said: dear as Ailill was to me, he was a king, and would do what he must, most of all, I suspected Ferdiad was angry with himself.

For failing as a guard so he must now prove himself; for accepting the promise of Finnabair, though that alone had not been enough to sway him; or, perhaps, for choosing his troth to Connacht over his love for his friend.

'Will that anger strengthen his hand against Cú Chulainn, or weaken it?' I wondered.

"Lóch always said..." Suithchern swallowed, looking over the side of the chariot. "He always said that it didn't matter why a warrior was angry, that when the fighting began, it was strength as long as he could keep his head and not let the anger drive him to rashness." She swallowed again. My arms were full of Conall, but as close as we were, I could give her a comforting nudge with my hip.

"I didn't realize I was speaking," I admitted. It was a risky habit in fili or drúi: I would have to watch carefully to make sure I did not do it again. Suithchern looked up at Ferdiad.

His chariot had moved ahead of ours; all we could see was the bright red cloak draped over his massive back and the gleam of the sunlight on his elaborate weave of golden braids.

"Still, he is magnificent," she said. "It is hard to imagine anyone defeating him."

Eochaid let out a little chuff of air, turning his head and cocking a black eyebrow sardonically at us. One slim-fingered hand left the reins a moment, moving in a quick flow of gestures that suggested a sling-ball, a spear-cast, and a large tree being chopped at the base, or a large man at the knees.

"I suppose I know little enough of fighting, at that," Suithchern said ruefully to Eochaid. "And I did not mean to suggest that Ferdiad is necessarily your better."

Eochaid smiled and turned back to his driving. The corner of Suithchern's mouth quirked as her blue eyes met mine. Though she did not say anything, traveling with Eochaid had sharpened my skills in reading unspoken thoughts from face and gesture:

Lóch had been a good-tempered man, but there were few warriors without a fair-sized spoonful of touchy pride mixed into their stew. Perhaps more, for a man who, like Lóch, was skilled, but not a great champion, or a man like Eochaid the Cat. It came to me suddenly that I had no idea how good a fighter Eochaid was.

He had, I was certain, been ready to fight Fergus on the spot, and much as I had come to dislike Fergus, I did not know another warrior in Maeve's army who would not have thought twice about such a challenge, though a Druid should be unassailable, there were always desperate men who cared less for the curse that might fall tomorrow than the gold they might gain today:

Eochaid would not have been sent alone with me if Cernach had not thought him well-able to deal even with a band of ruffians.

'Could he beat Cú Chulainn, if Ferdiad fails?' I did not know.

I did not have the right to command Eochaid to take up the challenge, and I did not think that he would if I or Suithchern and the children were not in danger; but I could not help wondering. We rounded the foot of the last of a line of hills, and suddenly the river was before us, the water flowing slow between the skeletal brown cat tails that fringed the edges of the low banks. The folk who lived here had kept the ford clear of reeds; the water ran more choppily over it, as though the shallows were full of broken stones. Cú Chulainn stood at the far side of the bank, tent and chariot behind him.

As I had heard those who knew him say, and seen in my dreams, he was short and slight. I could have looked him in the eye without tilting my chin up, and though his shoulders and chest were broad for his height, the hand that gripped the silver-bound shaft of his narrow spear was small and fine-boned as my own. He wore armor layered from pressed and waxed leather; a wide belt of thick boiled hide sewn with iron rings covered him from waist to armpit. His hair fell loose around his shoulders save for a narrow braid on each side holding it back from his face, and shone like polished dark wood, the sunlight catching tiny gleams of red and gold from its deep brown. At last I saw his face.

I had expected him to appear something like a younger version of Fergus, that fierce hunting-hawk arrogance sharpened by a youth's blossoming strength, undimmed by the shadows of time and sorrow that graved the older warrior's visage. Instead, I saw a young man whose beardless face was fine-shaped as one of the síd-folk, delicate features not yet thickened by manhood. There was something familiar about the sharp arch of his black eyebrows, the high cheekbones tapering down to a narrow chin, and the wide-set brightness of his storm-colored eyes, though I could not think what.

It seemed unreal to me, that this fair-faced boy should be the monster who had terrified our army by killing at our edges through dark and day, or the champion who had slain so many of the best in Eriu's host. As Cú Chulainn saw who had come to meet him, his eyes gleamed like bright blue-grey jewels against the pale winter-gilding of his skin. He smiled with brilliant joy, casting down his spear and opening his arms.

"Ferdiad!" He called. "I am so glad to see you again at last, my dearest friend! It has been so long, and I was grieved to know that you must march with our foes.

Come here, or I will come to you, and we shall eat and drink together, and speak of all that has happened since we last met."

My heart wrenched convulsively against the great vessels of my chest, sending a hard pulse of pain through my body. 'He does not realize! I thought. I would have him slain, for Calatín and Lóch and Orlamh, and because he must die or retreat for Maeve's sake...but I did not mean to bring this'.

Ferdiad's lips drew back in a snarl like that of a wounded hound tearing at its own hurt, teeth glistening from his short golden beard.

"Yield to me, Cú Chulainn, and I shall welcome you," he roared. "I have come to challenge you, and if you insist on trying to prove yourself the better, then you shall surely die."

Ferdiad had shouted bravely at first, but his fierceness faded like the glow of heat from molten metal, leaving his voice dull and hard.

"You cannot defeat me. When we studied with Scáthach, you were but my gilla: you fixed and honed my spears, and served my bed at night."

At Fergus' first words, the joy on Cú Chulainn's young face crumpled all at once like a butterfly smashed in a hard fist, his eyes closing tight as if he were fighting back a sudden rush of tears. When his eyes slowly opened, I did not see the anger I expected, only pain as naked as a blade's keen edge.

"That is true," he said, his voice shaking as if he were desperately clinging to the rope of his bravado with the last of his strength.

"That I did then because I was a young boy. You cannot call me that now: there is not a warrior in the world whom I am not able to face."

"I am that warrior," Ferdiad gritted. "And you are a fire without fuel; if you do not give over your boasting before me, you shall need a great deal of help if you are ever to see home again."

Now Cú Chulainn's delicate features were hardening with anger, its brightness flaring in his eyes as if it flowed through his limbs like a hot draught of strong mead against winter's ice.

"If we meet, you shall fall at a hero's hands, and never again lead men!"

I heard the iron and leather of Ferdiad's armour creak as the muscles of his shoulders bunched.

"Little bush, you have boasted and threatened enough: you shall get neither mercy nor victory here. I know you too well. You may have terrified and overcome others, but I remember when you were a clumsy and feeble boy, and easily frightened yourself."

I expected Cú Chulainn to roar back, to return Ferdiad's insults as men did when working up to a challenge. Though those who watched were few, between Fergus and myself, there was fame and power enough to make a good show of bravery and quickness of tongue worthwhile even for such heroes: that was how things should be done.

The Hound's wrath had already burned out, like dry dead leaves bursting into flame and falling as quickly to grey ash. His shoulders sagged, he seemed very small, standing across from Ferdiad's massive shape, and there was nothing left on his face but sorrow as he said,

"While we dwelt with Scáthach, we went into the fight as one man, with a single courage between us. My dear friend, my own heart's blood, dear above all...I shall miss you."

Ferdiad's jaw clenched, whether with grief or anger I could not tell.

"You make much of yourself, but the fight is yet to come. I shall not miss you: your head will come with me."

Cú Chulainn slowly bent to pick up the spear he had cast aside, but still made no move to cross the ford. "Ferdiad, you are only here because of Ailill and Maeve's ill-doing. I know they offered you Finnabair as a lure, but I also know that you will never have her. How many men now lie dead for her sake? Don't break our friendship and bond for this; don't break the oath we made once, all our promises and pledges to each other!

If they had offered Finnabair to me, however fair she is, and Maeve had smiled at me, I still would never have thought to do you harm, or touch the least part of your flesh." His voice caught, cracking for a moment into a boy's soprano before it settled to its depths again.

"When we were with Scáthach, didn't we always set out together, to battles and strife and dark places? Whether roaming the woods or after a hard fight, we made one bed and slept one sleep. How can our friendship mean so little to you now, when I still hold it so dear?"

"You yielded to Fergus before this," Ferdiad said slowly, his own voice choking in his throat.

"Will you not give way before me, and save both of us from this fight?" A surge of hope brightened Cú Chulainn's face, like a single ray of watery unlight struggling through a wind-torn mass of heavy clouds. "Will you do as he did, and swear to yield to me later if I give way now?"

Ferdiad drew a deep breath, and I heard the creaking of his heavy ancient armor again. For just a moment, it seemed to me that I saw huge dark shapes, like the shadows of men hacked out of great boulders, looming about him. I was of the druid, and I had witnessed his oath. Though I wished with all my heart that I could keep silence, I knew what I must say.

"By Aengus son of Umhor, who brought the Fir Bolg to Connacht, and the gods of your clan, you said," I murmured, barely loud enough for Ferdiad to hear. "Will you now vow to fail Maeve again?"

Ferdiad's head bowed as if I had struck him hard on the back of his neck; the breath sighed from him as though his lungs were collapsing in death.

"I cannot make that promise," he said to Cú Chulainn. "Give way before me now, or we must forget that we were foster-brothers, and our friendship be finished."

Cú Chulainn and Ferdiad gazed at each other across the ford. I held my breath, waiting. Then Conall yowled sharply: I had tightened my grip on him without noticing, hard enough to hurt. I eased up at once, stroking him in hopes of quieting him. Ferdiad shook his head, like a man shaking off the stunning dizziness of a heavy blow on his skull.

"We have talked too long," he said curtly. "What weapons shall we use, Cú Chulainn?"

Clothra began to wail in sympathy with Conall. I joggled him gently and petted him, murmuring softly and straining my ears to hear what the two champions were shouting above the babies' cries.

"You are the challenger; you have first choice."

"Do you remember the very last feats we learned from Scáthach and Aoife, that none of their other war-students could master?"

"I remember them well."

"Then let us set to them."

While Ferdiad and Cú Chulainn readied themselves, Eochaid spread a thick blanket on the dry frosty grass for Suithchern and I to sit on. Conall would not quiet, and finally Suithchern took him under her mantle to nurse, letting me hold Clothra.

I kept her wrapped well in my own cloak, a fold over her little head so that the cold air could not bite into her scalp, but I knew that the sprinkling of fine hair on her head would glitter like a dusting of gold. It might darken to her mother's honey-brown in time; I wondered if Ailill's red would show in my own babe's head at first, or kindle later; or if, like Finnabair, she would stay whitish-fair.

I already had a vision of her in my mind, a tall slim maiden with a rich flow of red-tinged gold hair, but I did not know whether that was true sight, or the wishful dream of my own mind, I was not even certain that I bore a daughter. It seemed to take an endless time for the Hound of Ulster to don his helm and for the two gillas to bring shields and armfuls of small javelins to their warriors; and at the same time, I was surprised by how suddenly Ferdiad and Cú Chulainn were facing each other.

Ferdiad's back was to me, but I could see Cú Chulainn's face beneath his helm. Whatever sorrow at their broken friendship, or ache of love, gnawed at the Hound's heart, he had walled it well away. Now his fine features were set in a mask of fierce intensity, as though the world around him had narrowed down to the single keen tip of a spear. I thought of the gestures Eochaid had made earlier, and wondered what Ferdiad had been thinking, to begin the contest between the two of them with weapons that would, it seemed to me, be to the advantage of the smaller and lither man. Should he not have chosen swords, to bear Cú Chulainn down with his strength and weight?

When I quietly asked Eochaid that, he shrugged and shook his head, lips curving in a mirthless smile as he made a gesture of casting something away.

"I don't understand."

His smile widened, and he waved his hand, as if to say, 'you will'.

The flash of Cú Chulainn's first dart came so swiftly I nearly missed it, a streak of silvery light glimmering across the ford and a sharp ting! As it bounced off the bronze boss of Ferdiad's shield. Less than an eye blink later, Ferdiad's javelin sang through the air, whirring a finger-width above Cú Chulainn's head as the youth dived into a mid-air roll beneath it, coming up with another dart in each hand and casting as his feet touched the ground again.

I could only stare with my mouth open, watching the two of them leap and whirl in their dance across the ford, the sharp javelins falling like a sharp rain of silver, when they were not caught in flight and hurled back. Cú Chulainn moved as though he were no more than a ghost of water and wind, his little wiry body spinning between darts that often seemed to miss him by no more than a hairsbreadth; but watching Ferdiad was like nothing I could have imagined.

It was one thing to see a small lithe man twist and coil in the air to dodge one weapon even as he threw another. For all his massive size and heavy armor, Ferdiad seemed no less agile or lightly bound to the earth: it was as if a great stone had suddenly gained the power and grace of flight. Gradually I overcame my awe enough to mark more subtle signs of their skill: how, for example, not a single tip had sunk into the wood of a shield, but every cast that one of the combatants did not dodge glanced off the bronze boss or iron rim.

Though I, peasant's daughter and student drúi, knew almost nothing about fighting, even I could guess at the unbelievable ability that must require. They went on and on, and after a time I understood what Eochaid had been trying to tell me. This dart-casting was no more than a game between Ferdiad and Cú Chulainn, showing off what they could do, and perhaps warming their blood for the real fighting, as I might chant and cast herbs onto hot coals to ready myself for a work of prophecy or enchantment. The Sun was nearing midday when Ferdiad held up his hand.

"Look at the javelins on your side, Cú Chulainn!" He called. "Every one over here is blunted, and we have not so much as drawn blood. Let us break off with these weapons: we'll settle nothing this way."

"Very well, let us break off," Cú Chulainn answered. They laid down the darts they still held, and their gillas came up to gather the ones on the ground.

"What weapons shall we use next, Cú Chulainn?" Ferdiad asked. His voice had lightened, almost laughing: I could only guess that they had cast javelins like this as a game when they studied war craft in Alba, and that, at least for a little time, Ferdiad had been able to forget the grim bones that lurked beneath their weapon-play.

"You still have the choice until nightfall," the Hound answered soberly.

Ferdiad let out his breath in a long hissing sigh, and his voice was quiet when he said, "Then let us give over this children's play with darts, and try our strong casting-spears bound with the tight flax."

Even I could tell at once that this was a more serious contest. They were throwing harder now, but less often, standing and watching each other for several breaths at a time before casting, and they had almost entirely given over the amazing leaps and rolls of the previous combat, swaying or stepping aside instead. I saw Ferdiad's shoulder twitch minutely, and Cú Chulainn's shield flicked high, then dropped again as the spear flew from Ferdiad's hand towards his leg, just barely deflecting the weapon. Eochaid nodded, a satisfied look on his face, and I wished briefly that he could speak so he could explain the fight to me. Some of these casts were getting through.

Ferdiad's armor covered his body and thighs, but I saw the blood welling from several grazes on his arms and lower legs, and one spear jutted from the hard leather between the iron plates on his chest, not a deep wound, the tip had barely pierced the thick leather; but when he wrenched it out, a red trickle of blood flowed after it. Cú Chulainn had taken at least one wound to his shield-shoulder, a few bright drops spattering every time he twitched his shield to block a throw. I watched carefully, hoping the injury would slow him; but if it did, it was too little for my inexperienced eyes to notice.

I thought surely Ferdiad and Cú Chulainn would wear each other down until one or the other missed a fatal cast, but though I could hear Ferdiad breathing hard after a while, they kept going with no sign of weakening that I could see, and after a while Ferdiad said,

"Cú Chulainn, we shall not decide the fight like this: let us break off now, and fight again when we have eaten."

"Very well: let us break off, if it is time."

Each of them handed the spear he held to his charioteer. I expected that Ferdiad would come back to his own chariot for food and drink, or to us or Fergus. To my surprise, he waded straight out into the ford, the clear water eddying just above his knees. Cú Chulainn came out to meet him, though the river reached halfway up the smaller man's thighs.

They spoke quietly for a little time: I could not hear what they were saying to each other. Then they put their arms about each other's neck, and each gave the other three kisses, before they parted.

'They have decided to stop the fight', I thought in a shameful wave of relief and disappointment.

Ferdiad walked directly over to me, his face set and calm.

"Fedelm," he said, looking down at me. "Bind my wounds, if you will, and then I would have you go to Cú Chulainn, for you are a more skilled leech than his charioteer. I would not have it said that I held an unfair advantage."

I closed my mouth, staring up at him. Only long training kept me from blurting out, ' I thought you both had decided to give over!' Gradually I regained control of myself.

I could not help feeling Cú Chulainn's pain at having to fight his dearest friend, as I had not been able to help my sympathy when I saw him wounded and forlorn in my dreams; but I did not want to give any aid to the man who had brought such sorrow to Ailill and Suithchern and myself. Still, 'You are here to kill him', I wanted to say. I could not: if Ferdiad had anything in his heart that gave him the strength to slay Cú Chulainn, I saw now, it was this belief that he was fighting to measure himself against his friend's boasts, not moving by his queen's will like a dog moved by an upraised stick on one side and a piece of meat on the other. If I wanted him to win, I could do nothing but agree.

"I will tend him as I tend you," I promised.

As I had thought, Ferdiad's wounds were all minor. Two of his gashes needed a few stitches, but there was nothing that would keep him from fighting, or even hamper him. When I was done, he thanked me and rose, going over to Fergus without looking back to see if I would keep my word. For a moment I wavered, but Eochaid was looking at me, his green eyes steady on my face as he lifted my chest of healing supplies onto his shoulder.

I followed him to the edge of the river, the sludgy mud sucking wet and cold at my shoes as I neared the water. Eochaid glanced at the ford, then turned back, crouching to put his free arm about the backs of my thighs. I wrapped my own arms about his neck, and he heaved me up one-handed as if I were nearly weightless, walking steadily through the water and raising me higher as it deepened. Cú Chulainn was sitting in front of his tent, his armor off and his fair-haired charioteer bandaging his own wounds. Cold as it was, his hair was already hanging lank and soaked with sweat; his crimson silken tunic was dark and wet as if it were soaked with blood. It clung to his body, and I could see every muscle etched against the wet silk as though it were a second red skin.

He might be slight, but I had never seen a human body so perfectly carved, as though Goibnu the Smith had chosen to shape a figure that would show in deep relief where each line of muscle should lie on a man. Calatín had been as lean, but his musculature had been stringy, not this unreal blend of curves and sharp lines. It almost surprised me when the Hound moved, as if the twining lines of a piece of fine gold work had suddenly begun to flow and coil living about each other. Cú Chulainn glanced up at me in surprise. "What are you doing over here?" He asked.

"Ferdiad asked me to tend your wounds as his own, lest it be thought he had taken unfair advantage."

The Hound's blue-grey eyes squinted closed in pain, as if his charioteer's clumsy fingers had jarred one of his cuts. "That is very like him," Cú Chulainn sighed. "You are Fedelm of the síd, are you not?"

"I am."

"Cathbad warned me to beware of you. If Ferdiad sent you to me, then I must trust you. Do what you came to do."

I breathed deeply, suddenly aware of the rich scent of roasting pork from the small joint over the Ulstermen's fire. There was bread laid out as well, not the flat journey bread and oatcakes that had made up most of our meals, but proper wheaten bread, risen and newly baked.

We were still in Ulster, after all, and those folk who had hidden when our host marched by were friends to Cú Chulainn: of course he would have the freshest and best of food to sustain him in his duels. None of Ferdiad's casts had pierced the heavy leather armor covering Cú Chulainn's torso, but he had taken several scratches to the arms and legs, and one nasty, if shallow, gash furrowed the outside of his shield-shoulder, just below where the layers of stiffened leather gave way to the finer and more flexible hide protecting his arms.

His charioteer had stopped the bleeding and sewn it roughly, but I thought the stitches would rip out when he went to fight again. I sorely wanted to leave it as it was. Though, unlike Ferdiad, I had not sworn a mighty oath by my ancestors and gods, I had given my own word to him. I would not have let Ferdiad go back to the ford with a wound so clumsily patched.

"Your charioteer is no healer," I said. "I will have to take these stitches out and resew the wound."

Cú Chulainn twisted his head, looking down at the little loops of fine sinew straggling down his shoulder.

"Do as you must."

"And you," I told his charioteer, "fetch a new tunic, and some cloths to dry him with. You cannot leave him to sit wet in the cold like this: even a hero's muscles may stiffen, or sickness creep into him."

Cú Chulainn blinked up at me as I set to snipping and pulling the little threads through his skin.

"You are giving me tender care, for a foe."

"It is not I who cares for you, but Ferdiad," I answered. That was surely true. I had played my part in bringing Ferdiad to the ford. I did not think I regretted having done it, but now I grievously regretted having had to do it.

'If only Fergus had not interfered, or egged Fiacha to aid you, I thought, you would be guesting with your father from the síd, or in the house of Donn. Perhaps gathering your strength to come back to this world, or dropped as a worm in a maiden's cup to enter her womb and be born again. Calatín would still live'.

My anger at Ferdiad in Maeve's tent had not been feigned; but it had not been he, after all, who was its true target. Despite the fact that he had been sitting in the icy winter cold with nothing but a wet tunic on his upper body, Cú Chulainn was not so much as shivering. Instead, the heat from his skin warmed my hands as though he had just emerged from a nest of thick blankets and goose-down pillows.

Beneath my touch, his naked skin felt like living silk stretched over smooth warm stone. With his arm laid still by his side, his muscles were harder than another man's would be when clenched tight. A strange tingle ran through my fingers and palms, the same I had felt when Cernach gave my weaving-rod into my hands, strange, but familiar at the same time, as though I looked on one whom I had not seen since early childhood. Cú Chulainn's face was set and still as I slipped the thin needle through his skin. The pupils of his storm cloud eyes were wide, as though he had been inhaling those herbs that aided a seer's trance. It came to me, then, why he looked familiar.

I had seen fine-boned features very like his, broad forehead tapering to a pointed chin, sharp-arched black eyebrows over wide-set blue-grey eyes, in the mirror in Alba, and their sharpened reflections in my dreams in the Cuailgne mountains, when the siabra sang to lure me: Cú Chulainn might have been my brother, or at least a cousin. Fedelm of the síd, I thought, and shivered.

The Hound was the son of a smith from Meath and Conchobar's sister, I the daughter of a Connacht farmer, with no great blood as far back as my kin could remember. Lugh had claimed to be the Hound's síd-father. Now I wondered if my own gifts had truly been given when I saw Rucht with his swine, or if that had only awakened something that had lain coiled in my blood like a great serpent beneath a pool.

A faint shiver ran through Cú Chulainn's body. I felt it through my hands rather than seeing it, but I knew that he must be sensing something similar.

'No wonder I found it so easy to see you in my dreams and trances!' I thought. For a moment, it seemed to me that I stood in a strange world of reflections, shaping and opposing each other: fair Rucht and dark Friuch, the White Bull and the Brown; Maeve and Conchobar, Connacht and Ulster, and myself and Cú Chulainn, struggling and yet bound by a yoke that could not be broken.

Wondering, I finished stitching Cú Chulainn's shoulder and bandaged it carefully. Calatín had taught me how to wrap a strip of linen so that it would hold a wound, and yet not hamper the movement of a fighter's limbs. It was not uncommon for a warrior to come from the battlefield to be patched up, and insist on plunging straight back into the fray. I hated the thought, but Calatín had assured me that there was no way to keep a man from fighting if his heart were set on it: all we could do was send him back with the best chance possible, he might have been speaking from his own experience as a warrior, not as a Druid.

'I wish that I did not have to aid my teacher's slayer with his gifts', I thought unhappily. I took a few stitches in the bandage to keep it tight without having to pull and knot it. As I rose, Cú Chulainn touched my arm lightly. Even through my white linen robe, hallowed with the smoke of mistletoe and vervain and water mint, I could feel the thrill of his fingers running up my arm as though he had tapped me with a Druid's wand.

"Thank you, Fedelm," he said softly, looking up to me. "I know you hate me for killing your teacher. What else could I have done, save die or betray my king?"

I met his blue-grey eyes for a moment, feeling the undercurrent that played between us like lightning glimmering through the depths of a storm bank.

"Fergus talks too much," I said, and turned to go before I had to answer his question.

I am Fedelm: I hide nothing, and I could not hide from myself the truth of what Cú Chulainn had said. When Eochaid set me down on the other side of the ford, I looked back. Cú Chulainn's gilla was just putting a fresh tunic over his head, Ulster's champion had no trouble raising the arm I had sewn and bandaged; I felt a twinge of disappointment twined with pride. They spoke a moment; then the charioteer took the roast from the fire, cutting it in two. He filled a large wooden platter with fresh meat and fresh bread, and carried it over the ford one-handed, with a great jug in the other.

"Cú Chulainn sends you this, for he knows that the victuals of a marching army are not as fine as those of one's homeland, and he would not have it said that Ferdiad lacked anything that he had himself. All of you are welcome to share it."

Whatever the charioteer, Láeg, that was his name, lacked in healing skills, he made up as a cook. The pork was tender and delicious in my mouth, the scent and taste of the fresh-baked bread almost intoxicating after eating journey bread and oatcakes for so long, and I could almost feel the strength flowing into my body as I drank a long draught of the creamy rich milk.

The milch cows we had taken on the raid had been allowed to dry, so that they would reach Connacht in good health in spite of the long march, and most of them were with calf in any case. Then it was time for Cú Chulainn and Ferdiad to fight again. They were done with casting at each other: they took up broad-bladed thrusting spears, and I knew they would be fighting in earnest.

"How do you think this bout will go?" I asked Eochaid.

The Cat shrugged, making a wavering motion of his hand: 'Who can tell?' Since he could not explain, I was left to watch and make my own guesses. I had never seen two spear men fighting before.

I had expected them to stand off and thrust at each other with the killing tips, or else close with a shortened grip to wrestle and stab. Now and again a lightning-thrust flickered out between them: but, to my surprise, they fought as much like peasants with heavy staves as anything, swinging the thick spear-shafts in shattering arcs and smashing out with the bronze butt-caps as often as they stabbed with the keen blades on the other ends. Once Ferdiad's left hand flashed from his own weapon's haft to grip Cú Chulainn's just below the blade, lifting Cú Chulainn off his feet and flinging him through the air like a bundle of hay caught on the end of a pitchfork.

The Hound kept his own two-handed grip on his spear-shaft, twisting about it in mid-air, and managed to wrench it away from Ferdiad's grasp as he landed. Brutal as it was, there was a strange beauty in this fight. Even had so much not been at stake, I could not have torn my gaze away. Both champions moved with a smooth graceful precision and power that, I thought, the finest dancers could not have matched, the shallow water frothing about their ankles as they circled and lunged at each other. As the duel went on, even I could see that they were both beginning to tire.

I saw the tip of Cú Chulainn's spear rip a deep gash between the iron plates shielding Ferdiad's side, the blood flowing out to drown the glimmering stones. The butt of Ferdiad's spear caught Cú Chulainn a staggering blow in the ribs: the Ulsterman rolled from it with a great splash, warding off the killing stroke even as he came to his feet again. I heard the loud crack as the Hound's shaft struck Ferdiad's left arm, and despaired as Ferdiad's hand dropped empty. Our champion had the strength to wield his weapon one-handed as another man might with two; and after a few parries, Ferdiad took his two-handed grip again and began to press his foe the more fiercely. Now the blood was flowing freely from both, enough that I could not clearly tell when another wound was opened.

It seemed to me that Cú Chulainn was getting the worst of it: Ferdiad might have been cut more often, but his mass and heavy armor let him shrug off blows that would have shattered most men's bones, whereas, though Cú Chulainn was able to partially slip most of the strokes that landed on him, he was simply too small to take the same battering that his friend could withstand. 'Finish it, Ferdiad, I urged silently. You have the advantage; finish him!. Cú Chulainn slipped to the side, switching his hand-grip and whirling the butt of his spear in a short hard shocking stroke to the back of Ferdiad's right knee.

The large man did not go down or drop his defense as he turned, but he stumbled, and Cú Chulainn dodged back out of range.

"Let us break off from this now, Ferdiad," Cú Chulainn called, the words barely intelligible through the hoarse panting gasp of his breath.

"We are equally matched, and equally hurt: we shall not come to a conclusion with these weapons."

"Very well, let us break off," Ferdiad rasped.

Bloodied and battered, they laid their spears aside, embracing and kissing each other again. I shook my head: I would never understand how two men could strive so fiercely to kill each other, and yet love each other so.

Perhaps Calatín could have explained it to me; but now I would never know. Fergus came over to help take Ferdiad's armor off so that I could tend him. He glared sidelong at me, but spoke no word until I had smeared the gash in Ferdiad's side with ointments and herbs that would keep it from festering, if he lived, and help it heal, then stitched it up. As I ran my hands over our champion's massively muscled body, trying to feel beneath the red welts of his bruises to see if any ribs were broken, Fergus grunted,

"Perhaps it is as well you came."

I nodded, but did not answer him: I could almost feel my tongue like a sac of black poison, ready to sting and spurt its bale into Fergus' veins. 'This is your fault, yours and Fiacha's'. After I had tended Ferdiad's wounds and given him a drink of herbs that would dull the pain a little without slowing him, I once again let Eochaid carry me across the ford to see to Cú Chulainn. As I had thought, the Hound had taken the worst of it in this last fight.

Though he had no single wound as bad as the one in Ferdiad's side, nor as disabling as the blow to Ferdiad's knee, I was certain several of his ribs were broken, and from the faint gasp that hissed between his teeth when I pressed gently on the huge lumpy welt on his left forearm, I thought the bone of that arm was cracked as well.

His torso and shoulders were a mass of darkening bruises, face pale from loss of blood, his light winter-tan like a faint scattering of golden pollen dusted over bone. I tended him as well as I could, stitching his wounds, giving him the same ointments and healing herbs and medicines that I had given his friend and rival, and sewing the bandages carefully to support his injured ribs and arm without hindering him. Cú Chulainn stood, swinging his arms in slow circles as if to test my work.

His calm face showed no sign of pain, but I winced for him.

"Will you not give over, for a day or two at least, and begin again when the two of you are fit to fight once more?" I asked. I thought of Maeve's army, marching at its best pace.

As evenly matched as Ferdiad and Cú Chulainn were, if the two of them could be talked into resting and healing for a little while between each savage bout, we might escape Ulster before the challenge was fulfilled. The corner of Cú Chulainn's mouth turned up in a wry sad smile.

"What good would that do? We might fight thus from now to Beltaine and neither of us be proven the better, but even if I won the duel, I would have lost the war, for Maeve's host would be long gone." He paused, looking down with his sweat-soaked hair hanging over his face.

"And," he whispered, so softly that I could hardly hear him, not even see his lips moving, only the stirring of a few wet dark strands as his breath sighed past. "If I stop now, I shall never be able to bring myself to fight Ferdiad again, and I must."

I thought of all manner of things then. I thought of the friendship the two of them had shared friendship, and more. Young warriors learning their skills together often share their bodies for a time as well; from the words they had exchanged, I thought it might have been so with Cú Chulainn and Ferdiad. If I could have been certain of taking the Hound's heart from him by speaking further of their friendship, I would have done so.

There was warrior's pride in the matter, and deep betrayal as well. Though Cú Chulainn, even young as he was quite a man for women, and I had seen the love and passion Ferdiad felt for Finnabair, the bond the two young warriors, lovers or not, had shared could not break without cutting their heartstrings at the roots; and Ferdiad had chosen to lift the knife.

"Well. I can do nothing more for you now."

"Thank you," Cú Chulainn said. He lifted his head, brushing the wet hair back. "Tell Ferdiad that if he wishes to halt for a time, I shall agree."

"I shall tell him."

Ferdiad's hair had long since worked loose from the braids Finnabair and Maeve had plaited that morning, swept up in a dark golden mass of sweat-soaked tangles. Drops scattered from the ends of the twining tendrils as he shook his head.

"We must go on," he said briefly. "We are too well-matched, but I can take more than he." And that, I had seen already, was true.

Whatever weapons they fought with, a blow that could crack one of Ferdiad's thick bones would do shattering damage to Cú Chulainn's lighter frame, and a cut that would bite deep into Ferdiad's flesh would slice to bone or entrails on the Hound. It seemed to me that Ferdiad's blue eyes were dulling; and while I knew it was only sweat that had darkened his fair hair, it looked as if a shadow lay over his head.

"You would do Maeve's host as much good by halting as by going on. If you are stronger than Cú Chulainn now, you will still be stronger tomorrow." And, I thought, the effects of the battering Ulster's champion had taken would be the worse tomorrow, when every bruise had swelled and stiffened.

Ferdiad shook his head again.

"It is not for Maeve's host that I do this," he said.

Once more the two champions walked out to meet in the shallows of the ford. Ferdiad was still limping, but I did not think Cú Chulainn's injured arm could stand another blow. 'Maybe Ferdiad will kill him after all! I think it must be easier to win a fight with a sore leg than with a broken arm'.

"Ferdiad," Cú Chulainn said, "you have an ill look about you now. I think it was your doom when a woman sent you here to fight against your foster-brother."

"Cú Chulainn, you are wise enough," Ferdiad answered heavily. "A true hero, a true warrior; but you know everyone must come to the sod that is his final bed."

Tired and wounded as the champions were, they were both speaking loudly and clearly, as if to make sure that those of us watching from both sides of the river could hear. A little shiver tingled up my spine as I realized that they were doing just that. Whichever of them died, if either lived, they would have these words remembered, and retold.

"Maeve's daughter Finnabair, however fair she may be, did not come to you for love, but to make you use your strength against me."

I could not see Ferdiad's face, but I saw the twitch of his shoulders.

"My strength has been well-used by now, dear Hound. Never, to this day, have I found or heard of a man braver than you."

Cú Chulainn sighed deeply, a glimmer of pain rippling across his face as the breath pressed on his cracked ribs.

"Yours is the blame for what must follow, for you came at a woman's word to cross swords with your foster-brother."

Ferdiad made a sound that might have been a short bitter laugh, or a cough.

"Sweet Hound, although we are foster-brothers, if we part now. Think of my ill-fame and shame at Cruachan before Ailill and Maeve. Would you have your foster-brother named an oath breaker?"

The Hound stepped forward, laying one hand on Ferdiad's big forearm and looking up into his face. This time he spoke more softly, but I could still hear every word.

"There is no man who ever ate, nor any man ever born, and no joyous son of king and queen, for whose sake I would do you harm. Give over now, and come with me. The ties of oath and service are strong, but the ties of kinship are greater still. Few would reproach you for it."

Ferdiad's head lowered.

"Cú Chulainn, tide of bravery," he said sadly. "I know that Maeve has ruined us. You will win victory and renown: no one will think you at fault."

Beside me, Eochaid made a muffled noise, and Suithchern murmured a soft curse. Staunchly as Ferdiad had spoken to us, it seemed to me that the heart had gone out of him; and if it were Ferdiad's ability to bear his wounds that could make the difference in this combat, then he might be lost already. Our only hope, it seemed to me, was that, once they began, Connacht's champion might forget his sorrow in the intoxication of fighting as I might forget my own in trance or song; forget that he faced his dearest friend, and remember only the dance of weapon and shield until Cú Chulainn was dead.

"My high heart is a knot of blood," Cú Chulainn mourned, "my soul is tearing from my body. I'd rather face a thousand battles than this fight with you, Ferdiad."

Ferdiad shook himself like a horse plunging up the steep bank from an icy river.

"I have chosen our weapons thrice. Now it is your turn."

"Very well. Swords and shields; and let us fight in the deep ford-water."

I looked at Eochaid, and so did Suithchern. A warrior's wife, she knew better than I how to voice the question in my mind.

"Why does he want the deep water? It will be nearly all the way up his thighs, while Ferdiad will be far less hindered."

Eochaid mimed ducking and swimming, then pointed to the back of his own right knee. I understood: Cú Chulainn would be able to maneuverer in the water more easily than his opponent, and perhaps take advantage of the injury he had dealt Ferdiad's leg. Now the two of them had their swords and shields, blades and gilded bronze work winking bright in the sunlight. Cú Chulainn waded more slowly towards the middle of the ford than Ferdiad, but in a moment I saw what he had planned.

As Ferdiad reached the deepest point, the Hound flung himself into a great leap, striking down over the edge of Ferdiad's shield at his head. I gasped; but Ferdiad blocked the blow with his sword and punched out with his own shield, knocking his small opponent back through the air. Cú Chulainn splashed down, vanishing beneath the water for a moment; it was only luck that the powerful swing of Ferdiad's blade passed just short of his head as he rose again. Cú Chulainn's charioteer laughed, the loud scornful sound carrying easily over the river.

"Ferdiad shook you as easily as a mother shakes a babe!" Láeg shouted. "He pounced on you like a hawk on a wren! From this day forward, little siabra, you have no right or claim or title to great deeds or daring!"

Cú Chulainn leapt up again, his sword flickering out like a kingfisher's wing in a backhanded cut at Ferdiad's face. As Ferdiad blocked it, the Hound made a great whirling leap to Ferdiad's right side, bringing his sword down from above his foe's head again and crashing his shield down on Ferdiad's own to keep it from stopping the blow. Ferdiad managed to wrench his sword into the way of Cú Chulainn's stroke, and all the Hound's weight was not enough to keep Connacht's champion from flinging him off with his shield and into the water again. I had seen Cú Chulainn's warp-spasm with the eyes of the Otherworld.

On this green earth, it was no such monstrous transformation. It seemed that Ulster's hero swelled within his armor, and beneath the iron rim of his helmet, his face contorted with rage like nothing human. His eyes bulged hugely, black and empty as cave-mouths; froth and blood streamed from his snarling mouth, and he moved as swiftly and fiercely as though he had never been wounded. He flung himself on Ferdiad, who held his ground, his sword-strokes speeding up as if to mirror his foe's.

The two of them began to hack at each other in earnest, and I
understood that even the brutal spear-duel that had gone before
had only been play for these two warriors. Their bronze shield-
knobs grated and shrieked as if a host of bocánach and bánánaich
and siabra surrounded us, howling in pain and glee; the thunder of
blades against shields rolled booming over the river, fiercer than the
lightning-riven heart of any storm. Great drops of blood spattered
into the river again and again, but so closely did Ferdiad and Cú
Chulainn fight, that I could not even tell who was wounded, let
alone how badly.

Then my heart leapt like a salmon in my breast, Ferdiad struck
at Cú Chulainn's thigh. The smaller man dropped his shield to
block, but Ferdiad's sword swerved like a bird in flight, arching up
to plunge straight over the rim into Cú Chulainn's chest, sinking
through all the layers of hide to bite in deep. Blood poured over the
Hound's armor as Ferdiad withdrew the weapon and struck again.
Cú Chulainn just managed to get his shield up again, but the force of
the blow drove him to his knees.

"Láeg!" Cú Chulainn barked, an awful shouting cough; blood
drizzled from his mouth. The sword had dropped from his hand, he
kept his shield up, turning it to glance Ferdiad's next stroke.

He did not even turn his head, but his empty sword-hand shot up
to catch the black barbed javelin flying from the shore behind him.
Grasping the weapon, Cú Chulainn dived beneath the water for a
heartbeat, and then Ferdiad screamed, the most awful sound I had
ever heard. The shattering agony of his cry reverberated about the
inside of my skull in sharp pain-bursts of light.

His body stiffened, a great gout of blood spurted from his mouth,
and he toppled like a felled oak, hitting the river with a mighty
splash and sinking beneath the froth and blood that streaked the
water's roiled surface. Fergus leapt to his feet, running towards
them. Though I knew already that I could not save Ferdiad, I was
only a few strides behind him; I gasped as the brutal ice-chill of
the river bit into my feet and legs, the water slowing my stride
like a nightmare, but I did not stop. Then Cú Chulainn's head and
shoulders rose again from the water. He was on his knees, holding
Ferdiad's lolling head up as well and weeping in great shattering
bursts.

"Stay back," he coughed to Fergus. "Don't touch me. I love you,
but I'll kill you if you touch me."

Fergus and I stood there together with the cold river-current tugging at our legs as Cú Chulainn whispered his last words to his slain friend, the blood coughing out of him with each breath.

"Ferdia, you are dead and I must live to mourn your loss. I thought, when we were with Scáthach, that our friendship would hold unbroken until world's end. I loved the noble way you blushed, your flushed sweet cheek and fine form; I loved your blue clear eye, your curled golden hair like a fair jewel, your way of speech and all your skills. Never till this day did I find your match for great deeds in battle. You are brought to death by deceit.

Maeve's daughter Finnabair, whatever beauty she may have, Ferdiad, she was an empty offering, a string to hold the sand. If you had met your death when we fought as companions, I would not have outlasted you; I would have died by your side. Misery has befallen us, Scáthach's two prize students: I, broken, blood-red and raw, you lying stark dead by my hand. You dead and I alive, bravery is battle-madness!" Cú Chulainn gave a gurgling cough, spat a mouthful of blood into water.

"All was play, all a game, until Ferdiad came to the ford. I thought my beloved friend would live forever after me. Yesterday, a mountain-slope; today, but a shadow. Now the blue cups of your eyes are empty where you once beheld me; but never a king's son has deserved fairer fame than you."

Slowly Cú Chulainn slumped back into the water. I did not know, and do not know, whether I would have let him die then or not, but Fergus leapt forward to scoop the unconscious body up in his arms and carry his foster-son to the bank on the Ulstermen's side.

"Help him, the gods curse you!" Fergus grated between his teeth as he laid Cú Chulainn down beside his own fire, drawing his own belt-knife and cutting the layers of waxed hide-armor away from his foster-son's chest with a desperate haste that left a few shallow cuts oozing blood behind the blade's track.

"For Ferdiad's sake, don't let him die!"

The blood was bubbling in the wound Ferdiad had dealt his friend, a sickening sucking gurgle hissing out with every slow shallow breath. Still, I held back a moment, shivering in the cold wind that tugged at my wet robe. My knees were weak and my back soaked with sweat as if I had been fighting myself; I wanted to sag down and not rise again. Nevertheless, I stood there, looking at the man who had done us so much harm.

Ferdiad had pierced his lung; how badly, I could not tell. Cú Chulainn would die if I did nothing. If I tried to aid him, he still might die, and if my hand should slip as I worked, it would kill him, and no one but myself would know whether it was by choice or chance.

Then it seemed to me as though a man's strong hand gripped my shoulder, pushing me down towards the youth who lay dying there. Perhaps Ferdiad had not begun his journey to the house of Donn, and perhaps, if I did not do my best for Cú Chulainn, he never would. I had reminded him of his promise, and brought him to his death. Now he was reminding me of mine: if I did not fulfil it, I would never be free of his sorrow. Maybe, if Ferdiad's ghost moved me, it was from love. If I saved Cú Chulainn now, he must live and bear his own sorrow, as I did, as did Suithchern and Ailill and Maeve and all the others he had bereaved.

And that might be revenge more fitting than his death. Whether it was compassion or vengeance that moved me, I knelt and laid my hand over the wound in Cú Chulainn's breast, lifting a little as he breathed in, pressing tightly to seal it as he breathed out.

"Get my chest of healing tools," I said to Fergus without looking up.

As the trance of battle had taken Cú Chulainn and Ferdiad so that they became heedless of their friendship, so the trance of healing was taking me now, leaving me heedless of our enmity, of all that had passed by his hand on this raid, and aware only of the guttering life beneath my hand and my need to do what I could to save him.

I waited for a time that seemed to span half the day, though it could not have been longer than the cuckoo sings in summer before Fergus was back. I grabbed the older warrior's sturdy wrist, pressing his palm down over the wound. One of my small sharp knives split away a layer of waxed leather from the flap Fergus had cut out of Cú Chulainn's armor; I smeared the edges with ointment to seal it, leaving one corner open to let him breathe, and pushed Fergus' hand away to press it down. For a moment I thought the bandage would not work; but then Cú Chulainn's chest heaved, the air flowing cleanly in, and when he breathed out, I did not hear the sucking burble I had feared.

"That will hold him a little time," I panted. "Get back, and let me work."

"Why did you save him?" Suithchern asked plaintively as we drove slowly back towards the host. We sat in the bottom of the chariot, she on my chest of medicines with the two children, myself cross-legged on the floor.

"Even with Fergus there, you could have..." She did not finish; but I knew what she meant to say: had I not thought the same?

"Because I had to," I answered dully.

I felt like a cold cinder, charred beyond hope of flaming again. Suithchern had made me get out of the wet robe and wrap myself in dry cloaks and blankets; she had heated the last of the milk Cú Chulainn had sent for me, and ordered Láeg to give her some honey to stir into it as well. I was still shivering, drained as if I had been in the fight myself.

"He may yet die. He lost a great deal of blood, and for all my skill, when the lung is pierced, the chances of even a strong man surviving are less than even. Should he live, he will not fight again until long after we have left Ulster; he may lose his wind, and never fight again. I promised Ferdiad. I had done him enough harm already. Should I have broken my word to him as well, once he was dead?"

Suithchern looked down at the two babes she held, for once both sleeping peacefully in her lap. They had been awake and wailing during most of the fight, though I had hardly noticed them. Now I wondered if they could possibly remember anything of it when they were grown. At least they would be able to say they had been there when Ferdiad fought Cú Chulainn at the ford. That would be as mighty a boast as anyone could ask.

Finnabair

The sun was lowering in the west; Finnabair thought her mother was getting ready to call her army to a halt, when she saw the three chariots ahead. Fergus rode in his; Fedelm, Suithchern, and Suithchern's two babes were still crammed in behind their mute driver, but Ferdiad's was empty.

Finnabair reined their golden horses in so sharply that the chariot almost overturned. She dropped the reins, turning to her mother.

"Ferdiad is dead! I told you..."

Maeve took her daughter in her arms, holding Finnabair as her shoulders shook with deep sobs.

"Hush, hush," she crooned, as if Finnabair were still a child. "We don't know that yet. He may be only wounded, or staying the night by the ford to fight again in the morning."

Finnabair wanted to believe her mother's words, but knew better. If Ferdiad were wounded too badly to ride, Fedelm and Fergus would not have left him; if he had chosen to stay the night, his charioteer would be with him.

She clung tightly to Maeve, her head buried damply in her mother's shoulder.

"Ferdiad is dead," she repeated, her voice muffled in Maeve's mantle.

'It was my fault after all, because'

"I didn't want to marry him. I didn't want him to die either! He loved me, I sent him out to die like the others, every man who loves me dies!"

'If I had truly loved him, would he be alive now? If, in my heart, I had wanted any of them to defeat the Hound and hence wed me. Was it some unknowing ill-wish of mine that slew Ferdiad, in the end?'

"It is over now," Maeve murmured. "You have done your part. I will not ask you to lure another man to meet Cú Chulainn at the ford. Nor, though Ferdiad desired you, was it for you he died, but for his own pride and honor. You carry no part of his doom."

Still Finnabair wept on her mother's breast, until the three chariots came close enough to speak. Then she pulled away, composing her features as best she could. There was no body in Ferdiad's chariot, but one look at Fergus' face was enough for Finnabair to know what had happened. His craggy hawk-features were set, but tears still ran slowly from his grey eyes down into his close-cropped beard.

A sudden flicker of hope glimmered in Finnabair's heart, shifting like a flame crawling from twig to twig. Did Fergus weep for one fosterling, or for two?

"Ferdiad is slain," Fergus rasped. "Cú Chulainn lies near the doorway to the house of Donn. Ferdiad pierced his chest; but Cú Chulainn struck him from beneath with the gae bolga. There was no hope of saving him."

"Where is Ferdiad's body?" Maeve asked.

"At the ford. Cú Chulainn awoke long enough to ask that I leave his friend to him for honoring, and I could not deny him. If he dies, his charioteer will lay them in a single bed as they lived and fell."

"That was well enough done," Maeve said. "Will you tell us all the tale this night?"

"Let Fedelm tell it. That is work for a fili, and I have no more tales in me." Fergus looked at Finnabair for a moment, and she felt as though her skin were scorching away beneath his glare. "Perhaps it is ever my fate to lose those whom I would protect to the madness a woman's beauty brings, as Deirdre lured Noisu to his death."

Finnabair gasped in pain, but Maeve spoke first, her voice deathly quiet.

"Ferdiad went to the ford from pride, not desire for my daughter. Had you aided Deirdre when Conchobar would raise her as his bondsmaid, Noisu and your sons might yet live. Mourn as you will, few have better right, but do not try to cast the guilt on Finnabair for Ferdiad's choice, nor on Deirdre for what Conchobar forced her to do."

Fergus turned and walked away, and Maeve embraced Finnabair again.

"Fergus is in great pain," Maeve said softly. "I think he feels that he should have halted this day's combat; and when such grief and guilt is upon a man, or a woman, it seems easier to bear if the blame can be laid upon another. Pay his words no heed; there is no truth in them."

Finnabair bit her lip. "Perhaps not this time," she admitted. "The others…"

"Hush, hush. It is over, and shall never be asked of you again."

A freezing rain fell that night, spattering noisily against the leather and wool of Finnabair's tent. Exhausted from worry and weeping, she turned uneasily in her sleep, too tired to think or rise. The rain was still falling by morning, the frozen ground beginning to soften into mud. Emerging from his own tent, her father turned his face up, sniffing the wet wind with a grin, and said,

"'Raw and cold is icy spring', but at least spring is coming!"

Maeve, sitting by the fire with a half-eaten bannock in her hand, looked up in alarm.

"We had best hasten, if we wish to be away before the men of Ulster have risen," she answered grimly.

Ailill raised a bright eyebrow.

"Cú Chulainn will fight no more for a time. What else do you know?"

Maeve paused, and Finnabair suddenly understood. The words of the curse she had spoken together with her mother and Fedelm at the beginning of the raid had flown past her ears like ravens then. Now she heard the black flapping and croaking again, and knew that Maeve did as well. 'Ceasing not in frost-hold. Frost-hold keep you fettered. Fettered, hosts of Ulster!' Finnabair wondered if her mother would tell her father what had passed, at last, and felt a sudden urge to press her hand to Maeve's mouth. Maeve said only,

"I know that Macha's vengeance has been harsh, but will not last forever. What began with the winter may end with it as well."

That evening, Maeve called for Flidais, Ailill, Fergus, and Finnabair to attend her in her tent. Finnabair was the first there, waiting with her belly tight from apprehension as her mother finished her rounds of the camp; her father, Flidais, and Fergus joined her a little later. Fergus did not apologize for his words of the day before, but his gaze slid away from Finnabair's when she stared straight at him, and she began to let herself think that her mother had been right about him.

"Well, Finnabair," Ailill said when Maeve came in and settled herself among them at last. "It seems your man has come for you."

Finnabair glanced dubiously up at her father. Ailill was grinning, his voice light, but that told her little. She could not suppress the warm spurt of hope in her heart, but she did not dare to trust it.

"Has he?" She asked. "Or does he only want to do battle?"

"Both, most likely," Flidais told her calmly. "If he is worthy of you, he will be ready to defend his king. Mac Roth says his host is large enough to slow and weaken us, but not so large that he might defeat us by himself. He may well be hoping that he can both do his duty and win you afterwards. Or he may have some thought of stealing you out of our camp, against which we must guard."

Finnabair's glance flicked unwillingly towards the tent-flap, as if she could see through it and into the darkness about the royal enclosure where Ferdiad could no longer keep his watch. She thought about all that had passed before; thought about going home to Cruachan, still its inheritor; still the lure to death or the prize to be won.

"If Rochad is slain in battle, I will not wish to live either," Finnabair stated flatly.

"We will do our best to keep that from happening," Maeve assured her. "If you have any thoughts as to how we might manage it, then it would be well to speak them."

Finnabair bit her lip, looking down at the little gold buckles on her shoes. She had been thinking on it since that morning, since she knew that Rochad would soon have to gather his host and come against her mother's army.

"If I sent him a message, that I wanted to meet him alone. He would come to me, I know he would. I have had enough of warriors and their gods-cursed pride and honor! I would be happy enough, if I only knew he would be safe, and he would be safe enough if you captured and held him until this raid is over."

Her mother looked at her father. Ailill shook his head, the gold wires woven into his red-gold braids flashing in the torchlight.

"He would never forgive you for that," her father said gently.

"He would, I know it!" Finnabair insisted. "He would understand that it is only because I love him."

"Finnabair, my dear daughter," Maeve said. "Do you believe that I have seen more of men, and know more of how their hearts work, than you do?"

Finnabair twisted the fine blue wool of her overdress between her fingers. She did not want to admit the truth of what her mother said, *because it is one more thing in my way?* There was no doubt that Queen Maeve knew the ways of men better than any woman born. Finnabair nodded reluctantly.

"Then believe me when I say that he would not truly understand. He might say that he forgave you; he might even think he had. The thing would ever lie between you, a shadow on your sun. Yes, such shadows fade in time, as grief does, but, like grief, they are never truly gone." Maeve paused.

"You have more than earned the love you want. Though I would rather have seen you with a greater man, I cannot stand in your way now, after all that you have borne for us. I would see you happy with what you want, not drinking the cup of marriage only to find its sweetness tainted by a bitter drop of deceit and betrayal. For that is how Rochad will feel if we do this, however much he loves you."

"It is true," Flidais put in. "Men will forgive almost anything from a woman they love, except for being kept safe when they would be heroes, especially when there is deception in the matter. Perhaps it reminds them of being children beneath their mothers' will; I do not know. If you want to live long and happily with Rochad, you will forget this at once."

"You are also assuming that he is an idiot," Fergus broke in sharply. "What manner of fool would leave his army alone, because he received a message saying that the woman he loves wants to speak with him? When she is the daughter of the foes' war leaders? Do you really think that Rochad is so stupid? I will agree that he is not the wisest of men, but surely even he could smell the ruse there."

"Rochad is not stupid!" Finnabair flared. "Perhaps he is not as swift of tongue as some, but I have never heard that any woman loved Bricriu for his clever speech."

'And, unlike most men, including you, Fergus! He thinks before he speaks, and thinks deeply'. She remembered how he had considered his words to her at the fair, how he had seemed to understand from the beginning what it was to be beautiful, and a great queen's heir, and how hollow it had begun to feel after the first pleasant flattery of men courting her for those things. Rochad had not bothered with fine words, but had laid out his heart for her, and trusted her in turn to deal kindly with him.

"So we may leave that plan aside," Maeve said. "Perhaps we would do better to offer him Finnabair in the light of day and seal a truce thus...but then we should have to deal with the Munstermen."

"I do not think Rochad would take it," Fergus mused. "As I said, he is not known for his great wisdom, but he is as loyal as any man born. I do not think he would betray his king, even for his dearest love, would he, Finnabair? Would you have him if he would?"

"He is loyal," Finnabair mumbled unhappily, staring down at her feet again. "However worthless of such trust Conchobar may be, he would never betray his king." Rochad had told her that, too, when he apologized for making her an offer of marriage that would mean she must leave Connacht and its sovereignty if she accepted him.

She had known that a man who was so true to his oaths and land would be just as true to his love.

"Then," Maeve said, "it is best that Rochad has no reason to think that you are part of any plot involving him. Finnabair, will you trust me when I say that I will do my best to bring both you and Rochad safely out of this and see you wedded to him?"

Finnabair looked closely at her mother's face. Maeve's blue eyes met hers without the least flickering; she looked sad? Resigned? Finnabair thought of the speech they had held together before the raid began, how her mother had confided in her as a full woman for the first time, trusting in her to understand, and do what was needed, 'and if you could trust me so...'

"I will trust you, Mother."

"Then go to your tent, and go to bed. If Rochad has blame to lay when all this is done, it is best if your father and I are alone in bearing it. He will live, and if you and he want each other, then you shall have each other, if it is at all within my power."

"May it be so!" Finnabair said, trying to keep her voice from cracking. She rose, and went to her tent, lying fully-clothed under her blankets. She knew that she would not sleep.

'Rochad, she thought. O, Rochad. If this can bring us together at last, then maybe all I have done, and suffered, will be worthwhile. If you still want me!'

Maeve

"What are you thinking, Maeve?" Ailill asked as soon as Finnabair was gone. "Are you going to follow our daughter's plan, after all?"

"No. Cú Chulainn is not the only one who can sneak into an enemy's camp at night, and Rochad's host has far less cause than we have had to keep his encampment as a fortress under attack."

Matters went swiftly after that. Even Fergus agreed that Maeve's plan would be the best thing, though Maeve suspected he was more concerned with protecting the Ulstermen in Rochad's host than with preserving what remained of Finnabair's tender heart. Their other choice was simple: to rouse their warriors and fall on Rochad's men in the middle of the night.

That would be red slaughter, with the little Ulster army outnumbered and taken by surprise; this way, the matter might be resolved with no blood spilled, and Maeve able to make unhindered for Connacht once more. When Ailill, Flidais, and Fergus went out to quietly find the men they needed, Fedelm rose to go, but Maeve gestured her to sit again.

"Can you cast some spell or charm on our raiders, so that they may go unseen and pass unseen and come back unseen again?"

Fedelm frowned.

"I think I can. It would be more effective if I went with them myself…"

"Absolutely not! It will be hard traveling to get there and back before daybreak. If you don't wear your Druid's robe, you will be a target for weapons, and if you do, even on a stormy night, it will stand out in the darkness. You are not battle-trained, and you are carrying a child."

"I am only a month or so along. I am past the time when a babe may easily shake loose of the womb, and it will be several months before I have to worry about straining myself. if my spell is well-wrought, I will never be seen by the foe."

Fedelm was staring up at Maeve with the same intense gaze Maeve had seen on her face when she had insisted on seeking the Brown Bull in visions, even though the effort was wearing her to the bone. It was the same look Maeve had seen on any number of young warriors demanding to take the fore in battle, and several of those men who had first volunteered to face Cú Chulainn at the ford.

Maeve knew that if Calatín were still alive, he would have insisted on joining the raiding party.

'He was still an able fighter, and Fedelm is bearing a child'. Maeve knew that was the heart of her objection; even she had never gone to battle with a babe in her womb. 'That I knew', she amended reluctantly. If Fedelm were not a seeress, or perhaps if Calatín had not only been a very skilled Druid, but many times a father as well and hence keenly alert for the first signs of pregnancy in a woman with whom he lived closely, she most likely would not know herself: certainly Maeve would not.

Maeve still did not know herself whether her awareness of Fedelm's pregnancy had moved below her thoughts when she stepped between the young woman and the Brown Bull.

She would never know that, but now she was certain that she did not want Fedelm to risk herself in this raid on Rochad's camp, though it might make the difference between getting her host safely out of Ulster and being delayed long enough for Conchobar to recover and gather his army. 'Macha's pangs are easing as the winter fades and the frost's grip loosens', just as Fedelm said. Rochad's presence was proof enough of that.

"I do not want you to go. It is too dangerous for you; it will be enough to do what you can here."

"And if it is not?" Fedelm demanded. Then she lowered her voice. "My queen Maeve, I know you do not wish to command me to go. You have told me that you care for me, and shown it even more clearly. Did you not offer your own life to the Bull in place of mine? While I have been less help to you than I wished. it is my own choice to go with the raiders now. If my spells fail and ill befall me, I say now that there will not be the least guilt on your head."

Maeve's mouth twisted into a wry smile. "There will be guilt there, whether you would free me of it beforehand or not, because I could have stopped you, and did not."

"Yet it is my choice. Isn't it?"

'It is my duty to protect you', Maeve thought. 'My subject, my Druid and seeress, my friend, my husband's adaltrach, whether you will marry with us now or not, and the mother of a child who will be my kin thereby. I am a warrior, who took up the risk of battle-death when I took up the sword and spear, while you are not'. It seemed to Maeve that every instinct she possessed shouted at her from bone and blood that she must not let Fedelm do this thing.

Yet she remembered her days in Ulster, where Conchobar shouted and the women whispered that it was not seemly for a queen to fight. She remembered, as well, the helpless sorrow on Ailill's face as he looked down at the infant suckling its slain mother's breast, her blood and milk both on its face. How even he, the best of men, had spoken from his heart in that moment, doubting that women should bear swords. The right to rule was the duty to protect; but the duty to protect also led to the right to rule.

And it seemed to Maeve that, as the two sprang forth together from one root, they must also end in the same place: there was a ford in every soul which another should not cross.

'If I hold Fedelm back now because I would keep her, even for her own good, from her right to choose her way, how then am I different from Conchobar?'

"It is your choice," Maeve admitted.

Then the words flowed from her: somehow, as before, she found that she could speak to Fedelm more freely than she had ever spoken to any other save Ailill.

"I have sent my sons to battle, and lost one thereby; I have come near to breaking Finnabair's heart. Fedelm, I love you as a daughter or sister, and I wish with all my soul that you would stay here in such safety as there is… if you feel that you must go, I cannot compel you to stay.

I will send you with my blessing, and pray to Brigit and the gods of the Cruachain that you come home safe."

Fedelm rose, and Maeve embraced her closely, feeling the young woman's heart beating quick beneath the small breasts pressed under her own.

"I will be careful," Fedelm said, smiling wanly. "I am Calatín's student, after all. Though I yet lack the understanding of much of his lore, still I have learned much: you may trust in his teaching."

"I will trust in you," Maeve said. She did not fail to hear the ironic echo of the words that Finnabair had spoken to her only a little while ago. 'If the gods are kind to us, both Fedelm and I will be able to make that trust good!'

Maeve knew she would not be able to sleep that night.

Thus, after Fedelm and the small group of chosen men had departed, she and Flidais set about preparing her tent for what she hoped would take place. She would have had her own gold goblet on the table, but she feared it would remind Finnabair of the other men to whom the girl had given mead from that cup; she borrowed Flidais' best bowl instead, an ancient thing of thin hammered gold with a handle in the shape of a stylized horse's head at the end of a long ringed neck.

Suithchern was loath to invade Fedelm's supplies of herbs, nor could she read the scraps of scratched wood attached to each waxed cloth bag, but when Maeve quietly explained matters to Eochaid, he smiled and sorted through the Druid's chest to gather a small handful of sweet-scented dried leaves for her to scatter about the floor in place of summer's rushes and strewing-plants.

Maeve wanted to dress Finnabair in her finest clothes and jewelery, to plait her daughter's pale hair and adorn it with gold and help her to touch her eyes with blue powder and her cheeks and lips with a dusting of madder. In her secret heart, she feared that to promise too much now would somehow bring her plan to disaster, and she was already afraid enough that Fedelm would come to harm, or that she would break the trust Finnabair had promised her.

In the end, once all the preparations that Maeve dared to make had been made, she and Ailill and Fergus and Flidais simply sat and talked quietly through the night to the sound of the rain pattering on her tent. It seemed to Maeve that they had somehow rolled back the river of time to the friendship the four of them had held before any of the things that had led them on this raid had come to pass, and she felt her heart easing as it had not eased for far too long.

Half a day's walk, Mac Roth had said. Though the year was turning upwards towards spring, Imbolc was a few days away; the nights were still very long, and the daytime short. Maeve guessed that dawn was still some time off when she heard Fedelm's voice speaking to the guards outside,

"The queen and king are expecting us. Stand aside, and let us pass."

Maeve's heart leapt with relief and hope, but she forced herself to fold her hands in her lap and sit, waiting quietly, as the tent-flap opened. Fedelm walked in, her delicate triangular face alight and blue-grey eyes blazing with triumph as she cast back her dark hood and let her black mantle fall open to show the glimmering white of her Druid's robe beneath.

Her cheeks were pink as foxgloves with cold and excitement, or perhaps from a hasty scrubbing; there was still a faint smear of dark pigment along her left cheekbone, and traces of more about the edges of her nostrils and the line of her jaw. Behind her came the five men Ailill and Flidais had chosen, their own faces still blacked like Samhain mummers; and between them they carried a long bound figure.

"Lay him down on the bed," Maeve said, feeling her mouth spread into a grin. "Free his mouth, but do not unbind his hands. You shall all be well-rewarded for this night's work."

Maeve had half-expected a torrent of shouts and curses, but Rochad lay silent, only glaring up at her. Looking at him now, she still could not imagine what Finnabair saw in the young man. He was very tall, as tall as Ferdiad had been, but all long scrawny limbs. He might be a proven warrior, but he still looked like a boy at the age of choice, whose bones had stretched towards manhood far too fast for his flesh to fill out over them.

Even set in anger, Rochad's face was pleasant enough in a homely sort of way, wide-mouthed and long-nosed, with a tangle of deep brown curls falling about it. Maeve guessed that his hair would not stay tidy no matter how tightly it was plaited, and the torchlight brought out the faint pocking of healed spots over his cheekbones.

His little chin-beard, as brown-haired men's sometimes were, was a violent shade of orange, and still had the tufted and fuzzy look of hair that had not been growing for long.

'Finnabair could have had Fraech; she could have had Ferdiad, and Connacht's rule with them. She could have almost any man in Eriu she desires.

What can she possibly want with this long funny-looking tangle of reeds?' Maeve wondered. Then she had to laugh at herself, a quiet inward chuckle. No Druid, however old and wise, could understand all the ways of love. She did not always know all her own heart: what made her think that she could fathom every depth of her daughter's?

"Well, Rochad," she said. "You are captive here, but we have not yet fallen on your army, and for that you may thank the fact that Finnabair has set her heart on you. Would you see her?"

Rochad's hazel eyes stared searchingly at Maeve.

"Did she have any part in this?" He asked quietly.

"She did not even know that we were thinking about it," Maeve answered.

"She begged us not to let you come to harm; she said she did not care to outlive you. Hence, we have gone to some trouble for your sake. We could have fallen on your host easily enough, and slaughtered it all, but instead we will offer you a chance to live, you and all your men, and Finnabair to wed, if you still love her."

"Of course I do!" Rochad answered hotly. "I have not so much as glanced at another woman's breasts since I met her at the Samhain fair before last. Finnabair is the only woman in this world for me, but what do you want in return?"

Maeve could not help glancing sideways at Fergus, a small smile curling her lips. She had wondered if he had been deliberately baiting Finnabair when he suggested that Rochad lacked wit; now she knew.

'What a powerful team we are, when we pull in harness together', she thought; and could not help, just for a moment, wondering how it would be now if Fergus had been Ulster's king instead of Conchobar when she had reached the age of choice.

"Take your host, and go home, with Finnabair at your side," Maeve said. "Swear not to lift arms against Connacht again, or at least until this raid is done. We shall not ask for a coibche of gold or silver, cattle or land: that will be bride-price enough for us."

Rochad grimaced.

"Would you have your daughter wed a traitor to king and homeland?"

"We are not asking you to fight against Conchobar," Maeve pointed out reasonably, "and we have already given you your men's lives this night, when we could have destroyed them and taken you with little loss to ourselves. Is your first duty not to those who follow you, rather than him who commands you?"

The young man's thick brows furrowed in thought; he did not answer.

"Go in peace, with neither of us doing harm to the other, and let Finnabair rejoice that all has turned well in the end," Ailill added.

Rochad thought a moment longer, but at last shook his head.

"If you do not slay myself and my men, then assuredly Conchobar will. If I and those who follow me must die, I should prefer that it be at the hands of Connacht rather than the hands of Ulster." Quiet as his voice was, Maeve could hear the granite bedrock close beneath the soft surface. Reluctantly, she began to admit to herself that Finnabair might not have chosen her love as badly as she had first thought, and that the wisdom of her daughter's choice was doing her no good at all.

"Is that so, Fergus?" Ailill asked. Maeve could have answered the question, but she was too busy wishing that she had known what her husband was going to say so that she could have stamped on his foot before he opened his mouth.

"It is," the exiled Ulsterman answered. "Conchobar does not deal well with those he thinks traitors. Whether treason was so much as thought of, or not," he added bitterly.

They all stood silent for a moment. Maeve considered threatening Rochad, but she suspected it would only make him more stubborn, even if she brought out the willow-withes and laid about the soles of his feet. Finnabair was lying in the tent next door. Awake or asleep, she had put her trust in her mother, and Maeve had feared enough to break it by mischance; she would not do so by choice. Fergus leaned forward, stroking lightly at his short beard.

"It may be that there is a way that, while it pleases few greatly, will not harm us nor bring down Conchobar's wrath on Rochad and Finnabair," he said at last.

"Rochad, if you will swear to take your troops back to your own fortress, and not raise sword against Maeve's army until and unless Conchobar's host marches against them. Then it is a matter for your fates, or the gods, as to whether Connacht's army will reach home again before Ulster's king arises from his bed and gathers his men. if you march with Conchobar in his need, he cannot be too wroth with you; and if you stand out of our way now, I think Maeve and Ailill will consider that a fair coibche for their daughter, will you not?" He added, looking at Connacht's rulers.

Maeve met her husband's blue-green gaze, considering. She was no Druid, to pluck Ailill's thoughts from the bone bowl of his skull. As long as they had been wedded, she could read his face as clearly as the tiniest movements of a foe's shoulders or eyes in battle, her body answering before the knowledge surfaced in her awareness. Fergus' suggestion was less than they had hoped for, but far more than they had feared, and it would give Finnabair, at least, what she had dreamed of and so sorrowfully earned.

"We will," Maeve said.

"Aye, we will," Ailill agreed, the grin spreading slowly across his face.

"But," Maeve told Rochad, "you shall have no claim on Connacht, unless Finnabair herself chooses to take up the queenship; and if she does, it shall be she who holds the rule."

"I wouldn't take it if it were offered," Rochad replied staunchly.

'Easy words to say, for a man bound and captive', Maeve thought. Yet she also thought he was telling the truth.

"Nor shall your sons have any right to rule in Cruachan. If Finnabair bears a daughter, we shall speak on the matter again."

"I only want to hold what is my own in honor, with Finnabair beside me," said Rochad. "That will more than suffice me."

"Well, then, we are understood," Maeve said. She drew her belt-knife and cut the bonds of twisted leather that held Rochad's wrists and ankles. He was not too proud to rub at the chafed marks as he sat up, but, slow and sure as dawn, a smile was beginning to cast its glow upon his face, brightening his irregular features almost to handsomeness.

"Ailill, call Cairbre and Dáire in from the guard, and wake the other boys, while Flidais and I prepare Finnabair for her marriage. Fergus, our guest has had a rude beginning with us. See if you can make up for it now!"

Finnabair

Finnabair lay staring into the dark, trying to make sense of the muffled sounds that came through the walls of her tent. Several times, she thought she had heard voices, but she could not even tell who was speaking, let alone what they were saying. Her thoughts circled in confused tracks, like travelers following a siabra's deceptive light through mist and bog, seeming to find a path and losing it over and over again.

'Rochad, Rochad. What have my parents planned?'

Would they ask what she would not; would they offer him land in Connacht as her bride-gift, if he would turn away from Ulster and Conchobar? And would he come, when the choice to win her or not truly lay there? Fergus had left, and Cormac, Conchobar's own son, with no stain on their honor; why not Rochad?

'And yet, if he comes to us, then I must still be queen. I must do as my mother does, and many more deaths be on my head. It would prove that he is not, after all, the man I believe him to be'. Or would they try to take him by force, and risk his death? Would it be an accident? Finnabair knew that her parents would have preferred her to marry Ferdiad, or Fraech...' they are both dead, and no champions of Connacht live who could match them, save perhaps my brothers'.

She heard footsteps, and silence; more footsteps, and silence again, and the low muttering of voices once more. At one point she was certain that someone was approaching her tent, and stiffened in the darkness, but the sounds died away. Finnabair did not know whether she woke or slept, until sudden torchlight dazzled her eyes, and she flung the covers back.

"Are you planning to sleep full-dressed like that with Rochad?" Flidais enquired. "You had best not, or he will be leading sheep by Beltaine."

"Is he here?" Finnabair asked, her heart pounding dizzily. "Will he...?"

"He is, and he will," her mother answered gladly, grinning. "Get up, let us braid your hair and touch your face with color, though your cheeks hardly need it, the way you are blushing," she added.

"Then we shall give you to your husband, who has promised us peace unless Conchobar's full host should rise and attack us on the way home. That," she added more soberly, "we could not gainsay, for your sake more than any. For if you would dwell with Rochad, you must also live under Conchobar's rule, and it would be an ill end if he slew you as a result of the truce your husband made with us."

Finnabair's body seemed weightless, her heart swooping as she lunged across the small tent to embrace her mother.

"O, thank you, Mother. Thank you!" 'I should never have doubted you, after all!.

Rochad was there, sitting on Maeve's bed. He was rubbing his wrists: Finnabair could see the red marks on them as though he had been bound, and his shaggy brown hair needed plaiting, but his dear face lit with a smile of dizzying ecstasy as his hazel eyes met hers. Finnabair's joy swept over her like a huge wave of sweet mead; she knew she was grinning like a fool, and did not care, for he was here! Rochad rose, clasping her hands between his in a strong grip, tears of wonder pooling in his eyes.

"Finnabair, my Finnabair," he whispered.

"I dreamed of you so long. As I lay in the pangs of Ulster, and thought I must die, you were my only hope."

Finnabair cringed within. She had never thought, as she lent her voice to cursing Conchobar, that Rochad would suffer as well. 'Would he hate me, if he knew? She wondered. Will his love fail, when he learns all I have done on this raid…Though at least he will never learn of my part in the curse on Ulster, not him nor any man, if Mother would not even speak to Father of it.' In that moment, looking up into Rochad's eyes, even the direst worries and guilt seemed very far away.

"You are here, and I for you," Finnabair answered. "May we never be parted again!"

Large as it was, her mother's tent was packed very tightly when everyone had assembled: the army's four leaders, Finnabair and Rochad, Fedelm, Cormac, and the six Mainí. Cairbre and Dáire, fully armed and armoured, stood at the tent-flap; Ceat, Feidhlim, Eochaid, and Sín were all crowded onto the bed together, silver goblets in their hands and their bright hair, in its various shades of gold and red-gold, gleaming like flames in the sunlight.

Cormac sat between them, and though he was bronze to their gold, the kinship in the faces of Finnabair's brothers and half-brother was as clear as if Conchobar's seed had melted away entirely in their mother's womb. Fedelm sat on the edge of the bed, softly playing her harp in rippling joyous strains.

Maeve had heaped a high load of treasure on the little table by her bed, but it was almost hidden by the crowd.

"So, Rochad mac Faithemain," Maeve said. "Your kin are not here to speak for you, but I think we can manage well enough all the same. Here we have myself and Ailill and my own sons as witnesses for Connacht; Queen Flidais for Meath; Fergus, king by birth and right, for Ulster; and Fedelm of the síd, seeress, ban-fili, and student of the Druid. You could hardly ask for better, though you would wed a queen's daughter. Now for our part, we will send with Finnabair these treasures here."

Maeve nodded to Fedelm, who recited a description of each of the pieces of gold, and silver-work. Finnabair paid no attention: the bride-gifts had to be witnessed, so that portions could be settled in the event of divorce, but that meant nothing to her with Rochad's long fingers wrapped warmly about her hand.

"Twenty-five of the finest heifers from our plunder, each of them in calf to the Brown Bull of Cuailgne; and these shall be chosen by Fedelm and Flidais, who are vowed to select the best for our daughter. As coibche for us, you shall take your host homeward, and make no move against the host of Eriu until and unless Conchobar should rise against us himself with his army.

At which time, lest you arouse his unjust wrath, you may join his host; but you shall not strike against myself, nor Ailill, nor our sons; nor, for friendship's sake, may you raise a hand against Flidais or Fergus. Is that agreed before these royal witnesses?"

"It is agreed," Rochad murmured, not so much as glancing at her mother.

"And will you hold to this as well, Finnabair Inghean Maeve?"

"I will," Finnabair breathed. She almost feared to speak too loudly; she could hardly believe that this was not a dream, and if it was, she would not risk waking herself. She lifted Flidais' gold bowl from the table and bore it to Rochad. "Drink of the sweet mead, my husband and love; let us pledge a long and joyful life together, with many children to come."

Rochad drank without taking his eyes from Finnabair's own, a gaze so deep that his hazel eyes seemed to reflect a glimmer of her blue like a forest pool mirroring a glint of sky.

"As long as I live, I shall never fail to do all I can to bring you joy and keep you safe, and our children as well, may Brigit grant us many!" He promised.

Rochad passed the bowl back to Finnabair.

"For my part," she answered, "I shall love you with all that is in me as long as I can draw breath; I shall bear your children and no others, and never fail to do all I can to bring you happiness." She drank as well.

Her tears of joy brimmed over her eyes and splashed like bright crystals into the golden mead, the sound lost beneath the silver ripples of Fedelm's harp. Ailill raised his goblet.

"To Finnabair and Rochad, the gods witness: a long and happy marriage!"

Everyone echoed the toast, Finnabair's brothers shouting it out exuberantly. Even in her trance of gladness, Finnabair could not help cringing inside. The guards outside would hear, and the news could not be kept from the whole camp for long.

'It could not have been anyway; and even if the Munstermen pack up and turn straight for home now, we can probably be out of Ulster before Conchobar can rise and raise his army, before Rochad has to face my parents in battle'. A breath of cold air cut through the packed warmth of the tent, blowing the torch-flames into shivering smoky trails.

"A long and happy marriage," Connla said sarcastically through the open tent-flap. Rain dripped from the ends of his dark hair, and his silver circlet sat askew on his brow. He looked as though he had dressed in haste, and Finnabair saw the dark gleam of ring-mail at the neck of his silver-embroidered blue bratt.

"How sweet! One of my guards awoke me to tell me that there was something happening here, and I merely thought that you were leaving me out of some important council again. I did not guess that you were quietly shattering all the pledges you gave me, or that Finnabair was at her whoring once more." He shot a dark venomous glance at Rochad."

"Did you promise to murder the Hound of Ulster as he lies wounded? Or was there something else? Perhaps to stand as a rear-guard for the host of Eriu, lest Conchobar catch us on the way?"

Maeve's face reddened and she drew a deep breath. Ailill laid a hand on his wife's arm.

Finnabair thought her father meant to try to calm the angry under-king, but before Ailill could speak, Maine Cairbre burst in, his tender cheeks flushed with mead and high feeling.

"Yes, my sister is married to a better man than you, little weasel in the grass, you nightshade among the cress! And glad she is of it, that you will no longer be slinking about trying to buy her heart with trinkets, as if it were she you loved, and not the hope of becoming Connacht's king. Finnabair told us often enough how it sickened her to put up with your fawning and pawing. Now she is free of you, and I hope that we soon will be as well! If you don't like that, then draw your sword and meet me like a man."

Both in heart and in looks, save the fair mustaches marking his manhood, Cairbre might have been their mother in her youth, all fiery speech and readiness to fight, long yellow hair streaming loose from beneath his helmet like a scalloped mantle of golden silk. The words he had spoken were surely what Maeve would have said, had Ailill not restrained her.

Finnabair found herself shaking with anger, hoping with more ferocity than she had known was in her that her brother would kill Connla, as if all the shame and sorrow she had suffered could be washed away by the Munsterman's blood. Connla only turned his glare on Finnabair.

"Does this poor fool know how many men you lured to their deaths with that same wedding-cup, you lying bitch-whelp in heat? How many champions have passed through your friendly thighs already?

Nath Crantail and Fer Taidle; the sons of Búachaill and Lecc, of Durcride and Gabal, and all the others, Ferbáeth mac Firbend and even Cúr mac Da Lóth, whom all men loathed. Ferdiad as well: no doubt four men could go at once into the gate where he passed and not even touch the sides."

Finnabair stood up very straight, shaking with anger. She grabbed the silver pitcher of mead on the table, drawing her arm back to throw it at Connla. Cairbre was closer, and quicker; his left fist smashed into the Munster under-king's sharp face, knocking Connla out of Maeve's sight even as the Maine's sword appeared in his right hand.

"Guards, to me!" Connla shouted. "Munstermen, arise, to me! There is treachery here, the host's leaders have betrayed us!"

Like a tangle of dry branches bursting suddenly into flame, the shouting arose all around the royal tents. Finnabair realized, horribly, that Connla had not come alone. Maeve was already grabbing for her helmet and shoving it onto her head, snatching up her shield while Finnabair's brothers scrambled for the spears that lay by one wall of the tent. The cries and sounds of fighting outside were rising to a thunderous rumble as the Munstermen shouted their under-king's words.

"Guard Finnabair and Fedelm!" Maeve panted, even as the sound of rending cloth and leather came from one side of the tent, then another. "Get them in the middle, stand around them."

Flidais had managed to get one of Maeve's heavy thrusting spears. There was no room inside for her to turn its length, but as the first Munsterman burst through the hole he had made, she drove the bronze butt-knob into his face with all the power of her heavy shoulders and sturdy hips.

The little bones shattered with a dry-twig crackling, and he dropped like a sack of grain. On the other side, Fergus brought his wooden club-sword down brutally to smash another man's sword-arm even as Cormac ran the attacker through with a slender casting-spear.

'Thank all the gods it is raining, they cannot fire the tent', Finnabair thought, half-paralyzed with terror.

Then she saw one side sagging, and realized that their foes could still cut the ropes and catch all of them like so many badgers in a bag. She pointed, crying out wordlessly; Ailill glanced up.

"Get out of the tent!" He shouted. The fighters gathered in a tight knot around the two unarmed women. Her father did not bother with the tent flap, where most of Connla's men would surely be waiting; two quick slashes of his sword opened the side where the first attacker had come in, and they burst out the side into the rainy darkness.

"Connacht, to us!" Maeve called, her voice cutting high and clear through the sounds of fighting; and Finnabair heard Fergus' bass roar, "Ulster, to me! Ulster, to Connacht; Munster are our foes!"

A knot of shadowy shapes lit by a single waving torch was running towards them. Finnabair could only huddle close to Fedelm and watch as Maeve, Cairbre, and Dáire crouched to brace their shields, meeting the attackers' rush and stopping it dead. Then attackers and defenders were pressed shield to shield, and Finnabair could see nothing beyond the backs of her protectors save the red glints of blades in the torchlight.

All she could do was huddle next to Fedelm, praying for her brothers and parents who stood between her and the foe and hoping that the ban-drúi's inviolability would protect both of them if the Munstermen broke through. She heard the cries and muffled grunts, the crashing of shields and swords and the axe like thudding of weapons biting deep into flesh, and trembled in terror. Then her brothers moved forward. Finnabair could see that Maeve was still up, and there were no more enemies in front of them, but Fergus was shouting a little distance away.

Armed only with his wooden sword and a large silver platter he had snatched from the table with Finnabair's bride-wealth, he was battering his way through another small group of attackers with simple, brutal efficiency while Rochad, who had managed to grab a sword and shield from one of the fallen, guarded his back.

Finnabair had never seen Rochad fight: the younger man's lanky limbs moved with surprising grace, whirling and lashing like tree-branches in a storm. 'O, he is beautiful!. She thought, her terror forgotten for a moment. 'And he is coming to keep me safe'. Every one of Fergus' swift blows cracked hard into a Munsterman's arm or shoulder or head. 'Why is he using a wooden sword?' Finnabair wondered.

Those Fergus struck on the limbs fell back cursing and clutching useless broken arms; those he hit on the helms wavered limp-jointed and half-stunned, and where he struck a head, that man dropped, skull shattered as lethally as if Fergus had wielded an edged weapon.

The Ulster exile was using the battered plate to parry with, though Finnabair saw it flash as he whipped the edge across one man's eyes, until Rochad won a little space to toss Fergus his shield and grab up another one from the ground.

Fergus called something to his countryman that Finnabair could not hear; Rochad turned and leapt back towards the women's group in two great bounds, but Fergus dodged aside from a spear's thrust, lowered his shield-shoulder and rammed his way through the wicker ring. Blood sheeted down Rochad's slashed cheek; he panted,

"He's going to gather the exiles," and stepped in front of Finnabair with his shield overlapping Cairbre's.

The sound of children squalling split the air; Finnabair turned and saw Fedelm's friend Suithchern with her two babes stumbling to join herself and the ban-drúi, the Druid's mute guard taking his place in the shield-fort next to Dáire.Finnabair thought the fighting was still spreading, a ceaseless roaring and smashing in her ears.

Above the sounds of men's cries and clashing weapons, a great deep bellow shattered the night: the Brown Bull was calling out in rage. Then all the warriors in front of them were shouting,

"Maeve, Maeve!" The defenders lowered their weapons. As far as Finnabair could tell, there were only Connacht's fighters left alive in the wreckage of the enclosure. All the tents had been felled, the wicker fence smashed to pieces.

"What is happening outside?" Maeve asked.

"Fergus is rallying those loyal to us, Leinster and Meath, the Ulster exiles and the Galeoin," a woman's husky voice gasped. Finnabair recognized the voice and the short wiry silhouette:

Ailbhe, the leader of one of Connacht's smaller troops. "It's dark madness out there, trying to fight in night and rain, but the Munstermen seemed nearly as surprised as the rest of us."

"Ailbhe, you and your men stay here, just give me five of them," the queen ordered. "Cairbre and Dáire, you come with us; the rest of you, get your armor on and protect Finnabair and Fedelm. Anyone who is hurt, let Fedelm see to your wounds. Come on, move!"

"Maeve!" Ailill shouted. "Armour up first!. Finnabair's mother was already running, sons and guardsmen hastening to catch up with her.

"Gods curse it, Maeve!" Ailill sighed, staring after his wife as she disappeared into the darkness; then, under his breath,

"If you had any sense..." Her father straightened, speaking louder.

"Well, boys, you heard the queen: armor up! Rochad, take Connla's hauberk, it's the least of what he owes you for this, but I think we'll have trouble getting more out of him now." Ailill laughed grimly, an unusual note of anger clashing in the sound.

"Guards, if we have any wounded out here, pull them back for Fedelm to tend."

"Rochad's wounded!" Finnabair said.

Her husband, my husband! Turned to her, his teeth gleaming through the blood that covered his face.

"It's only a little cut, nothing to worry about. You can see to it when we're sure you're safe."

You're still bleeding, Finnabair thought, anguished. Still, she had been told often enough that if she wouldn't learn to fight, then all she could do when fighting came to her was help the wounded and not interfere with the warriors.

Finnabair waited with the ban-drúi and her friend behind the shield-fort of Ailbhe's troop while her father, husband, and brothers armoured up, taking it in turn with the Connacht woman's fighters to guard the three unarmed women and get a tent raised. She could only see flickers of torchlight glimmering from the occasional silhouettes of men and blades past where the wicker fence had been. The shouts of "Munster!" And "Connla!" And "Cumail!" Were already fading, overwhelmed by the roaring of Leinster and Meath, Connacht and Fergus' followers. The Brown Bull bellowed once more, his great voice drowning all the warriors' cries; and Finnabair thought she heard a note of triumph, as if he had just battered down a mighty rival.

'At least he is safe; the Munstermen would not have risked killing such a great prize'. By the time Ailill's tent was up, the fighting around the royal enclosure had stopped entirely and Maeve's maidservants Fearbh and Liadain had crept out of hiding. Ailill set the women to sewing up the rents in Maeve's tent while Fedelm's mute guard fetched the ban-drúi's medicines. Then, at last, Finnabair could tend to the slash on Rochad's cheek.

She supposed it was a slight wound, as warriors thought of such things, but when she washed it with the concoction Fedelm gave her, she could see the white gleam of bone below the red meat before the blood welled again. Finnabair gritted her teeth and kept working.

'The free-running blood will help wash it clean, if too much be not lost', her mother had told her. She could hardly bear to push the ban-drúi's fine needle through her beloveds skin, but though Rochad closed his eyes, he showed no other sign of pain. 'Like sewing a fine garment', she reminded herself, each stitch pulling the edges of the gaping cut close together. There would be a scar, and she would always remember that her husband's first act of their wedding had been to fight without armor in deathly battle to protect her. Finnabair's brothers had taken a few cuts as well, but nothing too serious. Ceat was the worst-wounded, with a deep slash running the length of his left biceps, but Fedelm assured him that he would mend.

"The cut goes along the grain of the muscle: nothing worth mentioning was severed. Don't use the arm until I say you can, and put this salve on four times a day to keep it from festering." Ailill had gotten a nasty blow from a spear-haft or shield-edge to the side of his knee, and when Fedelm had sewn up the various slices, she took the king's trousers off and propped his leg on the table to rub salve into it.

Finnabair blinked. The ban-drúi's slow caressing touch on her father's body made her wonder. She could hardly imagine the self-collected Druid lying with any man, but Fedelm stroked Ailill like a lover, and he looked down at her so tenderly, though his eyes kept flickering towards the tent-flap, and Finnabair knew that he was desperately worried about her mother. Then, completely without warning, Finnabair found herself crying hysterically and shaking. Rochad's arms were about her in a moment, his shaggy brown hair falling half over her face as he rested his unwounded cheek against her head and murmured to her.

"It's all right, it's all right, Finnabair. Your mother is a great warrior, with her folk about her; no harm will come to her."

Finnabair huddled close to her husband. She was shivering with cold, but she could feel the warmth of his body under the looted ring-mail, 'the least Connla owes us, indeed! Rochad held her and caressed her, whispering quietly until her shakes began to ease. In a little time, Maeve came back in with Cairbre and Dáire behind her. Finnabair breathed a deep sigh of relief: all three were bloody from fighting, but none showed any sign of being wounded. Maeve looked at Finnabair and smiled.

"Rochad, maybe you should take your bride to your own tent for a time. I will give you a chariot to bear her home in, but I think that Finnabair needs rest and comfort, and none can give her that better than you."

"I hope so," Rochad said. "Come, Finnabair. The bloodshed and danger are past now; let us see what joy we can find in their wake."

Finnabair's own little tent had been raised and cleaned, with a fresh torch lighting the neatly arranged bed, and Flidais' golden bowl sitting beside the little keg of wedding-mead on the table beside it. Rochad did not hasten to undress, but drew Finnabair down to sit on the bed beside him, filling the bowl and passing it to her. She sipped deeply, the mead's golden glow calming the last of her shakes, then raised her face to meet Rochad's warm lips.

Her new husband kissed and stroked Finnabair slowly and gently, until it seemed entirely natural to slip off her bratt, and Rochad bent to let his ring-mail slither into a jingling heap on the floor. Only two layers of linen parted the tips of Finnabair's breasts from her husband's hard lean chest, and she was moving her hands under Rochad's tunic to lift it from his body when she suddenly burst into tears again. 'If he knew'

She had never touched any man so closely, but the number of times she had lightly brushed against a victim, like Ferdiad, in order to lure him, arouse him...

"Finnabair, what is it?" Rochad asked. "Are you? This was your first sight of fighting close-to, wasn't it? If you only want me to hold you, I will. We shall have plenty of time together, all our lives, I hope."

Finnabair shook her head, not trusting her voice. She wanted to embrace him fully, to hold him within herself as though their bodies could never be parted. it seemed to her that the reproachful ghosts of the men who had gone to the ford for her sake whispered her guilt all around the tent, and "You could have been killed!" She burst out. "You could have been killed, and it would have been my fault, like all the others..."

Rochad held her as she sobbed out her grief and guilt, telling him of each man she had brought to his death.

"Connla, even him, I hated him, but he died because of me after all. Because I had to lead him on, to win his warriors for our raid. If not for me, he wouldn't even have been there, he wouldn't..."

Finnabair's husband waited, stroking her gently until she had finished and sat snuffling in his arms.

"What a cruel thing for your parents to have to do to you," Rochad murmured. "Can you wonder, that I was so glad when you said you had no desire to be queen in Cruachan after your mother?

It is hard enough to command a troop in battle, to know that however well you array your forces, some of your own will die at your word all the same. To rule a province, that would be beyond me."

"You don't hate me for it?" Finnabair asked. "Others will say, as Connla did, that I whored myself although I never gave my body, and if one of them had killed the Hound, I would have had to. My parents wanted me to wed Ferdiad, I could not have gotten out of it."

"Hush, my love. You did what you had to, at great cost to yourself, out of love and loyalty to your kin. How should I think the less of you for it. I am glad that I can bear you away from such sorrows now, if you will be content to dwell in a small chieftain's hill-fort with a man who bears no great fame and can claim no mighty hero's deeds."

"I wish nothing more," Finnabair said, and kissed Rochad again. Then it was easy to strip away the layers of linen between them, to run her hands over his long lean-muscled body and arch into his soft caresses.

Though, as older women had often warned her, his first thrust into her was a sharp pang of pain, Rochad held still until her body eased, then moved slowly and carefully until Finnabair found herself moving with him and softly crying out his name.

Fedelm

The battle with the under-kings of Munster cost us most of a day's travel, and close to a tenth of our host dead or too wounded to fight. It was not as bad as it might have been, for Connla had died in the fighting around the royal enclosure, and Cumail had been slain trying to steal or kill the Brown Bull, so that many of the Munstermen had given over quickly. Much as it grated me to admit it, Fergus had played the largest part in that, by rallying the loyal hosts so quickly and thoroughly that they could fall on the Munster camps in at least a half-ordered mass. Nevertheless, we were slowed at a time when we could ill-afford it. We were still well within Ulster on the eve of Imbolc, and that night, I dreamed.

I saw a short man with long dark hair and the massive shoulders and chest of a blacksmith hastening through the first gates of a great fort, shouting, "Men murdered, women stolen, cattle raided!" He gave his first cry from the slope of the hill above the outer palisade; the second within the inner ring of logs that circled the hill's height, and the third from the mound that stood beside the king's great hall itself. It seemed to me that, beneath his pointed dark beard, he bore a certain resemblance to Cú Chulainn, though his features were rough and heavy, dirtied with ingrained coal and scattered with the tiny burn-scars of flying sparks: this, then, must be Sualdam, the Hound's earthly father.

No one answered, even when he stepped within the great hall itself. There, though there were many warriors within and a few women nervously bringing them food and drink, all was silent. Now I saw Conchobar for the first time. He was sitting in his high seat like a propped wicker man. His long craggy face was pale as death, drawn and haggard, the bruised lids drooping over his eyes; though his fair hair was neatly plaited, the braids bound with gold and held back from his forehead with a gold diadem made of swirl-embossed rondels riveted to a slim band, it was dull as though a scattering of grey ashes had just been cast over it.

For all his cloak of many-striped silk and huge gold brooch, his silken tunic of gold-embroidered purple and the massive gold bracelets on his wrists, he looked less like a king in his power than a man who had long lain in bed with a terrible crab gnawing his entrails. However unwillingly, I had felt compassion for Cú Chulainn, even in my dreams.

I felt none for Conchobar, and even less as he glared down at the smith who had come to bring him the ill tidings, then glanced at the man who stood beside him. As Cathbad had warned Cú Chulainn of me, Calatín had warned me of Cathbad. I recognized the old Druid at once. Like Calatín, he was lean, tall, and stern-faced, but there the resemblance ended. Where Calatín had been wiry and strong, still moving with a warrior's ease even in his sixties, Cathbad looked like a white robe draped over a frame of sticks to scare the birds, and leaned upon a carved stick that burned too brightly for me to see its graven shapes.

He was older than Calatín had been, his face seamed with a deep tracery of wrinkles, and his broad white mustaches did not hide the harsh furrows about his mouth, the marks of a man whose face had set in a frown of disapproval or anger for far too long. His hair was altogether white and very thin, sleeked closely to his pale scalp, and there was something disquietingly adder-like about the way his narrow head moved on his long neck as he met his king's glance, then tapped his stick sharply on the floor.

At that, every head in the room came up, though the warriors all seemed as pale and ravaged-looking as the king himself. I had heard that no man in Emain Macha was allowed to speak before Conchobar, and that even he must wait upon the Druids. I had never quite believed it; but now I saw it for myself.

Cathbad's voice came out as a rough hiss. "Who is robbing and stealing and plundering?"

"Ailill and Maeve of Connacht, with the knowledge and aid of Fergus mac Roech. Cú Chulainn, "and here I heard the lift of a father's pride in Sualdam's voice, though mingled with grief and desperate worry, "has harried and held them through the three months of winter, that they not escape your vengeance and bear our treasures and cattle and women away. He is grievously wounded, and can fight no longer. Arise, now O king, and make good your champion's striving and trials and suffering!"

Cathbad looked at him as if he were a turd floating to the top of a cauldron of simmering herbs.

"This man," he said coldly, "is annoying the king. By rights, he should be put to death."

"It would be fitting," whispered Conchobar, his voice almost a moan. I could see the echoes of the great and long pain he had suffered; but I felt no pity for him. His weary gaze swept over the hall.

"It would," the pale and worn warriors there chorused raggedly. Several of them surrounded Sualdam, grasping him by the elbows and shoving him to the door. His mouth gaped open in disbelief; he seemed too stunned to protest or struggle, although he looked hale and they were clearly weak.

Cathbad tapped his staff on the hard-packed earth of the floor, and they halted at once.

"Still, what Sualdam says is true. The hosts of Eriu have been overrunning our land throughout the winter."

Slowly a muttering began in the hall, the low susurrus rising quickly as anger brought a little color back to the white faces of the men who had so lately crawled from their pain-beds. Conchobar lifted his hand, and the hall fell silent again.

"What's all this uproar?" He said.

Though his voice was still weak and rough from long screaming, there was still a certain calm strength beneath its hoarseness.

"Have they not still got the sea before them, the sky overhead, and the earth underneath? And unless the sea rises to whelm us, or the stars fall shattered from the sky upon us, or the earth cracks open to swallow us, I shall beat them in battle; I shall bring every cow back to its byre, and every woman back to her hearth."

His voice gained power as he spoke, and he no longer slumped in his seat, but sat straight, blue eyes blazing angrily from his haggard face.

"Rise up, and call to me my loyal warriors! Call Deda from his bay, and Laegaire the honey-mouthed from his hearth; call Laeg from his causeway and Gemen from his valley; call Senall Uathach the Hideous and Cúscraid Menn the Stammerer. Call..."

I heard no more, for then Cathbad looked straight at me. His green-flecked hazel eyes, smooth and cold as ocean-pebbles, caught my gaze. The corner of his mouth turned up; he raised his stave, its brilliance darkening to a red-shot cloud of violet light. I knew that I could not withstand that blow. I fled swift as I could, hearing the storm of his power thundering after me.

By luck or my own strength, only the edge of it caught me; but that was enough to tumble me dizzy and wild for a moment before I could catch at my own body, clinging to it as if I were tosse. Drowning in a river's full flood and it were an overhanging tree-branch, a solid rescue by which I could pull myself back to earth and safety. I woke sitting bolt upright, my own cry still echoing in my ears as the two babes woke and began to scream in chorus. I heard Suithchern and Eochaid bumping about for a few moments; then Eochaid had a torch kindled.

"Give her some oatcakes and honey, quickly," Suithchern ordered above the crying of Conall and Clothra as she joggled one of them on each hip. "Fedelm, what have you seen? What is happening?"

"Conchobar has arisen, and the hosts of Ulster are gathering," I said. "I think we shall have to do battle with them, after all."

Maeve

Maeve stood on a hilltop at the edge of the plain of Meath with Ailill and Fergus beside her, looking down at the hosts of Eriu and Ulster. Conchobar's warriors had traveled fast and light, unburdened by the wagons and servants and herds of Maeve's host. It would not be enough for her army to escape Ulster: Conchobar would have battle. The emissaries of Ulster had come yesterday, agreeing on the ground where they would fight and swearing truce until morning.

Maeve suspected that they were also seeking to discover where she kept the Brown Bull. She had already sent him ahead with fifty of his heifers and a troop of herdsmen and guards; and if any of those folk thought it strange that she had spoken to the great beast as though he were a champion or fellow king, telling him the roundabout route through hill and wood to Cruachan and warning him of the dangers that might lie on the road, they had held their silence. The two armies were drawn up with bare brown winter ground between them.

Maeve had her own reserves and rear-guard hidden behind the hills on her side, and she did not doubt that Conchobar had the same; but for the most part, it would be a straightforward battle.

And, as the deep music of the trumpas and booming drums roared out over the plain, echoing from hill to hill,

Maeve felt suddenly glad. She had tried as best she could to avoid this fight, but now that it was before her, she could feel the blood rushing hot and tingling through her veins, her hand eager to grip the hilt of her sword.

The rain had halted, but great white-gray boulders of cloud still tumbled across the sky, driven by the same strong wind that set Maeve's crimson bratt fluttering about her shoulders and whetted her face with its damp cold. Bronze and gold and steel flashed as the sun's morning light came and went through the fast-moving clouds; the warriors' cloaks were an array of bright colors, blue and purple, crimson and yellow and green, like a meadow in full summer flower.

'I see them crimson with blood; I see them bathed in red'. Fedelm's words, haunting as the faint music of a bone flute above the earthshaking blast of trumpas and rumble of drums, came back to Maeve, a keen chill stroking down her spine. Now it was time to fight: if need be, to die. If she had good fortune, Conchobar would lie in his cairn by the time the sun rose again tomorrow.

"Now, Fergus," Maeve said, "it is time for you to take your place. For the vengeance you owe Conchobar, you shall stand in the fore at the center of the host, while Ailill takes the eastern wing and Flidais the western."

Fergus drew the broken stub of his wooden sword from his scabbard.

"I shall gladly do as you say in this. If I am to strike down Conchobar, I shall need a better weapon."

Maeve looked at Ailill. Her husband's eyes were wide, the sunlight glimmering from the narrow blue-green rims around his black swollen pupils as though it struck through clear shallow water; and though he turned his gaze on her, Maeve was not sure that he really saw her. Ailill often laughed as he sparred, sometimes even as he fought in earnest. More often when he held an edged weapon, he seemed to become a different being altogether, not through a warp-spasm like the Hound of Ulster; more like a Druid's trance, his human mind elsewhere as his body whirled and struck by deep instinct. Ailill shook himself, his pupils contracting slightly.

"Cuillius," he called to his charioteer who waited behind them, "bring me that flesh-piercing sword. I swear, by the gods of my clan, that if its bloom has faded since the day I gave it to you in Ulster, not all of Eriu will save you from me!"

Cuillius reached down into the bottom of the chariot to withdraw a long bundle, leaping down and trotting over to his king.

"If you can find one flaw or speck of rust upon it, then I deserve to leave my head on the ground right here!" He replied.

Ailill unwrapped the wool, looking carefully at the sword. It seemed to Maeve that she could see the keenness of its silver edges from where she stood, the blade polished as if it had come fresh-made from the smithy. The gold-bound bronze man whose head and arms formed the pommel, body the grip, and spread legs the quillions, glittered and seemed to wink in the sunlight, as though he, too, were eager for the fight. Fergus closed his hand reverently about the hilt, holding the blade aloft, then bringing it suddenly down to slice through the air with a singing hiss.

"You have kept it well, at least. Now you shall see its worth, and the worth of my aid!"

Maeve, Ailill, and Fergus mounted into their chariots. The horses neighed, pawing the ground, and then they were off, bearing the host's leaders to their places. As Maeve had said, Fergus was in the front line, beside Cormac and his purple-cloaked champions.

She herself was in the middle of the center: from her chariot, she could see above the heads of her warriors and judge what was happening, and should she be needed in the fighting, she could leap down and take her place in the fore.

The Mainí would fight with their father and the Leinstermen that day; the center was largely made up of Connachtmen and Ulster's exiles, those who had the most cause to hate Conchobar. Conchobar's trumpas and drums fell silent for a moment, and Maeve's followed.

She saw the flash of Conchobar's bronze standard, and lifted her own gilded pine-marten's pole from the socket that held it at the corner of her chariot, flourishing it high above her head. The trumpas roared once more, a single deafening blast; the armies rolled towards each other. As always, the first clash was shockingly loud, the shouting of thousands of warriors almost lost beneath the hammering clamor of swords on shields.

Maeve kept her shield high against stray sling-balls, turning her head from side to side. As they had planned, the right and left wings were spreading wide and curving forward, forcing the sides of Conchobar's host to turn and face them. The center was holding hard, and then Fergus, in the middle of the front line, pressed forward. He had dropped his shield, holding his sword in his two hands, and even in the midst of the battle, Maeve had a moment to be awed by his skill.

As Fergus had said, the thrilling feats of a young man were long behind him: now he made no move that was not deadly, shifting his body just enough to let the strokes of his foes pass by him; and each time his weapon whirled to knock another blade aside, it ended by biting into another man's flesh. Cormac, beside him, was a deadly whirlwind of slashing steel, his height and reach serving him well in this close fighting where he could strike easily over and past the heads of his companions.

Ulster had put their best to the fore as well, and though Fergus and Cormac were wreaking a deadly slaughter, they could not quite break through the solid lines of men. Maeve threw back her head, her long golden braid whipping against her armored back, and laughed as her own battle-wildness rose to her head like a draught of winter mead. Sword in her right hand, shield in her left, she said to Munremur,

"Take me to the front!"

Her chariot lurched forward, spear-armed warriors parting around it. A few lines from the fighting, she leapt down, pushing her way in beside Fergus and Cormac. Now none could stand against them.

The shock of her blade biting through flesh and bone, the heavy blows landing on her own shield, sang thrillingly up Maeve's arms, urging her onward. Hot blood splattered her face, salty-sweet in her mouth, the sharp coppery scent filling her lungs with every breath, and she cried out in wordless exaltation as another warrior's helm shattered loudly beneath her sword's fine Gaulish steel. The Ulstermen were backing away now, and Maeve charged forward again, driving them back. It seemed to her that she could feel each of her warriors as if they were all part of her body, pounding into the Ulstermen again and again. Three times she surged forward, and thrice they retreated.

Then they fell back further, the shields opening to let the spear men through. A silver hail of javelins hissed through the air; one banged off Maeve's helmet, showering bright sparks through her skull, and another screamed gratingly across the linked iron rings over her right shoulder. Now Maeve was facing a wall of spears, and even in her battle-frenzy, she knew she must fall back and let her own javelins and slingers deal with the unshielded warriors. Maeve shouted her own advancing spears forward, and retreated through them, leaping into her chariot again.

As she looked over the field, the blood drying on her face cracked away from her grin: Conchobar's standard had moved forward, almost to the front of his own host. His spear men and javelin-casters had pulled back to let the shields close once more; but Conchobar was taking the field now, Fergus chopping his way grimly through to meet him.

Only a few men stood between them, and not for long. Maeve cursed, realizing that she would never make her way through in time to aid Fergus, 'but so long as Conchobar dies, it is enough! And', though she was loath to admit it, 'he has a better claim than I'. Now Fergus and Conchobar stood face to face. The other warriors had drawn away from both of them, leaving a clear space in the middle of the battle. Those closest had stopped fighting to watch, though they held their weapons in readiness.

Fergus struck at Conchobar, so swiftly his blade seemed a shining silver fan. Conchobar's gold-adorned shield boomed like a drum as Fergus drove him back, the blows rumbling through the sounds of combat. Great warrior that he was, Conchobar was not even trying to strike back, but he defended himself so ably that not a single one of Fergus' deadly strokes got through. As if by some silent agreement, Fergus suddenly took a pace back, calling out to his foe.

"What man of Ulster holds that shield before a rightful king?"

"A better man than you," Conchobar answered.

His voice was deeper and hoarser than Maeve remembered, but it still held the same sharp edge, a tonality that grated across her nerves like a rasp drawn hard over bare skin. Once that voice had echoed through her nightmares; now she held tight to the hilt of her sword, cursing the chances of battle and fate that kept her from plunging through her own lines to strike at him.

"One who drove you out into exile to live with wild dogs and foxes; one who will stop you with all his battle-deeds today before all the men of Eriu."

Fergus leapt at Conchobar again, whirling his sword in great two-handed strokes that set the gold-wrought shield booming and shivering once more. Again, Conchobar managed to fend off every blow, until Fergus hammered his pommel hard into the top of the Ulster king's shield, driving it back into Conchobar's face as Fergus hooked his heel behind the taller man's knee. Conchobar fell, and Fergus lifted his sword for the final stroke. Then Cormac leapt towards Fergus from behind. He had dropped his weapons; he grabbed Fergus' wrists in both hands.

Maeve's eyes squinted tight shut for a heartbeat, her whole body convulsing in dismay as her son, and Conchobar's, called,

"Ulster's honor shall not be cast off today! Leave us, Conchobar: this man will pour out his rage on Ulstermen no more."

Fergus cried out, a great horrible roar of anguish that shattered through all the sounds of battle. He wrenched free of Cormac's grip as Conchobar rolled to his feet, and drove his blade down at the earth before him with all his strength as though his foe still lay there, his sword sinking its full length into the ground. Fergus dragged it loose and hacked down again and again, screaming all the while. Then Conchobar was gone, vanished back into his own lines. 'I should have known better than to put Cormac in the front by Fergus, Maeve thought despairingly. The boy-troop of Emain Macha was too much for him. Though he bears Conchobar little love, how should I have expected him to stand by and watch his father slain?' As if a síde-spell of timelessness had suddenly broken, the warriors who had stilled their combat to watch the duel between the two royal men of Ulster began to strike at each other again.

Fergus got his sword up barely in time to slice through the shaft of a spear that darted at him from the left; then he was driving Conchobar's line back once more. Maeve turned her head, looking at the flanks of her army. Flidais's line was holding solid on the west, keeping Conchobar's warriors bound up on that side. Ailill seemed harder-pressed: he had drawn his forces into a tight block, shields overlapped before the thrusting-spears and javelins arching over their heads from behind.

Maeve thought that Conchobar's eastern wing had no more chance of getting through than a dog had of pushing its nose through a hedgehog's spikes, not unless Conchobar turned his entire army in that direction and overran them with brute numbers.

Fergus was hacking through the Ulster line thrice as ferociously as before, and Cormac was right beside him, as if he could lose the memory of what had just happened in the fierceness of the fight. Maeve was not surprised when Conchobar's men drew away from the two exiles, but she was surprised when she saw the Ulster line part to let a chariot through, and heard a low voice shouting above the battle-din. At first she could not make out the words, and Fergus paid no attention, turning to the side to charge at his enemies again. Then she heard the chariot's rider clearly.

"Come here, friend Fergus!" He shouted. "I swear by Ulster's gods, I'll churn you like foam in a pool; I'll batter you as easily as a loving woman slaps her son!"

Fergus drew back.

"What man in Eriu speaks to me like that?" He cried angrily, his voice a horrible hoarse rasp.

"Cú Chulainn, Sualdam's son and Conchobar's sister-son. Give way before me now, Fergus!"

Fergus lowered his sword slowly. Maeve strained her ears, just barely able to tell what he was saying. "I swore to do that."

"It has fallen due," Cú Chulainn answered.

Fergus' shoulders heaved. "As you say. You gave way to me then; and now you are bloody and weak with wounds. I shall give way now – but you, my foster son, go back to your rest, and heal!"

Fergus turned and walked away as Cú Chulainn drove back, the Ulster lines closing behind his chariot. Although Fergus' sword was down, and the clumsiest fighter might easily have run him through, no sword struck nor spear jabbed at him: he seemed to walk through the battle in his own island of peace.

"What, by Crom Cruaich, was that?" Maeve asked Fergus when he halted beside her chariot.

The Ulster exile coughed, spitting a gobbet of blood-tinged froth onto the trampled brown grass.

"The price for what you asked me to do, when you sent me to meet Cú Chulainn at the ford. He yielded to me, though I bore only a sword of wood and would not lift even that against him. I swore that I would give way before him some time when he was bloody and riddled with wounds. At least he will take no more part in the battle: you can be glad of that much."

On the last words, Fergus' croak failed altogether, and he lifted his hand towards his throat. Maeve had skins of water and watered mead in her chariot. She gave him the mead now, and he drank deeply, though she wondered if his voice would ever be the same. Though it seemed as if only moments had passed since the battle began, the Sun was near her noonday height. Ailill's tight formation was still defending itself effectively, though it could do no more. Flidais' line was starting to curve inward as Ulster's weight bore to the west. Armies move to the right, Maeve thought, and turned to the men arrayed behind her.

"Ruirec, Bresal, and Aed, take your troops west to support Flidais – hurry! Laegaire, take your fighters and call Coirpre and his troop from the reserves, then form a wedge and go to the east; I want you to break through to relieve Ailill: he is still hard-pressed."

Maeve's belly tightened in a sudden cramp, but she ignored it. It was no strange thing, for a fighter's body to try to empty itself in the midst of a battle. There were many warriors, and some of them great champions, who came out of every victory with soiled breech clouts. Though Cormac could not press onward without Fergus beside him, he and his men were holding the front line solid. That was well, for Maeve had sent as many fighters to the relief of her wings as she could possibly spare. Still, Flidais' line was straightening again with the weight of the reinforcements, while the troops assailing Ailill's walking fortress were scattering beneath the wedge of Laegaire and Coirpre's men, struggling to regroup in bunches. This time, the cramp that racked Maeve was a monstrous bolt of pain through her belly. She clutched herself, bending over; an acid line of spew etched its way up her throat, dribbling from her lips. She could only shudder and wait for it to ease.

'Poison?' She thought, spitting and grasping for her water skin to rinse the foul taste from her mouth. That was unlikely. Bad water, or dried meat that had gone off.' Brigid grant that it is only I who got it, and not anyone else, or our host will melt before Ulster like frost in the sun!'

The third cramp sent an echoing pain shuddering down between Maeve's legs, the petals of her female parts aching as though someone had given them a sudden brutal squeeze, the way Conchobar had sometimes done.

Then she felt the wetness soaking through her breech clout, and knew what was happening. Often a woman's courses would stop and start again several times before her womb dried altogether. Now Maeve's, though two months delayed, were on her once more.

Slowly Maeve's womb unclenched; but her bladder was throbbing like a great swollen boil in the depths of her body. 'I can't turn away while my folk are doing battle! She cried silently. Brigid and Morrígan, help me now! Help me hold this off, so I can do my duty as queen and war leader!' No answer came, and when the next cramp racked her, Maeve leaned over the edge of her chariot and moaned, pressing her thighs tight together to keep her piss from spurting out. Bitter as the realization was, she knew she could no longer hold the command.

"Fergus," she moaned, "my courses are on me. You must take over here, until I can come back."

Fergus looked up at her, his sweat-drenched face twisting as if to echo the pain on her own.

"By the gods, you have picked a bad time for this!" He croaked.

"I can't help it!" Maeve shouted at him. "Choose someone else to be your voice to the army; but by all the oaths you swore me, and any love you ever bore me, you must hold here now."

Fergus stared at her for a moment, grey eyes wild and haunted, like the gaze of a broken-winged hawk staring up at a cliff's rocky heights.

"Go," he rasped. "I will hold."

Maeve managed to keep herself upright until her chariot had rounded the hill where the rear guard waited.

Then she curled into a ball in the bottom of the vehicle, pressing her lips tightly to keep from crying aloud. She had never felt such pain from her courses before, only a little cramping and tightness, but Finnabair often suffered greatly when the moon-tide was on her; and perhaps it was no surprise, after the long delay.

"What's wrong with the queen?" Voices were asking. "Is she wounded, get her out, let the ban-drúi see to her!"

Strong hands lifted Maeve out of the chariot. She staggered away, squatting to pull up her skirts and tear off her blood-soaked breech clout. Piss spouted out of her in a great hot river, foaming over the dead grass, and she gasped in relief, until the cruel talons clenched within her again, and she could only moan.

Then a small warm hand grasped hers. Squinting up through her haze of pain, Maeve thought at first that Finnabair had come to the battle with Rochad and somehow made it to the Connacht rearguard.

The young woman's streaming hair was more gold than pale, her eyes blue-grey beneath dark brows; and as Maeve's vision cleared, she recognized Fedelm's face.

"I thought, I told you to stay well back from the battlefield," she gasped.

"Hush, hush now," Fedelm crooned. "Hold onto me, I know it hurts."

"Can you give me something? I have to get back, I cannot leave my warriors to fight without me."

Fedelm shook her head, her delicate features sadly compassionate.

"No, it must all come out. Your other commanders are skilled enough to win the victory, or at least hold until you are able to return."

Maeve tried to keep from crushing Fedelm's slim soft fingers in her own sword-callused hand as the next cramp racked her body. Fedelm drew a sharp breath, but squeezed back with all her strength. It seemed they held each other a very long time, while the pain wrenched Maeve's entrails in great crushing waves.

'I would rather have been wounded, Maeve thought vaguely. Only giving birth ever hurt like this.' Wave by wave, the tide of agony slowly began to ebb, and the roaring of blood in Maeve's ears to give way to the sounds of battle beyond the hill. As she recognized the noises, it seemed to her that the shouting and clanging were suddenly closer than they should be. Blinking her eyes back into focus, Maeve looked around. A small troop of Ulster's men had somehow gotten around the main host; behind Maeve, her rearguard were all fighting. Before her loomed a chariot glittering with bronze and silver and gold, drawn by two huge stallions, one grey and one black.

The slight beardless youth who stood behind the driver held a silver-bound spear upraised, ready to drive it down at her. Her shield was gone; she scrabbled at her sword-hilt with nerveless fingers, but her hand lacked the strength to draw it, and the cramps still racked her so hard that she could not stand or even roll aside.

'Conchobar has no female warriors, he does not let his women fight, she thought dizzily. How unfair, that I should be killed by a boy too young for battle.' Then Fedelm stepped between Maeve and the chariot's rider, gold-inlaid weaving rod upraised and white robe gleaming bright in the sunlight. The spear point shifted, aiming at the ban-drúi's breast.

"Out of my way!" The youth ordered, his voice surprisingly deep and clear. Maeve knew she had heard that low voice before, but could not remember where. "I have killed Druids before!"

"Hold your hand, and lower your spear, Cú Chulainn!" Fedelm cried.

Maeve drew a deep breath, pressing both hands hard against the racking pangs of her womb, and looked up into her foe's face. It was little wonder, she thought through her daze of pain, that she had mistaken Ulster's champion for a maiden. Cú Chulainn was no taller than Fedelm, and, save for the breadth of his shoulders, no more heavily built. His blue-grey eyes blazed like storm-clouds with white lightning flaring within; but the ban-fili met his gaze with equal fierceness, her own eyes like polished steel flashing back the hot blue of a summer sky. Though Fedelm's hair was golden and the thin braids that hung in a curtain beneath Cú Chulainn's helm were dark, Maeve realized in astonishment that they could almost have been brother and sister.

The same triangular face and delicate features, the same sharp-arched black eyebrows, and it seemed to her that the same halo of unearthly brightness hovered around them both, as if they had just stepped from the depths of a síd onto the green earth.

"It is only fair that I slay Maeve now, for all the harm and sorrow her pride has brought to myself and my land," Cú Chulainn answered. "Again I say, step aside!"

"I shall not!" Fedelm said. Though she held no sword, only her glittering weaving-rod, a chill ran through Maeve's fevered body as she stared up at the young woman. Earlier, seeing Fedelm's anger, Maeve had thought her dangerous; now the ban-drúi stood fair and terrible as a goddess before the hero's wrath.

"You, Cú Chulainn, you were able to stand against us because Macha's pangs could not touch you, whose father was not of Ulster. Would you take them upon yourself now? You slew Calatín, who was my teacher, and for that his children shall be your doom in time; you scorned the Morrígan, and she will croak her laugh as you stand bound to the pillar-stone because your own legs can hold you up no longer. Your fate is heavy, with sorrow enough for a dozen men. Claim no more this day!"

Cú Chulainn stared at Fedelm a moment longer, then drove his spear into the ground in a convulsive motion, so hard that Maeve heard the shaft crack in its silver bindings.

"I suppose it would not be fitting for Ulster's champion to slay an unarmed woman," he said, the sharp scorn of a boy edging his voice. "Perhaps there will be another meeting between us."

"Perhaps there will," Maeve whispered. "For now, go your way and leave me be."

The Hound nodded to his charioteer. His mismatched horses wheeled, pounding away. Seeing him go, the warriors who had been keeping her rear-guard busy broke away from the fight, gathering into a tight knot bristling with spears, and marched off behind him.

Maeve's womb tightened again, but this time it was only an echo of the grievous pangs that had racked her. When it eased, she rasped, "So that was Cú Chulainn, who caused our host so much trouble."

"It was," Fedelm said. "Are your pangs lessening?"

"Yes."

"When you are ready, you may return to the battle. If they grow stronger again, or if your flow bursts into sudden flood, you must come back to me at once. Now, I think, it is safe enough for you to clean yourself, and I shall bind some cloth into a clout for you."

Fedelm

To my surprise and some awe, Maeve climbed back into her chariot without help as soon as she had cleaned and bound herself. Perhaps I should not have been surprised, for I had seen before how her will was strong enough to overcome the failures of her body. Several men of the rearguard were lightly wounded, though Cú Chulainn's followers had come only to keep them occupied while the Hound fell upon Maeve. I cleaned and bound their wounds, then walked back to the place where my queen had squatted in her pain.

The large dark stain on the grass stank of piss and woman's blood, but I had smelled worse on this raid; indeed, I smelled worse every time I changed Conall or Clothra. I reminded myself as I shuddered at the slimy touch of the thick blood-clots on my skin, I had touched worse as well. I knew the thing I sought as soon as I felt it. It was thicker and more resilient than the other clots, which fell apart like rotting mushrooms beneath my fingers. I wiped the dark blood carefully away, revealing a tiny red sac.

Within, as I had expected, a pale little creature, not quite as long as a finger's joint, somewhere between a worm and a long-tailed fish with four minute fins lay curled on itself.

"Maeve must have gotten you at Midwinter," I whispered to it. "I am sorry."

I touched my own belly, the tears rising to my eyes. My own child would be the twin of the little thing in my palm now; but she, Brigid willing!, Still lay warm and safely anchored within. I bowed my head over the tiny being that would have been Maeve's child, and gave myself altogether to weeping. My tears splashed down onto it, hot and salt as the inner sea in which it had been swimming. I wondered if Maeve knew what had happened, or if she only believed she had suffered an exceptionally painful bout of her courses. 'She is a mother nine times over; she must have guessed', I thought. If she had, would she have been so swift to return to the battle? I did not know.

"I am sorry, little one," I said again, gazing down at it through the brilliant blur of my own tears. "This was not your time or place. May you come back safely in a better!"

Then it seemed to me that I saw the little finned worm's shape stretching and blurring, becoming a tiny fish. The fish leapt from my hand, growing to a flashing silver salmon in the air; the salmon touched earth, and became a high-horned stag, and the stag's shape drew into the form of a man. Him I saw clearly, as though the bright water of my tears had become a crystal burning-lens. He was tall, strong-built but lithe, clad as a prince, with a mantle of every color over a tunic of crimson silk.

Gold-flecked auburn hair, held back by a gold diadem, tumbled about his broad shoulders; a glimmer of summer bluebells warmed the flint-gray of his eyes. His nose was arched like a hawk's beak; his face was rather long, but fair and tender. Maeve's son, but not Ailill's; the circlet he wore was the rondel-adorned diadem of Ulster's king, the crown Conchobar had usurped from Fergus. His eyes met mine, and a warm tide of sadness swept through me.

"Oró, prince who might have been," I murmured. "King who has died for thy folk. Hail, and farewell: may you come again!"

The unborn prince raised his hand to me, a warrior's salute. He turned away, and was gone, leaving me to weep a while longer over the little dead thing that he had left behind. After a time, I moved away from the bloody stain on the brown grass.

I cut the sod aside and dug a hole, laying the worm that might have become Maeve's child carefully into it. I covered him over as gently as if I were wrapping Conall against the night's chill, then walked back to the guardsmen.

"You, you, and you," I said, pointing at three of them. "Do you see that spot where I was digging?"

They nodded, looking at me warily.

"Gather stones, and build a cairn there. It need not be large, no higher than my waist, perhaps, but it must be sturdy enough to last."

"Ban-drúi," one said respectfully, "we should not leave our post."

"You need not go very far. Nor will you find that you are needed to rescue our queen or king. Whatever passes in the meantime, this day will end in a truce between Ulster and Connacht."

Had the fates of Fergus and Maeve been different, the prince I had buried might have grown to bring a deeper and more lasting peace between the two provinces.

His life had been spilled into the earth, all the same; and this much would be accomplished by it. As I had foreseen, the battle ended that day in some confusion, with no clear winner.

That evening, one of Ulster's emissaries, a stocky red-haired man with a mouth puckered as though he had just bitten into a large handful of sorrel, came to Maeve and Ailill.

"Although our king has beaten you on the field, and could certainly destroy you on the morrow, the Druid Cathbad has advised him to spare you now and allow a truce," he said. "It is our men who will go back to Emain Macha full of their great triumph, as it is."

Ailill laughed.

"If Conchobar thought that he had won any great triumph, he would not ask for a truce! He knows he has gotten the worst of it, and would again if he were to press to battle tomorrow."

The emissary's mouth tightened.

"Boast as you will; but will you make peace, and swear to leave the north in peace seven years, and return those cattle and women and treasures you have stolen? If so, Conchobar will allow you and all your men to live despite the insults you have given to Ulster."

"Allow us to live?" Maeve said.

"I think not. Nor shall we return so much as a bent copper pin or a hoof-paring.

Perhaps, and my reasons for it are nothing for you to know, nor have they aught to do with Conchobar, we shall allow those noblewomen taken into bondage to return with your host."

Lochu had been a chieftain's daughter, and I knew that her death still preyed on my queen's mind.

"Seven years is too long, but since Conchobar has whiled a hard winter beneath Macha's pangs, we shall allow three years before we ravage him again. Take those terms, and tell him to be grateful."

Ulster's mouthpiece had to make several more trips, but we all knew the matter had been decided when Cathbad spoke. As Maeve and Ailill did not and would not. It would only cause them pain to no good purpose, I knew why Conchobar's Druid had advised his king thus. I am Fedelm: I hide nothing, but I do not necessarily reveal all to everyone either.

Maeve

Although the rain beat on the thatched roof so loudly that Maeve could hear it above the sounds of laughter and talk and singing, the great hall of Cruachan was warm and bright. As many chieftains and nobles as would fit were crowded along the benches, and the door was propped wide open so folk might come and go freely between the hall and the large feasting-tents set up outside. She had drunk well, though not too deeply; her body was comfortably loose, the ache gone from her strained hip and the sting faded from the various small cuts and bruises she had suffered in the final battle.

The Brown Bull was safely ensconced in the ring-ridge below the hall. He had reached Cruachan before Maeve's army: the first sight to greet her on her return had been the Bull standing like a king in the ring-ridge below the great fort, his little heifers, red and white and spotted, all gathered about him like summer blossoms about a broad-spreading oak. Now and again she could hear him lowing lovingly to his cows, the sound a comforting rumble beneath the joyous sounds of feasting.

'And why should we not be joyous? Maeve thought. The raid is over, and so is the winter. If we were not able to defeat Ulster in battle entirely, we were not beaten'.

Orlamh was not there to bellow out songs in his loud, if not particularly tuneful, voice, nor did Ferdiad's golden hair shine above the heads of the other men in the hall. With so many folk gathered to eat and drink and celebrate, Cruachan should not have seemed empty. Yet, for all the merriment, it seemed somehow hollow to Maeve; as though, should she turn her head or blink her eyes, she would be standing in a dark echoing space with only cobwebs and dried leaves to keep her company.

"The raid is done!" Maeve whispered fiercely to herself. "It is done, and I have triumphed."

"No," Senchán's deep voice rumbled at her elbow. "The matter that sent you on it is not done, nor have you triumphed yet."

Maeve started, looking wildly about before her eyes settled on the old Druid. Senchán looked no different than he ever had, sturdy as an ancient oak. If he ever grew more wrinkled, the curly white beard that covered his cheeks almost to the eyes and the mass of white curls falling over his deep-tanned forehead hid it, and his massive shoulders bulked out his loose white robe as solidly as ever.

"What do you mean?" She asked. "I have gained Finnbennach's match – the Brown Bull is below, and won much plunder and renown, as well."

"You have won plunder and renown, but you have also given up a good deal of treasure," Senchán told her.

Maeve knew that was true. She thought of her great gold brooch which she had pinned on Ferdiad's cloak before she sent him out to die, now lying under a cairn by the ford where he had fallen. She and Ailill had supplied Finnabair's bridal portion equally, and they had both dealt out gifts with open hands; but she had lost Baiscne, while Liath still rested his shaggy grey head on her husband's thigh, rolling his brown eyes to cajole meat from Ailill's plate.

As the army had drawn closer to Cruachan, Maeve had begun to hope her black hound would be waiting there renewed for her. Baiscne had not come, no more than a young pine marten had scampered afresh, to claw its way up her dress, nor her wren fluttered reborn to her shoulder.

"I have seen the Donn Cuailgne myself now. So far as I can tell, there is not a hairsbreadth of difference between the Brown Bull and the White. If you are no longer lesser than Ailill, you have not proven yourself the greater either."

Maeve blinked. She had almost forgotten that her husband's boasting had sent her on the raid to begin with. The storms of the journey had quenched even the deepest embers of her anger at Ailill.

"Then what can I do?" She asked. "If I am not sovereign in Cruachan, then all that has passed has passed for nothing."

Senchán stroked his thick white beard thoughtfully.

"I can think of only one answer. Many would say that it is a grievous waste. Then," he added, "there are those who would say that of your entire cattle-raid on Cuailgne. Yet, for all you lost on the way, you did not find it so, did you?"

"Tell me," Maeve ordered.

"Very well. When two men are so equally matched, there is no way to find the better save to let them fight it out. So it is with the Brown Bull and the White." He smiled. "In truth, I think you will have little choice.

It will not be long before every heifer who is not already with calf will be coming ready for covering. Then the Bulls will hear each other bellowing, and I do not think the fence has been built in Eriu that would hold either of them."

"And will you judge between them then?" Maeve asked.

"Not I," Senchán said. "Nor Fedelm either, for all folk know by now that she is loyal to you beyond reason. No: I would say that we should send to Bricriu mac Carbad, Bricriu the Sharp-tongued, for he favors his friend no more than his enemy."

Maeve thought with a pang of Etarcomol: it had been said more than once that he was studying to be a second Bricriu. Though there were no bare spots on the crowded benches, Maeve knew her foster-son's absence had left an empty place there. There might be men sitting shoulder-to-shoulder where Etarcomol had once lounged alone, but the cold hollow still lurked below the hall's lively surface. She stood.

"I shall send for Bricriu this night. If he will come at all, he should be here before the hosts of Eriu have gone home: let all folk see which of our beasts has the victory at last!"

The chill rains of early spring had turned the roads to mud, but the way to Bricriu's hall lay along the long log causeway that began in the bogs north of Ai Plain. If Mac Roth was displeased to be sent on another cold wet journey the morning after he had gotten home, he did not show it, only stroked his red mustaches and said,

"Two days for me to get there, and three more for Bricriu to get here in his chariot. I would choose to run ahead on the way back, rather than suffer the edge of his tongue!"

"Do as you please, but get him here as swiftly as you can," Maeve ordered.

Mac Roth proved as good as his word: he was back in four days, with the news that Bricriu was following behind him. As long as they had been away, none of Maeve's host were willing to leave before they had seen the battle of the Bulls. It was no easy thing, guesting so many for so long. Maeve and Ailill were at least able to slaughter most of the oxen they had captured in Ulster; but it would go hard with Connacht if the grain harvest were bad that summer. Bricriu arrived late in the afternoon. The satirist was a slim red-haired man of middle height, with a fox-sharp face, small pointed beard, and quick-darting green-gray eyes.

There always seemed to be a little smile on his face, though not an entirely pleasant one, as though he were secretly laughing at everyone around him. Knowing him, Maeve suspected that was indeed the case. Certainly, no matter what the occasion, he had a sharp-edged jest for it, and usually one that would prickle under his victim's skin like the lingering brush of a nettle for weeks to come.

"Are you going to offer me Finnabair for this work?" Bricriu said almost as soon as he had stepped from his chariot and accepted the cup of strong cider that Maeve bore him.

"Or is that only if I promise to give the judgement that pleases you?"

Maine Felimidh and Maine Ceat, standing beside their mother, growled softly, but Ailill gave a hearty laugh.

"You are known throughout Eriu as a satirist. If you had the tongue of a true fili, with a soft side to it as well as a rough, you would have far less trouble finding a woman on your own," he answered. "You are too late for Finnabair, but I am sure that there must be a bondsmaid or two in our hall who would be willing to sleep with you, assuming that you will wear a muzzle."

Bricriu's face reddened until Maeve could hardly see the spattering of freckles over his sharp cheekbones against his flush.

"Leave off now, Ailill," she said. "Bricriu surely knows that he who would deal out insults must be prepared to receive the odd one in turn. He is a guest in Cruachan, who has come to do us a favor." 'And Finnabair, who would be far worse hurt by his words than we, is safely away and happy with Rochad'.

"As you say," Bricriu muttered. "Very well, where are these famous bulls? Hiding beneath a fallen leaf, perhaps?"

"Come with us," Maeve said.

The edge of the man-high ring-ridge that formed the Brown Bull's paddock was so crowded with watchers that the Mainí had to shove and elbow a path forward for Maeve and Ailill. Fergus and Flidais were already on the ridge, standing on either side of the wicker-fenced gap. Senchán and Cormac stood by Fergus, and Fedelm beside Flidais with Eochaid and Suithchern. Each of the ban-drúi's companions held a swaddled babe. Maeve remembered that they had taken the infants to witness the fight between Ferdiad and Cú Chulainn, as well. 'Those babes must grow up to be great heroes, or else Druids or bards, she thought. Who else has seen such mighty battles at such a tender age?'

The Brown Bull paced about the inside of the ring, his platter-sized fore hooves scraping deep grooves in the churned mud. His great horned head swung from side to side, and Maeve saw a red gleam deep in his dark eyes. She also marked that, whenever he came near the edge of the brown-grassed ridge, whoever came under his gaze drew back. Well they might: the Bull would only have to reach a little for his high horns to hook or gore a man on the top of the ridge.

"He knows that his rival is near," Flidais remarked softly.

"Aye, no one could sleep for their bellowing last night," Ailill agreed.

"It is a pity that one of them must die," the milk-queen said, tossing her thick copper braid back over her shoulder. "If it were my choice, I should keep them half Eriu's width apart and breed their calves together each year. Then there should be fine cattle in this island!"

"Well, we have plenty of calves out of both," Ailill said. "We can still breed those. Maeve is set on knowing which bull is the better. Few folk would not come to watch this fight if they could!"

As Maeve had ordered, Finnbennach had been penned as far from the Bull's Fort as possible in a futile hope that the two bulls would not be able to hear each other. Finnbennach's bellow was a distant thunder-rumble; but the Donn Cuailgne lifted his head at the sound, and his roar seemed to shake the timbers of Cruachan's palisade and echo from the low mountains to the east. Finnbennach answered, already sounding nearer: the herdsmen must, Maeve thought, be running full-out in hopes of keeping up with him..'They want this battle more than we do, Maeve thought. We could just have turned one or the other loose, and they would have found each other and fought all the same'.

The Brown Bull bellowed once more, and the White Bull replied, again and again, until it seemed to Maeve as though she stood with a trumpa-bell pressed against either ear and both players blasting as hard as they could. Flidais shaded her eyes, gazing westward.

"Here he comes!" She exclaimed.

Finnbennach had outpaced his herders, thundering straight across the fields towards his rival. Before, the White Bull had always seemed sweet and mild, but when the Donn Cuailgne had dwelt in his mountains, with only his heifers and herdsmen about him, he had let small boys play on his back. Now both bulls were roused, swelling and rumbling with fury.

Finnbennach's hooves tore great divots of mud out of the field as he charged the Bull's Fort: the two wicker gates burst to around his shoulders. The Brown Bull lifted his head. When he and Finnbennach bellowed together, the sound struck Maeve's ears like two sledgehammers smashing into her ears at once. For a few heartbeats, she saw nothing but darkness lit by a shattering of falling stars; and she did not know if the thin high wailing in her skull was the crying of Suithchern's children beside her, or only the echo of the Bulls' roaring.

Finnbennach and the Donn Cuailgne circled each other for a moment, one glimmering white as a specter in the grey cloud-light, the other gleaming black as a bog pool. Senchán was right, Maeve thought in her sound-struck daze: 'there is not a hairsbreadth of difference' to be seen between them. The Brown Bull's horns were longer, but the White Bull's were broader. Both stood as high as a tall man's head at the shoulder, and even a tall man could not have spanned the chest-width of either with his arms.

Maeve knew that she had never seen anything as magnificent as the two of them in her life. She did not know whether she longed more greatly to part them again, that both might live, or to see their battle. That choice was not hers, or any humans, now. The Bulls lowered their heads, charging straight at each other. When their huge skulls struck, the echoes of that clash shook up through the turf-covered stones of the ridge ringing them, shivering in Maeve's bones.

It felt as though the very earth beneath her cracked from the thunderous impact. For a heartbeat, Finnbennach and the Donn Cuailgne pushed against each other, their great hooves sinking deep into the mud. Then the Brown Bull shifted to the side, letting Finnbennach surge past him and swinging his horns about to gore his foe. The spear-sharp tip of one tore a long gash across Finnbennach's side, and blood streamed jewel-red down the bull's pearl-white hide. Bricriu was standing in the gap where the wicker gates had been. 'No one likes him, but no one shall say he is not brave', Maeve thought.

"First blood to the Donn Cuailgne!" He shouted.

'Come on, come on!' Maeve's nails dug cruelly into the palms of her clenched hands, her sweat stinging harsh and salt in the tiny crescent wounds, and every muscle in her body was wound so tight that she might have been locked in the grip of a great cramp.

Though the Brown Bull fought for her, and the White for Ailill, she still felt strangely torn between them. Finnbennach had betrayed her, trampled her queenship beneath his hooves, but he was born of Cruachan; the Donn Cuailgne was a beast of Ulster. She had won his loyalty herself, and set her feet back towards regaining her rule thereby. The White Bull wheeled swiftly and charged again. His head crashed hard into the Brown Bull's flank, a blow that would have smashed a man to pulp. The Donn Cuailgne staggered and shook his head as if to rid himself of an annoying horsefly, but did not go down.

When he opened his mouth to bellow again, Maeve prudently pressed her fingers into her ears, but it made no difference: her skull seemed to catch the huge sound like a trumpa's resonating disk, echoing it longer than seemed possible. The Bulls snorted and stamped, butted and gored, the awesome sound of their battle breaking over Cruachan plain as though the sea had risen to whelm it in great crashing waves of wrath.

At one point, Finnbennach blundered into the gap. Out of the corner of her eye, Maeve saw Bricriu flying back, and Fedelm hastening down to him, but that could not draw her attention for more than a breath or two. Streaks of blood brightened the Donn Cuailgne's deep brown sides and shone in brilliant stripes against Finnbennach's whiteness, until the glowering light of the setting Sun through the broken western clouds reddened Finnbennach's fair hide and gleamed ruddy from the Brown Bull's dark coat.

Sunset darkened to twilight, and twilight to black rain-drenched night; and the Bulls fought on. Maeve could no longer tell how much of the crashing thunder in her ears came from the mighty battle below her, and how much was only echoes hammering through her skull. She thought that lightning was flashing above her; she hardly noticed the heavy rain pounding down on her head and shoulders. A few times, someone tried to bring a torch up, but no fire could burn in such a storm. There was no way to see what was happening below: only the roaring and clashing of the Bulls, and stone and earth shuddering beneath Maeve's feet.

The faintest trace of grey was just glimmering in the eastern sky when a huge bellow of pain and triumph, far louder than any had sounded that night, shattered the black rainy air into a mass of bright sparks in Maeve's vision. She blinked painfully, squinting down into the ring. Only a single great shape still stood, its head grossly misshapen. It took a few moments for Maeve to realize what she was seeing. One of the Bulls had the other, dying or already dead, uplifted on its huge horns.

'Which one?' Maeve thought desperately. Which? By the time the last evening light had died, Finnbennach had already been more crimson with blood than white, and the Donn Cuailgne more red than dark.

She was soaked to the skin, shaking like a birch sapling in a high wind. Hard as she tried to make out anything that might show her whether it was the Brown Bull or the White which had triumphed, the dim grey light in the east kept fading to black in her eyes. Now Maeve's knees were giving way beneath her. She felt herself slumping down...and her right hand fell on something warm and strong and solid. She braced herself on it, pushing herself back to her feet again.

Her weary heart struck a sudden hard beat against her ribs: her fingers were sunk deep in shaggy fur. Although another wave of darkness swept across her vision with the movement, Maeve carefully inclined her head to look downwards. Her hand rested on the back of a great black wolfhound. The dog turned his head to gaze up into her face.

Even though he was hardly more than a deeper shadow against the darkness, Maeve knew that trick of movement, and the white-fanged flash of the canine grin.

"Baiscne," she whispered, and the tip of her wolfhound's powerful tail thumped hard against her right leg, even as little sharp claws dug into her left calf.

Very, very carefully, Maeve reached downwards without looking. The fingertips of her left hand touched a streak of silky fur and muscle. She lifted the pine marten to her shoulder, where it crawled under her sodden hood and curled warm as a heated bed-stone against the cold wet skin of her neck. Exhaustion and fear and pain all forgotten, Maeve raised her gaze. Her ears were ringing too fiercely for her to hear the chirp of her wren, but she felt the brush of feathers against her cheek, and little bird-feet tugged at her dripping hair.

The Brown Bull bellowed a final time. Perhaps Maeve's hearing was only stunned, but the sound seemed weaker now, ending in a deep gurgling cough. Slowly he bore Finnbennach's body across the ring. The dawn-light was still too uncertain for Maeve to be sure, but she thought she saw something dangling from the Donn's belly. Still, his heavy tread was sure and steady as he walked out through the gap, turning towards the north and continuing onwards until Maeve could no longer see him.

"It is over," Maeve whispered, still leaning on Baiscne to hold herself up.

"Yes," croaked Ailill, "it is."

Even in the early morning dimness, Maeve could see that her husband was swaying where he stood, as exhausted as she herself. She took a cautious step towards Ailill. He reached out, taking Maeve's hand in his. Together they tottered down the steep ridge and back up the hill to Cruachan fort, the height of Maeve's strength; the heart and seat of her rule.

Fedelm

Eochaid, Suithchern, and I walked up the slope between the two doubled ridges of the Black Boar's furrows. Suithchern carried Clothra, I bore Conall, and Eochaid carried a small wooden chest for me. The winter's grip was breaking, but the early morning wind on the hill was still raw and cold, and I snuggled Conall more closely under my cloak to keep him warm – and to keep myself warm as well. He squirmed in my grasp. He was able to raise his head now, and I thought that he wanted to see around himself.

"Do you remember this place from before?" I asked him. "Or is it all new?"

"I think," Suithchern said suddenly, "that I should like to go somewhere new. I cannot bear dwelling in the house of our marriage without Lóch. I cannot cook a meal without thinking how he would have liked it, even as I tell myself to remember to make a single portion; I cannot go to sleep without listening for his footsteps at the door, or wake without thinking how early he must have risen, to leave his side of the bed cold.

Fedelm, may I go back to Alba with you? I shall cook for you, and clean and wash your clothes, and help with your babe and make sure you eat when you need to. I know Eochaid came with you from the school there, so they must allow folk who are not of the Druid, even if only as servants and guards. Will you let me follow you?"

I blinked. I had never thought that Suithchern might be willing to uproot herself thus. It was true: the school did have servants and guards. Most often folk like Eochaid, who had no place elsewhere 'Yet where is Suithchern's place, with her husband dead, if she does not mean to wed again soon?'

"I...had not thought of it. You will find the speech of the Cruithne hard to understand," I warned her. "They say penn for cenn and such, and their grammar is odd. Some of the Druid there, both students and teachers, are from Gaul: their speech is even stranger."

"I will learn to understand them," Suithchern vowed, "and I have nothing to keep me here, but you are my truest friend. I think that you need me, or at least will be happier with me than without. After all, " she smiled, "you will soon have a babe to tend, and that is easier for two than for one."

As she spoke, I realized that Eochaid the Cat was staring at me intently as well, his eyes wide and unblinking as those of his namesake, or perhaps his former shape. I looked from him to Suithchern. Yes, it might be hard for her to live in Alba. She had followed Lóch on the raid with a babe at her breast; she had borne the rigours of the long winter journey as well as I had, if not better. Our servants and guards did not have to live chiefly on beans and black bread, nor sleep on hard pallets.

"Yes. If you will come with me, then I will be glad to have you."

Suithchern's blue eyes brimmed with joy. Though the babies we held made it awkward, she embraced me for a long moment. Over her shoulder, I saw that Eochaid was smiling as well, his green eyes glowing like summer leaves touched by a sudden shaft of sunlight. My heart swelled with a sudden spurt of happiness, and I blinked wetness from my own lashes.

Suithchern's grief for Lóch would linger as long as she drew breath, but would fade to a shadow in time, and she might not always be a widow. When we reached the edge of the grove at the top of the hill, I handed Conall over to Eochaid, taking the chest he held in turn.

"Wait for me," I said to Eochaid and Suithchern. "I would be alone a little time."

The gnarled oaks, tall grey ash-trees, and tangled clumps of thorn were all still bare, their bark damp from the cold rains of early spring. It seemed to me that I could already feel the sap surging up from their roots, the life thrumming through mossy trunks and leafless winter branches. Soon enough, the buds would sprout and unfurl, opening a shifting canopy of green leaves to roof the grove. Each breeze would scatter golden sunlight across the ground-ivy and bluebells, pale primroses and wide-leafed arums beneath. Now, as much as a holy place might belong to any human, this grove belonged to me by my queen's word.

Some of the trees would have to give their lives in the next ten years, but they would be reshaped and reborn into Mannanán's fortress, the school for Druidry that Calatín had hoped to build. There was a small clearing in the center of the grove. I halted there, kneeling on the wet covering of dead leaves and twigs, and opened the chest, taking out what I had kept carefully within. Despite the oils and herbs that Calatín had shown me how to use when we preserved Orlamh's head, the old Druid's skin was still a little withered, his eyelids sunken and wrinkled. As I stared into his lean aged face, I thought his lashes stirred, drawing back a little; I saw the dark gleam of his eyes through the thin slits, looking at me in approval.

Then it seemed to me that the bare winter trees around me were become the pillars of a great hall, their branches thickening to the slope of a roof; that I felt the warmth of a holy fire, and smelled the herbal smoke of mistletoe and vervain and water mint. I could see the shapes of white-robed figures all around me, some weathered and gray-bearded, some almost heartbreakingly young; a faint strain of harp-music glittered silvery in my ears. The skin of my own hands was the fine-wrinkled silk of an old woman's, the knuckles gnarled knots on the delicate twigs of my fingers, and the hair that fell about my face had faded from gold to shining silver.

A single huge oaken pillar stood behind the hallowed flames in the middle of the hall. Just above the height of my head, a deep niche had been carved in it. In that niche rested Calatín's head, his eyelids drooping in the half-dreams of the Otherworld as he watched over our school, ready to give counsel or warning, and I knew that my teacher's wisdom would guide me as long as I lived. As I gazed upon Calatín's face, the vision faded around it, leaving me sitting in the bare grove with his head in my lap again.

"I shall grow into the inheritance you left me," I murmured, "and when we come back, we shall fulfill your dream, father of my soul."

Epilogue

The Reclaiming of the Táin

After the time of Maeve, the tale of the Táin bo Cuailgne or Cattle-Raid of Cuailgne was lost. Some say that this is because of the deaths of Roen and Roi, Connacht's chroniclers, on the raid. It is, in any case, certainly known that the seventh-century poet, Senchán Torpéist, sought to recover it. He gathered the poets of Ireland about him to see if they could recall the Táin in its fullness between them, but none had more than a few fragments.

Thus Senchán asked which of his students, for the sake of his blessing, would travel to the land of Letha to find the version of the tale that a certain sage had taken eastward with him. Emine, the grandson of Ninéne, set out for the east with Senchán's son Muirgen. It chanced that their road passed the grave of Fergus mac Roech, and they came to the gravestone at Enloch in Connacht.

Muirgen sat down upon the gravestone, and his companions left him to seek out a house for the night. Muirgen chanted a poem to the gravestone, as though he spoke to Fergus himself. He said to it,

"If this royal rock of yours were you yourself, Fergus mac Roech, we sages who have halted here seeking a roof would recover the Táin bo Cuailgne, plain and perfect."

Then a great mist formed around him, and for three days and three nights he could not be found. The figure of Fergus approached him, fierce and majestic, with a head of brown hair, wearing a green cloak and a red-embroidered hooded tunic, with gold-hilted sword and bronze sandals. Fergus recited the whole of the Táin to him, and told how everything had happened, start to finish. Then they went back to Senchán with the story.

Death is nothing at all.
I have only slipped away to the next room.
  Níl an bás ar chor ar bith.
  Níor shleamhnaigh mé ach go dtí an chéad seomra eile.

I am I and you are you.
Whatever we were to each other, That, we still are.
Call me by my old familiar name.
  Is mise agus is tusa. Cibé rud a bhí againn dá chéile,
  Sin, táimid fós.
  Cuir glaoch orm le m'ainm sean-eolach.

Speak to me in the easy way which you always used.
Put no difference into your tone.
  Labhair liom ar an mbealach éasca a d'úsáid tú i gcónaí.
  Ná cuir aon difríocht isteach i do thon.

Wear no forced air of solemnity or sorrow.
Laugh as we always laughed at the little jokes,
we enjoyed together.
  Ná caith aon aer éigeantach sollúntachta nó brón.
  Gáire agus muid ag gáire i gcónaí ag na scéalta grinn beaga,
  bhaineamar taitneamh as le chéile.

Play, smile, think of me. Pray for me.
  Seinn, aoibh gháire, smaoinigh orm.
  Guigh domsa.

Let my name be ever the household word that it always was.
  Lig m'ainm riamh an focal teaghlaigh a bhí ann i gcónaí.

Let it be spoken without effect.
Without the trace of a shadow on it.
  Lig é a labhairt gan éifeacht.
  Gan rian scáth air.

Life means all that it ever meant.
It is the same that it ever was.
There is absolute unbroken continuity.
Why should I be out of mind because I am out of sight?
  Ciallaíonn an saol gach rud a bhí i gceist aige riamh.
  Tá sé mar an gcéanna go raibh sé riamh.
  Tá leanúnachas iomlán gan bhriseadh ann.
  Cén fáth ar chóir dom a bheith as intinn toisc
  go bhfuil mé as radharc?

I am but waiting for you.
For an interval.
Somewhere. Very near.
Just around the corner.
All is well.
  Tá mé ach ag fanacht leat.
  Ar feadh eatramh.
  Áit éigin.
  An-ghar. Díreach timpeall an chúinne.
  Tá gach rud go maith.

Historical and Other Notes

Maeve's Raid is more a reinvention of the Táin bo Cuailgne than a retelling. The original is presented primarily as a celebration of Cu Chulainn's heroism; Maeve is more often shown an arrogant, bloodthirsty, and treacherous. I realized how unfair this was when I read a reference to the Old Irish law which states that rule in a marriage is based (regardless of gender) on which partner brings more wealth to the marriage. This transformed the "pillow-talk" argument from the marital spat of a shrew and a man with a penchant for annoying teasing to a deeply serious challenge launched against a land-goddess queen's rule, and inspired me to tell Maeve's story.

The Táin bo Cuailgne or Cattle-Raid of Cooley, Ireland's "national epic", is part of a massive cycle of stories dealing with Maeve (Medb), Ailill, Conchobar, Fergus, Cú Chulainn, and their associates. While these stories were useful for many elements (Maeve's brief unhappy marriage to Conchobar and the subsequent rape; the mounting tension and aggression between Maeve and Ochall, etc.), Students of Irish literature will be aware that they are neither consistent nor chronological.

For instance, the Táin bo Fraech is a characteristic Celtic romance dealing with Fraech's courtship of Finnabair, including many typical heroic and folkloric incidents (Fraech battles a water-monster, a gold ring is thrown into the water and recovered from a salmon's belly at a key moment, and so forth). It concludes with Finnabair and Fraech's betrothal and Fraech's decision to go on the Táin bo Cuailgne.

This is obviously inconsistent with Finnabair's long-term romance with Rochad in the latter; in the Táin bo Cuailgne, Fraech is simply a fairly minor character who fights Cú Chulainn in the water, dies, and is collected by a group of side-women, with no relationship to the other story stated or implied, except for his presentation as a water-fighter connected to the side (his mother is a river-goddess in the Táin bo Fraech).

In the interests of presenting a coherent story, I have used the Táin bo Cuailgne as the final authority. The original Táin is no more internally consistent than it is coherently structured. For instance, it has Rochad killed in the fight with the kings of Munster and Finnabair committing suicide from shame, but Rochad appears as a participant in the final battle, and the text states that Finnabair stayed with Cú Chulainn afterwards. In such instances, I have felt quite happy to ignore or revise the messy original text.

I sincerely hope that no one will cite anything directly from this book until they have checked the original sources: I could have made it up. For the curious readers who want to know more about things turned out for the main characters in the Connacht/Ulster cycle (and a few of the ones I invented): Cú Chulainn was killed by Calatin's posthumous children, whom Maeve sent to the Druidic schools to learn magic for just this purpose (real story). Fergus was killed by Ailill when Ailill had finally had enough of him sleeping with Maeve (real story). Maeve was killed by her nephew in vengeance for his mother's death (real story).

Finnabair in the original text, as mentioned above, committed suicide after Rochad's death fighting the kings of Munster, then stayed with Cú Chulainn after the final battle, in which Rochad took part. A more coherent logic suggests that she went home with Rochad and faded into happy domesticity. Flidais, to the best of anyone's knowledge, lived a long and happy life, and continued on (or still) to be worshiped as a goddess of cattle and deer. She may have started as a goddess of cattle and deer to begin with; her association with the Táin is probably due to her relationship with Fergus, which is just as explicit in the original Irish texts as it is here. Fedelm's story is not told by anyone after the Táin bo Cuailgne, as far as I know.

In my personal version, she goes back to Alba to graduate (and bear Ailill's child), then returns to Cruachan and founds the Druidic school at Rath Manannan (later Caiseal Manannan, or "Manannan's Castle"; this is traditionally remembered as quite a famous Druidic school). Suithchern eventually married Eochaid, and both came back to Cruachan to help Fedelm found her school (characters and events both mine).

King Ochall met his untimely end as a result of planning to destroy Maeve and Ailill. Maeve's man Nera, who was wedded to a síde-woman, had a vision of Ochall entering Uaigh na gCat with the heads of Maeve and Ailill. When his wife told him that this would happen if something were not done, he went to his queen and king; Maeve responded by leading her warriors down Uaigh na gCat and wiping out Ochall and his tribe. Real story. Uaigh na gCat (the word is literally "cat", but probably actually referred to the "tree-cat" or pine marten) is a real cave and traditional gateway to the Underworld, too.

Although the part of the passage which used to lead under an earlier burial mound was accidentally collapsed by Ireland's electric company a few years ago, it is still possible to go down into the first section, so long as one is polite and respectful to the farmer on whose private land it stands (or, more accurately, hides).

Bring a flashlight and don't wear shoes with slippery soles. It's not for the claustrophobic. Conchobar was shot with a brain-ball by the Connacht warrior Ceat mac Magach. According to an eleventh-century story, the brain-ball stayed lodged in his skull for several years, until a day when the sky darkened and the earth trembled.

Cathbad told him that this was due to the crucifixion of a good man named Jesus Christ off in the east; Conchobar sprang up in anger and the ball fell out of his skull, causing his death; but the blood from his head baptized him before he died, making him the first Irish Christian. He amended his attitude towards women in his later years; his daughter became a noted champion.

Geography and Archaeology

The geology of Ireland has not changed since Maeve's time. One can see the physical features of Maeve's Raid simply by coming here and driving or cycling the "Táin trail", a pathway which follows the entire raid from Cruachan around the Cuailgne peninsula and bac. For the archaeology of Cruachan, I am greatly indebted to Bernadette Dalton and Laura O'Brien of the Cruachan Ai heritage center.

The Cruachan royal site is a large complex of Iron Age monuments near the town of Tulsk. The key ones for the purpose of this book were the Mucklucks ("Boar's Furrows" –there is some evidence that religious rites did take place here), Uaigh na gCat, and Rath Cruachan (the big mound, which is apparently an Iron Age barrow. It was certainly used for ceremonial purposes, but there is some question as to whether it was ever inhabited above.

Nevertheless, I have chosen, for reasons which should be clear at this point, to use this as the site of Maeve's palace rather than the somewhat more probable "fortress mound" which actually boasted the wooden watchtowers by the entry path).

Cnoc síd Una (Knocksheegowna) is within sight of my hometown Shinrone, "throne of the hairy man", which I envision as the seat of the herd-goddess Flidais and her hairy husband Adammair. Early Irish Fighting: For those who find the female fighters of the Cattle-Raid unrealistic, it should be noted that such accounts as survive suggest that the Irish fighting style was one relying largely on agility. The heroic battle-feats that can be identified are triumphs of gymnastic skill, not power; and it may be worth noting in this context that Cú Chulainn is the one European hero traditionally described as smaller than average.

The weapons of this period, in particular the very short swords, also bear this out: one archaeologist described early Irish combat as a sort of "ritualized farce". The heaviest armor (romantic descriptions of Ferdiad's harness aside) was probably chain-mail, an early Celtic invention.

This permits the possibility that early Ireland was one of the few before gunpowder cultures in which women could commonly have excelled as fighters, just as the older stories suggest (as contrasted, say, to the Norse materials, in which women assist magically in battle, but are very seldom shown taking up weapons).

Language and Name-Forms

The nominal time period of the Connacht/Ulster cycle is around the beginning of the Common Era. Ireland's inhabitants at this point were probably speaking some form of early Celtic, which may have sounded more like Gaulish than anything heard in Ireland later. I have generally used Old Irish forms in order to keep the familiarity of the original text and because reconstructing possible proto-Celtic names was an infeasible task. The main exception to this rule is, embarrassingly, Maeve, for whom I have used the modern spelling.

I cannot apologize enough to any of my readers who care about philological consistency for this. However, there seemed insurmountable practical issues in using the correct form, Medb (pronounced "Maeve"), for the title-character in a book meant to be published outside Ireland. I have also used the more familiar "Deirdre" for the difficult form "Deirdriu".

Druids

There has been so much, I'm sorry, but there is no other word for it; bullshit written about these folk it is indescribable, and I have probably unknowingly added more in this book. What is actually known about them is roughly: the rigorous 21-year training course and existence of several "Druidic colleges", which interacted and took students from the Celtic areas from Ireland across the continent; the practice of sacrifice, including human; the belief in reincarnation; the use of magical herbs, most notably mistletoe, vervain, and water-mint; the probability that they wore white robes for rituals but dressed as nobles the rest of the time; the inclusion of poetry (filidecht) and musical skills in the Druidic curriculum, and the belief that they were practitioners of magic, of which weather-control, illusion, prophecy, and transformation seem to be the most constant themes, along with the use of a wand to effect spells. They used the script known as "ogham" for inscriptions, usually memorial, but were strongly in favor of memorization rather than writing things down (the Irish tradition of unbelievably accurate trained memory continued in more rural areas into the twentieth century).

The combination of the human sacrifices and the role of the Druids in supporting Celtic unity inspired Rome, usually pretty tolerant of other people's religions, to make a concerted effort to wipe them out. This clearly had not become quite enough of a problem yet to involve Fedelm's school in Scotland (set where St. rews University stands now, as a tribute to that wonderful place of learning, though the lodgings and food are considerably more comfortable these days).

One of the few things we can say about the Druids with some certainty is that they were not shamans! The Celtic culture was not, by any reasonable stretch of definition, a shamanic culture, nor does the fact that shamans use common magical techniques make everyone else who uses those techniques shamanic. If you think that "Celtic shamanism" is anything other than an annoying oxymoron, please go look up the definition of shamanism in a real academic work on the subject.

From his humble beginnings, Gundarsson (Stephan Grundy) would make his mark on the world by writing on the most rare and obscure myths breathing new life into them, for a new generation of readers. His fictional works written under Stephan Grundy focused on mythology and history and were met with international success. Along with his fictional works, Gundarsson made a name for himself writing books on Germanic Paganism (also known as Heathenry) and Germanic Culture.

He has fought for equality in transgendered communities, as well as fighting for the acceptance of Loki. Gundarsson has shaped Heathenry through his numerous academic and fictional works as well as his extensive articles, thesis papers and his creation and sustainment of the lore program within The Troth. His hobbies included wood working, jewelery making and gardening as well as historical re-enactment. He is currently attending medical school in Ireland supported by his loving wife Melodi where they maintain a local hof called The Tribe of Thor

The Three Little Sisters

The Three Little Sisters is an indie publisher that puts authors first. We specalize in the strange and unusual. From titles about pagan and heathen spirituality to traditional fiction we bring books to life.

https://the3littlesisters.com